D1300712

THE CONSPIRACY OF THE CARPENTERS

Historical Accounting of a Ruling Class

By HERMANN BORCHARDT

Translated by BARROWS MUSSEY

Foreword by FRANZ WERFEL

For if a power or an order does not sanctify
itself, how shall it hope to survive?
—INSCRIPTION OVER THE PORTAL OF THE MINE
COURTHOUSE AT MARIENHALL

SIMON AND SCHUSTER, NEW YORK

1943

ABOUT THE APPEARANCE OF BOOKS IN WARTIME

A recent ruling by the War Production Board has curtailed the use of paper by book publishers in 1943.

In line with this ruling and in order to conserve materials and manpower, we are co-operating by:

1. Using lighter weight paper which reduces the bulk of our books substantially.

2. Printing books with smaller margins and with more words to each page. Result: fewer pages per book.

Slimmer and smaller books will save paper and plate metal and labor. We are sure that readers will understand the publishers' desire to co-operate as fully as possible with the objectives of the War Production Board and our government.

MANUFACTURED IN THE UNITED STATES OF AMERICA
AMERICAN BOOK–STRATFORD PRESS, INC., NEW YORK

Dedicated to
Rudolf K. Kommer

FOREWORD BY FRANZ WERFEL

I AM TO have the honor of presenting to American readers a new author and a new work. The new author is one of the numerous Germans who have been driven from home by the brown Satan, and he is one of the few Germans whose intellectual and human incorruptibility have fully earned that brown Satan's hatred.

The new work itself is one of the rare species, oblivious of success, and audience, or the book market, that attempts nothing more or less than realization of a highly individual, world-spanning vision. In proof of this it may be mentioned that Hermann Borchardt originally cast his work in the form of a gigantic epic drama some two thousand pages long, and only yielded much later to the urging of his friends that he tear down this amazing skyscraper and rebuild it with the artist's honey-bee industry into the far-flung but orderly structure of a novel.

I do not know whether it was a gnostic, an Oriental philosopher, or a modern astronomer who expressed the following ideas. In the universe, wherever rays of light speed through it, he felt that everything must have its counterpart. Every star and every planet had its mirror star and mirror planet, on which its entire vital process, its entire history, was repeated. True, according to this theory the primary process and the mirrored process are not the same. Between our earthly planet and the mirror planet lie infinities of space, which subject the light ray and the life it reflects to refraction, deflection, change, and distortion. Hence the history that takes place on our globe and the history of the mirror globe are indeed similar, but not identical. They bear to each other not the relation of a mathematical equation, but rather that of a poetic simile, a metaphor, an analogy.

I could not help thinking of this thesis when I first read *The Conspiracy of the Carpenters*. The novel seems to take place in a world like ours, but not identically like it. To be precise, it takes place in a Germany at the beginning of this century, in cities, villages, landscapes that appear vividly before our eyes, and among lively, sharply outlined persons (a huge number of them) who are clearly impressed upon our memory as individuals. And yet this Germany is not the real, the actual Germany, and its history is not the real history of Germany in the last forty years, but rather a musical variation upon the elements of that history.

Let no one suppose that Borchardt's novel is among the phantasies and Utopias copied from Edgar Allan Poe or the young H. G. Wells, which make daring play with reality. *The Conspiracy of the Carpenters* is a perfectly realistic book, its every line breathing the plainest common sense. Never for a moment does it swerve from its reality; only this is never a mere smooth repetition of a familiar and familiarly tagged reality.

With great productive energy Hermann Borchardt builds up for his own purposes a private world, a private state, a private society. Only the nation that forms this society, and that this state unites, is unquestionably the German nation. Here is a dangerous undertaking, in which both the author and reader balance on the razor's edge. But so much the greater is the success when we find ourselves compelled after a very few pages to take the book's presuppositions for granted and not to question them further.

The author begins by leading us into a world already on the brink of the abyss. The conservative forces of society, however, are not yet broken. They are embodied in the strongest personalities of the book— Adam Faust, the President of the Republic; Augustus Beyer, his successor; the bishops, mine owners, and banker princes. But already the torrent of mud, the bog, is sweeping onward.

Whereas almost all modern literature does homage to determinism, portraying man as the puppet of social and economic "natural laws," our author is an indomitable devotee of free will. He pronounces guilt, and he lays bare the roots of this guilt. One root lies in the fact that the conservative forces of society have lost faith in themselves, and are some of them coming to terms with their murderers. The other root lies in the false doctrine that has for decades been flooding the country.

One of the finest features of the present work is that it elevates the teacher's calling to be the supreme function of mankind. But by "teacher's calling" Borchardt does not mean education in the ordinary sense, but the reception, keeping holy, and presenting undefiled of that which God has revealed and continues to reveal to the illustrious spirits of a nation, its priests, scholars, poets, and artists. If the teacher's calling among a people has been corrupted by lying, fear of truth, feebleness of spirit, and cowardly lip service, then that people is close to destruction; then the bog is advancing.

And the very epitome of false doctrine is the desecration of man, garrulously professing to consecrate him. The very epitome of false doctrine is the attempt to persuade man that he is the innocent victim of the existing social and economic order, and that he must therefore unite into one gray, monstrous mass so that by surrendering his own thoughts and feelings (in short, his own soul) he can cast down that order by sheer force of superior numbers, and deliver himself from earthly sorrows. At first, false doctrine—I still follow Borchardt—treads lightly on velvet liberal and humanitarian paws. But when its historic moment arrives it bares its tiger claws, the whole murderously inhuman radicalism inherent in every true heresy. The historic moment invariably finds its own historic man, the somber flower of the stinking bog begotten by a materialistic civilization. This man's name in the actual Germany of the last twenty years is Adolf Hitler. In the Germany on the mirror planet where *The Conspiracy of the Carpenters* takes place, the man is called Urban.

The perseverant planning and waiting, the masterly undermining, the struggle, victory, and defeat of Urban and the Urbanites—these form the substance and carry the far-reaching plot of our many-sided novel. It is all very like and yet quite different from the way it happened in reality; but precisely this likeness and difference are not only most attractive, proving the author's unconfined power of invention; they also obey one of the most important laws of art, which ought to be not a journalistic copy but a significant parable of life.

It is in the explanation and development of Urban's defeat that Borchardt quite naturally departs furthest from the reality we know. For Urban's victory over his own nation is not so complete as Hitler's. Accordingly, he is not beaten down by a coalition of world powers in a foreign war, but by the forces of good deep in the soul of his own nation, which wages a civil war against him.

At this point many readers are likely to mistake the peculiar reflection of history in our novel for some retrospective Utopia. Who, after all the crimes and deeds of violence that have defiled the German nation for ten years past, can still faintheartedly suppose this nation to have any depth of soul, let alone any forces of good? Is this, perhaps, not a just parable, but rather a wish image that the author has smuggled into his indictment of his nation? Is he possibly harming his own cause at this tense moment of the war by conceding any national virtues to the dragon foe of the world?

On scrupulous examination I can answer these questions in the negative. Borchardt's work contains no hidden defense of present-day Germany; indeed, not even of yesterday's Germany. On the other hand, the good forces that the author conjures up, and that are embodied in the secret "League of Carpenters," are not an invention, not a wish dream; as a perennially active principle they reach far back into the remote European Middle Ages.

The brotherhoods, guilds, chapels, artisans' leagues, as they existed in Germany from the eleventh to the eighteenth and even into the nineteenth century, are the legitimate fruit of the union of the Christian spirit with the Germanic temperament. Primarily they serve the religious purpose of "being in earnest with the gospels," so to speak. We must not forget that for a thousand years, from Charlemagne to the Napoleonic age, the Germans lived in a political structure that went by the official name of Holy Roman Empire of the German nation. This empire was felt as a successor appointed by God to the Imperium Romanum that was transformed and renewed by Christ. If the Pope of Rome was the spiritual vicegerent of Christ on earth, "the German Roman Emperor" was Christ's temporal vicegerent. The Holy Roman Empire of the German nation developed out of a conscious attempt to realize Augustine's *Civitas Dei* at all four corners of the earth. It was not the Italians and not the French, but the Germans, who dreamed for centuries the holy dream of a political system founded on Christ, and paid for it in unparalleled national and governmental impotence, even at a time when Louis XIV had already centralized France and transformed it into a modern power state.

All the more demonic, morbid, and abominable, then, the apostasy of the German people from its Christian mission today, with its horrid witch dances of homicidal mania, insanity, and spurious science.

In his novel-parable Hermann Borchardt reflects this deviltry page by page. But he does not stop with that. Only the caricaturist confines himself to devils and fools. The true epic and dramatic writer knows that every play of force has its counterplay. Therefore our author displays not only the infernal powers that steam up out of decay, not only the half men, the irresolute, the germ carriers more dangerous than open hell; he also shows the healing forces that the bubbling bog cannot drown. These healing forces live in the superb idea of the "Carpenters," which is by no means a phantom, but a historical fact of the past, and perhaps of the future. Once stamp out the insane modern notion that man is no more than a fraction of an oceanic, "formless mass," and perhaps despite all our motorized progress the miracle may happen, and "brotherhoods" will be formed again to reconcile the exigencies of life with Christian love. And particularly in a shattered and disarmed Germany that is rechristianizing itself, surely the "small unit" or independent brotherhood must be the guiding principle of reconstruction.

The Conspiracy of the Carpenters is not only a great novel, but also an important political work. We must recognize the enemy whom we would strike dead; and I can think of no other aid toward recognizing the German character that I would place above this myriad-figured, fantastic, and precise vision.

TABLE OF CONTENTS

BOOK ONE

THE GEISENHEIM DISTURBANCES

BOOK TWO

THE BOG

BOOK THREE

GOLIGHTLY'S JOY PREVENTED

WELCOME NOTE FROM THE CHRONICLER
TO THE READER

FOR twenty years the ruling class of my country, which is now called the Carpenters' Land, fought for the preservation of its riches and posts of honor with such determination that I take up my pen to tell the tale. Our fathers shaped the story that follows with their own heads and hands, charging us, their children, to transmit it so that what was to them the tremendous present day might tower ominously into the future like the teacher's monitory forefinger, warning the nations not to let the security they now enjoy tempt them to worship it, that is, to grow sluggish and self-satisfied. "Let our life be like the whirring arrow, sped by the tension of the bow."

In the following pages, accordingly, the loves and sufferings of our fathers outside their own history will not be mentioned unless some episode is told to show the character of the older generation in a clearer light. For instance, it may be asked whether a story of the mighty, who have never tasted poverty, is the proper place for so poor a girl as Margaret Witt, the daughter of miners, a maid and shopgirl, who runs through the entire narrative: first as the chance mistress of the great banker Jacob Willert, the country's richest man; then as a hairdresser and lady's maid, the confidante of the grand Mrs. Willert; later as a nurse and assistant to the millionaires' physician in ordinary; and finally as the wife of a kitchen-chair manufacturer by the name of Heide; after which she finally seems illegitimately to revert to Jacob Willert, surreptitiously of course, and without running any risk. But the reader who has followed all the convolutions will, we are quite sure, exclaim: "It is the very place for her! The conduct of the great toward the little people, and the way the latter behave in collision with the powerful, must certainly be told; otherwise the ups and downs of the battle would take place invisibly, among specters in a frosty, vacant firmament."

Pious they certainly were; if they had not been so rich, we might imagine their pantaloons worn through by constant kneeling. They were, furthermore, a generation "with as many sins as they had hairs on their heads." Indeed, Margaret Witt's poor brother, Tobias Witt, was sent to his death by his commanding general, Otto von Hesse, a warrior of the Lord and a bishop's son, in order to gain possession of the poor man's widow, the dovelike Veronica. (Warriors of the Lord did the same in Biblical days.) All in all, though hymns and prayers flew as lightly from their lips as the leveled bullet from a service revolver, they were no hypocrites. Hesse, for instance, the commander of the Federal Police—the most aristocratic brotherhood in the Christian fellowship of Carpenters—could not be called a hypocrite merely because he some-times doubted the existence of God, but never the existence and power of Antichrist. No historian hitherto has recounted the episode in which Jacob Willert brought the devout police commander, Hesse, before the Archbishop to accuse him of an ambition dangerous to the state. The command of the army that defended the capital, he said, must not be entrusted to such a man. "Does this Hesse even believe in God?" asked Jacob Willert, as the spokesman of the Conservatives.

"No," replied the Archbishop, exaggerating slightly, "he doesn't believe in God, or only seldom; but he hates evil. *Hatred of evil is the ladder to God.*"

All the accounts of those twenty fighting years written since that time begin, not with the first year of the presidency of our Adam Faust, President of the Republic and intellectual chieftain of the Conserva-tives, who foresaw their own downfall "unless everything is changed"— not with his first year, as one might expect, but with his eighth; what precedes is known as the era of "invisible preparation."

For here is the amazing, nay almost the unique, accomplishment of our fathers. In times of unshaken strength they foresaw their fall; and instead of smiling, making witticisms, and belittling the enemy, as all previous ruling classes had done; instead of amiably supplying fuel, as all other governing castes had done, to those busy, sulphurous imps, the children of envy, those who kindle fires under the thrones of the mighty—instead of doing this, they recognized the danger when it was still so small that to speak of it would have seemed laughable; they recognized it and pondered means to resist.

Our Adam Faust spent seven years getting the army and administra-tion into his own hands. That he was exerting great efforts was obvious; why, remained obscure. During the eighth year he launched two blows in quick succession at his two mighty antagonists: first, at "impartial science," that world-wide spirit of the times which also goes under the name of freedom and civilization, progress, enlightenment, the technological era, or modernism; six weeks later, at the greatest demagogue and mass leader of his time, Dr. Urban. Neither blow was decisive; nor did either one seem intended to bring a decision, but rather to give notice, to warn all enemies: "Make no mistake—you are known!" and to all well-wishers, "Be prepared!"

We may compare what follows after these two events, the intellectual jousting before the Natural Science convention and the bloody night of Carolswald, to the growth of a rolling avalanche; it requires no explanation from the chronicler. But since this account treats not the adventures and metamorphoses of private persons but the adventure and the metamorphosis of an entire commonwealth, we have appended a list of persons to the end of the book.

BOOK ONE

THE GEISENHEIM DISTURBANCES

ADAM FAUST AND HIS MEN

I

BY THE time the President of our Republic was seventy-eight and had governed for thirty years, no one could remember his surname, for the people never called him anything but the Fat, John the Fat. Before he laid himself down in his mansion by the river and peacefully died, he urged his chosen successor upon the nation, which picks its ruler by direct secret ballot.

This man too was not thin, nor young either; on the contrary, he was tall and broad, with a large head and white mustaches; he was worth a hundred million thalers, perhaps more if you counted in his machine factories in the east end of the capital and his mines in the mountain province, in the southwest of our country. His name was Adam Faust; he was sixty, a widower, and head of the Conservative faction in the Senate. His sons, Bernard, manager of the mines, and Adam Augustus, manager of the machine factories (both already married), took no part in political life.

The Senate parties presented their candidates. The President must belong to a family of Senatorial rank; otherwise any upstart might come forward! Or else he must prove himself possessed of ten thousand thalers, because he who has property at least shows that he has not drunk it up, while with the poor man, where should he have learned responsibility?

By rights the President was bound to be a liberal: for one thing the Liberals were the strongest party in the Senate; for another they were conciliatory, open-minded, above suspicion from any quarter, and averse to revolutionary change; and for a third it was hard to imagine such a thing as a foe of liberalism. Could any normal, right-thinking man *not* be liberal?

This was the argument of the Liberals. They had four excellent candidates: Arthur Kuehn, a man of the people, who had created a pre-

3

viously unknown industry, the furniture industry, destroying a hundred thousand master cabinetmakers, and exporting his patent health kitchens as far as the southernmost cities of Africa; George Susemihl, a fruit importer with foreign connections in South America, and incidentally of an old-established Senatorial family whose seat was in Scottish Widows' Lane; thirdly the locomotive and cannon king, Borstel, an uninhibited liberal, but sickly, while his son Alois was still too young; fourthly, old Lienhardt, the mining king.

First old Borstel dropped out of the running because of an inadequately functioning gall bladder; then Arthur Kuehn, despite his humble origin, because, having been seduced by a female employee, he had been sentenced to pay for the support of the child. This left only George Susemihl, the lemon millionaire, whose cargo ships plied upon the seven seas, and Lienhardt, the mining man, as Liberal candidates.

Both Susemihl and Lienhardt passed for atheists, which was indeed not baldly and publicly announced, but was counted to their credit. It was to be supposed that our workmen and poor folk would rather elect an enlightened man as President than the high-church candidate of the Conservatives, Adam Faust.

After two months of busy intrigue Lienhardt, the mining king, became the Liberal candidate, thanks to the eloquence of a foreman from his great estates in the south, Dr. Urban by name, who had established a League for Enlightenment and Economic Peace and denounced the red unions in enthusiastic speeches for "using the right to strike as a means of tearing our national unity to pieces."

If only to spite the Sunday-only Christians and fashionable hypocrites, our workingmen would gladly have elected an "enlightened" President; but an antistrike law for economic peace alarmed many: industry was still thriving, and the fighting spirit of the poor remained unbroken.

Against the Liberal Lienhardt, the "Yellow," as he was now called, and his propaganda orator, Dr. Urban, Bart Plambeck, the "honest seaman," head of the Revolutionary Workers' Party, was fighting from the left flank, so to speak; on the extreme right was Adam Faust, candidate of the churches and the Conservatives.

Although a millionaire lady of revolutionary views had deposited ten thousand thalers at the State Bank for Bart Plambeck, he would have needed the help of a miracle, since not even the industrial workers conceded him any chance; accordingly every ballot wasted on him counted in favor of the antistrike Lienhardt. And him they feared worse than the devil; even the atheistic Free Unions took as their watchword, "Not a vote for Yellow Urban"; because, they said, he as the leader of the Yellows would rule the country if Lienhardt were elected.

"Heaven is high and God is far away," exclaimed a certain journeyman cabinetmaker and atheist, "but Urban, the estate foreman, carries a riding whip. Sooner a reaction and prelate rule than subjugation to Urban!"

Three events contributed to improve the initially very slight prospect of the candidate of "prelates and reaction," Adam Faust. First, the propaganda tour of the country conducted by a professor of political economy at a small university, whom the liberals derided as the "stage manager of reaction." His admirers, on the other hand, called him "the discoverer of medieval society," and a story was current that Adam Faust had learned the professor's books, *The Metaphysics of Reaction* and *On the Character of my Countrymen,* by heart, and recited his teachings in schoolboy fashion.

The second event was an anecdote that we shall recount in a moment; the third the dedication of a new office building at Faust's machine factory in the east end of the capital.

So far as the professor was concerned, he was named Andrew Zorn, wore a reddish-gray beard, and was accompanied by his young son; he did not deny at all that he was a reactionary, but on the contrary asserted it in every speech, even adding that his "esteemed audience" were likewise reactionaries, but simply didn't know it. He possessed what might truthfully be called a Satanic skill at making his "reaction" appetizing to the poor.

If Adam Faust was elected, he said, the Mining Law would be immediately promulgated, applying at first to the ore and iron mines, and reading as follows:

PREAMBLE

That class distinction exists is undeniable and natural. That a violent and belligerent conflict of classes exists is an invention of the demagogues.

A healthy social policy depends on the workingmen's realizing that the word "employer" indicates not a part of the population, namely the rich, but a state of mind and a consequent mercantile faculty, namely the capacity to imagine and organize the production of goods *and* their distribution as one integral task.

A healthy economic policy depends on the employers' realizing the fact that they cannot be allowed to carry things to extremes: it depends, in other words, on low interest rates, high wages, stable prices, quality work, and the general reassurance deriving from a fair and adequate social-security system.

1. The enterprise or plant conducted by the employer is to some degree his child, and he loves it. The employee looks for his daily bread from the employer, and his sense of honor bids him fulfill the labor contract conscientiously. Accordingly a natural harmony between the interests of employer and employee *does not* exist.

2. The workingmen and employees of a coal- or ore-producing enterprise have the right to set up autonomous unions independent of both the employer and the state, on the one condition that the leaders or officials of these associations shall be elected for two years by universal, equal, direct, and secret suffrage of the members themselves in plenary session.

3. The groups mentioned under Article 2 are recognized as representatives of the employees and the workers, respectively.

4. Twenty-five per cent of the so-called operating reserves appearing in the annual statement of each enterprise are to be transferred under the name of "Social Reserves" to the associations mentioned under Article 2.

5. In order to supervise the setting up of the statement, delegates elected through direct universal ballot by the associations mentioned in Article 2 shall inspect semiannually the books of account kept by the enterprise.

6. The autonomous associations mentioned in Article 2 shall form a corporation, without prejudice to the independence of any individual unit. At its own request this corporation may be temporarily or permanently joined to the corporation of the employers, without prejudice to the independence of both in their own concerns, forming a Mining Community.

7. The engagement and discharge of labor, the policy of the enter-

prise in regard to pensions and social matters, and the supervision
of the institutions for security are functions of the mining community.

Skilled debaters sent by the Liberals to Zorn's meetings asked him
why Adam Faust had not introduced the Mining Law in his own
Johanna Mine, particularly since a younger man, Augustus Beyer, had
gone before him in this daring innovation.

Augustus Beyer, known as "the great textile magnate," owned the
largest textile mills in the country.

The professor, hesitating a moment and clearing his throat, replied
that Adam Faust had not been *allowed* to introduce the law: John the
Fat had forbidden him.

People understood. The old President did not want his presumable
successor to earn the dislike of the industrialists.

Then they demanded a statement from Zorn as to what he really
meant by "Conservative."

"The Christian state."

Amazement, and another question: What was that?

"A perpetual league of autonomous communities," said Zorn.

When the Urbanite agents thereupon burst out laughing, shouting
such abuse as "Medieval! Witch-burning! Inquisition! Serfdom!" the
above-mentioned journeyman cabinetmaker and union speaker came
unexpectedly to the professor's rescue, saying that the autonomous communities were at least autonomous, and therefore not Yellow!

So much for Andrew Zorn.

The anecdote so helpful to Adam Faust records that on his election
tour he had come to Geisenheim, the capital of the mountain province.
An hour from the town, in the hills, lies the Johanna coal mine. Adam,
the story goes, was walking along in his top hat, looking at no one,
as usual, through a large group of workmen who were standing around
the pit entrance, where a little miner named Harry Tuerk, whose constant complaints were notorious, stopped him.

"I'd like to make so bold as to complain that the diet kitchen don't
issue me no buttermilk, with all I can't eat meat nohow on account of
stomach pains."

"*That's nothing to me,*" retorted the head of the concern.

"Is that so?" asked Tuerk, pretending to be surprised—but anyone who knew him was aware that he was putting on a show. "Who is it anything to?"

"To you, Mr. Tuerk," Adam said. *"I* don't need any buttermilk."

The crowding workmen laughed loudly, to the annoyance of the complainant.

"But I've complained everywhere—in the kitchen, to the company doctor, in the office. I just get thrown out everywhere!"

"Of course you do," said Adam. "If you get buttermilk today, Mr. Schwab will be around tomorrow asking for roast goose."

"Well, then I guess I'll have to bring suit!" said Tuerk with assumed naïveté, in order to get the laughers on his side.

"If I'd been you, Mr. Tuerk, I wouldn't have waited to be thrown out three times; once would have been enough. Then I'd have gone to my lawyer."

"Done!" said the unabashed Tuerk. "I'll go to your lawyer, then!"

"To *mine?* Well, Mr. Tuerk, if you go to a lawyer who's hand in glove with your opponent in the suit, you're bound to starve to death from sheer stupidity!" said Adam, tipping his top hat and going on.

The journeyman cabinetmaker and union speaker who had helped out the Conservative candidate against the Yellow Lienhardt and his "riding-whip foreman" Urban—his name, incidentally, was Hildebrand, and he rose to high rank—told the dialogue with Harry Tuerk around everywhere; later it was to be found in the history books under the title: "The Anecdote of 'That's Nothing to Me.'"

From Geisenheim Adam went back to the capital in order to dedicate his new office building by the broad east arm of the river that encircled the city hill, and at the same time to make the reputations of two men: the obscure painter and sculptor Rudolphi, of whom so much will be told later, mostly his antics; and the turner or lathe operator Anton Koerner, the organizer of the metalworkers, and a pietist.

As other rich men collect canes, stamps, pictures, or coins, Adam Faust collected gems of thought from ancient writers, the Bible, the *Pensées* of Blaise Pascal, the writings of the Danish seeker after God, Sören Kierkegaard; and he used his collection for inscriptions painted or chiseled in public places. He was also very fond of high reliefs and statues with pediments.

He wanted a high relief with an inscription put up over the main entrance to the office building; he even announced a contest, promising a large first prize to attract the best artists. A jury was appointed, and the theme was set: "The Praise and Glory of Industry." No small indignation prevailed in the Capital City Art Association when Adam subsequently paid the first prize, but rejected not only the work thus crowned but all the others recommended to him, and purchased a design by an utter unknown, who, on top of everything else, had apparently not grasped the prescribed idea—"Has missed the subject," as the judges said: he bought Rudolphi's design, *Equality*.

The dedication took place one sunny fall morning. The plant fire department, whose band "rendered lively music," accompanied by the flapping of the flags, was drawn up in the asphalt courtyard and to the left of the main entrance; next stood the delegates of the workmen; opposite was a deputation from the Johanna Mine—pitmen and carpenters, the latter in their ancient costume. Directly in front of the entrance, facing the marble high relief, stood the invited guests. The fat band leader raised his baton, there was a loud flourish, a white ribbon fluttered to rest before the steps to the main entrance; everyone looked up, and machine operators, pitmen, and carpenters, forming a semicircle held back behind the guests by the fire department, crowded forward to decipher the "story" represented by the fully rounded and more-than-life-size figures on the marble slab. For this was the period of genre painting, of episodes told through shapes and surfaces.

Across a field strewn with mounds and spaded up, two men were going toward a constellation that radiated beams, above which floated a dove with outspread wings. Some of the beams, proceeding from the upper center, took the shape of a trumpet, which emitted strong curves like tones. One of the men, obviously a gentleman, in a long frock coat and neckcloth, was carrying his top hat in his hand, and looked like Adam Faust; he seemed to be hanging back. But the other, short, broad, sturdy, wearing a cap and a workman's apron, was grasping the personage by the hand, pulling him onward, and apparently encouraging him to answer for himself to the constellation, at whose center, below the dove, an eye was visible. Under this scene a title was carved across the slab: *Equality*. No one except the initiate understood the "story," although both figures in the relief, the rich man and the workman as well, were portrait likenesses; and since it would hardly do to renew the argument in the presence of the crowding smiths and miners, silence prevailed. The three Fausts, father and sons, shook hands with Rudolphi the sculptor, a young man but already a widower, who stood there rather embarrassed, already a trifle fat, bareheaded and with a blond forelock. The plumes on the ladies' hats billowed in the autumn wind, the bunting flags flapped against the poles, and the elderly mayor was starting to clear his throat when, mercifully, the band struck up. The fire-department band crashed out the *Onward March of Industry,* which the wretched pianist in the Municipal Opera orchestra had cobbled together on behalf of an enterprising music publisher for this purpose and for thirty-five thalers.

Then, at the expense of the scenario (for the mayor was done out of his carefully rehearsed speech), people passed into the museum hall, which had been cleared and transformed into a banquet room; the employers went first, the workmen followed. Along the side of the room, up two steps to the platform at right angles to the gigantic horseshoe table in the hall below, stood the table for the patricians, who thus sat facing the workmen at dinner, after the fashion of a presiding table; because of this arrangement they had to address their toasts and speeches not to one of the two classes, but to both rich and poor simultaneously. This was the first prank played that day by Adam Faust; the second was so surprising and so costly that our *Town and Country Intelligencer* declared one was reminded of the days of the Caliph of Bagdad. For although there were only eighteen gentlemen at the presiding table, while more than six hundred workmen and foremen sat in the hall below, not only the chairs, tablecloths, dishes, flowers, bowls of fruit, candlesticks, the food and drink were exactly the same above and below, but even the number of liveried footmen was in exactly the same proportion to the number of guests waited on by each.

The workingmen at the lower end of the table looked up at the personages to assay them. Names were mentioned, fortunes estimated, and there was brisk argument about whom Adam Faust would take as advisers if he should be elected. Obviously nothing could be expected of Adam by those who were seated farthest away from him (so that he should not have to talk with them), and were invited not as friends but only as representatives of commerce and industry, like lemon Susemihl, furniture Kuehn, and Alois Borstel, son of the locomotive king, who was already growing spherical; least of all, naturally, by the three young brothers yonder who were apparently trying to get drunk out of boredom, the sons of Yellow Lienhardt, the mining man, sov-

ereign of the mountain province: John Theodoric, who pursued the
miners' sixteen-year-old daughters, Gregory William, the agriculturist,
and Peter George Lienhardt, the youngest, a lieutenant in the army.
Politically they would all be finished, the company around the horseshoe agreed; and justly so, for in those men's eyes independent unions
interfered with "national unity."

"They'll plunge into the cold depths of oblivion," said another guest,
the journeyman cabinetmaker, Adolf Hildebrand, nodding.

"And others will rise—that's life for you!" replied a young bookkeeper, pointing to a man with a reddish-gray beard who sat next to
the Archbishop. "He's been plaguing the students in that seaside
hamlet long enough, but his bags are already packed."

Yes, no doubt Andrew Zorn would be called to the University at the
capital now, or even appointed to the Academy of Twelve, the President's inner council.

"Funny way we have," remarked a pit inspector from the Johanna
Mine. "Anyone who's going to become a great man has first to disappear for years, vanish in some little hole of a town, and read books
or write them, or do nothing, God only knows. Suddenly the *National
Gazette* says: 'Professor Andrew Zorn'—everyone scratches his head
and tries to think who in thunder that can be—'has been elected to the
Academy of Twelve.' "

"You mustn't exaggerate, my dear fellow," said the bookkeeper.
"Zorn reformed the Conservative Party—don't forget that. They used
to have just money; now they have a program, in fact one that the
little man can understand."

"You mean the Mining Law?"

"That too. But the fine thing about their program is that some sentences in it make you think—I might say sentences that invite you to
smoke a pipe and do nothing but reflect, just as if you were not a
workingman but a human being. For instance, I remember a question
right at the beginning of the program, among the principles: 'If the
railroad takes four hours to go a certain distance, why should I not
rather spend a week covering it?' "

"But isn't that reaction, my dear fellow? Just think!"

"Reaction is dangerous, that I admit. But can you kill off a reflective
question like that with a word—with the abusive term 'reaction,' I
mean? After all, anyone that tosses me grand words—'There, eat that!'

—is treating me like a dog; but anyone that allows me to reflect is treating me like a human being, and, you might say, bowing to me. Am I right?"

Aside from Andrew Zorn there were only two men at the high table whom everyone was sure Adam Faust would not quarrel with. One was that lean, long-faced fellow there, everything about him long— legs, arms, hands, nose: Augustus Beyer, the great textile magnate, with cotton plantations in America as big as provinces; for it was he, taciturn and indifferent to praise or blame, not asking permission of John the Fat, who had introduced the provisions of the Mining Law in his business; he was not doing at all badly in the process, and so far, at least, the fear that the workingmen would finance strikes from the Social Reserves had proved unfounded. On the contrary, they were starting to build housing developments. Adam Faust would have no quarrel with him, through respect for his capacities; nor would he with the second man, sitting next to Beyer, quite different in looks— but with him it would not be from intimacy. He was a brown-haired, handsome man, everything about him broad and stocky—shoulders, back, face, hands; only his nose was not, but resembled the Beyer nose, and no wonder, for the two were cousins, descended from two English sisters of fabulously exalted lineage. His name was Jacob Willert, the banker prince; the Queen of Sheba had not so much money as he. Because he was much younger than Adam, enough so that the latter might have been his father, the intimate friendship between the two had led to whispering; finally people decided that the mercurial Adam Faust was still boyish at fifty, while at the same time the twenty-five-year-old banker was already ripened and solid.

A romantic affair brought the two yet closer. For at fifty—that is, ten years before John the Fat's death—while his sons were growing up and his wife was still alive, Adam Faust fell in love with the twenty-year-old Elizabeth Sparangapani, a proud blonde with a pair of famous eyes that could dart glances like Persian arrows—one of the Sparangapanis, immigrants from Venice centuries before, who now kept confectionery shops and almond-paste bakeries all over the country. Their old ancestral mansion was next to that of the Susemihls (opposite a house of ill-fame at the sight of which the governesses in charge of millionaires' daughters cast down their eyes), in Scottish Widows' Lane, our quietest and most expensive business street.

Whether the splendid Elizabeth refused to enter upon an affair, or whether John the Fat made the man whom he was "holding in reserve" see reason, at any rate one day Adam appeared in the presidential mansion just after the midday meal. He said to John, who was resting in his armchair and using his silver toothpick: "I'm going to marry Elizabeth left-handedly—I mean in such a way that when my first wife dies she will have a sort of option on me by contract."

"You might have done that four hundred years ago—not today," said Fat John. "Let her marry and get pregnant, and then you won't love her. Marry her off!"

"To whom?"

Groaning, the President tossed his toothpick into a glass bowl, took a leather notebook full of names and addresses out of the table drawer, looked through it, and said: "To your friend Jacob Willert."

Adam scratched his head and went home. For Jacob Willert, twenty-five at the time, was keeping a milkmaid as an alleged secretary, to the chagrin of his countess mother, the Englishwoman; he dressed the peasant's daughter in silks and satins, and had vowed to marry her.

The "Triumvirate" was formed, if the conspiracy of an elderly man and two elderly ladies can be so called. Jacob's mother, the steeple-chaser, who broke her neck not long afterward; Elizabeth's mother, old Eugenia Sparangapani, laden with diamonds; and Adam Faust; all convened and whispered. They had a man in readiness for the lovely milkmaid—her commonplace name was Dorothy Thiess—they hounded her with threats until she grew afraid, and gave her ten thousand thalers. Dorothy Thiess fled from the Willerts' country house by the river; Jacob, convinced that she was unfaithful, married Elizabeth Sparangapani.

The confectioner's daughter punctually became pregnant. Out of pride and boredom she transformed the white palace of finance on Lady Square into a gambling den, so that Jacob, returning from a trip abroad, slapped his wife savagely, and would have injured her if Adam Faust had not flung himself between the two. Fright and pain caused a premature delivery, which turned out successfully and presented the firm with its heir, little Henry. The friends of the house doubted the premature birth; they said little Henry had not been born too early, but his parents had married too late. At any rate, the splendid Elizabeth was spoken of as "the defeated" after that.

While the soup was being served and heavy red wines were being poured at the horseshoe table in the hall, the guests remembered with relish this and other tales from the fabulous house of Willert. True, there were no women in the hall, but two Willert women had been outside before Rudolphi's high relief of *Equality:* the splendid Elizabeth, holding her ten-year-old Henry by the hand, and the "Beloved," Elizabeth's stepmother-in-law, who had just arisen from childbed, pale, delicate, and young. Everyone had seen her kissing little Henry, Elizabeth smiling, and the boy looking enchanted at his young grandmother and stroking her. This adventure, the love affair of an old man, seemed to have reached a happy issue. For old Melchior Willert, Jacob's father, after the fatal fall of his English steeplechaser, had indeed turned over his business and posts of honor to his only son, but had set tongues wagging by a second marriage at fifty-nine: this was impossible, they said; he must be restrained!

She was the childless widow of a small suburban shopkeeper, thirty years old, without a penny, uneducated, Anne Mary by name; Melchior, as if in defiance, then and later called her "the Beloved." He married her in the Church of the Saviour amid a pomp already outmoded, with three hundred guests, and retired to the country.

John the Fat died, Anne Mary gave birth to a daughter in the Willerts' city mansion, and was seen arm in arm with the splendid Elizabeth in Scottish Widows' Lane. When Rudolphi's high relief was dedicated and the guests went into the hall, two Willert ladies and the child Henry went back home with old Melchior.

"Ssh! Quiet!" At the millionaires' table above, Adam Faust had tapped his glass. He proposed his toast to the builders of the office building and the creator of the high relief, *Equality*. He would leave it to his "friend and fellow worker," Anton Koerner, turner by trade and president of the metalworkers' union, to speak on equality itself, what it was and what it was not.

"Friend and fellow worker" sounded very much like electioneering. But when Koerner's speech was over, when years passed, when a book entitled *Speeches and Opinions of Anton Koerner the Turner* had appeared in print and been forced upon the war colleges as a textbook, the mockers realized two things: firstly, that the lathe operator had prepared his speech alone, needing no outside help, and secondly, that the intellectual structure which people called the "Faust system" had

been built by professors, bishops, turners, and journeymen cabinetmakers.

Old Anton Koerner, with his gray, pointed beard, stood up, made an
angular bow toward the personages, cleared his throat, and said:

"When one looks at this monstrous dinner, course after course, wine
after wine, more and more until a man of our sort almost has to
unbutton his vest, any normal person must realize that there can be
no thought of equality between rich and poor." For, he went on, the
poor man could not afford such a dinner even after christenings or
funerals; in fact, he could not so much as dream of affording it, not
if relatives and friends were to club together and stump up two weeks'
wages. "Those are the facts."

The Archbishop, in his regalia and wearing the cross upon his breast
on a gold chain, gave a short, dry laugh, perhaps because the speaker
had glanced up from his manuscript for a moment, and added the last
sentence on his own account.

"Contrariwise and on the other hand," Anton Koerner went on,
"there is no equality among the poor either, not even in what they
require of life. If each one were asked individually what he regarded as
a happy life, no two answers would be alike; whereas if we could
question a hundred canaries, probably they would show that they had
reached a much higher level of equality, though not so high a one as
the ants. The lower the order a living being belongs to, the greater the
equality among the individuals: *complete* equality can be found only
in inanimate nature, among machines and their parts.

"And why does so little equality exist among us workingmen, while
there is so much among ants? Answer: because we are men and not
ants! Which irrefutably proves once and for all that ants should be
treated as ants and workmen as human beings!"

There was a roar of applause throughout the hall, and the people
looked up at the table occupied by the rich men.

Anton Koerner found himself obliged to hand over his manuscript
and glasses to a neighbor, and start speaking extempore, so undig-
nified did docile reading from the page seem to his fellow workmen.
And so the organizer of the lathe operators, gesturing—when his coat
sleeve slipped back one could see that he wore no cuffs—and frowning
with intense concentration, never deviating from his subject, rose to
enlarge upon the theme in a way that won profound admiration.

"Well, then, variation is the same thing as humanity, and if they all want the same thing—that is, if they all want equality—they are scattered to the four winds, as we see in the building of the Tower of Babel. And yet an equality must exist among men, a perfect equality, much greater than what we see in this hall today, where those condemned to labor sit in the same chairs and eat the same costly dishes as the employers and prominent personages. You see, it was not for that reason, not to set up a sham equality of rich and poor, that Mr. Faust and his sons arranged to have everything up there and down here alike to a hair. Nor was it to 'put us in good humor'; but simply because they wanted to do us honor—the honor of being the Fausts' guests!"

Everyone clapped; Koerner, with an angular movement to the right, bowed toward the presiding table. The Fausts, father and sons, got up and returned the bow. Courtesies of that sort were taken for granted in those days, and attracted neither attention nor suspicion. What Koerner's reference to "putting them in good humor" signified was perfectly understood both above and below.

"An equality must exist, a perfect equality, I said, and I mean to prove it; but first I must correct a misapprehension. Recently, and not very surprisingly to us older men, there has arisen a theory so pitiless, bloody, and vile that simply hearing it makes our flesh creep. This theory says, 'A man is worth as much as he accomplishes,' and I call you gentlemen to be my witnesses that we union men began to defend ourselves at once and with all our force (which unfortunately is small) against this newly invented vileness and its consequence, piecework. Kindly do not try to trip me up with trifles! Who would deny that piecework may sometimes have its place—for instance, when a delivery date is approaching, and large sums are involved? Not that; but when I was a young fellow at night school, a teacher taught us the saying: 'Nip things in the bud!' "

"Get on with it!" cried a youthful voice at one end of the horseshoe.

"What do you want? That *is* equality," cried the turner. "That is the kind of equality attainable on earth: everyone—you too, young man —is worth no more and shall receive no more than the equivalent of what he does! Do you think that I, after spending my whole life at the lathe, propose to stand here and speak for idlers, for those who complain of their low pay because they are unwilling to improve their skill?

Obviously an instrument-maker earns more than a stoker—that is not what the new theory means; it means that you are an ant! The king of the ants cannot have invented this theory of attainable earthly equality, so I suppose it must have been invented in hell."

"Very true," came the Archbishop's clear, matter-of-fact tones in the midst of the deep silence, the footmen having ceased to serve.

"So I have excluded that kind of equality too, the ant equality according to which I am worth only as much as I can accomplish, and must starve or be eaten if my eyes fail me. Nevertheless, an equality, a complete equality, must exist; for if it did not, the strong would long since have devoured the weak, and the human race would have destroyed itself in a free-for-all fight."

The footman filled the speaker's goblet with champagne and made an inviting gesture. Anton Koerner, looking blankly at the man in livery, drained the glass, and went on: "Perfect equality may be compared to a bell hanging down into our lives; but the hook it hangs from has never been seen, unless by the eye that looks upon the guilty and demands an accounting, in Mr. Rudolphi the sculptor's carving. This bell, or the earthly echo of a voice that is not of this world, we call conscience. We call an employer who believes in nothing but his business, and thinks he owes no one anything but money, a conscienceless employer, because the only voices he hears are of this world; and those voices can indeed speak of profit and loss, and how you are worth what you accomplish: but of guilt and responsibility they know nothing. There is, then, one equality, one complete, indistinguishable equality of rich and poor: that of the voice hanging down into our lives and demanding a reckoning; and this equality is so great that the sculptor has even given me, the turner, a little advantage over my master, having me grasp his hand and encourage him before the judgment seat. That, gentlemen and fellow workmen, is what I have to say about equality."

The impression produced by the speech of the old agitator and pietist was so deep that all the Fausts came down the two steps from the platform and went over to congratulate the foreman, who was stowing away his glasses and unused manuscript in a coat pocket. At the same time the chief could not quite restrain himself from delivering a little concluding speech. With one hand on Koerner's shoulder, with the sly twinkle that had become second nature to this toastmaster of uncounted dinners, he said—and now the attempt to create good humor was obvious: "You realize, gentlemen, that we could not invite the ladies for want of space. But now, as if to see that justice was done, the house steward tells me the dessert wines and pastry have scarcely been touched. And so I do not believe I shall offend against etiquette if I make bold to send the sweets and the port wine home for my married guests."

Four weeks later the presidential election took place. Adam Faust was elected over the opposition of the "progressives," who had formed a solid unit for the first time.

Hardly was he installed in the supreme office before the "personal rule" that the Liberals had predicted began. The papers asserted that none of his predecessors had rewarded his campaign followers and pushed his enemies out of office with such barefaced impudence. Within a year the appointment commission whose duty it was to nominate civil servants had been packed with Adam's followers; a network of employment inspectors to report on the health of the industrial population was spread over the country in order, as the Liberals put it, "to harass free enterprise." Anton Koerner, the speaker at Adam's unveiling banquet, became employment inspector of the mountain province, and an uneducated pit inspector by the name of Lange— "church attendance excellent, spelling unsatisfactory," as the *Intelligencer* described him—was Koerner's first assistant. Materialistically enlightened pastors and heads of seminaries were constantly urged to take up some other occupation, until they finally did so to avoid being thrown out; and to the magazines' complaint that liberal theology was in danger the President replied that there was indeed a threat to those seminary teachers and pastors whom God had intended neither for clergymen nor for teachers at all, but for office clerks.

As President of the Academy of Twelve he appointed Andrew Zorn, with Jacob Willert as his deputy; a young doctor, student of the natural sciences, and pupil of Zorn's, whom the all-powerful professor had recommended, became secretary of the inner council and privy physician. His name was Dr. Daruhi.

Starting with the President's third year in office a decline of the frontier fortifications was observed; people laid it to the "shift of generals," the change of personnel in the officers' training schools, and to the new strategy, which Adam's adherents kept secret, not even mentioning it in the military journals. No reports of maneuvers were allowed, no foreign observers were invited; but the President was away from the capital from three to five weeks a year to attend the training, and as long again to inspect the army schools. New names made their appearance; a colonel in the foreign service, Frohwein, became Chief of the General Staff, and a military historian and theorist in the science of attack, Kaempf, was made Inspector General of the military training system. From general to company commander, from provincial governor to village mayor, the country sensed the new tone and the personal rule, without clearly recognizing the purpose of the changes and unrest thus produced.

In the President's fourth year the disaster to the Willert family took place.

Anne Mary Willert, "the Beloved," had left the city mansion and was living at the great country estate that stretched for miles along the riverbank an hour from the capital. Even here she chose, not the house by the river, prepared for guests, but "the little house" by the pond that later received the name, after her monument had been set up among the reeds and water lilies at the narrow lower end, of Madonna Pond.

One morning when the child was three years old it was playing in the sand by the bench where she sat with some needlework; she sent the little girl's nurse on an errand to the neighboring forester's house. The nurse reported that the cries of someone struggling with death had summoned her back; but the black and muddy water had already sucked the two of them under, mother and child.

Old Melchior's life was blasted. "It's awfully easy to say, 'He was hard hit'!" said Dr. Kuttner, the surgeon at the Women's Hospital, afterward, "but here was a chance for you to see what it looks like when a man is *really* hit!" The old man's limbs shook with such spasms that two male nurses had to hold him to prevent his falling out of bed. The doctors, in the prevailing confusion, having summoned colleagues and consultants, swarmed like bees through the house, and were bowed out by Jacob Willert, who thought it cruel to insist on bringing back to life a man who obviously longed for death—bowed out all but one, whose old-fashioned and quacklike laying on of hands and rubbing with aromatic essences, accompanied by incantations, seemed to please the patient. This was Dr. Daruhi.

That he cured the man without the use of poisonous medicaments is not, as Jacob pointed out, in accordance with fact: once a normal pulse was restored, morphia was injected in order to produce (in Jacob's words) the "glorious drunkenness" that lays open the mind and makes it amenable to the "incantations." These were simple enough: God would let no one, living or dead, look over His shoulder; he who felt Judgment Day drawing near, or even so much as caught sight of the moving finger, should recall his own past, making no resistance whatever.

In this fashion Melchior Willert was led to reflection—that is, back to life; for two years longer he walked, leaning on his cane and the arm of his valet, John Huebner, along the banks of the Madonna Pond, not avoiding the spot where "the Beloved" had gone down; he commissioned and unveiled the monument to her with the child in her arms, which gave its name to the pond; and thus he brought lasting fame to another man besides Daruhi (whose celebrity was thenceforth assured)—Rudolphi, the sculptor and painter.

Jacob Willert's fortune, consisting of the bank, securities, and real estate, was estimated at two hundred million thalers when he came into his inheritance. In addition, Melchior on his deathbed, cared for by Daruhi, "the man who made dying easy," was said to have bequeathed four pieces of advice to his son:

1. Don't give up; preserve what you have, and avoid installment transactions.

2. Be careful in trying to conciliate your enemies, lest your friends forsake you.

3. You will store up guilt in your soul, and hatred as well: keep constant watch over this account, and employ a spiritual adviser.

4. Try to be faithful to your wife, but never let her or any other woman of your household show her breast or wear silk stockings when the weather is cold.

With the exception of the last, Jacob followed all this advice, as will be seen. The dying man's statement that his son should be slow to reconciliation, but should curb his hatred, referred to the combinations resulting from the death of Anne Mary, "the Beloved." The most widespread suspicion, believed even in the highest quarters, namely that Melchior himself had pushed his young wife into the water, was a piece of sheer malice. The nurse's story, that the child had trustfully walked into the water to try it when its mother did not happen to be looking, and that Anne Mary had drowned in trying to save it, seems likely. Jacob, however, knew from his father that the young wife had been mortally insulted. At an evening reception in the town palace, under an arbor in the garden, the drunken Lienhardts had asked Borstel, the old locomotive king, while Anne Mary was listening, whether he knew what a madonna was.

"Oh, yes! A woman who doesn't know where her child came from!" the old cynic had replied, and all four had roared with laughter as if at a preconcerted signal.

So much for the suspicions about how "the Beloved" perished. Jacob Willert became an admirer of female beauty; it is said that not one of the twelve servant girls in his household was ugly, and not one wore woolen stockings even when the cold was arctic, for thick ankles were an abomination to him. He was familiar with love, not with hate. Yet, admitting all this, we shall see that the three young Lienhardts who laughed in the garden all came to violent ends.

BOOK ONE

THE PROFESSIONAL OPINION OF DR. DARUHI

II

THE President's eighth year in office brought the first onslaught of the Faustites upon materialistic enlightenment.

At that time such wanton high spirits prevailed that the ladies in our best circles would go shopping with young kangaroos trained to carry small parcels in their pouches; the kangaroos died in swarms during the biting winter weather. The President of the Republic, on the other hand, was accused of demagogically favoring the poor because he forbade army officers to breed race horses. Servant girls, old and young alike, wore elastic-bottomed flannel drawers and home-knitted woolen stockings under skirts of utterly imperishable material, and ancient crones were laid to rest in the same dresses they had expectantly donned as brides. Any festive meal had to include fish, game, poultry, cheese, dessert, and at least three kinds of wine in addition to soup and the entree. Peasant weddings lasted three days, and there was hardly a baptism that did not end with some accident due to drunkenness; for the three basic forms of strong drink—whisky, gin, and orange liqueur—were within reach of the common people. The night watchman at the village of Liebenau quite simply expressed the popular feeling when he told the itinerant cattle dealers who treated themselves to red wine and him to brandy that wine was for the rich man, distilled spirits for the poor.

This, then, was the time when Adam Faust invited a few rich men to his friend Jacob Willert's house in order to ventilate the question of whether to embellish the First Public Convention of the Society for Natural Science by making an appearance, or to ignore the modernists, "leaving them," as Adam put it, "to stew in the ink that is their natural element." For the Society, although they proclaimed with resounding vociferousness the recent discovery that man was descended from monkeys, and other such advanced talk, had very little money; chiefly for this reason, but also through an overweening confidence in their own cause, it was supposed, they had invited the Society of Friends of Paracelsus (a body that our best people traditionally belonged to, dating from the time of the romantics and mesmerists) to follow the public reading of each important paper with a speaker of its own who would offer a rebuttal, enjoying absolute freedom of utterance. In return the Paracelsus Society would assume half the expenses and the entire rent of the hall.

Following a telephone conversation with the President, Jacob Willert suggested consulting Dr. Daruhi, the presiding officer of the Paracelsus Society, for an opinion on the Natural Science Society. Adam Faust made no objection.

The merry chatter of sparrows in the trees and shrubbery of Lady Square came in through one of the three tall windows of the conference chamber, half opened by Jacob's butler; the bronze chaplet of Our Lady, whose figure surmounted a small column in the middle of the square, gleamed when the sun came out from behind the clouds. The wooden pavement of the roadway before the white palace of finance swallowed the clop of the horses' hoofs, and there was such a pervading air of quiet opulence that the ensuing prophecy of doom must have struck the richly successful governing personages who heard it as springing not from present reality but from a realm hidden behind the high white brow of the man who was leaning forward on his hands at the end of the table, delivering his professional opinion.

"When the soul of the people is gripped by an undefined fear," declared Dr. Daruhi, Professor of the Occult Sciences at thirty-five, "it remakes the surrounding countryside through actions and dreams." Once upon a time, he continued, the ordinary city—to say nothing of rural neighborhoods—had presented the same appearance for three hundred years. Today it would be past recognition within thirty. This transformation, induced by the forlornness, anxiety, and feverish unrest of the individual, and hence abnormally speeded up, was described as "progress"—a euphemism that indicated the soul's striving to conceal from itself a horrifying state of decay. At the same time it was not true that this frantic anxiety, expressed in blind bustle, would attack first a single person or small group, and only afterward the many, like an epidemic; no, it would descend like a fog from unknown regions on whole countries or continents simultaneously. And the professor cited a report written seven years previously by General Frohwein, a former officer of our colonial army, and Bishop Hesse, stating that the young Malays who were wealthy enough to make acquaintance with modern civilization at our universities spread unrest after they came home.

His listeners said nothing. At last, putting down his cigar, the elder of the Faust brothers said: "I don't see how we can charge the Natural Science Society with this disturbance and frantic change that you have been discussing."

Said Daruhi, with a look of suffering: "But, after all, they maintain they have unsettled what is fixed and certain, what has always been accepted within the memory of man. And they *have* unsettled it, with their big mouths—not from love of knowledge, that is, and in fact not from love at all, but from envy. That is not enlightenment; it is preparation—preparation for overthrow."

"Maybe everything actually has grown uncertain," said the joviaı President, shrugging his shoulders. "In the immortal words of Socrates, you don't know nothing for sure." Occasionally Adam talked like this for diplomatic reasons, but if ever a man was devoted to orthodox Christianity, and regarded fixed laws and established authority as the way out of all difficulties, it was our Adam Faust. To right and left of him sat his two married sons, Augustus Adam, in command of the machine-factory section east of the capital, and Bernard, the younger, who had charge of the southwestern mines. Down the table sat the Archbishop, a man in his fifties, with the face of a sea captain, in mufti, and below him, face to face, the two leaders of the Conservative element in the Senate, Jacob Willert, the banker prince, and Augustus Beyer, the great textile magnate. The lower end of the table, facing the President, was occupied by the speaker of the day, Daruhi, physician in ordinary, explorer of souls, and Professor of Occult Sciences.

"The warmth of the home fires is sure, and love for children," he replied, and added with bent head, "and the disquiet of these fools who fill the earth with the glory of their names is sure also."

The younger of the Faust brothers whistled through his teeth, stopping the moment the hypnotist looked at him. "Yes, I am suffering, Bernard Faust," he seemed to be saying, "I admit I am suffering, but not from envy. Don't undervalue me."

There seemed, however, to be another member of the little group who also mistrusted Daruhi's dislike of the "modernists." Old Maier Herschel Simon, whose ancient, wasted face was covered with a taut skin quite devoid of color, cast a glance of his watery eyes at Jacob Willert, his more influential rival. The look said: "If a poor and talented man wants to climb by the help of the rich, he does well to denounce progress and advancement. Anyone who publicly charges progress with all the vices is at least free from suspicion of being a revolutionist. But this Daruhi fellow is carrying obsequiousness to the point where his listeners are beginning to shake their heads—too far, in other words. The man who makes concessions is the one who seems to merit belief."

Jacob Willert caught his glance, and did not return it. He was thinking, "You old fraud, you're asking me why I invited you here when you have no influence on the government and haven't even got into the Senate. But for that very reason your ambition is unlimited; and if you had been slighted, wouldn't it have pushed you over to the Natural Science people, who could then, armed with your check, have bid defiance to all opposition?"

And as he motioned to the butler, who came in pushing a tea cart of drinks, Jacob thought of the Senators whom he had not invited, because his hatred of them had come down to him from his father

Melchior: the Lienhardts, mining kings of Geisenheim, and the Borstels, the outstanding locomotive builders. It was true that, unlike old Simon (to whom everything was "all one" because he had ceased to understand what went on), the Borstels and Lienhardts, leaders of the Liberals in the Senate, would mean to stick by the radicals through thick and thin; but their hearts, soft as greasy dishwater, were not of the stuff for rash and revealing enterprises. They would never give a penny to the Natural Science people.

Just then Augustus Beyer (who was not yet old, had never been young, and was always ailing) looked up and said, "I'm not interested in whether man is descended from monkeys. That's just the same sort of clever remark as Daruhi's saying that monkeys are descended from a degenerate race of men. Do I look like a monkey?"

Bernard Faust, the mine operator, began drawing little men on a piece of paper, tittering softly; but his father, after brusquely inquiring of Beyer, "Are you trying to make difficulties?" gave the floor to the Archbishop, as if everything were all signed and sealed.

The bull-necked Archbishop, in mufti as always, asked who were to be the speakers for the rebuttal. The Natural Science Society, surprisingly—or rather treacherously—had announced a paper on economics, and another on the social question, just as if the distinction between natural and social sciences had already been argued away. If religion should happen to be included also, he would offer his own services.

To everyone's surprise Bernard Faust spoke up to suggest that the rebuttal on the social question be presented by a pit inspector from his Johanna Mine, a young man by the name of Theodore Lindbrecht who had organized the carpenters of the mining district, under the guidance of Bishop Hesse, the revivalist preacher already mentioned, into an independent fellowship. His name was familiar to the others, and it was agreed that the pit inspector should be summoned to the capital and examined by Professor Andrew Zorn, the political economist, who was to conduct the rebuttal on the third day.

Accordingly, Dr. Daruhi having finally convinced even the ailing Beyer that it was necessary to stand up publicly against the monistic apostles of enlightenment, the conference ended with a unanimous resolution that the Paracelsus Society should accept the challenge of the Natural Science Society.

The President and his sons were the first to leave; the half-blind

Simon was led to his carriage by two footmen, and Beyer, the textile magnate, greeted in the hallway his grand-nephew Henry, the sole heir of the Willerts, a blond young man of seventeen who shook hands stiffly and timidly with the Senator.

Only the Archbishop remained. As leader of the Christian Middle-Class Party he had some influence on appointments; and it appeared that the Senator in Charge of Police and Federal Commissioner of Public Safety, Baron von Brick, was still conducting his grain business, but that through good nature and unhappy family circumstances he was leaving his police duties to unsuitable subordinates. Order still prevailed; a respected Conservative member of the Senate could not as yet be casually removed from office; and besides, Brick himself had asked for an adjutant, adding, with an apologetic smile, "An energetic one." For evidently the speed with which the tall, long-bearded, muscular Baron lost control of his wife and two children, who forced him to stand helplessly aghast at impudence, unruliness, and misbehavior, thus increasing the domestic anarchy, exactly matched the decline of his resolution in public affairs.

BOOK ONE

START OF THE DEBATE

III

GLEAMING chandeliers; the buzz of voices; fluttering plumes on the hats of our ladies in the banquet hall of the Palace Hotel. Yes, we took the most expensive hall—money doesn't count when the Paracelsus is in on it: this had been the talk among the Natural Science people, and their great day was here at last.

It almost failed to arrive. Three days beforehand a deputation of ladies arrived at the presidential mansion, led by the intrepid wife of Beyer, the textile magnate, whose word carried great weight with us because she was English by birth. The people of the capital, impressed

by her figure and her lineage, never called her anything but "Lady
Beyer." Adam Faust telephoned to his favorite, Professor Andrew Zorn,
for help, and the following conversation took place.

Lady Beyer: "A piece of impudence, Mr. President!" She pointed
with her lorgnette to the newspaper that Adam had spread out before
him.

The impudence consisted of a satirical article in the *Intelligencer,*
entitled "The Paracelsus Society, Its Manners and Customs." Sixty years
since, said the unnamed author, when the ladies had given one another
the shivers with magnetic circles and sleepwalking, the entertainments
of the Paracelsus Society had at least been entertaining, and under
pretext of magnetism the young people whom the mothers in our best
society had paired off could hold hands and step on one another's feet
under the table. But in later times, while some five-thaler speaker
delivered a harangue from the stage, "No pretexts were even invented
any more for bridge-playing, society gossip, and matchmaking in the
auditorium."

"That sentence might interest the state's attorney," said Lady Beyer,
who had three daughters to marry off; and the young wife of Senator
Kuehn, the furniture manufacturer, announced her attention of sub-
scribing to the complaint, "because otherwise anyone might go and
start spreading public slander."

The "public slander" was an anecdote printed at the end of the
article, and demonstrably true: Kuehn, the manufacturer, being elected
to the Senate and invited to join the Paracelsus Society, had said:
"Later. My daughter is still too little."

Adam Faust showed the ladies a letter from the Natural Science
people declaring that they had no connection with the anonymous
author, and promised his "most serious consideration." Thus the complaint went off to the satisfaction of all; it was agreed that the session
should take place, and the government should emphasize its impartial-
ity by not attending.

At home Mrs. Beyer told her husband and daughters that by way of
punishment for that impudent article the President had forbidden
government officials to attend the Natural Science Congress. Augustus
Beyer, the textile magnate, did not bat an eye.

It had been sensibly decided not to parade the heavy artillery of
science until later, but to make the first day "a truly popular event."

(*National Times.*) Accordingly, the subject of affirmative and negative speeches was, "The glorious present, the more glorious future," and the price of admission was reduced by half. The young poetess, Diana Rose, founder of the League of Revolutionary Writers, recited a prologue of her own composition. But the affirmative address of our Alderman Heidemann "won the admiration of the entire country," starting out by way of antisepsis, the ophthalmoscope, and Riemann's system of mathematics, and going on to proclaim the defeat of the medieval concept of "eternal verities," the now unassailable triumph of materialistic monism, and "the deliverance of the masses, formerly cheated of happiness, through science and technology." Behind him on the wall of the hall, which seated a thousand and was overflowing, hung a more-than-life-size painting by the progressive artist, Felice Gasparra. On a gently rising, flower-sprinkled meadow it showed a group of unclothed men and women of all ages embracing one another, each raising his unoccupied arm to greet the sun rising on the horizon. In order to make the symbolism of the picture plain, the master had chosen as a title the refrain of a song often heard at the time, and had carved on the bottom of the frame:

> *Strive toward the sun and freedom,*
> *Brothers, strive toward the light!*

Not a single member of the government had appeared, and of the twenty armchairs upholstered in yellowish brocade that the proprietor of the hall had ranged in the front row facing the speaker's desk—in his opinion only citizens of Senatorial rank were entitled to brocade armchairs—most remained vacant. Modesty led young Borstel to take the seat at the extreme left: Alois Borstel, the heir of the locomotive king, and already well on his way to becoming spherical. He was an adherent of progress who reached a ripe old age despite innumerable follies, perhaps because he was not among those who had laughed over Anne Mary Willert that night in the garden.

To the right of the center aisle sat Augustus Beyer, dressed in black, tall, emaciated, pale-faced, with his lady. In the midst of the thunderous applause for Heidemann's affirmative speech, the Senator beckoned to a blond young man; from the whispering behind fans, while the ostrich plumes and flower arrangements of the ladies' millinery brushed

one another, one could gather that the textile magnate was bestowing
the honor of his company on Dr. John Henry Merckel, senior assistant
master of the Girls' Academy at the capital, and son of a washerwoman.
Merckel took a pencil and pad from his coat pocket.

"Well, now look at that," said old Mrs. Susemihl to the diamond-
bedecked Eugenia Sparangapani, Jacob Willert's mother-in-law, leaning
forward to catch what the President's favorite might have to discuss
with this son of the proletariat.

"You've got white, Senator," whispered the young headmaster, and
Beyer leaned back, folded his hands, shut his eyes, and said: "*E 2—e 4.*"

"*E 7—e 5,*" repeated the washerwoman's son, his eyes downcast, and
wrote something on the pad.

"*F 2—f 4.*"

"*D 7—d 5.*"

"*E 4 takes d 5.*"

"*E 5—e 4.*"

"*D 2—d 3.*"

"Knight *g 8—f 6.*"

"What language is that?" old lady Susemihl asked her neighbor.
"Esperanto?"

"It's chess," replied the white-haired Eugenia Sparangapani snap-
pishly, for she was sure that she herself would be gossiped about for
sitting next to the mother of Senator Susemihl, the head of the firm,
who had campaigned against Adam Faust in the election eight years
before, and had recently carried his progressiveness to the point of
supporting the "notorious adventurer," Dr. Urban. There was also
another reason for caution: old lady Susemihl would have loved to
chatter about the rumors linking the penniless Dr. Merckel with the
youngest of the Beyer girls, Kate, the consumptive, who was barely
eighteen, and had chosen the thirty-year-old schoolmaster for her
traveling companion, with the consent even of her English mother, on
going abroad in midsummer to a sanatorium. If the parents don't
mind, whose business is it, Eugenia thought, remembering her own
difficulty in marrying off her daughter Elizabeth.

Now there was a silence, a fluttering of the plumes, a whispering:
the Archbishop had entered the hall. As he strode along, of more than
middle height, red-faced, his sandy hair brushed back, clean-shaven,
wearing no insignia of office with his heavy checked woolen suit, there

was little about him that recalled the prelate. Beside him, in a wrap of iridescent silk, walked the woman who had once been called "the Splendid," Elizabeth Willert, née Sparangapani, the wife of the great banker.

"Church and moneybags arm in arm!" said Felice Gasparra, the creator of the heroic painting, *Strive Toward the Sun and Freedom,* in a stage whisper to the progressive poetess, Diana Rose.

Edward von Brick, a bearded Wotan figure, our Federal Commissioner of Public Safety, rose to welcome them. He had already reached such a pass that he fled to the solitude of music halls and great public gatherings: the trills of suburban songstresses and the ripple of speeches, the commands of the plate-laden waiters as they kicked open the kitchen doors, and the bawling interruptions of drunks filled his soul with the peace of oblivion.

The Bishop took a seat in the very middle, next to Mrs. Jacob Willert, who fell asleep before he could speak to her; and Dr. Daruhi, the rebuttal speaker and president of the Paracelsus Society, mounted the speakers' platform. People had watched him filling a slip of paper with notes during the affirmative speech of our enthusiastic Alderman Heidemann, but he interrupted only once. This was when Heidemann, mentioning modern mathematics—which, he said, had "far surpassed the naïve Euclid, as one would expect of our dynamic age"—introduced the extended axiom of parallels: "Two parallels intersect at infinity."

"And what about the circle?" cried Daruhi. "Supposing we take a circle of infinite extent; are all the points on its circumference still equidistant from the center?"

"Of course not!" cried the intrepid city father without a moment's reflection. "Because presupposing an infinitely large circle, its center may be assumed to be anywhere, at any point within the circumference."

"Ah, most consistent!" murmured the hypnotist, while this hint of the grandeur of the century made the ladies' hearts shiver with awe.

Now that Daruhi was on the platform, reaching for the glass to take a sip of water before starting his speech, the solitaire on his right hand sparkled, and the ladies raised their lorgnettes to look at the "mountebank." The dark-brown hair above the powdered face with its piercing eyes rose in curly waves; the pince-nez on the black ribbon dangled over the high-buttoned white waistcoat with its double row of dark-red glass buttons; there was an orchid in the lapel of his long frock coat, and in the bulging cream-colored ascot that filled the opening of the waistcoat was a dark pearl set about with diamonds. The spiritual adviser and protégé of our conservative families had no very scientific look about him. And he made a bad start as well: confused by the hissing of a dozen young people whom Dr. Urban, the "political adventurer," had sent to the meeting, he felt obliged to apologize for the large bills he submitted to his rich patrons.

Then, turning toward the Bishop, he retracted a statement censured by the *Church Times;* he had meant to say—but how hard it was, even for an author, to express such a complicated relationship!—he had meant to say that an undefined fear descended upon mankind, not *as* a fog, but like a fog, or comparably to a fog. To regard conscience as gaseous was the way of the materialists, not his way—just as he had never asserted that the cheese had considered the matter, or that hope was rectangular.

At these words Senator Beyer opened his eyes, turned his head toward his partner, and asked: "What do you call that?"

"An unexpected thrust in the opening gambit," replied Dr. Merckel, smiling.

"Since the human soul, or, as people evasively call it, the psyche," Daruhi went on, "is found in continual contact with mundane objects —in direct contact with certain parts of the gray cortex, and in indirect contact with the nervous system of the body and thus with objects outside the body—my statement regarding an ethereal fog whose descent I said caused the 'undefined fear' that oppresses us is not beyond the bounds of possibility. I made this statement, however, not because it expresses something possible, but in order to call your attention, ladies and gentlemen, to the dreadfully and mysteriously *simultaneous* appearance of very different symptoms, all indicating a mortal sickness of the spirit. Within fifty years—simultaneously, from the historian's point of view—civilized man has accepted the following dogmas, and proclaimed them as science:

"1. The real is spatial. The nonspatial does not exist. (This is materialist monism.)

"2. Man as a social being acts according to his material interests.

That which proves expedient for his preservation and advancement he calls 'truth.'

"3. 'Eternal verities' spring from the efforts of a ruling class to maintain its sovereignty.

"4. The Euclidean system of geometry, regarded but yesterday as absolutely certain and 'eternally true,' is antiquated. Parallels meet at infinity. The center of an infinite circle is not equidistant from every point on its circumference.

"Of these four assertions, which together are called 'the foundation of modern science,' only the first, although no less false than the others, is at least of ancient origin. But it isn't the origin of the others, and indeed no one of the four originally led to any of the others; on the contrary, they were all enunciated and believed simultaneously—as if a fog had descended, or the indwelling spirit of the world had resolved to unmask our mechanically inventive century as the stupidest and lowest within the memory of man."

And Dr. Daruhi began his analysis of the four assertions: "The mistaken opinion," he said, "that the world is an 'infinite space' or an enlarged nursery furnished with bodies and intervening spaces, derives from the preponderant part played in the life of every human being by the senses of sight and touch. It is quite true that with our five senses we have only sensory perceptions; we perceive only what is corporeal or spatial and its attributes—in other words, objects. And it is thousands of years before man discovers his five senses and their meaning: but once having discovered them, he supposes that what can be learned through the senses and through instruments constitutes the whole of reality. This is a childish belief, and not without its dangers; for if it is taken seriously and proclaimed (under the name of 'materialism') as a science, the learned child promptly aims his telescope upward, and insists on finding God where He is obviously not to be found—in space.

"And yet if our mechanically inventive century had but a trace of the honesty and good will possessed by our forefathers, we might discover precisely by means of its instruments what naïver men have long known—that reality is not fully described by simply listing physical bodies and their relationships. Yes, my dear lady," cried the hypnotist, fixing the sleeping wife of the great banker with his eye, "why not summon our machinery to your assistance? If your finger hurts, examine every tiny cell of the painful spot with a supermicroscope to enlarge it a billion times, and see whether, for instance, the intervals among the vibrating atoms house the pain, whose reality you will not deny, at least so long as you are the sufferer!"

Applause broke out in the rear rows, was hissed down, and swelled again, re-enforced by stamping (a form of scholastic approval in favor at the time). On the broad window sills of one of the casement windows that reached almost to the floor sat a broad-shouldered lad with a strand of blond hair hanging down. His high forehead was covered with beads of sweat; his square chin and firm mouth emphasized the lower part of his face. Daruhi motioned to him; the student called: "Quiet!" Ladies' hats pivoted. The applause stopped. It seemed to be understood that as the clapping died away, the hissers must also quiet down.

And, starting with physical pain, which he said could be discovered neither within nor without the body, or in other words nowhere, and which yet was an indubitable reality, the hypnotist discharged dart after dart at the materialists.

"For, speaking not delicately and foggily (or, in other words, fraudulently), but rudely and plainly, bringing sense and nonsense out into the daylight, the materialistic monist cannot but maintain that the brain exudes ideas, indeed that the brain exudes love and hatred, unbelief, confidence, and certainty; and since these exudations are of the brain, that is, corporeal—otherwise there can be no monism! —they must have physical attributes: extent and form, at the very least. If this is the case, gentlemen, then please do say rudely and plainly what I said to begin with: that hope, for instance, may be rectangular, the will bright red, confidence pot-bellied, or that certainty smells of violets, and despair has reached a height of five hundred feet, or disappointment has gained four pounds. If, on the other hand, the psychic is asserted to be an attribute of the physical, we must concede that the cucumber salad was firmly resolved, or that the cheese had considered the matter: there is nothing else behind your monistic assertion that 'matter thinks.'"

The rebuttal speaker had shouted out the last sentences like a child reciting the catechism. The rich Beyer asked for the second time, "What do you call that?" and the young schoolmaster replied: "A breach in the middle game!"

Alois Borstel, not yet quite spherical, and with nerves already weakened, although in addition to locomotives he also made cannon, wiped the sweat from his chalky face and beckoned to an attendant. He was led out. In later times, with a better knowledge of his own constitution, he would leave voluntarily whenever the discussion rose above the level of ordinary amiability. "Everyone must bow to science; that's my motto!" he used to say. He loved high-flown talk above all things, and achieved mastery in it; but he favored his heart, and kept his friends.

"Dogma Number Two of the apostles of enlightenment, that man acts 'according to his interests,'" Daruhi went on, "is based on the superficial view that we can see behind our desires—or, putting it another way, that we can watch and supervise ourselves. I would point out to the government that this doctrine tends to deny demons, or, if you prefer, instinct. It is therefore dangerous: the hound of hell will not submit to being chained for the cream puff of persuasion; he comes to heel through fear."

Here there was a great outburst of noise; Daruhi leaned forward, listening to the yells: "Boo! Scared cat!" He was, they shouted, calling for the police to stop free investigation.

Mrs. Willert awoke and looked around her distractedly; the student watchman on the window sill restored quiet.

Daruhi promised to skip over assertion number three, saying he thought it was too silly, but he would like to know what sovereignty the Egyptian garret mathematician was trying to defend when he discovered the "eternal verity" that the sum of the angles of a triangle was equal to two right angles!

"It isn't an eternal verity at all!" yelled Heidemann. "Old fossils!" said someone else, and one of the political adventurer's young men stirred jubilation in the rear benches by saying, in a grandfatherly bass, "If we had some ham we could have some ham and eggs, if we had the eggs!"

"Not an eternal verity?" asked Daruhi.

"No, because the spherical triangle—" yelled Heidemann, but got no further, because Daruhi retorted: "Was Euclid talking about the spherical or the plane triangle?"

The president, jingling his bell, announced a ten-minute intermission. While he personally preferred excitement to monotony, he said, still the speaker as well as the gentlemen interlocutors and the guests in general must be allowed a chance to wet their whistles at the buffet. Indeed he could not but include among the "eternal verities" the familiar saying:

> *For the scholar to wassail is proper and right:*
> *If. the lamp has gone dry, can it give any light?*

This was the first cheerful moment since Daruhi's appearance, and people applauded as if relieved of a burden. Police Senator Baron von Brick, convinced that all was over, made good his escape.

BOOK ONE

THE EXTENDED AXIOM OF PARALLELS

IV

ALL attempts to arrange a "friendly mingling" of the Paracelsus people with the apostles of enlightenment along the buffets in the white dining room next door were given up, to such an extent had the first part of the rebuttal spoiled people's good humor. No one had any doubt that it was altogether Daruhi's fault, not even the ladies and gentlemen who asked for introductions to Mrs. Beyer in order to establish their claims to an invitation. What could one do, however, against this man whom the Bishop had shaken hands with as he left the platform, and who sat on the hostess' right at the great Willert dinners? Certainly he was being pushed ahead. And while the conversation, circumnavigating the reefs of the assigned subject, turned toward family events, people thought gratefully of Alderman Heidemann, who had cast no suspicion on anyone, offended no one, but innocently celebrated the "more glorious future" out of a heart overflowing with contentment, and radiated confidence and a pleasant glow to the assembly.

Among the Natural Science people, the least attention was paid to Dr. Urban's group of young people, who jeered at Daruhi as a moss-backed old bore, and promised to spit upon him "until he was under water." The professors were standing around Professor Bock, the industrial chemist, coinventor of a world-famous poison gas: "Daruhi goes back to fundamentals, like his teacher, Andrew Zorn. That was modern too, a hundred years ago; but research today is concerned with results—with results, gentlemen, not fundamentals. On the contrary, I judge by the results whether the fundamentals are still valid, or have begun to grow shaky. Besides, if the psychic element isn't present anywhere, as Daruhi himself says, then surely I have a right to stick to its physical equivalent, haven't I? I can't experiment with nothing, now can I?"

Only the small group of authors gathered around Professor Schiele, the editor of the monthly magazine *Freedom and Culture,* his son Nicholas Edwin (an essayist who seemed to justify great hopes), the dramatist Mark Antony Perlotta, and the graceful Diana Rose, scented the political significance.

"What's he trying to do—attract the government's attention?" said the fragile Nicholas Edwin indignantly. "To what? Himself?"

"No, you!" said Mark Antony Perlotta.

"I can dispense with the honor, thank you," hissed the little man. "I think he's improper, absolutely improper!" And he made a violent gesture of vexation with his hip.

"Old Daruhi's making himself ridiculous!" said Professor Heidemann, joining the group.

"In whose eyes? Only in ours, unfortunately! Not in the eyes of those who matter," observed Mark Antony.

"We don't matter?"

"No, unluckily."

"And who does?"

"Those who have the power—the government, that is, and the General Staff."

"Intellect doesn't matter?"

"No, unfortunately."

"Listen to him! An intellect libeling the intellect!" twittered the graceful Diana Rose. "Isn't he delicious?" She tossed the dramatist a glance.

"You don't think Daruhi's finished, do you?" Mark Antony went on. "Why, he's only begun; naturally he's holding his best number, the extended axiom of parallels, for the third act, the clever rogue. Remember his interruption about the circle."

"Honestly, now, Mark Antony," said Schiele senior, "who's interested in this whole debate, anyway? How many of the audience—two, three, four?"

"Less than that," said Perlotta. "Naturally Daruhi is talking out of the window; but tomorrow evening millions of people will be reading what he said, and since he speaks in a popular way, millions will understand him."

"I doubt it."

"All right, they may not understand, but they'll sniff the air: they'll sniff and see that as of today the wind is blowing from a new quarter."

"Putting it bluntly: that the government is going to interfere, you mean?" asked Habermann, an art historian whose trousers were too long.

"Naturally, you simple Simon!" said Perlotta.

"I think the government would be biting off more than it could chew!" threatened Nicholas Edwin Schiele, clenching his tiny fist. "Against the iron phalanx of intelligence——"

"Where is this phalanx?" asked Perlotta. "Where, I ask you?"

"If it *isn't,* it *will* be!" cried the little man. "For there are bounds to the power of the tyrant."

Just then the chairman's bell rang, the audience slowly filled the hall, and Daruhi, accompanied by the young man who was directing the applause of the conservative students, came out of the speakers' room, and sat down on a bench against the platform.

"Come and sit down, Bruno," he said. "In my egotism I forgot to ask about your new invention."

"The Zorn signal light," said the young man, beaming. He was a son of Andrew Zorn, and had studied at the technical academy in Mittelburg; he had already sold two inventions to the Northeastern Railway.

Elizabeth Willert, thirty-seven years old, defeated but still beautiful, approached, held out her hand to Bruno Zorn to kiss, and raised her celebrated eyes. Jacob had recently averred that they were mechanical, like a doll's, and if he had known it sooner, he would never have married her. These eyes she raised to the counselor of consciences.

"You wizard," she said, "you have flung everything down before you again."

"Excepting my friend Elizabeth," replied Daruhi. "Because she was asleep."

She slapped his face with her glove, widened the mechanical eyes again, and went to her seat, for the bell was sounding its third summons.

Welcomed by a brief, loud stamping, Daruhi proceeded, as had been foreseen, directly and without preamble to the axiom of parallels.

"When the teacher says, 'Draw a straight line on the board,' we know that what the pupil draws is not a straight line, nor even a surface, but a body consisting of chalk. We see this body, but we can see equally well what the teacher calls a straight line, namely the length or edge of the body. We cannot draw an edge without drawing something that has an edge: but we *see* the edge; we *see* the line! We see ideas. The whole substance of gometry is ideas that we see, or, in other words, it is universal and immutable. The theorems of geometry are not individual and variable statements, but definitions of quantitative, universal, and immutable attributes—that is, laws. Here or on the planet Sirius, in hell and along the Milky Way, the sum of the angles of a plane triangle is two right angles: for locality is foreign to the triangle.

"Before a human being appeared on the earth, the sum of the angles of a plane triangle was two right angles, and the center of a circle was equidistant from every point on the circumference. Time is foreign to the triangle, as it is to any other mathematical figure. And the relationships among mathematical figures—for instance, the equality of the alternate angles formed by parallels and a diagonal—*are;* they neither come into being nor pass away. They *are*—no matter whether any consciousness discovers and expresses them or not. Accordingly, the laws of mathematics are 'eternal verities.'

"If the teacher were to say to the pupil, 'Suppose you draw one parallel on the board!' the whole class would laugh. But when world-famous scholars talk of *two* parallels (which after all is equally stupid), and proceed, piling up mountains of nonsense, to have the parallels running (as if a mathematical figure were mobile), running on side by side like two tireless old nags until they reach infinity, or in other words nonsense, for the word 'infinite' has no positive significance—

when they do this, no one has the grace to laugh any more, so rotten has our century become.

"What does 'parallel' mean, ladies and gentlemen? 'Parallel' means an identity of distance separating several lines, no matter where I may measure that distance—on the planet Sirius, in fairyland, or in hell. If 'parallelism,' then, means that the distance separating several lines is the same, no matter where measured—and the word 'parallel' means nothing else—what am I to think of a generation that describes as *parallel* two lines that meet somewhere—in the Hereafter, for all I care? For my part I believe such a generation belongs under police supervision."

When the chairman had restored order, Daruhi went on: "That was not a threat. Now if the doctrine of 'intersecting parallels' were merely a scientific mistake, like the doctrine of 'infinite space,' or if at least it were a product of the imagination, like our forefathers' belief in monster ash trees that grew into the sky, Midgarth serpents that encircled the earth, and fire-breathing monsters, I would not have wasted an unkind word. Mistakes and figments of the imagination go with us through life; the latter, incidentally, always express something possible, never complete nonsense. But there are a few simple matters in regard to which neither mistakes nor imaginative activity occur. If a healthy, full-grown man asks me to explain 'right' and 'left' to him, or says he doesn't know what 'round' means, then that is not a matter of error or imagination, but hypocrisy. Parallelism is something just as simple as yesterday and tomorrow, round and blue: and both error and imagination leave simple things untouched. That a monstrous serpent might encircle the earth, I can imagine. That parallels should touch or intersect is something a person can only *say*, but not *imagine*.

"Accordingly, an 'extended axiom of parallels' must have some other origin than misconception or fantasy. It is an invitation to mankind to regard an unmeaning sequence of words, i.e., nonsense, as truth. It is an invitation to mankind to learn brute assertions by rote, and to submit to arbitrary authority. It is an invitation to mankind to worship what has never yet existed, and to despise the accustomed order because of its antiquity. It is an invitation to mankind to betray conscience and reason to the phrasemaker."

Thus ended the rebuttal speech on the first day. Daruhi's motion that the government be petitioned to remove the "extended axiom of parallels" and its corollary theories from the curriculum of the academies was defeated.

Six weeks later the Senate increased the Federal Police by 64,000 men, violent debates having preceded.

THE GEISENHEIM DISTURBANCES

V

WHILE the police bill was still under debate bloody disturbances broke out in the southern mining province, the old hotbed; the miners' villages of Bergdorf and Carolswald went up in flames, the Lienhardts' château near Marienhall was blown sky-high with dynamite supplied for mine blasting, the eldest of the Lienhardt brothers was pulled out of the brook bordering the estate with two stab wounds in his temple, and murders of such cruelty occurred that the age of witches and flagellants seemed to have returned. When the number of victims passed three hundred, the governor, a Mr. von Radowitz, declared martial law and ordered the expulsion of all persons without passports or the right of domicile. Radowitz was immediately relieved of his post; Count Bessonoff, commander of the Geisenheim infantry brigade, took his place as provisional administrator of the province, and a Senate investigating committee, headed by Beyer and Jacob Willert, set out for Geisenheim, the provincial capital.

Outside the station, which had been built away from the town in order to preserve the scenery, stood kerchiefed, dark-eyed girls with their sweethearts, mothers and children, and pupils from the schools; but "in view of the shameful outrages so recently perpetrated" the city had not been allowed to offer the Senatorial committee a festive welcome, although the head of the diocese, the highly respected Bishop von Hesse, had bombarded the President with telegrams. Had there not been at least partial expiation already? Three hundred dead, the Lienhardt mines closed, families dependent on charity! If the government were to march in as an angel of atonement a week too late, the distress would simply be made worse by the departure of those who were here on holiday, taking the cure!

Despite the order prohibiting a reception, Bishop Hesse had posted on the open platform, with white dresses and bouquets, his two grand-daughters, Eva and Claire Crémieux, the children of his eldest daughter, who was married to a Lyon silk manufacturer. As the train, winding its way up Chapel Hill, came out into the straightaway, they waved their tiny kerchiefs; the schoolboys clambered up on the fence and the plum trees along the line, waved their caps, and shouted.

"This is a tender sort of view, somehow," said Jacob Willert, who was standing with his cousin Beyer at a train window. "If things are as they should be, all the girls here must be beautiful."

The experts and secretaries in the next compartment put on their hats.

"The loveliest are the women of forty," said Beyer. "You'll see."

"Why?"

"Because the softness is gone, and the contours stand out. I mean the Roman shape of their faces. Of course the young lads are all born with a knife in their boot, and it was some Helen or other that they destroyed Carolswald for."

"And Bergdorf," Jacob added. "The Helen's name was Kate Schwann."

The train rolled slowly to a stop, guards in Sunday uniforms opened the car doors, the schoolboys raced around the station and crashed through the shrubbery to the fence in order to exercise their critical faculties on the panting locomotive. Eva and Claire Crémieux spoke their piece and had their heads patted; Count Bessonoff, the newly appointed governor, gray at the temples and wearing the ill-fitting mufti of an old officer, said something that sounded like, "Welcome, gentlemen, we shall soon see," and was addressed by Jacob as "neighbor." The Bessonoffs' town house in the capital was on Lady Square next to the Willerts' palace. Then the mayor stepped forward, a true son of the region with his brown, weather-beaten complexion, his angular aquiline nose, his drooping mustache; Jacob thought of the "knife in the boot," and felt it would have been more interesting to see this man's daughters than Mr. Crémieux's chicks.

The descendant of the Roman frontier guards said he hoped the gentlemen would be satisfied with their quarters at the Black Eagle; rooms were reserved for the rest of the party at the Crown. Outside stood his best three carriages, his pride and joy, he added with a broad smile: "I hope you gentlemen will use them for sight-seeing trips and to see how well the guests of our health resort are looked after."

He was a prosperous carriage builder.

Finally old Hesse, who had been Bishop of the mountain province for seven years (the Protestant ecclesiastical heads of provinces carry the title of Bishop), introduced his younger son, Otto, a lieutenant in the Federal Police. He shook hands with the Senators and departed. "They've got enough to keep them busy," his father said. "The jail jammed, questioning going on until far into the night."

"He makes a good impression, your youngest," observed Beyer.

During the drive, the two emissaries rode in one carriage with Count Bessonoff and Hesse. The governor told in a halting voice about his predecessor, Radowitz. Immediately on receiving a telegram from the capital to ask whether he wished to take a leave of absence, he had requested his dismissal. No one had heard the slightest word of resentment or complaint from him. "His virtue (and fault) of making no enemies, his belief that everyone is right in his way, was what brought his downfall. He didn't want to do anything arbitrary—that was all."

"Unfortunately, he never wanted to do anything at all except attend functions," replied Beyer, "because he made two mistakes. No. 1, he thought a conservative politician was one who left everything as it was. No. 2, he thought if he didn't do anything, everything would stay as it was."

Darkness was falling as they drove in through one of the arched gates to the city, and although because of the resort traffic the town council had ordered the cobblestones smoothed off as well as possible, the rubber-shod and excessively high carriage wheels bounced up and down enough to disrupt the conversation. Jacob Willert, a lifelong lover of beauty, admired the century-old houses. "They're alive, they're alive," he whispered: "That there is a nose, that's a handkerchief," and he nudged his elder cousin Beyer in the ribs.

"When you see the place by day and on foot, Senator," said Hesse, full of local pride, "you'll feel that the streets are alive too, and the bridges; in fact, even the quarters of the town are like a family of lanes, squares, fountains, and bridges—at odds, as families often are, but families nevertheless."

"Deceased families lying in state," observed the sober-minded Bessonoff, "embalmed for the spectators. The town has lived on tourists for a hundred years."

"Not even half the town," retorted Jacob, and an argument ensued between him and the governor.

"These lanes are melodies. Our modern cities are sets of false teeth, with big gaps everywhere."

"No doubt, Senator. Nevertheless, they live by working. And what does Geisenheim live on? On the rich people who come from elsewhere and buy places here to die in. You've heard the name of Crémieux. Radowitz is a stranger too; that patrician house of his on the market place belongs to his wife. But the rats would have chewed it up, house and wife both, if Radowitz hadn't come thirty years ago and married both of them."

"Did he marry in order to die here?"

"Certainly!" And at last, thinking he sensed a change of mood, Bessonoff came out with his request. Mr. von Radowitz would be greatly pleased to welcome the Senators to dinner. The only other guests would be Hesse and his Catholic colleague, Bishop Oriola. The former governor regarded himself as a private citizen—no politics, no evening clothes, a little music in the drawing room after dinner. He himself, Bessonoff, unfortunately had to work.

The invitation was accepted. The carriage turned in under a dark, narrow archway that echoed to the noise of the horses' hoofs, and stopped in the central courtyard of the inn.

DINNER AT OLD RADOWITZ'S

VI

HALF an hour later the two emissaries welcomed the officially humiliated man, who had accepted his "leave of absence" with a haste that seemed to tell against him. But when he left, a man of almost seventy, "to make a few more preparations—men do the cooking here!" he added with a smile as proud as if he were about to entertain barbarians—the two were no longer so sure that he and Lieutenant Colonel Laurenti could have prevented what had happened "by the application of energetic official measures."

That evening they dined at the patrician mansion of the Radowitzes that "the rats had almost eaten"—"They'd already begun to gnaw a little!" whispered Jacob to Augustus Beyer, for the old lady was spare and bony. Bishop Oriola, a tall, distinguished man with the Roman nose common to the natives, began telling anecdotes "to make the gentlemen from the north feel at home in our mountains."

The "mountains" were a range of hills 125 miles long, none really high enough for a mountain, with many outlying spurs, and forested with evergreens.

"One fine day Anton Schwann, the father of our poor Kate and of the possibly innocent Albert, goes to see a patient. He's a follower of the revival mission, and cures by prayer and laying on of hands."

"But you're libeling me after all, you old Jesuit," interrupted Hesse. "We had put a stop to Schwann's doctoring long since."

"Not so long," retorted the Catholic leader. "For it was seventeen years ago, and Schwann went in to see Sister Antonia, a young farm woman who was in bed with a hot brick on her stomach, suffering from cramps. When he came in, the pain eased a little. 'The devil went out of me when he saw you,' said the grateful Antonia. Schwann, first feeling under the blankets to see whether the brick, wrapped in cloth, was hot enough, went over to the window."

"This is certain to be something indecent," said Mrs. von Radowitz. Her white hair was parted in the middle, wavy at the temples. A large knot at the nape of the neck created the impression that it was abundant.

"Please have a moment's patience, dear lady," said the priest. " 'Aha!' cried Schwann, 'do you know where your devil went to? Come and look at him jumping around!' And he pointed to Antonia's one goat, which was walking placidly around the yard. A sense of modesty kept the woman from getting out of bed."

"Dear God, what a lie!" said Mrs. von Radowitz in a stage whisper.

" 'Get that goat away from the farm,' cries the practitioner, 'or the devil will find his way back!' And he waved to his son to put a rope on the goat. 'I'll see what I can do,' Schwann reassured Antonia, 'but if the devil doesn't go out of it, it'll have to be butchered and the meat burned.' And so he acquired the goat, but he wasn't satisfied with that."

"Just what I thought!" whispered the old lady. It was well known that she snapped at all women, and did not feel comfortable except among men.

"While our friend is still looking out into the yard and thinking things over, the brick cools off, and the pain comes back. 'Damned rascal, I'll pull you out, never fear!' cries Schwann, meaning the devil, runs over to the bed, throws the brick on the floor, and . . . uh . . ."

"Didn't I say so?"

"You hit the mark, Madam," the Bishop agreed.

"She didn't, Anton Schwann hit the mark!" cried the former governor, his eyes twinkling at his guests, and his round face with its white pointed beard was sheer merriment.

"*Assez,* Bernard!" said the old lady. "I'm afraid our guests will get the wrong impression of our local ways."

Jacob Willert, reaching for a peach, inquired whether this method of cure had been "Effective—I prefer to avoid the word fruitful."

"Oh, yes, in court, because Antonia was a widow," replied the priest. "You finish the story, Hesse."

"We threw him out of the brotherhood——"

"For twelve months," Oriola pointed out.

"Yes, for twelve months."

"Because of his methods of cure?" asked Beyer.

"No; for impropriety in court. He didn't deny it at all. He testified under oath that just at the moment when the goat was being led through the gateway Antonia's devil left it, and entered into him to tempt him. He said the devil had been extraordinarily strong, even stronger than his fear of God. And so, although he had prayed and trembled until he broke out in a cold sweat, he had succumbed to the tempter."

Bishop Oriola's long, muscular face quivered with suppressed mirth. Mrs. von Radowitz had to put down her coffee cup to keep from spilling, and she said, hiccuping and holding her napkin to her mouth, "He hasn't so much as a word of defense for a brother revivalist!"

"There's nothing to defend," said Hesse, "and not much to accuse, either, I must say."

A silence followed, during which Jacob Willert looked in amazement at the two jolly clerics: a painful tension while everyone tried to discover some subject of conversation remote from the dreaded theme. In vain: Beyer was already asking whether the two missing ringleaders, the youngest Lienhardt and Dr. Urban, had fled or were being hidden.

"Hidden?" asked Count Bessonoff, changing color; he had come in for the music. Just then Mrs. von Radowitz broke up the dinner, saying they would take coffee and liqueurs in the music room. The doorbell rang. The expected pair of artists had arrived, accompanied by the singer's father.

The musical evening went off without incident; the Senators promised to receive the singer, who complained of discrimination, during office hours.

This was on a Monday. On Thursday Jacob Willert sent his first report to the President.

BOOK ONE

JACOB WILLERT TO THE PRESIDENT

VII

MY DEAR OLD FRIEND AND WELL-WISHER:

As my travels so far have always taken me northward, never in the opposite direction, I have been seeing such things as never were. What do you say to a hotel where you don't go in at the front, like a decent citizen, but from the back, through the courtyard, after driving under an echoing arch as if you were going straight into an old ballad? The courtyard is surrounded by wooden balconies on two stories, supported by columns, which make arcades covered with vines. The latter, to say nothing of the roofed balconies themselves, darken the rooms that open on the courtyard, just as if twilight was the natural light for anyone who stays in a room, because in them things are not done but committed, things that people of past centuries apparently never got enough of; for all the rooms of the amazing old-fashioned houses, even Mrs. von Radowitz's (whose husband, by the way, is innocent), are darkened by oriel windows, broad window sills, and preposterous panes.

In view of such circumstances, and because the air resounds with memories—of violent passions, I mean, which are fed bloodily in broad daylight, *and* in the twilight—the disturbances seem to me natural and in harmony with the local tradition of the country. So I advise you not to pay too much heed to the legalistic scribblings of the experts we have brought with us, but to wait for the inclusive report of a native, Matthew Brandt, the town clerk and archivist, of whom I have carried away an excellent impression. This Brandt—now please don't say *aha!*—has a daughter Louise, a singer, aged twenty-nine, who sang for us our first evening here; she's married to the conductor of the resort band, Richard Hofer, a fashionable kept man, I should think, though faces sometimes lie. She's a ripe strawberry blonde of heroic stature, with a flawless silvery alto voice; why did she ever marry that fellow, who will never do anything but let her womanly charms work for his comfort? But of course women do run after band leaders (poor von Brick!). In short, as she begged me on bended knees when I saw her during my office hours, I shall promote the pair to the capital, with the ulterior purpose of putting this Hofer in place of Hollberg, who is such a trial to our Police Senator. Anyone who looks smart and can read a page of music can lead a band—we needn't fool ourselves about that. So far as the strawberry-blonde Brünnhilde is concerned, in order to show you that I have no entanglements, I shall recommend her to Hans Simon, Maier Herschel's art-loving son and heir.

One thing more: the idea that religious conflicts had anything to do with starting the disturbances is sheer nonsense. Owing perhaps to Hesse's old-fashioned Christianity there are no conflicts between Protestants and Catholics here, indeed scarcely any differences; to judge by a story that Bishop Oriola told at Radowitz's house, you would think Hesse's Protestant revivalists, also known as pietists, were more Catholic than the Catholics.

Last but not least: in the five-minute interview you gave me before I left, you spoke of the "great moment," of "now or never," but unfortunately you were in a state of enthusiasm that added little or nothing to the intelligibility of what you said. You said we would have an opportunity to turn the united mines into a vest-pocket model of Zorn's ideal state. That was all; and I, being polite and in a hurry, said, "All right," not stopping to think that your enthusiasm was bent on the awakening of a "new life" from the ruins of the mining villages. Arriving here and trying to get the lay of the land, I discover in the transactions of the court an artifice, secretiveness, and obfuscation that I do not like: I hate to be thought gullible. Please be kind enough to enlighten me; if you send the letter by one of the special couriers, Messerschmidt or Bogatzki, nothing can go wrong; I'll send it back to you, sealed, by the same man. I'll stick by you through thick and thin, but I do like to know what goes on. As matters now stand, I cannot rid myself of a suspicion that Augustus Beyer knows more than

Your old friend and pupil,

JACOB WILLERT

CONFUSION IN COURT

VIII

THE blind burning and destruction had rendered homeless half the 2500 inhabitants of the two mountain villages; they were bedded down in the barracks, in the Convent of St. Odilia, and in the gymnasium of the commercial school. Four hundred suspicious characters went to jail.

But as so often happens after sanguinary outbreaks, the longer the hearings went on, the more complicated and confused became the motives, and anything that was not brought to light, with no great effort, within twenty-four hours was obscured by contradictory testimony. The youngest Lienhardt, Peter George by name, and his friend Dr. Urban, founder of the League for Enlightenment and Economic Peace, were not to be found; all fury was therefore concentrated on them. But the investigation by the President's personal jurist, Supreme Court Justice Holzkopf, from the capital, made so little sense that people began to whisper and spread rumors that the celebrated illuminator of criminal obscurity had been dispatched to the mountain province in order to conceal the political background underlying the bloody acts.

Jacob Willert, at all events, refused to believe that the President's legal adviser was as poorly informed as he pretended to be concerning the life and doings of the "Carpenters," who had started the trouble. Favoritism, accordingly, must be involved: the Order of Carpenters, an autonomous brotherhood by now not entirely secular, brought into being by Andrew Zorn, developed and pampered by the bishops, must be shielded from scandal.

"I do not wish to know, Defendant Charles Froehlich," the judge shouted, "I am not at the moment interested in knowing, what brotherhood you belong to, whether you are an agricultural laborer, miner, or carpenter. I want to know why you rang the church bells on the evening of October ninth at Carolswald."

"Because young Schwann, the bookkeeper, said to me: 'Ring the bells immediately!' because when the bells are rung hereabouts, all the men assemble in the Church Square."

"In other words, if any private citizen tells you to do something, you do it?"

"Albert Schwann isn't a private citizen, he's a brother."

"What kind of brother?"

"In the Fellowship of Carpenters."

"But confound it, you aren't a carpenter."

"No, but I'm a brother, a lay brother, and—not yet of equal rank with Brother Schwann."

"Where are you a lay brother?"

"In the fellowship."

"Mr. Magistrate," said the presiding judge in an exasperated tone, "please don't take up the court's time with half-baked cases. Take the man out! I want to know within twenty-four hours what system of obedience existed there, and the bylaws of the fellowship are to be placed in evidence."

When the defendant Charles Froehlich was about to be led out, the presiding judge called him back.

"One more question. You were a sort of writer of petitions and legal adviser?"

"Yes, Your Honor."

"You have clients in both villages, in Bergdorf and Carolswald?"

"Yes, Your Honor."

"Did all your clients know that you were a lay brother in the Order of Carpenters? Be careful that you tell the truth: I have a hundred witnesses at hand."

"Not all of them knew it."

"Who did *not* know?"

"The Urbanites."

"Aha! Please remove the defendant. Next!"

Bishops Hesse and Oriola concurred in testifying that the Christian Workers' Fellowships were not secret bodies, and maintained no secret service. Nor had any officer or member of the board of these fellowships given any encouragement to violence. The newly admitted members were called novices or lay brothers, but not a word of the bylaws indicated any requirement of obedience. If Brother Charles Froehlich nevertheless believed he must obey Brother Albert Schwann, then ancient customs must have been revived without the knowledge of the officers.

"But if they find out about it, what do the officers do?"

"The officers can advise the members, but they are not there to police them," replied Hesse.

"What have you got to say about it, Bishop Oriola?"

Oriola asked to have the courtroom cleared, and testified in secret session that the murders of Kate Schwann and Theresa Froehlich proved that the Fellowship of Carpenters was being obliged to act in self-defense, and probably had been on the defensive for some time. Accordingly, the fellowship, as a living organism, must be conceded a right to defend itself by the same methods its enemies used.

"But that's sheer feudalism," said the Supreme Court Justice, controlling himself with an effort. "That's anarchy."

The two clerics said nothing, and while Holzkopf was readmitting the public to the court, Jacob Willert asked his brother-in-law, Odo Sparangapani, an expert in penal law, to take his place, and went out; he was confused and agitated, for it seemed to him as if the two bishops, talking so cheerfully and laughing so amiably, were living in a world unknown to him.

BOOK ONE

THE STATIONERY STORE

IX

JACOB went down Linen Lane, banging the iron tip of the alpenstock he had bought on the steep pavement, his hat pulled down over his eyes and his broad shoulders hunched together to shrink away into insignificance, if only for today, before the looks of women through windows and in Philadelphia mirrors—alas that there was no such thing as a cloak of invisibility!—to shrink away into insignificance at least for today, before public curiosity. How the court disgusted him, all this secretiveness of the assessors, acting as if they "just didn't want to talk," this dragging on and on of the nonessentials, this mutual lurking in wait and this artificial confusion!

Why? Why?

Why could the Carpenters, in costume as if it were Sunday and as if the government had ceased to function, bar the entrance to the Lienhardts' property, refusing admission to anyone, so that the papers were beginning to say quite openly that the mines were on the verge of being flooded? Why were police and the military kept in their barracks?

Jacob had meant to go to his hotel to fetch a forgotten bottle; when he looked around, he found himself on the way to the upper town, where stone steps led up the hill to Bread Lane, which ran parallel. Cats lay there as long as the sun shone and the stones were warm; the air smelled of kitchen herbs, and as one climbed one could see into the side windows of the houses.

This was the beginning of the poor quarter; here were the little shops where anything could be bought—thread, wooden shoes, clothes-lines, imperishable sausages, love-letter writers, and chewing tobacco. Here no one knew him, no one wanted anything, no one spied upon him. Incidentally, he must buy some writing paper. He was in urgent need of writing paper and sealing wax, but first he must get chocolate for her who perhaps no longer expecting him. And he thought of "his Roman lady" as if it had been twenty years before, and the world still young.

He had discovered her on a stroll with Beyer through the upper town, in the pointed little corner shop that sold "official school copy-books," ink, erasers, pens, but also dolls, toys, and cigars; in the show window, decked with pink ribbons and bows, stood cardboard boxes of writing paper, and on real tracks outside a tiny station was a tin train, rather dusty, with a motor that wound up. The man with the red peaked cap before the station was holding up his staff. When the two entered the shop, she was standing on the ladder, stretching at arms' length to get some kind of paper, apparently printed forms, out of their box on the shelves. With a quick glance Jacob took in the slim ankles, the knot of brown hair fastened with cheap pins above the brownish neck, and the arms, thin, but not weak, for she picked up the box without effort; her fingers were long. She tossed the printed forms on the counter, put the box back into place, and climbed down. "A Roman lady!" thought Jacob, looking at her. "That's an old family's nose and chin." From the middle of her short, pale upper lip protruded two front teeth a trifle too long, which, while the customer was looking at the paper, she polished with her tongue, whether from shyness or coquetry. Her hands and the wrinkles in her neck were dusty, like the counter, but her brown hair seemed to have been washed; it gleamed. She had noticed the arrival of the stranger out of the corner of her eye as she came down the ladder. While the girl was wrapping her paper and talking to the customer, Jacob drew his cousin toward the front window, pointed to one of the gift packages, and whispered: "Like her?"

Beyer shook his head.

"I do, though!"

"Then I'll run along."

"I'll be back for dinner," said the youthfully ardent banker, and Beyer followed the purchaser of forms out of the shop.

Jacob was about to take a beribboned box of writing paper out of the window when he sensed that she was standing behind him. "I'll give you a better box, sir. That one there is for the window," she said. Her voice was soft and deep, older than her face, with a hint of dialect. "She knows men," he mourned, and turned to watch her take a box with a wide pink ribbon from a shelf at the side, and blow at it. "Twenty-five sheets, twenty-five envelopes, gentlemen's size, cream," she said, mentioned the price, and polished her front teeth with her tongue.

"Yes, thank you," Jacob agreed.

"What else can I do for you?"

"Do you keep perfume?"

"I'm sorry. But in Broad Street, across from the Crown, you can get marvelous perfume—French." For the second time she beamed at him; her eyes, her half-open mouth, seemed to yearn for the beauty of the world.

Here was the bond between them, the banker felt. He could come back tomorrow and bring her an expensive perfume. He said with a light heart as she wrapped up the box: "And I'd like to buy the train you've got in the window, with the station and stationmaster."

"The train?" This time she was honestly surprised.

"To tell you the truth, I'm here for my health. I'm staying at the Lamb, and beginning to find it tiresome. So I feel like playing with the train for a while of an evening before I go to sleep."

He gazed into the face turned toward him; not a muscle betrayed the swift calculations that youth and poverty were pursuing through her mind: have I really caught the great fish? Dear God, let me have him for five minutes! I know perfectly well that he'll be swimming away soon enough! Just a little while, *please!*

And without stopping to consider, while her face paled, she took the offensive: "Why tell a falsehood, sir? If you want to talk to me, you easily can without lying! You aren't here for your health and you aren't staying at the Lamb. You're staying at the Black Eagle, in the royal suite."

"Completely wrong! The Eagle has no royal suite."

"In the first place it has, and in the second place your picture is on display at the photographer's in Long Lane."

"There are a lot of pictures on display there."

"So there are; one of them has your name under it."

"You're mistaken, young lady!"

"Your name is Senator Jacob Willert. I didn't mean to offend you, Senator, God knows I didn't. Forgive me!"

Jacob reached for his bundle. "I ought to apologize to you, not you to me. Don't misunderstand me: if one mentions one's name, one gets stared at. It's very disagreeable in the long run."

As he put the money on the table she drew back the package: "Of course you needn't carry the package; my lady will send it to your hotel by messenger."

Jacob: "Fine; you send me a messenger."

Her eyes were downcast as he shook hands with her and left the shop.

Late that evening, for sheer impatience, Jacob Willert wrote his second letter to the President, complaining of the danger to the Lienhardt mines, the withholding of the Federal Police, and the confusion in court, and saying that a possibly hidden hand, Urban's or the remaining two Lienhardts', was involved. At last there was a knock; a young lad in the customary jacket of the province, his cap under his arm, came in: he had two packages and a bill to deliver.

"From whom?"

From his sister.

Jacob looked the messenger in the face. Sure enough, it was she, or her boyish image.

"What's your name?" asked the Senator, while in response to his gesture the boy put the parcels on a side table.

"Tobias Witt."

"And your sister?"

"Margaret Witt."

"How old?"

"She's eighteen, two years older than me." Too timid to sit down on the silk sofa, he pulled up a chair, and, holding his cap and the bill in his hand, told about his life as an office boy under Bernard Faust, the mining magnate.

Yes, he was living with his parents in Marienhall. Father, invalided as a result of a mining accident, belonged to the Revival Mission and to the Carpenters. It was undoubtedly the fault of the Urbanites, but strange ones, who weren't known here. They must have come by rail and gone by the evening express, after the murder of Kate Schwann. No, his sister wasn't only a salesgirl—the shop didn't bring in enough for that—but a maid-of-all-work to the owner of the house, a Widow Mantels, who lived on a little income, the shop, and by letting out rooms.

The next three days, said Jacob after a while, leafing through his calendar, would be occupied with inspections. "Four or five days from now I shall go myself and pay your sister for the toys she has been kind enough to send me. Will you tell her that for me?" He gave a thaler to the boy, who said, "Gladly," and got up; bidding him enjoy a supper that was ready for him in the dining room, he returned to his letter.

"There are movable mirrors fastened to window frames," he wrote, "which permit the housewife in her living room to watch your friend and pupil going about his business, yet do not discover the observer, who need not even change her position. This inequality of opportunity is beginning to embitter me; I am considering coming home, and would like to ask your approval." He sealed the letter and went downstairs to hand it to the President's courier, First Lieutenant Bogatzki, who was playing cards in the private drawing room of the hotel with Odo Sparangapani and Beyer.

Now the four days were up. He could have been at liberty sooner,
but very young girls are precisely the ones to look down on a man
who shows impatience. On the other hand, making her wait longer
might be interpreted as pride. Or was she by chance not waiting at
all, but flirting with young lads and boasting that she had conquered
the rich Willert? Who could say? Jacob threw away his cigar. The
perfume, of course, he had forgotten—not to buy, but to take with
him; perhaps that was just as well. The words, "If you want to talk
to me, you can easily!" had sounded whorish and not much like love;
but a bar of chocolate could hardly compromise him. He bought a
reasonably good brand in a basement, with hens cackling outside.
The place smelled of herring and cheese; Jacob began to be hungry.
If she's sensible, he thought, I'll take her out to eat.

When he looked across the railroad and the pink bow into the
stationery store, no one was there, but the rear door leading into the
house was wide open, and he could see down a narrow hall, narrow
and bright, into the yard. The yard door was open too. Was the house
empty? He opened the shop door; an abominable bell, jangling im-
pertinently, tore the silence. At this—Jacob's face lit up with delight—
shoes rattled on the stairs, she ran in, recognized him as he stood
before the counter, and then, sobbing and swallowing like a child
when the pain is almost over, leaned forward on both hands; her
tears fell on the counter.

"What are you crying for?" asked Jacob, clasping her hands.

"I thought you weren't coming."

He raised a hinged flap in the counter, stepped through, and touched
her shoulder. She held out a tear-stained face to him. Joy and youth
were both blotted out.

"The door to the yard is open, Margaret; is your lady out there?"

She pulled away, locked the yard door from the inside, ran back into
the shop, hung a sign, CLOSED, BACK SOON, on the front door, locked that
too, seized Jacob by the hand, and hissed: "The old lady's gone out.
Come!"

When Jacob found himself in her bedroom, he took time to notice
that it was a neat and pleasant little room, and sat down on the bed
beside her; she, with her arms around his neck, whispered: "So you
did come after all?" and he could feel the deep childlike sobs shaking
her afresh. In silence he took the ugly pins out of the knot of hair,

while she helped him. He kissed her fingers, her mouth, her eyes (which were reddened), her neck at the hairline behind the ears. Stammering, pale, shuddering, with swimming eyes, she surrendered herself.

The Senator awoke to find himself alone. He noticed, abashed at his own pedantry, that the dark suit he wore to court, and had not wanted to get crumpled, was hanging over a woman's clothes hanger on the wall. Then the cover over the keyhole moved, the door was unlatched, and Margaret came in. She poured steaming water from a big pitcher into her washbowl, put a half-filled pail beside the bed, and asked him—he had sat up—whether, seeing that it had been a dusty walk, he would like to wash his feet, or she would do it, "very gladly." Jacob thanked her, but said he had taken a bath.

"So did I," she laughed, "in the washtub."

"How completely changed you are!" he said.

"For the worse?"

"No, only changed back to the way you were when I saw you first." She seemed disappointed, and he added: "Even lovelier, in fact; your neck was covered with dust then! Let's see your neck!" She leaned down; he kissed the lobe of her ear, and tried to pull her down to the bed.

"For goodness' sake, the old lady's coming in half an hour! You'd better get up, Senator."

Jacob looked at his watch; it was half-past two. He had slept almost two hours. How pretty the girl looked! She was wearing a black cotton dress, probably her confirmation dress, remade with flounces sewed on below; over this was a white apron newly washed and crackling with starch. And our lover of life, refreshed by his sleep, assured her— laughing merrily in her face—that he was not afraid of old ladies; he had one himself; as a Senator he was obliged to, that was the rule; was she old?

"My old lady? Almost seventy," said the girl. "She's kind to me— she needs somebody to talk to; but if there's a gentleman up here, she'll throw me out." While Jacob was dressing, which she helped him do, he boasted that he would conquer "the old lady." He had been taught as a schoolboy that "you captivate the old ones with gold, the young ones with vows."

She took out the dirty water, and came back bearing an enamel tray with coffee in a plain little pot, milk and sugar.

"Nothing to eat?"

The morning's rolls were eaten up, Margaret confessed. She could run over to the baker's.

"There's no need. Do people here in the upper town know you?"

"No, you see I come from Marienhall. Only the neighbors know me."

He thereupon invited her to dinner.

"When?"

"Tonight, at the Lamb."

She took off her apron and asked whether the dress she was wearing was "good enough."

"Very lovely, but too grand," Jacob talked his way out. He would send her four dresses to choose from, size eighteen, from Stern's Specialty Shop. She was to keep the prettiest two, and send the others back by the messenger.

"But not from Stern's! Stern's is too expensive!"

"For you, but not for me!" he laughed at her, and then apologized by little touches of flattery.

She accompanied him downstairs, opened the shop door, removed the CLOSED, BACK SOON sign, waved to her new friend, and began to consider, as she sat on her stool behind the counter, what sort of fairy tale she must tell the inquisitive old lady when the messenger came with the dresses. The Widow Mantels was an easygoing woman, good-natured, indulgent, and as much of a matchmaker as befitted her years, but an incorrigible gossip. "Well, now that gentlemen's cream writing paper," she said, "if mine weren't better than what Thiele on the market place keeps, I don't suppose Senator Willert, with his four châteaus and ten million thalers, would have needed it...."

Jacob, after getting something to eat at an unpretentious restaurant, marched cheerfully toward the center of town, savoring in advance the fashion-shop atmosphere (which fitted him like a glove), and the conversation he would have with the supervisors. He was not disappointed; the competence of old Mr. Stern, "forty years in this line," was famous throughout the province. The moment the Senator's arrival was announced to him over the house telephone, he sent for Miss Schiller, who, although thirty-three years old, had been honored with the beauty prize of the Geisenheim Carnival Company, and was, in his experience, "the smoothest article you ever saw."

She entered in a high black afternoon dress with a low Russian collar, the gold cross on her breast as blond as her hair, long-legged, eyes downcast, a regular demonic Gretchen.

"Off with those rings, you side-show barker!" the head of the house yelled at her as she came in; she, with a shrug of the shoulders and a haughty smile that said, "Why, you plebeian, you have no idea what handsome means!" stripped the gaudy imitation jewelry from her fingers; a single hoop on her engagement finger remained.

"You will have the honor of waiting on Senator Jacob Willert," said Mr. Stern, reverting to propriety and circling about the saleslady while he picked bits of lint off her dress. "If I told you how much money he has you'd do a double flipflop."

"Pooh!" said Trudy Schiller, disdainfully putting the hand with the ring on her hip. She had been engaged for six months to a widowed clerk in a bank.

"But this honor is also a test, yes, I tell you, a test of your ability, young lady," Mr. Stern went on, while Jacob in the lobby was occupied with the low neck of a dress worn by a saleslady who was bending down to him where he sat in order to explain a "Fashion Album for All Occasions."

"Yes, I say, a test! You haven't got your Mr. Ehlert yet, because, God help him, he belongs to the type of people that are born so careful they turn around at the altar, right before God's face, you might say, burst out of the church door, and are never heard of again."

Good God, I'm not even going to have as much of an adventure as that in my life, thought the prize-winning beauty. She was utterly sure of Mr. Ehlert, the bookkeeper.

"On principle, let me tell you: to a forty-year-old millionaire you couldn't, even *you* couldn't sell what *you* want, but what *he* wants. So the logical result is: you listen, just once in your life for five minutes, not to your own gab, but to the customer—no matter how hard it is! Just *once* for three minutes of your life, don't be selfish!"

That was asking too much on her ridiculous salary, said Schiller.

Sighing deeply, he promised her five per cent, called her his song-bird, his tree of paradise, the prop of his old age; then suddenly, while the clock on the wall struck four, he declared that tomorrow morning he would throw out "all the thirty-two bloodsuckers that fattened on the sweat of his brow," because he was "flat broke anyway." Burying his face in his hands, he predicted that her forwardness would drive away "the best customer anyone ever saw," called her a nail in his coffin, and invoked curses on her posterity.

Gertrude Schiller fled, ran lightfooted down the marble steps, looked in the mirror to see whether the gold cross was hanging straight on its ribbon, made an appearance before Jacob, and implored him, in a voice that had unjustly received no prize, "Will you be so kind, Senator?" The tribe of salesgirls scattered; Gertrude, when she felt she had waited long enough to be noticed, raised her eyes to look full at him. The banker, believing he recognized this mechanical eye opening, was reminded of home, and surveyed the supervisor suspiciously.

Damn! I haven't made an impression! thought Schiller. She was right. His days of being led astray by nurses and madonnas were behind him, and he had gone back to nature.

This left a businesslike manner, a distant and distinguished bearing and the divining of the customer's wishes, or, in other words, a great deal—so Gertrude's fifteen years of experience told her as she accompanied him into the dress department.

But Jacob, confronted with the night- and morning gowns, the lace chemises, drawers, trinkets, toilet articles, and jewelry that filled the displays on the ground floor, confronted with all this trifling and enchanting tinsel, cheap, utterly cheap, but naturally and properly the end and aim of a young girl—Jacob changed his mind. Why should he not outfit his brown Peggy as the servant girls of the Willert mansion were outfitted when they left to get married? He reflected that his wife's most recent hairdresser had already been two years in the house, and could be set to doing some other work, looking after the silver and linen closet, or temporarily doing some light gardening at the palace by the river, and that his once-splendid Elizabeth had even learned not to be surprised when Jacob informed her that a better hairdresser, already engaged, would take up her duties shortly. In a good humor, pleased with the continuation of his adventure, he expressed a desire to buy some underwear and a few of "those shiny things." Which particular ones, they would have to try on and see: for a dark-haired, dark-skinned lady of twenty, size eighteen, shoulders, arms, and hips more powerful than the average, height only half a head shorter than his own.

"Miss Pauli, please," said the supervisor in a low voice to a boy after she had listened attentively to the customer. The boy rushed off and Miss Pauli appeared, an unattractive, painted brunette with Peggy's outlines. Jacob expressed his thanks and satisfaction. By the time he left the store, the happy Schiller had relieved him of a hundred and fifty thalers, earned a commission of two gold pieces herself, and secured his permission to put a ticket, "Purchased by Senator Jacob Willert," into the main show window along with a number of model dresses (of size twenty, it was to be noted). The white-bearded Stern hugged her, and Miss Pauli got a bonus.

Jacob, in festive mood, was awaited at the hotel by the special courier with a message from the President. He invited Mr. von Bogatzki into his rooms, and read the letter, whose envelopes bore three seals and the notation "confidential."

BOOK ONE

THE PRESIDENT TO JACOB WILLERT

X

My dear boy:

You cling to tradition and are slow to make up your mind, two excellent qualities: accursed are the hasty! And so it was that *I* hesitated for a long time about initiating you into my untraditional intentions; but now that you have asked about the "hidden hand" responsible for the confusion and the "flooding," listen to this and decide for yourself:

You see as soon as the first news of the villages' burning came in, I began to consider acquiring the Lienhardt mines—firstly, in order to push the Lienhardts out of a highly civilized province and back to the sheep pastures and cow barns of the south, where they originally came from and where they certainly belong; secondly, because mining, considered as an investment, is a good thing, far too good in any case for this rustic family, who have always exuded an odor of leather, brandy,

and manure pile wherever they made their appearance. The third
reason is Dr. Urban!

The Lienhardt Mining Corporation was a prosperous enterprise, and
its stock stood correspondingly high. So I had to make up my mind
that we would capture the whole affair just as old Lienhardt captured
it before us: by means and in the course of an earthquake on the stock
exchange. And because all things come to him who waits, Albert
Schwann, a bookkeeper, lay all day in a state of deathlike trance, and
then on the evening of the ninth hit upon the notion of seizing the
Lienhardt works by means of the captured arsenal belonging to the
Urbanites. So he had the bells rung, occupied the pit heads, stopped all
work—and the "flooding" began.

What had preceded is partly familiar to you. I requested the perfectly innocent Radowitz to resign, appointed Brigadier General Count
Bessonoff, and instructed him secretly and in strict confidence to give
all possible support to Schwann—that is, to the armed miners and Carpenters of the anti-Urban movement. Bessonoff's having got the Lienhardts' château blown up in the process is just like him. It took place
without my knowledge and is quite immaterial. A person can sleep
quite nicely on straw, particularly if he comes from the country.

Well, when practically all the papers picked up the false report of
the flooding of the mines, naturally panic broke out, and old Lienhardt,
dying by inches in the same foreign sanatorium where his wife died,
offered his shares through intermediaries, in order to rescue half his
capital, at least.

Your remark about "darkened rooms" makes me suspect that you
have been putting one of the "roses that bloom by the way" into your
buttonhole again. Returning to the Senatorial world, you will learn,
with satisfaction I hope, that Lienhardt Mines have fallen from 175
ten days ago to 95 today, or below par. Tomorrow they'll be 90; then
we'll take hold, "we" being a syndicate consisting of Adam Faust, Jacob
Willert, Augustus Beyer, Hans Simon, and Count Bessonoff. Your
assistant general manager (the head one is too old—you should pension him off), Mr. Mueller, executed a dance of joy when I took him
into the secret, and quite understandably too, because if *we* go in, the
Lienhardt mining shares are bound to rise to their old level very
quickly, so that the whole thing will fall into our hands for a bagatelle.

To save you the work of writing a letter, please wire me your acceptance. Your Mr. Mueller tells me that so far as your share is concerned he will have to raise only four million at most, a mere trifle.

The unavoidable cry about "misuse of official power for purposes of private gain" I shall shoulder for the time being. In the first place *they* have no proof, and in the second place *I* am not afraid of threatening gestures on paper. And in the third place, as soon as you get back, in about a fortnight, we will start preparing the Zorn Mining Law—a law, my dear fellow, that will make the thoroughly dishonest shouters' "tongues freeze to the roof of their mouths," in the words of First Lieutenant von Bogatzki, who brings you this letter by direction of

Your old teacher and friend,

ADAM FAUST

Jacob, his face darkening, folded the letter, put it into the official envelope that was ready, and, while the courier impressed two seals on it (for confidential letters were to be returned without delay), asked that he have the kindness to send the President a telegram in cipher: "Agreed. Many thanks!" Left alone, he pondered the injustice done him by Adam Faust's reference to the "roses that bloom by the way." True, the old man was almost seventy. But even in his earlier days he had had a strong inclination to think himself above his equals, and since he had no sense of humor he did not mind forgetting the point in telling a joke, or applying quotations in the wrong place. When had Jacob ever "put a rose in his buttonhole"—that is, abandoned a girl he had once loved, if but for an hour? Friends and foes alike exaggerated the number of his affairs. And he remembered with spiteful satisfaction his frequent opportunities to laugh at Adam Faust, who upon being asked his opinion would amaze the dinner guests in the midst of a conversation or after some anecdote (since he never listened) with a perfectly senseless quotation such as: "The fame that comes after is oblivion" or "Frailty, thy name is woman!" True, there was behind all this a certain guile, a guile of which the didactic old man was so enamored that his favorite pupil, the dry, crafty Augustus Beyer, was beginning to copy it—pretended stupidity, letting oneself be laughed at: the capacity of a destined ruler to give all the trumps to his adversary, very likely a perfect blockhead, making him the center of things, letting him sparkle and rise like a bubble in a glass of champagne, in such fashion that on returning home to the privacy of the bedroom this adversary could report to his proudly listening spouse: "I had Adam Faust with both shoulders to the mat this evening. An awfully nice fellow, but oh, so stupid!"

At any rate, he would pay Adam back for that quotation about the "roses," as inappropriate as anything imaginable, unjust, and a sheer display of senile presumption. "He doesn't need to stir up my conscience—it's never right anyway," thought Jacob, and telephoned to the Upper Town Casino, known among the natives as the Lamb, to order a dinner for two.

"At eight-thirty—I can't make it any earlier." What was there to eat?

"Venison soup with dumplings, brook trout, filet of buck with cream sauce, wild mushrooms, salad, greengage compote, Camembert cheese, dessert."

"Excellent. Half-past eight."

In the restaurant downstairs Jacob found, in addition to Bogatzki, Major von Leugenfeld sitting over his beer, with the conspicuous epaulets of the artillery; both had their belts buckled, with the courier's pouch attached. The little band, consisting of pianist and fiddler, was playing a frivolous waltz.

"Well, well, Leugenfeld!" the Senator greeted the major, "whom have you been giving the honor?"

"The governor, but I'm not supposed to tell."

"Having told one secret, you know-it-all," said Jacob, sitting down at the couriers' table, "why did Bessonoff's wife run away from him, the beauteous Ida? Is it true that she's hidden herself?"

"They've even searched her house," replied Leugenfeld, a favorite of the President's, speaking the abominable dialect of the capital, "but they didn't find a 'certain party,' because you see he's abroad with old Lienhardt."

"Urban?"

"Yes." And, he went on, Dr. Urban was known to have left long before the disturbances broke out. For three weeks he had been seen daily, wrapped in blankets, with snow glasses, beside the mortally ill old man on the open balcony of the sanatorium, ten thousand feet above sea level. In the first place, he could not possibly have had anything to do with the disturbances; in the second place, he could not have been lying hidden. Logically enough, Bessonoff had asked for his discharge because of the affront to his wife—of course it would have been impossible to keep the search of dwellings, stables, and barns on the Bessonoff estate a secret—but the President, tearing out by the roots the last ten hairs on his head, had begun with a disciplinary transfer of the commander of the Eastern Federal Police Division, a man much too young.

"Do you suppose it was altogether without reason and out of whole cloth that this young fellow . . . ?" Jacob inquired.

"Not at all. The beautiful countess, not inaccessible—to modern ideas, and perhaps rather young for her husband, who by the way, being an old instructor at the staff college, will certainly fall *up*stairs. . . ."

"Frailty, thy name is woman," Peggy's lover quoted, getting up. He took his leave, and sent for the mayor's closed carriage, the one with the rubber wheels. He remembered how all color had drained from the face of honest Bessonoff when Beyer had asked about Urban's "hiding place" that evening at Radowitz's.

BOOK ONE

TÊTE-À-TÊTE

XI

MEANWHILE John Christopher Laemmle, host and chef of the Upper Town Casino, tasting the almost black venison soup, said to his apprentice, "Flour always makes second-rate thickening—a rule with no exceptions; and if you weren't such a rascal that it would be a waste of powder I'd send you to my friend Guillemin, the chef at the Hôtel Malesherbes in Paris, to tan your tail. Come on with the Madeira!"

The order was addressed to Josephine Laemmle, a small, bustling woman completely under the thumb of her noisy braggart of a husband; she was rushing back and forth, the bunch of keys jingling at her belt, between kitchen and public rooms. As she unlocked the cupboard of southern wines, her unlucky star brought Jacques Scholz, the postmaster and a regular patron, into the spacious kitchen, whither he had been lured by John Christopher's generous voice; and now, like the noble race horse turning into the stretch, the white-clad chef in his tall cap was no longer to be restrained.

"God in His wisdom has given women weak arms, so that they can't move skillets," he roared, adroitly flipping a huge iron pan so that the fried potatoes whirled like snowflakes, turned over, and fell back as he raised the pan to meet them, "but in the barbarian countries where the skirts can do as they please because religion is held in contempt, they are even tolerated in the kitchen, and not merely for menial services, with the natural result that the men, weakened by fat and insubstantial food, degenerate into buffoons. What do you say, Scholz?" he went on, while Josephine, in contemptuous silence, poured Madeira into a little jug. "Suppose I present a memorial on the subject to the General Staff?"

"A splendid idea," the postmaster agreed, winking at Mrs. Laemmle, who had poured him a glass of Madeira. "In this matter we would make an alliance of the countries where the men do the cooking, and then, with united forces, undertake a crusade against the defamers of religion."

"Scholz, friend of my bosom, do we or do we not understand each other?" asked Mr. Laemmle, spreading his arms.

"Two minds with but a single thought!" declared the postmaster, raising his glass to the host, and then returned to the public rooms.

Originally the inn was named, "At the Sign of the Lamb," and the natives call it that even now; but one fine day mine host's subtle and ingenious brain conceived the idea of pulling down the rear wall of the structure and building a glassed-in veranda directly on the edge of the rock, on the "yawning abyss" whose sides echoed the ripple of the river Geise flowing below. The veranda was as long as the building, and two rooms deep; the glass windows, extending up to the slate roof, were made to slide, so that on fine days the "first-hand ozone, well known for its curative properties," would pour in upon the patrons; the whole room was to have heating, so that the incomparable view could be enjoyed in the cold season. This gave to the Lamb, as viewed from the street, three successive large public rooms: the restaurant, where service went on all day; the back room, to which the privileged characters withdrew for a nightcap and a game or two, occupying the same seats at certain tables for the whole of their natural lives; and, adjoining these, the veranda, where screens were set up as required because of its spaciousness, and in order to form "cozy nooks," particularly of an evening.

Ten minutes before half-past eight Mr. Laemmle inspected the corner of the veranda prepared for the Senator and his guest. The stove was giving off a moderate degree of heat; nevertheless, mine host opened a window in the farther glass wall to its full width. "Naturally, since the guest may be a lady, it mustn't be cold," he said to his wife and the head cook, who were standing in the veranda door, "but the air has got to be fresh, continually fresh, without change of temperature. Therefore, an eye must be kept on the stove." Remarking that "claustrophobia or fear of confined spaces" was a Senatorial ailment, he had the screen shoved back, doubling the size of the "cozy nook." Finally he inspected the serving table, an open, four-level buffet pushed against the veranda wall near the main table, which was set and decorated with flowers. On the top level were extra plates for cold entrees and dessert; on the second shelf, in covered dishes, salads and an assortment of cheeses; on the third, preserves, compote, *petits fours,* an orange cream cake, and native marzipan; on the bottom level were bottles and champagne buckets full of ice. Madame Josephine had her own bedroom rug spread under the table; she said the veranda was cold to the feet.

When the Senator's carriage drove up and he got out, the regular patrons noticed that he was alone and sent the carriage back. Mr. Laemmle, in an oxford-gray frock coat, escorted him to the table, returned to the restaurant, shouted into the kitchen, "Pull yourselves together—he knows what's what!" and replied to the inquiring looks of the regulars, "Either he's a hotel man himself, or his father was one. He saw everything with one look—the stove, the open window, the carpet, the flowers, the crystal goblets, the roll in the napkin, the plate warmer—with *one look!*"

"But he had the screen put away!" interposed Borst, the apothecary, whose wife had charged him to "find out everything, particularly what she has on."

"Naturally," replied Laemmle, "which once more brings home the wisdom of the proverb that you're never too old to learn. Because I guessed right that there's a lady coming; in fact, one from town here!"

"You don't say!" exclaimed Westphal, the architect.

"So of course I said, 'Senator, the screen means that the guest doesn't want to be observed, which is well within his rights, and makes the dinner taste better too,' and he said to me . . . well, what do you suppose he said?"

"Don't talk riddles to us, Laemmle!" cried Dr. Gaul.

" 'My dear Mr. Laemmle,' he said, lifting up his finger like this, 'if you don't want to be observed, you shouldn't be an alderman or a mayor or a senator!' The man's no fool—am I right!"

At that moment there was a sshhing; horses' hoofs sounded on the stone driveway, Laemmle ran to the door, and "she" came in, her face hidden from recognition under a half veil; she was led through the darkness of the back room to the veranda. Borst, the apothecary, noted like lightning: heavy, high-buttoned double-breasted wool coat of Scotch plaid, mannish cut, wide collar, horn buttons half as big as your palm, matching cap of the same material fastened with a diamond brooch, sea-green taffeta dress, light-colored silk stockings, shoes of gold braid.

She threw back her veil, opened her coat, made her escort feel the silk lining, called attention to the scent of his perfume on her breast, and would have kissed his unwilling hand, regardless of mine host standing ready with a coat hanger, if Jacob had not whispered to her, "Wait!"

She sipped at her champagne, asked for cold water, and was so busy talking that she passed by the hors d'oeuvre, caviar, jellied salmon, preserved olives, and even the *ragout fin en coquilles*.

She said the old woman had crossed herself over and over again when a beautifully dressed young lady arrived bringing the packages to the house from Stern's Specialty Shop. Margaret had had to try everything on, and the young lady, Pauli was her name, had measured and pinned and fixed, and taken along everything that didn't fit; Margaret was going at the end of the week to try on what had been fitted, and the alterations were free.

Jacob, surprised at her perfectly natural behavior and her disregard of appearances, asked whether she had a fiancé or admirer.

Peggy, her eyes cast down, said, yes, an admirer; but he had been called to the capital to deliver a lecture, and had been kept there ever since. "He's ten years older than I am, and he really was in earnest—his father and mine were old friends—but now that he's having a great career, naturally he forgets about me." He had not sent her so much as a line. And, she added, looking the Senator very seriously in the face to see whether he believed her, "And, anyway, we weren't so intimate."

Was she hoping to see him again?

"No; later perhaps, but I'm not going to run after him. Why do you ask?"

"Because I know him," replied Jacob. "His name is Theodore Lindbrecht, and he was a pit inspector at the Johanna Mine."

"Good heavens, how could you possibly know him, in that big city?"

To the waiter Jacob said, "Please tell Mr. Laemmle the soup was excellent; the next time I come I'm going to ask for the recipe."

Then he explained to her that Lindbrecht, after addressing the Natural Science convention on the social question, had been invited by the Archbishop to join the board of the Christian Unions. It was, he said, a safe career, but not a great one.

Following the Hôtel Malesherbes tradition, every main course was offered twice; when the waiter appeared for the second time with the celebrated brook trout, Jacob declined, and Margaret ventured to say that she would have enjoyed some more fish.

"So would I," whispered Jacob, "but we mustn't hurt mine host's feelings. Look at your menu." And he showed her that the next course was "Fillet of young buck Laemmle, wild mushrooms, cream sauce, *pommes frites,*" mine host's trump card, a dish that they must both take two helpings of to reward Laemmle's effort and loving care. Farther down the menu, also, she must not overlook the fact that among the desserts the orange cream cake was marked *spécialité de la maison,* which was the way that the mistress of the establishment chose to show she was doing her part toward honoring the guests.

Three dishes were specially singled out: the soup, the roast, and the cake. "Everything else, the menu says, you might eat elsewhere."

"How about you and me?" asked Peggy. "Must we go by Mr. Laemmle's taste?"

"Absolutely!" And as the head cook was approaching with the roast, and setting the covered platter on the serving table, Jacob added in a lower tone: "Take very little the first time, and more the second. It's so easy not to offend people!" To the cook, who was bending over the serving table, slicing the saddle of venison, which had been removed from the bones: "Thin slices, sir! Let us try it first. You know the old saying, 'What the peasant doesn't know he won't eat'!"

"Quite so, Senator," agreed the cook, laying one slice on each plate.

The waiter sparingly dispensed wild mushrooms and golden-yellow sliced potatoes, and covered the meat with thick, grayish-brown sour gravy.

A few moments later the chef appeared in the veranda door.

"Heavens above, I'm certainly going to overeat myself on this!" Jacob Willert called to him. "How long did your buck hang?"

"Ten days, Senator."

"I thought as much—the meat melts in your mouth."

The enraptured Laemmle vanished; Peggy, feeling her way in an unknown world, and striving to shun all missteps, said in a tense voice, "Governing must be hard."

"How do you mean?"

"I was just thinking. Now, you take my father—suppose he were to strike it rich, and order this same dinner here at the Lamb. It's ridiculous, of course, but suppose he did. . . ."

"Yes; then what?"

"He wouldn't see the same meaning in the menu that you did."

"Probably not, for the simple reason that he's not used to being honored and thanking people for it. He'd soon learn; but what's that got to do with governing?"

"I don't quite know, but it has," the girl replied, her brow clouding; without preamble, peeping frequently to see how her rich companion handled his fork, she began to talk about her life.

After school and confirmation, she had been a dishwasher at a canteen for some time. Then the skin of her hands had suffered from the strong acids, and she had taken a job in the artificial-flower shop.

"Was all this at Marienhall?"

"Yes. I've only been in Geisenheim six months."

The work on the artificial flowers was not hard, but the Urbanites predominated, so she was pushed out; the next two years she spent at home, helping her rheumatic mother. She said this period had been like an apprenticeship: through her father's conversations with the two Lindbrechts—the old man and the young one who was having such a great career—she knew about the Fausts and the Lienhardts and conditions in the mines. In fact, even Matthew Brandt, the town clerk, had sometimes called on her parents in order to argue with the Lindbrechts.

"What did they argue about?"

"About Dr. Urban."

The Senator pricked up his ears. He had had the President's report, he was expecting the archivist's "objective account," and he knew what the bishops thought. What would this fourth voice say, this "voice of the people"?

"As a scholar, Matthew Brandt always wanted proofs, but the Lindbrechts laughed at him."

"Why?"

She hesitated: "When you go back to the capital, you can ask Lindbrecht."

Jacob leaned forward: "If I were to get you a job in the capital, possibly as a hairdresser—some easy kind of work . . ."

"Seriously?" Peggy reached across the table for his hand.

"Listen: if your lady leaves on a trip," he whispered, keeping his eyes on the veranda door, "but in good time beforehand, you go to the post office and send me a telegram, just a few noncommittal words. I'll come to your place, and we can talk everything over. Now tell me about the Lindbrechts."

"She's going by the day after tomorrow at latest. Well, about Matthew." Of course he had not treated the Lindbrechts as though he were something better and they "just workmen." "Matthew isn't that big a blockhead."

"Nowadays there are people," Jacob interposed, "who tell the workmen, 'You aren't *just* workmen, you're *even* workmen.' Are they blockheads too?"

"We know all about them—they've been agitating here. But Father says they're swindlers, not blockheads. And, anyway, they couldn't get anywhere at home, because they tried to put on our mountain province accent, and they pronounced it wrong. They called themselves 'the Revolutionary Workers' Party,' and they were all swells. Urban is a swell too, but he never talks dialect. He treats the workmen loftily— very . . . well, the Lienhardts' men aren't used to anything else. But— how shall I put it?"

She squinted up her eyes, pushed away her compote dish, and polished her front teeth with the tip of her pointed tongue.

"'But Urban succeeds all the same,' you're trying to say," Jacob explained. "He succeeds because the workman will let people treat him as an inferior. Condescension, now—and, after all, speaking dialect without understanding it *is* condescension—*that's* what the poor man up here in the mountain province won't put up with. That's what you mean to say."

"That must be it," Margaret agreed with an apologetic smile. "I just can't express it."

"You said the Lienhardts' men were treated like inferiors. Aren't Faust's? Aren't there any tales hereabouts of old Faust's pride, and of Mr. Bernard's?"

The cheese dish was passed, and the waiter, looking as if he personally would not be able to resist them, indicated the greenish Roquefort, the Camembert ready to burst, the Brie in tinfoil.

Out of the question! They asked for coffee and the cake.

Suddenly Peggy beamed: "I've got it!" she said. "I know about the proofs. I don't believe there's a man in the country whom so many stories are told about as Adam Faust; you could 'prove' his pride with a dozen anecdotes. There's only one thing you can't prove: you can't prove that he ever spoke or behaved differently to a rich man from what he did to a poor man. That much is certain—if he's proud, he's proud to everyone."

"Is that your own opinion?"

"All Faust's men think that. Once just before he was elected President, Urban proved at a public meeting that Adam Faust didn't care for his workers. At that old Lindbrecht got up, and agreed with everything Urban said: 'Quite so, Faust doesn't care; he doesn't look into our chimney corners, our stewpots, or our conversation. It's absolutely true that he doesn't know a single worker. All he knows is Mr. Koepke or Mrs. Koepke, Mr. Meier, Mr. Schmidt, Mr. Lindbrecht, Mr. Tieck, Mr. Bickel. He doesn't even know the word *worker*. He knows that a man is a blacksmith or a carpenter or a miner, but he doesn't know that a man is a worker—he's as stupid as that.' Of course by this time there was loud laughter, and since then there hasn't been any debate allowed when Urban has spoken."

She sat bolt upright, one hand on her breast; her face was flushed, her eyes sparkled.

From behind his screen of cigar smoke Jacob teased her, suggesting that once she got to the capital she would probably run to Lindbrecht's meetings to hear him speak. He meant young Lindbrecht, he said, Theodore. And as she did not answer, he whispered, "What are you thinking? A penny for your thoughts!"

"I was wondering whether you'd be a little jealous."

"We'll go together, Peggy—nobody'll know us. I've learned something here in Geisenheim."

"Really?"

"I've learned here that I still have a lot to learn."

He paid the check and asked the waiter to convey his thanks to mine host and Mrs. Laemmle.

"But you didn't need to learn from us," Margaret flattered him as they waited in the darkness for the carriage, "how to manage people."

"It may well be that I have underestimated the old gentleman," said Jacob, tipping his hat, for the carriage was driving up and the coachman saluted him, "Faust, the old joker." He opened the carriage door. "Anyway, I did like the idea that the workman is not a worker. I owe you something for that."

They shook hands; Margaret, one foot already on the step, turned so that the carriage lamp lit up her profile. "Day after tomorrow," she whispered, and disappeared.

In high spirits over the bracing air, the star-spangled sky, and the pleasure he had given the girl, Jacob set out for home. The curtain was rising; the backgrounds of the hatred that had destroyed a château and two villages were coming into view.

BOOK ONE

THE BLOODY NIGHT OF CAROLSWALD

XII

THERE follows, in eleven sections, the report of Brandt, the Geisenheim archivist, concerning the cause and outbreak of the disturbances, critically revised and supplemented by many details that did not come to light until afterward.

I. RESTORATION OF THE ORDER OF CARPENTERS

On an April morning of the year before Adam's election to the presidency, Mr. von Hesse, Bishop and head of the Revival Mission, had finished the services in the Geisenheim Mountain Chapel, and had gone into the vestry to remove his ecclesiastical vestments, when his sixteen-year-old son, Otto, who had been poking around with youthful curiosity in an old iron chest, called his attention to a heavy, dusty, worm-eaten trunk of pigskin.

The rusty iron lock refused to open, although there was a key sticking in it. Otto forced it with a crowbar; dust, bugs, and documents once tied with crumbling string spilled out.

In this way the documents were discovered from which it appeared that the Mountain Chapel, four hundred years before, had been both the church and meetinghouse of the pit carpenters, a half-secular, half-religious brotherhood, as was at first supposed; since then Andrew Zorn had proved that the former organization of the Carpenters belonged entirely to this world, though it was a world shone upon by God's sunlight.

Of course everyone remembers how the celebrated Zorn appeared in our Geisenheim the following winter, and managed by means of money that he begged, argument, and the support of influential quarters, to induce first the Carpenters, then other groups of wage earners in the mining region, to restore the brotherly fellowship that had been forgotten for centuries.

At this time one of the rich newcomers, moved by love of our happy river valley and the Bishop's daughter, distinguished himself by an act of great generosity. He bought the Mountain Chapel from the city of Geisenheim, and presented it and the meadows beyond it in perpetuity to the re-established brotherhood. Thus the Carpenters regained their meetinghouse; and in order both to honor the giver and to add a light touch to this account, I will record the answer given by Crémieux, the Lyon silk manufacturer, to his wife, née Hesse, when she asked him why he regularly spent his holidays in her native country, not in his: "I have two businesses, my child: our plant and your father!" The rumor that Hesse extracted large sums from his son-in-law for the brotherhood and for missionary purposes is thus seen to be founded on fact.

Our mountain province, bounded on the east by the stream that flows northward, embraces the broad, level, western half of the valley and the mountain chain rising abruptly from it, out of whose clefts spring mountain brooks that form ponds and lakes in the lowlands, and finally empty into the river.

At the point where a broad mountain brook called the Geise emerges from the foothills, we find the city of Geisenheim, nestling against the heights and going uphill, spreading into the plain with the new part of the town, and numbering some thirty thousand inhabitants. The traveler walking upstream along the banks of the Geise, into the mountains, arrives in about two hours at Marienhall, long and narrow, crowded by the steep sides of the valley, where the air is strong with the scent of spruce forests, and on still mornings, with white smoke scattering over the rooftops, the hills opposite give back the sound when the brother from the Revival Mission sounds a hymn from the overhanging Bloody Cliff.

The cities of Geisenheim and Marienhall and the villages, watering places, and sanatoriums scattered along the heights are the center of our resort travel. Half an hour by rail farther south, in the wide valley of the Eller, the coal region begins; not far away are the mountain villages of Carolswald and the somewhat larger Bergdorf, both villages inhabited by miners and officials at the mines. But several pit trains leave the cities of Geisenheim and Marienhall every day and bring the miners home again in the evening.

When the Reformation took place in the sixteenth century, the cities of the mountain province became Protestant, but the peasants from the villages, when they rose against ecclesiastical rule—the gentlest ever known—suffered a bloody defeat. So it happens that even today the Protestant population predominates in the cities, the Catholic in the villages.

Under these circumstances it was fortunate, when the Protestant municipal authorities of Geisenheim declined to turn over the Mountain Chapel to the resuscitated brotherhood except for exclusively Protestant services, that Bishop Hesse intervened.

"If the chapel remains city property," he said at a meeting of the town council, "the rain will surely be coming in through the roof." But, he said, if the municipality cared to sell the old ruin, it would be relieved of responsibility for anything that might later take place there. The Brotherhood of Carpenters, newly founded and too weak in numbers and finances to keep the building in condition, already had Catholics, Protestants, and freethinkers in its ranks. Accordingly, if this house of Christian worship were turned over to a single sect, the union would be deprived of quarters that all its members respected, and so they would be unintentionally but effectually divided and scattered. The Catholic diocese (Oriola) and the Protestant Church would have to exercise a joint protectorate as long as the Carpenters could not stand on their own feet, and an agreement had already been made by which Protestant and Catholic services would alternate in the chapel. In fact, even the members of the brotherhood who had conscientious scruples against belonging to any church must not be excluded from the enjoyment of the chapel as a place of assembly.

At the time, although one of the aldermen reproached the Bishop with seeming less interested in the propagation of his Protestant faith than in the preservation of this union that showed every color of the rainbow, the city fathers had nevertheless begun to suspect that Hesse was introducing such dangerous innovations not on his own responsibility, but under orders from the Archbishop; a good many had some idea of the connection, and the opposition died down. This took place during the second year of the presidency of our Adam Faust.

2. NOTES ON THE HISTORY OF THE POOR IN THE MOUNTAIN PROVINCE

For the struggle had already begun, and its purpose was not the accustomed and visible one of gaining lands and cities or property. Instead, just as preachers, students, and clerks of court had wandered through the province four hundred years before, rousing burgesses and peasants to arms against the old religion, so in our day the struggle for the poor man's soul was being renewed.

Since the reporter cannot go back to the past, he would now recall three facts, never quite forgotten:

1. The carpenters, miners, and laborers in the mines during the Middle Ages were united in brotherhoods that made their own laws, and thanks to this union they were protected against want and unjust treatment.

2. No master, either lay or clerical, in those days disputed the right of the men to lay down their work.

3. No tyrant, even the bloodiest, in the Middle Ages could compel a poor and helpless man—helpless because he did not belong to one of the brotherhoods—or his wife and children to work. It remained for our enlightened century to see the wives and children of the poor

sleeping in factories, under the spinning jennies or the power looms. "The mass execution of the weak and helpless in the ministerial wars of the eighteenth and the industrial establishments of the nineteenth century is an invention of modern intellect." (Andrew Zorn.)

In our province as well as elsewhere the miners lived worse than cattle for half a century, harassed by the exploiters of the mines, and resembling them in having no fear of God and in skulking abjectly before the powerful.

Religious faith had died out. But since Christianity still survived, shriveling away under such names as "humanism" and "the rights of man," but nevertheless survived, rich private citizens, well-disposed hatchers of schemes, those who simply pitied, and ultimately the churches as well, came to the aid of the downtrodden. This was the first stage of improvement.

They had sunk very low indeed. The "illumination" that had begun to cast its rays in the sixteenth century shone only upon those who could read and write or were at least not too exhausted to listen—that is, upon the rich. Only one well-gnawed bone from the tables of learning was thrown to the working people: the idea that there was no God. And the very moment when godlessness became the "public property of enlightenment," the whip flew off the wall as if of its own accord, and the poor man was scourged to work on the estates, in the penitentiaries, and in the army. He had become "the masses," like cattle.

Then, in this first stage of improvement, those who felt pity discovered that the poor man was human. After the softhearted came the socialists to discover that he was a citizen.

But if he was a citizen, then he had rights—for instance, the franchise —and as a voter he could express his wishes. In fact, since the poor man, by his predominance of numbers, dropped more ballots into the box than the middle class and the rich together, sooner or later he was bound to gain power and overwhelm his tormenters.

The socialists, proclaiming that the poor man must not accept acts of charity but must possess himself of the government, pushed the philanthropists aside, and sang:

> *None else can free us from our thralldom:*
> *That is left for us to do.*

They held great public meetings, and wore red carnations in their buttonholes. And to show that they would capture power not by blood and violence, but through the franchise, they used to get up from their seats at the close of a meeting and sing:

> *Upon our victorious banner*
> *See our watchword: votes for all!*

Two young men in our mountain province particularly distinguished themselves by their talents as agitators: Theodore Lindbrecht, pit inspector in Faust's Johanna Mine, the "bishops' man" and speaker for the Christian unions, or, as they were called for short, "the Christians."

The other, Adolf Hildebrand, had always worn a red carnation in his buttonhole; but although he could never, even in his mature years, quite choke back such phrases as "science is on the march," and "the rosy dawn of technology"—in this he was like a wound-up music box—nevertheless, he had many sensible discussions with the bishops, encouraged the pious Lindbrecht to make bolder demands, and was neither a fool nor a seeker after power, not even a swindler. In his first talk with Hesse and Oriola, who were co-operating in their social endeavors even then, and whose workmen's associations were superior in numbers to Hildebrand's, the young atheist is said to have put forward the following argument: "You gentlemen offer to let me sit among the devout in church, and attend to your sermons. If I will agree to sit below and listen while you stand above in the pulpit, you will even elevate me, and I am to have a chance, as your equal, to preach from the pulpit of the Mountain Chapel that a millionaire has given to you. In reply to your offer I have this to say: I won't be made a fool of, and I won't be made an accomplice of. If I sit below and listen to you, you will be making a fool of me, because, after all, you can read and write, and you don't believe in God any more than I do. But if I stand up high in a Christian pulpit, and preach, then you'll be making me your accomplice."

He took his hat off the hook, remembered his manners sufficiently to say: "Good day, gentlemen!" and left the room.

"If that's honestly meant and actually true, about his refusing to be made a fool and accomplice of," the surprised Oriola said to Hesse, "we can work with the fellow. The enemy is at the door."

3. ORIGIN AND PROGRESS OF DR. URBAN

The "enemy" was an agitator of a new stamp, of uncommon industry and guile, and at the same time gifted with a medieval vigor of speech: Dr. Urban, organizer of the proletarian agricultural workers, president of the People's League for Enlightenment and Economic Peace, adviser to the Lienhardts. A file maintained by the secret police described him as the son of a peasant, born in a village on an estate in the south. An estate manager in his early twenties, later a student at various academies and member of a socialist secret society, he made an unexpected appearance in the insurgent region when the agricultural workers rebelled. He stirred the workers to enthusiasm by forceful speeches, negotiated secretly with the landed proprietors, induced both sides to yield, and quieted the tumult in a fortnight, thus preserving the agricultural south from immeasurable losses.

After uniting tens of thousands of agricultural workers in the Patriotic Farm Laborers' League, which the socialists called a Yellow union, he turned to the industrial workers, organized them on the same principles, which will be discussed later, and, despite the resistance put up by both the "Christians" and the "Independents," gained great success, particularly in the concerns whose masters would previously have shouted for the police to help them against any attempt at association among their workmen. The so-called seasonal workers, who are unemployed for part of the year, like the painters and the men in the building trades, poured into the party of "our Dr. Urban," and he not only promised these poor people help but actually helped them by means of a system of factory policing that he had devised.

This system was what originally created the disturbances.

It began on the great agricultural estates of the south, in the wheat and sugar-beet regions, and had existed in a primitive form before Urban served there, first as a manager, then as an employment agent.

One of the great estates belonging to the Lienhardts or the Oriolas, for instance, covering many square miles and burdened with mortgages, cannot support throughout the year the great numbers of hands needed in the harvest season, least of all when Faust, the machine king, is President, and a city-bred government keeps down the price of grain, potatoes, and sugar. In times like those, moreover, the farm laborers are paid their wages in provisions produced on the estate, and they hardly see any money at all. When the wheat and beets are harvested, most of the hands are discharged, leaving only a so-called "staff" to care for the fields and buildings. Obviously, this system depopulates the country; for the farm laborers, originally peasants "freed from feudal oppression," go to the cities as industrial workers, and do not come back to their rural homes even for the harvest. Accordingly, the proprietor turns to an intermediary, a labor broker, who, armed with power of attorney and money, sets out for our backward, agricultural, neighboring country, recruits a sufficient number of poor hands and girls, and brings them back across the border in batches.

When they arrive at the estate, their personal papers and passports are taken from them, while the local constable searches their pockets. Then the director of the estate explains to them what the broker had concealed: that if they should attempt, leaving behind the wages that are withheld, to escape and "take to the hills," they will be fired on. More humanely inclined managers have been known to take down such speeches in shorthand and give them to the newspapers.

"You see around here we do things in an orderly way," says the director or his representative, Mr. Urban. "We do not run a pigsty, the way they do in your precious country. If you by any chance think you can sneak off by night through the fields, or that my men will fire over your heads, you'll find out something. But even supposing somebody manages, with his skin half full of lead, to hook on to the train and get to Geisenheim or Marienhall: do you think you can find work there, in the woods, or in the mines? You won't even be able to find a place to stay! Not so much as a whore will take you in for a single night without a passport and identification papers. No, the Federal Police on the platform will bust you one right and left until false teeth fly in every direction, and then they'll send you back where you came from, and you'll return to my open arms. What will happen then I don't know, but just take a look at these fellows!"

And amid the laughter of his young men, who have buckled on holsters for this ceremonious reception, he sends his long riding whip whistling through the air to slap against his high boots.

"On the other hand, this is a Christian country, not a land of Hottentots like where you come from, and so long as everyone does his duty you'll get first-rate treatment here, and not eat rats like you do at home—roast pork on Sundays, and on weekdays stew that will leave you licking your fingers!"

The poor people's faces beam. They like to hear about food, and they do not believe the threats. Last winter, in their thatched cottages, a man who could read showed them letters from relatives who had escaped from the estates in the mountain provinces—letters from those who "took to the hills." Besides, there is a rumor that the mining Lienhardts keep spies on the Oriola estates to help the runaways reach the mining district in safety: new blood intimidates the miners when Hildebrand and Lindbrecht have stirred them up.

"So far as rations go, you will get punctually the bread, fat, and cheese allowances called for in the contract, and also a quart of skimmed milk a day, malted coffee beans, wood, coal, kerosene, and the reapers can always have as much sweet brown beer as they feel like drinking. I can tell you if anyone had offered me that when I was young, I'd have worn through my leather breeches kneeling down and thanking God. Speaking of wearing through breeches, or, in other words, manners and morals, I tell you quite plainly that both are to be strictly observed here. No paternity and support suits shall be allowed, and any girl who gets herself in a family way will have to take the consequences when she gets home. Dismissed!" (From the *Marienhall Messenger,* Sunday Paper for the Christian Home.)

It was on the great estates in the south, then, that Dr. Urban learned from the directors (who by comparison with the young manager were great men and deserving of his admiration) the habit of being surrounded with armed men. It was there also that he got the idea of training seasonal laborers, who could not be deported across the frontier because they were citizens, as a sort of police in their free time, arming them and offering them as factory police—under contract and temporarily—to the industrialists. It was down in the south that he learned to treat men as "material."

On the other hand, it became clear to him during the hands' uprising that a workman who prefers vengeance and death to life is not material, but an injured human being, and, what may be more dangerous still, an unmanageable one. This realization changed him, almost overnight, into a social reformer and friend of the oppressed, so that when Adam Faust assumed the presidency there were already three competing associations of "friends of the oppressed": the "Christians," the

Hildebrandites, and the Urbanites. The struggle for the soul of the poor man had begun.

4. CHARGES LEVELED BY FAUST'S MEN AGAINST THE LIENHARDTS AND URBAN

The inhabitants of the villages of Carolswald, the western fringe of Marienhall, and the suburb of St. Dorothy in Geisenheim are predominantly Faust's miners and employees of every class. They look down superciliously on the Lienhardt men who live in and around Bergdorf, because their masters, the Fausts, have always had their mines in the family, have always been mine operators, and because they are city men. The Lienhardts on the contrary, they say, are from the country. Partly by stealing church property, it is asserted, partly by thimblerigging, they became great landowners, and then gradually sold half of their fifty estates in order to edge into the more profitable mining industry; but they have maintained their rustic habits of despising and treading down their people. The Lienhardt "shop" was a corporation and a dividend mill; the Lienhardts' move toward social improvement was due not to reason but to fear, and was conducted by a Dr. Urban, a former slave trader, merchant of souls, and riding-whip manager—the familiar rural mixture of threats and promises, sweetmeats and the lash. The "jolly evenings" organized by Urban, with orchestral music, lectures, sandwiches, and free beer, were not for jollity, but for supervision and to spy out the men's sentiments. Under the pretext that gymnastics and marksmanship were good physical training, Urban had tempted the young people to establish "sports divisions," and the Lienhardts, usually closer than the bark to a tree, had supplied expensive uniforms, high laced boots, and arms gratis. Only their cowardice prevented them from giving to the sports divisions of the pits their right name of company police. What, except fear and a guilty conscience, had caused Urban, and of late the youngest Lienhardt as well, to surround himself with armed men in uniform whenever he appeared at meetings or at the free-beer evenings? Even the mine doctors were wearing those ridiculous private uniforms. Who had ever seen a doctor with a pistol under ordinary circumstances?

5. URBAN'S INDISPUTABLE ACHIEVEMENT

Obviously, the Fausts' workmen would not have talked so disdainfully of the Lienhardts without some guidance. The accusations against
the neighboring Yellow or Economic Peace establishments betrayed
the voice of Hildebrand the agitator. There was envy, too, of the successful competitor, the spellbinder and darling of the ladies, Urban,
who drove to workmen's meetings in his employer's four-in-hand, and
never unaccompanied; when he appeared in the hall the band of the
sports division would sound a flourish, and the miners stood up. Had
not Brigadier General Count Bessonoff himself invited him to dinner?
The poor simpletons trusted him because he had raised their wages,
shortened their hours, made their evenings pleasant, and had so much
improved their outward lives in ten years' struggle that they were no
longer inferior to the Fausts' men. He had even succeeded in turning
the Lienhardts into affable personages who slapped the poor on the
back; and the influx from the agricultural south, awaited with dread
every fall, failed to arrive if the employer was satisfied. Urban's voice
could be a great roar, and it could sound like a cooing dove. The poor
loved him, the rich asked his advice. There was no one whom employees and employers, men and women, lettered and unlettered alike,
heard with such pleasure, and understood so easily; no one could explain so convincingly that it was not the individual who counted, but
the plant—not the worker *or* the employer, that is, but the solidarity
between the two: for this harmony produced the wealth whose just
distribution was not the business of the rich *or* the poor (both, if left
to themselves, would be unjust), but the affair of the state, which, once
he, Urban, controlled it, would banish insecurity and fear of starvation
to the museum of antiquities.

6. THE PERIL OF THE RED CARNATION

In the fifth year of our Adam Faust's presidency his "partisan and
autocratic" conduct in office, as people called it, had produced such
discontent among the propertied classes that the Industrialists' Association invited the founder of the League for Enlightenment and Economic Peace, the "leader in the struggle against socialists and men of
darkness" (*People's National Times*), Dr. Urban, to explain his basic
principles in a lecture. He had never done so before, nor did he do it

then, but he delivered his much-admired speech on the "peril of the red carnation," creating such enthusiasm and bewilderment that shrewd, cynical pessimists (like Hilgenfeld, the poet) shortly afterward declared that "in view of the hopeless state of public opinion" he would attain power within ten years. Whether this prophecy was accurate, only the future can show; for the time being his denunciation of the "red carnation" drove the previously wavering Hildebrand-ites, that is, the independent unions, into the camp of the "Christians." Two years later, when the church bells were rung and the drums beaten, there was no further friction or ridicule between the bishops' and Hildebrand's men: they marched against the Urbanites as if they were a single brotherhood.

As a proof of the great extent to which Urban lost the confidence of the "Independents," let us take the following extract from the examination of Hildebrand before the court on October 14 and 15.

JUSTICE HOLZKOPF: "How long has the enmity that you speak of between the members of your union and the Urbanites existed?"

HILDEBRAND: "Since Urban's speech about the red carnation."

HOLZKOPF: "Will you please give us your views on the subject?"

HILDEBRAND: "Urban is a conspirator. Neither in his earlier days nor since has he said anything definite about the ultimate purpose of his agitation or his view of the ideal world. This concealment of what will happen if he secures a free hand is enough in itself to keep our suspicions alive. But until that notorious speech, we had in common with him our faith in progress, in science and invention; yes, we shared this faith with him, important and conciliatory in its effect as it was—this and our aversion to the prelates. Till that time it would have been possible for us to unite with Urban against the reactionary church in our fight for enlightenment and progress. But then, before the richest two hundred of the rich, Urban branded us as liars, saying we were now too cautious and hypocritical to wear the red carnation in our buttonholes, but if anyone cut open our hearts he would find the feeling for which the red carnation stood, namely an avid desire to ruin the man of property and divide his possessions among ourselves. Therefore, no one must ever believe us when we said that strikes were necessary to improve the lot of the poor. It was not to help the impoverished that we propagated strikes, but to ruin those with property. In fact, our purpose was not to better the condition of the workingman, but to plunge him deeper in misery, hatred, and animal fury, so that he would at last exchange the tedious wage struggle for a bloody uprising, and cut down his employer. The Christian unions, Urban said, were pursuing exactly the same object—after all, the primitive Christians had been communists! And there was just one slight difference between them and us: while we would establish a tyranny of union leaders once we had been victorious, the goal of the 'Christians' was the sovereignty of the prelates. Having slandered us and the 'Christians' in this way, he explained his own attitude. It was a basic principle of his policy that any businessman, small or large, had the same right to defend and augment his property as the least of his workmen. And in secret session he advised the rich to make use of his works police.

"Every one of us remembers how the Senate lowered itself when it resolved to enter the part of the speech dealing with 'the equal right of all to property' in the *Golden Book of Speeches and Statements,* and how, as tradition demanded, Urban was permitted to read out the passage before the assembled Senators. They actually applauded!

"A week afterward Bernard Faust distributed *The Conservative* magazine in the workmen's and office workers' canteens. We read with satisfaction what Professor Andrew Zorn (whom we had long despised as a man of darkness) had to say there about Urban's speech on the red carnation, and about the self-degradation of the Senate.

"Certainly, Andrew Zorn wrote, there are strikes aimed at the ruin of the employer, but they are instigated not by the unions, but by the very few union leaders who are members of a secret conspiracy—the same secret group of conspirators that produced Mr. Urban and taught him his conspiratorial tactics. The aforementioned group of conspirators, a combination of ambitious and dissipated literati with other idlers from among the enlightened *bourgeoisie,* had meanwhile crawled out into daylight, and presented itself to the public as the 'Revolutionary Workers' Party.'

" 'The equal right of all to property' is an empty phrase intended to confuse. The possessions of the poor, articles of everyday use, cannot be compared with machinery, money, and wheat fields.

" 'Equal right to property' means exactly as much as 'the equal right to health'—in other words, nothing!

"In the conclusion of his article Zorn spoke scathingly of the applause accorded by the Senators, our ruling men, to Urban's treacherous phrase, as follows: 'And the same city rabble that is in the habit of clapping the gestures of actors showed its rhythmically regulated approval. One might have supposed they were happy. And indeed perhaps they were: what do they care if the state is outraged?' Not he himself, Andrew Zorn wound up, was the author of these words, but the Roman Publius Cornelius Tacitus, on an occasion almost two thousand years before, when another Senate had plunged from freedom into slavery."

So much for Hildebrand's speech to the court, and the common enmity of Hildebrand's and Lindbrecht's men for Urban.

7. THE LOVERS

A girl with good physical health and strict principles, who has aimed too high in her first youth, scorning a would-be husband and later, out of pride and shyness, a lover, will fall in her twenty-seventh year: this is the experience of the mountain province, and this is what befell the tall, blonde, muscular Kate Schwann, residing and domiciled at Marienhall, left homeless after the death of her God-fearing parents, and performing the work of a chambermaid at the Lienhardt château, when she was deceived by the untrustworthy protestations of love uttered by the eldest of the brothers, a shriveled, yellow-faced creature. The spacious house, its rear façade touching Bloody Cliff, was adjoined by a gloomy and extensive park full of old spruces and beeches, through which the Geise flowed between abrupt banks, hidden in their turn by thick masses of alders.

She had hardly been working there a week when one day she was busy making the beds in one of the chambers, and unexpectedly John Theodoric Lienhardt, the old chief's eldest, familiarly called "the eroticist," appeared on the threshold, as thin as a rail, a schoolboy in stature, his face already a ruin. He inquired after Albert, her only brother, a bookkeeper for the Fausts; delightedly repeated her name— Kate, Katharina, Katya, Kitty; and told her, first having asked her to sit down, about his never-to-be-forgotten Kate, poor but honest, who had betrothed herself to him, and then ruined his life by dying. And, stroking her bare forearm, "If Cupid's arrow were ever to pierce me again, it could only be for a Kitty," he said, gazing fixedly at her already heaving bosom; he got up with the words, "No, or it will be too much for me!" and he moved to a few paces' distance. On the threshold, while she sat motionless, staring at her lap, he turned back, and whispered as though all were lost and he were looking into his own yawning grave: "An implacable fate has sent you here. You are not only called Kate, you are she herself. What is to become of us?" And, as she moved her arms in a helpless gesture, he came closer again, pushed her gently upon the bed, did with her as tradition demanded, and repeated the same three times weekly during the next two months, until in early autumn he asked a newly hired milkmaid what was to become of them now that fate had brought him and her together.

At length, after he had presented her with a pocket mirror, a hand-bag, an apron, and a notebook, Kate discovered that she had been deceived and was pregnant. John Theodoric declared in poetic terms that "the iron hand of necessity and unforeseen circumstances" had compelled him to betroth himself to the old and ugly Frederica von Oriola, the daughter of the landowner, who had been left on the shelf. But since by destiny his heart belonged to a Kitty, she was to say nothing and have no fears. At the same time he gave her ten thalers and a letter to Dr. Gaul in Geisenheim.

The doctor, having examined Kitty, shrugged his shoulders: "Too late!" She must not ask him to commit a murder, perhaps a double one. So saying, he held young Lienhardt's letter over the open fire until it was reduced to ashes.

At this the girl began to feel the desire to bear a child and go on living. But because John Theodoric's affair with the milkmaid, which she had found out, had shaken her confidence in her lover, she went over Grace Hill one evening to Carolswald, to see Charles Froehlich, the petition writer and legal adviser. He was a gigantic young man with a blond beard, who had been unable to find work because he had served a prison sentence.

Were there any witnesses to her intimate relationship with John Theodoric, the unofficial consultant inquired. Yes: in the first place, Froehlich's own sister, Theresa, who was also in service at the château; in the second place, the uniformed Urbanites, the Sports Club members, to whom John Theodoric had boasted quite openly of his affair.

"He'll give you a hundred thalers hush money—that's his price!" said the blond-bearded giant, pacing the room.

"To the milkmaid, not to me!" cried Kate Schwann. "And what will happen to the child?"

"The child will be a charge on the parish where it is born."

"A pauper child? And its father a millionaire? No, my dear sir." How much did she ask, Froehlich wanted to know.

"Nothing. Just for him to admit the paternity."

"That will be the best way—for you, not for him!" he said, and explained the state of affairs to her. Old Lienhardt, already half dead, uneasy about the great sums of money he had invested, on Urban's advice, first in the mines and then in the Sports Clubs, and alarmed, furthermore, lest after his own demise Urban should completely clean the three brothers out, had reached an agreement with the multi-millionaire landowner, Oriola, that his own eldest, John Theodoric, should marry Oriola's Frederica, much his senior and lame in one hip. Old Oriola, a thoroughgoing swine, had no objection, and the man-crazy Frederica still less; but both of them, half-insane bigots that they were, would be quite sure to reject a son-in-law and husband who had to support an illegitimate child. Consequently John Theodoric would be ready to pay more money rather than to acknowledge the paternity. "That is why I advise you to begin by having an amiable talk with the father of the child and finding out what he will do of his own accord. If he offers too little, we can bring pressure to bear on him." With these words, declining the proffered thaler, the legal adviser dismissed her.

On her way home Kate Schwann recalled the hatred of Oriola, the landowner, for his cousin and namesake, the Bishop; she also remembered the reason.

At one of the Catholic crèche festivals before Christmas, which Hesse and the leading brethren of the Revival Mission usually attended also, for reasons of interchurch harmony, Bishop Oriola, the mayor, Dr. Gaul, and the rich Crémieux had all been sitting around a table, drinking wine, and, jokingly spending the Lyonnais' millions, they decided to establish a "Museum of Hypocrisy." When it came the Catholic Bishop's turn to say what he would present to the museum as a concrete and instructive exhibit of hypocrisy, he replied—and his answer flew like the wind through the province—"The Christianity of my cousin Oriola."

If Oriola's son-in-law remained obdurate, she could always throw herself at the feet of the Bishop.

John Theodoric Lienhardt almost wept over "the ingratitude and wickedness of the world" when Kate asked him in reasonable language to acknowledge the paternity. Why, did she take him for an unnatural father? Of course he would acknowledge it, orally and in writing, as soon as he had married Oriola's daughter, and her dowry had been paid out to him.

Good; she would keep the written acknowledgment secret until he was married. The paper could be turned over in trust to a notary, with instructions not to make any premature use of it. "But give me the paper! Give me the paper!"

"Impossible. After I'm married, if the notary brings suit on the basis of the paper, my marriage could be dissolved because I'd 'concealed an essential circumstance.' Take pity! Do you want to ruin my life?"

"But it's all right to ruin the child's life?"

"It isn't living yet."

"It will, though."

"Never. There are nervous pregnancies, just the same as there are barren eggs. Get your stomach flushed out. I'm impotent."

"Too late, my dear boy!" Whispering scornfully, she recalled his words of love: "Fate has brought us together. What is to become of us?"

"I meant it honestly, and you didn't—one begins to see that now!" he cried. Rolling his eyes heavenward in anguish, he threatened to flee from the faithlessness of men to his estate in the south, to the depths of the forest:

> *"Far from the madding crowd's ignoble strife*
> *Their sober wishes never learn'd to stray;*
> *Along the cool sequester'd vale of life*
> *They kept the noiseless tenor of their way.*

So speaks the poet! Golden words!" he finished his declamation.

But Kate remained cool. "The paper! The paper!" she cried. "And then you're free."

Then he came closer to her, and looked at her as he had on the first day: "My own Kate, I should have thought you were wiser. Do you suppose I can ever love again? No. Just as the month of May comes but once a year, so love flowers but once in life, and it is love, not Mammon, that makes life beautiful. Do you want our young love and its sacred memory to be destroyed by an ugly scrap of paper?"

When he touched her hair, she softened. He laid her down upon the bed and slept with her. The days passed, he came again, and, although Kate had no thought but "The paper! The paper!" she felt it would be unkind to remind him.

8. THE CONTRACT

Meanwhile certain changes took place both in the château itself and on the farm belonging to it, which was situated on one side at a point where the park grows thinner. Theresa Froehlich, the servant girl, the sister of the legal adviser, disappeared without taking leave; the milkmaid, whenever Kate crossed the farmyard on some errand, would stand with arms akimbo, singing the song of "Maytime" that "comes but once a year" in her very face and eyes; and outside the gray building where the help were housed stood armed men whose faces were unfamiliar to the pregnant girl. They wore the familiar private uniform of the Urbanite Sports Divisions, holsters, and high laced boots; and shots echoed on the rifle range in the valley bottom between Grace Hill and the village of Carolswald more often than they once had—usually about noontime. A "sociable gathering for target practice" became an almost daily pastime.

One evening Kate, uneasy and curious, crept across hill and valley to see her brother Albert, a bookkeeper at the Faust mines. She worshiped her brother, three years her senior, the only blood relative she had left; and as a matter of fact, although his looks and manner seemed to indicate a fondness for ease and comfort, he had distinguished himself among his fellows. For when Hesse, with Andrew Zorn's help, found out after his great discovery that a life in accordance with the rule of the medieval carpenters could not be combined with the intolerant and overzealous activities of the Revival Mission brethren, he abandoned the work of his manhood, and induced many of the mission brethren to help build up the Order of Carpenters. A man of action, of quick, often precipitate decision, he declared out of hand that the word "carpenter" must be taken symbolically, and that it really meant follower or successor, i.e., of the Saviour; over the entrance of the Mountain Chapel he had the words carved: "Jesus was a Carpenter."

The practical purpose of this interpretation was to unite all classes of those employed in the mines, grouped according to their special trades, in the Order of Carpenters, and under the roof of the Mountain Chapel. Once Hesse had turned his back on the Revival Mission (under Oriola's influence, it was asserted), it declined into a mere minor sect. Both bishops seemed inspired by the bold and ambitious idea that the Carpenters should be the model and advance guard for all associations of Christian workmen. Except on great holidays a nonsectarian service was held in the Mountain Chapel; Hesse called the brethren "soldiers of the Lord," and a fast-day sermon by Bishop Oriola for some miners was the origin of the medievally rugged statement that it was "unfortunately necessary to give decaying Christianity a kick in the rump to make it get up from its deathbed, and rise to its full stature and militancy before its pygmy contemporaries." Being asked to apologize, Oriola said he had not been talking to the sheltered sons of ladies and gentlemen, but to the children of the people, in the language of the people, which last was indeed not the language of gentility, but the language of poetry.

In this work of reorganization Stark and Lorenz, two country schoolteachers, Lindbrecht, and also Schwann, the bookkeeper, had assisted the bishops; consequently Schwann occupied a high rank in the Brotherhood of Carpenters.

When Kate went into the little house she found the bookkeeper sitting under the hanging lamp at the dining table, which had already been cleared, and letting the baby, a two-year-old girl, make scrawls on a piece of paper. She screeched with delight and held out her tiny arms to Aunty. The poor betrayed girl, overwhelmed with apprehension as to whether she would ever have a home, or her child a father on whose knees it could play, halted at the threshold.

"Come in and take off your things!" said Annie Schwann. She belonged to the more austere wing of the Revival Mission, and was pregnant.

Of course there was nothing to hide here; they knew everything, Kate's misstep, her consultation with Charles Froehlich, her futile struggle for the "paper." They regarded the affair as in good hands because the ex-convict owed a debt of gratitude to the bookkeeper: Schwann had endorsed Froehlich's request for admission into the Carpenters' Brotherhood. Of the fact that Kate had resumed her intimate relationship with her seducer, and had even, through weakness and calculation, let him have his way under the open sky on a bench in the alder thicket of the park along the Geise, they knew nothing.

While her sister-in-law put the child to bed, the deceived girl made coffee in the kitchen, and asked whether the people of Carolswald were perfectly willing to have the Urbanites banging away on the rifle range even by torchlight at night. Didn't they hear the shots?

"Perfectly plainly," replied the bookkeeper; but so long as the Lienhardts themselves allowed this nuisance on their own property, nothing could be done except possibly by the police.

"But nobody knows them—they're all strange faces!"

His wife came back and poured coffee.

"They're probably runaways that Urban has smuggled into the province from the south," said the easygoing Schwann. "They can't find a job in the mines, so they're being trained."

"To shoot," said his wife.

"Naturally, to shoot."

Now Kate finally came out with her fears: "In that case they'd have to be recruits. But recruits move differently. These are men that have seen service, Albert, strangers, brought in from somewhere else —a guard, for protection. The clouds must be getting black!"

"Whom would they be protecting? John Theodoric?" asked Albert; but his wife, clutching his sleeve, implored him: "Don't keep anything from her—she's your own sister! She'd better sleep here in the kitchen, and look for work in Geisenheim, as far away as possible! If only we could raise the fare, we'd send you a long way off, and let Brother Froehlich carry on your case meanwhile; he won't miss any chances, and will take every advantage, you can depend on that."

"Because they won't give me my rights *I*'m supposed to hide?" cried Kate. "If he doesn't do what he promised, I'll kill him!"

"Easy, not so proud!" her brother quieted her, and the couple explained to her what she had not known: surely she would not set up to be Charles Froehlich's equal either in bravery or in physical strength, and yet he had taken his sister Theresa away from the

château, not because she could "better herself"—she had no place yet
—but because she was a witness!

"Because she's a witness?" asked Kate, turning pale. "Does that
mean because her life's in danger?"

"I don't say they mean to kill her right away," replied the easygoing Schwann, "but since she is a witness, Froehlich suspects that
they want to damage her credit. She has not only seen and heard too
much, but has talked too much in Marienhall."

"Don't go back to the château—stay here and sleep on the sofa!"
Schwann's wife begged.

"Tomorrow! Tomorrow evening surely," Kate promised, and, suddenly bursting into tears, she confessed that John Theodoric had
softened: "Yes. I've brought him to the point. He'll admit he's the
father."

The husband and wife hid their incredulity behind exclamations
of surprise.

"Is that so? He's going to pay?" asked the bookkeeper at length.
"Does he know what the new law for the protection of children provides?"

"*He* knows, of course," the sister-in-law corrected, turning to Kate.
"But do *you?*"

Yes. The counselor had told her: according to the new law an illegitimate child must be brought up to the standard of living and station in life of whichever parent was the better situated.

"True enough," Schwann agreed. "The consequence is that the
judge can make a millionaire pay enormous sums for support."

"Can? Has to! He has to! That's why I keep saying that Kate
ought to disappear!" urged his wife.

The pregnant girl looked down at her lap with a smile. If it was a
boy, the cradle of the newborn child would be decked in blue silk
bows, and the baptismal dress would be made of lace.

"Listen to me," she said confidently, "and I'll tell you word for
word what happened. Of course I could never have persuaded the fellow, but he went on a trip, and when he came back he was entirely
changed. So he must have talked to his lawyer, and of course the
lawyer knew about the new law. 'If you want to see reason triumphant,' John Theodoric said to me, 'then come to the park this evening.
No one will eavesdrop there.' I could hardly say no to that, and at

the bench under the alders he told me what the lawyer had said: he would have to pay, there was no help for that. Did I want to arrange things so that the Oriolas wouldn't find out? Of course I did: even Charles Froehlich had advised me to do that. So he said—I'm telling you in his very words what he told me: 'Kate,' he said, 'passion vanishes, love must dwell; the flower withers, the fruit must swell. Am I right?' How could I argue with that? 'Accordingly, calm consideration and reason must prevail,' he said. 'By the law of nature you must seek your own advantage, and by the law of nature I must seek my own.'"

"He really said that very prettily," nodded her sister-in-law, "just the way the tenor at the opera sings and the Hofer woman listens to him, with one arm in the air. And what about this?" and she made the gesture of counting out money.

"Listen: I'm telling you his very words," Kate went on. "'Do you remember, my child, what the law provides?' he asked me, and then he said himself, '. . . to the *standard of living* of whichever parent is better situated!'"

Albert Schwann laughed aloud, and they all remembered the abominable meanness of the Lienhardt family. All Marienhall knew that John Theodoric used to go to the canteen assigned to the help, on the pretext of trying out the food, in order to get his belly full. He would go up with an enamel bowl, like any workman, to the big soup kettle, say in an undertone: "I'd like some from the bottom!" in hopes of getting a few scraps of meat, take a tin spoon from the basket, eat at a remote table by the window, and ask for a second if there was any left. When his father was still in good health, and had to go by tram, he would ride to the last stop "to use up the ticket," and walk back on foot from the extreme western end of town, out by the Federal Police Barracks, to where he was going. When he had to go to the most expensive of the mountain sanatoriums to die, he boasted that he had never given away a penny to the municipal tramway.

"Well, congratulations!" said the bookkeeper. "According to his standard of living John Theodoric spends thirty thalers a month, tips included."

"That's just why the judge would have a hard time making a decision," said Kate, "and at most I might be given a hundred thalers a month for a period of twenty years."

"Twenty times twelve hundred makes twenty-four thousand thalers! I'd be satisfied with that," Albert said.

"He'll give me half, but right away, tomorrow evening, in return for a written and notarized statement that I've been indemnified, and will never demand anything more, not even acknowledgment of the paternity. Shall I do it?"

"What does Froehlich say?"

"He says I should. With the twelve thousand thalers in my hand, I can marry, and have my husband adopt the child."

And she took out of her handbag (John Theodoric's gift) the formal statement, written and authenticated by the local notary, that "the undersigned," etc., was fully indemnified.

"Where is he going to give you the money?"

"At the notary's, when I turn over my declaration to him. I'm supposed to meet him first, at the bench under the alders, and sign something else, more private."

"What?"

"That I will never, either directly or indirectly, approach the Oriola family, or communicate with them in any way. He's going to have it drawn up as a sworn statement, and I'll sign it, of course. The notary isn't supposed to know anything about that."

"Why not?"

"How do I know? Maybe because it's not his notary, but mine."

"How much have you got to pay the notary?"

"Nothing! He said to me, 'My dear Miss Kate, if you bring John Theodoric Lienhardt here to my desk with a check for twelve thousand thalers in his hand, you're a Sunday child! I won't take anything from Sunday children, because they bring luck.' "

"Well I'll be damned, Kate," said the bookkeeper, looking at his sister, "if I remember rightly, you *are* a Sunday child!"

She had in fact been born on an Easter Sunday. Since both contending parties, furthermore, had used common sense and overcome their passions, a successful outcome of the adventure was to be expected. And so, having cleared the table and expressed her thanks, Kate went back to the Lienhardt château. It was taken as settled that the moment she received the check for twelve thousand thalers at the notary's, she would move to her brother's and sister-in-law's, and look for a husband among the lower clerks at the mines. She could

be sure of the good offices of her brother, who was highly respected
in the Order of Carpenters.

9. FATAL OUTCOME

The following morning Theresa Froehlich, the servant girl, who
was temporarily working for her brother, the legal adviser, noticed
on leaving the house to fetch milk that a cross had been chalked on
the front door. She was alarmed, said nothing, and removed the mark
with a wet rag. An hour later, through the indefinable channels of
rumor, the people of Carolswald learned—and passed on the tale with
relish—that the servants' building and outbuildings of the detested
Lienhardt château had been searched by a patrol of six members of
the Federal Police. Charles Froehlich thought of his client, closed his
office, and went to see Albert Schwann in the office building of the
Johanna Mine. Even in those days it was his habit to hide his long
blond beard by turning up his coat collar. Although it was Saturday,
payday, the bookkeeper got up at once from his swivel chair, sent
Froehlich back home, instructed an office assistant what was to be
done, and knocked at the office door of his superior, the mine office
manager, von Lindequist, of whom, although he was respected for
his universal friendliness, people said he "didn't kill himself with
work." In reality the man, still young, was an administrative genius,
whose article on "Inspiring the Office," printed in the *Official Gazette
for the Province,* had produced a minor revolution and brought him
a letter of approval from the School of Administration at the capital.

[The peculiar circumstance that Albert Schwann did not go on his
journey of investigation with Froehlich, the unfortunate Kate's legal
adviser, but sent him home, and turned to his superior, the office
manager, remains unexplained in the Brandt report. Evidently the
town clerk thought it premature to reveal the hierarchical structure of
the Carpenters. For Charles Froehlich was a novice, while the office
manager and the bookkeeper were of the same rank in the brotherhood.]

Mr. von Lindequist maintained in his article that an office worker
who complained of too much work or too little time must either be
unfitted for the job, because he tended toward disorder, or else a liar.
Mr. Lindequist, I say, had not only plenty of time, but even more
inclination, to play truant. "Office work," he used to say, "is the ideal

profession because anyone can be replaced by anyone else, so that you, my friend, with your hankering after real life, can run off at any moment and have someone take your place."

No sooner said than done. When the bookkeeper and the office manager went out upon the sunny open grounds before the buildings, the yellow carriage of the Carolswald mine doctor was standing there, and the beautifully groomed chestnut pony was eating oats mixed with chopped straw out of a nosebag.

"Look at him cheating!" said Lindequist, pointing to the pony. The chestnut, occasionally turning his head to see if anyone was watching, puffed into the nosebag through his nostrils, so that the chopped straw flew out, leaving the heavier oats behind. "Just wait, my friend, you're going to take us to Marienhall!" threatened Lindequist; he lifted the strap of the nosebag off the pony's head, stowed it away in the back, mounted the driver's seat, and undid the ribbons, which were tied around the whip socket.

"You're crazy," said Schwann. But the adventurous young man cried, "Giddap!" and instructed an emerging office boy to tell the doctor that Lindequist had had to go to Marienhall—on police business. Not touching the village, they drove a little way across country, plunged into the bushy hollow that hides the rifle ranges, turned uphill into the ravine, and then the driver had to touch up the horse, which had dropped into a walk on the soft, rising forest path. The hills rise steeply right and left, green with underbrush and spruces. After a scant ten minutes of hard going, the ravine slowly descends to the valley of the Geise; the carriage rattled across the wooden bridge, the farm and outbuildings of the Lienhardt château came into sight on the right, and they turned left on the main highway, where the frame houses of officials and *rentiers* rose from among trees and shrubs on both sides.

Long, low, and white, with rows of flowers and vines before the windows of the third story, the customary archway through the middle to the central courtyard, surrounded by stables, storerooms, and offices —this is the Federal Police Barracks at the extreme west end of the town, peaceable, with sleepy cats outside the archway, all the windows opening southward, toward Carolswald, Bergdorf, Schenkendorf, Tann, where the humble miner picks the coal out of the living rock.

It may be remarked here that our most widely circulated paper, the *Mountain Province Advertiser,* sharply rebuked the inactivity of the

Federal Police in a series of articles. "Is it the sole duty of the imposing green-clad equestrians," writes the literary stylist of the local section, "to adorn the landscape? Ninety-nine out of a hundred of us never come in contact with these splendidly uniformed and well-fed police, since they are not authorized to take charge of traffic, fire prevention, or disturbers of the peace at night; in fact, not even to regulate the prevailing immorality and crime of every description. But what, then, is all this splendor? as the poet says. To anyone who may suppose that our Federal Police is the standing army of the Commissioner of Public Safety, and that its sole duty is to protect the life and property of the citizenry against political assault, I would point out that the regiment of mounted chasseurs commanded by Lieutenant Colonel Laurenti at Marienhall and the infantry brigade at Geisenheim are both of them almost as unoccupied as the mine office managers or the preachers."

Our friends Schwann and Lindequist, who were far from identifying themselves with the views of the newspaper paragraphist, found the police barracks in a state of tranquillity. This seemed to suggest that Sunday had already arrived, and no one, neither the officer on duty in the guard room nor Captain Heinz in the regimental offices, knew anything whatever about any dispatch of a patrol to the château, or any search of the Lienhardts' premises. Troops were being drilled in the riding school; anyone who was not riding out into the country on a regular police detail was required either to be doing stable duty or to be drilling with the squadron on the big drill ground.

The two Carpenters went down the stone steps and through the archway into the inner yard. The broad ground, rendered pleasant by its surrounding row of horse chestnuts planted in front of the buildings, lay quiet in the autumn sun; an oval of dark, trodden soil, the summer riding school, stood out against the bright surface of the sand. Now and then a white dot would come out of the building on the far side, grow as it came closer, and turn into an orderly in white drill uniform with gold buttons who had some business or other at the main building. At the left, on a bench against the wall, sat Lieutenant von Hesse, bare-headed and with his tunic unbuttoned, sunning himself, drawing figures in the sand with his riding quirt, watching a detachment of recruits who were being taught how to curry horses by a noncommissioned officer. The gleaming bays, switching their dark tails to drive off a gray horsefly now and then, stood as patient as donkeys in the sleepy autumn sun, quite accustomed to being curried the wrong way by recruits at the same season every year. Occasionally, when a curry-comb going the wrong way across their bellies tickled them, they would indulgently shift a hind hoof. If Hesse gestured with his riding quirt, the noncommissioned officer would come over—his drill jacket, unlike the short ones worn by the recruits, was cut like a tail coat—receive some instructions in an undertone, and pass them on in the same tone while he seized a currycomb, gathered the men in a semicircle around him, and did the currying himself.

The two truants had stopped in the shadow of the archway, and watched the training without themselves attracting notice.

"It's just like church," whispered Schwann; "the Bishop's son can't stand any loud noise."

"That's because he served for a year under Bessonoff," Lindequist returned. The aristocratic reserve of Count Bessonoff was smiled at all over the province, and his instructions regarding military discipline were passed around as jokes: "A man who shouts loses his dignity, appears vulgar, and destroys the respect due to a superior." Or: "No noncommissioned officer is to approach within ten paces of a private. Going closer creates intimacy. Intimacy is prohibited." Or: "The non-commissioned officer speaks, the captain whispers, the colonel gives his orders by gesture, eye, and in writing." Thus Brigadier General Count Bessonoff. Lieutenant von Hesse worshiped him.

"Good morning, Otto," cried Lindequist.

"Sit down," said Hesse after a glance at the two, without getting up. "What's new?"

"There are six Federal Police over yonder at Lienhardt's farm outside the help's quarters."

"Nonsense," replied Hesse, "somebody's been seeing ghosts again. People wish we'd clean house over there. What you guys wish for, you see—forgive my saying 'guys,' but it's true."

"People might be right, at that," observed the placid Schwann. "Federal Police, Chasseurs, Urbanites—three uniforms in little Marien-hall! I'm sure we could do without one of them."

As the Lieutenant shrugged his shoulders and motioned to the non-com, the two took their departure; after traveling a short distance toward town, they inspected, through the completely run-down hedge that enclosed the château park, and through the alder thicket, the

bench that John Theodoric Lienhardt had indicated to Kate as a nocturnal rendezvous. From the old wooden bridge, keeping under cover
like boys playing Indian, they scanned the château farm. Not a uniform
was in sight; Hesse was right.

Except that it would sound utterly fantastic (for what could a Lienhardt have to fear from a housemaid who had already been made to
see reason? And what, on the other hand, had she to fear, having
agreed to his proposal without stipulation or objection?), except that it
would sound like sheer gratuitous nonsense, one might say that this
bench, with the alder thicket on both sides behind it, directly before it
the steep, rocky declivity at whose bottom the Geise rippled—this bench
could bear witness to lovesick murmuring, and to bloody retribution.

Making their way in through a hole in the hedge, while crows
flapped away, the two friends found to their satisfaction that not a
dry leaf rustled under their cautiously advancing bodies, and not a
twig snapped: the underbrush was wet and slippery, the ground soft
with decaying vegetation. They crawled back, brushed each other off,
and decided to hide in the bushes at the appointed hour that evening
so as to hear Kate's negotiations with John Theodoric. The unfortunate
girl's anxiety for the future of her child was justified, and her demands
were modest when one reflected that Oriola's daughter had a dowry
of almost two million thalers; what was a ridiculous twelve thousand
to this? What, on the other hand, about John Theodoric, the son of
the man who rode to the end of the line and walked back to "use up"
his horsecar ticket—what could be expected of him?

At the château, meanwhile, Kate Schwann finished washing her
dishes and went to her bedroom for a short rest during the noon hour;
there she received by special messenger a letter from her legal adviser,
saying that she should pack her things at once, leave the château, and
come to see him. She obeyed on the spot, hurried to Carolswald with
her bundle on her back, left it with her sister-in-law, appeared at
Charles Froehlich's, and promised to take all his warnings to heart;
only one thing she never had done and could not do: leave her work
without giving notice. She would go back to the château, finish her
work, and appear punctually at the appointed rendezvous, the more
so since in Froehlich's own view John Theodoric would be coming off
very well indeed if the evening's encounter ended amicably, and once

her release was handed over, there was no objection to be feared from the Oriolas either.

"No, if you simply keep your word you have nothing to fear from John Theodoric. He's well out of it."

"I don't even recognize his vile face any more. By tomorrow I'll forget his name," she gritted out, "and when my sister-in-law takes me in I'll study the pictures in church by day and remember them by night, so that the child shan't look like him!"

"Remember two things: first, leave the money with the notary. Don't carry it around the streets. Your brother won't take any money from you; your sister-in-law can't, as a mission sister. Second, if John Theodoric has been lying to you, if by chance he should toss you scraps of paper instead of the money, and laugh at you besides, because he thinks he can get out of it still more cheaply—no matter what he does, keep perfectly cool; don't say a word, turn your back on him, and be off without giving the château another look; or, better yet, go to the guard room of the Federal Police, and ask for a place to sleep. The color sergeant or sublieutenant on guard duty will have been informed in the meantime, and will show you a room. Have you got everything well in mind?"

"God will repay your kindness, Brother Froehlich," she said, shaking hands and taking her leave.

At five in the afternoon Otto von Hesse, already dressed to go out, received a written communication signed by Carpenters Schwann, Froehlich, and von Lindequist. He turned over the letter to Color Sergeant Laurenti, the eldest son of the commander of the Chasseurs, with orders to house and look after "Sister Schwann."

At about the same hour, Schubert the coachman set out from the Lienhardt farm with a box cart such as is used for transporting cattle, drove down the Geise through the town, turned into the highway that runs parallel to the Carolswald road (that is, southward) at the eastern end, and handed to the commander of the Sports Division at Bergdorf, a butcher's son, sealed orders requiring him to take a detachment of men "without passport or right of domicile" and occupy the range of low hills that cut off the rifle ranges on the south, and to keep away strollers or the curious. This order, which had been issued on other occasions also, was due to the fact that Carolswald common extends to the ridge of the low-lying hills, and the hostilely disposed

villagers had often annoyed the Urbanite Sports Divisions at their
target practice. The order was signed: "Peter George, Chief of Staff."

Peter George was Peter George Lienhardt, the youngest of the three
brothers. The eldest, John Theodoric, too much of a weakling for
marches and military exercises, was never seen in uniform; he
"directed," if one cares to call it that, the paternal mines. The second,
Gregory William, lived in the south as master of an estate, and was
unknown to the people of the mountain province. It was under him
that Urban had served as a manager. The youngest, Peter George,
thirty years old, and the strongest of them all, had been called to
account by Bessonoff as a young lieutenant "for misuse of authority,"
and been cashiered from the army; he now did nothing at all, unless
his playing soldier as "Chief of Staff of the Sports Divisions" and his
suspicious interest in corporal punishment be considered an activity.

By the light of a candle (for darkness had already fallen), Kate
Schwann made herself beautiful before the mirror: she wanted to
appear with John Theodoric before the notary in her Sunday best, her
hair done, wearing coat, hat, and gloves, to deposit the twelve thousand thalers in safe hands, and then await the birth of the child at her
brother's, conscious that she was a "good match." But how about signing? Oh, it was perfectly all right to sign, Froehlich had said, so long
as there was nothing more in the document than her promise never
to communicate with the Oriolas. "Take a good look, read over what
you're going to sign! Many a man has looked too late, and found he
had signed his own death warrant!"

Ah, she would take good care that no slippery trick should be worked
on her. And as the darkness thickened, she lit her farm lantern, a
handy one of antique make, its pierced shell of wrought iron forged
by a good workman into the long, thin, jagged leaves of a prickly
tropical plant that stores up water.

Schwann and Lindequist, wearing high boots and country jackets,
crawled with the agility and caution of young Mohican scouts through
the hedge and underbrush to the very edge of the abyss where the
Geise flows. Facing them on the other bluff, higher up and no more
than thirty feet away, stood the bench, the scene of the rendezvous,
surrounded by a semicircle of alder thicket. The château behind it
shone through, because the light of a carriage lantern fell on the wall.
So there must be a wagon standing ready on the drive in front of the

château, the two decided, and as an ordinary wagon has two lanterns, the one on the side toward the alder thicket was being darkened. The friends grew uneasy, and they reflected that while their hiding place was excellently adapted to eavesdropping, since even whispers from the other side could not escape them, it was not at all advantageous for helping anyone who found himself in danger on the farther bank; the gorge was too wide to be jumped. Besides, the footing for a leap was slippery, and the far bank was the higher.

John Theodoric came first, put his slouch hat on the bench, and made gestures of salutation toward the copse on his right. He was being guarded, then: this craven with the brain of a toad was afraid of the girl, whose own hands were trembling in a fever of scared expectation as she crossed the drive from the château and followed the narrow path through the thicket toward the scene of the forthcoming decision, lit by the swaying light of the farm lantern.

She put the lantern down on the ground before her; as he was looking into the gorge, one hand at his mouth with the expression of a thinker, she sat down beside him, and said with a voice full of humility: "You were going to give me a letter, sir, that you were to write and I was to sign. I'm ready."

"Do you know what I've just been doing?" John Theodoric asked, turning toward her.

"No."

"I've been looking into the abyss."

He took an open envelope from his overcoat pocket, unfolded the letter, and asked her to read it very carefully, and, just in case she wanted to unburden her conscience, to sign it.

The letter was a statement under oath before a notary by Schubert, the coachman, Matuleit, the farm dairy hand, and Leschinski, the assistant forester, that each of them had repeatedly had sexual commerce, in the stable, the quarters for the help, the barn, and on the bench in the alder thicket, during the months of July through September, with Kate Schwann, chambermaid, of Carolswald. Under the clumsily written names of the three there was a space, terminated by a ruled line. Under this were the words: "The truth of the above is fully attested by: . . ." No signature. Kate saw that "in order to unburden her conscience" she was supposed to sign this.

This had been bound to happen. She had never believed it would come out right. What was it Froehlich said: "If he tosses you scraps of paper, and laughs at you, don't say a word; turn your back on him; go to the Federal Police." She trod the letter into the dirty leaves (to which circumstance its preservation is due), picked up the lantern whose light she had read by, arose, turned to the right, and started off along the path.

She had hardly gone three paces before John Theodoric also got up, and said: "The barn for you! Get the bull to kick you in the belly, you blackmailer, and bury your bastard under the straw!"

He should not have said that: it was too much. They were his last words. Kate turned, swinging the lantern, and drove the wrought-iron points and the crashing glass into his face. His blood spattered her dress; gurgling, he staggered toward her, received a terrific blow of her fist, and went over the edge into the gorge, his arms upraised. The body thudded on a boulder and rolled slowly into the brook.

The bookkeeper tried to jump up, but Lindequist pulled him back into hiding by his leg. "Shut up!" he whispered. "His goose is cooked."

Then the Yellows sprang from the bushes on the far side, felled Kate, and thrust a knotted cloth into her mouth; while two of them relit the lantern (which still worked) to fish John Theodoric's body out of the water, the rest flung Kate with curses and commands into the wagon that stood on the drive.

Schwann and Lindequist, who abandoned their place of concealment at this moment in order to reach the Federal Police Barracks before the Yellows did, and if possible to secure their arrest, both afterward testified separately that in the light of the relit lantern they had recognized Peter George Lienhardt, the "Chief of Staff," who had been missing since the night of the murder. After Kate Schwann, overpowered and lying on the ground, had been abundantly treated to kicks, they said he had knelt down and sung in the half-unconscious girl's ear, incidentally in a firm, strong voice, the following rhyme:

> *Hurrah, hurrah, the dead child is there,*
> *The dead child is cheering, I do declare!*

The nineteen-year-old Color Sergeant Laurenti, meanwhile, was sitting in the guard room of the police barracks, reading *Ivanhoe;* the letter from the Carpenters he had covered with a paperweight. Ah, when he was of age he would be admitted into the brotherhood where the humble called the great by their first names without envying them, where one man helped another, and all had vowed to "avert harm and misfortune from one another."

About this time the wind rose, blowing strongly from the north-west, from Marienhall toward the mine district, so that shots, cries, and commands on the rifle ranges were blown toward the villages of Carolswald and Bergdorf, but were not heard in Marienhall—a circumstance that contributed, along with the customary Saturday leave given to many commissioned and noncommissioned officers of the police, to the failures of that night. Not even the departure of the box cart, on whose floor the unlucky Kate lay tied up in a flour sack, was heard by the two friends as they hastened away. If they had listened for but a moment or two, great disasters might have been prevented. But as it was, assuming that the Yellows would turn over Kate to the Federal Police as a murderess, and eagerly hastening to forestall them, they never noticed that the wagon at the western entrance of the park did not cross the bridge and go up the main street, but turned in to the ravine that Schwann and Lindequist had traversed in the opposite direction that morning.

The adventure-loving color sergeant, glad that his captain and the lieutenant were absent, immediately on hearing the news ordered out the emergency squad, which was kept ready for duty day and night, and had the little squadron carriage made ready for Schwann and Lindequist, the bearers of the news. Through the western gate of the park, which the box cart, traveling in an unsuspected direction, had left twenty minutes before, they raced into the courtyard of the Lienhardt château—a patrol remained at the gate, which was closed. The frightened farm people, who were standing around whispering, were formed in two lines and guarded; the rest of the squad occupied the exits.

Thus for the second time the Carpenters pursued in the wrong direction the box cart in which Peter George and his band of murderers were carrying poor Kate Schwann to the rifle range in order to set her up as a living target. It was this second mistake that Lieutenant Hesse had in mind when he said later that it was a guilty responsibility which to make good would require a whole lifetime of police work.

But a grotesque spectacle awaited the color sergeant, the two friends, and a few noncommissioned officers when they were led into the castle itself by the old farm overseer. In the middle of the great entrance hall, covered over, the dead man lay on a raised bed; around him and along the walls a carouse was in progress. The whole "Sports Group" stationed at the château, and now assembled as a guard of honor, had fetched beer, sausages, pork, and bread from the cellar; they were drunk already, and one, standing on the table, brandished his side arm as a baton while they sang marches and love songs by the light of candles that they had stuck into bottles. The man who had been sent to town to get the doctor for the post-mortem examination did not come back, and the six "noncommissioned officers" who were lined up with drawn bayonets to right and left of the dead man's bed as a guard of honor had grown bored: pulling up chairs to sit in, they had great piles of beer bottles before them, and were brawling noisily. When the Federal Police came in, silence fell, and the Yellows tried to adopt a military attitude; it is a principle of the Urbanites not to provoke trouble with police or the military.

Where had the box cart with the girl gone? the color sergeant barked at them. Schwann and Lindequist had paused at the door to the hall.

They knew nothing about it. The Chief of Staff had himself chosen the men detailed to transport the murderess to prison, and ordered those remaining behind to lay out the body in state, and to inform the hospital guard, which would see to everything necessary. All yelling at once, they told what they suspected.

"So! And you're guzzling here with the corpse!" yelled the color sergeant to hide his embarrassment. The adventure was getting out of hand.

They mumbled something about wakes, funeral banquets, and ceremonial.

In the judicial inquiries it appeared that these wretched, misguided creatures, seeing their master's corpse come to the surface of the water and apparently move an arm of its own accord in the ripples, had fled into the bushes, a prey to terror and superstition, and could only be induced by the promise of a "funeral banquet with beer" to help retrieve the body.

The trampling of horses was heard in the courtyard: Captain Heinz with two squadrons occupied the château. The homicide commission of the criminal police turned up in their antiquated coach; the Urbanites were locked in the stables, and the official machinery began to grind.

Suddenly, while Captain Heinz was in the act of questioning the mine office manager and the bookkeeper in the presence of the doctors, the southern sky turned red, the window rattled with explosions, and Lieutenant von Hesse rushed into the ground-floor steward's room where the questioning was taking place. Behind him, hatless, with tangled hair, came blond-bearded Charles Froehlich and two messengers from the embattled men of Carolswald.

"Bergdorf is on fire!" The miners of Carolswald, commanded by Stark, the schoolteacher, had cleared out the village mayor's big barn, the arsenal of the Sports Divisions. But the Carolswald men were being pushed back; in their retreat they had blown up the barn.

How about the fire department?

No; Bergdorf was past saving—the wind was blowing straight into the village. But Carolswald might be saved if the police hurried, the last messenger added. Laurenti asked if he might inform his father, and raced off when the captain shrugged his shoulders.

Hesse suggested mounting three squadrons.

"With two thousand people shooting at each other, young man, you'd better not get between them," said fat Heinz, "or you'll be riddled in short order."

A sergeant of the mounted Chasseurs reported and was admitted. He said the governor had already ordered out the Geisenheim fire department and the infantry ambulance corps. The Chasseurs had taken to horse in order to shut off the battleground on the south and east, lest people from Karlsbrunn and Tann should mix in. Help had been requested by telephone from the Carolswald village mayor's. "The Lienhardt men are pushing in to Carolswald."

At this Captain Heinz changed his mind. "I'll take the dirty work on my shoulders," he said, turning to young Hesse: "You have the first and third squadrons get ready. Ride over, establish contact with the Chasseurs, and put an end to this village war. You privileged characters from Carolswald," he instructed Carpenters Schwann, Lindequist, Froehlich, and the two messengers, "since you don't know anything anyhow, may as well follow. I'll stay here at the telephone, but you'd better not dream of bothering me!"

John Theodoric's corpse was taken to the hospital, and the captain drew up a preliminary report with the doctors. The head wound, inflicted by two sharp points of the wrought-iron leafwork, was enough to have caused death. The twelve-foot fall on boulders had resulted in spinal injuries and a broken rib.

Lastly they discussed the removal of Kate Schwann; the captain detailed for the first time what the mayor of Carolswald and, later, the stationmaster of Marienhall had reported to him concerning the outbreak of the disturbances.

The box cart with Schubert, the coachman, the firing squad of six men, and probably Peter George, the Chief of Staff of the Sports Divisions, had transported the unfortunate woman to the rifle range, at whose eastern end, next to a box for the scorekeeper, the targets stood. Here Kate was roped naked to a post, set up as a target, and shot at with small-caliber carbines according to a system derived from Indian stories, by which the captive suffers protracted torture before being killed. Probably, it seemed, they had begun at the feet, and put one shot above another up the legs. The arms and legs were so torn that the hits could not be counted. In doing so they took time to listen to the animal screams emitted by their victim. Torches and hurricane lanterns lit up the living target, and the strong northwest wind that carried shots and screams to the villages must have been weaker in the hollow, or else have passed unnoticed by the men in the excitement of the tortures they were inflicting.

The awful, long-drawn screams reached Carolswald, whose inhabitants rushed from their houses under arms. "It is difficult," the captain declared, "to break these poachers' sons of using weapons." Determined not to be driven back as heretofore by threats or warning shots, they advanced upon the rising bushy ground in two columns led by the gigantic Charles Froehlich and Principal Stark. Both leaders had secured mounts, and indeed with the help of the women every possible object capable of being used as a weapon, every horse and vehicle, had been brought out of stables and sheds in anticipation of strong resistance. The defenders on the ridge of the slight rise, hopelessly inferior in numbers (apparently no more than half a file of thirty-two men), and these furthermore in the light of torches and hurricane lanterns from the bottom of the hollow, had no chance, despite superior equipment, against the great waves of their assailants.

Just then the Lienhardt men from Bergdorf came to the assistance of their companions; Principal Stark had to swing the right wing of the Carolswalders around to the east, and although the latter drove the enemy back, they suffered delays and losses in the exchange of fire that developed. The firing squad in its box cart, however, found time to escape from the hollow. Half an hour later the stationmaster telephoned police barracks to say that eight noncommissioned officers of the Federal Police in uniform had left by the evening express. When the train was searched at Geisenheim, no one wearing a green uniform was found on board. The murderers of Kate Schwann had escaped.

After a brief skirmish the surviving defenders of the rifle range hung a white rag from a withered pine on the height, threw down their arms in despair of breaking through, fled to the thickets of Grace Hill, and stole to the rear façade of the Lienhardt château, hoping to creep back through the cellarways into the servants' building. They were apprehended by Federal Police patrols.

The Carolswald men of the attacking left wing charged into the hollow. Kate Schwann's body, head and chest fallen forward, covered with blood, her limbs in shreds and already stiffening, still hung at the stake. The miners, small farmers, hands, and artisans, having tipped their caps and looked at one another mutely, left a guard with the dead woman, and followed the advance of their right wing. They pushed into Bergdorf, looted the arsenal of the Urbanites, set fire to houses, barns, stables, and dispatched three messengers in succession to ask help from Marienhall when the Yellows, re-enforced meanwhile, drove them back out of the burning village toward Carolswald. First they sent Froehlich, then the other two.

10. SPEECH ON THE PARADISE OF THE TORMENTOR

Under the gas lights of the great yard in the police barracks the noncommissioned officers and sergeants major were shouting at the top of their lungs and bustling about to make good the voices and function of their fellows who were absent on leave; Hesse, however, aged twenty-six, trembled for his first command when the man on guard duty in the office called him to the telephone. It was the major. Thank God (the young man thought) the governor's uncertainty seemed to have infected the police commander; he said once or twice,

"Oh, do you think so?" urged moderation on the lieutenant, and promised to appear within an hour on the battlefield, "Or, to be exact, at the office of the mayor of Carolswald."

The two squadrons took the carriage with the five "privileged characters" between them, galloped across the Geise and through the ravine at such a rate that the old wooden bridge echoed, and came to a halt at the end of the ravine. Here the remaining detachment of Carolswald men had posted a few guards; old Fuchs, the wheelwright, shading his eyes, held a lantern aloft and, in a quasi-military attitude (for he had been in the service), made his report to the lieutenant. Hesse, leaning down from his horse, learned that in expectation of the homicide commission and its photographers they had not ventured to go near the dead woman. Beyond question Peter George Lienhardt, "the well-known beast," was responsible.

"Have you got torches and candles at hand?" Hesse asked.

"Yes, sir!"

"Then please have the place lit up, Mr. Fuchs—the post and the corpse. We want to take a careful look at it." And to the astonishment of the Carolswald men the lieutenant ordered both squadrons to dismount and draw up in an open square around the martyr's stake, where he delivered the speech published in the *Official Gazette* a few days later to refute some malicious exaggerations, which was severely criticized by the public for its dry and sarcastic tone. "What says the ceremonious Count Bessonoff to this barrack-yard jargon of a minister's son confronted with the majesty of death?"(*Geisenheim Daily Times.*) "Promoted to be an officer in his early youth through paternal influence, and not dreaming of the nearness of that which is divine, he did not order his men to remove their helmets or kneel down. Not a sigh, not a sign of emotion was to be observed, nothing but the command, 'At ease!' and then, in the rasping voice of a top sergeant, a didactic statement so truly military in its presumption that it could not possibly have been uttered in any other country. Mr. von Hesse himself set a perfect example of callousness. He stepped up to the tortured figure, put two fingers to the visor of his cap for no more than a second—as one lieutenant might greet another on the drill ground—and studied the wounds; then he turned to his men, and delivered his exhortation. We have been hearing for seven years that the President is concentrating his efforts on improving the officer class. Is this the result?" (*The Beautiful South,* official organ of the Chamber of Commerce.) "Coldness, hardness, contempt for the truth, distortion of the facts, irony and absurdity in face of a most mournful spectacle—this is what our ruling class has come to. Why do they not at least proclaim their intentions, at long last, by forbidding the intellect, and setting up in its place their own ideal of humanity, the top sergeant? Ah, but in a few years even this will not be necessary: as the fast-day sermon delivered with impunity by Mr. von Oriola proves, even the bishops have already begun to talk like top sergeants. Destroy language and you destroy civilization!" (Nicholas Edwin Schiele in *Aurora, Monthly Review of Art and Life.*)

The original version of the speech, not modified for publication, was as follows, according to a transcription by Sergeant Benjamin Werner, a member of the Carpenters:

"Members of the first and third police squadrons! Lest the picture that you see before you now should ever fade from your memories, I shall ask my rich brother-in-law to donate three hundred copies of the picture of this victim of a sadistic murder that will be taken by the criminal police, and I shall even ask him to contribute the frames, so that each one of you may hang the framed picture in his quarters, and never forget or rub out, let alone deny, what he has seen tonight. I am not thinking now of the dead woman. She is already confronting her God, whereas we are confronted with the perpetrator. We were confronted with the perpetrator when she was still screaming and we heard nothing. No, we heard nothing; we were deaf—not by chance or because of the northwest wind, but so as to take upon ourselves a guilty responsibility which to make good will demand not weeks or months of police work, but our whole lifetime.

"What is the meaning of those pitiful screams? It is double: the perpetrator wanted to hear them; in him they produced a paradisiac ecstasy, the supreme and only ecstasy that no effort, no journey, no adventure, no crime, and no trouble will prevent him from tasting. Whatever enjoyment this life can offer him, he enjoys when the tormented creature cries out. The scream of the victim is the paradise of the tormentor. The devils of hell, particularly the smaller ones, the downtrodden firemen and stokers—why, men, if you stop to think it over sensibly, you cannot but conclude that the devils have begun to find it tiresome after thousands of years down below, and are coming out into the light, preparing to buy a pleasant little villa on the Geisenheim highway.

"Why don't they do it? Think it over! Use your reasoning powers! They don't do it because they are quite sure of the single minute that will repay them for a thousand years' hard work: the minute when the tortured victim screams. For during the moment that the scream lasts, the devils are in paradise; no sacrifice is too great for the enjoyment of that moment, as the poet affirms:

> *A single moment's bliss in Paradise*
> *Is not too dearly bought with death itself.*

"This is what the scream signifies to the perpetrator. But what does the tortured victim mean by her scream? Surely not the pain alone; she cried out for help. She was screaming for us, for us, men, for our well-aimed volley that would have laid her tormentors low. Why did we stay at home? Never mind the west wind; dig deeper for the real reasons. We came too late, that is evident. But would we have been in time an hour sooner, a day, a week sooner? For the poor victim, no doubt: what interests us policemen, however, is not the dead woman, but the killer. As a policeman one cannot be proud of catching and wiping out the tormentor red-handed, at the most innocent moment of his life. For the evildoer unmasks himself before the world *when* he does his deed; he presents himself to the police, throws away his disguise, makes himself honest, and the kindly volley carries him off. It is the evildoer who does *not* commit his deed who is dangerous, a dreadful foe and worthy quarry for the police. For he gives us no rest; he puts us on the rack of expectation, because we know one thing certainly: his life, whether he be in the Senate or the tavern, whether speaking or playing cards, every moment of his life is a preparation for his misdeed.

"The tormentors have escaped, as you know. If we had caught them and shot them, they would have died calmly and gladly, as indeed any man dies contentedly when the meaning of his life has not been withheld from him. The meaning of life is paradise: but the criminal's paradise, as I have already said, is the moment when his victim screams. Anyone who does *not* wish to hear the cry of torment is quite uninteresting and not a criminal at all.

"The tormentors have escaped, and just as their past life has been preparation, so too their future life will be preparation: the criminal always has this music sounding in his ears, the cry of the anguished victim, but imaginary music does not satisfy him; he must hear it from without. We policemen, therefore, with the framed picture of the dead woman before our eyes, will atone for our guilt, shooting down the tormentors wherever we find them, at the inn or in parliament, working in the fields, in bed with their wives—because their every act is preparation. If anything is not clear to anyone he may ask now. No one? Squadrons—march!"

II. TOBIAS AND VERONICA. THE LIENHARDT CHÂTEAU IN ASHES

In moments of peril, in darkness and confusion, the man of highest resolution comes to the fore. Accordingly, before he knew it or could get a good general view of the situation in the burning village of Carolswald, Otto von Hesse found himself commanding a mixed troop of Chasseurs and Federal Police; he attacked the Bergdorf men and the uniformed Urbanites mercilessly, pushed them out of the village, and had already done great execution among them by the time they sent a flag of truce, asking time to get their wounded out of the line of fire. But Lieutenant Colonel Laurenti, commander of the Chasseurs, who had arrived at last to relieve the young police lieutenant of the responsibility, laughed at the man with the white flag, and demanded absolute surrender within ten minutes. And so the men of Bergdorf, whose blazing village was gutted down to the last cottage, had to surrender before they could administer the same medicine to the hated Faustites of Carolswald; for the wind, blowing steadily from the northwest until after midnight, was away from the village, sweeping smoke and sparks from burning buildings into the faces of the invaders, and hampering their progress.

There was a moment's embarrassment when Laurenti ordered a bugle call to announce the cessation of hostilities; the regulations provided no call for civil disturbances, and the Lieutenant Colonel, a smooth-shaven, pedantic man in spectacles, rejected as improper the suggestion that the call for the end of maneuvers be sounded. Finally the infantrymen who had come with their ambulance corps sounded retreat; the call traveled clear and joyful through the night, and the work of the doctors, nurses, and ambulance men began at the same

time with the arrest of the survivors from Bergdorf. As the expected
rain did not materialize, work went on at the first-aid stations and
field hospitals until noon of the following day. At about this time
the martial law proclaimed early in the morning by Radowitz was
ended by the newly appointed governor, Count Bessonoff; no expulsion of the "persons without passports," or, in other words, the runaways from the south, took place—nor could it, since most of them
were under arrest.

At two in the afternoon of October ninth, the day following the
bloody night—320 dead had already been counted—government headquarters issued the following order, which caused much shaking of
heads: "Quiet is restored. The military and the police will return to
their barracks." Protests from the mayors of both mountain towns
that this order would give the troublemakers an opportunity to resume
their vengeful work went unanswered.

Our people distinguish very sharply between a natural death suffered in combat and an unnatural death due to murder. And so even
during the bloody night itself the unexplained disappearance of Theresa Froehlich, the "witness" in the abortive lawsuit that Kate Schwann
was to have brought, attracted attention. She had told her brother
Charles in the late afternoon, as he was about to leave her on his
way to meet Lindequist, of the white cross chalked on their door.
She thought it must have been a death sign put there by order of
John Theodoric. Accordingly, since she did not seem to be safe in the
legal adviser's cottage, he took her for the night to the so-called town
offices, and the mayor's family received her. At eleven o'clock at night
—of course not a soul was asleep, for the Bergdorf men were charging
on Carolswald—she had gone out in the yard to get wood from the
woodshed: strong coffee was to be made for the major of police,
who had promised his assistance and a visit. She did not come back;
a vain search went on all night. At seven in the morning some ambulance men of the Chasseur regiment found her mutilated body in
a copse near Bergdorf. She had been attacked innumerable times
before her skull was crushed, said the doctor who made the post-
mortem. Her brother Charles, seeing the dead girl, made the strange
statement that he "must change his life." Two days later, while the
bells of all the churches in the province rang by government order,

all vehicles stopped, and work was halted, she and her fellow worker Kate Schwann were interred in the Carolswald cemetery.

A heavy sleeping potion had been given Albert Schwann, the book-keeper, on the morning of the ninth; his companion, von Lindequist, sat by his bedside. He woke up toward evening, sent his friend off, washed carefully, and began to put on his Carpenter's costume. It was a Sunday. He took the shirt out of the box—a black shirt of stout, shiny material, the breast decorated with embroidery, and closing at the neck with a dark-red silk cord with tassels. The smooth black trousers hug the legs tightly, flaring at the calf, and dropping in wide bell bottoms around the ankles, leaving the double-soled laced shoes free. Finally he put on the short, close-fitting jacket, made of the same smooth material as the trousers. It buttons with a double row of big black buttons, each button with four holes, and its sleeves are so short that the flounces and ruching of the cuffs on the silk shirt show below them. The soft, round black hat has an unusually broad brim, slightly turned up. This, then, is the uniform of the Carpenters; Schwann, however, buckled on over it the wide brown belt with the holster that the captors of the Urbanite arsenal had given him as his share of the booty. Crossing the street, he pulled at the bell of a house on whose door a white cardboard placard announced the office hours of Counselor Charles Froehlich. The mayor's daughter opened the door, wiping her mouth with her apron: she had cooked the lone man's supper, and was eating with him. Schwann, not taking off his hat, ordered "Brother Froehlich" to ring the church bells and tell the Carpenters they were to fall in on the highway before the cemetery, armed and in costume, within a half-hour.

And with a wrinkled brow, slightly embarrassed when Froehlich, in some surprise, asked why, the bookkeeper confessed he had dreamed that the "well-known beast" had been hidden in the Lienhardt mines. Since "the governor hesitates to use force," then, they would have to take matters in hand themselves. The legal adviser obeyed at once; Albert Schwann, taking off his hat and saying a short prayer, ate up the supper with the mayor's daughter.

They were not finished, and Schwann was just praising the elderly maiden's work, the crisp potatoes, the poached eggs, and the way she had managed to fry the fat out of the bacon, when Tobias Witt, the apprentice, came out of the bedroom giving on the yard, greeted his "uncle" Schwann, said, "She's asleep!" and sat down at the table, resting his elbows on the table top and burying his face in his hands.

"Sit up properly!" said the Carpenter. "You'll learn to control yourself yet."

"Never!" the boy wept.

For Theresa Froehlich, the dead woman, had had by a journeyman mason, who had "gone on a journey" and never come back, a child now eleven years old, the sandy blonde, angelically beautiful Veronica. One day when she was four she had come running to her mother, who was then in service at Carolswald, and had not yet given up hope of seeing her lover again. "Is it true that Father got drowned?" the child asked. Theresa screamed, and found out from her neighbor that for a joke the village children had asked Veronica where her father was, and had immediately answered themselves, copying an ugly phrase from the grownups: "Your father got drowned in the buttermilk." Thus Theresa discovered that cruelty was at work poisoning her child, and she sent her away to a childless couple in Karlsbrunn. These farm people adopted the child for her beauty, but she went to see her mother whenever she liked, and Theresa herself went over to Karlsbrunn every Sunday with some little present.

Now it happened that the fatherless girl had been a great friend of Tobias Witt, the apprentice; from the time she was nine. He was her first male playmate, but so tender and careful that when the rumor of Theresa's awful end flew through the villages, he rushed over at once to Karlsbrunn lest his "little sweetheart" should find anything out, and induced the frightened peasant couple to let him take Veronica to her uncle Charles' in Carolswald. We may well be astonished at the boy's delicate perception, which told him that after the terrors and bloodshed they had gone through the people of Carolswald would not repeat the joke about the buttermilk. On the way, since her mother's death could not be concealed for a day, he told his little friend that Theresa, carrying munitions to the battling brethren, had fallen "like a brave soldier." And, holding hands, while the wind blew across the fields, they sat down at a meadow's edge and wept.

"You mustn't ever be a soldier!" Veronica begged.

"Never!" young Tobias promised.

Incidentally, even as early as that Sunday, October ninth, it was apparent that the Urbanites had received a blow from which they would find it hard to recover, at least in our region. For when the Carpenters led by Schwann and Froehlich, armed and in costume, approached the gate of the Lienhardt mines in the darkness, the clerical force had already abandoned the office, and the watchman with his lantern stood outside his hut, leaving the way open for them.

"What do you mean by letting us in?" Schwann asked.

At this the watchman let slip that the management had known an hour previously that the Carpenters would be coming, and had asked assistance from the new governor—or else the right to fire upon unauthorized intruders. Enough blood had been shed already, Count Bessonoff had replied, and military assistance would come too late. At this, the watchman said, the bosses had "seen which way the wind was blowing," and had made off.

Schwann gave the old fellow a cigar, ordered a search of the buildings, and, when this proved fruitless, telephoned to government headquarters. With many protestations of submissiveness and polite expressions of regret he explained two things to the governor. In the first place, the culprits might be hidden below ground: so no more lifts could go down. Accordingly, the mines would have to suspend operations and be kept under guard.

"How long?" asked Count Bessonoff.

"Until the murderers come to light."

"I see. And what's the other thing?"

"Secondly," Schwann replied, "a sense of common justice requires that the Carpenters be not refused permission to search the Lienhardt château at Marienhall from roof to foundations, as well as the alder thicket."

Bessonoff agreed. He would be at Marienhall himself within an hour, bringing a company of Chasseurs.

Whether it was through clumsiness or by intent no one has ever discovered, but at midnight, after the explosion of a box stored in the cellar, the Lienhardt château went up in flames, and, the fire departments being still busy in Bergdorf and Carolswald, burned to its foundations. Two Chasseurs of the First Company were injured severely, and Lieutenant Colonel Laurenti slightly.

On his porch in the high mountains, meanwhile, old Lienhardt, with blue lips, whistling breath, and half his mind, died cursing his enemies, after having rescued seven million thalers at the last moment

from "the stinking syndicate of robbers and arsonists" that was pocket-
ing his mines, and having received extreme unction.

Dr. Urban, in the full-dress uniform of a general of the Sports
Divisions, with his new "Chief of Staff" at his side, for Peter George
did not reappear, delivered a funeral oration "for that merchant
prince, that Maecenas of science, that father of the oppressed," which
seemed to lend wings to the very air, and made three ladies swoon.

BOOK ONE

GOOD WILL AND RECONCILIATION

XIII

D URING those weeks, while the light, brownish, efferves-
cent, slightly sweet new wine that is called "Feather-White"
was being served in the south of the country; while our
Jacob Willert, strolling, drinking, arguing with the bishops,
with Matthew Brandt, with Peggy, found himself unable to part from
the tenderness of the wine-loving province, admitted that he "still
had much to learn," and therefore, as a pupil of life at a trout dinner
with John Christopher and Josephine Laemmle, and an astonished
listener also at the meetings of the Carpenters, stayed on and on,
whereas the Senate delegation had long since returned to the capital—
during those weeks the vanquished rebel, Dr. Urban, sat idle in his
mountain hotel, cursing the dead eroticist, John Theodoric, and (himself in turn cursed by his own followers because he had "forsaken
them in their hour of need") watched his party in the mountain
province disintegrate.

The married men in the former Lienhardt mines, intimidated by
Hesse's partisan action during the bloody night, being discharged
from the jails and received with tears and howls by their wives
because, after losing all they owned, they were now housed in wooden
barracks and fed from the kettles of the poor relief, began to hold

whispered meetings. They sent delegates to Bernard Faust, who declared that the Mining Law then in preparation forbade him to employ workmen whose organization was "hand in glove with the employer." They thereupon went out one Sunday on the Carpenters' meadow behind the Mountain Chapel, and publicly burned their uniforms except for the boots—the caps, the badges, the mementos of their membership in Urban's League—and asked for admission to the Order of Carpenters after a period of probation. The heads of the secular and Christian unions met: Hildebrand, who had declined "to be made a fool or an accomplice of," warned against immediately re-employing the Urbanites in the mines, and gave important reasons. Theresa Froehlich, he said, had been carried away from the mayor's farm—that is, from a part of Carolswald that the Bergdorf men had never reached; which proved that Urban could plant members of his secret service among a perfectly loyal population without having these agents give themselves away or be discovered. "Does any of us know how many Carpenters or how many independents are in fact Urban's secret agents? Who marked the white cross on Theresa's door? No one from Bergdorf, no Lienhardtite, but a Carolswald miner, above suspicion by any of us! Well, if you take the homeless people of Bergdorf into the mining community today because they burned their Sports uniforms yesterday, and tomorrow half the Johanna Mine blows up, then what? Then day after tomorrow Dr. Urban will be on the spot, recalling the 'peril of the red carnation'!" And Hildebrand proposed employing the homeless for the reconstruction of the village, and watching them carefully.

Bishop Oriola opposed this, asking that the poor people who had shown their good will be not turned away. "Man can endure cold, poor housing, and bad food for a lifetime, but being an outcast he can endure for not more than a week at most. Those who are cast out from freedom immediately form groups in prison. Surely, gentlemen, you do not yourselves believe that the people of Bergdorf are Urbanites from conviction! And even if they were, heavens above, 'conviction' hangs about an ordinary person's shoulders as loosely as a rain cape."

"Christian conviction too?" asked the "implacable atheist" Hildebrand, with a mocking smile.

"Naturally! Or do you think a man isn't a Christian any more if he forgets his catechism? For instance, Mr. Hildebrand, your conviction that you *aren't* a Christian hangs very loose indeed!"

"Not in the least! You needn't trouble yourself!"

"From those whom we take into our fellowship," Oriola went on, "we have very little to fear, but from the outcasts, everything. If anyone comes to me from the barracks in the mountain meadow, and asks to be taken into the association of Carpenters, I shall favor it as a matter of course, without catechizing the man. In case Bernard Faust asks me what to do with this man, a proper organization member, who has reported for work, I shall tell him, 'Put him back at the job he had before, just as if nothing had happened. If there is to be no forgiveness after such grievous blows, grudges and rancor are bound to remain.'"

So Hildebrand, losing his case, gave in: the former Urbanites, even "the people without passports or right of domicile," were employed in the mines after they had applied for membership with the "Christians" or the "independents."

Dr. Urban, however, beyond the frontier, was waiting for "his moment."

BOOK ONE

ON A SILVER SALVER

XIV

HIS moment came. For the transaction by which old Lienhardt and his "rustic family" had been ejected from the mountain province, and the rich mines turned over to Adam Faust's "stinking syndicate," could not be long kept secret. Even the first report of a decline in the Lienhardt mine stocks on the Amsterdam and London exchanges, about the middle of October, aroused suspicion. How's this? people said. How can the mines be flooded when the governor announced as early as the ninth that order prevailed, and the police and military were to return to their barracks?

How can the mines be flooded if order did prevail?

When the Lienhardt château blew up on the night of the ninth-tenth, so that the governor appeared to have been mistaken, the great newspapers sent their correspondents to Marienhall, and for a week Mr. Laemmle's veranda over the abyss was turned into a journalists' café. But, damn it, quiet did prevail, and the storm against a President who allowed a band of black-clad, sinister-eyed artisans to occupy his competitor's plant would have broken out at once except that the three stormily mysterious murders, of John Theodoric, Kate, and Theresa, offered sufficiently interesting subjects for headlines and stories, each trying to cap the one before. For a week they reveled in sin, vengeance, and vows of love; the illustrators showed the gloom of the park, the bench in the alders, and the horror of the abyss; the eyes of the guards gleamed in the underbrush, and the flickering torch-light fell on the martyr's stake and the shattered woman screaming with mouth wide open.

This theme was scarcely exhausted before they assaulted Hesse's speech to the squadrons. It was, as Nicholas Edwin Schiele put it, "a joy to be alive." "The battle is still raging in the paper forests," wrote the essayist in the wine-red ladies' lobby of the Crown Hotel, "but the iron phalanx of intelligence still stands resolute and unshaken, intellect against force, its banner on high though the man may fall!"

THE PRESIDENT TO THE GOVERNOR OF THE MOUNTAIN PROVINCE,
COUNT BESSONOFF

MY DEAR FRIEND:

If you can scare up a few more corpses for the journalists, it would help me out. Because of course the headline "President Steals Lienhardt Mines" is already in type, and has simply been put aside as long as the corpses are fresh. Now, it is true that I have a new headline under my hat, which will knock all the others dead—to wit, the Mining Law; but Zorn's fellows are still monkeying around with it, and I've got to go the rounds to inspect the officers' training schools. I have sent for old Zorn, Hilgenfeld, and young Dr. Merckel, Beyer's reader, to tell the papers the truth about our alleged theft of millions: that the profit is on paper, and could be realized only if we were to sell our shares. But that is precisely what we are not going to do, in accordance with the Mining Law.

So far as the gossip about your wife is concerned, you have my sympathy. Whether you should get a divorce, with two sons in the army, I don't know: I'm against it. Leave her alone for a while, and come here. If you want to be head of the Staff College, just say the word to

Your old friend,

ADAM FAUST

P.S. Matters are even worse at Police Senator von Brick's.

At the end of October the "storm of indignation" actually broke out, with such force that the President postponed his trip of inspection. He flung two hundred thousand copies of Matthew Brandt's report to the "enraged beast," recalled his personal jurist, Holzkopf, from Geisenheim, published Hilgenfeld's, Zorn's, and Merckel's opinions as paid advertisements, and, since no agreement had yet been reached upon the wording of the Mining Law, exhausted the government's and his own personal account for press relations.

Nothing did any good. The "Iron Phalanx," already in process of foundation upon the enormous resources of Oscar Koenig, the millionaire newspaper and book publisher, dug long-forgotten crimes of the old man's out of their files: why, he was a gambler! Sixteen years before, when the splendid Elizabeth had turned the Willert palace into a gambling hell, had he not held the bank at roulette? Had he not, as a man already fifty-one years of age, entertained such relations with the young wife that when Jacob came back, and, despite her pregnancy, slapped Elizabeth's face so that her powder dusted across the table, he could venture to fling himself between them? What respectable patrician house had he not outraged in company with his fellow topers? "The man attained the summit of hypocrisy, however, when, accustomed as he was to dragging in the dust the things most precious to the human bosom, he set up to be the leader of the Conservatives, who, after all, even admitting their narrow-minded backwardness, are at least family men of the old sort." He made a great to-do about his Christianity, they said, but he had never disavowed the statement ascribed to him that ninety out of a hundred

Protestant ministers were office clerks who had missed their calling. He had shown his respect for public opinion by his repeated assurance that he was not to be intimidated by printed threats. And under the title "Barbarism on the March" Nicholas Edwin Schiele reported in the evening paper that the President had called liberty an animal with a thousand snouts, and culture a lady.

"But the proletariat has awakened!" wrote Mark Antony Perlotta in *Liberty and Culture* magazine. "The working masses of the mountain province have a few tales to tell of Town Clerk Matthew Brandt —for instance, the number of bottles of cherry brandy, 38% alcohol, that Governor Bessonoff sent to the old sponge in order to put him in a condition to prepare his groveling, Machiavellian report."

In the *Criminologists' Weekly Record* an attorney named Dr. Tadd, legal counsel for the Koenig newspaper combine, demanded disciplinary action against Lieutenant von Hesse, with the object of dismissing him from the service for encouraging the squadrons to murder all suspicious characters unconvicted of crime, at an inn, in parliament, in the fields, or beside their wives in bed.

Tadd's law partner, Pole, accused the governor in the *Law Journal* of having sent the case of dynamite to the Lienhardt château on October ninth by a teacher named Lorenz, and accused Matthew Brandt of withholding this circumstance despite knowledge to the contrary, after giving a receipt for the bribe offered him, in the form of an advance, out of Adam Faust's discretionary account.

Adam Faust was lying on his veranda, watching the movement of the autumn sky above oak forests and river. At the word "bribe" he sprang up as if a viper had bitten him, and, on the strength of a long-since-forgotten decree from the days of the monarchy, which had never been repealed, caused ten leading writers, among them Professors Habermann and Schiele, Mark Antony Perlotta, Diana Rose, and as many editors, including the powerful Oscar Koenig (the Liberal leader in the Senate since Lienhardt's demise), to be sentenced to prison terms "for slander and libel upon the head of the state."

In this way he did indeed fulfill a wish of the higher army officers that had come to him in many telegrams assuring him of support, but he provoked the Senate. His friends, among them Jacob Willert (who had returned to the capital on the fifteenth, sending Margaret Witt ahead of him), had all warned the old man against lending weight by his own interference to the outcry—a weight that neither the "man in the street" nor the higher administrative officials attached to it. No minister or governor had offered his resignation; the poor, on the other hand, indifferent to wrangles among the great sharks, and also not stultified by "enlightenment" and the reading of half-baked journalism, but with that natural intelligence which is sharpened by the struggle for a livelihood, had scented for some seven years past the march not of "barbarism" but of a "revolution from above" advancing step by step. The people had passively approved the filling of the civil service and the General Staff with Zorn's followers and Zorn's ideas, as well as the inscriptions that the President had had placed on public buildings. The inscription on the Staff College, for instance, taken from a novel by a Russian writer:

If there is no God, what sort of Captain am I?

This had been sneered at by the enlightened Urban, and called hypocrisy by the literati. But the people did not understand the sneers; they understood the inscription, literally, just as it was, and would have none of symbolism or hypocrisy. All they wanted was "to see it acted on." This was just how the President understood it. The high relief of *Equality* above the Faust administration building, and Koerner's speech concerning it, had not been forgotten. Nor had the inscription engraved across the ancient gable of the Supreme Court of Arbitration for Labor Disputes:

Thou shalt not muzzle the ox when he treadeth out the corn.

It was very little use for the leftist liberals to write, "In the eyes of the enlightened section of the population the workers are not oxen." The people did not understand this witticism of the "great minds"; they understood the inscription, and wanted it carried out.

Nor had the "That's nothing to me!" episode been forgotten, which had taken place in the yard of the Johanna Mine when Adam was campaigning for the presidency.

And so, because the people had thought him capable of masterfulness, of overstepping the mark, but not of anything wicked, the assertion that he had robbed the dying Lienhardt made the unsentimental poor, unschooled in the law, laugh out loud. "Everyone knows he's a man-eating shark—among other things," wrote Hildebrand in the *Labor News*.

Whether this defense did not satisfy him—"For," he said, "sharks eat herrings, but I never ate a little man!"—whether his gray head was forgetting how strong his position still was, or whether his pride required vengeance, no matter: those who had libeled him went to jail, and at the instance of the Liberals the Senate declared that "the constitutionally guaranteed freedom of research and criticism was being endangered."

At this he presented the Mining Law to the upper house, believing that silence would ensue. The very opposite took place; indeed, the bill did not even reach the house, for the committee on new legislation returned it to the presidential chancellery as "on the whole not deserving of recommendation." Thus the Senate paid back the impudence that Matthew Brandt, the favorite, had allowed himself in preserving Zorn's insulting quotation about the "city rabble" from oblivion by putting it in his memorial.

The President immediately struck back, appointing the obscure town clerk as Teller of Great Deeds. Not since the days of the kings had this medieval title been bestowed; it opened to its possessor the secret archives and the gates of the Academy of Twelve. A man of the pen can rise no higher than this: the Academy, developing out of "the monarch's inner council," and recast in a republican mold, included the twelve most important men of the nation—scholars, statesmen, and soldiers. The power of appointment to fill out the twelve when a member dies is reserved to the President of the Republic.

Here, incidentally, a constitutional detail should be added so that the distribution of power in our fatherland and the struggle over the Mining Law may appear to everyone in its true significance. After the great revolution three hundred years ago had replaced the absolutism of the monarch with the absolutism of parliament, we found ourselves entangled in a series of costly wars by the eloquence of city-bred lawyers and ambitious ladies, so that finally, when sensible men discovered that neither monarch nor parliament but the absolutism of one or the other was responsible for our plight, an intermediate form was established. The entire executive power was transferred to a president elected directly by the people. His election was indeed for life, but he was obliged to resign if both houses of parliament, the lower house and the Senate, simultaneously gave a two-thirds majority showing lack of confidence. He shared the right to initiate bills with the two chambers, and ordinarily the law was enacted by the approval of both houses and the president's signature. In exceptional cases, however—this provision sets our constitution apart, and increases the president's power—he does not even need both houses of parliament, but only one in order to promulgate a law, provided that a three-quarters majority of the Senate, in addition to the Academy of Twelve, supports the president's proposal.

The Mining Law had only a bare majority behind it in the Chamber of Deputies, and no majority at all in the Senate. Adam Faust now realized that the "families of Senatorial rank," that is, those having at least four thousand thalers' annual income and holding real property, were revenging themselves on him for everything he had been guilty of in seven years: for the statue of *Equality* and the preferment of Rudolphi, for the appointment of Andrew Zorn and the inscriptions, for the stiffening of the examinations for officers and the stamping out of excesses in the barracks, for the order prohibiting the clergy from disguising their voices and their manner, "in order to combat the popular belief that religion is the art of speaking unnaturally," for his discrimination in favor of the independents and against the Yellows, his childish literalness in understanding Christian dogmas, his disdain of culture and soaring flights, his cynicism, his pride, and his popularity among the lower orders.

Not heeding Daruhi's objections, not believing Jacob Willert's warning that he was about to make a second irreparable blunder—"Compromise is better than defeat, and out of sight is not out of mind"—without asking the Archbishop's advice, Adam resolved to annihilate the Senatorial families, and published in the *National Gazette* his appeal to the people, "The inexhaustible source of common sense, goodness, and justice." It lay in his power to compel changes in the constitution by direct referendum of the people, against both houses and the Academy of Twelve. He proposed, then, to give up the plutocratic principles as a requirement for the Senate, and to replace it by the principle of "worthiness": particularly deserving men, rich or poor, were in future to constitute the Senate, whose membership was to remain fixed at seventy-five. The right to nominate candidates was to be entrusted to the corporate bodies of the employers, the workmen's organizations exclusive of the Yellows, the Academy of Twelve, the Staff College, and the provincial synods.

No one had any doubt that the people would legalize by an overwhelming majority the proposed *coup d'état*. The people would really have preferred to abolish the Senate altogether, but a reform along the lines of Adam's proposal was better than nothing. So that the liberals could have no cause to complain of being crippled during the weeks of campaigning that preceded the referendum, the President pardoned the writers and editors whom he had imprisoned. "If they hate me so much that they stand up for the old Senate," he said, "they're done for." This was certainly true; the Iron Phalanx of Intelligence, welcomed out of prison with wild enthusiasm and flowers, unanimously supported the Senatorial reform.

Adam, however, unable to check his senile fury, was determined "to put a spoke in their wheel": restoring a second forgotten title, he appointed the black reactionary Herbert Hilgenfeld, the "slanderous Aristophanes," who had something wrong with his nervous reflexes, and was beginning to limp, as "Clerk to the Government," with a stipend of nine thousand thalers. Under the kings it had been customary to employ a man to stylize the language of government decrees, and he had borne the above-mentioned antiquated title.

And so everything was beginning to move obediently in the direction of the President's wishes when at last Urban appeared on the scene. His hour had struck: if he had sat by and watched Lindbrecht and Hildebrand entering the Senate, while the League for Enlightenment and Economic Peace was put away empty-handed, the great popular orator would have been finished for all time.

It did not turn out that way: crossing the frontier, he marched, surrounded by his adherents, into the mountain province, and blood flowed at once; an old enemy fell forward with throat ripped open, gurgled, and died—the strongest and most successful of all his old enemies, Bishop Immanuel von Hesse.

THE SHOTS AT DAMMERKERK

XV

IT WAS not by chance that Dr. Urban was known as the ladies'
darling; he was tall and slender, with pleasing, manly features, brown-haired, blue-eyed; his reddish, roughened skin
showed the effect of wind and weather; he moved with the same
self-possession and assurance among rich and poor. Merckel and young
Hesse later insisted that his gestures and utterances showed "falseness
of heart," but their judgment seems to have been warped by hatred;
Jacob Willert, at any rate, whose supposed eye for people rests to some
extent on documentary proof, considered Urban a "great man" down
to the crucial days, and was for taking him into the government, as
we shall see. The popular leader was distinguished by an unusual even-
ness of temperament; he was reflective, nay skeptical, at the summit of
his success, and imposing in his downfall; no one ever saw him jubilant or despairing. Women were devoted to him because he was a
soldier, and his uniform fitted him as naturally as a cat its fur; men
loved him because he was a dreamer. It was in the realm of dreams
that his first speech moved, the first speech he made in the school
meadow at Blendheim, before three thousand men of his Sports troop;
by his side stood the new Chief of Staff, Count Oriola, and an artillery
captain by the name of Justus Thomas who had left the army to join
him. His secretary, Weisse, a young steward on the Lienhardt estates,
was in mufti as always.

As the sun was shining down brightly on the gently sloping
meadow, Urban wore dark glasses. He stood on the wooden judges'
stand of the football field, before him a desk brought from the school;
when the band had blared out a welcome to him, he ordered, "At
ease!" and, not referring by so much as a word to the defeat of his
people in the mountain province, he said:

"There are only two true-born worlds, mine and his: all else is
falsehood or slime. My world is quiet and kindly, his is full of trouble

and darkness, because he is trying to find the secret of something that does not exist."

Applause broke out here, although no one yet knew what "his," "he," and "something that does not exist" meant. It was only the following sentence that showed Adam Faust was indicated; "something that does not exist" referred to Christianity.

"And because this President of ours with his celebrated sense of justice is wandering around in the fog, he cannot distinguish, as a perfectly shallow person like Lawyer Tadd or his partner Pole can without the slightest difficulty, between friend and enemy. He throws the weight of his prestige and the votes of the little men against me, as if I were the only enemy. If he had more imagination, he could now picture to himself the two chambers of parliament as they will be, thanks to his blind dislike of me, six weeks hence; he might yet call a halt. Mohammed said to the mountain, 'Come here!' Since the mountain was unreasonable enough not to come, Mohammed went to the mountain. And so I shall go to the advisers of the President, first to old Hesse, and I shall try to tell the balky horse as kindly and gently as I can what he does not know:

"It is futile to fight against me, because I am inevitable. I am Siegfried, the man of light—the future, the peace of the human race. I am the deliverer from trouble, even from forsakenness, as Messrs. Daruhi and Hilgenfeld and the Academy of Twelve will not realize until it is too late. They are shrewd enough to suspect that I am not slime or mud or the Iron Phalanx of Intelligence, but they still refuse to admit to themselves that I am not falsehood either.

"And so, while they are bringing all available guns to bear on me, the Yellow, in their blind zeal they are overlooking a breach in the walls through which the Reds are breaking in, the perjured swarm of rats with which, to my shame be it said, I associated in my foolish younger days—not for long, of course, because when I discovered that what this swarm says, nay that the swarm itself is falsehood incarnate, they drove me out. Today, ten years after, this agglomeration of as yet unrecognized parlor lions and unapplauded actresses calls itself 'the Revolutionary Workers' Party'; and since the President is calling all hands to man the walls against me, that party is going through the aforementioned breach into parliament, in order to turn the latter into a rostrum for fine phrases and a ladies' drawing room.

"This is the first and last appeal I shall address to Adam Faust, and also to our people, the people who the flatterer boasts are 'the source of common sense, of goodness and justice.' My League for Enlightenment and Economic Peace, once the blast of propaganda against it is stopped, will be the more ready to reach an agreement with the President concerning the Mining Law, because after all it expressly recognizes our principle of the owner's right to his property.

"Why it is that, after this concession, we are still called 'the Yellows,' I shall ask Bishop Hesse; I am now leaving for his farm near Dammerkerk, accompanied only by half a file of the Sports Divisions. I instruct the rest of you to return to your quarters, and to protect the speakers of our League from the violence of their opponents during the election campaign."

The Urban who delivered this address (which, it turned out twelve years afterward, represented his real and undisguised opinion) was the same Urban who had delivered the eulogy of the dead Lienhardt in which, as Daruhi rightly observed, "every single word and comma was a lie." Incidentally, he was right: the Urban League, assailed from all sides, managed to get a single candidate, Weisse, the League Leader's secretary, into the Senate, while the Revolutionary Workers' Party marched into the reformed upper house with nineteen members. This shows the intense hatred of the time for the Yellows; it was increased, and in many people's eyes justified, by the clash of the Urbanite half file and the Federal Police at Dammerkerk.

They had followed the "father of the Yellow Associations" on bicycles as he drove in a hired carriage through the village and into the farmyard. They drew themselves up at the gateway while Bishop Hesse welcomed his adversary in an arbor at the rear.

It has already been observed that the outcome of the referendum as to whether or not the Senate should be reformed was a foregone conclusion. Consequently the bodies from which the reformed Senate was to emerge immediately met to appoint their candidates. The results of long habituation to parliamentary democracy were immediately apparent: the above-mentioned bodies broke up into party factions, and in reality the candidates were decided on by these factions, and only formally by the associations of workmen, employers, or the provincial synods. Thus, although our Adam had appealed to the entire people, "the source of all . . . , etc.," the popular speakers acted as party orators, the old party venom reappeared, and everywhere there were noisy quarrels, clashes, and bloody noses.

Accordingly, it seemed the part of precaution for Lieutenant Otto von Hesse to betake himself to his father's farm with a group of Federal Police. They stood around smoking and talking beside the arbor, paying no attention to the uniformed men by the gateway, while Urban argued with the Bishop. After about ten minutes, the leader of the Peace League having presented to the astonished Bishop the arguments he had put forward at Blendheim, besides others suggested by the exigencies of the moment, in a low voice and so intensely that his forehead was beaded with sweat, the old man said at length: "But that would mean everything was quite all right, and I could join your League, or you could join the Carpenters!"

"Without a moment's hesitation!" replied the desperate Urban.

"Let me tell you," replied the Bishop, "let me tell you what an honest man once said to me: 'I won't be made a fool of, and I won't be made an accomplice of!' I think that is sufficient answer. It is not important what a man says, but what a man *wants*."

Suddenly Otto von Hesse was at the entrance of the arbor: "Perhaps it's even more important, Dad," he said, "what a man accomplishes, whether he wants it or not. What that gentleman has accomplished is target practice with a living mark."

There was no time for a reply. The policeman's words turned Urban's followers, who had been standing quietly by the gateway, into a howling mob.

"He means Kate Schwann," yelled one. "What do we care for that old bitch?" said another.

"Arrest that man!" cried Otto von Hesse, flinging up one arm, and Color Sergeant Laurenti ordered: "Ready!"

Two shots flashed, the crack was drowned by savage yells, and Fritz Laurenti, nineteen years old, sagged to his knees.

"Fire!" yelled Otto, racing across the yard, and the massacre began. It was scarcely twenty seconds before Dr. Urban, seeing the old revivalist preacher (who had come out of the arbor) fall on the cobblestones with his throat shot through, took out a police whistle and blew it. His men, better posted from the outset in the shelter of the huge gateway, leaped upon their bicycles and fled, leaving their dead and wounded behind. They were overtaken, and, attempting to escape, were shot down.

Thousands passed by the body of old Hesse as it lay in state. The women wept; so did the little children. When the Archbishop delivered the funeral oration for the dead Bishop in the Mountain Chapel of Geisenheim two days later, even the side portals had to be left open for the benefit of the listeners on the meadow and the forest path, for the little chapel was filled with Carpenters down to the last seat. Those parts of the memorial sermon that emphasized the accomplishments of the revivalist preacher received little attention in the press; all the more was devoted to those "that, apparently imitated from the notorious address of a certain police lieutenant, had a taste of blood" (*People's National Times*), and, as a matter of fact, what he said on that occasion about the "howling and burrowing beasts of the abyss, which could only be chained, but never converted," did sound like the pamphlets of the Reformation.

Among the papers of Bishop von Hesse were a sealed letter addressed to "Mr. James von Frohwein, Chief of the General Staff," an unfinished "Instructions Regarding Practical Piety in the Police Service," and a "Possible Joint Divine Service for Protestants and Catholics," worked out to the last detail, and ready for print.

BOOK ONE

THE CLERK TO THE GOVERNMENT

XVI

WHEN the two houses of the Diet were reconstituted in February of the following year, the ninth of our Adam Faust's presidency, and the shift in power came to light, the whole country was horrified—no, this was not what they had wanted! A previously unknown group of cold, sarcastic men of darkness, bitterly hostile to property, the family, and the Christian religion, the Revolutionary Workers' Party, had arrived as the second strongest party in the Senate and lower house alike. True, it had been foreseen that the Conservatives, the party of the mine robbers and the much-envied Andrew Zorn, would emerge damaged from Adam's mine transaction and the furious revelations of the Liberal press, and logically the Liberal assailants and exposers, "banner on high, intellect against force," were bound to carry off the victory.

They, however, were the very ones who came near to being crushed: of their twenty seats in the Senate they kept seven; the lost thirteen went, not to the moderate left, but at one fell swoop to the swarm of rats denounced by Urban, the Revolutionary Workers' Party, which also picked up another six seats among the malcontents of all parties. Hildebrand's independents and the Christians joined to form a Democratic Reform Party. The result of the election was meager—ten seats in the reformed upper house.

Praise be, Adam's provincial governors and their officials in the medium-sized towns, particularly in the lowlands, still had sufficient resources at hand to intimidate the voters: accordingly, the Conservative group, though weakened, was, with its twenty-one seats, still the strongest in the Senate; taken together with the Archbishop's Christian Middle-Class Party they had a small majority, and when joined by the Reform Party a large one.

The Senate was ranged as follows:

Conservatives (leaders, Andrew Zorn, Augustus Beyer, Jacob Willert)	21
Revolutionary Workers' Party (leader, Bart Plambeck, the "honest sailor")	19
Christian Middle-Class Party (leaders, the Archbishop and his nephew, Brother Henry, a Franciscan monk)	17
Democratic Reform Party (leaders, Adolf Hildebrand and Theodore Lindbrecht)	10
Liberals (leader, Oscar Koenig, President of the Iron Phalanx of Intelligence)	7
League for Economic Peace (Urban)	1
Total	75

But human behavior in face of measurable successes and defeats is so illogical that the most frequent butt of campaign insults, who had been

able to take but a single seat, was at the same time the only one whose
power appeared unshaken, his prestige assured—Urban. Had he not
predicted the victory of the Reds at Blendheim? Had not the fruits
of the hatred sown by Adam's faithful against Urban been harvested
by the enemies of home and prosperity? Had he not offered to work
with Bishop Hesse? That he was not responsible for the clash at
Dammerkerk had now been judicially ascertained, and the crimes of
the Lienhardts, the eldest and youngest of the brothers, were not his
crimes; on the contrary, if he had been in the country at the time he
would have prevented the eroticist's contemptible craft and the sadist's
maniac murder. Herbert Hilgenfeld reprinted the essential part of
the Blendheim speech in *The Conservative;* Alois Borstel, the locomotive and cannon king, pointing out that everyone must bow to
science, that was *his* motto, announced his adherence to the League
for Enlightenment and Economic Peace; the popular *People's
National Times* passed into Urban's hands and became the official
League organ. Immediately, in his very first editorials, the League
Leader showed his enormous shrewdness: the Conservatives, who had
cursed him at a thousand meetings as an abominable "concoction of
disease and crime"; Lindbrecht's and the Bishop's men, who called
him Satan and Antichrist; the Hildebrandites, who carried in their
parades pictures of Kate Schwann at the martyr's stake with the
caption, "The Ideal Aim of His Existence"; all were magnanimously
forgiven. The victorious Reds, however, did not even receive the
honor of being mentioned at all. He flung himself with all his
strength upon the unfortunate Liberals, decimated in the election,
upon the Iron Phalanx of Intelligence, and charged them with having
brought about the Red victory by their own money and the behavior
of their papers. He admonished the newspaper editors of the Koenig
combine to confess that no payment had ever been demanded for the
advertisements, often pages long, of the Revolutionary Workers'
Party. In proof he quoted the libertarian poet Mark Antony Perlotta's
phrases about the "awakened proletariat," and Nicholas Edwin Schiele,
who had attributed the President's excesses and looting to the "desperation of capitalism."

Again, as in the Blendheim address, the "Leader" rose to prophesy:
"The Liberals, who have no cause of their own left to defend—except
for the one that has always been theirs, namely showing off and getting

themselves talked about—will now slip into revolutionary costume, and proclaim their new aim for humanity, the downfall of the *bourgeoisie* and of capitalism, with true Perlotta uproar—not because they are convinced of it, for they are convinced of nothing except that they are the elite of the intellect, but because any scribbler no matter how unimaginative can put himself in the foreground by 'solidarity with the disinherited,' and, puffing his own high principles with the shamelessness of a whore, can put down genuine talent. For the man who has nothing to offer can only resort to the livelihood of a swindler. Liberalism has nothing left to offer, and I therefore predict its future: it will glorify freedom and bring about oppression."

Thus Urban. And, amazingly, nay incredibly, the hated Yellow, the atheist and inciter of murder, the loser of the election, found support in the group that hated him most, the Conservatives.

It happened in this wise. One morning in the proletarian eastern quarter of the capital, where the gray lines of treeless streets, broken by treeless building lots and factory grounds, disappear into the pauper parks along the river, the doorbell rang on the fourth floor of one of the houses, each as much like the next as twins. Hilgenfeld, the ailing Aristophanes (past sixty, and never prosperous because he was not enough of a windbag), went to open the door, wearing an old woolen shirt and a wet rag around his head, while his wife was putting the bedroom in order. He found an officer of the First Guard Regiment, whom to study more carefully he put on his spectacles. His unkempt gray hair hung down over his ears.

"My name is Lieutenant Messerschmidt," said the dazzling young man, lifting two fingers to his cap and bowing.

"Charmed, I'm sure. Unfortunately I can't receive you!" replied the author, who never saw anyone at his apartment, and seldom went out now that his gait had grown unsteady. He and his wife had had five children, two of whom had died, three married and gone abroad, whence they sent begging letters at regular intervals to their parents. The old woman, first having counted up to see how much could be spared, would run to Lawyer Held, a fellow writer, and weep until she had stopped the mouths of her "abominable children." "Herbert isn't making anything at all any more!" she would sob, "and the doctors . . ." But *The Conservative* paid its editor three hundred and fifty thalers a month.

"Come right on in, Lieutenant!" cried Mrs. Hilgenfeld from the bedroom opposite, without emerging herself. "You can go into the dining room—that's been straightened up."

"Thank you, Madam," cried the young man, instantly aware of how incongruous the word "madam" sounded in these surroundings, "but I've got somebody else with me that's waiting downstairs."

"Who is it?"

"The President of the Republic."

"What shall we do now?" Hilgenfeld asked his wife, who had meanwhile finished buttoning her blouse.

"Why didn't the President tell us before? Then we could have had something in the house!" she said to Lieutenant Messerschmidt.

"He doesn't need anything; he's had breakfast, and is sitting in the carriage downstairs. May I bring him up?"

And so Adam Faust, having trudged slowly, panting, up the stairs, came to the writer's dwelling for the first and next-to-last time, greeted the old couple, and said: "You really might live a little better than this, Hilgenfeld."

"It doesn't make any difference where a person lives, Mr. President."

"But I hear there are bugs here."

"You get used to that."

"Write it down!" cried Adam. "Write it down—for the staff officers that are asking for more living allowances. Will you?"

"Certainly. In a fortnight."

"Under what title? You've got to find a title—for a separate reprint, do you understand?"

"Perfectly. 'Against Overrating Externals' would seem to me a suitable title."

The President assented, arose, and in the resounding phrases of the past—while everyone stood, including Mrs. Hilgenfeld—informed the writer of his appointment, hastily adding, so as not to disappoint a man already too old to be vain, that there was a stipend of nine thousand thalers, and that a secretary had been provided for in the budget lest he be burdened with work. It was to agree on the choice of a secretary that he had come, Adam said; but the old lady felt sure the President had come out of curiosity.

"Whom do you want for a secretary?"

"Albert Ackermann," replied Hilgenfeld after everyone had sat down.

"Who's he?"

"The one that writes the stories about girls."

But old Adam no longer read anything he had not read before.

"They're good stories," said the invalid, "solid, tender, and cool, yet not sticky if you look at them in perspective; retrospective, without the shadow of disappointment. Ackermann teaches at the girls' academy; he's a colleague of Merckel's, but no money, and married."

"How old?"

"Twenty-six."

"Good. Congratulations, Mr. Hilgenfeld," said Adam, taking his leave.

Of course the moment she had finished coffee Mrs. Hilgenfeld ran over to old lady Merckel, the washerwoman, who had given up washing, to tell her the news piping hot. The Widow Merckel in turn put on her rain hat, donned her quilted coat and rubbers, because there was snow on the ground, and paid a morning call to Mrs. Ackermann, young Elsie, who "could get along on that money perfectly well, but doesn't want to." The young woman, always in terror of bills when the doorbell rang, cried for joy and hysteria at the news. Now at last even she, Cinderella that she was, would receive invitations and be a person of consequence.

"You'd better be a little saving, Mrs. Ackermann, the extra fifty thalers won't pull you out," said the Widow Merckel, and almost instantly regretted it, for there was a chorus of shrieks: the pretty Elsie, pale and irresponsible, her lips blue, rolled on the floor—as her husband was not at home she could allow herself to—and the babies, Paul, two, and Frieda, three and a half, flung themselves on top of her, screaming.

"All right, all right, go ahead!" the old washerwoman consoled them. "I've got to go now and get dinner for my John." Dr. Merckel, the senior assistant master, Beyer's chess partner, protégé, and reader, answered, as we know, to the name of John Henry.

But scarcely was Hilgenfeld solemnly invested as secretary to the Academy of Twelve before he reprinted Urban's speech on the future of the Liberals in the Proceedings of the Academy and in his magazine,

The Conservative, accompanying it with admiring commentary. As
no one contradicted the Clerk to the Government, an alliance of the
President's followers with the murderers of Bishop Hesse and Kate
Schwann seemed to be in preparation.

BOOK ONE

BISHOP HESSE TO HIS SON

XVII

INSTRUCTIONS REGARDING PRACTICAL PIETY IN THE POLICE SERVICE

MY DEAR OTTO:

I am giving you this letter as a guide that you will need in the
capital, for there you will not have to carry out the orders of an experienced superior, but to beg, extort, and wheedle for your own orders
the signature of a commander no longer capable of action. Mr. von
Brick really ought to be retired; a man who begins by succumbing to
petticoat influence at home, and has to pay so enormous a price for
emancipation from it, cannot properly fill any public office. But the
President has decided to keep him because after the bloody night of
October eighth no other member of the Conservative group was
willing to assume the office of Commissioner of Safety.

Long conversations with Supreme Court Justice Holzkopf, Senator
Beyer, to whom you owe your appointment, Oriola, Bessonoff, and a
few other insiders whose names you know have convinced me that you
will have to combat a mysterious group of conspirators, which, although in Urban's service, is nevertheless not directed by him, but
maintains a vigorous independence that might under some circumstances even be dangerous to the "Leader." The murders of Kate
Schwann and Theresa Froehlich are their work, and the insiders
believe that Peter George, Schubert, the coachman, and the other six
who escaped by the evening express have not gone abroad at all, but
are living in our midst, slightly altered in outward appearance, scat-

tered over our big cities, and awaiting new tasks. What these tasks are, who assigns them, whether the Peter George group forms a secret executive organ subordinate to and paid by the League for Economic Peace, or whether it is attached to the Sports Divisions—all these questions you will have to cast light upon; the gentlemen who promoted you expect it.

Perhaps they are expecting too much; perhaps the capture of the girls' murderers, who are watching you from the windows as you pass by, will in itself demand your life. If the gentlemen of the capital tell you that with the increase in the Federal Police force you have an army of 100,000 men at your disposal, tell them what you have already told me: one does not send soldiers against people who are hanging out of the front window smoking a pipe; one sends a neighbor, or their wives, who listen to them as they talk in their sleep.

So you must send a neighbor against the murderers, or the doorman and the listening wife—again not the wrong persons, in league with the murderers, but your own allies.

Sensible men like Oriola, Schwann, Lindequist, Stark, and Lorenz, then, are agreed that you must not meet the secret service of the Sports Divisions with a uniformed force, but with a secret service of your own, recruited from the Brotherhood of Carpenters.

Do not yield an inch in this demand that your basic troops shall be a Christian brotherhood; and if Mr. von Brick, a worldly man, should be against you on this point, call on General Frohwein for help; I am writing a letter to him. If you follow my advice you will have the three most powerful men on your side: the President, Senator Beyer, and Andrew Zorn. I don't know Jacob Willert so well; but he is still inclined to suspect that Christianity is "the art of speaking unnaturally."

You know I am not a hypocrite. I have never considered Christianity a sort of science or doctrine that could be put in the form of questions, sung, or enunciated; nor have I ever asked a man his "faith," because that is, after all, the stupidest and most barbarous of ways to test a man's Christianity. I have taught you from childhood that the sectarian differences to be found by question and answer have nothing to do with Christianity; for that reason you should use the "joint service" at the meetings of your Carpenters. I am having it printed. I have taught you from childhood that if you want to know whether a man is a Christian you must watch his daily life for at least a week.

You must do the same in order to discover whether a man will make a proper Carpenter.

For the weakness, I may say the Achilles heel, of the Urban troops is their worldliness, or, in other words, the fact that they are not a brotherhood. Because they are not a fraternity but an association devoted to certain purposes, in order to hold the individual members together and create a travesty of brotherhood it is necessary to use such desperate expedients as joint crimes. These methods, even the girls' murders, are quite unsuited to creating a brotherhood, as Andrew Zorn has shown by hundreds of examples in his book, *On the Character of My Countrymen,* the same in which he defined the conservative state as "a perpetual league of autonomous brotherhoods." The reasons he cites in support of his definition are very simple; I will recall them to you.

A brotherhood, he says—by contrast with an association, a league, or a union—has no purpose. Like weeds, it has no purpose at all, and wherever (ignorant of its own nature) it mentions "aims," these are revealed on closer inspection as ways and means of brotherhood. For that is the very thing that distinguishes it from any conceivable association: it is in itself a final end, an ultimate end, or, to use the ordinary inexact term, an end in itself. It seeks nothing but its own preservation. Brotherhood strives for brotherhood, the brothers seek to be brothers—that is all. Because the preservation of itself is the sole possible end of any brotherhood, and preservation its first and last idea, Zorn calls it the "organized form of conservatism," and, he says, the ideal state of the conservatives is one made up of associated brotherhoods.

So long as you stick to Andrew Zorn and act in accordance with his views, my dear son, nothing can happen to you, for Adam Faust would sooner resign his office than be false to his teacher.

Be careful if by invitation or by accident you should fall among the great mockers who surround the President—the Zorns, Hilgenfelds, Merckels, Daruhis; on the outside they appear cynical, but they are the touchiest of men on subjects they do not make game of—for instance, the inscriptions or the Mining Law.

Smile, say yes, agree with those who hate you, and never express your own opinion at a gathering of the "Conservatives"; for with five or six exceptions there is no such thing as conservatives in the world.

The rest are not real, and even Jacob Willert, although on his way toward us, has not arrived, and never will. The so-called "Conservatives" are in reality enterprisers, capitalists who have their minds on their business, including both liberal men who do not grudge their neighbors and the poor their rights (i.e., Jacob Willert), and reactionaries like Kuehn and Lienhardt, whose world ends with their mothers-in-law.

Adam Faust too has his mind on his business, but for a conservative purpose: that is, he looks toward the preservation, I might almost have said the perpetuity, of his business. How naïve and lacking in guile, in other words, how honorable the man is, you can see from this: "I shall present the Mining Law to the people who accuse me of having stolen the Lienhardt mines," he thought, "because this law will enable them to see through my intent. The Mine Law transforms my enterprise into a small-scale model of the conservative ideal commonwealth, a community of entirely different yet autonomous and allied brotherhoods. The mining community recognizes the interests of the wage earners, which differ from the 'interests' of the owners, as a natural difference; that is why the brotherhood of miners must be just as independent and autonomous as the brotherhood of mine owners. Any person of normal intelligence who has followed me thus far will see that I threw out Lienhardt not to enrich myself but because he is a protector of the Yellows, and accordingly cannot be a member of a community consisting of allied brotherhoods. For as a Conservative, which I am, I envisage a lasting alliance, not a sham that will blow up tomorrow."

By this argument the guileless Adam thought he could win over the majority of the Senate; but he did not even win over its Conservative faction. They would more readily—indeed, with a merry twinkle of the eye—have forgiven him for stealing whole provinces than for being so dangerously naïve as to make the conservative principle of preservation a reality.

In later times the historian, who describes an earlier era, say, as that of agriculture or predominantly of city dwelling, will refer to ours as predominantly the era of the lie.

I now come, my son, to your own affairs, the first of which is the recruiting of the 64,000 men approved by the Senate. This figure is much too large, and irrelevant in any case, since you must first recruit and train small troops of tried-and-true brothers, so-called cadres. Within six months the cadres should be able to furnish adequate personnel for training. At least two thousand recruits, all members of the Order of Carpenters, will volunteer at once in our neighborhood alone, in Geisenheim, Marienhall, and the mountain villages, if we summon them; naturally enough they would prefer the enviable posts of policemen to the heavy labor of the mines or a humiliating life on poor relief. You should leave the choice and training of the cadres of future officers and noncommissioned officers in the Federal Police to your captain, my old brother Heinz, who will get intelligent assistance from von Lindequist, Schwann, the bookkeeper, Stark and Lorenz, the schoolteachers, and finally from me and Oriola.

You should devote your attention to the cadres in the north, where Zorn's pupils, the Archbishop, and Lindbrecht and Hildebrand will help you choose the *right* people, that is, the ones who will be possible in a brotherhood, from among those who volunteer. Look around for yourself among the workmen and employees of Faust's machine plants in the east end of the capital, and call on old Klingenberg, the former organizer of the bakers. Never forget for a moment that the fearful and treacherous enemy whose secret service you are to extirpate has one weak point: worldliness. Accordingly, the ultimate purpose of any Urbanite League is not the holding together of the members; the latter, rather, is never more than a means to accomplish something with united forces. A worldly league holds together in action, but in times of quiet the advantage, or, as the world characteristically puts it, the sense in holding together, is not obvious; the members therefore yield to whispered demoralization and bribery.

For that reason *your* police must be a Christian brotherhood. Brotherhood knows nothing of purpose or advantage, not even the advantage of holding together, because there is no visible "aim" beyond the brotherhood. It is its own ultimate; and so that each of you may be daily reminded that he has one foot already in eternity, I have represented in the attached Order for a Joint Divine Service the reciprocal flow and commingling of police service and divine service, of worship and command, of choral singing and reports in the line of duty, displaying them all by practical examples. By these you are to live, and by the rules of the Carpenters; for that reason I recommend introducing the

Carpenters' costume for the plain-clothes agents of your secret service when they are not engaged in a special assignment.

As a brotherhood you seek no *gain;* but having a *task* is a different matter. When I asked you what function you thought to perform with the brethren, you said, "We'll be the Lord's gendarmes."

So I will explain to you, at least as I see it, how the "gendarme of the Lord" differs from a worldly policeman: not in "religion," of course, which even you sometimes possess and more often, like the worldling, do not possess; you differ not in that, but, naturally, in your daily life —that is, your behavior toward the brethren of the brotherhood and also toward those you pursue, arrest, or imprison.

About your behavior toward the brethren I will say nothing: this you have lived ever since you could walk.

Your relationship to the offender, no matter what his offense, derives from one dominating feeling, to wit, that the criminal is your equal, your equal absolutely, and you are his equal without excuse or limitation: you are, among others, John Theodoric the liar, Peter George the murderer, Dr. Urban the tempter.

From this it follows you must show no mercy and inflict no punishment upon yourself, I mean upon the criminal; for you are not the Lord, but only His gendarme. Nor are you to carry out His vengeance or administer correction: vengeance and correction are the Lord's. You must seize the offender and deliver him up to the Lord: that is your task.

Supposing you had caught Peter George and his marksmen torturing their living target to death; would you not have shot the tormentors on the spot, and no questions asked? I hope so: a murderer caught red-handed expects death, but an immediate death that will deliver him —not a slow death after examination, trial, sentence, and religious hocus-pocus.

Supposing you had indeed caught Peter George red-handed, but had not shot him on the spot; in that case he must have been let live, and you would have only to deliver him up to God, who would fix the time when he was to die.

So far as your secular position is concerned, you are an official under the Federal Commissioner of Public Safety; the criminal police is no concern of yours, and its methods are not yours if you mean to be a gendarme of the Lord. Therefore you must not turn over your prisoners to any court, but to the Lord, either directly by shooting the criminal in the act, or indirectly—in which case not you but the Lord determines the moment when your captive is to die. In such a case, logically, you have no right to meddle in the fixing of the moment by cutting short the life of the offender.

What, in fact, does it mean to "deliver up the criminal to God"? Ponder this question. . . .

At that point the letter broke off. A carriage rolled into the yard; Dr. Urban asked for a brief interview. Fifteen minutes later Bishop Hesse was dead.

BOOK ONE

URBAN'S INTERVIEW

XVIII

THE general dismay at the victory of the Reds in the parliamentary election turned the eyes of the small property owners and the middle class toward the President.

Surely the man who had been strong enough to snatch the mountains from the mighty Lienhardt without a single voice being raised in criticism throughout administration and army, the centers of power, must be the person to show his teeth to those who, when they came into power, meant no doubt to dispossess all property owners, but to begin with the biggest.

One tingling cold February day Adam Faust summoned the twelve of the Academy to his house; more reserved than usual, without a jest, already remote, it seemed, from earthly battlefields, he invited "his friends" to go with him to the city of Geisenheim. The members of the mountain community, brotherhood after brotherhood, would be sworn in by Hesse's successor Kessel and Oriola in the chapel under the provisions of the Mining Law; so too would the mine owners. The freethinkers and those who were unwilling to swear had agreed to give a promise of similar tenor on the mountain meadow before the governor, laying their hands upon the flag of the Carpenters. No one, he continued, was preventing him and the syndicate from applying the Mining Law (which was bound to displease an unprepared public) to their own property. On the spot where the Lienhardt château had stood the mine courthouse was to be built, and the landed property of the Lienhardts, 15,000 acres reaching down into the plains, would be purchased from the funds of the Office of Public Safety, and fenced at first, then walled in. That which was to go on within this walled area must remain secret "until the murderers are surrendered."

The eleven—Hilgenfeld did not appear—had premonitions of what this would mean. On their promise to keep it secret, the dead Hesse's letter to his son Otto had been shown to them.

Before the altar of the Geisenheim Mine Chapel, their faces turned toward the provincial governor and the bishops, while the deputies of the two brotherhoods, garbed in Carpenters' costume, and the twelve of the Academy rose from their seats, Adam Faust and his syndicate took oath "faithfully to keep and care for their property, and not to let it fall into the hands of one unworthy of it; at all times to respect the rights, liberties, and ordinances of the allied brotherhoods of the masters as well as of the men, and in no way to infringe upon the independence of the last-named; but to avert harm, misfortune, and dishonor from all the brethren of the alliance jointly." The employees and workmen of the mountain community (the very numerous former members of the Revival Mission having refused for religious reasons to take an oath) promised "at all times to respect the rights of the proprietors, and to defend the law of the community and the ordinance of the brotherhoods with their blood; but to avert harm, misfortune, and dishonor from all brethren of the alliance jointly." Twice a year the governing bodies of the unions were to have access to the books of account.

With a suddenness that not even Daruhi could explain, the public temper changed, and the provincial press, damned by the bright minds of the Iron Phalanx as "unintelligent, stultified, stultifying, bought and bribed," took the President's side. These thousands of little sheets, conducted by little men, presented the ceremonies of consecration in the mining community to their readers with a wealth of detail such as had not been devoted to any political event in years; in their largest type, frequently in color, they printed the promise contained in the oath of the miners and clerks "at all times to respect the rights of the proprietors." What employer, they asked, "except for our President," enjoyed the confidence of the workmen to such a degree that he could expect them, and even make them promise under oath, to defend the "law of the community," which, after all, did include his own property? From this time, and particularly from the first application of the dreaded Mining Law, dates the provincial taproom regulars' confidence in Adam Faust as "the right man" with the strong hand: again and again the venerable master bakers, butchers, tailors, mechanics, barbers, and *rentiers* emphasized in their discussions that a miner who spoke out of turn now might cool his heels in jail for breaking his oath. The circumstance that the proprietors too had raised their right hands and affirmed rather costly promises under oath was barely mentioned or entirely passed over.

Jacob Willert had kneeled most reluctantly; the operatic manner of a proceeding no longer in tune with the times went against the grain of a forthright nature like his, and *The Free People,* the newspaper of the Revolutionary Workers' Party, wrote: "Capitalistic terrorism and the backwardness of our institutions have, we hope, reached their peak in a scene where the horrified miners, bent under the police lash and faced with a prison embracing 15,000 acres, had no choice but to swear, 'Thralldom for us; for the proprietors, property for all time! Amen.' "

The Conservative deigned not reply a word either to this rough demagogy or to the subtle sneers of the Iron Phalanx at the "Godly hypocrites"; Urban, however, fluttered the great sharks with a factual report, quite devoid of criticism, on the ceremony at Geisenheim. It will always be remarkable that a man cheered by the masses at a thousand speeches in public squares, market places, and speakers' platforms should have revealed his inner heart almost never—once at the beginning and once at the end of his extraordinary career. For that reason we include here the interview that he granted to a foreign journalist at the time.

His headquarters were near the capital, in the large, prosperous farm village of Liebenau, a favorite resort and picnicking place, in the former manor house, now transformed into a hotel and belonging to the town, and rather ludicrously called the Grand Hotel Liebenau. This piece of ostentation was due to two prominent farmers, Schmalz, the village mayor, and Alexander Kersting, who called himself an "estate owner," and was a great hand at incurring debts.

Here, in a hall-like room, walking to and fro with his hands clasped behind his back, Urban said to the foreign newspaperman:

"The Liberals smile at the solemnity of the Geisenheim affair, and the syndicate kneeling before the altar. But a man who kneels is very strong to begin with, because he is professing submission to something —much stronger, of course, than a man with a smile. What happens to me is that I feel secure among strong men, while among people with a smile I grow embarrassed, and don't know what to do with my hands and feet, like a girl at her first dancing class; and because I'm not twenty years old, this embarrassment rouses hatred for those who put me in so disagreeable a situation—in other words, the Iron Phalanx. For I can see them smiling all the time; I can see them still smiling if I take away their pocketbooks; indeed, I can see them still, utter paupers, smiling at me because I am *mere* power, whereas they are intellect. What 'intellect' is, I can't tell you at the moment, but I shall give it some thought; if it is the quality of a man with a superior smile, I shall stamp it out along with the smile, that much you may be sure of. I have no intention of blushing like a schoolgirl, and hiding my hands and feet."

"Does that mean that you will approach, uh . . . the Conservatives, Mr. Urban?"

"I should like to. Old Adam not only has strength, but he knows where it comes from—not from superior reflection, as the people with a superior smile suppose, but from the irrational. This syndicate of lawbreakers, kneeling with uplifted eyes before a god who they know perfectly well does not exist, but who, if existent, would condemn their lawbreaking, and, if he had but the strength of a sparrow, would send the kneeling figures to hell—that syndicate is enormously impressive to me; to a certain extent it gives me aesthetic satisfaction, whereas I suspect the Liberals and revolutionists of having bad breath—forgive me."

"Not at all. Will you and the Conservatives, then——"

"No, I can't. To my mind they don't go far enough. They don't smile, and they don't talk empty chatter; when they say, 'Lienhardt must go,' villages start to burn—excellent. They kneel and indicate submission—splendid. Peace through submission is, after all, the end and aim of all human striving: write that down, because I shan't say it again. But one must be absolutely honest in meaning it. For what does 'submission' signify? It signifies bowing to arbitrary authority; that is how the word has always been understood; there is no will above God's, and His ways are called 'inscrutable,' so God is, in a word, arbitrary authority. But the Conservatives, and especially the leaders, Adam and his bishops, have abolished arbitrary authority and substituted for it a so-called law—the immutable divine will. Utter nonsense: a god who cannot alter his purpose every day is no god at all, but a prisoner of his very human obstinacy, or else the mere popinjay of a very human lawgiver. Submission, the end and aim of all human yearnings, means submission to arbitrary authority. Anyone who surreptitiously introduces a law in place of arbitrary authority either wants or brings about not submission but its very opposite, rebellion, the root of all human suffering. Since I am called to deliver from suffering, or (which comes to the same thing) to receive submission, I have no choice but to be arbitrary authority, because the old arbitrary authority that was once called 'God' has been unmasked as fictitious. I am real, not fictitious: accordingly, to put an end at long last to this brawling, I must be God. Do you see?"

"Pretty well; but five minutes ago, Mr. Urban, you said God would condemn their lawbreaking."

"Never."

"I seem to remember that you did."

"Then I didn't mean God, but the gossamer modern creature of reason that the bishops worship, which even the Liberals could worship if they were not so dismally, God-forsakenly stupid."

"Many thanks. How about your practical policy for the immediate future?"

"If I join the Conservatives, then the Liberals, soft as a pulp even now, will be squashed within five years between us and the revolutionists. If I go over to the revolutionists, adding my strength to their duplicity, then strength and duplicity together will smash the Conservative party. Adam and his men know that; so they will pay me tribute to keep the peace; and as long as they keep on paying, there will be peace."

"And how are you thinking of using this tribute? To strengthen your position, or——"

"That, I regret to say, is my business; anyway, it's of no immediate interest, because there is a long period of peace ahead."

BOOK ONE

SOCIAL CALLS

XIX

OLD Hesse's funeral took place on the eighteenth of December. Two days later his son Otto, having traveled up with the Archbishop, arrived in the capital and reported, with the two stars of a captain already on his epaulets, to his commanding officer, the Federal Commissioner of Public Safety.

Mr. von Brick received his new adjutant in the bare office of the Commissioner in the department building. Involved at the moment in a dispute with Rudolphi, the painter, he sat at his desk, gigantic, Wotan-bearded, as broad as a tile stove, and dressed in a far from citified, high-buttoned jacket; instead of a collar he wore a white-silk neckcloth. But his forehead was high and clear, his eye direct: no one seeing him like this could have guessed the depth of his ignominy. The heavy Empire desk, with one end to the wall between two windows, filled half the width of the room; on the end wall, so that von Brick's eye was bound to fall upon it as he looked up, hung a huge painting, a wheat field in the bright sun, smudged in with romantic French unction.

The Police Senator, standing up, towered half a head above his slightly built adjutant. Rudolphi, sandy-blond, broad and obese, appeared smaller because of his slovenly dress.

"You've come at just the right moment," said von Brick when Otto sat down. "They're all beginning to think they can use me for a football."

"I don't," said the painter.

Suddenly the Senator's face changed color, shrank, his mouth hung open. He bent down to Hesse, and whispered, as if he must unload a burden that could not be borne for another second: "She's beginning to be seen in the East End now, in the cabarets with Hollberg."

Otto, shaken more by the other's whispering and his anguish than by the words, lowered his face toward the helmet that he held between his knees, and made a conventional remark: "Terrible."

"No, young man," said von Brick, who sat with sunken shoulders, "what's terrible is that she drags her son along, her eighteen-year-old son—and mine!"

Rudolphi made as if to go.

"I can't help it if Kate Schwann's murderers haven't been caught yet, and if no one knows who abducted Theresa Froehlich—or can I?" von Brick turned to his adjutant.

Otto shook his head, and the Police Senator realized he had made a mistake by mentioning the subject in the painter's presence: "How do you like that picture?" he asked, pointing to the painting. "I've only had it three days, and already this gentleman here is running it down to me because his competitor Gasparra, the progressive, painted it."

Otto turned. "Don't look at it, Captain," said Rudolphi, "it isn't worth while, not even in winter, when you might be quite glad to see that sort of thing."

"He's joking," von Brick smiled, but Rudolphi went on to Otto: "If I should have the honor of making your closer acquaintance—portrait in uniform or of your charming bride-to-be cheerfully executed at all times; the Senator is smiling because he's a millionaire by trade—well, if I should have the honor, Captain, you would discover in five minutes—oh, a policeman's eye would not need that long: in a minute or two—that I am humble beyond all measure; humility is my way with everyone; but calling me a competitor of this fellow whose total absence of character will allow him to do anything, French, Spanish, ancient Chinese, religious, modern, whatever the market or the customer demands, is really going too far."

"That's what he calls humility!" said Wotan.

"You really don't need to look at it, Captain; please look out of the window, and just tell me one thing: should a man be given government commissions whom well-founded suspicion would prevent you from commissioning to drop a letter in the mailbox? Because, stopping to consider what he will get out of it, either he will not send the letter (on principle, because he never does anyone a service except himself, and the mere idea of 'serving' makes him sick) or else, if he does send the letter, he will have opened and read it first, because after all, you never can tell . . . Assuming that Gasparra, the painter, is that sort of man, his heart fatty with dishonesty down to its innermost recess, scornful of anyone who ever lets slip a word of confession, of honesty, such as you have just heard the Senator say: are you in favor of giving a government commission to a man like that?"

"No," said Otto for the sake of peace and quiet.

"All this is about the familiar project of tearing down the dirty old part of our city, and putting up a Palace of Justice across from the town hall," von Brick informed his adjutant. "Rudolphi wants to cut his competitor out of any competition. But he can rest easy: the police reform comes first."

"The police reform won't be cheap," Otto von Hesse observed almost bashfully. "No, not cheap—very expensive indeed."

"Then I wish you luck with the Senate, Captain," said Rudolphi, getting up. "I'm a poor man; but for *that* fellow"—he pointed to the wheat field—"not a penny!"

When the painter had left, and Otto, being questioned about his bodily welfare, said he had come from the station and did not know where he would be living, the Senator showed him a slender book bound in leather, and entitled *Against Overrating Externals*. The fine paper, the large type, and the decorated initial letter of each chapter did not strike Otto as being in accordance with precepts of moderation; but, presuming that his superior was a bibliophile, he spoke highly of the edition. At the bottom of the title page, where the publisher's name usually stands, were the words: *Privately printed by the Library of Hans Simon.*

"We can talk about our business later," said von Brick, "or else we won't: you need expect no trouble from me, nor from the Senate either for the time being; they've had a good fright. But to show my good intentions I'll describe the people you'll have to deal with here—or has the Bishop already told you his sad story?"

"No."

"Not anything at all on that long trip?"

"No; he was talking about other things, half religious matters, half police."

"May I ask what?"

"Oh, all purely theoretical," Otto reassured his superior, who had given him a mistrustful look. "He explained to me the meaning of the words 'deliver up a criminal to God.'"

"I see. Well, that's theology, of course," said von Brick, heaving a sigh of relief. "The things I'm going to tell you are worldly, but interesting. Point one: I shall furnish you as my adjutant with horses and a carriage and liveried footmen—correctly rating externals. You will be seen in the equipage for a few days before I introduce you to the staff, so that they will know which way the wind is blowing. Point two: you're going from here to Beyer's, aren't you?"

"Yes."

"Very good. Then please tell him that it was I, with true presidential disdain for externals, who advised you to live at the old washerwoman's."

With a shrug Otto asked to be enlightened.

"If you follow out to the letter what I tell you to do, you will kill more birds with one stone than I can possibly count up at the moment. Point one: the President does not wish the staff officers to move into villas or splendid apartments, where they can hold receptions, and criticize the government. That was why he had Hilgenfeld write this little book *Against Overrating Externals,* which all the training schools and officers' clubs have been obliged to buy, and which by now is even part of the curriculum at the academies. The officers are not supposed to withdraw themselves from the very people whom they will have to lead in war. Point two: fashionable quarters and anterooms attract callers who have the best intentions toward themselves alone, and of whom you never know who may have sent them. You will do well to limit your associates to the people who are irreproachable followers of the President. Everything you do at first will be laid to me; I can't carry more than I'm carrying now, and besides, I want to maintain my position, which is being disputed because of something that I am innocent of. I'm not the only one with an unfaithful wife; the old days are dying, and the so-called cream of society is to be found at that old bawd Madame Kittelsen's 'House of Dreams.' Hypocrisy is trumps, my young friend! Point three, but please keep this to yourself: among the President's intimates, the most intimate is the ostensibly ailing Beyer; I will say no more. Beyer has a reader—and prompter—who of course is a pupil of Zorn's, and gives a couple of history lessons a week at the city academy for girls for the sake of appearances. His name is John Henry Merckel, and he's the son of a washerwoman and rooming-house-keeper whom Adam regards as practically a saint because she lets out rooms without having to. In reality the same disorder prevails there—these are times of disintegration, my dear sir: let them pull their own noses for a change, instead of mine!—the same disorder that you will find at Rudolphi's, Hilgenfeld's, Ackermann's: the women can't get along on the money they have, and if you were to give them an extra thousand thalers, they could get along on it even less. Scarcely was the Rudolphi woman married before she had to 'keep a grand house.' They shan't get another penny from me; I don't care if they go to Hans Simon and abuse me for a skinflint—my money is going to my daughter, who, thank God, is still with me. Have you ever seen . her?"

Otto shook his head, and Mr. von Brick told the servant who answered his summons to call Alexandra.

"Where was I?"

"Point three," young Otto recalled.

"Well, point three, the Widow Merckel, washerwoman, saint, and landlady, who can't get along on the money she has, has two rooms vacant. The third is occupied by Charles Emil Koehler, the director of the Municipal Electric Plant, and a steady patron of old lady Kittelsen's; the man has looked suspicious to me for a long time—he doesn't make as much money as he spends at the 'Castle of Dreams.' In a word, please tell Senator Beyer that on my advice you have rented the two connecting furnished rooms at the Widow Merckel's; there are no bugs, and the bathroom is half a flight downstairs, on the landing."

Alexandra von Brick came in: dark, big-eyed, thirteen years of age, with the long, straight nose of the south from which her mother came. Otto arose and bowed; she nodded, let him look into her big eyes, and, suddenly covered with confusion, hugged her father.

"Have you been racing around again? Your heart's beating so hard," said the happy man, and then cried, "Madame Fallières!" touching a bell on his desk. No one answered; Alexandra, nodding to Otto, fled, laughing.

At Senator Beyer's house our young friend, having been presented to
the "Lady" and the youngest daughter—the elder two were in Scotland
looking for husbands—received some words of praise for having preferred simple quarters in the poor East End to a more comfortable
dwelling, and was assured that Brick's suspicion and uneasiness were
unfounded: no one grudged him his post. Even Bessonoff, who had
been put in an impossible position by his wife's outrageous behavior,
for she was conspiring with an enemy of the state, would nevertheless
be continued in service: marital troubles, so long as the husband secured a clear-cut separation, not a divorce, did not greatly concern the
President. The pair of white horses, the coachman and footman, incidentally, created a good impression.

Otto, breathed upon by the chill breath of diplomacy, was not much
the wiser as he departed to give his father's message to General Frohwein. He could have sent the letter by mail; but the art of opening and
reclosing letters addressed to prominent personages without injuring
the seals was one very successfully cultivated at the time.

Frohwein, the Chief of the General Staff, put the letter from his
dead friend in a desk drawer, and said, "I spent some good days with
your dad among the Malays—the best days of my life." He looked out
into the snowy garden, and suddenly asked, as if his memory had
suffered and he were listening to the report of a subordinate: "Anything else?"

At this Otto took out the manuscript "Instructions Regarding Practical Piety in the Police Service" from his leather dispatch case: and as
the old man immediately opened and read it, he spent the time playing
with the reddish-gray cat, which had a tiny military belt buckled
around its neck.

Finally the general finished, put away his spectacles, and wiped his
eyes: "I used to believe all that too, in the days when we wrote our
pamphlets about 'Dangers Overseas,' and put the motto on it: *Humana
mens naturaliter christiana.* Today I believe in Daruhi's fog, and I am
sure we shall be done for within ten years, killed by the rabble, as
Hilgenfeld and Held have prophesied. They'll leave us to die, if we
haven't fallen in battle, in a tower full of snakes, like the King of the
Goths. What was his name again?"

"Gelimer."

"Yes. Gelimer."

"It seems to me that Your Excellency and the President have done a good deal at least to postpone that event."

The general's mouth hung open with astonishment: "What, you young rogue, have you a courtier's talents too?"

"I really meant it quite honestly," said Otto.

"To think there are such things in Geisenheim! Well, *you* can't possibly go wrong! Did you show the manuscript to von Brick?"

"No."

"You'll have to eventually. Listen to me: there is here in town a man half as rich as Willert, which means very rich; he's suspected of having helped finance Dr. Urban. His name is Hans Simon—a big banker, book collector, and a man with all kinds of notions; he has the finest private library anywhere around. You go to him and tell him the President has established a committee to assist in clearing up the murders of Kate Schwann and Theresa Froehlich; among others Generals Frohwein and Kaempf will be members. Speaking of Kaempf, you've got to go see him, today, or he'll be jealous. He's a schoolmarm, and is sure to give you a history or geography lesson; that aside, he's a sensible fellow and will be useful to you if I die. So you ask Simon if he will join the committee—it's going to be started, Adam has announced it—and if Simon turns around and asks what he's supposed to assist, you show him your father's manuscript. That first sentence, with the attack on Brick, I think I'd cross out—shall I?"

"Please do."

The old man seized a preposterously fat red pencil, and crossed out the sentences aimed at the Police Commissioner.

"There, you can still read the words—just so that Simon shan't be suspicious. Now listen carefully. You can tell him that no one is going to know about your father's . . . well, more or less last will and testament, except the members of the committee; and if he asks who sent you to him, don't hesitate to mention my name. I'm willing to bet that the man can be snatched away from that great scoundrel even now if we take some trouble about it; but he wants some place to go. If he refuses, we'll know how things stand, which isn't so bad either."

"What shall I tell General Kaempf?"

"That his men, including the majors, are all going whoring at Madame Kittelsen's."

"For God's sake!" Otto ejaculated.

"All right, then let me be! Good-by!"

General Kaempf was the director of the Staff College, and, like Frohwein, a member of the Academy of Twelve.

"You can see for yourself that this used to be a high-class house, I mean, for high-class people with seven-room apartments," said the Widow Merckel, showing Otto to the tripartite bay window of his living room. "Common folks have no bay window, and the stoves are Renaissance style, which is very nice in summer, but in the winter it takes more coal. Of course Kuehn has gone and spoiled our view with his furniture factory, but anyway, the hammering and sawing and pounding and creaking, he had to move that back off the street, because the people around couldn't sleep, because their night's rest was disturbed."

And, continuing her observations on impermanence "in this changing world of ours," she showed the police captain the back room belonging to Mr. Koehler, the director of the electrical works, "A real gentleman, very seldom at home, and he pays extra for coffee and rolls," the two rooms occupied by her son, "The doctor, but he bothers too much about politics," and the common living room, which also served as a dining room "If the gentlemen take board too, which I don't suppose you'll be doing, Captain, on account of having your duties elsewhere"; and the shining kitchen with pantry and linen closet. "As I say, it's a high-class house, but nowadays the big apartments are almost all being divided up, because otherwise the rent is so high that everything stands empty, and they have a sign out the year round, 'Apartment to rent'; but you know my son, the doctor, he says it really ought to say, 'No apartment to rent,' because if there's always a sign out, anyone can see that it isn't a place anyone would want to rent."

Otto inquired whether his pair of white horses with the two men in livery would not be conspicuous in the neighborhood.

"It might have once upon a time, but not now," replied the Widow Merckel. "Old Herbert Hilgenfeld lives not far from here in a regular tenement of fifty families and three hundred children. But there's a double guard outside the building day and night even so; in fact, it's two noncoms, because Hilgenfeld belongs to the Academy. So people have got used to it."

Either the President's injunction not to overrate externals was meant for the lower ranks alone, or else the upper ranks ignored it. Kaempf, like his older colleague in the army command, lived in the quiet West End of the city, which was full of gardens, parks, and country houses; he occupied a little château with a big yard and stables, hidden from the street in summer by an old stand of trees and the shrubbery planted amongst them. Dressed in mufti, with a fur coat, a brown bowler hat on his head, he was in the front hall picking out a walking stick with a long iron ferule from the collection in the stand when the young man was announced.

Otto, hastening toward the general, begged his pardon and promised to come again later.

"How about your coming with me?" asked Kaempf. "I must admit it'll be a long walk, because this is my day for a haircut, and my barber is on Cathedral Square. Or can't you do your errand except indoors?"

As our friend immediately accepted the invitation, his carriage was put up, and the two went out on the street. The general, a thickset man in his fifties, with reddish mustachios and gold-rimmed spectacles, really did look like a village schoolmaster. Seeing the black band on the young man's sleeve, he expressed his sympathy: "There's something prophetic about names—that's an old discovery. People called your father a soldier of the Lord, and he did die like a soldier."

In the light of the wintry early afternoon they went up the broad, gently rising, tree-lined Blue Griffin Road. Strollers were few; dogs barked in snowy front yards when a jingling sleigh passed by. The general began to talk about his days as a color sergeant; he said he had been an infantryman, and had carried a rifle for a whole year, though only with a lieutenant's pack. "We've done away with that. The color sergeants carry a full pack now; one can certainly stand it at twenty, and they cheat with the makeweight sandbags anyhow. On long marches I always used to try to get next to a man who was talkative by nature, like Sergeant Strege, who knew two hundred dirty limericks by heart, and was constantly reciting them. He's still living, on the coast, a tax collector at Neuhafen. Why not, for that matter? I'm fifty, so he must be sixty. Because it isn't the weight of the pack that makes the march painful, it's thinking about the weight and trying to shift it. It's your spirit that makes it light or heavy: why does your rifle suddenly weigh a scant half pound when the band marches up, posts itself opposite the company, and starts blaring away? Why? Because your thoughts aren't occupied with your rifle, or with your aching shoulder, but with the music. They're writing whole libraries now about the 'economic insecurity of the masses'; the same thing is true of that. But if somebody does something in his own group to combat the insecurity, the whole world rises up against him—I don't mean the Mining Law, but myself."

And he recalled his abortive effort to turn the army corps into self-supporting bodies, with a central supervisory system to equalize surpluses here and shortages there. "We could buy run-down big estates cheap everywhere, and produce everything for ourselves, from feed for the horses to the Sunday goulash, wool, wood, and leather—almost everything except metal. And the service wouldn't have suffered; even the reservists' families could have bought potatoes, bread, meat, sausage, and flour at their post exchanges, for cost plus ten per cent. What an uproar! Some of them called me Urban the second, and the rest said I was a revolutionist!"

Von Hesse remembered that his father had called the general "tireless in thinking up schemes." And, urged to "contribute something to the conversation" in his turn, and feeling secure in Kaempf's own frankness, which inspired confidence, he told of his call on Chief of Staff Frohwein.

By now they had reached the broad and bustling carriage road known as the Outer Boulevard, which girdles the west side of the city in a flat curve; the smell of hot asphalt drifted toward them from a swarm of workmen who were repairing the roadway. The general sniffed, and pointed to a bench: "This smells good, and we get heat for nothing!" As they sat there facing the asphalt-coated street, the tree-lined bridle path, the sidewalk beyond it, and the shops on the ground floor of the apartment houses, many of which had a half-rustic air as if built by farmers trying to be worldly, Otto remarked that the city must once have ended here, and been prevented from growing further by fortifications.

Yes, said Kaempf, the remains of the old Outer Bulwark had been leveled off, and this splendid street, the Outer Boulevard, had been built out of them: "You may have noticed that we are ascending a gentle rise. The flat top of the hill with the cathedral at the inner town, the old core of the city, is 18,590 feet from where we are now sitting."

He hailed a cab that was swaying on its leisurely way, and told the driver, "Gobiert the barber, corner of Triumphal Lane and Cathedral Square," but instead of continuing his geography lesson he began to talk about Hans Simon, and Otto soon scented out that the general was one of those originally poor officers who, marrying into money, always remained unfamiliar with their own wealth, and were accordingly the more assiduous in preserving it. Naturally he defended his wife's banker: "Did you ever hear the term 'integrity provision'?"

Otto said he had not.

"Well, in that case let me tell you that Simon is the only banker in the country whose loans contain a *provision* as follows: if the borrower becomes guilty of any infringement of the law or of commercial ethics, the dates specified become invalid, and the loan is payable on the same terms as a debt for a bill of exchange; that's the substance of it, though I'm no businessman; but a banker who can impose such stiff terms as that on his clients must certainly be a man of integrity."

"I understand Simon has retired from the business," Otto said.

"From railroad and government loans, yes; but on the other hand he administers all the greatest fortunes. If you give Simon a hundred thousand thalers to handle, of course he can't put it in his sock—he's got to lend it out; but to whom, there's the question. Answer: to people who are willing to face ruin if they can be proved guilty of an infringement of law or ethics—just think, of *ethics!* Could there be any greater security? So it's pure nonsense about Simon's financing Urban —or do you think Urban would sign the integrity provision?"

Von Hesse, astonished at the naïveté of the general and contriver of schemes, was about to point out to him that money supplied to Urban was not a loan, but a contribution, and that the giver would expect political favors instead of interest and repayment; but, reflecting that such statements cannot be directly made without offense, he turned the conversation to the private editions, Hans Simon's well-known hobby.

"Do you know what? I've got an idea!" said Kaempf suddenly. "We'll run over to Simon's, and I'll introduce you." He called out the address to the cab driver, and the carriage turned into a side street on the right, rolled along the quiet bank of the canal for a few hundred yards, and stopped in front of a five-story house whose reddish brick façade was adorned with arches and columns in the Florentine manner.

The doorbell was a gilt lion's head, holding a brass ring in its mouth.

"Let me ring," said von Hesse, and told how that had been his mother's dream in the days when they were still on short commons before his eldest sister married—a gilt lion's head for a bell at the front door.

The maid who opened the door, powdered and gray-haired, wore an apron over her high-buttoned black dress. Otto scrutinized her for a fraction of a second, and searched his memory. Behind her in the hall appeared the house steward; while the general was whispering to the young man, "Shiny elbows—even at the richest houses they have shiny elbows!" the enormous, fat, pale man approached them with a gesture of apology: "Reception day—have you some identification and a number, gentlemen?"

"You must be new here, aren't you?" Kaempf asked the servant rather roughly. "You tell Mr. Nessel General Kaempf and Captain von Hesse from the Federal Police want to pay a call."

"Certainly, gentlemen," panted the fat man, motioning to the maid to take the callers' outer garments.

"Dr. Nessel, Simon's private secretary and librarian, the private-editions man, and of course a pupil of Zorn's and a member of the Clique," Otto was informed in a whisper. "The very few writers, six or seven, that Hilgenfeld allows to write for *The Conservative* are known as the Clique. I had the honor of being in the thick of things there when I wrote my articles about provisioning the army," the general added. And Otto remembered a truth uttered in jest by his father: to count for anything in the capital, you had either to have a double guard outside your door, or to be received by Hilgenfeld; the man who had accomplished both was "first-rate."

They sat waiting in ample leather armchairs, and at the rear of the hall a door opened; a confused sound of talk, as of people quarreling, could be heard; a little man scornfully waved his broad-brimmed black hat toward the room he was about to leave—evidently the waiting room for the petitioners—and called back in a bleating voice, "Have you read my drama, *Theodoric the Titan*? What do you think of the title? Grips you—strikes a spark, what? My time has come, let me tell you, Mr. Mark Antony!" He slammed the door (which was apparently heavily padded, for the babble of voices died away instantly), and went out through the hall, giving the captain and the general each a glance of understanding. Under the dwarf's broad-brimmed hat a

pale, clown's nose and a billy-goat beard of the same color were conspicuous.

That was the look of an accomplice or of one who was offering himself, Otto felt, and he asked: "Do you know him?"

"Not personally, which incidentally I regret, because he's mad. But
as an instructor at the college of course I have to be familiar with con-
temporary literature. His name is Léon Léonhard—a pen name, of
course—he's been carrying the manuscript whose title grips you and
strikes a spark around with him for ten years (the paper is spotted and
soaked with grease by this time), offers you fifty per cent if you'll get
it produced, which has been prevented by the priests, and proclaims
after every political upset that his time has now come. He was supported for years by Hilgenfeld, who used to use him as a model—if
you can call it 'supported': Mrs. Hilgenfeld would invite him to supper,
or, in other words, for a sitting, and when he left she used to give him
a thaler at first, then half a thaler, then fifty pennies, and finally the
tram fare. When she wouldn't give him even that any more, because
her daughter who was still at home then complained he had laid hands
on her in an improper way—he's an incredible swine—he threatened to
sleep on the sofa!"

"How can a banker get involved with such people? Even the house
steward doesn't look like a house steward—more like . . ." Otto checked
himself: at the fat colossus' side a man of about thirty approached, with
tousled brown hair above a smooth-shaven, slender, delicate face. The
general stood up, Otto followed his example, and the suspect house
steward pulled out a third armchair.

"Oh, Your Excellency!"

"My dear Nessel, it doesn't make the slightest difference—I've been
having a splendid time. This is Captain von Hesse, good old Brick's
right-hand man."

"Welcome indeed to the capital. Won't you sit?"

The three sat down, and Simon's private secretary was lavish in his
praise of von Hesse's address to the squadrons.

He doesn't seem to be quite normal either, thought Otto. He had
long since come to regret the address: his father had objected to its
"conspicuous arrogance."

"Still, Captain, if you will forgive my being personal," said Nessel, "it was an important moment in your life, and, it seems, not in yours alone. Was it not as if Destiny had allowed Hercules at the crossroads but a single second's reflection?"

"I didn't reflect at all," said Otto.

Kaempf kept silent. From Bessonoff he had heard that the military doctors' judgment of the swiftly promoted adjutant was unfavorable. His weak heart was perhaps not serious; but the head physician at Geisenheim, an old practitioner, regarded the notorious "address" as the outpouring of a man in a dream. "In this category of patients," the doctor had declared, "the guardian power of reason suddenly ceases to function, and for an hour or sometimes for half a day at a time they will live in a state of waking dream during which they seem outwardly normal—and there's the danger. I would not entrust the command of any body of troops to an officer who gives orders while in a waking dream, that is, while ignoring the external world." This opinion was presented to Daruhi, who declared it was sheer Philistinism: no normal consciousness, he said, remained uninterruptedly under the so-called control of reason.

"Precisely because you didn't reflect," replied the librarian, pedantically riding his hobby, "the result was a mixture of command and poetry, a product, most attractive to the great banker and to me as well, of—what Daruhi would call the 'unknown intermediary regions.' In a word, Captain, would you allow us to issue an artistic private edition, strictly limited, with drawings by Rudolphi?"

"By thunder!" cried the general with a laugh that freed the two young men from their embarrassment, "he's off!"

"The copies would be kept under lock and key, and issued to no one without your permission," Simon's secretary continued his urging.

"Since you regard the address as poetry, that is to say, don't take it seriously," said Otto (courteously interrupted by Nessel's ejaculation, "Captain—please!"), "I'm willing." And he made his request for an interview with Mr. Simon.

"Not today, I beg of you! You gentlemen can come any day you please, any except Wednesday, the petitioners' day. If I were to open that upholstered door over yonder—I had almost said the padded cell —you would both have to admit that this place is a madhouse."

"We've already seen one madman," Kaempf observed.

"There are fifteen of them in there, all insulting one another; but when Simon lets them in to see him—one at a time, of course—they go crazy. Lou Hofer sings ballads of unrequited love at him, and expects him to melt away into a grease spot. Her husband, answering to the name of Richard or Ricardo, swears he will shoot himself by tomorrow noon unless he has been made municipal opera conductor by then. Léon Léonhard vows his time has come, and offers the banker a fifty per cent interest. Alderman Heidemann wants to become mayor by the help of the Liberal faction, and very humble people; the only ones who are ever quiet can't buy a coffin for their dead children. It goes like that every Wednesday from three to nine; tomorrow Simon will swear he's going to drop it all, but he won't do it."

"Why?"

"His father died on a Wednesday."

Now the General reminded Otto of the "Instructions Regarding Practical Piety in the Police Service," and Otto took the manuscript from his pocket. Would Mr. Simon be willing to join the Committee to Investigate the Women's Murders?

He could promise them that, Nessel said.

"In that case I will leave with you my father's letter, which no one is to read except the members of the committee, and we'll come back day after tomorrow."

"The document will be kept under lock and key in the safe," said Nessel, accepting it.

"Please tell Mr. Simon this: what my father wrote there is the result of elaborate deliberation, it's not poetry. Those 'Instructions' will be followed to the letter—just as Simon himself seems to follow his father's will to the letter."

The secretary thanked them for the honor they had done his employer. He would see that all the messages were transmitted.

The farewell civilities had already been exchanged when Otto, his helmet already on his head, turned back: "Mr. Nessel! Just a moment. Will you step outside the door with us for a second, please?"

Outside, the cab driver was lighting his two carriage lanterns. It was four o'clock, and growing dark.

"What's the name of that powdered, gray-haired maid who opened the door for us?"

"Claire Mill," replied the astonished librarian.

"Has she a lover?"

"The steward, I'm told, but I don't know anything definite."

"Do you know who Claire Mill is?"

"No."

"A former stewardess and fellow worker of Dr. Urban's at one of Oriola's estates called Albertsdorf. If you'll call on me at the Commissioner of Safety's office, I'll show you her photograph."

"Impossible, Captain!"

"Careful, don't leave anything lying around! She was a wild girl in her day!"

That day von Hesse grew fond of the red-mustached general and schoolmaster for his very human garrulity. "Another one with no false face about him," he thought, remembering the fatherly warning against those literary and political salons where moral pessimism was the accepted thing, and a visitor suspected of meaning what he said rendered himself ridiculous. Nothing was so well looked on at the time as witty remarks about the degradation and decay of the age; writers who wallowed in decadence, artists who cast satirical sidelights, were highly paid, and palmed off as moralists into the bargain; on the other hand, Hilgenfeld's reputation as a "reactionary nincompoop" and, worse yet, a "creature of the President's" was assured the moment he declared in *The Conservative* that all this "decadence" would vanish, like cooking odors when the windows are opened, the moment the moralists and revolutionary millionairesses (in skirts and in trousers) were deported across the frontier under police guard.

"Who is that pale, fat man, Simon's butler and Claire Mill's lover? Where does he come from?" Otto asked his new friend, the general, when they drove along the quiet canal bank toward the city.

Kaempf, as a "walking town history," of course knew the story of the fat house steward and how Simon had engaged him. He reported that the banker's one hobby before he devoted himself to book collecting had been strong men and wrestling: no matter where these Herculeses appeared, even at the amusement parks of the proletarian East End, Simon, lean and narrow-chested like his father, had been a well-known and (since he always treated the performers to several rounds of drinks) a popular figure.

One day the despairing proprietor of a booth issued an announcement to say that he had, at great trouble and expense, induced the former world champion, Frank Jaeger, also known as the Caucasian

Oak, to return to the art of wrestling, and that the champion, appearing on such-and-such a date, would pay to any adversary who could pin his shoulders to the mat the sum of two hundred thalers in the presence of the assembled public. The proprietor of the booth had no hesitation in guaranteeing the above-mentioned sum, as the Caucasian Oak would employ a new technique of his own invention.

In the amusement parks on the edge of the circular green surrounding the War Memorial, in the poorest part of the East End, the sport enthusiasts who paid their ten pennies' admission fee had long since grown accustomed to any possible piece of impudence from the booth owners and fight managers. But this impudence very nearly went too far. Although "Frank Jaeger, the Caucasian Oak," an obese and gigantic printer's helper, had lost what little money he had to the owner of the booth, he had never so much as seen a wrestling match in his life.

This privately reached the ears of our Emil, the subsequent house steward, at that time a male nurse at the madhouse, in whose presence the lunatics became reasonable through fear of his strength; and partly from a love of adventure and partly for the two hundred thalers he offered himself as a contestant. The proprietor appointed him "Ab del Kadr, the Lion of Afghanistan."

Hans Simon appeared in a white waistcoat and gray top hat, flourishing a bamboo cane with a gold head, and his popularity rose to new heights when he stood even the younger members of the audience a round, and treated the ladies to raspberry soda pop.

Frank Jaeger, the printer's helper, is reported to have trembled with fear while his adversary was having his tights put on: he regarded Emil, a perfect stranger to him, as a wrestler, and the proprietor did not enlighten him. The audience shouted to Frank, urging him to show his "new technique," and he, half swooning with terror, pounded and trampled Emil, who had at least expected some sort of fair play, with fists and knees; amid the derisive cheers of the experts he had already reduced the latter to a mass of ruins when the platform collapsed. The Municipal Police ambulance transported the unconscious Emil and the victor, who had suffered a skull fracture in the fall, to the near-by hospital. The defeated "Lion of Afghanistan" was discharged five days later, covered with court plaster; Frank had to spend eight weeks in the hospital, consoled and loaded with presents by the witness of his triumph, Hans Simon. It was during this time that the sharp-witted and not altogether untrained printer was supposed to have extracted from the banker a promise to set him up in business, in a "nice little shop, a poor thing, but mine own": a calling-card and advertising printing shop with a modern press, whose owner was on the verge of bankruptcy, could be bought at a bargain.

Not long after this, "Frank the Printer"—he no longer bothered with his surname—issued to the public an invitation, of his own printing, to honor him with its commissions: "First-class execution assured." And on a stiff, gilt-edged card he proffered his services not only to print but also to compose original wedding poems, with suitable humor. In the upper left corner of this card a winged cupid, clad only in a loincloth and a wink, was discharging his arrow; on the back, framed in roses and greenery, was the poem:

> *You'll find I have mastered the art*
> *Of verses for summer and winter;*
> *My sentiments goes to the heart—*
> *Very truly your friend Frank the Printer.*

Meanwhile the two had moved on from the quiet residential district along the canal, where there are few shops and hardly any children at all, into the so-called "city," always following the broad Blue Griffin Road, which the driver had turned back into after the call at Simon's. Otto showed his surprise at the length, regular width, and straightness of the road.

"Yes, this is our only avenue of invasion," the general explained, "and the word 'invasion' is in fact to be taken literally, if I may permit myself a little discursion into military history."

"Oh, with great pleasure," the young man flattered, while the driver slowed his pace as if anxious to listen.

"This is the road they attacked on, you see, the so-called enemy— that is, the burgesses of the good city of Mittelburg, leagued with the Counts of Neumuehle and Niederwesel and a few lousy bishops, some four hundred years ago. All those towns are across the river to the west, none of them more than thirty miles away—a happier age!"

"Why happier?"

"Because the world was bigger. Just think, if a lad in those days said

to himself, 'I'm going out into the world and conquer strange king-
doms!'—he went out at cockcrow to one of the city gates, and there the
world lay before him. And by the time the sun had reached high noon,
he was already journeying through the next kingdom, as strange as
Siam, and as familiar as his nursery, because after all he was a dreamer.
At that time this where we're driving now was all virgin forest, and
the Blue Griffin Road was an open glade, in which before sunup our
city army, two hundred patricians and a thousand foot soldiers, were
moving westward from the hilly plateau down, in the opposite direction
from what we are going; so we expected to attack the enemy along
the river at crack of dawn. And we wanted the sun (which, as you
may have heard, rises in the east) to be shining in the enemy's face, so
'that he, dazzled, would miss us as he swung. An excellent plan; and
we met the enemy where we sought him, just short of the Liebenau
bridge, which is there to this day, and were terribly thrashed, for reasons that are at the moment no concern of ours, but only of my class
in the history of warfare. Sixty dead strewed the field of battle around
Hinrich's Gardens and Tavern, and the battle was fought with such
plebeian savagery that as much as a hundred years later the poet sang:

> *Bloody and pale they lay there sixty strong;*
> *Before each man found his dead master oft was long——*

and so on, because in the old days you didn't kill your enemy, but
knocked him off his horse, took him prisoner, and demanded a pretty
penny for ransom. What was to be done then? The foot soldiers scattered down the river to southward, in the direction where Willert's
property is now; the knights and patricians faced about and galloped
back into the city, which, in no condition to defend itself, was spared
upon one humiliating condition: it must open up the forest glade from
the river to the West Gate into a triumphal avenue, so that the counts'
fat horses could march in more comfortably. To this day the part of
the road we are driving along from the old West Gate to Cathedral
Square is called the Triumphal Way; but the humiliation was proper,
I mean to say it was a warning: the enemy has never marched in
since."

They drove across the busy Augustus Square, at whose center rose the Municipal Theater, copied from classical models; on the pediment was a golden inscription not put there by Adam: *Artem non odit nisi ignarus.*

"Left, left!" cried Kaempf to the driver, "we want to go round by Scottish Widows' Lane, and then back into Blue Griffin Road."

Scottish Widows' Lane, into which were crowded the small and exclusive shops where Elsie Ackermann had not even ventured to price things, had a history of its own. In the first century of the progressive era (the age of railroads and the telegraph), architecture as an art vanished from the earth as Greek fire and the secret of Chinese lacquer had vanished before it. It had indeed left great traces behind, but even the most recent of these, the last humble witnesses to architecture—unpretentious cottages, pavilions, stone stairways, entrances, and gates to gardens and enclosures—had already begun to resemble documents from ancient times or a puzzling script in some mysterious character, products of a will that no longer existed. True, the talent of photographic imitation did subsequently develop; but even the best imitations, making no pretense to "an idea of their own," shared the fate of the originals they were copied from, in that they were a sort of writing that is considered "beautiful," but is meaningless because no one can decipher it. The architects and their contemporaries no longer lived on this earth. This monstrous transformation took place as all monstrous things do, unnoticed.

Decades passed. Then, long before Zorn and Daruhi, conscientious men were horrified to see the products of the young architects who had carried out their own ideas "in accordance with our dynamic era"; and the Senate was induced to declare Scottish Widows' Lane a "protected historic area," in which, when repairs or new construction proved necessary, original ideas were prohibited, and only the copying of outworn models was allowed. Since that time there had been more English than the native language spoken in the Lane and shops during the autumn tourist season; fire-insurance premiums and shop rents rose to unreasonable heights; it was forbidden to drive faster than a walk on the ancient cobblestones; the cab drivers, using their whips as pointers, acted as guides; starling houses and swallows' nests were put up under the rain gutters, and lorries were excluded. Dark archways led into courtyards with roses creeping over green shutters in which a heart was sawed out; gray and weathered benches stood around weeping willows and little fountains; the scrawny Englishwomen jumped when a ripe horse chestnut plopped on the ground.

The general, declining the driver's services, pointed out to Otto the corner mansion belonging to the Susemihls, the rich fancy grocers, "who became great by importing oranges and lemons"; in the show window a long-mustached Chinese was shaking his head at measured intervals over a copper bowl full of tea; next door was the shop of Levin, the jeweler, where "the daughters of the Sparangapanis and Beyers beat down prices with an impudence one would never suspect to look at them." Suddenly the man on the box cleared his throat; Kaempf, winking, nudged his young companion; on the left, above the door of an unadorned, three-story white house, was a flourished gilt inscription so small that one had to look closely: HOUSE OF DREAMS.

"Madame Kittelsen's brothel?" Otto inquired.

"Heavens above! Surely you aren't a fanatic?" replied the general. "Of course it's not a brothel, or a wench would be looking out of the window now. It's what our more lighthearted forebears called a 'bagnio,' a place for men, a discreet, harmless spot with a little stage for singing and dancing on the ground floor——"

"And Mrs. Kittelsen's willing ladies!"

"Not at all, the ladies stay on the third floor, and no one who doesn't care to ever sees them at all."

Before Sparangapani's café the driver stopped and watered his horse at a trough.

"A two-hundred-year-old café, the oldest in town, still owned by the same family—you know Odo, Jacob Willert's brother-in-law," Kaempf explained. "The splendid Elizabeth is pregnant for the second time, after fifteen years—she may work her way up again!"

They turned back into Blue Griffin Road, and passed through another quiet backwater, Lady Square, with the Willert and Bessonoff houses; suddenly the noise of the wholesale houses and provision markets was all around them; then a broad strip of green opened before them, poverty-stricken, swarming with children, with soda-water stands, street candy sellers, greasy smells, playgrounds, couples embracing—the Inner Boulevard. Not far from the sidewalk, in the dirty, snow-covered green of the dwarf spruces, stood park-department toolsheds; there was an old wooden pavilion, its walls covered with far from ambiguous drawings and verses written by schoolboy hands; and there were brown-painted public conveniences of corrugated iron.

Otto reminded the general that he had started to tell about Emil, the fat house steward, and then, diverted by the similarity of the two, had talked of Frank, the printer, instead, who was obviously another one of Simon's satellites: the banker and steady patron of wrestling shows, he said, was becoming a most interesting figure.

"Do you by any chance suspect him?"

"Not in the least; but how did he happen on Emil?"

"Quite simply: through the woman."

"Claire Mill?"

"Exactly." Alarmed by the bickering of the petitioners on Wednesday afternoons, she had requested a "strong man," who could be at once house steward, bouncer, and quieter-down: she knew of a male nurse who wanted to better himself. And so Simon had engaged Emil for fear of losing his housekeeper.

"Triumphal Way!" said Otto, pointing to a street sign. Going straight ahead, they had crossed the Inner Boulevard, filled with the noise of children, driven into the Old Town, and three minutes later they found the broad Cathedral Square with the cathedral and the Gothic town hall before them.

BOOK ONE

HEINZ'S TRANSGRESSION AND THE HOUR OF WEAKNESS

XX

I N THE dark of early morning—the stars were still twinkling when she went to the window—Claire Mill rose from the couch of the Lion of Afghanistan. It would have been unwise to encounter a spying chambermaid a little later in the corridor of the third floor or on the landing. As she put up her hair at the mirror, the house steward's gray mass of flesh stirred. He watched her projecting shoulder blades for a while; the madness of a world where vitality continued undiminished, without aim or purpose, in such an aging bag of bones caused him to belch.

"Where's the sodium bicarbonate?" he asked.

"On the bedside table," replied the housekeeper, absorbed in a few tiny hairs on her chin, without turning around.

"If I were in your place, I'd be out of here pretty soon," said Emil, leaning back after taking a drink of water.

"Out of the house? So that Diana Rose can come to see you, I suppose?"

"Where's the package that Hesse gave Nessel?"

"In the safe, but it's nothing to me any more," she said, turning her powdered face toward him.

"Is that so?"

"No; and recently I've begun to believe in God, too."

"You must have got a fright, I should think."

"Not because of that," whispered Claire, listening in the direction of the door, "but if you get found dead in a ditch, great gob of fat that you are, do you think everything's finished?"

"Yes, unfortunately."

"It can't be, though, because if everything were finished, then you or anyone else could dare to do exactly what they pleased."

"Why, you're trembling."

"Me? Why should I?"

Emil sat up to bring himself closer to her face: "Because Hesse recognized you. But you knew days ago that he was coming. Why did you open the door for him?"

"Because I'm finished, if you want to know! And if he hauls me up, I'll admit everything, because I want to live, but not a hole-and-corner life, here today and gone tomorrow—I'm fed up!" She fell down before his bed, and stretched out her thin hands to him.

"He'll end up in an asylum, Hesse will," said Emil at last in order to put an end to a disagreeable situation. "I looked him in the eye, and I know what lunatics look like."

"But *we*'ll end up first, and do you know how? The way the half file did—the best half file in the guard regiment—when that accident happened at Dammerkerk. They didn't do anything wrong: they sim-

ply fought back when they were attacked, and old Hesse was shot by
mistake—Hesse says so, and he's no liar."

"How about the half file? They were arrested while fleeing, the
paper says," remarked Emil, as if the matter did not interest him.

"Not one of them is alive!" whispered the housekeeper, slipping out.

Her fear of being summoned before the Commissioner of Public
Safety and forced to make confessions that would necessarily bring
with them the vengeance of the Urbanites proved unjustified, either
the next day or afterward. Emil, on the other hand, was surprised to
see how her body changed after her fear of the "lunatic adjutant" had
led her to cast the burden of espionage service from her soul. She gained
weight, her skin grew firmer, and the natural color returned. Dr. Kuttner, the Simon family physician, however, triumphantly reported the
success of his blood remedy, Phocasan.

In the years with which our story deals, or at any rate in our fathers'
time, moral concepts were more complicated than they are today.
When Jacob Willert came back from Geisenheim, the splendid Elizabeth confessed to him that she was pregnant. He embraced his wife,
doubled her allowance for the duration of her term, and, in accordance
with the usual conscience of his time, was unable to continue his marital unfaithfulness, begun with Peggy, until the child begotten in wed-
lock should be born. To what superstition it was originally due that a
husband was obliged to be faithful during his wife's pregnancy has
never been explained: the rule was followed almost without exception
in the upper and middle classes, more rarely by the poor. On the other
hand—and therein lies the complication of our fathers' moral views—a
visit at Madame Kittelsen's was not regarded as unfaithfulness, but as
an escapade, diversion, or recreation.

Margaret Witt was the one chiefly concerned in this austerity of
morals, and she grew reconciled to it when she met Otto von Hesse
in the hairdressing salon of her master, Mr. Gobiert, on Cathedral
Square. True, Hesse became neither a fiery nor a generous lover, and a
prouder girl would have interpreted as disdain his cigar-smoking taci-
turnity when they sat in the darkened depths of the Café Sparangapani.
Peggy had never been pampered, with one half-forgotten exception;
she suspected, furthermore, that the overfed and muscular gentlemen
with bowler hats and overcoats that were too tight who instantly ap-

peared and began acting casual wherever her fellow provincial might be sitting or walking were secret police, in whose presence the object of their vigilance would not become very intimate. He, on the other hand, liked her chatter, the familiar ejaculations and the conversational tone of back home; the voices of the north had a cold sound to his ear. She asked whether he had seen Senator Willert.

Rumor had it that the shots at Dammerkerk and the disappearance of the Urbanite half file after an unauthenticated attempt at flight had made Jacob Willert thoughtful; he was said to have locked himself up with John Huebner, the manservant, who had served his father before him, and to be studying both Testaments; for "a time of lawlessness had begun," and the turmoil was great. That was why he had begun reading the Bible; either that which had been formerly revealed was all nonsense and superstition, in which case he, like Borstel, would approach Urban; or else the revelation was not all nonsense, and then it must also contain the remedies. He did not propose to continue along the road that had been followed since old Hesse's death, answering crime with crime and diverting the ordinary course of justice.

For in the meantime the violent outcome of the bloody encounter at Dammerkerk, which had been kept from the newspapers, had come under discussion in the Academy of Twelve, and Adam Faust had been obliged to submit the report of Captain Heinz. It stated that the police group stationed at the farm under the command of young Hesse had been in communication by field telephone with a detachment hidden in the ditch by the road outside the village, under Captain Heinz. When the Bishop and Color Sergeant Laurenti had fallen, and the Urbanites had fled on their bicycles, they were not pursued at all; Otto had telephoned word to his superior. Heinz, his report asserted, had loudly ordered the group of cyclists, upon their approach along the highway, to dismount. Instead of obeying, he declared that the leader had fired at him, and all had increased their pace, so that "there was nothing to be done but shoot them from their wheels." In this way, regrettably, the criminals had all been killed without exception.

At the word "regrettably" Jacob Willert sprang up and denounced it as hypocrisy. He was not chickenhearted, and must decline to let His Excellency the President count him in the category of "ladies," but if any police captain was in future to be allowed to shoot down men like partridges, then governmental authority would in actual fact cease to exist. This, he said, would be no more than feudal law, or anarchy, as Justice Holzkopf had remarked on an earlier and similar occasion. Mr. Heinz's marksmen should have punctured the tires of the bicycles and arrested the culprits.

Otto got up, and although von Brick tried to push him down in his chair, although the President and Beyer warned him by their glances against bringing up the subject again, he asked for the floor.

Before he could speak, Jacob addressed him: "Of course I shall be grateful for further information, but I am familiar with the 'Instructions Regarding Practical Piety,' etc., and I agree with them all but the point about 'Delivering up the criminal to God,' which no one has been able to explain to me; incidentally, the 'Instructions' expressly say that the gendarme has no right to cut short the life of a criminal. The men who were shot were not even criminals."

"If this respected gathering is of opinion," the young adjutant replied almost bashfully, "that governmental authority, that is, publicly controlled machinery, can combat Urban's secret service, and that the methods employed heretofore, arrest and interrogation after the fact, will suffice to combat it, then I would humbly request my dismissal. I respectfully remind Senator Willert of the passage in the 'Practical Instructions' that says: 'So you must send a neighbor against the murderers, the doorkeeper, and the listening wife,' which, after all, is as much as to say that the ways and means of defense against an Urban cannot be the ways familiar to us all, which, being old, seem morally above reproach."

"That last point I am quite ready to admit," cried Jacob Willert, "but what does the shooting down of the twenty-five on their bicycles signify?"

"A symbolic act, Senator. The shooting signifies that the time for formalities is past. Urban will never again bring a half file with him for an interview with any governmental or ecclesiastical functionary."

"Do you know the saying: 'Do unto others as you would have them do unto you'?" Jacob asked. "Not only Urban but the Bishop also had a half file for his protection."

Otto, disconcerted, looked at the President, who replied: "I take the point of view that Captain Hesse will need about ten years to get a proper anti-Urban corps in working order. We shall have to have patience even with transgressions and unjust executions, which may occur often again; but, after all, this is a jungle fight. Injustices, excesses, and crimes committed by the fighting police will certainly create a tempest in a teapot—in the newspapers, I mean to say—and will be completely forgotten when the constructive accomplishment of the group becomes evident. Jacob, are you willing that we should give the Commissioner's Office and Mr. Hesse two years to prove themselves, after which he will have to justify his actions?"

Old Adam having added a few more civilities, Jacob Willert expressed his agreement.

The President had originally shared Jacob's view, and had meant to punish fat Heinz, especially since the men shot had belonged to very respectable middle-class families, and none had any previous criminal record. But then Senator Beyer had urged political considerations, and Bishop Oriola, summoned to give his report, had cited religious grounds in the police captain's favor.

The textile magnate and confidant of the President said in substance what follows: the duration of the reformed parliament was six years, just time enough to turn von Brick's run-down office into a useful instrument. The Conservatives, the Episcopal Party, and the Reform Party of the independent unions were ready to vote the money that von Brick asked: the three groups together controlled forty-eight votes out of the seventy-five in the Senate. In the lower house the majority of the three was greater still—for the next six years, it must be remembered! "It is not our business," Beyer went on, "to drag out the transgression of our adherent Heinz into the public view, carrying confusion to the ranks of the parties allied with us, and thus weakening our numerical superiority in the two chambers. If the Reform Party falls away from us because we leave a friend in the lurch owing to moral scruples, we have just *one* vote more than Urbanites and leftists together. In the second place, it is not our business at all to make things easy for our enemies, but to keep our friends' courage up. Fairness to an irreconcilable adversary is an ideal for after-dinner speakers in search of popularity."

Oriola's opinion was as follows: "Against an enemy who need subject himself to no limitations in the choice of weapons—for in his interview he called God an 'unmasked invention'—any means that promises success must necessarily be permissible. If it were not permissible, we should from the start be voluntarily conceding to our adversary a

superior strength that would assure his victory. He who supports the
enemy in a holy war shows not his morality but the very opposite."

Accordingly, the actual course of events was concealed, and only a
"regrettable attempt at flight ending in the death of all those involved"
was made public.

Although the semiofficial communication did not even try to sound
convincing, the attack of the humanitarian press, dominated by the
Liberals, was feeble and disunited. True, the Iron Phalanx, recently
founded, had spread to neighboring countries; it never printed "attempted flight" except in quotation marks; nevertheless, either the
dainty young men and Diana Rose must have squandered their energy,
rage, and self-assurance in the struggle against Adam Faust three
months before, or else they did not think a similar exertion worth
while so soon after an election.

At a secret session of the Academy of Twelve, Professor Daruhi cited
the "law of habituation": "A party whose actions show that it will
stop at no crime intimidates its adversary, and leads him to doubt the
success of his own resistance." The torture of Kate Schwann had been
an attempt at intimidation. Naturally the first reaction was a fierce
outcry of indignation; but if the same crime were to be repeated, the
outcry would not have its original force, and by the sixth repetition it
would be no more than a dull whisper.

A government, then, once having undertaken the task of reconstituting a nation that was becoming unhinged, could derive a comforting
lesson from the law of habituation. After Adam's mine enterprise there
had been a hurricane; Heinz's twenty-five-fold murder still raised a
small storm; the next act of violence would be in small type under
Local News.

Adam Faust cleared his throat, and asked whether the law of habituation had paralyzed the pens of the Urbanite editors, who had not mentioned the event at Dammerkerk at all in the League's own organ,
The People's National Times, except in the announcement section
under the pungent heading: "Died Like Heroes in the Fight at Dammerkerk," followed by twenty-five names.

"No!" cried Otto von Hesse in a loud voice. "Urban's headquarters
at Liebenau are under observation day and night from our 'doorkeep-
ers and listening women.' A young N.C.O. of the so-called 'guard regi-

ment,' with whom Urban spends his nights in periods of depression, has furnished a detailed report."

"How much did it cost?" asked the nephew of the Archbishop, a monk in the cowl of a Franciscan.

"The young Adonis draws a monthly salary from us," replied Captain Hesse with a smile.

DR. URBAN IN PRIVATE

It is definitely known that the situation regarding the difference of opinion in Urban's camp over the ways of publicly exploiting Heinz's mass murder was as follows:

The League Leader read books, fat ones for preference, but no newspapers. He found out what was going on in the world in three successive stages during the morning. The two bath attendants who gave him a treatment of Swedish gymnastics at half-past eight in the morning, massaging him, soaping him, and giving him a shower, played the part of "voice of the people," telling him the latest political occurrences. At nine came Gretchen with the coffee, Gretchen Demuth, a natural daughter whom old Lienhardt had bequeathed to him, and who was supposedly, for publicity's sake, joined to the leader by a "secret love": she supplied housekeepers' chatter of domestic events in the first families—anecdotes polished up by Weisse and intended to produce merriment. Urban's third informer was his barber, Willie Gaedicke, an N.C.O. in the guard troop, the very Adonis mentioned by Hesse—a vain, avaricious, femininely beautiful and unscrupulous roué who had affairs with both men and women, and a barber's helper by profession. He grew rich on bribes coming in from every direction, and through blackmail practiced upon Senators' sons, high officials, and sixty-year-old millionairesses. In his riper years, when he would rather have done murder than fail to find his picture in the papers, he devoted himself to the cultural life and liberation of the proletariat, with the financial support of a brewer and a Hungarian dancer. At fifty, in the days of the decisive struggle between the Conservatives and Urban, he died in the capital of a southern kingdom while fleeing the daggers of Urban's secret service. That Urban could not only bear to associate with such a person, but even confided his most secret thoughts to him in moments

of spiritual weakness, is a dark blot upon his character; and Hildebrand, the union leader, no philosophic dialectician and dreamer like
Lindbrecht, but a sober, everyday sort of man, as his words to Bishop
Oriola show, steadily concentrated his blasts against Urban on this one
dark spot, driving home by tireless and convincing repetition the idea
that the figure of the League Leader and his companions proved the
truth of the saying, "Show me your friends and I'll tell you who you
are."

The "Darling," as those who knew him called him, was of no use
even as a soldier or messenger; on the other hand, his mastery of an
art related to his own trade of barbering was superb—the making of
masks. He could make durable wigs, mustaches, and whiskers so true
to nature, and put them on so fast, that people whom he instructed in
the art and supplied with materials could go into a small railway toilet
as soldiers, and come out three minutes later as sixty-year-old deacons.
He would smile at you as a young lover, pass his hand over his face,
and there, slack-jawed, drooling, chewing on spittle, would be a professor of history whom death had forgotten. He would get up, stretch,
lift his head, raise his left arm, clenching his fist, and there was the
model for the heroic-sized statue of the *Awakened World Proletariat*
that the Feminine Friends of Armed Rebellion had commissioned from
Felice Gasparra.

So far as the "most secret thoughts" were concerned, which the
League Leader confided at moments of weakness to this Narcissus, the
stupid booby, understanding not a word, passed them on to Hesse's
secret service in a form so distorted that Schwann and von Lindequist,
who had been summoned to the capital to help with the organization,
and even Hesse himself, lying on the sofa at the Widow Merckel's dining room, assisted by the doctor and Albert Ackermann, often conjec-
tured in vain what might have been intended.

The moment of weakness came when Urban's backers, whom he
hated, Senators Borstel, Susemihl, and Kuehn, decided to "make a
great play" with Heinz's crime, fanning world-wide sympathy for the
innocent victims and world-wide indignation against the President's
clique of robbers, murderers, and arsonists. Urban did not hate his rich
patrons for their wealth; he had loved the still richer Lienhardt, forgiven him everything, and called him his "father." He hated them for
their ulterior motives; Urban was convinced they followed him not

because he was the deliverer, but because he was the Yellow, the founder of the economically peaceable workers' associations that Adam Faust derided for choosing a lawyer who was hand in glove with their opponents.

Urban told himself, and in fact believed, that his backers were Yellows out of sordid greed, while he was one through idealism: he wanted to bring peace to the world, while they only wanted to pay lower wages. He told himself that he rejected Adam's commonwealth of brotherhoods as a matter of philosophical insight, while the employers did so because a brotherhood can go on strike. He was not thinking of money, but of peace, and of the fact that Adam Faust's ideal world was as different from his own as fire from water. Who was to hold together the thousands of autonomous brotherhoods? The common roof that had once sheltered them all had now collapsed, and Adam's celebrated "sense of justice" was a cobweb roof compared to the old God who dispensed punishment in the thunder and lightning. Yes, it was fear of "Him" in this life and the "hereafter" that had held them together. But the universal fear of what may come after was gone: nothing at all would come after the body dead in the ditch. Accordingly, anything was permissible to the strong man (for nothing came after him): therefore "brotherhood" is a survival from the days of priestly de- ception.

Thus Urban. What he would not see was this: in those days the employer was not by any means a Yellow from sheer sordid greed. Kuehn, Borstel, and Susemihl did not grudge their workmen a comfortable life: but they wanted the workmen to be *their* workmen, and to accept what they received as a kindness, not as something earned for which they owed no gratitude; and brotherhoods were to be forbidden not because they ran counter to Urban's vision of the world, but because they were cells of secession, of criticism and rebellion.

Looked at in this way, Urban could not boast that he was different from the hated employers: even they by that time regarded their forebears' striving for money, jewels, and fine houses and food as antiquated and ridiculous. They wanted not to exploit but to subjugate the workmen and the people. They were modern by then, at least in this country. The old conquerors subjugated a people in order to enrich themselves; the new ones take a people's wealth in order to subjugate it: whether their own treasuries fill up or remain empty in the process is to them a matter of indifference. Urban attained his great power because he was intrepid enough to recognize that money no longer rules the world: "The love of the subjugated," he said, "is my treasury." Or: "He from whom I have taken away everything, money and conscience, is bound to love me, for I have relieved him of his burden." Or, in later years, to his secretary Weisse: "Man wants not to give but to receive. He who is allowed to hold up his hands in expectation of a gift, like a child, knows paradise. Take everything from them, and then they will be recipients."

After the passage of many years we can see more clearly the similarity between the wish dreams of the rich people and of their Dr. Urban: neither party wanted wealth of their own, but a world given peace through subjugation. They were pacifist Yellows, going out to do battle with their original and archenemy, the militant Christian.

Borstel, Kuehn, and Susemihl, as they themselves admitted, had "contrived matters splendidly." Even the Iron Phalanx of Intelligence had been let into the secret, and won over after initial resistance. True, it was anything but easy for the literary gentlemen, and a whole week was spent whispering and negotiating in the offices and conference chambers on the fashionable bank of the canal. What? They, the representatives of liberty and culture, were to support the man who had called them a swarm of rats, swindlers, unrecognized parlor lions, actresses, and suppressors of talent? This was really going a little too far —indeed, a little further than humanity demanded! None other than this very Urban, whose interview had shown the whole world that he had a screw loose? "We think he's improper, simply improper," lisped Nicholas Edwin, "and if his low origin and lack of education did not excuse him, why . . . !" Wounded feelings robbed him of speech, and he made a violent gesture of annoyance with his hip. Why, this farm hand who called himself a doctor had not even attended a higher academy!

But at this the president of the Phalanx intervened. His name was Innocent Isabella Rex, and he was a fat, popular, talkative man, a former journeyman mechanic and talented mediator between irreconcilable opposites. Because of his elasticity, the Revolutionary Workers' Party had dispatched him to the heart of "bourgeois culture" to spread disintegration. When *The Conservative* accused him of being a revolutionist, he threatened suit against Herbert Hilgenfeld as a "liar, slanderer, spy, and syphilitic." The old man made no reply. Innocent, giving him one for good measure, justified his own hard-earned and unoffending livelihood as a writer in a biographical novel entitled *The Life of My Grandma, Asleep in Christ and the Catholic Faith.*

Innocent, then, intervened. He did not have a higher academy behind him either, he said, and still—"Of course I didn't mean it that way," Nicholas Edwin apologized—"and still I would like to point out to you learned gentlemen," continued the mechanic, with a pleased smile from Senator Kuehn, who had not gone to a higher academy either, "to point out to you gentlemen that another such opportunity to pull the provincial press out of the President's camp into the camp of culture may not occur again. Provincial housewives read the local news and the magazine section first. Accordingly, our provincial syndicate service must try to regain its lost customers with exciting and touching short stories about the lives and sufferings of the twenty-five victims, with a religious touch of course, which I shall be glad to contribute. For every dead man, family included, I reckon three stories, which makes seventy-five altogether, and since the writing of the stories can be entrusted only to first-rank writers, as otherwise the irresistible emotion of the lady reader cannot be guaranteed a hundred per cent, I consider an average price of sixty thalers per story suitable, and indeed moderate. After all, we are not interested in making money, but in recapturing the provincial press as a step toward the victory of culture."

Kuehn and Susemihl, who had been prepared for some perfectly shameless demand, heaved a sigh of relief. Innocent, observing this, pointed out the "emotional religious inspiration," which he would have to add to each finished story, adapting it to the particular subject, for an extra charge: his novel, he said, had proved that he was an expert at this.

Let him name a lump sum, the alarmed grocer requested.

The president, since he had to divert 33⅓ per cent of his extra income to the Revolutionary Party treasury, had to resort to pencil and paper; he asked for time to think it over, and finally, in a tête-à-tête discussion, by alluding to his shattered health he induced the understanding Susemihl to promise that he should have three hundred thalers for his "religious endeavors," but should give a receipt for only a hundred.

By the time of the final conference the following day, Mark Antony

Perlotta had a finished short story with him, which was approved with unanimous enthusiasm. As the writer had neither had time nor been interested in any of the bodyguards who were shot down from their wheels, he had chosen Countess Ida Bessonoff, who had not returned to her husband's house, for his central figure, and had depicted her adventurous escape "through cold water" from the minions of a capitalism ripe for destruction. Everyone admired his skilled hand: there was no lack of either the emotional touches calculated for the provinces —"Her tears fell on the newspaper, for here it was bringing her a message from her childhood home"—or the realistic and ironic features that showed the author's objectivity and moral pessimism: "Ida discovered that a fire in the fireplace may be replaced by omitting to bathe, and a roast chicken by cheese parings. Poverty is an illusion."

Spring, meanwhile, had come to the farm village of Liebenau across the river, two hours from the capital. Snowdrops, crocuses, daffodils, and tulips were blossoming in the rich peasants' gardens; the blackthorn was blooming in the hedges, the old established pair of storks had arrived on the roof of the schoolhouse beyond the cemetery, and the ancient lindens in the garden of the aristocratically withdrawn Grand Hotel, as if remembering their younger days, were putting out incredibly bright green buds. When some prosperous farmer (for example, the loose-living Kersting or the pompous village mayor, Schmalz), some blue-faced cattle dealer, or an unpretentious summer visitor from the capital, forehandedly tending to his holiday accommodations, came driving along the single, long main street, and turned off the rough middle roadway to the sandy summer road beside it "in order to save his bones," the dust was already beginning to fly in clouds.

As quietly as spring itself, a species of men hitherto unknown to the region, young, black-clad, speaking oddly, had moved into the village on the edge of the hill—the Carpenters.

The first to start it, of course, was Alexander Kersting, who came sailing back one day from a conference with "his banker" (but everyone knew what was behind that). He returned to the village in his shooting cart, which was ridiculous enough in itself, for he had no shoot, nor was he an estate owner (which he was fond of pretending to be), but a peasant, and up to his ears in debt besides. And as for his quite undeserved good fortune in having a wife who had once been

Jacob Willert's mistress some twenty years before . . . well, that could hardly go on forever; and he and none other was the target of the pastor's remarks on Sunday when he said that anyone who stands rounds in the pubs after he has pawned his wife's jewelry, anyone who tries to look like more than he is, will be "overtaken by poverty like a horseman, and by want like an armed man." Such was the village talk about Alexander Kersting: nevertheless, there was some astonishment when the people sitting outside their doors—for it was evening—saw the "black man" on the box of the shooting cart, holding the reins; a pale face and sandy hair falling over the ears could be seen under a queer black hat with much too wide a brim. In the dark days of the Middle Ages people would have thought it was the devil coming to make a seven-year contract with the avid Alexander, upon the expiration of which the dissipated and uproarious man's neck would be wrung, with a smell of sulphur. But starting the very next day the black man worked in a light-colored, faded, patched drill suit, whose military origin was obvious enough, on the farm and in the stables, like a farm hand; he wore his neat black costume only on Sunday, in the morning at church, where the pastor now refrained from any insinuations about the Kersting family, and in the afternoon while strolling through the fields. He did not go to the inn of an evening, but could be seen smoking a pipe around the scattered buildings at the lower end of the village, sometimes even with a girl. Before long, the example set by the proud and deeply involved Kersting was followed by other farmers: they would hire a Carpenter as a farm hand from an employment agent in the capital; and if old lady Wenzel had none on hand, she would promise "delivery within three weeks." They all spoke a strange dialect, and from reading the papers people knew that they had destroyed the village of Bergdorf, and blown up the château at Marienhall. But when asked they denied this; and although they did not say where they came from, or ever receive letters at their village addresses, word soon got around that the pastor and the schoolmaster were sure they did not come from the mountain province.

Now Yellow headquarters, as has already been mentioned, were in Liebenau at the time; Urban had rented the whole Grand Hotel, and since he was by no means stingy, the village had profited by it. Thus it was that the farmers began to feel an entirely new uneasiness when Schmalz, the mayor, who was friendly to Urban, announced in town meeting that the League Leader's adjutant had threatened to move headquarters elsewhere if the Carpenters did not go.

So far, Schmalz said, they had got along together well: Urbanite farmers and hands had sat peaceably at Freddy Ritter's inn side by side with those who thought otherwise. The Blacks were disturbers of the peace. He, the mayor, had told the adjutant that the Carpenters never went to inns; and it was a fact, well known to all the villagers, that "those who thought otherwise" among the farmers had moved over from Freddy Ritter's to Wernicke's inn since the arrival of the Carpenters, and were holding secret conclaves there with Alexander Kersting. It had also come to light that these conclaves disturbed the peace, and so had their true purpose: for if some perfectly innocent person should venture to spit in the vicinity of a Carpenter—and surely it was legitimate to spit, or what was one to do with all the saliva that collected in one's mouth from all the glands, and particularly when smoking a pipe?—suddenly there would be three or four men standing beside the Carpenter, as if they had sprouted out of the ground, threatening the man who had innocently and legitimately spat because he just happened to feel like it. Such a threat to freedom as this had surely never been known: our forefathers had died for freedom, and the grandsons would show themselves worthy of the example.

There was applause in the taproom as Schmalz described "these conditions." Fat Fred Ritter, related to the mayor through his wife, invited all those present at the meeting to be his guests, and filled the empty glasses up without being asked.

"Surely it is enough to make one laugh in our telegraphic age," continued the village mayor, already encouraged by a glass or two, "when —though not in our enlightened and illuminated village of Liebenau, at any rate in Molkenberg, Primm, and all the way down to Neumuehle and Niederwesel—old women and soothsayers maintain that the Carpenters have no home at all, and no families, and that none had ever been seen to die: so they must come from the Hereafter, and be messengers of the Last Judgment! Isn't that enough to make one laugh? For a man who is enlightened because he's learned some education could even tell you the street and number two hours from here by rail where the carrier picks up once a week the letters written by living families to the Carpenters—letters that they read in secret, answer in secret, and send their answers to by their regular carrier, not to the

Hereafter, but to the mundane addresses of their fathers and mothers. Messengers they are, true enough—not from heaven, though, but from a Federal Commissioner's office ruled once upon a time by intelligence and moderation, but now by a well-known madman."

Thus spoke John Schmalz, and the farmers, although they realized that their village dignitary was not "plowing with his own heifer," but had borrowed this intelligent flow of oratory from headquarters in the Grand Hotel, would have been very much inclined to reach an understanding even so. The rumor was already current that, just as rats depart when the cat appears, the Urbanites would fade away wherever the Carpenters grew numerous. The League Leader thought it not yet time to take up the struggle with them, so soon after his defeat in the elections—particularly since the force and fury with which "the well-known madman" would fight back were incalculable because of his very madness. And probably some compromise acceptable even to Dr. Urban in those months of modest simplicity would have been arrived at, if only the farmers who had hired a Carpenter and changed their regular inn had bickered intelligently with the village mayor. But they had not put in an appearance at all; they sat at Wernicke's inn as if they did not care a damn for the town meeting, drank dark beer served by Annie and Clara, and played cards.

This was the state of affairs in Liebenau when the three millionaires arrived at the Grand Hotel for a consultation with Dr. Urban: Borstel, Susemihl, and Kuehn. Then and later, perhaps to his own loss, no scheme or plan of campaign could ever be presented to the League Leader until the discussion, which he never took part in, was finished, and even then he would hear only a broad outline, without detail. "Anyone who talks longer than five minutes is trying to confuse me, or else he doesn't know what he wants," he said, and he had already refused to receive the "three tiresome fools" when the Ordnance Master pointed out to him that the three had only recently agreed to stand good for the purchase of a hundred thousand knapsacks, pairs of boots, and carbines.

The Ordnance Master, who, like Justus Thomas, the adjutant, had switched over from the army, a dry, perpetually coughing man, author of a *Strategy of Attack Against Superior Numbers,* arranged folders and pencils around the circular table in the little conference room on the second floor, which looks out from the gable end of the house.

Thomas and Weisse were talking in an undertone; Urban was standing at the window. "Let the rascals wait!" he said without turning
around, and, looking out at the cemetery that spread before the window as far as the church wall, he decided for the hundredth time to
move his headquarters away from peasants and dead men to the county
town of Mittelburg—decided and discarded the idea again, because he
might be accused of fearing the Carpenters, but actually because the
view of the cemetery, instead of wearying him, always calmed his
nerves.

"Did you know that there are still tribes to this day who know nothing of death?" he asked. "They sniff at the corpse for a moment, leave
it lying, and go on."

"Yes. In the Australian bush," replied the adjutant.

"It'll come to that again, in the cities first—not *exactly* to that, of
course, because it makes a difference whether you know nothing of
death yet, or whether you no longer know it. I see three stages in the
development of mankind: the age of barbarism, in which people know
nothing of death *yet;* the age of Gods and religions, that is, of superstition; then people are acquainted with death. But the third, the coming one, is the age of civilization: then people will no longer know
death, which will come about quite naturally. First, for sanitary reasons, because corpses are poisonous, burial will be prohibited, and
cremation will be required. For a while people will go on collecting
ashes in urns, and then they will stop, because it's nonsense—they
might just as well collect cigar ashes. So the ashes will be scattered
wherever they may chance to go. Meanwhile the cemeteries will decay,
and when the gravestones have been used for paving they will be
turned into parks, or built up. Finally every cellar will have its inciner-
ator, supervised by the municipal board of health, and if your wife
dies, all you do is call up the janitor: he takes her down and chucks her
in. When the world advances to that point—we will leave the folly of
working against the future to the Conservatives—it will be a world of
the living at last, and not of the dead."

"But tiresome, tiresome!" murmured Justus Thomas, pulling at his
cigarette. He could allow himself to say what no one else dared utter.
"To you, Justus, not to mankind—mankind will have no time to be
bored. Pipe all hands! The land of Cockaigne was the dream of the
second period, like cemeteries and the Gods. What are Gods? Dead

men living in memory. *Work* is the ideal of the future, for labor is life. Do you know what the land of Cockaigne is? The realm of shades, the land of the dead."

"The three gentlemen have been waiting for fifteen minutes," reported the Darling, coming in.

"Not long enough!" Urban snapped at him. Willie Gaedicke disappeared.

"Tiresome," repeated the adjutant, well knowing that his contradiction would lend wings to the great man's thoughts.

"To you, I tell you! Not to mankind."

"Then I don't belong to mankind?"

"I hope not! No, Justus, luckily we don't. We have no illusions about this rabble called 'mankind.' We don't establish brotherhoods as Adam Faust and his syndicate do, with Tom, Dick, and Harry, in order to halt the inevitable. The third age, which no longer knows Death, is inevitable: I don't say that I'm sailing before the wind, because I know how to tack also, but I know the wind. The Conservatives know the wind too; but they think it can still be turned back."

"If I don't belong to mankind . . ." Justus Thomas put his finger to his nose.

The League Leader burst out laughing: "But you're going to have your cemetery, stupid, naturally—in our own walled, guarded, and hidden precincts. It's with me, you donkey, not with mankind that you'll have everything and find everything familiar—the cemetery, the chapel, bells, quiet, and that fellow Johann Sebastian Bach's funeral music. While those fools out yonder are whizzing in express trains through dynamited cliffs, faster and faster, no peace anywhere, work is life—*we*'ll be standing on the edge of the plowed field as the sun rises, admiring the glitter of the dewdrops, or, guarded at a thousand yards' distance by our faithful machine gunners, we'll be watching the wild rabbits playing around their burrow. Are you going to pray to me when I'm dead?"

"Definitely!"

"Then we're agreed. Let the three scoundrels come in!"

Borstel, Susemihl, and Kuehn, warned and instructed, but unfamiliar with military reporting, entangled themselves in explanations.

Urban was persistently silent. He had looked for a moment at Borstel, who spoke the preamble, and then folded his arms. His intimates noticed that his eyes grew dim and fixed, either because there was a nervous attack coming, or because he was moving in regions of his own, remote from the subject of the conference. For months he had been tormented by uncertainty as to whether it was better to pretend quiet, to arm, to wait until the reorganized secret service under Peter George should be finished with its preparations—but what did "finished" mean?—or whether, before the enemy grew strong enough, he must strike out at Hesse, the "well-known madman," who, lying on the Widow Merckel's sofa with a wet compress on his chest, was spreading unrest, dismay, and legends throughout the country. In all the provinces, even in the quiet land of Guldenberg, walls and machine-gun turrets were sprouting up, enclosing broad areas of forests and fields, guarding them and cutting them off from the busy world. At the same time these Carpenter fellows began to appear everywhere in their challenging costumes, unquestionably for the purpose of tempting the League Leader and his followers into "spitting" and striking the first blow. But if they struck, then the madman would have the legal pretext he wanted; he could give free rein to his fury, and fill up the fenced forest districts, popularly called "the lunatic villages," with innocent people; surely the notorious phrase in his "Address to the Squadrons" had no other meaning, when he said that the man who "does not commit a misdeed" is a worthy quarry for the policeman. Certainly it was Hesse's strategy to lunge at the secret service before it had shown it was ready. But suppose he, the League Leader, did nothing but wait and stay out of sight, while the other's strength grew visibly before everyone's eyes? Then what? One thing was sure: if you took the offensive, you would have to be very strong indeed. The defeated aggressor accumulates the hatred of all—he has "disturbed the peace," according to the uninformed world.

Suddenly Urban opened his mouth, waited a moment until Borstel, who was speaking, fell silent at a sharp "Sh!" from the Ordnance Master, and said: "The blockheads point the finger of scorn at the man who started it, and excuse the ones who 'just defend themselves.' If a man doesn't even defend himself, they acquit him entirely! Just as if some guilt were involved—the guilt of the aggressor—and some innocence, the innocence of the defender! There is no such thing as guilt—if there were any, of course the loser would be guilty: but that's nonsense."

Smiling absently, he looked for a pencil, nodded his satisfaction when the adjutant said, "Ready!" and went on: "Take this down. There is no guilt in aggression, and no innocence in defense, because the world consists of centers of force. If the tension decreases in one of the simultaneously vibrating fields of force, a vacuum is created, and some neighboring outside force rushes in, irresistibly drawn to the region denuded of force, for nature abhors a vacuum. He who does not defend himself is a vacuum, and nature abhors him. Then what becomes of your innocence?"

"Ready!" said Thomas, who had been writing shorthand.

"I was a high-tension center of force. I allowed a vacuum to be created, and the Carpenters immediately rushed in. Victory is the rushing in of force into a space denuded of force: for nature abhors a vacuum. So I must restore the old tension around me by denying the defeat I have suffered. He who disputes his defeat is sure of victory, because his denial proves that he is gathering force. Yes: he who denies his own defeat is gathering force. Got that, Justus? Thank you. Now will you please tell me what you have to say, gentlemen? I've been listening for half an hour, and I haven't heard anything."

Susemihl patiently repeated the "costly" arrangements made with the Iron Phalanx to arouse world sympathy, and stiffen the world's indignation over the "stinking syndicate" into a hurricane. He had not been speaking for quite three minutes when Urban's intimates noticed that their leader was growing pale, and his hands were trembling. The Darling, standing motionless on guard by the double door to the stair landing, pressed a buzzer. A second door, in the middle of the short wall behind the leader's seat, was opened wide, giving a clear view into his bathroom. It was like the operating room of a clinic. The two bath attendants carried in a white-enameled armchair, to each of whose arms was fastened a basin full of water with chunks of ice floating in it. They motioned to Urban to stand up; he obeyed immediately; they pushed his chair aside, and put him on the enameled steel seat. He rolled up his sleeves, and dipped both hands in the basins.

The Ordnance Master asked the grocer to abbreviate his proposals.

Susemihl said, "Willingly, willingly," and got no further; Urban, looking at the table top before him as if he were ashamed to look at anyone else, had already begun to reply. "I understand," he whispered, almost unintelligibly, for the whispering turned to a hiss. "I'm supposed to beg for pity, and bewail my dead. I'm supposed to hold out my hand like a beggar, and implore sympathy; I'm supposed to bewail my dead like the vanquished, or like a man expecting his own defeat."

"Good God, no!" Kuehn ventured to contradict. But Urban snatched his hands out of the basins, clutched the edge of the table, and spasms distorted his face as he yelled: "Did you scoundrels ever hear of a man who was expecting to win counting his dead? You want me to be the laughingstock of the world because I put people under arms, and then wipe away a tear when they fall?"

"I take the liberty of making some protest against the word 'scoundrels,'" said Alois Borstel firmly, getting up and waiting to see what the effect of his reply would be.

"Quiet! Away with you!" yelled the League Leader. "You want me to be despised by the whole world, don't you, because I stand by and weep when my bodyguard are shot down like partridges! Of course—that's just what you want! I'm supposed to protect you rich scoundrels from the greed of the poor, and when I've restored quiet, then I'm to beg for a discarded pair of trousers!"

Now Kuehn and Susemihl too got up to leave the room.

"Halt! Stay where you are! None of you is leaving! You want to humble me, see my humiliation, and then turn your backs on me? None of that! Who could be lower than the mendicant? And you want me to beg for the cheapest thing there is, for ladies' tears and the humanitarianism of the sensation-mongers?"

Weisse, his secretary, stepped up and put the raging man's hands back in the basins.

"I'm perfectly calm. But surely I have the right to tell the truth in my own house. Yes, it's true: I accepted the shooting down of the twenty-five passively. For a little while, gentlemen, for a very little while—make no mistake! This very day I shall consult with my friends upon vengeance, the manly answer, the answer of the victor: a man replies with vengeance, a woman with tears!"

"But what about the world's outraged feelings?" the furniture manufacturer shyly interposed.

"Shut up when I'm talking!" screamed Urban. The bath attendants, held back by Weisse's eye, came in and stopped on the threshold. The leader, turning to Justus Thomas with a scornful smile, pointed to the millionaires: "Did you hear that? That high-brow flow of words in the editorial leader is what they call 'outraged feelings'! And they profess to be comrades of mine!"

"Why shouldn't we bewail the dead?" asked Alois Borstel, shrugging.

"Don't you read anything? Don't you know anything about human beings?" asked Urban in reply, apparently quite calmly; but his eyes had changed. "To keep my enemies from getting a head start, I have to read the Bible, stupid strong stuff that it is. If anyone in the Bible mourns the dead, he's beaten, or else he's expecting defeat. David mourned Saul and his sons, the ones killed on the hills, not because they were dead, but because they were defeated. But when he was the victor himself, did he ever bewail his dead? Now I ask you, if every one of them had fallen, leaving him alone, but victorious, would he have counted his dead? No: if my faithful ones are falling all around me, but I am carrying off the victory, I shall order the sun to stand still upon Gibeon and the 'moon in the valley of Ajalon'! The prophets bewail the future dead because they foresee their defeat. A learned rabbi, by the way, once told me that the prophets by no means whimpered in querulous, womanly tones: 'Woe, Jerusalem'—the way you want the ladies of the whole world to whimper over my dead half file. No, they hissed scornfully, warningly, with satisfaction because God's vengeance was at hand: *'Ai waih, Jerushalayim.'* That means: 'Watch God shatter you, thank God, and very rightly too!' or, as applied to me: if I mourn my dead, that means I am defeated or expecting defeat. If I beg for the world's pity, that means that I am not a fighter but a mendicant."

"Unfortunately, the short stories are already ordered!" said Susemihl in an undertone to Weisse.

Urban straightened as if being raised on a rope; his jaw worked, his face was white. Before the bath assistants could jump to help him, he bent over to Justus Thomas, managed to shape the words: "He's regretting his thousand thalers!" and fell back into the arms of the masseurs, who, grabbing his armchair, now carried him out in a state of collapse.

The three millionaires, returning to the capital after a few words of sympathy, told one another their suspicion that the great man's health must be affected.

"Yes, you know, his nerves!" Kuehn nodded.

"Open the windows, and a glass of water before going to bed," Susemihl recommended, and Borstel added: "And above all, no excitement! Excitement is the most dangerous of all, because it affects the gall bladder."

It was thus, and accordingly not pursuant to the law of habituation, that the Urbanite papers printed only the one pungent line in small type in the announcement section: "Died like heroes in the fight at Dammerkerk . . ."

MAN'S JOURNEY HOME

XXI

D URING the following year, Adam's fourteenth in office, a dreadful blow befell the Yellows. Bruno Zorn, the inventor, Andrew's favorite son, being elected to the Senate at a by-election, and thrust forward by the President of the Republic, offered a bill to supplant the previously independent municipal police of the cities, which had been under the mayor's control, with the troops of the Federal Commission of Public Safety, or, in other words, the Carpenters. And the Senatorial majority of forty-eight (Conservative, Episcopal, and Reform Parties), still as thick as thieves, passed the bill. Accordingly, the municipal police, who had hitherto been friendly to Urban in many localities, were either received into the Order of Carpenters and made federal policemen after six months' constant observation to see whether they were fitted for it, or else they took up other occupations. It was a heavy blow, very slightly eased by the quite criminal bureaucratic lightheartedness with which Commissioner Lindequist handled the transfer to other occupations of those rejected by the Order of Carpenters. These disappointed men, being obliged to give up their agreeable duty as policemen, were turned over to the municipalities and assigned to the municipal gas and electrical works as office employees and workmen. It was not hard for Peter

George to form from among them a terrible criminal group known as the "Gas-House Boys," who would have plunged the country into ruin except that a premature "trial mobilization" revealed them and Peter's secret service to Hesse's intelligence department. But this came later: for the time being the not particularly courageous town councils had the impression that Urban, who had been gaining influence in all quarters, was dislodged from a position that he had held so far. And such was the case: even the capital, dominated by Liberals, gained nothing by its appeal to the "guarantee of municipal freedom." All around the center of the city rose the fortresses of the Carpenters, with low, white administration buildings, living quarters, and stables enclosing a broad inner courtyard, a copy of the Marienhall police barracks. One was on the fashionable bank of the canal opposite the Federal Chancellery, one on the Outer Boulevard, where Blue Griffin Road comes in, the third in the proletarian East End, at the green opposite the War Memorial by the garden restaurants and amusement parks where Frank, the Caucasian Oak, had once defeated the Lion of Afghanistan.

As Otto von Hesse was well guarded by the stout gentlemen in the tight overcoats, and also by agents who were quite unrecognizable, Urban demanded the death of Bruno Zorn, who had introduced the bill. The three intimates asked time for consideration, asked again, and finally, when the chief disappointed them in their hope that he would forget the matter, presented their arguments against it: in the course of the five years during which the League had pursued a policy of peaceful propaganda and "elastic phraseology," offending no one and satisfying almost everyone, the number of large backers had been multiplied tenfold, the army of the Sports Divisions had doubled, and instead of the old wooden clubs they were now equipped with the most modern carbines and light Maxim machine guns. In three by-elections against Red opponents, they said, the Urbanites had emerged victorious, and by what a margin! Only one more year separated them from a new general election, and their rise to power.

"Correct! But the secret service is rotting in idleness," Urban objected.

"Hesse might say the same of his Carpenters," Justus Thomas replied.

"But that's just what he can't! They have their own criminal police, and a halo has already been put around their stupid heads. Think of *Man's Journey Home*."

Man's Journey Home was a children's book illustrated by Rudolphi, depicting the appearance of the Carpenters "on earth" and life in the lunatic villages. It was a success such as the author, Herbert Hilgenfeld, had never known and never was to know, for, unable now to enjoy the long-desired glory of being a popular writer, he was dozing away his last days at one of Faust's estates by the sea. The book fell in with the popular superstition, already deeply rooted, that the Carpenters were heralds of a tribunal whose influence issued into earthly life from a transcendental sphere. They appeared without parents or children, taciturn, helpful, playing wooden instruments of an evening before the doors of the lunatic villages, where criminals listened to them. When they made their first appearance, descending to "men" from the primeval mountains of the north, chattering magpies and turtledoves showed them the way, and they introduced themselves and their mystery with a song to a tinkling accompaniment:

> *Our messengers have winged their merry way,*
> *And now the guilty wait the verdict just.*
> *A call has brought us here and bade us stay;*
> *Before the lofty Caller we are dust.*

Later they appeared everywhere at once: in the turmoil of the cities, among the farmers, in prisons and beside sickbeds, as messengers of accusation, counselors of the accused, and as judges receiving confessions. Their counsel was always the same: "Give an accounting of yourself!" or: "Have you forgotten?" or: "Summon back the memory, degraded man, of your happy years!"

Finally they built the lunatic villages—first the walls around a field and forest region of some 5000 acres, then houses, mills, monasteries, villages, railroads, guards' cottages, all built from the timber of the felled trees, with the help of murderers who had been condemned to life imprisonment. The walled precincts seemed to be their goal and final abode; outward sanctity and power fell away from them—costume, messengership, counseling; all that they kept on with was their piping and tinkling at sundown, when work was done; nothing else distinguished them from the murderers, conspirators, and burglars who listened, stretched out on the ground, smoking home-carved pipes, to the tinkling music.

The story was a graceful mixture of invention and fact; but nothing that was said about the lunatic villages was invented. True, those visitors who were permitted, members of the government, the Academy, and clergymen, had pledged themselves to silence; even so, a good deal leaked out through an unexpected channel. For criminals guilty of grave offenses and sentenced to more than six years' imprisonment might apply for transfer to one of the lunatic villages, which were officially called "delivery precincts." Anyone who applied was informed of the conditions:

1. He would receive no word from the outside world, neither from family nor from friends. He would hear nothing of what took place beyond the walls. Nor could he send out word himself, not even if he fell ill or was dying. There are no newspapers there; all the books tell of the past. In the delivery precincts time stands still.
2. By day he must ply the trade he had learned, or work in the woods. A moderate stint of work was prescribed; the workmen were not driven to their tasks.
3. Loud talk was forbidden, whispering allowed.

These were the conditions. The first criminal to apply was an abnormal murderer, a sickly wheelwright in glasses, who had killed two children. After him came hundreds of others; but it was precisely the first one of them all who could not stand it: in the penitentiary, he said, he had been allowed to see his wife and mother once every three months; he was too young to bury himself alive.

The village elder in his precinct, a Carpenter, asked him whether the work was too hard.

"No, it's easy," replied the murderer.

"The food?"

"As good as Mother's own," said the man, and still insisted on returning to "the world," which, after all, was the penitentiary.

"You'll be back!" said the Carpenter, passing on the word. As the murderer's abnormal mental condition had saved him from the guillotine, he was given his own way. He was allowed to go back to the

walled building in the capital; but, being questioned about life in the
lunatic village, he made obscure replies: "The trees rustle very loud,
the sound of the fountains can be heard far around, and you jump at
the cries of the birds. Clouds and wind are disturbing. The noises of
work are pleasant—and wholesome."

"Wholesome?" asked the fellow prisoner, tapping his forehead.

"Yes. Like ointment, or men's voices, if you prefer," he said.

"Speak up, man, so that a person can understand you!"

"You did understand me," whispered the murderer.

"Was your village elder a Carpenter?"

"Not any more. He had been one."

His fellow prisoners reported to the warder that the "child lover,"
who had always been half crazy, was now crazy altogether. But the
question addressed to the Academy of Twelve by the President of the
Republic, whether Hesse had "delivered up his prisoners to the Lord,"
was answered in the affirmative.

BOOK ONE

INTIMACIES

XXII

NOW and then Otto von Hesse would inquire after the
health of his fellow provincial, Margaret Witt. For more
than three years now, since finishing her two years' apprenticeship, she had been in the Willert household, where
she was now promoted to the post of confidante to "the Madam."

"When you get to know her better," said Peggy of her mistress to
Otto in the half-darkened rear of the Café Sparangapani, "you'll find
she isn't any different from the Widow Mantels at Geisenheim: she
gets up early and writes his letters."

"Whose letters?" asked the astonished Otto.

"Why, Jacob Willert's—all morning! And do you know what's the
craziest thing of all? You know he had a first love, of course, when he

was young, a milkmaid by the name of Dorothy Thiess, who afterward married Kersting, the farmer, the roué of Liebenau. She writes sometimes, for money, I suppose—isn't ashamed at all; but who reads the letters and writes the answers?"

"Jacob Willert," said Otto, not to spoil the girl's pleasure.

"Missed it that time!" cried the delighted Peggy. "It's she, the Madam, the splendid Elizabeth, that writes the answers to her husband's first love! Did you ever hear the like?"

"And what does she do in the afternoon?"

"Then Rudolphi, the painter, comes, and talks gossip."

"Gossip's nice," replied Otto in the provincial dialect, surveying, as he smoked, the enormous back of a stout gentleman whose overcoat was too tight.

"Yes, I admit it is," nodded Peggy, giving him a lovelorn glance, and thinking to herself: He's still the same Marienhall boy he was—now there's a man you can talk to. And as she compared him with Theodore Lindbrecht, who had forgotten her, although his father was only a poor devil like her own, the girl's soul was filled with bitterness. Either she would marry Major von Hesse, and be Madam Major —or not anyone. Why shouldn't he marry her? Melchior Willert had married "the Beloved" at sixty—she knew all the secrets by now—and Jacob at twenty had wanted to marry a milkmaid, and actually would have if she hadn't run away with handsome Alexander Kersting.

The waiter put the evening paper on the table. Peggy, walking like a kitten around the hot soup of the subject, told about the peculiarities of the family she served.

"How old is the boy—Henry Willert, I mean?" Otto asked.

"Twenty-two, or a little more."

"Has he a mistress?"

"His mother takes care he shan't, so that he won't do like his father and grandfather."

"What do you mean, 'His mother takes care'?" Otto asked.

"Well, things are simply different with rich people—not the way we imagine."

"Before, you said Elizabeth Willert wasn't any different from the Widow Mantels."

"The women, no, but the men," she whispered, for the fat gentleman had turned around. Otto nodded to him; he paid elaborately, went out, and another, who might have been his twin, came in and sat down, paying no heed to anyone, with his back to the two fellow provincials.

"Common everyday people keep their skirts clean," Peggy went on. "I mean, if a man has had a mistress, when he gets married there's an end of it, and every recollection is wiped out. That's true of the Willerts too, but only outside, for the public. Secretly the men do as they please, and their wives are supposed to shut up. Every month Jacob Willert goes to Liebenau to see his first love—what do you say to that?"

"And the boy, Henry?"

"*She* looks after him!" Peggy pointed toward the front door. "Old Kittelsen—can you imagine that? She gets her instructions from my Madam!"

"Amazing," said Otto, thinking of General Kaempf, who had called him a fanatic and the House of Dreams a pleasant place of sojourn for men. "There's simply a different air here, colder than what we're used to, Peggy," he added, and looked at the paper.

He knew more about the Willerts than the girl did. For when Dr. Urban could no longer possibly doubt that the fugitive Darling was a traitor, his domicile "among peasants and dead men" suddenly disgusted him, and he moved his headquarters to the county town of Mittelburg, which was friendly to him; the Carpenters, on the other hand, established their "interrogation depot" in the deep basement chambers of the Grand Hotel Liebenau. And so Hesse had repeatedly visited the friendly village, a resort for the lower middle class of the metropolis; and soon Wernicke, the innkeeper, had revealed to him (highly receptive to gossip as he was) in the reserved back room and "strictly between ourselves, of course," the secret of the great banker, converted to God and religion by his old manservant.

Almost half the farmers were his friends, and in debt to him; Jacob Willert called the carousals (not uncommon even in Melchior's day) that were held in Wernicke's back room "cultivating his clients." One evening, in fact it was after midnight, with only Jacob Willert and Alexander Kersting left, the other topers' wives having dragged them home, the following conversation had taken place in the innkeeper's presence, with Jacob sitting huddled in a heap, drinking strong coffee. Kersting, tall, spare, with little of his youthful good looks evident in his face by now, got up, swaying to and fro against the edge of the table, and said: "I'm a great scoundrel. Admit that I'm a great scoundrel, who leaves his family to starve—admit it to me, Wernicke, or else you're my enemy, and I won't associate with you any more!"

"Obviously you're a great scoundrel," admitted the innkeeper.

"I'm also a rogue and blackmailer, because I extort money from this rich man here, my only friend—everyone else can go to hell! Am I right?"

"I understand that's true," said Wernicke.

"Is that so? Can you prove it?" asked the drunken farmer truculently.

"No, I can't prove it," said Wernicke.

"All right, then *I'll* prove it. A quarter of a century ago, this young man, this rich man, I meant to say, loved Dorothy Thiess. But she loved me, and I married her, my dear wife, the mother of my children George and Elspeth—that's the kind of scoundrel I am!"

He sat down and began to sob.

"But there isn't any rascality about that," the innkeeper soothed him.

"Be a man, Alexander, even if it is hard work," said Jacob suddenly, refreshed by the coffee.

"There isn't any rascality about it," howled Alexander, "when I extort money from the rich man that's my only friend—everyone else can go to hell—if I extort money from him because a hundred years ago my dear wife and mother, who pinches every penny, while I sit here and booze like a scoundrel——"

"You're a great scoundrel, Alexander," said Jacob, holding out his hand to the farmer, "but are we friends?"

"My only friend," sobbed the drunken man.

At this Jacob Willert showed that he too was tipsy: "You're such a great scoundrel," he said, "that you sell your harvest on the stalk."

"Never!"

"You'd sell your wife and children, as God is my witness," yelled Jacob. "But listen to me and swear to me: before you sell your daughter Elspeth, five minutes before you sell your daughter, you great scoundrel, bring her to my house, where she'll be safe! Swear to me!"

"I swear it to you, Jacob!" the farmer was said to have replied, and then to have fallen asleep.

His daughter Elspeth was not living at home at all just then. Sixteen years of age, she was attending the Academy for Girls at the capital, and was a pupil of Dr. John Henry Merckel.

The smile on Hesse's face as he remembered the two drunken men's pact suddenly vanished.

"Something wrong?" asked Peggy, startled.

"Urban, Urban, nothing but Urban," said Otto, shaking his head as he leafed through the newspaper. "A thousand meetings a month, and the halls are so jammed wherever he appears that they have to hold parallel meetings in the street outside."

"What do you mean, parallel?"

"The speaker out in the streets reads off a manuscript the same speech that the League Leader is making in the hall at the same moment. It's a trick of the parallel speakers to introduce every platitude with the phrase: 'It is the Chief's *conviction* that,' and applause breaks out instantly, for minutes on end, as if they didn't want to hear what the Chief was convinced of—implicit agreement in advance! So this is the results of fifteen years of Adam Faust."

"What actually is Urban's conviction?"

"Urban's 'conviction' is adapted to the listeners on each particular occasion. His own people call that 'elastic phraseology.'"

Otto's eye had fallen on an announcement occupying half a page of the paper: "Let's go, Peggy!" he cried, handing her the paper.

She blushed, and said, "I don't mind, Otto, if you'd enjoy it. I'm not going to run after him."

The advertisement announced a speech by Senator Theodore Lindbrecht. Subject: "The Convictions of Dr. Urban." Sponsor: Coalition of Independent and Christian Unions.

As the stout gentlemen and the inconspicuous ones had to be informed and to communicate among themselves, there was such a considerable delay that Otto and Peggy did not get into the enormous assembly hall, where cigar smoke rose to the arc lights, until Lindbrecht was half finished.

They only arrived in time to hear the following words in his flexible, sonorous accents: "Yes, the temptation is great, and yet, my friends, you should resist it! You should no longer attempt, not even once, to convince an Urbanite that his convictions are wrong.

"Oh, I don't blame anyone for his convictions. There is scarcely any nonsense so great that we would not all allow ourselves to be convinced of it, if only our liking for the person who convinces us is sufficient. For it is not arguments that convince us, but emotions, especially love and hatred. Now, it is quite true that we love not only people but causes; otherwise it would be impossible for a perfect stranger, of no interest to us, to convince us. What, then, does it mean to say: 'A perfect stranger convinced me'? It means I agree with the stranger in what he loves and hates—in fact, that I did agree with his love and his hatred before he spoke his first words to me.

"To you, who know me, I can say almost anything, even something wrong, without your having any doubts; in fact, if I were to utter an obvious lie, you would deny to the last gasp that it was a lie, and maintain it was a joke. That is because you, my friends, agree with me in one basic feeling, in a love of freedom, which is love of submission to the old law, or—to put it differently—a hatred for arbitrary human authority. Love of freedom and hatred for arbitrary authority: these are not two different feelings, but two expressions of the same feeling. We are agreed, then, that we will submit to God, but to no one else: and now the understanding between us is so great, the bond connecting us is so strong, that you will believe everything I say. Incidentally and by the way, your acceptance of everything I say is by no means unreasonable—not because I am a wise man or a Senator (the latter I am, the former not yet), but because the argument, on the basis of which you trust me, is a very strong argument. For you reason, and quite rightly: stupid Lindbrecht may be; but stupid enough to tell us a lie and thus to break the bond between himself and us, the bond that makes him respectable and his life secure? No one could be as stupid as that!

"Well, Urban and his fellows are connected by an equally strong tie, and so it cannot be made up of convictions: for the 'tie of common convictions' is not a tie, not even a thread, a cobweb! Accordingly his, like ours, is made up of shared love and shared hatred, a bond strong enough to outlast the living, the shifting suns, the shifting moons, shifting convictions. For it will last as long as shared love and shared hatred, which I have already said are one feeling.

"This feeling that unites the Urbanites is the exact opposite of ours: it is unruly, defying danger and death—a love of submission to arbitrary authority, or, in other words, an unruly hatred of the liberty that submits to no one except God. The Urbanites, who have as much brains as we, know as well as we do what freedom is—voluntary submission to the old law; and what slavery is—voluntary submission to arbitrary authority.

"That is why we—the bishops for a long time now, myself quite recently, and of late even Hildebrand—have been urging you not to engage in any discussion with the Urbanites, except about cookery and gardening, and to avoid even that if possible. For how can I hope to convince anyone of my feelings—for instance, that my sweetheart is beautiful—of a feeling that I have and he has not? And supposing I do convince him that my sweetheart is beautiful, what difference does that make? None at all, for he is simply convinced, but does not love her! As long as the earth has existed no man has ever fought or died for a conviction. Both have been done for love and hatred.

"Who, then, can uproot Urban's hatred of freedom, his love of slavery, that is, of submission to arbitrary authority, from the millions of souls for whom everything that Urban says is true, just as everything that I say is true for you? Who can uproot them? Counterargument? No, my friends: perhaps force of arms, and perhaps time."

This year brought the disappearance of Urban's Darling, the barber and mask-maker, Willie Gaedicke. For the League Leader, failing to win the approval of his three intimates for the "punishment" of Bruno Zorn, the inventor, in a weak moment expatiated upon the desired murder to the Darling. The stupid booby, as he "had always served Hesse's men honestly," asked only a hundred and twenty-five thalers to betray the attack on Bruno Zorn, which had indeed been considered, but not decided on: and he noticed at the last moment, almost too late, that the safeguards with which the inventor was promptly surrounded had caught the eye of Urban's secret service. None but he could have been the traitor: he must flee, then, disguised and masked!

But who can describe the impudence of this barber fellow? Only four months later—everyone was preparing for the election campaign —he returned to the capital under an assumed name, with a pointed beard, Windsor tie, and broad-brimmed slouch hat. In the meantime, at the most fashionable beach resort, he had subjugated a fat brewer, and initiated with him and his young wife, a Hungarian dancer, a marriage for three. His new calling was the liberation of the proletariat from the chains of the capitalist Moloch. At the start of the fall season the three of them, at great expense, remodeled the Gambrinus

Cabaret by the circular green in the East End, and rechristened it the Proletarian Revolutionary Theater. The first presentation was a prologue by Diana Rose, which won thunderous applause.

Later the Perlotta brothers and lawyers Tadd and Pole became partners in the enterprise, rescuing it when the brewer sulkily withdrew after the dancer had proved a disappointment on the legitimate stage.

It was at that time, too, that the poetic Diana, dissatisfied with Mark Antony Perlotta, and yelling at him: "I want something solid!" gained an ascendancy over Simon's house steward, Emil, the Lion of Afghanistan, whom she had known at the Wednesday afternoons. This was too much for Claire Mill, released, rejuvenated, and feeling more beautiful; in an unjust fury she accused the poetess of having "something virginal about her."

Diana slapped the housekeeper's face, whereupon the latter went out to Liebenau, flung herself at Senator Weisse's feet, and ascertained that she would have nothing to fear if she should catch Emil out.

One day she reported to the horrified banker that his house steward was being paid by the Iron Phalanx for espionage. Fat Emil, called to account by Simon, departed of his own free will, having assured Claire Mill that she was a bag of bones and a dirty sow whom it made him melancholy to live with. He moved into the artistic studio of Diana Rose, made cozy by colored pictures, silk lampshades, and broad divans; and he became a merchandise inspector in Roland Perlotta's wholesale and retail ladies' garment establishment, where we shall shortly encounter him. Claire Mill, incidentally, had been telling the truth. The former madhouse attendant was actually an adherent of Marxist doctrines.

From now on events crowd one another in the documents preserved in the archives; and the behavior of Albert Schwann (now promoted to be a captain) and his Carpenters against the agents and "Gas-House Boys" of Dr. Urban can no longer be excused by the interests of the state, by current moral ideas. What took place here, not even always secretly, was no longer the struggle of a federal machine responsible to the Senate against the organs of a party aiming at rebellion: it was a reciprocal throttling of two class, mortal enemies, each outdoing the other in craft and implacability. Sometimes the mortal enemies seemed to agree on something. Both, for example, allowed Willie Gaedicke, the Darling, to go on living—either because he made himself ridiculous, allied with millionairesses and actresses in "fighting for the proletariat," and so speeded the downfall of the Reds, or because both sides still hoped to use him. Nor could it but attract attention that Charles Froehlich, the former legal adviser, leader of the Carolswalders and brother of the horribly murdered Theresa, having moved to the capital because he felt he "must change his life," neither joined the Carpenters nor resumed his old profession; exploiting his tall figure and prophet's beard, he seemed to live by posing (alternately to Gasparra and Rudolphi) and by odd bits of occasional business. For whom he was spying never came out; he left his niece Veronica at home, under the eye of the farmer couple and Tobias Witt, who had sworn never to become a soldier.

One afternoon Roland Perlotta—already a respected name in the ladies' garment industry—had arrived for a business conference with Jacob Willert, bringing along for moral support his celebrated brother, Mark Antony. The latter, deserted by his secretary, Diana Rose, for lack of manhood, was at the zenith of his fame. His libertarian drama *Gisela Goes Her Own Way* had brought him the World Peace Prize. Henry Willert, sitting opposite his father at the spacious desk in the private office on the third floor, regarded the poet without affection. For two years the heir of the Willerts, now twenty-three, had been initiated by his father personally into the rules and secrets of the banking profession, and summoned to all conferences. He resembled his father, was slim, blond, sage and earnest in his demeanor; he spoke the various modern languages fluently, and had spent a year with a friendly firm at Edinburgh, being mothered by Mrs. Beyer's relatives. He admired his father so devotedly that the experienced Jacob, fearing a relapse, side-stepped the dangers of intimacy, and apparently did not notice his son's private life. Quite understandably his mother, the once-splendid Elizabeth (who in spite of the birth of the little girl seven years before had never regained the authority once lost), intervened in the matter. Fearing that the retiring, pedantically honorable and idealistic youth might become infatuated with some poor girl, as his father once had with Dorothy Thiess, she invoked the help of young men friends to direct his natural inclinations toward the harmless, carefully inspected, and trained creatures of Madame Kittelsen. The latter, her beringed hand upon her bosom, had assured the vanquished Elizabeth that she would spare no pains or expense, because her own heart beat—like a mother's, of course—for the young man, who was the very image of his mother. In reality Kittelsen herself, a plump widow at forty, was young Henry's first mistress. Elizabeth Willert made no objection.

As long as Roland Perlotta was putting forward his business explanations, mingled with bits of practical philosophy, Henry sat silent and erect, watching alternately the garment merchant and his father.

Finally Jacob said: "Let's get to the point, Mr. Perlotta. You want to expand your garment business in blouses and coats for ladies, wholesale and retail—to expand it tremendously."

"Exactly! Perfect!" said the plump-cheeked and fashionable Roland obsequiously.

"And for this you need a long-term bank loan," Willert senior went on. "That's the first thing. Secondly, you want to rent for your concern the Château Rouge, the big business premises in Linen Lane. But the owner of the building, Senator Beyer, wants his rent guaranteed for the duration of the contract."

"A mere formality," Roland declared.

"By your leave, it's not a formality. Because if you, for example, Mr. Perlotta, should go bankrupt——"

"God forbid!"

"—after two years, then whoever had agreed to guarantee the rent would have to go on paying the full amount to Beyer for three more years."

"There's a little misapprehension on your part, Senator. Mr. Beyer, who is having difficulty in renting that big, antiquated building, has already made concessions. The guarantee is to run concurrently with the loans I need."

Jacob Willert looked out on Lady Square, said nothing, finally puffed out his breath, and his mind was made up: "Well, Mr. Perlotta, I can't make the deal."

As the garment merchant, whether surprised or dissembling, sat agape, Mark Antony asked in a tone of impertinence that young Henry never afterward forgot: "How so? Isn't it the economic function of the banking system to expand industry?"

As he spoke he looked at his elder brother, who returned: "And that's the special function particularly of an industrial bank!"

Jacob, after looking for a moment at his son—his glance said: "See, that's the way they talk!"—handed to the author an unopened envelope: "You, Mr. Mark Antony Perlotta, wrote on behalf of your brother a letter that I return to you herewith in order to spare you the sleepless nights that you would have if it got out that the fighter for freedom and leader of the oppressed had sent a letter of appeal to the capitalist money-grubber—to me, who am mentioned every day in your papers as 'the old cutthroat' who has 'amassed a hundred million by sharp practices.' Every day I'm astonished all over again——"

"At what, may I ask?" asked the author, offended by Jacob's scornful glance.

"At the profound ignorance of the human heart—at the remoteness from humankind, I might call it, of the radical papers. You won't find *Urban* stupid enough to go right out and advertise old Willert!"

"Advertise?" Mark Antony smiled.

"Certainly, sir. If some poor devil comes back from a meeting or from work, and reads at dinner about the 'old scoundrel that has amassed a hundred million by sharp practices,' what does his wife say?"

"Organize! Fight!" whispered the libertarian writer.

"Preposterous—if you'll forgive me, young man. 'I wish,' says the proletarian wife to her husband, 'that you could amass just a thousand thalers by sharp practices!' And he feels the same. For an old scoundrel that has amassed a hundred million by sharp practices, a proletarian feels——"

"Liking, by any chance?" asked Mark Antony, this time with disdainful superiority.

"No. An admiration bordering on reverence," replied Jacob, "in respect to which I admit that the reverence is less for me personally than for my destiny, my good fortune in life. Because that's what the human heart is like, Mr. Perlotta!"

"But why do you refuse me credit, in spite of the best recommendations and references?" the disappointed businessman finally put in.

They had all got up. Old John Huebner appeared at the door, which led out to the central corridor and the marble staircase.

Jacob shook hands with both Perlottas: "I have nothing against you personally, gentlemen, let me assure you, lest any bitterness remain in your minds. But I dislike to assist a business built up on cheapness and a mass market."

Henry, the boy, put in the first words he had yet spoken: "Why, actually?"

"Because if everything grows cheap, my son, the buyer will grow cheap too. And if the buyer is cheap, do you know who will buy him?"

"The one who can pay for him, which is to say the capitalist," the dramatist replied in Henry's stead.

"No, Mr. Mark Antony," said Jacob with a smile, "not I. I've never bought a man yet. The demagogue buys the cheap buyer. Yes, sir, that's who buys him, and cheapness will end in rivers of blood. Good day, gentlemen." And he was still standing in the middle of the room looking after the departing callers as the door closed and Henry silently began clearing the desk. Jacob Willert had changed. He was beginning to age, beginning to discover the meaning of the Scriptures; and Urban's success worried him.

On Sundays in the Church of the Saviour, the Archbishop, before horrified listeners, invoked God's mercy for the capital, and compared it to Nineveh, "that great city in which lived more than a hundred and twenty thousand persons, who did not know any more than we do which was right and which left, along with many animals."

The afternoon of that same day Jacob was sitting upstairs in his seven-year-old daughter Elizabeth's room, helping her to scrawl the alphabet, when Henry knocked and announced that Hans Simon, the banker, was on the phone: "He's offended that we sent the Perlottas to him."

"But we never did—they made that up," said Jacob, going out on the landing and paying no attention to Elizabeth's screams.

"Simon wants to make the deal on condition that we come in on it. He wants us to guarantee the rent; it'll bring us five per cent."

They went down the bright, curving stairs to the second floor. The old man halted on the wide landing with its milk-glass door panels.

"I'd decline," said Henry. "Those fellows are most unattractive."

Jacob appeared to have heard nothing: "Did you ask if Perlotta would have to sign the integrity provision?"

"Yes. He's got to, and he will," replied Henry.

"In that case I can't say no without offending Simon. Go and tell him so. But our guarantee isn't to run any longer than Simon's loan."

Three months later Perlotta's ladies' wear establishment opened its doors at the Château Rouge, and became one of the sights of the capital. There was even a refreshment room at the rear of the main floor, in a palm garden provided with evergreen plants and cozy nooks for lovers, and roofed with a glass dome. Stretching along the whole end wall, covered with white and nickel, with high red-leather stools before the bar, was an unheard-of novelty, the soda fountain, where an unknown drink "with fizz" was on tap in tall lemonade glasses: a mixture of vanilla ice, raspberry sirup, and soda water, which travelers declared had been imported from America.

Quite possible. For to the citizens of the capital the advertising that Roland Perlotta bombarded them with also seemed American: monstrous full-page advertisements (as if Simon's loan were an unending stream), with red headlines, and the phrase coined by the publicity manager, which spread like wildfire: "Meet me at the soda fountain!"

BOOK ONE

JACOB WILLERT AND HESSE BEFORE THE SENATE

XXIII

FORESEEING, meanwhile, that after the general election an unfriendly parliament would refuse to approve his expenditures for the Federal Police, and also at the risk of diminishing the Conservative Party's election prospects, Adam Faust presented the electricity bill; and his intimates flogged the law through, welding the forty-eight together for the last time, by various dodges such as breaking up the printed draft into a hundred sections, so that everyone was scared off reading it. Seven pages of small print and a legalistic style that was positively ridiculous had been employed to express the simple idea that dating from the enactment of the law the generating of electric power was to be an exclusive prerogative of the state. Opposition came less from interested parties, since no electrical industry of any consequence yet existed, than from quibblers over ideas, who quite rightly pointed out that this electrical monopoly, from whose profits the President could meet some of the federal expenses, would undermine the right of parliament to approve the budget. "In the years that followed," wrote Matthew Brandt, "our commonwealth was like a steamer whose drunken deck hands are breaking one another's heads on the upper deck in the sunlight. But the helmsman is not drunk, the stokers go on working, ignoring the tumult above, and a powerful engine keeps the vessel on her course. Our ship of state, despite the parliamentarians raging on her decks, was held to her course by the electrical monopoly."

The new general election did break the President's old majority in both chambers, but Urban's Yellows, who were returned as the strongest party, could not form a majority except by uniting with those upon whom they had heaped unforgivable insults, the hated Reds and the despised Liberals. Even then the total seats stood at thirty-eight to thirty-seven: Urban's majority, possible under certain circumstances, topped the old presidential coalition by only one vote, as the following table shows:

League for Economic Peace	(Urban)	29
Conservative Party		15
Episcopal Party	(Middle Class)	12
Democratic Reform Party	(Unions)	10
Liberals	(Oscar Koenig and Right Wing of Iron Phalanx)	5
Revolutionaries	(Tadd and Pole, the Perlotta Brothers, Willie Gaedicke, Left Wing of the Iron Phalanx)	4
	Total	75

Adam Faust behaved as if nothing had happened, spent three weeks in the region where the fall maneuvers were taking place, and went thence to Marienhall, where, remembering a certain day and old Anton Koerner (who was still alive), he unveiled a high relief, created by Rudolphi, above the entrance to the newly built Mine Courthouse. It showed the syndicate kneeling before the altar of the Mountain Chapel as they took their oath, and below it was the inscription of Adam's choice:

FOR IF A POWER OR AN ORDER DOES NOT SANCTIFY ITSELF,
HOW SHALL IT HOPE TO SURVIVE?

In place of the late General Messerschmidt, his adjutant's father, he appointed General Kaempf Minister of War; brought Count Bessonoff, who had become reconciled with his wife meanwhile, to the capital as director of the Staff College; and appointed Bishop Kessel, Hesse's successor, provisional governor of the mountain province in spite—or because—of the fact that he was at outs with the Conservatives. On the newspapermen's asking him why he allowed the Urbanites to wear uniforms, which was forbidden even for soldiers off duty, he said: "All the better to count them," an answer that provoked country-wide laughter, for it was only too reminiscent of the wolf's answer to Red Riding Hood: "All the better to eat you with." When the newspapermen asked further what he meant to do with the profits from the electrical monopoly, he replied: "Tear down the old part of the city on Cathedral Hill, because vermin have got lodged there." More laughter, for the impoverished and filthy old town was a stronghold of the Urbanites. Finally the journalists asked whether he would not reshape his government in accordance with the newly elected parliament. "I shall proclaim the day on which our people freed itself from the absolutism of parliament," replied the President, "a national holiday." This time no laughter followed.

In the sixteenth year of our Adam Faust's presidency the Marienhall labor decree was issued, Police Major von Hesse was promoted to be a colonel, the little Church of the Carpenters in the capital was opened in the broad inner courtyard of the police barracks on the canal bank, and Alexandra von Brick, twenty-one years old, was seduced by John Hollberg, the son of her mother's gallant. The dovelike Veronica Froehlich married Tobias Witt, office employee at the Johanna Mine, and Senator Beyer disappeared from public life; Dr. John Henry Merckel, on the other hand, published his commentary on Cervantes' *Don Quixote,* and began to approach the Urbanite position; the lunatic villages, after a "trial mobilization" of Urban's secret service, were filled with captives, many of whom succumbed to the loneliness and the whispering. Urban's "elastic phraseology" had already confused the parliamentarians to such an extent that the League Leader managed to gather the necessary majority for a bill that he introduced, the so-called Urban Liberty Law; he had succeeded in the apparently impossible, forging a coalition of Reds, Yellows, and Liberals. The bill demanded "the liberation of our South Sea Islands from the alien yoke," or, in other words, from our own, and "self-government of the aboriginal inhabitants." It passed! When the President, now almost seventy-seven, refused his signature, thus tabling the law, Urban, at an audience granted to his "inner council," demanded a third of the government posts, urging that the people's will had given him twenty-nine out of seventy-five Senate seats, or more than a third. Since the election his party organ, *The People's National Times,* had carried the democratic motto: *Voluntas populi suprema lex.*

Adam Faust treated Messrs. Weisse, Justus Thomas, and the general with his notorious courtesy.

"If a man knew what he was doing," he said, "there are a good many things he would not do. I will even grant that you gentlemen have not carefully considered what you *want* to do. Your 'Liberty Law' puts the Malays at the mercy of a foreign power geographically closer to them, a power, incidentally, that has been proved—by the cheapness of its export goods—to have attained greater proficiency in the exploitation of man than any European power. Supposing this Asiatic power does not 'at once rush into the space denuded of force'—which is hard to believe, as 'nature abhors a vacuum': but assuming it does not, then, as you can discover by reading Frohwein's pamphlet *Dangers Overseas,* the aboriginal soldiers of fortune will." The old man laughed aloud.

"Secondly, I reject your democratic motto, *Voluntas populi suprema lex.* For there is only *one* supreme law, the Ten Commandments; any earthly law should be only an ordinance to administer one of the Ten Commandments. In this respect I am fairly well satisfied with myself, which is saying a good deal, as I shall soon be facing my God. You want me to be guided by the *people?* No, gentlemen, a captain must be guided by God, and a people forgetful of God must be guided by the captain, so that at least some indirect connection with God is left open. Any other questions?"

"Yes," said Justus Thomas, and quoted the inscription on the pediment of the Staff College: "If there is no God, what sort of captain am I?"

"A bandit captain," replied Adam, "that's perfectly obvious. Either I am God's captain, that is, an earthly steward of the divine will; or if not, who is to give me authority? Public opinion, the soldiers of fortune, the lyricists, the applause of the ladies? Don't take it amiss; remember that I'm only half here, a couple of hours a day: but if you try to set up parliamentary rule, there'll be a big bang. For it is better that the body should die than that a people should fall a prey to the devil."

After his success with the "Liberty Law" Urban's coalition fell apart, and the President governed with varying majorities.

Our Alderman Heidemann, portly and amiable, managing the Municipal Commission of Culture and Education in the capital, was an interesting figure. The splendor of the enlightenment that he had received, condensing in drops on his forehead, appeared to shine back from him; and politically he was on the extreme left wing of the Liberals, where they merged with the Revolutionaries. When the old mayor died, Heidemann was the only one who could be put up against the Conservative candidate, and he was in fact elected by the temporarily effective coalition of Urbanites, Reds, and Liberals at that moment prevailing even in the assembly of city fathers. Out of gratitude he now began to use Urban's "elastic phraseology"—had "always been a socialist" among the socialists, was a "liberal of the old school" among the Liberals, and called Dr. Urban "our Chief." He was equally close to the salons of the Iron Phalanx, smiling, despising, despairing on an even footing with them, and looking down with immense superiority upon "this age of intellectual mammals." *The Monthly Review of Art and Life,* welcoming the newly elected mayor, called him "one of the most amiable representatives of the progressive age." At one of his first receptions appeared Alexandra von Brick, only a few weeks past her majority, introduced by her mother (who was then living in the capital, separated from her husband's bed and board, but not divorced).

It was a splendid ball. James Hollberg, who had "fiddled his way" into the heart of Mrs. von Brick, Alexandra's mother, as she herself confessed, was directing the municipal opera orchestra, shaking his

silver-gray mane, and as slender as a boy; his son John, in the uniform
of an officer from the corvette *Swallow*, "breathing out the fresh salt of
the sea" (as Alexandra said at her first divorce proceedings), looked
into the eyes of the newly budded maiden more deeply than she could
bear. "He breathed on me and poisoned me," she confessed a year
later, still weak from the abdominal operation that Professor Kuttner
had to perform in order to save the poisoned victim. She confessed
it to her father, who, having forgiven her, was sitting by the bed
holding her hand. The result of the ball at Heidemann's was that
Alexandra ran away to marry her seducer. He went on board, came
back, concealed the nature of her sickness from his young wife, and
started out on a long tour of duty. Then Alexandra discovered herself
to Professor Kuttner, the director of the Women's Hospital at the
capital, who brought about the reconciliation with her father. Mr.
von Brick, once his daughter arose from her sickbed "robbed of possible children in the future," energetically prosecuted two lawsuits
simultaneously, and within three months he himself and his daughter
were both divorced. Mrs. von Brick in one case and young Hollberg
in the other were held solely at fault, and Alexandra returned to her
father's house. From now on the old man's indulgence toward his
adjutant knew no bounds. In gratitude for the saving of his "only
child," for the son had gone with his mother, von Brick endowed two
chapels for prayer, and gave the altar paintings to the little Church
of the Carpenters in the courtyard of Police Barracks I. The rumor
was current among officials that Otto von Hesse no longer needed his
superior's signature, but used a rubber stamp to authorize his own
orders, "to save worrying the old man."

Urban put forward his "trial mobilization of the secret service" as
a "spontaneous outburst of popular indignation at the President's contempt for the people." A few rows of streets in a half-dozen medium-
sized towns were destroyed because Urban's agents caused the underground gas mains to explode: from then on Peter George's men were
called the Gas-House Boys. The counterattack launched by Hesse bore
no relation to the property damage, which was soon repaired: even in
the Senate Club, the General Staff, and the Golden Eagle Hotel on
Cathedral Square the President's followers muttered that this was
going too far—the "well-known madman" had turned the Public
Safety Commission into a kennel of mad dogs. As Peter George struck

back, hundreds of Carpenters lost their lives in the course of a year; the Urbanite losses in scattered actions and the unsuccessful assault on the Guldenberg lunatic village were not made public. In reply to the anguished reproach of the Liberal press that "Barbarism had broken out in the midst of the progressive age," Professor Daruhi, editor of *The Conservative* since Hilgenfeld's death, quoted what the Archbishop had said of the "howling and burrowing beasts of the abyss, which could not be convinced, but only chained," as well as Theodore Lindbrecht's peroration: "Who can uproot the Gas-House Boys? Counterargument? No, my friends: perhaps force of arms, and perhaps time."

The pitilessness of the pursuit seemed to justify the common talk that had "spitting in the neighborhood of a Carpenter" being atoned for by a lifetime of whispering. One day the President's intimates, joking, laughing, and slapping each other on the back, decided to embarrass old von Brick, and so they sent him an official document requiring him to defend his adjutant's "mad frenzy" before the Senate. If the Federal Commissioner had not been a doubly humiliated man, made unsure of himself by the infidelity of his wife and the sufferings of his daughter, he would have paid as little attention to the letter as the President did to the Senate, which, the Clique said, was like a circus audience, being amused by talking clowns. Von Brick, having attempted with a frown to dictate a five-minute speech to his pale-faced secretary, sent for Hesse and showed him the letter from the President's chancellery. The colonel, only thirty-three, did not understand the joke either; but anyone who may wonder why he did not understand is touching upon the mystery of the changing generations. For the old people, the Zorns, Fausts, Willerts, Oriola, Hesse the Bishop, and Generals Frohwein, Kaempf, Leugenfeld, all were hatchers of schemes, inventive, broad, humorous, skeptical; they could take things as they came; and each in his own field of activity had spun out the idea of the conservative commonwealth much further than he dared to say. Only on his deathbed did the President admit his belief that churches, priests, and tolling bells were a misunderstanding: the conservative commonwealth—that is, the perpetual league of autonomous brotherhoods—was in itself Christianity, and all else was an eclipse of the true light. To such lengths did the old men go —in their heads: and to their sons they left the field of performance.

Whether for this reason or for no reason at all, in any case, the sons, like Henry Willert, Otto von Hesse, Merckel, Bruno Zorn, and the younger officers, even Bishop Kessel at Geisenheim, were more austere, narrower, more fanatical, and they discovered nothing beyond what the older generation had laid the groundwork for; their humor was drier.

Young Otto, then, ran up the stairs, entered, read the letter while the Wotan-like von Brick, leaning back in his armchair, looked at him, and said: "Very simple! Are you ready?" (This to the secretary.) And to his superior: "If you have any objections, speak up!"

As the old-maid secretary said, "Ready!" he began: "Nineveh was a great city where no one knew which was right and which was left. Our country is Nineveh, and our duty is to teach the blind that right is different from left. Obviously if everything is relative, then Peter George's right to destroy cities is as great as my right to arrest people; and, in fact, our idiotic nation looks upon Urban and me as two struggling but equally rightful adversaries. They simply don't know what is right and what is left, and accordingly we are Nineveh. Of course *right* and *left* mean good and evil, or justice and arbitrary authority, or God and Baal.

"How can I get this nation that thinks itself entitled to harbor Peter George in his thousand disguises and hide him from me, because 'he's human too'—how can I get this nation to distinguish the face of the murderer from that of the just man, and Baal from God? Will you tell me that, my honorable friends?"

"Ready," said the secretary.

Hesse asked: "Do you agree?"

"Go right on," replied von Brick.

"Since you can't tell me, gentlemen, I shall tell you. Because this nation actually cannot distinguish God from Baal, or the just from the unjust, I take the unjust and punish them so long, so thoroughly, and so often that the nation finally points its finger at them, and says: 'Look at the convicts!' If I didn't do this, the nation would point its finger at me, and say: 'That nincompoop pretends to be the police, but the gas mains in the neighborhood are blowing up!'

"I am acting according to the tenets of religion. For the prophet Elijah, having convinced the people by a miracle that God was more powerful than the Baal of the priests, was far from imagining that the people were convinced and could now tell right from left. For that reason—to make his miracle more forceful, and conviction more striking—he brought the four hundred and fifty priests of Baal to the brook Kishon, and slew them. Now at last people were convinced, and from then on, whenever a priest of Baal passed by there was a whisper: 'He will soon be slain.' And so, I hope, our nation will whisper from now on as a Gas-House Boy goes by, 'He will soon be delivered up.' In this inescapable way the nation will learn to distinguish right from left."

"Ready!" said the pale secretary.

"Make a clean copy and send it to the President's chancellery."

The speech pleased old Adam so much that it was actually delivered to the Senate and the crowded galleries. It was listened to in silence, for Hesse himself was speaking, and might possibly be offering provocation so that he could make some arrests.

In reply Weisse, the leader of the strongest party in the Senate, almost drowned out by the applause, said this was no more than he would have expected from a well-known megalomaniac like Mr. von Hesse—both well known and megalomaniac since his address to the squadrons. That, after all, was the excuse of all tyrants, that the people they had overpowered were guilty, and had not been overpowered, but punished: a person being punished must surely have been guilty, or he would not have been punished. The proof of guilt, then, came from the punishment inflicted! Yes, here was the familiar irony of all despots: on top of everything else they exposed their victims to public scorn, pointing to the blood of the murdered, and saying, "Must not the people thus executed have been terrible criminals?" "Our nation, far from the baseness that this favorite of the President imputes to it, does not regard those punished by Hesse as criminals, but on the contrary as martyrs of an autocracy ripe for downfall!"

Then Jacob Willert, the leader of the Conservative Party, arose and showed that he was learning: "If there is no God, then Mr. Weisse is right. If there is no God, then neither is there any difference between the police and a gang of hooligans that break into houses and hold people captive. If there is no God, then neither is there any difference between Mr. Urban and Mr. Hesse, or between the priests of Baal and the prophet Elijah. If there is no God, then the slaying of the priests of Baal at the brook Kishon was four-hundred-and-fifty-fold murder.

If there is no God, then there is no telling right from left, law from arbitrary whim, straight from crooked; for then everything is relative. If there is no God, then Count Bessonoff here beside me is a man who incites young men to study methods of mass murder.

"But if there is a God, my honorable friend Mr. Weisse, then the proof of guilt actually does issue from the punishment imposed, provided that the punisher is a servant of God, an earthly steward of the old law, i.e., a gendarme of the Lord. Hesse's assertion that our nation will despise the convicts, and by this roundabout way, namely through contempt for the convicts, will regain the highroad of esteem for justice, or, to put it differently, for the 'old law'—his assertion, I say, is correct if the man inflicting the punishment is a gendarme of the Lord in the nation's eyes. In that case all is put right: then the four hundred and fifty priests of Baal and the two thousand Gas-House Boys were not murdered, but punished. Up to now—I'm not speaking of tomorrow—up to now Colonel Hesse had proved that he is trying to be a gendarme of the Lord. A part of our nation, including a child murderer whom I personally questioned, believes so. And those who to this day cannot distinguish right from left will perhaps learn in the lunatic villages, as the child murderer did, to their own advantage; for it is not punishment, but rather wholesome discipline, illumination, and conversion that King Solomon speaks of when he says: 'A whip for the horse, a bridle for the ass, and a rod for the fool's back.' "

So saying, the great banker drove to the South Station and took a train via Geisenheim to Marienhall, where the old turner, Anton Koerner, had lived for more than seven years now with his almost fifty-year-old daughter in one of the country cottages surrounded by gardens. Adam Faust, after the establishment of the Mining Community, had appointed him Federal Conciliator of Labor Disputes and Employment Inspector. One winter day—he was still in bed with the gout that had prevented his attending the consecration of the Mine Courthouse—Jacob Willert came in unannounced, and asked the conciliator to look over a proposal from the mine proprietors and recommend it to the Colliers' Court before the Labor Decree should be published.

Hitherto disputes and complaints had been handled in three stages. First they came before the Colliers' Court, which transmitted its decision to a committee of the management, the so-called Proprietors'

Court. If the decision of the latter seemed unacceptable to the workmen, they summoned the conciliator, and at the same time went out
on strike. Jacob Willert wanted all disputes as well as the complaints
of individuals brought before the Proprietors' Court first: if the brotherhoods of miners were dissatisfied with the proprietors' decision, they
were to make proposals themselves, not to the proprietors, but to the
Federal Conciliator. In case the latter's decision displeased either the
miners or the proprietors, according to Jacob's proposal the dissatisfied
party could appeal to the Joint Court of the Mining Community, in
which the proprietors and miners had equal representation; the provincial governor presided.

This procedure, looked at from outside, prolonged the period of
peaceful negotiation, and considerably delayed the strike, which was
still recognized as the final and extreme method of settlement—delayed it and "pushed it into the background," observed Koerner, "for
presumably neither of the parties to the dispute would defy the decision of the Joint Court."

"If the two parties care more about quarreling than about peace,
more about victory than about justice, there's no brotherhood and no
league, and they might as well strike at once," replied Jacob. "With
this proposal we want to put our league to the test, to see whether
it is a league or just talk, and primarily we want to test the proprietors:
if they care about justice, then one court, the lowest, will be sufficient
to settle a dispute."

While Anton Koerner was still negotiating with the miners, Jacob
was recalled to the capital. The Perlotta scandals had broken out, in-
volving both brothers.

BOOK ONE

HEAT LIGHTNING

XXIV

FOR it was an act of plagiarism that threw the capital into turmoil: Mark Antony Perlotta, whose glory went beyond the continent, was asserted to be the thief; and he had not even had time to defend himself before Hans Simon, the great banker and financial administrator of our oldest families, and thus a conservative "by nature," threatened the writer's brother, Roland Perlotta, the owner of our largest ladies' wear shop, with destruction.

Mark Antony's transgression, hardly believed by anyone at the time, and furiously denied, is now perfectly patent. When Herbert Hilgenfeld died and his title of Clerk to the Government lapsed, young Albert Ackermann thereby lost his position as secretary and the fifty thalers a month that, as the Widow Merckel had prophesied, "had not pulled out" the high-spirited Elsie Ackermann—out of her debts, that is. In desperation, if we are to believe her, and provided with a power of attorney, she went behind Albert Ackermann's back and sold his play manuscript, *In the Middle of the Night,* to Mrs. Habermann, the professor's wife, the manager of the play department of the omnipotent Koenig Publications, for the ridiculous sum of eight hundred thalers. The manuscript was turned over by Mrs. Habermann to her party friend and associate, Mark Antony, who changed the names of the characters, watered down the dialogue, rewrote the third act, and submitted the whole thing to the Municipal Theater management under the title, *Secretary Kreisler.* Its success was so great that two critics who did not yet belong to the Iron Phalanx doubted Mark Antony's authorship. They were haled into court and sentenced to ruinous fines. On the day after the twentieth performance Elsie Ackermann, red-eyed, went to see Mrs. Habermann, and confessed, biting her pocket handkerchief, that Albert Ackermann would kill her if she did not "find" the "mislaid" original manuscript of *In the Middle of the Night* by tomorrow. It was handed back to her by a stenographer, while Mrs. Habermann regretted with a shrug having paid eight hundred thalers "for anything like that." Odo Sparangapani, the lawyer, brother of the once-splendid Elizabeth, being asked his opinion, declared after long study that no proof of Ackermann's original authorship could probably be offered, since the text of *Secretary Kreisler* agreed with Ackermann's original only in one unimportant point, and unfortunately the books of Koenig Publications showed that Mark Antony's comedy had been submitted two months before *In the Middle of the Night*. Elsie Ackermann accused the attorney to his face of being hand in glove with the Iron Phalanx, put on her lowest-necked afternoon dress, intending with its help to fascinate Dr. Nessel, Simon's librarian, and thus won a promise that the matter should be brought under discussion that very evening at Baruch Eisenberg's soirée. She would do well, he said, to send her husband, but not to appear herself: the sale of Ackermann's manuscript to Mrs. Habermann behind the author's back had created an unfavorable impression.

"But little Frieda had a toothache, and my Albert is the kind of genius who never has an inspiration if he has to smoke five-penny cigars. What else could I do if I was not going to steal?" cried the high-spirited Elsie.

The librarian showed her out with consolatory murmurs, and reported the occurrence to Hans Simon, who allowed his liking for Ackermann's stories about girls and a few scenes of an unfinished play that Nessel had read aloud to tempt him into a disastrous step.

In spite of a careful upbringing he was a moody and easily angered person, touchy and no man to accept affronts. When he came into the big back office, the pens ceased to scratch. "Miss Werner," he ordered, clasping his hands behind his back, and looking at the floor. The automatic smile of the dainty secretary disappeared as she heard the chief murmuring unintelligible words of vituperation.

"Take this down.

"Mark Antony Perlotta, writer and swindler, has plundered Albert Ackermann's comedy *In the Middle of the Night,* which Oscar Koenig's publishing house had bought for publication, in order to construct from it his piece of sentimental trash, *Secretary Kreisler.* So far the latter has earned 75,000 thalers, while Koenig Publications paid eight hundred thalers for the actual original, and has now, after the success of the theft, not only refused further payments to Ackermann, but has even declined to publish Ackermann's play, because it was 'outdated'—put 'outdated' in quotation marks."

"Right," said Miss Werner.

"All right. New paragraph: Thanks to a toleration on the part of the government that passes understanding, the fighters for freedom and culture united in the Iron Phalanx have brought their suppression of freedom to a point where no public print will accept even as a paid advertisement my forthcoming announcement of an impudent literary theft. In consequence I am publishing this notice myself in broadside form.

"Hans Simon."

"Hans Simon," repeated the secretary.

"Two thousand copies. Get it to Frank the Printer today. Let me see it again in five days."

"In five days," repeated Miss Werner, and was dismissed.

That evening at Baruch Eisenberg the antique dealer's, despite Nessel's promise to Elsie, authorship was not discussed at all; instead a violation of commercial ethics that Senator Lindbrecht accused Roland Perlotta of came under discussion. For the owner of the ladies' wear shop it was a question of whether to be or not to be: if the angry Simon invoked the integrity provision, the clothing firm, built on too small a capital foundation, would collapse.

BOOK TWO

THE BOG

Dullness and malice lechered there
Like dogs in the public street.

HEINRICH HEINE, 1844

DOLORES McCARTHY, THE BALLET OF THE LIFELESS BRIDES, AND THE KNIFE UP THE SLEEVE

I

TODAY, when anyone in danger of confusing right and left, black and white, good and evil, would instantly be interned as spiritually unbalanced—today we are amazed at the confusion prevailing in our Carpenters' Land but a few years since. For although no one, not even the Iron Phalanx, had any doubt that the Perlotta brothers, Mark Antony and Roland, were guilty, nevertheless it was not the guilty but their accusers who were the defendants, four previously irreproachable men—Hans Simon, the banker, for calumniation of and libel upon Mark Antony, the libertarian playwright; Albert Ackermann, writer and teacher, for slander of Roland Perlotta, the merchant, in his pamphlet *Man's Honor;* the former party leader and presidential candidate, Bart Plambeck, for a libelous article in the *Sunday Evening Post;* and lastly the proprietor and printer of the weekly paper just mentioned, Frank Jaeger, the Caucasian Oak. And even the latter's chivalrous opponent in the wrestling ring in the proletarian East End, Emil, the former house steward, the Lion of Afghanistan, being employed at the time of the suit as a merchandise inspector in Roland Perlotta's gigantic store, was involved in the trial: he pretended "morbid weakness of memory" and escaped unharmed.

All four accusers of the guilty Perlottas were themselves convicted, and this not through fraud or intrigue, but by due process of law; Ackermann, furthermore, was dishonorably discharged from the school system because of "proved association with a prostitute."

A seamstress, thin enough to have blown away at a breath, set the stone rolling.

Was it not Bishop Oriola, the leader of the Catholics in the moun-

tain province, who once said that man could endure bad food and
unwholesome quarters for a lifetime, but suffering for not more than
a few hours, and only by way of exception, so to speak? If this is true
—and Oriola, an honorable man, surely meant what he said—then the
seamstress family of McCarthys did not deserve such pity as they
received from the salons and the moralists later, when poverty and
dirt had already given way to better times. True, at the time we speak
of, in the sixteenth year of President Adam, the six McCarthys—
father, mother, three daughters, and the father's crippled father—
were living in one room and kitchen in the Old Town, under heaps
of silk and cotton stuffs, bows, buttons, scissors, and thread, bitten
at night by bedbugs, while even by day mice and cockroaches nibbled
the bread crusts and margarine; the doctor from the Welfare Department insisted that the dust from the material was not good for the
three anemic girls, aged fifteen, sixteen, and eighteen, and that the
lack of sunlight in their basement dwelling was positively harmful;
unfortunately, the family's earnings were insufficient to provide as much
milk as was needed for the affected lungs of the three girls—to say
nothing of the parents and grandfather.

One day things got to the point where the grandfather egged on
his favorite, Dolores, a greensick girl as thin as a rail, saying, "Things
have got to be differentest," or, in other words, rather more than
different. No matter what the consequences were—"You only die
once"—she should take the last place in line when the seamstresses
delivered their goods in the basement of the Château Rouge, and tell
Mr. Emil, the merchandise inspector, and James Unger, the cashier,
who handed out the pay envelopes, that "things have got to be differentest," and that he must make no deductions from the pay any
more, because after all there was a God in heaven who could not go
on watching such things happen.

The father, Joseph McCarthy, an unemployed carpet weaver, wax-
ing a thread, replied that heaven had been watching such things go
on for three thousand years; the tears of poor mothers had always
been woven into the carpets of the rich: "Why, they trample them
underfoot: a poor man simply has to organize."

Dolores said nothing. Her father knew as well as she did that Mr.
Roland Perlotta told his employees he had already built a theater
for the revolutionary proletariat, and was himself so far to the left that

anyone who organized or struck against him could only be doing it "from the right," with reactionary intent. The unions, Hildebrand's and Lindbrecht's alike, by their support of the President had "opened the eyes of the workingmen, and unmasked themselves as traitors to the proletariat."

When the poverty of a poor family has gone so far that they no longer see the dirt around them, and the men give up, the vigor and inventiveness of the female intellect come into their own. This was true of the McCarthys, and Dolores was the one who found the way out.

For that year, as epidemics do come and go, a wave of necrophily swept over our capital, a craving of the roués for emaciated, bony, pale, corpselike women. Madame Kittelsen, who regarded it as her duty to accommodate the above-mentioned craving, went on evening tours of inspection through the poor quarters, inconspicuously scraping acquaintance with ladies who excelled in hollow eyes and legs without calves. She soon assembled a small troupe, and got her friend Willie Gaedicke, the mask-maker, to write and rehearse a musical play: *The Tower Warder, or, The Ballet of the Maidens Carried off in the Bridal Prime of Life.*

It was a sensation, and Dolores McCarthy did not come home on Wednesdays and Saturdays until the morning after, "from a girl friend's house," she said, but with money! From now on they were able to have spare ribs on Sunday, and butter and sausage twice a week; the pale girl rightly suspected that her father's and grandfather's sudden refractoriness was due not to their misery but to their returning bodily strength.

The musical play was really most exciting. The dance floor in the middle of the great hall downstairs—older citizens still remember that it could be lowered, and that in the ballet of *The Water Nymph* a pond sparkled in place of the dance floor—the dance floor, I say, had been turned into a cemetery, whose white crosses—for the scene was at night—were lit by the ghostly glow of the moon. The orchestra played Chopin's *Nocturne*. At the edge of the cemetery, built of wood and cardboard, rose the tower, on whose platform stood the necrophile warder, his cheeks heavily rouged, with a long mustache, and resembling our Emil, the Lion of Afghanistan, who willingly accepted this agreeable way of making some extra money. He had felt un-

certain, unsafe, and off his balance since the time recently when he
had put Diana Rose out of her own house into the street at night
because she was "impudent": but, a devotee of poetry and romance
down to his old age, he played his part splendidly, stroked his mustache, and, anticipating adventure, rolled his eyes, peering down
restlessly at the graves, impatiently licking his lips and the corners of
his mouth, dancing about, and rubbing his hands. While he was
preparing, Madame Kittelsen herself behind a pierced curtain declaimed Goethe's verses:

> *The warder looked down in the deep of the night*
> *On the myriad graves as they lay.*
> *Every blade of grass shone in the moon's clear light,*
> *And the graveyard was brighter than day.*

At this moment the tense excitement of the audience was increased
by twelve deep strokes on a gong; out of the graves, raising the covers,
came twelve corpses, nine women, three men, which later one realized
were women in men's clothes. The resemblance of the painted faces
to corpses was incomparable; thin cheesecloth veils floated about the
slowly revolving figures, and Mrs. Kittelsen went on with the poesy:

> *A tombstone stirred here and another moved there;*
> *Up they came, men and women, so cold and so fair*
> *In floating and billowing garments.*

There was brisk applause; Madame Kittelsen bowed and retired
to her box as the curtain was drawn back. The orchestra played a
merry march, and the corpses, clasping each other's hands so that
rings and bracelets flashed, avidly circled the tower and its warder,
accusing Death in sprightly rhythms of having cheated them of "life's
meaning":

> *Scarce had love our bosoms kindled*
> *Ere he struck: our numbers dwindled.*
> *He snatched us from our darling and the light,*
> *Poor maidens in the long cold night!*

Whereupon the warder, one hand on his heart, sang the response:

Ah, how I famish for these dainty dead!
Sweet ones, shall our hearts be wed?
See what a man of might you've caught:
Without love life's meaning is but naught.

The arm movement with which Emil boasted of his might won applause and laughter. The music grew wilder, and the brides sang:

Those that stand and pant about your tower
Would see and feel some token of your power.
For but a single hour 'tis our right,
Poor maidens in the long cold night.

Then, with a terrifying leap, the gigantic Emil jumped down from the tower among the dancers, who scattered, shrieking; the light went out, and the music depicted the triumph of the corpses thus made happy.

Whether from pride, consequent upon her extra earnings, or for love of her strait-laced grandfather, from whom her expeditions had to be kept secret, Dolores actually did take the last place in line on delivery day, in order to protest against the customary deduction of twenty per cent from her pay.

The "blouse and coat basement" of the Château Rouge was two hundred yards long, almost as wide, and as high as an ordinary living room. From apparently endless rows of metal rods hung coats enough to fill half the basement; the other half was reserved for blouses and suit skirts. The windows looked out on the court, and the room was lit by glaring arc lights when the seamstresses arrived for the inspection and delivery of their finished products.

It was the usual show. The seamstresses tossed the blouses they had brought with them on the counter, and two apprentices held them up to the inspector, who, casually exclaiming, "Filthy work! Filthy work!" opened a seam or pulled off a button that he said had been "sewed on slapdash." Thereupon he would murmur, "Twenty per cent, or take it back?" And the girls, instead of taking their things back and being entered on the black list of recalcitrants, mutely accepted the twenty per cent deduction from their pay. The shriveled cashier, James Unger, at his little table near the front door, took a receipt from the girls and handed them their pay envelopes.

Today the head of the house, Roland Perlotta himself, had put in an appearance; he stood near his inspector, Emil, watching the delivery and chewing on a cigar, so that an almost solemn silence prevailed; and it was only when Dolores McCarthy's turn came and Perlotta was starting to leave (for she was the last) that the general harmony was disturbed.

"Filthy work! Filthy work!" muttered the Lion of Afghanistan mechanically.

"It is not filthy work!" cried the pale girl, fortified by extra earnings and sandwiches. "My sisters and I did a good job, and so did Mother, and Father waxed the thread."

"She wants to make a speech," said Emil to Perlotta, who turned and looked at the girl in amazement. "Want to take it home, then? Go right ahead!" the inspector went on, motioning to the apprentices to throw the blouses, which had already been hung up, back on the counter, "Please do! Everyone is perfectly free around here!"

"Absolute freedom of choice. No compulsion possible," agreed the elegant Roland.

There were red spots on Dolores' cheeks: "But how are we supposed to make new ones and repair the old ones at the same time? We work half the night as it is!"

"Please sign the receipt, Miss!" the little cashier urged.

She looked at the pay envelope: "Six sixty? All right, then give me six sixty!"

"You are being paid six sixty less twenty per cent for unsatisfactory work," said James Unger in a didactic tone.

Perlotta threw his cigar butt into a box marked FOR THE ORPHANAGE.

"But the work isn't unsatisfactory," cried Dolores, pointing to Emil. "*He* has a little knife in his hand to open seams and cut off buttons."

"Where?" asked Emil, causing the little knife to vanish.

"In his sleeve! In his sleeve!" cried the seamstress, with a glance at the chief to ask justice.

"Listen here, young lady," said Perlotta very quietly, "you're the last of thirty-five seamstresses that made a delivery today. Why didn't the others complain?"

"Because if they get put on the black list and don't get any more work, they'll starve."

This, however, was too much for our friend Emil: "No, you silly fool," he yelled at the girl, "it's because your fellow workers have studied economic conditions, and are well informed on those matters."

"This is what comes of reading novels," said the chief, without raising his voice. "If you'd ever poked your nose into socialism, you'd know why I make deductions. Did you never hear of the difference between fixed and variable production costs?"

And as Dolores shook her head helplessly, Emil added in accents of deep sorrow:

> *The enemy that earns our bitterest hate*
> *That chokes and hems us in with darkness dense*
> *Is popular stupidity, a grievous weight:*
> *Only the sword of knowledge can drive it hence.*

The chief, like a teacher who had not yet given up hope, presented a strong argument: "Only by reduction of the variable production costs—that is to say, the wages—can the goods be cheapened. Do you understand that?"

"That is the teaching of the venerable masters of the science!" yelled Emil. "Culture for all! High standards on a broad basis! Silk blouses for all!"

"Would you hold up the triumphal chariot of progress, young lady? Put a spoke in the wheel of history?" asked Roland, elevated now by the force of a certain enthusiasm.

"I should think it would roll right over you, the way you're built," opined Emil, studying her pitiful figure.

Dolores, helplessly confused, conceded everything: "I realize that perfectly. And I'm willing to sign. Only about the knife—that much you must admit, Mr. Perlotta, it isn't right."

"Oh, all right, Emil," said the good-natured head of the house as Dolores signed the receipt and took her pay envelope, "next time take a pair of scissors!"

Five days later at the House of Dreams the catastrophe occurred. Inadvertently and by chance Dolores McCarthy was sent to the top-floor room of Roland Perlotta, who had "devoted himself to the champagne" (*Intelligencer*) even during the Ballet of the Lifeless Brides. He flung his goblet in her face, and cried out that she was infecting his blouses and coats with the pox. Never let him see her face again! Tomorrow morning he would fetch the unfinished goods, and have them disinfected! Dolores and her family were to regard themselves as fired.

These were the reproaches of an amateur, for there was no house of a similar character where the patron could feel so safe from infection as at Madame Kittelsen's. Infections did not occur at all, owing to the supervision of the Sanitary Police and the keen eye of the proprietress. And in fact she appeared at once, led the indignant drunk downstairs to the vestibule giving on the street, which was furnished with a bar and a tobacco stand, and propelled her patron toward the front door. Dolores, afraid of losing even her extra income, slunk after, and leaned on the cigarette girl's shoulder to keep from collapsing.

"Beastly damn business, I tell you!" gritted the elegant Roland, totteringly threatening the seamstress with his cane. He had lost his top hat on the stairs.

With this old lady Kittelsen barked at him: "Loud talk is quite out of the question here—I am a house for the best society, sir, and anyone who can't stand a glass of champagne simply shows how he was brought up."

"Everything's going to be fetched tomorrow! Not another piece—abscess! Germ carrier!" stammered the merchant of ladies' ready-mades.

"You, sir," said old lady Kittelsen, in a low, menacing voice, "if you make any further allusions to infection or contagious diseases, we shall be seeing each other in court on a charge of damaging my business. Now out with you! If you want your couple of bob back, you're very welcome!"

And, without giving him back his money, she pushed the reeling man out of the door. A few "dainty dead," attracted by the row, had crept out of the parlors, and the favorite steady patron of the house, Charles Emil Koehler, the director of our formerly municipal and now federal electrical plant, had followed them; he put a hand under Dolores' chin.

"Did you ever hear such impudence?" old lady Kittelsen asked him, her heart running over. "First he deducts twenty per cent from the girl's pay, so that she has to come to my parlors and make a few thalers extra for the family; then he throws her out of work to starve *because* she's making a few extra thalers that she *has* to make extra, because he deducts twenty per cent off of her!"

But Charles Emil Koehler outdid even Perlotta's drunkenness: "Too complicated, mush too complicated—for thish time day," he blubbered.

"Perfectly simple, because he doesn't want to pay," the woman informed him.

"Want to pay?" said Koehler, frowning. "Out of the question. Charles Emil Koehler paysh f'everything. Waiter, want to pay my sheck!" And as Dolores sidled tenderly close to him, hoping to please Mrs. Kittelsen, he declaimed:

> *Old Koehler looked down in the deep of the night*
> *On the myriad graves as they lay!*

He freed himself from Dolores to offer Mrs. Kittelsen his arm; " 'Scuse me, I'm sure, young lady!" and, bowing to the cigarette girl, the barmaid, and the bellboy, who had come out of the main hall: "My friends, when I die, you'll see what you've lost. Everything but honor. *Mon coeur aux dames, l'honneur pour moi!*" He tossed his head, indicating pride, and vanished, piloted by Madame Kittelsen, behind the black velvet curtain. There was Charles Emil Koehler for you, the electrical director, a good soul at bottom, and quite without any suspicion that the head of our secret service, Captain Albert Schwann, superintendent of the Eastern Police Division, had already started a file marked "Koehler, C. E."

IN THE FRANCISCAN MONASTERY

II

WHEN Roland Perlotta's cashier, accompanied by a porter, appeared the following afternoon at the McCarthys' and took away the unfinished blouses, paying the contract wages without deduction, and showing a letter from the head of the house saying that the firm could entrust no further work to a registered prostitute, nor, since they were living in the same family with one, to the younger sisters or the mother, no one said anything for a while after the messengers of disaster had gone.

Not so much as a sigh was to be heard during these seconds of horror, until the pious grandfather opened his mouth and suddenly said: "This is perfectly simple." The younger sisters turned their heads toward the old man's bed; the mother kept looking into the courtyard as if something were to be seen there, but Dolores rightly guessed that this was only because she did not want to look at anyone, and if there had been any gas in the kitchen, she would have opened the cocks now.

Perhaps Grandfather really might know of something; anyway, Madame Kittelsen's was done for now too—she would write a polite letter to Perlotta: "Thus and so, the girl in question has been dismissed. Looking forward to the pleasure of your esteemed patronage, your obedient servant, Anna Amelia Kittelsen, Widow." Of course if she went and cried to her, it would certainly bring in a thaler, better than nothing at all—she did have pity, and pity is fine, but you can't put it on ice and keep it fresh, or pickle it like herring. What does Grandfather want? She knelt beside the bed.

"Take your misdeed, my daughter," said the old man, "take it, but take all of it as it lives and breathes, and lay it on God!"

Joseph, the father, heard his father's words. He was not without piety; sometimes these old-fashioned wise saws had a background that could bring salvation—who could tell? But what Grandfather was asking now was incapable of practical execution; the sound of the words pleased the carpet weaver, so he said: "Father, that is incapable of practical execution."

At this the old man spoke of Count Savoya, Dolores' father confessor, who had also confirmed her. He was the nephew of the Archbishop, the prior of the Franciscan Monastery, and was known among the common people as Brother Henry.

"But I haven't been to confession for two years," objected Dolores.

"That doesn't make any difference. He knows you. Lay your misdeed on him, but all of it, and if he asks how you expect to make up for it, tell him you and your sisters are looking for work, and if he should happen to have a carpet to be repaired, why . . . They have a great many carpets there."

Dolores snatched her confirmation dress out of the bureau. Mother had put on flounces a year ago. She washed her arms, neck, face, and hands. The army was looking for nuns to be trained as nurses, that she knew. It must be a good life—many of the nuns were fat; the monks were fat too, as you could see in the pictures, so piety must be endurable; a drunken fellow was not a pleasant sight either. . . . She was ready, shined her shoes with tissue paper left behind by Perlotta's men, stuck on her hat, thought, "He can't do worse than throw me out," called, "See you later," and then Grandfather said: "A lot of carpets. The Apostle Paul repaired carpets in Corinth; he didn't want to live by begging either. Tell Brother Henry that!" She was out of the house. She remembered a story where a fallen girl went into a convent, real touching and all in rhyme. How did those verses go when the unfortunate girl fell at the prior's feet? Thank goodness, she remembered them; she rang at the front entrance, ran down the hall, ignoring the doorkeeper's voice, and went across the corridor to the waiting room, where the blackboards hung with the regulations and hours. She knew that door—beyond it was the prior!

"What did you wish?" asked a black cowl.

"To see my father confessor."

"Which one?"

"Brother Henry."

"Oh, the prior? Well, then in the first place, you have to ask for an audience, and in the second place you'll get word from the chancery."

"How long will that take?" asked Dolores, fear rising in her throat.

"It all depends. Say five days?"

"And suppose I want to see my father confessor right away?"

"But the prior is busy, young lady."

"Is that so? I'll just see about that!" she cried, and pounded with the full force of both fists on the panel of the oak door.

Brother Henry, the prior of the House of Savoya, really was busy. He had fetched a pair of brown riding boots out of the depths of the cupboard, which contained clothing and the utensils for Mass, and was telling his uncle, the Archbishop, who was at the desk reading the paper, how to keep the boot leather supple.

"Bâle oil," he said exhibiting a vial. "What's good for living skin can't do any harm to dead skin." Just then the blows resounded from the door, and the Archbishop called, "Come in!"

Dolores ran mincing across the room, and fell to her knees while the surprised prior, the vial of oil in his hand, went over to the desk; she crossed herself and bowed her head as she had been taught to do.

"Unannounced? Get up," the Archbishop directed. "What do you want?"

Dolores stayed on her knees, and rattled off her verse:

> *To a convent, Father, I would go,*
> *A nun I would become!*

The prior, displeased, whispering to his uncle, "She's a poetess!" put the vial on the table, turned to the kneeling girl, and searched her face: "Will you please tell us what you want?"

Dolores, gazing at him:

> *To a convent I would go,*
> *A nun I would become.*

By now Brother Henry recognized her: "Aren't you Dolores Mc-Carthy, the seamstress?" he asked, pushing a wicker chair toward her.

"Yes, Father."

"Well, then get up and for goodness' sake tell us what you want!"

Dolores got up, folded her hands, and said, keeping her eyes upon her father confessor:

> *I would take the holy veil,*
> *Bid adieu to the world's travail,*
> *A nun I would become.*

This play-acting annoyed the Archbishop: "Look here, if you want to make fools of us," he snapped at her, "I'll have you chucked out— it won't take a minute."

Dolores, utterly astounded—both priests noticed that her amazement was genuine: "Funny how no one ever believes you when you tell the truth."

"Your truth is cheap and easy, my daughter," remarked the Archbishop, with scorn in his voice. "After all, then any girl that had lost her job, or that her sweetheart had got with child and then run off, could come and say: 'To a convent I would go, A nun I would become.' Sit down."

"Why shouldn't she come?" asked the seamstress, sitting down.

The Archbishop looked at her a trifle disdainfully: "Because a religious order isn't a tavern that you say good-by to after you've eaten. Within a month you'd be thinking, 'If I had the wings of a bird!' or, 'How I repent my holy vow, 'tis a whore that I'd turn now!'"

"I can't turn whore," whispered Dolores, remembering her grandfather.

"Why not?"

"Because I am one already."

"Weren't you a seamstress?" asked Brother Henry after a pause.

Dolores, with the feeling of one in a dream, plunging from a cliff and surrendering herself to the winds, told the story of how, being compelled by the twenty per cent deduction to go to Mrs. Kittelsen's, she had been caught by her employer and discharged from both places.

"What did Perlotta do to you at Kittelsen's? There are two priests listening to you, and no one else," the prior admonished her.

"He went and yelled at me that I was a whore and defiled his blouses and coats."

"And five days before—what sort of discussion was it you had with him then?"

"He gave me a dressing down for being a devout Christian and going to church every Sunday instead of reading those enlightened books by Marx and Engels, where it proves that the priests invented the Lord God so that they could have a soft life for themselves."

The Archbishop, writing a letter, glanced up at his nephew. "I wouldn't put that beyond Perlotta—either of them, for that matter," said Brother Henry of the House of Savoya. He was thirty-eight years old, schooled in the ways of the world, and was being "held in reserve" by the President's intimates for some high office.

"Were there any other witnesses to your conversation with Perlotta?"

"Emil, the merchandise inspector, and Unger, the cashier."

"Marxists?"

"Yes, Father."

The Archbishop finished the letter, sealed the envelope, and gave it to the girl: "In the refectory they'll give you dinner and a thaler. When you've eaten, you take the tram to the Union Headquarters Building, and ask to see Senator Lindbrecht, with my regards. You give him this letter. He'll look into your case and get work for you."

Dolores kneeled down and kissed the hand the Archbishop held out to her.

BOOK TWO

PEACE OFFERED AND DECLINED

III

THEODORE LINDBRECHT, the Secretary of the "Christians," being reproached in the letter for devoting himself too extensively to philosophy instead of thinking of the sweated home workers—a reference to his recently acquired habit of talking over people's heads—immediately ordered a carriage and, accompanied by his stenographer, called first on the McCarthys, then in the course of the day on eleven other seamstresses' families, and by late afternoon had in hand twelve signed and independent statements to prove that Dolores had told substantially the truth: they all confirmed the trick of Emil, the inspector, with his knife, the acquiescence of the chief, and the twenty per cent deduction from pay.

Dr. Nessel had just dismissed the high-spirited Elsie Ackermann and heard his employer dictate the broadside against Mark Antony when Senator Lindbrecht was announced. They sat down to the ebony table in the hall, where General Kaempf and Hesse had once sat; the librarian, after looking at the reports, said, "We'll have to disturb him after all," and showed the guest into the library.

Simon's private library, the largest in the city, was a room running the whole depth of the house, two stories high, its walls covered with books clear up to the skylight. At the level of the second story a gallery with a bronze rail went all the way around; wheeled ladders mounted on rails glided like toys along the bookcases, and the long, movable arms of electric wall lamps would cast the light either on the walls or on the reading tables, set thirty feet apart.

The banker offered cigars, read only two of the statements (as Lindbrecht told him that all twelve were pretty much the same), excused himself, seemed for a time to be occupied with his pencil— a gold mechanical pencil attached to his long, thin watch chain— and lost himself in reminiscence: "There were three of us children, one sister is dead, the second married abroad; and my father's oft-repeated wisdom whenever I suggested anything to him was, 'Let it be!' or, 'Do you need to do that?' He went to the office every morning at eight, but we children were supposed to have a comfortable life, and I in particular was always narrow-chested. On the other hand, my father also said, 'You can't worry everything all the way through,' which is wrong grammar, but meant that he couldn't guard the future of his children when he was dead. After all, it's no accident that both of these cases have been brought before me on the same day, within two hours' time—Mark Antony's plagiarism and Roland Perlotta's lack of honor. Why? No one would ever come to my father with such things."

Lindbrecht and Nessel, feeling that the naturally kindly banker was crouching to strike a fearful blow—why else this long preliminary? —said nothing.

"I'm simply cut off from the navel cord," Simon went on. "One can't worry everything all the way through to the end." He turned to his secretary: "Send Miss Werner to Frank the Printer, and tell him not to set the broadside until I give him word—not before to-morrow morning, that is. But get Mark Antony to come here at once, and Ackermann also. If he makes an honest man of himself here in my presence—Mark Antony, I mean—and at least recognizes Ackermann as co-author, fifty-fifty, I'll let his brother off with a bloody nose."

Nessel objected that Mark Antony would not allow himself to be confronted by Ackermann—it would be almost too great a humiliation.

"I don't want to confront him; the two aren't even to see each other," replied Simon. "I want Ackermann to demonstrate his art." And, the secretary of the "Christians" opening his mouth in amazement—for what had the misfortune of the seamstresses to do with art?—the banker explained: "Art, you know, is the ability to express a figure or a state of being in a naïve, immediately convincing way. The seamstresses can be taken care of elsewhere, and Perlotta's loans can be called in for violation of commercial ethics: or he can be let go, and I *shall* let him go if Mark Antony makes an honest man of himself. There's only one thing that can't be done: one can't wipe away such monstrous improbity by silence. Now of course I could speak, but I can't depict: I can't depict the figure and the state of being called Roland Perlotta in a naïve and immediately convincing way. That's why I want Ackermann here."

"Quite understandable," observed Theodore Lindbrecht out of politeness.

The banker, however, slipped back into the past: "I know that my father would not have done what I intend doing. Nor would he have dictated the broadside against Mark Antony, because the affair was no concern of his. His only concern was his family: where that stopped, his world stopped too. Was that a proper attitude?"

"Most people, in fact almost all of them, have the same attitude," replied the union leader.

Simon leaned over the table, and his voice was a hissing: "Almost all of them, my dear Lindbrecht, are fortunate enough not to be Jews."

Nessel looked at the clock and took his leave to carry out Simon's orders. When the chief was riding his hobby, it might easily go on far into the night.

Coffee and liqueurs were served, and later beer and cold cuts. Lindbrecht kept his seat.

"In the ghetto that was all right," said the banker. "In the ghetto our world left off where our family left off. But we ourselves are the ones who damned the ghetto, abandoned it, threw ourselves at the outside world, at alien peoples, amongst whom we shall perish, either by intermarriage or by persecution. Is that right?"

The union leader shook his head.

"It is right, Mr. Lindbrecht. The first Jews who abandoned the ghetto were absorbed at once—remember Mendelssohn's children. In the twelfth century the Jews fled from persecution into the ghettos. There they were safe for six hundred years; when they came out, persecutions began at once. Why? Because a Jew who lives in the world cannot live as if he were in the ghetto—as if, that is, the world left off where his family left off. The world of strangers in which I live has got to be my own world: I cannot meddle in the economy and the public affairs of the people among whom I live, I cannot meddle for the covert purpose of gaining some advantage for myself, my family, or my people, I mean the Jewish people. No nation will tolerate that—hence the persecutions."

"Then you're for absorption into the people you live among, for intermarriage?" asked Lindbrecht. By this time rumor had it that Louise Hofer with her reddish hair and her voice had made a conquest of the banker, and was preparing to get a divorce from her perpetually drunken Ricardo in order to marry the "great shark."

"No; for I see a third possibility. The Jews must serve the people among whom they live."

"They're doing that now; only they're going about it wrong," said Lindbrecht, remembering a witty outburst of the Archbishop's. "They behave as queerly as the famous violinist who asked a lady who was raving about his playing, 'But how were my bows?' He didn't think much of his playing, but he wanted to hear praise of his bows! It's

the same with the Jews: they don't want to be told that they are
doing tremendous things in commerce, and have built up a garment
and shoe industry that allows even the poorest to look decent. But
you take certain subsidiary occupations that gentiles can do as well
and better—for example, journalism, art, and science, occupations on
the fringe of life, whereas industry and commerce are its center—
the Jews are constantly boasting about those, like the violinist about
his bows, and thus obscuring their real merits. Am I right?"

"Yes, unfortunately, but I mean something else. The Jews can live
in the world without being absorbed only if they refuse to be outdone
by anyone in one particular point. The point I mean is their sense
of honor.

"You're staring at me, asking what a 'sense of honor' is, whether
it isn't simply a word shell, or, as Merckel says, a 'splendid phrase.'
No, no, my dear sir: I'll tell you what it is—I shall have to say it in
a sentence: a person with a sense of honor has an exaggerated idea
of the sensitivity of another man's soul. Yes, that's it exactly. If the
Jews were to carry this exaggerated and sometimes quite mistaken
idea of the sensitivity of their neighbor's soul with them as constantly
as they carry a wallet in their pockets, they could keep their breed
unmingled."

He speaks as if he weren't one of them any more, thought Lindbrecht.

"A gentile doesn't need very much sense of honor: he makes good
its absence by his own numbers. But for one Jew who has no sense
of honor a hundred thousand are punished. What possible idea has
Mr. Mark Antony Perlotta of the sensitivity of an Ackermann's soul?
What idea has Mr. Roland Perlotta of the sensitivity of a seamstress'
soul?"

"Perlotta will say that she's a prostitute."

"Well, then, of the sensitivity of a prostitute's soul? An exaggerated
idea, like the man with a sense of honor? No, my dear sir; that is
why I shall proceed against both brothers without scruple."

"Mr. Albert Ackermann!" announced Claire Mill, in a white ruffled
apron.

While Hans Simon was serving dinner, Nessel was facing the
rugged-faced, gray-headed Mark Antony, and withholding nothing.
The banker's broadside, which the papers would have to take notice

of willy-nilly, would be posted in all the public squares if Mark Antony did not at once change his mind. As the writer emitted nothing but a contemptuous grunt, the librarian reminded him of the danger threatening his brother Roland, namely that Simon would call in his loans and Jacob Willert would cancel his rent guarantee. "Within a week Roland Perlotta may be left with nothing but the clothes he has on."

"And I, provided I confess to plagiarizing from Albert Ackermann, may save my brother?" asked the playwright.

"You not only may, you definitely will," Nessel returned. "I'm empowered to promise you that. You will save yourself too, because if you come to meet us even a little of the way, the broadside won't be issued. The printing of it has been held up until tomorrow morning."

Mark Antony, playing with the key to the drawer of his desk, smiled such a long and amiable smile that the emissary was alarmed. "If you were to condemn not only my brother but my mother and sisters to starve," he said, "nay, if you were to drive me from the city, to pursue me through country after country like a hunted stag"— he enjoyed the image for a moment—"you still couldn't bring me to disavow my work."

"But you aren't supposed to disavow any of *Secretary Kreisler* that is your work!"

"Even if six Carpenters with iron rods were to smash my jawbone, the way they do in their interrogation depots——"

"I never heard anything of the sort," Nessel interrupted.

"—not a word, not a syllable, not a comma will I confess to borrowing; I shan't surrender five pennyworth of my celebrity as an artist to that nobody, not even on the rack." He pointed to a strong iron hook on the wall, pulled out his desk drawer, and showed his tormentor a carefully soaped rope: "Do you see this sealer of lips? You can't prove anything against me, but if, being hounded, I ever felt like talking, this mouth would be silent forever one minute before it spoke!"

He tossed the rope into the drawer: "So there's no use asking me to confess, Mr. Nessel. Sorry!"

The librarian, reflecting upon the half-hour conversation on his way home in Simon's pair-horse carriage, admitted to himself that

even so wretched and ridiculous a quality as vanity, if only it was
great enough, raised the vain man above mediocrity, and put him
in a condition that was frightening perhaps, but certainly not ridiculous.

The music room of Baruch Eisenberg's antique house in the Scottish
Widows' Lane was lit up that evening, as always, and Haydn's "Toy"
Symphony was being played on instruments made in the eighteenth
century; the guests, however, lacked both interest and gaiety. Hans
Simon avoided his friend Louise Hofer's eye and devoted himself
to listening. The wives of the three captains, Schwann, Lorenz, and
Stark, their necks framed in the wide, white, starched linen collars of
Revival Mission sisters, and by no means out of place in the plainness
of the room with its antiquarian furnishings, looked at the back of
Ricardo Hofer at the piano. Old Eisenberg had fallen asleep, and the
once-splendid Elizabeth, blaming Hans Simon personally for having
summoned her husband back from Marienhall, egged on young
Ackermann "not to do it cheap."

"What's the title of this . . . pamphlet that you're writing against
Roland Perlotta?" she asked.

"Man's Honor," replied Elsie's husband, out alone.

"Gracious, how tiresome!" slipped out of Elizabeth's mouth. She
instantly clapped her hand to her lips, declared that Ackermann
would be sure to make the subject interesting, and said he should
"make him pay through the nose." "If Simon wants to feed sugar
to his monkey, let him pay for it. Of course it's an honor that you
should be the one to write it, Mr. Ackermann—honor is a fine thing,
no doubt of that—but a married man has to think of his family's
living first of all."

As she gave him no peace, he finally satisfied her curiosity: Simon
had offered him a hundred thalers for two hundred and fifty words,
that is, for an ordinary manuscript page. He was intending to write
twenty pages, amounting to two thousand thalers—an enormous sum.

"But then you should write a *hundred* pages," counseled Elizabeth,
"far apart, with a lot of space between lines! Of course if you're the
kind of donkey that is put before a manger and won't eat, naturally
your wife has to sell plays behind your back, the poor, pitiable woman!
Frailty, thy name is man!"

At midnight in the Black Eagle at Geisenheim, where he stayed for the sake of the memories, Jacob Willert received a telegram. He had his baggage sent to the station and left early in the morning.

THE HONEST SEAMAN UNDER EXAMINATION

IV

FOR two months the President's legal authority, Judge Holzkopf, searched the previous lives of the four defendants.

The first testimony was taken from Bart Plambeck, who had written an article, "The Alteration of Dates in Oscar Koenig's Account Books," accusing the great publishing house of falsifying its records for the benefit of Mark Antony Perlotta.

Plambeck, who had run for president against Adam Faust seventeen years before as head of the Revolutionary Workers' Party, was treated respectfully. His examination took place at the Supreme Court of Appeals, in the paneled chambers of the presiding justice; no one except Holzkopf himself and the parliamentary stenographer, Benjamin Werner, was present.

"Very cozy," thought the former dockyard worker as he looked around from the depths of his leather armchair. A broad white tile stove near him, stoked from the corridor outside, radiated warmth, and three incandescent gas lights with green shades gave just enough light to read by for each of the three men that foggy March afternoon. But the little table set up before Plambeck was empty; the defendant had brought no notes with him, and occasionally as he talked he would run his heavy hand caressingly over the polished table top. At four o'clock Mrs. Holzkopf sent in coffee to the gentlemen, "With *petits fours* like what the Willerts have," she said.

The retired revolutionist was a tall, lean, red-headed man of fifty, well dressed, fond of women, fearless, drunken, and a gambler. He had initiated his employer, Frank Jaeger, the Caucasian Oak, into

the "better things." For a bottle of champagne in a night club, said
the Iron Phalanx, for the smile of a hundred-thaler woman and the
handshake of a general he would sell his wife and children; whereupon Plambeck retorted in the *Evening Post* that love of life, a national peculiarity of our nation, should not be discussed by those who
were born on the billiard table of an Odessa café supported by international brokers of opinion.

He had the ready tongue and imagination of the poor, the shamelessness of a woman in her home, and the clear understanding that
annihilates pedantry and is known among us as mother wit. He never
learned to speak and write our language correctly. That very lack
was what made him so perfectly at ease in facing the judge who was
questioning him.

The magazine articles in which he poured bucket after bucket of
revelations upon the heads of the Revolutionists, now that the party
had cast him out, did display his rude imagery and his sense of humor,
but not a single grammatical error, whereas they had the naïve and
solemn sentence structure that the President's chancellery had copied
from the late Hilgenfeld; hence a second author or at least editor
of Plambeck's output had necessarily to be assumed—and one so
highly placed that not even the Iron Phalanx dared mention his
name.

"Will you give the name of the man who wrote your article?"
Holzkopf asked.

"You know him as well as I do," replied the redhead, laughing
aloud. "He wears a teacher's white collar, is secretly engaged, and
likes to play chess with his secret father-in-law."

"Then will you at least tell the name of the employee of Koenig
Publications," Holzkopf probed further, "who told you the story about
altering the dates?"

"If I did that, I'd be a great scoundrel, God knows!" replied Plambeck. "Only a scoundrel speaks of confessions made by a lady in an
hour of weakness."

"Then you would take the punishment upon yourself, imprisonment or a large fine?"

"Of course. A gentleman holds his tongue and pays."

The judge leaned back and looked toward the stenographer's table.
"Got it," said Benjamin Werner.

"If none of you admits the truth," Holzkopf suddenly yelled at the defendant, "a highly respected man is going to jail."

"You mean Simon," replied Bart Plambeck, rather alarmed. "He won't care about that. He lost two hundred thousand thalers by Roland Perlotta's failure. He knew what he was going to lose, and still he didn't stop the failure. Two hundred thousand thalers is more than six months in jail."

"Whom does Frank's Printing Shop belong to?" asked the judge, turning to Plambeck.

"To Frank Jaeger, the printer."

"Don't lie to me!"

"Legally speaking, it belongs to Frank Jaeger; humanly speaking, it belongs to Hans Simon, due to the fact that he bought it out of sympathy when Frank was severely injured wrestling."

"Whom does the *Sunday Evening Post* belong to?"

"Legally speaking, it belongs to Frank Jaeger; humanly speaking, to Dr. Urban, because he founded it—at my suggestion, incidentally."

"At your suggestion?"

"Yes, Your Honor. The Revolutionary Workers' Party was an honest party as long as I was the head of it; they rightly called me 'the honest seaman,' although I never went to sea—my father did that. But when education and intelligence began to creep into the poor people's party, and tried to take over the controlling posts and editorships, I protested, and got chucked out. So I go up to Urban and I say: 'Doctor, I'm going to settle this swarm of Red rats' hash. I know more than what they can stand.' 'What will it cost?' Urban asks me, in that short-tempered way of his. 'Ten thousand thalers.' 'Done!' says the great man, whom even Hilgenfeld recognized. That's the story of the founding of the *Sunday Evening Post*."

"But Hans Simon puts articles in your *Sunday Evening Post,* people say. How does that happen?"

"One hand washes the other, Your Honor," replied the honest seaman, smiling.

"Now tell me the truth, Mr. Plambeck. Why won't you give the name of the woman who told you about the alteration of the dates?"

"Because I have to keep the confidences of a lady, Your Honor. For that matter, Simon can't be convicted anyway, because Mrs. Habermann and Diana Rose would have to deny the change of dates, *under oath.* That they can't do, with so many people knowing about it."

"Unfortunately, very few people know about it, Mr. Plambeck. That's enough for today."

That was the end of the first hearing.

THE CAUCASIAN OAK FIGHTS FOR HIS LIFE

V

EMIL and Frank, the first a former madhouse attendant, the second an unemployed printer, who met in the wrestling ring for pecuniary reasons as the Lion of Afghanistan and the Caucasian Oak, together tipping the scale at more than five hundred pounds—these two have been regarded by the public and the historians as Dioscuri, as twins, because in later years when Dr. Urban became prominent the two heavyweights stood behind him, like monstrous mastiffs, for his personal protection. But they were neither brothers nor alike. Emil was more manly, stronger, and more musical; the shameful and cowardly fashion in which Frank defeated him we have already mentioned; the conversation with Dolores and Roland in the blouse basement shows his revolutionary convictions, nay more, his knowledge of the party literature; his address to the Urbanites two years later shows his bravery; he never bore a grudge against Claire Mill for her treason, nor against Frank for his unfair fighting, thus showing that he was able to endure affronts; vengefulness was not his way; when the phonograph played *La Paloma,* he could not restrain the tears. His leaning toward domesticity, too, is remarkable; it was not because she had confessed to him her part in the fraud upon Ackermann that he threw Diana Rose out of her apartment at night, but because she did not come home until after midnight, without having cooked supper. Certainly, all proper respect to the "emancipation of woman"; this was a political conviction preached alike by the Iron

Phalanx and Urban. But when a man came home hungry from inspecting merchandise, opening seams, and cutting off buttons—to leave him standing humbugged before an empty larder, defrauded of food and domesticity, and furthermore to insult him two hours later by the statement, "An intellectual man isn't all the time thinking about his gut"—this cannot be called freedom, but unnatural behavior, and it was accordingly punished by the ejection of the emancipated culprit.

Quite otherwise Frank, the Caucasian Oak, master of the art of occasional poetry by natural talent, printing-shop proprietor by the grace of Hans Simon, newspaper publisher by the grace of Urban, roué in dubious cabarets, drinking companion of his make-up man and chief contributor, Bart Plambeck, the honest seaman—and yet neither happy nor successful. He made money on visiting cards, advertising printing, and wedding poems with erotic spice; he made money on announcements and advertisements in his *Sunday Evening Post;* he made a great deal of money on Plambeck's exposures, which he used to show, already in type, to the person exposed, promising to suppress the material "from a sense of delicacy"—in which case Plambeck got twenty-five per cent; he must surely have been a rich man, and yet remained a poor one, because the very thought of checking a bill made him break out into a sweat accompanied with heartburn, because the various Willie Gaedickes emptied his pockets, because his cashier, Ruth Westen, assistant editor of the revolutionary paper, *Onward and Upward,* falsified his books, embezzling incoming payments and drawing commissions from suppliers; finally, because Weisse, exploiting Frank's cowardice, had only to threaten a "white cross on the door" to extort "contributions" for Urban's party.

The *Sunday Evening Post* appeared on Saturday evening as a Sunday paper, with an abundant magazine supplement. Hans Simon paid Frank twelve hundred thalers for his promise to print Ackermann's essay, *Man's Honor,* eight pages long, uncut on two successive Sundays in the supplement. When Albert Ackermann's article did not appear on the expected Sunday, Hans Simon put in a telephone call to Urban's headquarters at Mittelburg, and, when the great man's intimate, Senator Weisse, answered, shouted into the instrument: "Frank Jaeger doesn't want to print Ackermann's article, although I paid him handsomely. Yes, the article is called *Man's Honor.* Frank pretends to be afraid of going to jail; he's not to be ridiculous! Will you tell him that?"

"I'll see that it goes through in proper order!" Senator Weisse shouted back.

On Monday morning he appeared, uniformed as a captain of the Sports Division, and quite official-looking, at Frank's dirty suburban plant; whitewash was peeling off the walls, hens cackled in the yard, meadows and dumps made breaks in the lines of streets; no bus went this far, and the open fields were in sight. The pounding of the presses came from the basement, and Frank, gray-faced, with an attack of heartburn, had to drink bicarbonate and water when Ruth Westen, the cashier, shouted down the basement stairs: "Captain Weisse!"

Every time that soldierly tread announced a visit from Urban's secretary, the whole staff from chief to compositor was terror-stricken, and in the grubby editorial room behind her little table with the cash register, the youthful Ruth Westen would say: "Oh, Mr. Plambeck, I think you'd better go into the library!" The library was a room crammed with old newspapers, used for dressing and hand washing.

Weisse, with a casual greeting, tossed his cap on the editor's desk, sat down at it, pulled out the drawers, and began to read letters; Frank the Printer, however, bewailing the state of his health, and clad only in a sweaty woolen shirt above his trousers, rolled his way up the worn basement stairs. Once at the top, he had hardly fallen groaning into an old wicker chair when the dialogue broke out: "You corrupt swine," asked the Senator, "why didn't you print Ackermann's article?"

"Albert Ackermann is a definite enemy of our Dr. Urban."

"Shut up! Oscar Koenig was here and offered three thousand thalers if that article against Perlotta didn't go in."

"It wasn't Oscar Koenig," moaned Frank, beads of sweat appearing on his brow, "it was his advertising solicitor, Dr. Grau, that was here."

"Oh, so *he* was? I take it His Majesty's is sort of getting on fire, then?" Weisse asked the cashier.

"I'm not acquainted there, Captain," replied Ruth Westen.

"He's looking for a job, Dr. Grau is," Frank interposed, exchanging glances with his cashier.

But the captain had already penetrated the glance and the printer: "Hand over the check Grau left here, or you'll know something's happened!"

"I'm telling the truth," Frank defended himself, swallowing and regurgitating. "In the first place, the check isn't signed by Koenig, but by his editor in chief, Hoppelkopf. In the second place, the publisher himself wasn't here, it was Grau. In the third place, he didn't pay three thousand, the close-fisted swine, but only two. In the fourth place, Dr. Grau is really looking for another job; the one at Koenig's is too commercial for him."

Weisse, instead of replying to this drivel, looked at the check carefully, made Frank endorse it and send it out to be cashed, and dictated a receipt to the cashier: "Received two thousand thalers for the party funds."

Frank began over again: "By the way, Grau asked me if there was any possibility of Dr. Urban's seeing him."

"Oh, you were supposed to be the go-between?"

"Not at all!" protested the printer.

"How much did he pay for your services? But don't waste my time, you cursed bore!"

Ruth Westen produced the check, and the Senator dictated: "Received three hundred thalers for the party funds." And, turning to Frank: "You can tell Grau he'll get an invitation."

"Yes, Captain!"

"Now listen to me, you cheap crook, but what I'm telling you is strictly confidential: Simon has made such a big contribution that all attacks on him have got to stop; and, on the other hand, Ackermann's article against Perlotta is going in uncut this next Sunday. Yes or no?"

"Yes, sir," Frank breathed, and the cashier nodded agreement.

Weisse rose, straightened his tunic, and picked up his cap.

"Even so I would venture to humbly remind you," said the Caucasian Oak, getting up with difficulty, "that Ackermann is known to some extent as an enemy of Dr. Urban's."

Weisse stopped on the threshold to consider: "What does all this mean that you're telling me about Ackermann? Does it by any chance indicate robbery? Have a care, my fine friend! Ackermann has a wife and three children, one of them sick. You haven't got so much as a rabbit, you pig, and your sweetheart Willie is on our black list. I'll tell you one thing before I go: if you cheat Albert Ackermann out of so much as a single penny of his fee, you've got me to reckon with. When *we* take money to do something, we take it to *do* it, and we stick to it, no matter whether it's Beyer or Simon! Have a care! Good-by!"

"Why, I wouldn't take anything away from a man that had a sick child," cried Frank after tne departing captain. "How would I even think of such a thing? Good God! Really, a person isn't utterly and completely heartless!"

As he closed the door, the telephone rang. "Ackermann is on his way here," Ruth Westen reported. "If the article doesn't suit, he'll cut it."

Frank went into the library, sent Plambeck out "prospecting," transformed himself by the help of a wash, shave, white dicky shirt, cuffs, collar, tie, and dark suit into a printing-house proprietor, and welcomed in Dr. Albert Ackermann, the senior assistant master, with the kindliness and worldly wisdom that a publisher displays to his author. Ruth Westen had disappeared into the "library."

"Come right in!" cried Frank, sitting at his desk, in reply to a knock. "The door's open." And, getting up with an expression of fatherly cordiality: "Where the heart is open, the latchstring is always out, right, Mr. Ackermann?"

"So I believe," smiled the writer, and the two sat down face to face.

"You came about your article? You can speak openly to me—I always say, heart and hand both open and both free. But now for your superb article!"

"Did you like it?" asked Ackermann. He was in his thirties, broad, of middle height, correctly garbed, the blond hair cut short and parted in military fashion.

Frank the Printer knew from experience that a writer has the deepest confidence in the man who flatters him most crudely. He replied, therefore: "Why, wonderful! The way you formulate the sentences and give the thing expressiveness—first-rate, I tell you!"

"Thank you very much; but judging by your expression, there may be two or three little changes wanted. Do please speak openly; I'll gladly——"

"What I mean is, from a human standpoint I'm sure you'll understand, Mr. Ackermann. I, at least, am primarily a human being, able to fully understand the human element, which is always the dominant factor, I'm sure you'll agree."

"Absolutely."

"I'm delighted, delighted indeed, and I'd like to immediately assure you that there can be no question of the thing going wrong, or, as Dr. Grau so well says, 'to negotiate with an intelligent man is a genuine pleasure,' due to the fact that when mind meets mind the flower of friendship and cordiality burgeons."

"So it does."

"Consequently, to a man who don't walk blindly through our world, but has gathered his lessons by experience, and keeps them collected like the lilies of the field in a bouquet—you see, I'm a literary man myself, and ready to absolutely match myself against the gentlemen of the Iron Phalanx——"

"I'm sure you are, Mr. Frank."

"My poems on solemn occasions are accepted in the highest circles— if anyone in your valued family has a silver wedding and should be in the market for appropriate humor with the genuine poetic touch— here's my card: the inscription, of course, is my own."

He handed to the writer his gilt-edged business card with the winking cupid and the inscription:

> *You'll find I have mastered the art*
> *Of verses for summer and winter;*
> *My sentiments goes to the heart—*
> *Very truly your friend Frank the Printer.*

Ackermann read it aloud, and expressed his admiration: "Marvelous, Mr. Frank! My respects!" He held out his hand across the table to the publisher, who grasped and shook it, making no effort to conceal his emotion: "Do we understand one another? Are we, then, to be friends?"

"Fellow servants of the Muses!" declared Elsie's husband. She had treated him with deepest scorn because, she said, not even a blackmailing sheet would publish his spiteful and incompetent stuff, not even for pay! And he added, terror in his heart: "Fellow fighters above all, Mr. Frank! I shan't take any payment from you, not a penny! Matter of honor!"

"Ah, let us not speak of filthy lucre!" Frank brushed aside the offer. "You make money, you lose money, but the human spirit is a lasting treasure. Such are my sentiments. I can no other. When emotion is in question, my heart flutters like a dove."

"Emotion? About what?"

"Look here, if you remained faithful to the title of your article, be-yond question an excellent title, *Man's Honor*—if you were to con-stantly remain faithful, and write generally about honor in general, so as to not give anyone grounds for unkind thoughts, or better yet to not give anyone grounds for any thoughts at all, but to simply fascinate them from the very first word with the beauty, the sweep, the depths—like our great writers write in the Iron Phalanx—why, Mr. Acker-mann, I would not hesitate to immediately lay five hundred thalers on the table. But you, my dear sir, have something particular to say. Why, every policeman making a report has something to say! Does that take art? Beauty? Cultivation of thought? And—careful, now, here's the main point: is it consonant with the dignity of literature to ruin a family? You never mention the name of Perlotta, but still the reader knows whom is meant. Can you as a man of culture and emo-tion ignore the tears of Mrs. Perlotta, the innocent children, the rela-tives, who—this is something to give your serious consideration to—extend far into the key circles of Koenig Publications? Do you not think a loving mother, a faithful wife, would sacrifice everything to save her chosen life's partner from shame, him having already sacri-ficed his fortune?"

"As a friend and colleague, Mr. Frank, I ask you, how much did Mrs. Perlotta offer you so that my article shouldn't appear?"

"Confidence for confidence, Mr. Ackermann; confidence is the music of the spheres, cementing soul to soul: those dirty scoundrels, those bankrupts whose meanness stinks to the vault of heaven, all the Per-lottas together offer fifteen hundred thalers. What do you say to that?"

The author took out Simon's check, the fee that had been paid him, which he had kept secret from Elsie: "We are informed, as you see. My party offers you two thousand thalers. Done?"

"Honor where honor is due," protested the printer with unfeigned emotion, accepting the freshly endorsed check. "Handsome is as hand-some does, that's my motto. The article will appear uncut on Satur-day. Good-by, brother in arms. It has been a pleasure."

When Ackermann went out, the cashier appeared from the library in hat and gloves, ready to leave for the offices of the militant revolu-tionary organ, *Onward and Upward*.

"You must think I'm hard of hearing," she snapped at Frank. "Do I get my ten per cent or don't I?"

Spitting contemptuously, he flung the check at her feet: "There! Cash it and keep your wages of sin, venal woman, you dirty slut!"

Twenty-four hours later the high-spirited Elsie learned from Simon that Senator Weisse had forced through the publication of the article on *Man's Honor*. She went out to Frank's, and by threats, showing him a railway ticket to Mittelburg, extracted from him fifteen hundred thalers, three quarters of the whole fee. Thus, lacking in steadfastness, easily shaken, and mistrustful in the management of his own good fortune was Frank Jaeger, the Caucasian Oak.

BOOK TWO

THE LIEBENAU STATEMENT

VI

IF HANS SIMON had really been guilty, and Mark Antony innocent, the case would have aroused little interest, and would soon have been buried as the "quick-tempered mistake of a busy man"; indeed, our spokesmen of freedom and progress would surely have had no objections to the acquittal of the banker, if only on humanitarian grounds. And, in fact, when Simon was already under prosecution, but before the truth had come out, an article by a leading female advocate of women's rights appeared under the title, "To Err Is Human, to Forgive Divine," defending the banker and speaking highly of his humanitarianism.

But the moment that Bart Plambeck, this time truly with tiger strength, tore aside the tissue of lies fabricated by the Iron Phalanx with his article, "The Alteration of Dates in Oscar Koenig's Account Books," so that there could be no further doubt of Mark Antony's theft, and in fact no one felt any, the situation was radically changed.

Mark Antony, after all, was not a nobody; for twenty years he had been one of the great spokesmen of the "rising masses," the champion in the struggle against yesterday. To leave him in the lurch, proclaiming him a vain and cowardly thief, was to throw one's ideals overboard, to desert the flag, to vanish into desuetude; it was suicide—not of the individual alone, but of our whole culture!

And so, pushed to the wall and fighting for their own lives, the intellectuals rose up against the drunkard Plambeck, bribed a hundred times over, Simon, the usurer and money-grubber, against that outcast, adulterer, pander, and police spy, Ackermann. What they urged on Mark Antony's behalf was not facts—these the dullard Plambeck had already assembled—it was something deeper—psychology! How could anyone believe that Mark Antony, who had convinced the world, not of his literary skill but of something far more venerable, his character —how could he possibly be called a cowardly rogue? No indeed: anyone who could read faces, allowing for all shortcomings of authorship, would still have the fighter, the intellectual, the monument to conviction. "A mere author might write a *Divine Comedy,*" wrote Nicholas Edwin Schiele, "but to rise to action, to help, to rescue, to put *Secretary Kreisler* in the limelight of world sympathy: for him, the highest praise!"

True enough, this "psychology," holding that fine feelings a hundred thousand times reiterated constitute a "conviction," that a man's character may be recognized from his "conviction," and that "convictions" influence daily action, so that a standard-bearer of culture perforce cannot be at the same time a self-infatuated cheat—this psychology was described by Faust's circle, in terms of unprintable obscenity, as smelling like an unventilated lady's bedroom. Nevertheless, it is not altogether remote from reality, but actually does account for certain facts proved by experience, particularly in Perlotta's case.

By the time a Mark Antony has repeated for two successive years the dogmas of enlightenment—that God is a bugaboo, the proletariat the mainstay of the future, and that the latter will be sunny—he may still have moments of reflection and self-criticism, in which he will confess (not to anyone else, but still to himself, probably with a smile of cynical satisfaction at his success) the fraudulent nature of his livelihood. But to keep oneself capable of this momentary self-criticism after five years of such a swindler's existence requires a power of isolation and of resistance to the outer world—in other words, a strength of mind—that a good many of the Carpenters, and now and then some great pessimist, may have, but never a Mark Antony. He, on the contrary, will grow into his lie; he becomes a part of it; out of intellectual weakness, the herd instinct, and vanity, he is finally bound to believe what he says. If subsequently, as in our story, the whole world changes so radically that the conviction opposite to his own becomes profitable, he will then begin in his old age to "lie" for the first time, because "a man has to live."

To Mark Antony's credit be it said here and now that in his days of defeat he did not commit this ultimate villainy of forsaking his life-time lie, his oldest companion: he preferred to emigrate rather than to join the Christian sects, the Disciples of Emmaus or the Penitent Congregation, which were then established "because a man has to live" by Innocent Isabella Rex, Professor Schiele, and Heidemann.

Twenty-four hours after publishing his assertion that Mark Antony deserved the World Peace Prize for his *Secretary Kreisler,* Nicholas Edwin Schiele was arrested in bed, blindfolded, and taken to the Carpenters' interrogation depot at Liebenau. When the closed carriage stopped, he walked along a gravel path, and felt that he was being taken downstairs to a basement that smelled of ether and chloroform. Suddenly he was ordered to hold on to a metal rod, and the blindfold, fastened with straps, was removed.

He then saw before him the rectangular operating room of a public clinic, with the rising amphitheater of benches for the students, who watched the professor's surgical demonstrations and listened to his explanations. On the other hand, there was something churchlike about the room—a stone floor, a vaulted ceiling, and in the middle, before the rising rows of benches, an altar, without an altar cloth, but with a silver crucifix on an ebony base. Furthermore, the onlookers were not students, but men in gray drill jackets with masks on their faces; many of them had their jackets open, and embroidered on the inside was a girl tied to a stake, from whose drooping hair drops of blood were trickling—the dreaded Kate Schwann badge of the Carpenters.

Nicholas Edwin closed his eyes for a moment to make sure he was not dreaming, and opened them again: this was not a hall, it was a basement with barred windows; the floor of the first story had been knocked out, and people were leaning over railings, so that the corridors must run around, and the "students" came down from there to the rows of benches: hence the twilight of artificial light above and natural light through the basement windows.

He ventured to look to the left, where the windows were nearest;

there, close by the metal chair that he was clutching, lay a man on the
narrow operating table, with two nurses at his head; he moved now,
and the man in the white coat, the same whom Nicholas Edwin had
thought "improper, simply improper" eleven years before, Daruhi,
turned to the audience: "You have heard that he is a Gas-House Boy.
I made this experiment so that you might see it; it can be used when
there is no time and the truth has to be discovered within twenty-four
hours. Success is uncertain, but not quite so misleading as a confession.
Confessions are so easy to obtain that they have very little evidential
value; almost any method is better than an attempt to extort confessions. The Maid of Orléans expressed it very well at her great trial: 'If
you torture me,' she told her judges, 'I shall say what you ask: I shall
deny my voices and God and the Virgin, for I cannot bear pain.'

"I would remind the great psychologists of today of the medieval
heroine's words: they are surprised when a person quite innocently
accused confesses as many murders as you please. The man of the
present day fears pain terribly, and death not at all; he would far
rather go to his death than across a red-hot metal plate. Indeed, it is
quite sufficient to keep him from sleeping for seventy-two hours in
order to make him seek and find the confession that means death: he
will describe the details of monstrous murders with a joy and inventiveness such as he has never shown in all his life."

At this moment the man sat up, raised his forefinger, and started to
deliver a speech; one of the nurses called to the other: "Lend a hand,
he's too heavy for me!" They lifted him down, he stood on his feet,
and Nicholas Edwin recognized the director of the city electric plant,
Koehler, Madame Kittelsen's steady patron, who seemed to be recover-
ing quickly from his artificial intoxication.

"Take him to the table—next!" Daruhi ordered; but the patient,
staggering slightly, raised his left arm; his face beamed with craft and
amiability as, pushing Daruhi aside, he addressed the audience:

> *Know ye the land where the cypress and myrtle*
> *Are emblems of deeds that are done in their clime;*
> *Where the rage of the vulture, the love of the turtle,*
> *Now melt into sorrow, now madden to crime?*

Why, that was used in *Persecuted Innocence!* The Carpenters laughed and clapped, and Koehler had an excellent exit; by the table at the right, however, on Odo Sparangapani's demanding his signature, he collapsed and was carried out. He would sleep for ten hours, and tomorrow, sober and quiet, would be doing his accustomed office work in the lunatic village near Mittelburg.

"We've delivered him up," said Daruhi, when there was a knock at the basement window. Someone in uniform opened it, and two flower-pots were handed in and put on the altar—roses trained on sticks. "We thank you!" said the man in uniform toward the window; Nicholas Edwin recognized the voice—Hesse; he must have been listening in the half-darkness, leaning against the wall. And see—the little man recognized them, and grew easier in his mind—those who sat on the first bench were not wearing masks, and in their presences Hesse could not quite go to any lengths he chose; the faces of Generals Kaempf, Leugenfeld, and Spitta were familiar.

The two nurses came back, and it was Nicholas Edwin's turn: "You can have your choice, Mr. Schiele," said Daruhi, "whether I am to pump the truth out of you the way I did out of Koehler (there are several methods, by the way), or whether you will save me the trouble."

"I'd like to sit down. I'll tell everything," replied Nicholas Edwin, sitting down in the nickel-plated chair.

"You can be at liberty in five minutes. I shall even have to write you a letter of apology and compensate you for having deprived you of your freedom for a morning. Those are the rules. Furthermore, your testimony, if true, will not be exploited either in private or pub-licly against you or those who hold your views. I will carry my con-fidences yet further: you were not arrested because you were guilty of anything, but because the federal government is embarrassed by an uncertainty of your making, which you can therefore also clear up."

"Please go ahead and ask! I'm rested now—I can stand," said Nicholas Edwin to the man in the white coat.

Daruhi pushed him back into his chair: "On the other hand, since we blindfolded you on the way here, you yourself will have no doubt that the matter is serious. The situation is as follows: every single one of you in the Iron Phalanx, every one without exception, knows that Mark Antony robbed Ackermann. And every one of you knows, too, that this same Mark Antony carries his vanity so far that he would hang himself with the rope that he showed to Nessel before he would confess the truth that he is guilty of plagiarism. Thus far everything is clear.

"Now, however, you turn up and write in one of the country's leading magazines that this man, whom you know as a vain cheat, deserves the highest honor, the newly established World Peace Prize. You wrote that quite gratuitously, for you did not need to earn money at all, since your father is a rich man.

"These gentlemen sitting here before you want to know why you wrote that. If you should make a false confession, thought up on the spur of the moment, the results would be sad indeed. Will you tell the truth now?"

"I will."

"Please do."

There was a pause. Nicholas Edwin's manner and motions were like those of a student caught out by the professor at an examination.

"Why are you struggling with yourself?" asked Daruhi. The generals smiled.

"Because everyone here is a layman," replied the little man, as if he had at last found an excuse in the examination.

"By your leave," put in General Kaempf, "I used to be a writer too."

"A military writer, Your Excellency, of course. But never a professional writer. What I have to say here in order to tell the truth, however, will sound perfectly natural to professional writers, but quite incomprehensible to laymen."

"How does that happen?" asked Kaempf, shaking his head.

"Because of the specialization in every trade, including magazines. Every good, more or less intellectual magazine is so highly specialized and has so pronounced a character of its own that it can be recognized at once. An intellectual magazine is not a source of information; it doesn't report facts, like a newspaper, or make revelations, like a blackmailing sheet. It creates opinion about facts. It is the mouthpiece of public opinion—not of all public opinion, of course, but of a small circle, narrowly specialized as it is. Thus *The Conservative* represents the mouthpiece of the Conservatives—not of all the Conservatives (since it is highly specialized), but of a small group, the President's own. Thus my father's magazine, *Freedom and Culture,* represents the opinion of a leftist group. The intellectual magazines, then, are smithies of the public opinion held by a certain level of the population: for instance, the *Monthly Review of Art and Life,* though akin to ours, is in its turn so different from other leftist organs that I can't write for it. The most sacred thing to any magazine is its own character. If it gives that up, it gives up its intellectuality.

"Of course there are also points in common: all rightist magazines are by nature against Mark Antony Perlotta, all leftist magazines are by nature for him. Therefore the question of why I defend Mark Antony is a technical or professional question: if I belong to *The Conservative*'s circle, my position against Mark Antony is obvious; if I belong to the circle of *Freedom and Culture,* then my position *for* Mark Antony is obvious too; it is only the layman who sees anything puzzling about it. Well, since *Freedom and Culture,* where I work, has always been very strong for Mark Antony's work, it is expected of me as the editor's son that I shall demand the Peace Prize for the writer in whom we specialize, so to speak, just as *The Conservative* would have demanded the same prize for Hilgenfeld, because *The Conservative* used to specialize in Hilgenfeld. That is the reason why I demanded the prize for Mark Antony Perlotta: I'm telling the truth."

"I'd like to ask a question," said General Kaempf. His mustachios now were more white than reddish. "Do you think Simon, the banker, will be convicted?"

Nicholas Edwin shook his head: "After Bart Plambeck's revelations? No."

The generals looked at each other, and Daruhi asked: "But we still have the penal law, young man. What have you to say about that? In penal law the oath of two witnesses is taken as proof if no other evidence is available."

"We don't think the court will hold to that antiquated provision; we think they'll acquit Simon."

There was a clearing of throats in the front row. Nicholas Edwin had touched on the bitter dispute between Jacob Willert and the President. "If an oath doesn't count for anything any more, then justice simply hangs in mid-air," was Adam's opinion; to the banker, however, it seemed monstrous that two perjurers might send an innocent man to prison, and he warned the President that he was going to "bring up this damned scandal in the Senate."

"If Simon is acquitted, thus more or less convicting Mark Antony, what will you write then, Mr. Schiele?" asked Kaempf as spokesman for the generals.

"That's a magazine question, Your Excellency. If I could work for *The Conservative,* you know yourself what I *would* write. As I do work for *Freedom and Culture,* it's equally obvious what I *shall* write."

"I mean, if Simon is acquitted," persisted Kaempf.

"Well, all right, if Simon is acquitted, naturally there'll be a storm in the papers, and I shall denounce the cultural reaction, plutocracy, and money-grubbing, because that's our speciality."

"But day before yesterday you replied to Bart Plambeck's revelations by demanding the Peace Prize for Mark Antony. Wasn't that a very inopportune moment to do it?"

"Because Mark Antony had just been guilty of plagiarism? No: professionally, speaking as a magazine man, that was exactly the right moment—the moment that will bring our magazine credit for having the courage to fight. Standing up for Mark Antony's character when it hasn't even been questioned is battering down open doors. But to demand the great prize for the same man when he has been unmasked as a thief—that means showing courage, steadfastness, and the individual character that is the pride of a specialized magazine. 'Banner on high, though the man may fall,' is our motto, and I followed it, by defending the man's *character* when the man himself was past saving."

He had spoken the last sentences in the higher key of enthusiasm. "Ready?" asked Daruhi. And the Carpenters' stenographer, Benjamin Werner, working behind his desk in the first row of benches, answered: "Got it."

"Then you can add that the man under arrest was discharged because he told the truth when interrogated. Sister Bertha, please show Mr. Nicholas Edwin Schiele the way out." And, clapping his hands: "Sister Margaret, the next victim of the reaction!"

"There aren't any more today," replied Margaret Witt, who, having had no luck with the "well-known madman," was being trained as a nurse, and already serving as a volunteer under Professor Kuttner at the Women's Hospital.

While the Carpenters were taking off their masks and departing, Hesse greeted the generals.

"Who gave you those roses, you old joker?" asked Leugenfeld, the artilleryman, who boasted that with his new howitzers he could shoot the weathercock off a church steeple.

"A Mrs. Kersting," replied Hesse.

"The one with the beautiful daughter?"

"The same."

"We really all ought to go and thank her," proposed the tall Spitta. "After all, she had the roses put right under our noses."

But Hesse declined: "You'd better go to Wernicke's instead. He's got lunch ready."

"You're right, Otto," said old Kaempf, while his footman helped him on with his overcoat. "Don't let them get in your way!"

BOOK TWO

ELSPETH KERSTING

VII

WHEN Otto von Hesse was still in school, his father used to get him out of bed in the summer at half-past five. At the point where the long-drawn town of Marienhall is narrowest, between the wooded hills, they climbed the precipitous Bloody Cliff, and the boy had to sing a hymn at the crowded roofs down below, while his father sounded the trumpet. Thus he became an early riser, tiresome at evening parties because drowsiness would steal over him at ten o'clock no matter whether he had slept all afternoon or not. But by five in the morning he was up, taking a shower and going out "to see the morning." Nothing but bodily sickness ever prevented him from enjoying the bright, greenish sky, the first twittering, and the indescribable scent of the fresh earth; but as he was a favorite of fortune, still living at a time when the story in which he figures was being recounted with all the adornments of fable, the vegetable women, bakers, and street sweepers of Marienhall saw him, a white-haired man, with his aged wife, his second, whom he married for propriety's sake after living with her for ten years, strolling up the easy path to the Bloody Cliff that the Town Development Commission had built.

Today, on a cool spring morning, he is thirty-eight years old, and has for eight years been the adjutant of the man with the rubber stamp; if we are to believe the catchwords of the Iron Phalanx, he is "the well-known madman," or "the Bloodhound," "Drawswords." The latter term of abuse derives from the perfectly proper military command, "Draw swords!" given on an occasion after a gigantic Urbanite meeting at Hinrich's Beer Garden down by the river (where the knights had once fought with the burgesses), when it was his duty to divert the Sports Division coming up Blue Griffin Road and singing derisive songs, to stop them at the Outer Boulevard, and keep them from entering the inner town.

Here (where General Kaempf, sitting on a bench and smelling the molten asphalt, had once taught him history and the geography of the capital) he received his only wound, being thrown from his horse after sustaining a volley of dirt and stones; and he would have been killed if Lindequist had not ordered, "Fire!" The Urbanites scattered: the bullets would be aimed over their heads only once, but not at the second command, as they well knew. But Otto von Hesse never forgot the songs in Blue Griffin Road, the Outer Boulevard, and the volley of dirt.

For two years he lived in the "high-class apartment" with the Widow Merckel, in the poverty-stricken East End; then, owing to the catchwords that were invented, and despite the double guard, the stout gentlemen and the inconspicuous ones, it grew too difficult to watch him; he moved to Police Barracks I on the canal bank. His father having taught him that a man's life grows impoverished if he keeps no symbols to remind him of the places where he once lived—and perhaps, also, through his own natural inclination to look back and hold together the time that was given him—he attended the weekly Thursday-afternoon coffee parties of the old landlady, where there was fresh pastry from Klingenberg, the baker, next door, and no one was invited except John Henry, the "son of a washerwoman" who was being held in reserve, and Albert Ackermann, a friend of the family.

"They've gone and thrown out Albert the Author," thought Hesse, strolling that spring morning along the edge of the Public Garden,

separated only by the width of the roadway from the horse chestnuts
that bordered the canal. The red thrushes and kingfishers were twittering a concert in the shrubbery; suddenly, in house doorways and
under the horse chestnuts, he noticed three, no, four "inconspicuous
ones" who were not his own. Looking around, he turned off to the
right on the paths of the Public Garden: the man there by the canal
railing, his broad back turned, that white-haired man in the green cape
and slouch hat—it had not yet struck six from the Church of the
Saviour—he probably wanted no society. It was Adam Faust, the man
at the helm, an utterly straightforward man, who yet never traveled
any but devious ways. What had he thought out now? Hesse would
learn today, Thursday, for Merckel had sent him a card: "Don't forget Klingenberg's good pastry! I've got some news."

Yes, the Disciplinary Chamber for Civil Servants had made short
work of Ackermann: "Proved association with the prostitute Dolores
McCarthy"—imagine anyone's daring to do that as a senior assistant
master, especially at the City Academy for Young Ladies—not for
Girls: we have changed the name, and raised the tuition, because
Young Ladies are grander than Girls. Of course Hesse took a hand,
going in full uniform to call on Heidemann: "Do you dare to tell me
to my face, Mr. Mayor, just between us two, that a senior assistant
master must not do the same thing that I would never dare forbid a
Carpenter to do?"

"In the first place, of course he can," the impudent fellow had replied, "only it mustn't be allowed to get out; and, in the second place,
it's nothing to do with Ackermann. The question is whether the city
can still discharge its own officials or whether the guarantee of municipal liberty is just on paper."

So it was a trial of strength; every word said was wasted, and no
help to be expected even from the President. Playing the fool in minor
disputes, letting his adversary rise "like a bubble," was one of his
devious ways. He had refused most emphatically to save Hans Simon
from the charge of slander and common calumniation by means of
any special court or "presidential state's attorney": "The man ought to
get five years," was Adam's opinion. "The more obviously the representatives of culture and freedom cheat, lie, swindle, and suppress the
truth, the more confidently I shall look toward the future." In fact,
with his passion for an illuminating exaggeration, he had deplored the

scarcity of great scandals: "That's just the trouble—so often our thieves
still confess that they were trying to get rich quick, and the murderers
that they enjoyed the sight of blood. We'd be a great deal farther along
if all thieves said they wanted to enrich the proletariat, and all murderers that they intended the deliverance of humanity. Then at last this
thick-skinned nation might realize that deliverers smell of blood, and
liberators are all born light-fingered. I can see the day—unfortunately
I shan't live till then, but you will—when some perfectly blameless
man, making a speech, will accidentally use one of the splendid
phrases, 'culture,' or 'freedom,' 'duty,' 'responsibility,' 'democracy,'
'solidarity,' 'the rights of man,' 'religion,' 'the family,' 'the fatherland'
—and the listening multitude will unhesitatingly drag him off to jail
because a man who fills his mouth with that kind of talk is absolutely
sure to be a swindler."

That afternoon at the Widow Merckel's, while she was busy making
coffee in the kitchen, and before Ackermann had appeared, Otto von
Hesse heard the news. Beyer, who had been retired for four years, and
living apparently in idleness, had suddenly turned up in the capital,
and had commissioned Merckel to ask a few trusted friends what they
thought of the President's plan. The seventy-seven-year-old Adam
Faust, foreseeing that after his own death (which could hardly be
more than a few years off) the people, bewildered by the splendid
phrases of the Liberals, would elect Urban as his successor, intended
(so the story ran) to have a council of physicians declare him a physical
bankrupt. The new President would then have to be elected within
three months, and Adam Faust could exercise the influence he still
possessed to put in his own candidate, Beyer.

The great textile magnate, informed by Messerschmidt, the adjutant,
forsook his lady without explanation, stayed under an assumed name
at a third-rate hotel, studied Adam Faust's *Instructions to My Successor,*
and had Merckel "sound out the general feeling."

Now of course, as will be remembered, the washerwoman's son had
been withdrawn from public life at the same time as Beyer; having
been obliged to approach the Urbanites, he had pleased the "great
man." Since that time the President and his intimates had known that
Urban abominated his forced confederates, the Liberals and Revolutionists, and would much rather have shared power with the Conservatives than have opposed the President in battle for the one third that

was rightfully his. Asked by Merckel what his attitude would be (supposing Faust should have to resign) toward the candidacy of a Conservative, possibly Jacob Willert, Urban, who continued to believe in the possibility of an understanding with Willert, in particular, up to the very moment of the breach, replied that he would not offer himself as a candidate provided even as few as three government posts, say Justice, War, and Public Safety, were conceded to him.

Beyer, when the message was brought to him in his hotel cubicle, informed the President that he would assure Urban orally of the three desired posts, and simply forget his promise after the election. This of course would mean civil war; accordingly, Commander in Chief Frohwein, Kaempf, the Minister of War, and Colonel Hesse would have to be ready and willing to fight. This was the present status of affairs, Merckel concluded; he had not yet asked any of the generals, and wanted Hesse's opinion first.

"Well, to give you my opinion before your mother comes in: *no!* In the first place, there are two variable quantities in your equation. Urban is willing to accept Jacob Willert; he didn't say anything about Beyer. The Yellows might possibly believe an oral assurance from Willert; from Beyer they are sure to demand a contract. That's the first point. Secondly, Frohwein is excellent for a foreign war; he'd be about as happy to fight a civil war as I would to take a cold plunge in the river in a snowstorm. Thirdly, you don't just surprise the Supreme Command with a plan like this five minutes before it's to be carried out."

"And suppose he asks when the Carpenters will be strong enough to put down acts of sabotage during mobilization?"

"Pardon me, but that question is backward. It isn't when *we'll* be strong enough that Beyer must ask, but when the Gas-House Boys will be weak enough so that they can't risk any further acts of sabotage. How do you propose to 'put down' an act of sabotage already committed, say a burning city without water? So you've got to arrest the saboteur, not when he has become one, but *before* he does. When I told that to the squadrons eight years ago, saying that the policeman's worthy quarry was the evildoer who had not yet committed a crime, you called me the well-known madman."

"*We* didn't. So what am I to tell Beyer?"

"That the apple isn't ripe. Let him come back twelve months hence."

As the coffee drinking went off rather silently, Mrs. Merckel tried to liven things up by spicy remarks: "Here today and gone tomorrow —that's how life is. I don't mean to console you, Mr. Ackermann, you'll make your way out all right, never fear—anybody with a man like Simon behind him is in clover—never mind about that, but I always say to my John, 'John,' I say, 'you look out for them girls, they'll be the death of you yet!'"

Dr. Merckel silenced his mother with a glance, and Ackermann said: "If you had to listen to my wife's curtain lectures about how I've 'brought shame to the whole family,' and how she doesn't go to the cemetery any more because she's ashamed to look at her parents' graves, and she's going to send our baby Hans, aged fifteen months, to the strictest boarding school she can find, because he's sure to have inherited his father's depravity, and he mustn't die in the ditch——"

The men laughed.

"And all this because the McCarthy girl got five shillings from me and aroused the professional envy of my legal spouse."

The old woman's face looked very sharp as she stood up to clear the table and fetch cigars, ash trays, and matches; she said: "I hope I didn't hear right, Mr. Ackermann. It can scarcely be true that you would first be unfaithful, and then accuse the mother of your three children of envying the five shillings to the girl you were unfaithful with."

"Why shouldn't it be true, Mother?" asked Merckel with a look of innocence, kicking Hesse under the table.

The widow disappeared into the kitchen with the coffee things. She had stood over the washtub for thirty years. If her son, in order to rise to the ranks of the gentry, had to learn the gentry's way of making game of old washerwomen, well, she would pay even that price.

"What did you ask Elspeth Kersting to come over at five for?" her voice came into the living room.

"Not for anything. She forgot her French composition," Merckel called back.

"Now, now, if only it's true! I don't begrudge her to the three of you, never fear!"

In reality she harassed her only son by her naïveté, her fear of life, and her mistrust of the "grand gentry" whom he served. She kept everything strictly in order, but no drawer of his desk, no manuscript, no sheet of notes, was safe from her curiosity. And, terrified lest her son, led astray by a schoolgirl, should lose his post as a teacher, she tried to marry him off to Marie Klingenberg, the baker's daughter, before the old man should sell the business for want of a son to carry it on. Marie, a gadabout spoiled by Urbanite ideas of freedom, would settle down if she were married, no doubt, and "a baker never starves." But most of all she was afraid of Elspeth Kersting, the sixteen-year-old schoolgirl who had "poisoned her poor boy."

"It would take something more than a chick like her," John Henry tried to reassure his mother. In his desk, however, was a drawing by Rudolphi of the girl whom the older schoolboys lined up along the sidewalk to see coming home from school; and the Widow Merckel was unshakably convinced that what "my son the doctor" had written at the end of his commentary on *Don Quixote,* in the *Appendix on True Nobility,* was drawn from the face and figure of this daughter of a bankrupt.

"Of course she's beautiful. Beauty perishes, but the hard cash thaler rules the world, and her old man can't even pay her tuition." This much the old washerwoman told her son to his face, wondering privately what could be good about the daughter of a man with a shooting cart and no shoot, an estate owner with no estate, who boasted about "his banker" without having any money, and stood treat for rounds that he still owed.

Elspeth lived with her mother's brother, the grocer, Charles Thiess, in his dwelling, adjoining the basement shop, at the corner of Canal and Broad Streets, diagonally across from Police Barracks I, and in the same building in whose garret (with a view over canal and Public Garden) Rudolphi had his studio. She helped her aunt wait on people when the shop was full late in the day, went out Saturdays to her parents', and came back Sunday evenings; finally, a few weeks after her father's drunken confession that he was "a great scoundrel and blackmailer," Rudolphi discovered her.

From then on (starting, that is, as a schoolgirl of sixteen) until the rebellion and her marriage, she posed for the sculptor's *Flora* for the Public Garden, the *Victory* in front of the Soldiers' Home, and the *Justice* in the great Hall of Assizes—always, however, in the presence of her aunt Mrs. Thiess and Mrs. Rudolphi: her aunt and uncle had forbidden her to enter the artist's quarters unaccompanied. Until the decisive turn of events in her twentieth year she had never set foot in the Willerts' palace on Lady Square, and had never known either young Henry, the heir, or his mother by sight.

She sweeps through the literature of the time like a monumental statue, a figure from classical antiquity; but then, would not any normal girl who was firmly convinced that she was being held in readiness and "destined for something" have maintained the same reserve? Pursued by the village youngsters at twelve, Elspeth was sent to the capital.

She knew perfectly well that her father could not afford it, and that some powerful protector, whose name was never mentioned at home, had made the move possible. She knew, too, that her uncle Charles Thiess had long been in communication with this protector, and in the course of years she discovered his name, and even saw him once for a few moments at Rudolphi's studio; but she was not allowed to set foot in Lady Square or its environs.

Leaving the academy at eighteen, and going back home to Liebenau, she helped her mother in farmyard and stables; she witnessed the domestic discord and heard her mother's threats that if "this shame" were not put an end to she would leave her home and family; she went through the bankruptcy and humiliation of the too-carefree Alexander Kersting. That year and a half brought a development in Elspeth's character, which her school reports had described as "reserved and self-assured."

And no matter what reproaches her mother might heap upon the spendthrift, the show-off, the drunkard and blackmailer, she took her oft-accused father's side. Her father, she said, was a gentleman, not a farmer, and he had a right to a shooting cart; and if he had no shoot, no estate, and no money, that was his misfortune, not his fault. When her mother insulted him, naturally he had to go and put one under his belt, and if her mother insulted him once more, she would go with her father to Wernicke's and come home just as drunk as he—she knew someone who would pay her score, she said.

Dorothy Kersting could not believe her ears—so this was how her Elspeth had turned out!

"You're going to come home drunk?" yelled Mrs. Kersting.

"You get drunk by drinking, that's a law of physics," replied the academically educated daughter.

"And who's going to pay the score?" asked Dorothy, sitting down and wiping her brow with her apron.

"First come, first served!"

"First come . . . Why, then you're a *fallen woman!*"

"No, Mother," smiled the wingless *Victory,* "I shan't sell myself, I shall let someone make me a gift. So I'm a gifted woman."

"Oh, God, that it should come to this," groaned her mother, who thirty years before had been Dorothy Thiess, the milkmaid.

She did not, as a matter of fact, accompany her father to Wernicke's, but only fetched him from there, and this at her mother's request. The first time all went well; Alexander rose and followed her home. But Elspeth's beauty, perfectly regular, very rare, and perhaps best described by Rudolphi when he called it "the model of Praxiteles" or "the classical canon," was bound to attract attention wherever she appeared, no matter how she was dressed; and she herself drew all eyes so completely that even in later years no one seeing her could ever describe her dress: yet she was very fond of jewelry and clothes, and used to boast of her finery, like the violinist of his bows.

No wonder the leader of the Urbanite Sports Troop in Liebenau, the rich village mayor Schmalz's plump and flourishing son Caspar— his "convictions" having snapped off as swiftly as a blouse button in Perlotta's basement—took his custom from Ritter's inn to the Faust-ite tavern, Wernicke's: a welcome and considerable addition, for he was not stingy. When Elspeth came into Wernicke's to admonish her father the second time, and stopped at the door of the taproom, signaling with her eyes, her shoulder against the door post, Caspar Schmalz's goose was cooked.

"Champagne!" he yelled. A hundred years ago today, he said, his grandfather had married his grandmother; anyone who cared to join in should be his guest. A white damask cloth flew over the table as if of its own accord; knives, forks, china plates, cut-glass champagne goblets, silver candlesticks glittered; Annie and Clara, serving in white aprons, showed what heights Wernicke could rise to. An imposing figure with his wide-spreading dark mustache, collar and tie under his jacket, Caspar Schmalz, rising from his chair and demanding "something decent to eat," arranged and commanded the line of battle. Hot sausages appeared in great bowls, then salads with mayonnaise, hastily roasted chops. Elspeth sat down in a dark corner of the room at a vacant table, as if the whole thing were nothing to her—which was dissembling on her part; she, who had posed for Rudolphi and walked past the lines of worshiping high-school boys, could not fail to see what was taking place in the soul of the mayor's son.

Now the champagne corks began to pop. "Come here, girl—you can't say no today!" cried Alexander Kersting, pulling her down in the vacant chair beside him. When she had touched glasses with everyone, and drained hers, Caspar Schmalz, trained in speaking and argument under Urban, turned his guns upon "Our fellow townswoman who, after six years' absence, a girlish bud that has blossomed out . . . indeed I may say the rose of Liebenau!"

Pouring of wine, smashing of glasses, steaming sausages, masticating jaws, emotion in the fatherly eye of the happy Alexander: "How do we live?" the gray-haired man roared. "Like princes! And how does your mother live? Like a dairymaid!" Whereupon the farmers, whose wives lived no better than Mother Kersting, shouted their approval of the proud Alexander. After a while, it is true, he began shedding a tear for "the solitary lot of my spouse, the mother of my children." Elspeth, however, though unused to strong drink, and obliged to ask Annie, the waitress, the way to the courtyard, where the stars wavered in a low sky, managed, after sobering up on coffee and cheese sandwiches, to stick to the old man while he embraced Caspar Schmalz (whose calash was waiting ready hitched up in the yard), welcomed him into the fellowship of the well affected, and called him his "only friend—everyone else can go to hell." She always defended her father's behavior, regarding it as dignified and natural; she mistrusted the "still waters" that did not drink and never laid themselves open.

"Button up your coat, Otto, La Kersting is coming," said Dr. Merckel, when the doorbell rang, to Hesse, who lay stretched out full length as usual with his tunic open.

Elspeth came in, dressed in schoolgirl fashion, and shy at the sight of the men, one of whom she knew at school, the other from the papers. Merckel took her composition, and as he started to read it at once, offering the girl a chair, Hesse asked her where he had seen her before.

Elspeth blushed with pleasure: "The children and we older ones sometimes stand in the archway to the barracks, and watch the riding in the courtyard from two to four."

"Can you ride?"

"No, but Father has taught me how to drive. I've seen you at home, too, Colonel, at the Grand Hotel in Liebenau. We have a farm."

She was, Hesse felt, like the bright greenish sky, the scent of the earth, like a beginning.

Ackermann asked: "Are you satisfied with Teacher Merckel, Miss Elspeth?"

She drew back her short upper lip in laughing, baring her teeth: "That's how it should be," thought the author of the *Appendix on True Nobility,* looking up from the copybook. "The teeth shine, but without being brushed. The dress, threadbare, unpressed, looks like a thousand thalers; the cellar bugs run across her skin without biting; she is clean without washing, and when it is hot she does not perspire."

Nobility—what it was, how mankind had lost it, and how it could be brought to return—was a subject of Dr. Merckel's investigation that had occupied Andrew Zorn himself in his theory of "substitute gods." Perfumed toothpaste, sanitary plumbing, the morning bath, the tailored garment—all these were substitute gods, which taken together constituted niceness, a modern substitute for the true nobility of an older day that had departed like Greek fire, architecture, and Chinese lacquer.

"Oh, Doctor," Elspeth laughed, "you really ought to ask how my teacher is satisfied with me."

"No, no, don't be evasive," Ackermann persisted. "What do you like best about Merckel's theory of the Middle Ages?"

"The story about the love of noble women."

Merckel pretended not to remember: "What story?"

"I can even recite the beginning by heart," said his pupil, almost whispering with reverence.

"Please do."

Elspeth put her handbag in her lap, folding her hands on the edge of the table: "Suddenly it occurred to the women that they were living in dishonor. And, refusing cohabitation, they demanded that their suitors should first love God and prove their love of God. From that time forward the term 'manly love' took on a new meaning. It now meant going adventuring, living in peril, protecting widows and orphans, delivering princesses, re-establishing exiled kings, and running footpads, the godless, and the envious through with one's lance."

All three men clapped, and Elspeth Kersting hid her face.

"Do you think that's true?" asked Hesse.

Elspeth got up to leave: "Yes, and that's how it ought to be, I think." She shook hands with all three, and then Hesse said: "Don't you want to marry me, Miss Elspeth? After all, I pursue footpads!"

To the surprise of them all, the girl showed no embarrassment, but replied, still holding the petitioner's hand in hers: "But not on my account. You'll have to marry the woman who bade you do it."

"Then I guess I shall stay a bachelor," laughed Hesse, and Mrs. Merckel, with a look that tried to be motherly and failed, came in and showed the visitor out.

That afternoon *The Pensive Watchman,* the official publication of the Federal Police, was founded, with Albert Ackermann as editor of the semimonthly sheet.

As her former tenant took his leave, the old washerwoman asked him: "Well, Colonel, what do you think of Elspeth Kersting? After all, you've got a policeman's eye."

"So I have, and you know, Mrs. Merckel," replied Otto, buttoning his gloves, "you're doing your son too little honor. It wasn't the youngster that poisoned him, it was he that poisoned her!"

"He poisoned her? With what?"

"He poisoned her with his theory of love—you wait and see!"

BOOK TWO

INCOMPLETE ACCOUNTING

VIII

ADAM FAUST watched the progress of decay with anxiety, and the fact that his advisers, Zorn, Frohwein, Daruhi, and Bessonoff, had foreseen it all was slight consolation, since the antidotes that his people tried either did not reach the "body of the nation" or remained ineffective. After all, he hated the parlor pessimists who toyed with "inevitable disintegration" no less than the optimistic blockheads with their progress, their "more glorious future," their "revelation of beauty through railroad building." The high tone and deep thinking of the *Monthly Review of Art and Life* smelled from afar of pretension, patent leather, lipstick, and stucco false front—but this was the very thing that was taken seriously. This fellow Bart Plambeck, who allowed himself first to be made an accomplice of and then to be bought, passed current as a fighter for truth; when one of the honest Urbanites was challenged for the shamelessness of the "elastic phraseology," he would say with a sly twinkle: "But that's politics, my dear fellow!" Roland Perlotta, the commercial adventurer, was not unique, not even an exception: in his field he was just as representative a figure as Mark Antony in literature or Dr. Urban in politics; and all three were simply different aspects of the same decline. Never before in human history had such an admiring to-do been made about works of art; but the producers of this art all over the world resembled the eel-like copyist, Felice Gasparra, or that resoundingly empty libertarian barrel, Mark Antony; the patrons of this art everywhere looked like Tadd and Pole or Gaedicke's brewer and Hungarian dancer.

The white-haired man by the canal railing began to have gooseflesh. It was not the morning chill; it was shame as he reflected that fools, accomplices, and swindlers were at large and being made much of while he had to be guarded by stout gentlemen and inconspicuous ones lest, because he had been steadfastly true and upright for the seventeen years of his presidency, someone should break his head. When he inoculated the General Staff with the idea that an army existed not to defend bridgeheads and fortifications but to charge the enemy; when he chucked out first the "defenders of the defensive," then the barrack-yard sadists, and finally the lovers of dress parade; restricted reviews; extended the maneuvers; and forbade the wearing of uniforms off duty; of course he was an "enemy of the army": his faithful helpers, Frohwein, Messerschmidt, Kaempf, and Kraus, had to do everything in strict secrecy so that this "breach of the peace" should not be noticed. When he cleared the pulpit, pushing out the speakers of fine phrases, the ecstatics, the seekers after power in sheep's clothing, and those who had missed their calling and were office clerks by rights, they shouted "Foe of religion." In the beginning his carved reliefs and Biblical inscriptions were smiled at as an aesthetic pastime: but when it turned out that he was literally and mortally in earnest with every word that he said or had carved, he was hated. As he was a good speaker himself he despised orators, kept propagandists out of federal offices, and called upon the silent ones, the specialists, the overgrown boys who made drawings in garrets, glued up models, and discovered little improvements. Thus he became an "enemy of the intellect," and the Iron Phalanx opened fire on him under the watchword: "For there are bounds to the power of the tyrant."

His quiet industry aroused such suspicion abroad that once, just once, he tried to divert it by a public utterance. This was the time when the case against Hans Simon for slander of the libertarian writer, the so-called calumniation trial, was preparing. Our previous scandals, Peter George Lienhardt's test mobilization, which amounted to high treason, Andrew Zorn's speech at Hilgenfeld's grave, which became public through an indiscretion, the Dolores McCarthy affair, and Roland Perlotta's bankruptcy had drawn little notice; but the trial of Simon attracted unexpected attention here, and abroad the dislike for Adam Faust, partly natural and partly artificially fomented, actually rose to the point of threatened war. We were accused of three improprieties: the defamer of the celebrated author was left at large, and said to be able, through his wealth, either to win over the witnesses or, that failing, to seek safety in flight; secondly, not the judge of the appropriate court but the President's own personal jurist, Holzkopf, had been put in charge of the trial; thirdly, the President's friend, Jacob Willert, had restored the declining prestige of Simon's banking house by entrusting to it the management of the Sparangapani fortune; Jacob Willert was connected with the family by marriage. This step was taken in concert with Eugenia Sparangapani, Jacob's mother-in-law, who died shortly afterward; it attracted the more attention because the state's attorney had already demanded Simon's arrest. Such a great proof of confidence, at such a moment, and bestowed without compelling reason by the more successful upon the smaller competitor, scarcely differed from undue influence upon the jury at the assizes.

So it was that, while the jury was being impaneled; while the Urbanites were maintaining a stony silence about the trial (we know why); and the Revolutionary Workers' Party was having its hands very full pillorying Plambeck, with his merciless revelations, as a liar, slanderer, spy, and syphilitic; a great number of foreign newspaper correspondents turned up in the capital. They filled Scottish Widows' Lane, Susemihl's Confectionery Shop, Baruch Eisenberg's showrooms, and the Café Sparangapani in the afternoon, and the House of Dreams by night, where Madame Kittelsen put on a ballet adapted to Western morality, *Persecuted Innocence, or, Bypaths to Happiness*. With quotations "of the time" it treated the life of a modern Maid of Orléans; unfortunately, since more important matters are under consideration, it must be omitted here. In it Emil rapturously played the part of a village seducer, and later (uproariously applauded) that of the King of France, an impotent old goat who could not be spurred on even by blows of a cane. Madame Kittelsen, an enthusiastic Faustite patriot, had sprinkled in political insinuations aimed at the defamers of our President.

Outside influences and our own backwardness combined to spoil the humor of the foreign representatives. For in those countries where the Iron Phalanx governed public opinion, and progress had gone deepest, Perlotta's plays were produced immediately upon the appearance of Simon's broadside, in order to defend freedom against Mammon. The plays were not, it is true, regarded as exciting, but as "cultural," for in civilized countries at this time, the utterance of fine sentiments was confused with culture, perhaps inevitably, because no other meaning of the word culture could have been discovered. Obviously the journalistic representatives of these countries arrived with a prejudice in favor of freedom and against the calumniator of the dramatist.

The Iron Phalanx did arrange great banquets and sight-seeing tours, but after two days the foreigners were tired of associating entirely with their own kind, and wanted to meet the writers and academicians of our country: the Iron Phalanx, they said, was something they had at home. But the twelve of the Academy and the Clique, the contributors to *The Conservative* and *The Pensive Watchman,* lived in various quarters; they had no club and no cohesion among themselves, but lived as Hilgenfeld had lived (by now, of course, he was a model and example for them all); only the rich members occasionally met government officials or officers at the Golden Eagle Hotel on Cathedral Square. The foreigners' hope of learning about the "Adam Faust system" by daily association with his intimates was disappointed. Unfriendly news stories by the journalists were the result; our Simon calumniation trial was presented to the foreign reader either as a struggle of finance capital against the libertarian dramatist, or as the march of reaction. The united strength of Mammon, the foreign reader was told, had managed to throw that father of the oppressed and founder of proletarian culture, Roland Perlotta, into bankruptcy. But the conscience of the world was awakened! The sentries of civilization, assembled in the capital, would carefully watch every move of the court that was ostensibly to convict Simon, but in reality to force the dramatist of world freedom to his knees; and they would spread enlightenment accordingly. Albert Ackermann was mentioned in the reports as "the convicted, disgraced, and dismissed defendant in a morals case," and he was denied the title of a creative writer because he had too obviously associated with the stout gentlemen in tight overcoats.

The greatest morning paper of our neighboring country to the west recalled the five shillings that he had "after all, probably not given for nothing" to a certain fallen woman, and added that Dolores McCarthy had not taken to a life of shame by necessity, for the whole family was in comfortable circumstances, occupying a bright three-room apartment. Of course Andrew Zorn's "Metaphysics of Reaction" and Adam Faust's "ideal conservative commonwealth" were ironically commented on. Of the latter an Iron Phalangist reported that Adam Faust's political ideal was "actually a league of autonomous brotherhoods—composed of prelates, bankers, and the ink-stained wretches of a well-known madman who was in the habit of arresting those criminals who had not committed a crime."

Finally the correspondents decided on a frontal attack, and informed Brother Henry, the Archbishop's nephew, who meanwhile had been promoted Secretary of State, that they wished an official invitation. Adam Faust complied at once, arranging an evening reception in his palace by the river for all the representatives of the foreign press. During the discussion of the ceremonial, the invited guests learned that the President must not be formally addressed, nor must there be a toast proposed, as he was too weak to reply.

Contrary to expectations, Adam remained seated at the table when the dinner was over; he had coffee served, and addressed the assembled company. He spoke haltingly, wandered, left sentences unfinished; for seconds at a time he seemed to have forgotten everything, and Daruhi would help him out. The following morning he asked to see the text of the speech, and wrote above it: "Incomplete accounting."

"You accuse me" (the speech went on) "of not having invited you here before this because I despise public opinion. There *is* no public opinion—I do not know how many times before in history it has happened that there was none. This is a very bad thing, for every nation that has lost its public opinion has decayed or been subjugated. The Chinese had a public opinion; it was: 'Honor the dead, and ply your trade well.' The Persians had a public opinion; it was: 'Tell the truth and shoot your arrows straight.' The Greeks had a public opinion; it was: 'Honor man, the image of the gods.' The Romans had a public opinion; it was: 'Thou shalt till the soil and respect the law.' The last public opinion—the opinion, that is, which young and old, rich and poor alike, agreed on as a precious common treasure—the last that I know of existed in Europe until about 1490; it was: 'Fear God and keep His commandments.'

"All the public opinions that I have enumerated perished in the same way: the rich and great began to despise public opinion, which is always a demand made upon everyone—to despise it first by deeds, finally even by words. As long as the ancient Greek nobility complied with public opinion, man was honored; the historian of Greek antiquity bestowed on Eumaeus the swineherd, a serf, the cognomen of 'the Divine,' which is a name for kings. Later the nobility worked the serfs to death in mills and mines, and immediately the mob leaders, the Urbans, appeared on the scene; the Greeks called them *tyrants*. Frequently they were murdered by noblemen. But the nobility decayed; the whole people, formerly held together by a public opinion, fell apart: *disjecta membra,* scattered limbs, the poet calls it. At this point—just before the final downfall, that is—the opinion-makers appeared, the orators, the sophists, the associations, and the ladies with their salons, who were called hetaerae in Athens. Then came the beginning of enlightenment, which was at all times the same, namely that there is no God, that beauty is revealed through railroad building, and that we have a more glorious future before us.

"The promisers of the future, also known as deliverers, fight one another with their tongues, and every few years there is a new 'public opinion,' which is the opinion of the opinion-makers. Anyone who brings it to mind that deliverance from disunion, fraud, avarice, and deception is not ahead of us but far back in the past, that it lies in reflection upon the old, all-embracing demand—in betrayed and forgotten public opinion—anyone who brings this to mind is 'behaving unsuitably, fouling his own nest,' and is thrust aside as a reactionary, a slanderer of the glorious future, a calumniator, spy, and syphilitic.

"In the sixteenth century of our era the little people tried to re-establish by force the public opinion of the Middle Ages, forgotten by nobility and clergy: 'Fear God and keep His commandments.' They were struck down, and the sophists of modern times, the Humanists, made their appearance, and along with them the opinion-makers, the orators, the associations, and the women with their salons and their moralists, whom we call madams and fine ladies. At the same time, as with the Greeks, there was an afterflowering of art. Later came the deliverers, who asserted that one must not look backward toward the 'dark Middle Ages,' but forward into the future, which was to be sunny. They killed one another with their tongues, exposed each other's machinations, and proclaimed that the opinion they made was public opinion.

"If this goes on, my honored guests, if progress progresses at this speed, the tyrants will spring up tomorrow. But as history, while it warns us, never repeats itself, the tyrannicides, the young people inspired to sacrifice themselves by a yearning for the old public opinion, will not be available this time.

"The public opinion that I am supposed to have despised—but can one despise what does not exist?—the last publicly and universally recognized opinion, 'Fear God and keep His commandments,' is what I have striven to restore. All the changes that I have brought about together make up this attempt. Those opinion-makers and deliverers who have not seen what I propose to do (namely to restore public opinion!) smile at me, and everything I do seems to them absurd, devious, dark, malicious, treacherous, and dangerous. But those who have seen through me, like Mr. Urban, those who know, therefore, that no deals can be made with me because I am childishly in earnest, are preparing for the struggle that must inevitably occur unless my pupils and young friends forsake me after I am dead. For eighteen years I myself have been preparing against this struggle; there can be no understanding between the opinion, 'Fear God and keep His commandments,' and the public opinion of the opinion-makers, for the simple reason that the opinion-makers, the salons, the moralists and their hetaerae are seekers after power, whereas I am a seeker after God.

"Nor do I despise anyone—please, my dear guests, believe me there! Contempt for mankind is the quality of upstarts, of the *arrivé* mob, the nice people, the salons, the moralists, who do look down on the people, as is shown by the word 'masses,' which they invented. I, on the other hand, depend on the people. I know that they will not fail the man who is not a despiser or smiler, but who tries to restore their public opinion, namely the Ten Commandments, no matter how much money and blood this recapture of the common heritage may cost.

"Naturally, if one is an ecstatic, turning fine phrases about the pacific little Lord Jesus, while the poor man's child has no milk—naturally if the President or the pastor tells a hungry man there will be pie in the sky, godlessness is bound to spread among the people. It is not true that the people hate the rich man or the aristocrat: they hate the hypocrite.

"I have never been a hypocrite, and so I am merry in my old age. For since the people know that I have been childishly and mortally in earnest in my intent to create respect for the Ten Commandments, they have gained confidence in me; and when I call them they will take up the position I order, instead of submitting to the tyrant."

BOOK TWO

THE FOX OF GOD AND THE SEVEN CAUTIONS

IX

JACOB WILLERT carried out his threat to Adam of "bringing up this damned scandal in the Senate": he offered a motion to abolish the oath of a witness as evidence in court. For if Mrs. Habermann and Diana Rose were to deny their offense, namely the change of dates in Oscar Koenig's account books, *under oath,* Simon was quite sure to be convicted. Jacob offered another motion as well: to enact the Marienhall Labor Decree by federal law for a preliminary two years in the mountain province only, and only for plants in the iron and textile industries.

When the two motions were sent in printed form by the Senate to Adam Faust, he sent word asking Jacob to drop at least the second motion. The limitation of time and locality, he said, made it so modest and harmless an experiment that it would no doubt be accepted if put forward at the right moment. But this right moment would not come till the head of the Liberal Party, Oscar Koenig, was griped "by a bourgeois-idealistic bellyache" owing to the conviction of Hans Simon, the banker. Koenig's and Senator Kuehn's votes, split off from the weak Urbanite majority, would be enough to turn it into a minority. Oscar Koenig's idealistic bellyache and defection from the Liberals could be the more confidently expected because, as stated in Nicholas Edwin Schiele's recorded testimony at the Liebenau interrogation depot, the Iron Phalanx was convinced of Mark Antony's plagiarism and Hans Simon's rightness. Oscar Koenig, said Adam, was too old and worn out to adopt Nicholas Edwin's justification based on "highly specialized magazines."

Messerschmidt, the adjutant, standing helmet in hand in Jacob Willert's private office, delivered this message while the banker and his son Henry listened.

Jacob pretended difficulty in understanding: "I keep hearing that Simon is supposed to be convicted even though he's in the right, so that the head of the Liberals shall be sickened by his own filth. Is that the idea?"

"Not as violent as that," Messerschmidt assured him, was urged to sit down, and then continued: "Good God, no! Six months might pass before the actual trial of the Simon case, and possibly the prosecution witnesses would have qualms of conscience some day. Though it must be said, if we voluntarily surrender so powerful a weapon as the sanctity of a witness' oath, who can guarantee that?"

"Do you hear that?" said Jacob to his son. "He doesn't even want me to make my first motion, for the abolition of the oath for witnesses."

"Why not?" Henry asked the adjutant.

"Because if Perlotta's witnesses don't even have to swear, they're perfectly sure to give false testimony—against Simon, that is. The matter is quite different if we *don't* impugn the sanctity of oaths. Before a normal person perjures himself, he will think things over carefully, and probably refuse to testify. And if Perlotta's witnesses, two employees of Koenig Publications, refuse to testify, then Simon will be acquitted: that's the opinion of Holzkopf, the presiding justice."

"But if those two females do perjure themselves," cried Jacob Willert, "then Simon is perfectly sure to be convicted."

"Yes, Senator, and if the sky falls it will flatten all the sparrows too," retorted Captain Messerschmidt. "Besides, the President can't see why you care so much about getting Simon acquitted. People in worse health than he have survived prison, and grown fat on it. With Simon in prison eighteen months before the election, the Conservatives can accomplish a good deal, among other things the Marienhall Labor Decree for the whole country."

"Thank you kindly!" cried the banker. "No, sir, I must say, this dizzy balancing on the thin edge of injustice—excuse me, but I think you must have the wrong address. We're simple people, we Willerts —I'm a moneylender, my wife is a confectioner's daughter; we always say, 'Do right, and fear no man.' Simplicity, straightforwardness, uprightness, looking the other man square in the face—that's my policy. I won't put an innocent man in prison just to give someone else a bellyache!"

Jacob had sprung up as if he had been personally affronted, and was walking red-faced about the room: "If you'd be good enough to take down what I'm saying now, Captain; I'm sure the President will realize that I'm not refusing just out of obstinacy."

Messerschmidt took out his shorthand notebook, and attempted one last objection: "But the public, Senator—what will they think if we abolish the oath for witnesses just before the Simon trial? Aren't they bound to think that Simon must be guilty, since we tried such a desperate remedy?"

"God knows he's right about that, Dad," said young Henry, now twenty-six and a confidential clerk of the firm. When a thing interested him he had the habit of sitting bent forward, his head raised, his hands on his knees.

The captain put his helmet on the floor, gave young Henry a twinkling glance of gratitude, and brought forward an argument that he had been holding in reserve: "Naturally the public will say that in a plutocracy the rich man is safe enough from going to prison. If the oath is abolished, the decision is in the hands of the judge, and of course he'll be one of the President's judges."

"Well, now what do you think of that?" cried Jacob Willert. His face was distorted in an arrogant grimace, and he bleated unpleasantly. "Pardon me for giving three loud laughs! Are you afraid of the word plutocracy? I thought Adam wasn't afraid of fine words—but that is one! There are rulers, *and* there are rich people: but where can you find rich people who rule? That would be wonderful, my dear fellow; the world would be perfectly all right if those who had to protect the weak and satisfy the people in order to preserve their own property were the rulers! But who rules our poor country? The lawyers and seekers after power in parliament, not a doubt of it; the corrupt ones because they have nothing and are incapable of earning anything; those with a craving for posts of honor because they were born in a cellar; the blowhards, the opinion-makers, the adventurers, the ones that like to look at themselves in the mirror.

"Where will you find the rich, if I may ask? Not, by chance, at the race tracks, in the night clubs, at art exhibitions—wherever they can be photographed? Not in luxurious vehicles and pleasure yachts, goggling at nature? Yes or no? But just you show me a rich man who will take the trouble to be a ruler! For, saving your reverence, this lurking behind the scenes as the Borstels and Susemihls and Koenigs do, thinking they're manipulating affairs, but really being manipulated by the Reds or Yellows, I don't call ruling; I call it conspiring. It may well be that there isn't such a thing as ruling any more, just as Merckel claims there is no more true nobility, and everything is a substitute, and what they call 'ruling' now would once have been called mendicancy and conspiracy. Naturally, if I were the people, I wouldn't allow myself to be ruled by some young whippersnapper just because he had money: but they're much too soft, too lazy, too vain to be rulers. Unfortunately, there's no plutocracy any more, Messerschmidt, any more than there's any architecture or Chinese lacquer!"

Stout and broad-shouldered the banker stood there, a patch of sunlight painting his trousers yellow; Henry signed to the captain that this was one of the outbursts, familiar to the inmates of the house, which one must listen to and allow to blow itself out, glad enough that it did not go beyond the four walls of the room.

"To look at, a ruler must be upright in word and deed, like a man grown straight," Jacob went on. "Would you mind moving for a moment, Messerschmidt? I've got to get something out of the desk." He took out a document, closed the drawer, and said: "Look here, I'll rub old Adam's nose in this."

Henry stooped over the paper, and the captain made a note in shorthand. It was the President's instructions to his successor, which Adam had distributed to the twelve of the Academy when he was planning his *coup d'état.*

"I'm sorry to be quarreling with old Adam," said Jacob. "I went through it all: I defended Hesse in the Senate when Weisse had run him down to nothing. When Adam called freedom an animal with a thousand snouts and culture a lady, to the horror of half the world, I called him the 'great President.' That's ten years ago—and now it has to come to this!" Sitting down on a Chinese taboret, he leafed through the *Instructions.*

"Why are freedom and culture so contemptible, anyway?" Henry asked.

"Because Nicholas Edwin Schiele lives on them—not *for* them, my dear boy, *on* them: notice the difference! A thousand Schieles live on it, as if from peddling sausages; in other words, freedom and culture today are a branch of trade. Merckel even declares that as long as freedom and culture existed, the words were never used at all, or very seldom: the words' being used so often today is due to the fact that the things they stand for no longer exist."

"I've got that, Senator," said Captain Messerschmidt.

"As far as I'm concerned you don't need to write anything down," replied the disgruntled banker, while the adjutant busily took notes. "I've already said what I thought, that I'm a simple man and my wife is a confectioner's daughter. And so, as a man who likes the straightforward way, and despises the devious paths and foxholes that Adam Faust grows fonder of as he gets older, I shall inform the Senate and the people of an important truth tomorrow, whether he likes it or not —an *important truth,* write that down! Tell him from me that the Simon affair has come to the point where the Conservative Party can't even save its face by publicly expressing approval of Simon's behavior. Adam Faust professes to be a 'Christian captain'—he says so here in his instructions to Beyer. And yet he has forbidden Conservative papers even to touch the Simon affair before the court hands down its decision. Why should we take the same attitude as Urban, who says nothing because he's been bribed? Simply because the Revolutionary Workers' Party and the Iron Phalanx have to be handled with kid gloves eighteen months before the election, so that Messrs. Koenig and Kuehn will come over to our side 'because of a moral bellyache'? That's the devious way of playing politics, which Adam Faust first chose eleven

years ago, during the Geisenheim disturbances, and since then—what's
the name of that river that winds like a snake?"

"The Meander," replied the adjutant.

"Right. Well, you write down that I won't concur in the meandering
subterfuges that the President favors because of his liking for baroque
gestures and clowns' faces. How can the same man who keeps twisting
like an acrobat, who preferred to be abused for a thief as long ago as
the Geisenheim disturbances, instead of telling the truth—how can he
at the same time issue these instructions, in which he is presented as a
monument of straightforwardness? Read out that first paragraph,
Henry, the one he calls the Preamble, so that Messerschmidt will see
what I mean."

Henry Willert, giving the adjutant a glance that asked forgiveness,
read:

"Preamble to the Instructions to my Successor.

"Time was when the wares were good and the show windows were
small; you could wear a tailor-made coat for thirty years, and you kept
your shroud in a chest. Today the house consists of show windows, in
which the most up-to-date thing is on display every day. Accordingly,
man too was bound to become a show window, with the most up-to-
date thing on display every day, so that the lady purchaser may be
satisfied. What Urban calls *vox populi,* what the salons call 'democracy' or 'freedom,' is a display arrangement of today's show windows;
tomorrow it may be filled with some still more up-to-date object, under
some such name as 'authority,' 'religion,' 'the fatherland.'

"The show windows are no concern of yours at all. The present age,
which keeps looking in the mirror and admiring itself, is nothing to
you; let the Perlottas and their ladies reflect themselves. You are supposed to be a Christian captain, and nothing more. As a Christian
captain it is your job to harmonize your commands with the commandments of God, which are published and well known. In other words,
you are to cherish justice, trespass on no man's rights, protect the weak,
not muzzle the ox when he treadeth out the corn, and, above all,
strengthen the army and police, so that your command and God's law
shall be respected, if not from love, then from fear.

"Do not be led astray by those who have devised substitute deities,
such, for instance, as culture, civilization, or progress. You must deal
not with substitute deities nor with the *vox populi,* but with God. For

if the people love freedom, the personal freedom that is given in the old divine law, not as a gift but as a duty, an achievement daily to be renewed, they will drive out the cheats who are trying to take away the old law from man because they mean to take away his freedom. If, on the other hand, the people despise God, because they wish to submit to the tyrant, then you must defend personal freedom *even against the people,* stand firm for your God, and fall under His banner sooner than give way before those who have been cheated.

"Whether you will have to go through periods of democracy or of dictatorship depends not on you but on the condition and will of the people. Either they will concur in the way of God, in which case freedom will prevail, or they will want to doff their hats to the tyrant and receive alms from him, in which case, a rod for the fools' backs!"

Henry looked up; none of the three said anything for some seconds, and Jacob began to pace the room: "Those are the words of an honest man, and if you can't be a politician and an honest man at the same time, but have to turn into a fox—don't hesitate to write the word 'fox,' Messerschmidt, it's the right word for Adam Faust—then I think I'd rather be a private citizen than a clown and tightrope-walker for other people. One thing more: Simon's conviction, if it takes place, will naturally be a moral victory for the Reds, a greater victory over us than the Revolutionary Workers' Party has had in ten years. Therefore, to speak the language of the fox, Simon must not be convicted for that reason if for no other! For no such stinking bog as the Iron Phalanx has ever opened up in our country; never before has the lie attained to such omnipotence as it has under Adam Faust—and why? Because in his blind hatred of Urban he refuses to see that the Reds and their Iron Phalanx are Enemy Number One, whereas after all Urban is an opponent with whom one can deal without besmirching oneself. As he has captured more than a third of the seventy-five Senate seats, his right to some posts in the government is undeniable. Urban is not an enemy of property, and passes for a friend of the workingman. I prefer an understanding with him to a civil war."

"Is that all, Senator?" the adjutant asked.

"Yes. Thank you, my dear Messerschmidt."

The President's messenger went out, but Henry, running down the open staircase, overtook him: "Please don't tell the President every-

thing that Father was croaking about. He's been sick ever since the
Simon affair, and he's never quiet for a moment—goes running through
the house, raving about punishments to come. Whenever he hears anything said about the Iron Phalanx, he yells that it's going to end in
baths of blood. When a man's nerves go to pieces, he isn't responsible
for what he says."

Messerschmidt shrugged his shoulders and left. Late that same evening he brought the reply.

ADAM FAUST'S LAST LETTER TO JACOB WILLERT

DEAR JACOB:

In this letter I send an enclosure to call you back from the soaring
flights of an honest man to the carpet of solid fact. By the testimony
of Nicholas Edwin Schiele at Liebenau, the so-called "Liebenau statement," please note the dirty solid fact that no matter how important
your truth may be, it will be throttled by someone professionally, speaking as a magazine man. By today's enclosure, please note the comforting solid fact that the seven years' dispute in the Academy, consuming
all my nervous energy, as to whether the Iron Phalanx of Intelligence
or Urban is the more dangerous enemy, may now be regarded as settled. Read the enclosure and judge for yourself!

In regard to your complaints of me: yes, those were good, honest,
brave, and easier days for a ruler when you could intimidate evil by
speaking its name out loud and calling the liar a liar. It is not my
office to "save face," but to be a Christian captain. This object is not
achieved by uttering or invoking it, as in the days of magic, nor again
by steadfast straightforwardness, but perhaps by meandering subterfuges.

What good would it have done me eleven years ago to say that the
Yellow was Antichrist, and therefore Urban must be thrown out of the
mountain province, the province of the key industries? What would
the result have been? Shaking of heads, laughter. The magazines would
have said I deserve to be committed, and if they agreed with me I was
altogether done for. "They know the art of grinding corn fine, and
making it into white dust," says the poet. What did I do? I traveled
along meandering bypaths; but Justice, when I looked up to her,
wringing my hands, nodded approval.

You'd better not display yourself to the Senate after all: in my palace by the river I'll give you a hall with mirror walls, where you can make a speech every day, and look in the mirror to see if you have "saved face."

On top of all this, you quoted me wrong: I didn't say I was a Christian captain, but only that I was an emulator of those who had gone before. To be a Christian captain nowadays, when you do not meet evil in a form that can be struck dead, but as cotton batting with sugar, as injured innocence, as a superior smile, as a hip motion of annoyance, as emotional indignation—you don't meet it, but step in something slippery as if into gathered, sweetened, and whipped spittle! To be a Christian captain in this world, you have to combine very different qualities—the broad shoulders and solidity of a piano mover and the agility of a tightrope-dancing clown.

You might have spared yourself that business about simplicity and the confectioner's daughter: your father had a hundred horses, and the house of Sparangapani is older than yours. I mention this, with my regards to Elizabeth (my old and forgotten love), because you as a cultured man have always overrated "culture" and accordingly regard the Iron Phalanx of Intelligence as Enemy Number One, because that ridiculous gang of opinion-mongers doesn't satisfy your cultured taste. But even if they were less ridiculous, even if they were not so cheaply purchasable, as they seem in the "Seven Cautions" included herein (read it carefully, please, and send it back!), even then they couldn't be a danger to the state; nor do they exercise any influence on our army or administration.

Now look at Urban, a man not only with more intelligence and courage than all the Iron Phalangists together, but also with millions of votes and an army of I don't know how many adventurers behind him! He says he wants three government posts, and you say he has a right to do so. Do you know what he wants to accomplish *with* those government posts (Justice, War, Interior)? But even that is of no interest; the thing that is of interest is what the spirit of history means to accomplish with the Urbans: do you know what that is? As a reader of Andrew Zorn you ought to know that Urban is everything we hate, and that the Red intellectuals are only his beaters or pullers-in.

When I had the Lienhardt château destroyed after the Geisenheim disturbances, I knew what it means when anyone tries to deny to the workingman the right that we industrialists claim as a matter of

course, namely the right of forming an independent body. What does
it mean when the Yellow convinces the industrialist that the workman
is his workman and his property, while advising the industrialist to
give his property, the workman, gentle, sparing, and kindly treatment?
What lies behind it? But the Yellow is an enemy of the workmen, say
the Reds; and from this in itself, from this blindness of the Reds, you
can see two things: firstly, their harmlessness as a movement on their
own account, and, secondly, what the spirit of the universe proposes
to do with them. For if the Reds loudly trumpet year after year that
Urban, as a Yellow, is an enemy of the workers, while the workingmen
see daily by their own experience that he is actually a friend of the
worker, nay a sympathetic and humanitarian friend of the worker,
what can the result be? The result is that Red propaganda drives the
workingman into Urban's camp: thus the Reds fulfill their historical
mission of acting as Urban's agents and beaters. For the workingman,
since he does not read the specialized magazines, can still recognize
truth, and still has the strength to shake off the liar.

So the Reds drop out, leaving two to struggle for the little man's
soul: the Yellow and me—as Urban himself admitted in his Blendheim
address in these words: "There are only two true-born worlds, mine
and his: all else is falsehood or slime."

What is Urban's world? He says to the workingman: "Hold out
your hat!" and to the employer: "Fill it generously!" He actually does;
according to Gaedicke's report, Urban said himself to his intimates:
"Man does not want to give, but to receive. Take everything away from
them, and then they will be recipients." Or: "He from whom I have
taken away everything is bound to love me, for I have relieved him of
his burden." The hat held out, the generous gift, the tear of gratitude
in the eye of him thus blessed—this is Urban's vision of kindness to
the workingman. No hunger, no disorder, simply the horn of plenty
emptied upon him who holds out his hat and offers thanks. And if this
Urbanite state is established, even you will love him, because he is sympathetic and lets you live—which, however, he might omit to do; for
you are nothing if you are a recipient of gifts.

Now, I am *not* a friend of the workingman; I have always hated the
hat held out and pity and charity. He who shows pity for the poor
man is my enemy, for he would rob a fellow citizen of his citizenship,
and cast him down into the depths where one holds out one's hat.

That is what Urban wants, and if you give him your little finger he will cast you down there too, because he wants to achieve, after all, the "equality of everything that bears a human countenance." He is Antichrist: such sober-minded men as Beyer and Merckel are of the same opinion.

So there is no question of whether you should oppose Urban; the question is, *how* are you to do it? In this connection, however, allow me to reply: it would suit the enemy to perfection if you were to oppose him like an honest man or like an honest confectioner's daughter. There is, on the contrary, no beaten path, no rule, and above all no rule of etiquette; I must not even save face, much as I would like to, for my face is not what counts, but the downfall of Antichrist.

This world is of the devil. If you walk the "straight and narrow path" of the honest man who says outright that he wants to fight the devil, the world will laugh—but its laughter will be dissembling, a sham, a mask, an excuse: for seriously, with clenched teeth, it will stay your hand, defending its ruler, Antichrist. That is why, in the Geisenheim disturbances eleven years ago, I trod the crooked path, and untruthfully told the world (lest it stay my hand) that I wanted to enrich myself. For that is what the world likes to hear; this it regards as "human and understandable," and besides, you give it a subject for indignation: and what does the world love better than a chance for indignation? It loves a President who will lower himself, also; if he lowers himself to the very level of a thief, there is a merry twinkle of the eye. Thus I amused the world—Nicholas Edwin wrote that it was "a joy to be alive"—and at the same time distracted it so that it should not stay my hand. I acted then as a Christian captain, that is, as a combination of piano mover and tightrope-walker: I let it be known, with excuses, that I was stealing; but before God—in truth—I hurled back Antichrist.

No, Jacob, I am no "lover of the workingman," and in fact I am against such expressions in general. I have always suspected that kind of love—especially love of humanity, love of the workingman, love of children, even love of rabbits. Unless you were keeping it in captivity in order to eat it, the rabbit could feed itself, and would not need your kindness; furthermore, I suspect the rabbit lover of caring much less about rabbit stew than about ownership of a victim upon which he can lavish his pity.

Of what consequence was the Marienhall Labor Decree? Very little. What is of consequence to me is to put away the outthrust begging hand, and to compel the poor man to be a citizen, with the rights and liberties of a citizen. For as long as he is not, as long as he wishes, deep down in his heart, to submit to the Red or Yellow tyrant, receiving his work and his wages too as charity, any labor decree is a scrap of paper. If you agree with me in this, then logically you must regard as your Enemy Number One the Yellow, the man who would urge the acceptance of charity; then you must not saw wood with a razor, as you are doing by allying yourself with Hans Simon against the Iron Phalanx. Are you a smaller and stupider man than Bart Plambeck? Hardly. Well, then read in the enclosed "Seven Cautions" what an unschooled dockyard worker thought of the Perlottas' intelligent flow of oratory long ago!

As Simon is trying to outstink that heap of dung, which is quite impractical, let him go on into prison; the consequences will be disastrous to the Iron Phalanx, and agreeable to us.

You call me a fox: that is no reproach, and I am not angry at it—by no means. On the contrary, I would be much pleased with the epitaph:

Here lies
Adam Faust
the Fox of God

P.S. I prefer the natural kind of intelligence that sees through men and situations to the profundity of the bookworm, which throws everything into confusion. For that matter, the bookworm too may possess natural intelligence, if Mother Nature has bestowed courage and honesty on him; how seldom that is the case, you know as well as I do. Bart Plambeck can neither speak nor write his mother tongue; but who excels him in intelligence?

Naturally when the Iron Phalanx found out by treachery about the enclosed document, they ejected its author, and themselves took possession of the governing posts and editorial chairs in the Revolutionary Workers' Party. What will be the result? The hastened downfall of the Reds, let us hope! For our proletarians are not yet stupid and degraded enough to submit in the long run to the leadership of literati and actresses.

ADAM FAUST

Enclosure (Please return by courier)

Secret order by the chairman of the Revolutionary Workers' Party to officers under him, issued in the year of the Geisenheim disturbances.

Re: Destruction of the liberal *bourgeoisie* by propaganda for culture and freedom.

THE SEVEN CAUTIONS

1. It is ordered to begin at once establishing nonparty clubs, associations, societies, evening parties, Christian sewing circles, five-o'clock teas, and world leagues, as it is necessary to win over to the revolution of the proletariat those spokesmen of the *bourgeoisie* who we know are still shackled to the golden chain of capital.

2. Doing this, care is needed to look out for the vanity of the painters, sculptors, writers, and other favorite clowns of the *bourgeoisie,* carefully keeping from them the genuine purpose of starting up the associations.

3. No one can escape the spell of progress and humanity. By reason of which these clubs, leagues, and evening parties are all to be described as *progressive,* inviting the revolutionary millionairesses to join up for the cause of humanity.

4. The vanity of the artists is to be flattered by furnishing galleries for the painters, and newspapers and publishing companies for the writers, so as to print their junk and raise the stock of the ones that get exhibited or printed in bourgeois public opinion. Obviously don't let just any painters' and writers' stock go up, only those that are at least progressive-minded and against reaction. The rise of their stock is to be assisted by us, like, for instance, having the ones that are printed praised by our friendly critics in the bourgeois papers, and called Tolstoy or Zola, whichever it is. We might have to grease their palms a little. When the painters or writers have risen with our assistance, they are to apply at once for positions in managing the art associations, clubs, leagues, or the publishing companies and newspapers and

CAUTIOUSLY

to work for the victory of the proletarian cause as secretaries to art associations, editorial readers, critics, teachers, or journalists.

The *first* caution is that, for instance, the publisher's reader or critic that has risen by our help must never accuse a reactionary writer of being a reactionary, but of being a liar, slanderer, spy, and syphilitic. Of course, a reactionary writer is a writer who doesn't sympathize with us.

The *second* caution is plain boycotting of reactionary writers by publishers sympathizing with us. The manuscript being submitted is to be copied and the copy handed over to a right-thinking writer for private poetic use, being paid for by a small contribution to the party treasury. The original is to be returned to the sender, asking him to work over it and increase the suspense and poetic power. This has the purpose of stalling off the reactionary nincompoop and stopping him from writing more junk that might do harm to the proletarian revolution. Publishers sympathizing with us are to put a heading of "cultural publications" in their catalogues, so as to identify them immediately. Meetings of clubs and leagues founded by us are to be called Cultural Congresses whenever they last several days, to make the police keep their hands off. At all of these Cultural Congresses a revolutionary millionairess must speak at least once, and there is not to be any suggestion what she has to say. It makes no difference anyway, because the illustrated picture story is the main thing, and besides, the lady has got to be allowed to talk for her money.

A *third* caution is the individualism which the painters and writers bow down to, so their pleasure must not be spoiled in it, but on the contrary we should convince these muckers that only the revolution of the proletariat can bring victory to *unlimited individualism*. For this reason the same must be announced in all the new clubs and societies as the main point in proletarian doctrine, what the proletarians march to triumph and death for. In regard to this, to flatter the artists' vanity we have already engaged Professor Schiele to formulate this matter of how and why the revolution means victory for individualism. The formula of Comrade Schiele, which is to be used to prepare *all club lectures,* is as follows:

"Under the tyranny of the capitalistic Moloch no man is equal to another in respect to prosperity, but on the contrary there is an outrageous inequality: intellectually, however, they are all perfectly equal cart horses before the triumphal chariot of capital, obliged to sing of the things that make a millionaire's life pleasant, namely female flesh, spring, the moon, and the fidelity of the oppressed to their exploiters.

"Under Communism, on the contrary, no one is richer than anyone else, and *consequently"*—this "consequently" must never be left out on pain of a hundred thalers' fine to the party treasury—"everyone is *unlike* the others: each one a creative ego, each an irreplaceable personality!"

This formula is to be announced everywhere, and everyone doubting it, much less saying it is on purpose for our party ends and to soft-soap the artists, is to be unmasked as a liar, slanderer, spy, and syphilitic, and sued in court.

The *fourth* caution is to keep absolutely secret this and all other instructions to our comrades working in the bourgeois cultural camp, keeping it away from bourgeois nincompoops and Hesse's Carpenters. But specially the aim and purpose of our cultural campaign is to be kept secret from the president of the Iron Phalanx, Oscar Koenig the newspaper magnate, as you can never tell what kind of mood he will be in, such as a bourgeois-idealistic bellyache; also he is already suffering from hardening of the arteries.

The *fifth* caution is to support unreservedly any philosophy and doctrine that claims everything is relative. Because if everything is relative, so is the Conservative Party and the *bourgeoisie* particularly. If the latter is first cautiously brought to realize for itself that it is relative, its self-assurance and determination to defend itself will be paralyzed, thus producing the weak will and toleration in the soul of the *bourgeoisie* that is necessary for our victory.

The *sixth* caution is for us not to attack the Christian church, but put them to work for us, by constantly goading the silly horse-collared crew into preaching tolerance as the chief Christian virtue. If tolerance is preached to the *bourgeoisie* in the churches, they will have to practice it on us. That is enough.

The *seventh* caution is unquestioningly to support and finance the Iron Phalanx of Intelligence, founded by us, which has already classed our party organ, *The Free People,* as the greatest artistic event of the last two thousand years. Letters from provincial comrades protesting against our attitude on the literary question are to go into the wastebasket. We alone know that there is no bourgeois group so full of contempt for the little man as the Iron Phalanx which considers us as the "masses" like a flock of sheep, and runs after every essay writer because he went to college. We know that; but we also know that the intellectuals who announce the dying of capitalism and the "new age of equality" can be bought cheaper and used more easily than other bourgeois literati, because they are vainer and more anxious for applause. So they are our men, and being as they will quickly seize upon any way at all of going up the ladder to bourgeois prosperity without work, they will do the job we have for them, softening up the bourgeois conscience by simply pouring scorn on the Adam Faust system more effectively than the protesting comrades in the provinces.

We know and they know that the Iron Phalanx principles of culture and freedom are all talk. But putting aside the fact that they make confusion, which is highly useful in itself, they have one principle that they do honestly mean: that straightforwardness and a sense of honor are reactionary prejudices. People like them can be used for anything— not in the actual action, because of their famous dishonesty and their putting a very high value on their lives, but during the period of preparation!

With a revolutionary salute!

BART PLAMBECK, the honest seaman
Party chairman

BOOK TWO

KING THRUSH-BEARD, OR, THE TRYING
OF THE HEART

X

THE Willerts' white palace on Lady Square was built in the eighteenth century, and the architect really had nothing in mind beyond the magnificently sweeping staircase that rose from the ground floor through two stories, with the broad skylight above it, making the Carrara marble of the steps and florid railings gleam on sunny days. The rooms, Rudolphi said, were "built around the staircase." Old Melchior, who did not settle down until he was sixty and beginning to love the Beloved, had always previously been a feudal lord; the forty rooms in the palace had scarcely been enough to house his banqueting and shooting guests, while the stables around the place and in the park had been altogether inadequate; for as a high stepper of the old days, he loved above all things the sight of horses, the smell of stables and leather tackle, the creak of saddles, the pull of the living rein, and the foam at the mouth of the heated animal. Jacob Willert liked to talk about questions of human beings with workmen like Anton Koerner, the conciliator at Marienhall; his father had talked with saddlers about questions of saddlery. So great were the changes that had come about.

Elizabeth Sparangapani, the confectioner's daughter, having paid with the now famous slapping for her mistake in supposing she must keep up the old-time splendor, furnished for herself and her husband a five-room apartment at the rear of the house, looking on the yard, a quiet, tree-shaded yard whose like was to be found only in Scottish Widows' Lane; and there they had lived since the birth of the heir of the family, now nearly twenty-seven. The old ground floor and several offices on the Lady Square side of the second floor were occupied by the bank. But as Melchior had enlarged the attic floor for his numerous staff, and had connected it with the staircase by a wooden stairway continuing the marble steps, there were fifty-six habitable rooms available all told, and at the very top, where the maids lived, a wooden railing, called "the Belle Vue Gallery," ran around just under the skylight in such fashion that anyone moving across the ground-floor lobby or up the open stairs could be observed and criticized from on high.

This method of building the interior of the house around the dominating staircase, and particularly the wooden circle of railing under the skylight, very seldom led to any happy event, but produced constant annoyances, encroachments, and complaints: during the pauses in their work—and in the Willert household there were more pauses than work—the twelve maids would stick their brown or blonde tousled heads over the railing, with light from above to make it worse, and scandalize the bank employees, both apprentices and gray-haired cashiers, curlyheads and baldpates, that moved across the ground floor and up to the second floor, by whispering and sometimes by audible remarks. True, it did occasionally happen that some dashing correspondent would make a quick-witted reply, resulting in a connection which to strengthen and render permanent was a favorite pastime of

the splendid Elizabeth; but far oftener notes fastened to fat knitting
needles were dropped, admonishing the passer-by to comb his hair,
shine his shoes, button his trousers, wash his hands, look handsomer,
use this or that beauty preparation, and insults of a similar tenor.
Often there would be ten heads leaning over the railing at once, and
many a bashful young man hurrying up toward the confidential clerks'
offices or the conference chamber on the second floor tripped and
stumbled, to the accompaniment of merry and resounding laughter, because his heart was beating like a soldier's on going through an enemy
barrage. Very seldom—but it did happen—some object of particular
love or detestation would be hit on the head by an orange peel. Once
or twice a day, of course, when the head of the house, young Henry,
or Elizabeth appeared on the staircase, the heads vanished like a flash;
also, because of her loud and piercing voice, the girls fell back before
Madame Fallières, the redheaded Frenchwoman, who had come over
from the von Brick household, and was bringing up the "chick," little
Elizabeth. These brief moments aside, the girls ruled the house, especially on the long summer days.

To quell this lack of discipline there were, of course, three house
stewards, not equal in rank, but all of them superior to the girls. The
first, Augustus Huebner, who, as the son of John (the old manservant,
Bible student, and Revival Mission brother), had grown up in the
house, was by trade a mechanic and wheelwright; he occupied himself
entirely with repairs, was married, and never looked at the girls. Usually
he was to be seen standing by a wall or on a ladder, his toolbox before
him, a nail in his mouth, his rule in his breast pocket; for Jacob Willert had a way of tugging at the heavy curtains and hanging mirrors,
and running white cotton gloves over shelves, door frames, and curtain rods in order to "halt decay."

Meyer, the second steward, was directly in authority over the maids,
and supervised the work of all except the first chambermaid, who kept
the mistress' rooms in order. Mrs. Wenzel, with a great sense of delicacy, had chosen for this office a man whose contrary leanings rendered
him unreceptive to girlish love. But his attempts to prevent the girls'
looking down from the gallery met with personal remarks, and his
dialogues with the undisciplined creatures were reported to the splendid Elizabeth, who emitted shrieks of joy at the recital. For Meyer, a
well-fed, plump-cheeked, beardless *bon vivant* with an unhealthy gray

complexion, and pimples on the back of his neck, tried to offset his lack of manhood by roughness, brisk motions, and a half-soldierly, half-ironical manner of speech interlarded with poetic quotations. For his assistance, and to do a favor to the firm's confidential clerk, Mr. Arnold Mueller, who was overseer of the poor in the district where he lived, Jacob hired the third steward, Andersen by name, a tall, brown-haired, handsome young man, quite useless for any sort of work, whom some person unknown, possibly his mother, had left at the door of the orphanage as an infant. In respect to love he was Meyer's exact opposite. It was on his account, to avoid falling from major to tramp, that Peggy Witt left the house. "The others only wanted to love me," she said. "He wanted to marry me, but I won't have him." Incidentally he pursued her even to the Women's Hospital, and was not honest in his new love for the first chambermaid, Emily, Peggy's successor.

Things were in this unsatisfactory state as the splendid Elizabeth awaited her husband at the breakfast table on the morning of the day that Jacob Willert had chosen to "bring up this damned scandal in the Senate." It was an old privilege of hers to spend this coffee hour, beginning at eight in the morning and often lasting until half-past nine, with Jacob, without other witnesses or interruptions. The banker read the business mail, already sorted, answered, and ready for signature, at eleven; private mail he did not read at all, but left it to Elizabeth to open the letters at the breakfast table, choose what she would tell him about, and ask his advice concerning the replies. The answers, some of which she wrote herself, others of which she dictated, but most of which she simply outlined in a few words to the secretary, occupied her all morning: every private communication, even if it was simply a begging letter, had to be answered, and signed in either the chief's or his wife's own hand. Only after the correspondence was disposed of, and never before nine o'clock, might the ten-year-old Elizabeth and her Frenchwoman come in; her father would then tell her a story, either out of the storybook or from the Bible, beautified or made wickeder, depending on Jacob's humor.

Today he will be late and "wickeder," thought his wife, her spectacles on her nose and a pencil in hand, reading a begging letter. From their common bathroom, its door ajar, she had seen him lying in bed, with the sheets of the President's letter scattered over the bedside table and the floor: he must have gone to sleep late, reading it. Old Adam has pinned both his shoulders to the mat again, she thought, and was glad of it, because the expression "confectioner's daughter," which he had used in conversation with Messerschmidt yesterday, had penetrated as far as the wide landing. All right, she was a confectioner's daughter: but his grandfather had washed Ewert & Hansen's windows as an apprentice!

Emily, the head chambermaid, came in bringing hot oatmeal, stewed prunes, and a storybook with pictures and a bookmark in it, which she put down open by the Senator's seat.

"What's this I see, Emily?" said Mrs. Willert, with a sidelong glance over the top of her glasses, handing the girl a letter of complaint from the chief confidential clerk, Mr. Arnold Mueller. The letter stated that when the author set foot upon the open staircase, a swarm of maids, their heads and necks depending from the gallery, had greeted, or rather derided, him with a long-drawn, ironical "Oh!" This disrespectfulness had caused his feet, incapable of further locomotion, to become rooted to the stone steps. Mr. Arnold Mueller, the chief's right hand in banking questions, supervisor of the Senate chancellery, and occupying countless positions of trust, excelled in the art of complicated sentence structure. This "Oh!" uttered in unison indicated surprise or displeasure. It also evoked the legend about the Women's Hospital, that old Melchior had founded in order to interrupt the pregnancies of his favorites. The story, passed on from generation to generation of the servant girls, had become part of the family tradition regarding the Willerts' paradise and the "Harem"—a tradition with no substantial basis except the wealth of the family and the easy life of the staff. Jacob, however, loved the Willert tradition precisely because it included not only flattering but criminal features: its credibility and venerability were thus assured, he said, and he kept it green just as he kept the twenty vacant and useless guest rooms of the palace fresh and ready, exactly as if the persons who had formerly been welcomed there, now long since dead, who had eaten and drunk with his father, were now invited to take off their hats and coats at any moment, and stretch out in a freshly made and turned-down bed, which even had a nightshirt spread upon it. The head house steward, Augustus Huebner, as the most dependable, with foot rule and pencils in his breast pocket and the awkward toolbox hung around his neck, twice a week inspected the twenty useless and closed rooms.

Accordingly it was an empty threat, already threadbare from use, when Elizabeth said to the pretty Emily: "You'll go so far that we shall have to clear out the rooms and fire you all! What did Arnold Mueller do to you?"

"But it wasn't him they meant at all, Madam. Deep in thought, goodness knows of whom——"

"Why are you heaving a sigh?" interrupted Elizabeth.

"—Andersen was coming up the stairs; Mr. Mueller was at the very bottom; just then one of us—I don't wish to tell on her—came down the stairs; suddenly, his left hand on the banister, he stretched out his other arm, and embraced her."

"Who, whom?"

"Why, Andersen the——"

"You, you! Be honest!"

"I am honest, but he isn't honest about it; he loves——"

"I don't want to hear about it; but the 'oh'?"

"Well, if he had his arm around me, I can't have been among the ones who cried 'oh': because they were shouting 'oh' at me, not at Mr. Mueller."

"Today at one you will show me a letter of apology addressed to Mr. Mueller, and signed by all of you, or Mrs. Wenzel shall get you!"

Emily, with a gesture of horror, promised to compose the apology on a specially purchased sheet of letter paper adorned with a picture and motto.

Going into service at the Willerts' was as good as life insurance; consequently the choice of applicants was so great, and Mrs. Wenzel's selection was made with such care, that no plain, clumsy, or gossipy girl ever came into the household. She who was once accepted and not exchanged after the two weeks' trial period belonged to the aristocracy of her kind; hence the self-assurance and the lack of discipline.

Elizabeth ate her oatmeal, and clipped together the letter and envelope of the day's second unpleasant surprise. Dorothy Kersting, née Thiess, had been heard from for the first time in ten years, and once more on the same business.

At that time—the Willerts' little daughter had just been born, Peggy had captured Hesse, and Jacob was drinking bosom friendship at Wernicke's with the carefree Alexander—Dorothy, the former milkmaid, had come to see the Madam in town, wearing peasant costume presumably on purpose, to beg forgiveness for her guilt, and "to put an end to this shame." She did not fall at the splendid Elizabeth's feet —her costume and the kerchief instead of a hat were humiliation enough. One saw by her clenched hands that the trip had been hard for her to make. Well, she said, she had not seen Mr. Jacob since his engagement, in fact, even longer than that, this she would swear to; anyway, if it hadn't been her, it would have been somebody else; rich gentlemen——

"I'm not reproaching you for anything, Mrs. Kersting!"

"But this shame has got to stop," moaned Dorothy. She had already quite crushed a lace handkerchief—perhaps one left over from Jacob's day?

"There's no shame about it," Elizabeth had said, "if my husband treats the farmers who are his clients. His father Melchior used to do it too."

"But the farmers don't believe in his 'cultivating the clients.' They think my own husband is offering——"

"Is selling you to Jacob? Why, that's ridiculous!" the daughter of the Sparangapanis had replied with hauteur.

"Not to the farmers that look at me like . . . like someone no better than she should be," said the victim of these insults, beginning to sob.

Elizabeth, with the comforting assurance that the other woman who could have been Mrs. Willert was grievously punished by having her handsome Alexander, promised to "forbid" her husband's drinking and treating at Wernicke's. That was that, and Jacob went on in his old way.

That night he had read the President's letter through very carefully three times; and he thought he found in it a complement to the "Incomplete Accounting," as in fact all the old man's recent utterances, even the governmental decrees, had taken on the character of retrospection and defense. But he found nothing to discountenance or contradict the speech that he had already worked out for the Senate.

Lying in bed with a satisfied smile, he came to the realization that a complete accounting was probably not possible in the world; for Adam Faust had not touched anywhere in his letter upon the great and important aspect of life to which his Senate speech was to be devoted.

At midnight he put on trousers and slippers, waked Andersen, the house steward, and sent him with a message to Arnold Mueller, the supervisor of the Senate chancellery: Jacob Willert would give up his two motions, but wished to make a statement, in his capacity as head of the Conservative Party, on the Marienhall Labor Decree, which had been publicly attacked.

Jacob awoke with pleasure, locked away the President's letter, and Elizabeth could tell from his greeting, "Morning, old lady!" that he was in a triumphant mood. Thereupon she hurled the "confectioner's daughter" at him.

He squinted as if to study her carefully: "Well, aren't you?"

"But we were making almond paste in Venice while you people were still eating with your knives and wiping them off on your trousers."

The banker, eating prunes and a slice of toast, remained perfectly cool: "They were leather breeches, Lizzy."

To pierce this lofty amiability she had to think up something improper: "Why, they smell bad," she cried, wrinkling her nose.

"Naturally leather breeches stink. Are you trying to spoil my good humor?"

"Why do you complain to Messerschmidt that you married a confectioner's daughter? Weren't you even going to marry a milkmaid? There! Please answer that one yourself!" And she handed him Dorothy's letter.

He pushed it aside: "Quiet down, now, Lizzy, and tell me what she wants."

"She wants you to put an end to this shame, and never to consort with Alexander Kersting again. If you do it anyway, she's going to take her son George and leave the house."

"What does this mean? I can't see it," said Jacob. "Is she forgetting that I set up her brother Charles Thiess in business, and paid for Elspeth's education? She ought to get a good hiding for being ungrateful."

"She wants to keep her house clean, Jack."

"I've been hearing that twaddle for twenty years now, but if I let go of Kersting he's done for! He can't even pay the interest on the second mortgage that old Schmalz gave him."

"At any rate, Dorothy has more sense of honor in her than you have."

"Pride, you mean she has in her—but she'll come around yet! I can see her just crawling—after her scheme blows up. Do you know what she imagines?"

"No, but please don't think anything up!"

"She thinks Hesse will marry her Elspeth, and she can drive a coach and four in her old age as the Police General's mother-in-law. That's what she imagines, and that's why she wrote the letter!"

Elizabeth raised her shoulders: "Have you any objections to Elspeth's marrying Hesse?"

"He can't marry her, because he's already sleeping with the other one, von Brick's daughter."

"I once heard somewhere that it had been known to happen," she retorted, looking excessively ironical, "for somebody to sleep with someone and marry the other one."

"Do you mean me, by any chance?"

"Heaven forfend, I never had any doubt of you," said his wife so sanctimoniously that Jacob himself had to laugh.

There was an agreement of about a year's standing that as soon as von Brick had resigned his office, and the Senate had confirmed Hesse's appointment as his successor, the formal engagement of our youngest general should be announced. The Senate as at present constituted could not, it is true, be expected to confirm Hesse as Federal Commissioner: Urban's coalition still held together against the "well-known madman," and the Clique of intimates as well as von Brick, though from different motives, were racking their brains for some way to break it up.

There was a knock; the redheaded Frenchwoman and the child Elizabeth, freshly washed, sweet, and saucy, came in to breakfast. "The story, the story!" cried the little girl, pushing her way between her father's knees. She knew the story; she knew all the stories he told; but by telling them differently each time, he kept the child's curiosity alive.

"Once there was a peasant's daughter," the father began.

"Wrong! A king's daughter," cried the younger Elizabeth.

"All kings used to be peasants once upon a time, my child; they ate with their knives, and wiped them off on their breeches."

Madame Fallières winked at her charge. "It isn't so at all!" she protested.

"The peasant's daughter refused all suitors. None of them was

handsome enough, not even King Jacob the First, although he possessed great riches."

"Tell your father," said the splendid Elizabeth to the child, "that
King Jacob just thought he was her first."

"Was King Jacob a peasant too?" asked the little girl.

"He was a peasant that had learned to be educated, as you shall
hear in a moment, but you must pay close attention. She made fun of
him, calling him Thrush-Beard. At this Thrush-Beard went to her
father, and the kings whispered together secretly. The following day
the father of the peasant's daughter summoned the monarch's inner
council, and asked what should be done to anyone who humbles the
child of another. 'He shall be humbled himself,' replied the Academy
of Twelve. And so the peasant's daughter was declared guilty of one
of the four great vices, and her punishment was decided. What are
the four great vices?"

Madame Fallières' mouth and nostrils gaped, and she looked at
Jacob as if to seduce him on the spot. The child gave her governess a
nudge in the ribs.

"Cruelty, malice, pride, unfaithfulness," Jacob answered himself.
"What vice was the peasant king's daughter guilty of?"

"Talk so the child can understand you," said Mrs. Willert.

"Pride," cried the child, "because she made fun of the king and gave
him a silly name."

Old John Huebner, sticking his head in at the door, announced that
the carriage was outside.

"Madame Fallières will tell you how the proud girl was punished,
and how she was finally rewarded for submitting to being humbled,"
said the Senator, going out.

BECAUSE HANS SIMON WAS MINDFUL OF PUNISHMENT

XI

THE so-called "reactionary extension" of the Mining Law, putting the Proprietors' Court in the foreground, had been presented, it will be remembered, by Jacob Willert, and later, he having left the city of Geisenheim because of the Perlotta scandal, it was approved by the assembled colliers. Scarcely two months later, the beneficial effects began to be felt all over the mountain province. The previously mistrustful industrialists and the smaller mine owners recognized the Mining Law as binding upon themselves, and applied for membership in the League of Carpenters.

Thus both the Red revolutionists and the Yellow economic peace-makers vanished from the mountain province: henceforward both, of necessity, hated the Marienhall Labor Decree, with its preferment of the Proprietors' Court and its postponement of strikes, as a bull hates a red rag. To Urban and the Reds the words "league" and "brotherhood" signified worldly associations with definite and strictly limited aims. The Urbanites and the Red unions, in order to underline their worldliness, called themselves progressive and scoffed at the Carpenters as "backward people" and "praying brethren." There was honesty in the Urbanites' opposition to the way of living reflected in the Carpenters' Rule, which began with the same words Adam Faust had used for one of his inscriptions: "For if a power or an order does not sanctify itself, how shall it hope to survive?" The "enlighteners" at that time, the Schieles, Heidemanns, Perlottas, and in front of them the Urban followers, could not see any meaning in the word "sanctify," so they called it a word ruin from the Middle Ages misused by our great sharks as a weapon in their fight against "inevitable progress." And, indeed, the brotherhoods of Carpenters, although they didn't call themselves "Christian" or "religious," were built up exactly in the way laid down by the late Bishop Hesse in his last letter to his son.

They assembled in chapels or churches, and there was a "reciprocal flow and commingling" of business matters and divine service, "of worship and discussion, of choral singing and reports in the line of duty."

What a strange behavior! The Urbanites could understand this as little as they could the calls of birds or the roar of the surf. For in Geisenheim the Mountain Chapel was the place of assembly for the brotherhoods; in Marienhall the Mine Courthouse; in the pit region, the administration buildings, where their rooms were those of the Board of Directors. If it was a league matter, they wore the costume of the Carpenters, without the badge embroidered inside their coats, which was reserved for the Federal Police, and could be bestowed on those who (like Tobias Witt) had distinguished themselves in the secret service. Hurried movements, quick speech, strong expressions, and attempts to drag out proceedings or to confuse an issue by talking were considered unseemly. On the other hand—which shows how hard it is to describe these quiet and passionate gatherings —there were strong expressions used, in fact very strong expressions whose use was ordained, for which reason the gatherings were indeed free of quarrels, but not always free of anger, and accordingly not without passion.

For example, the discharge of a workman or office employee was not called a discharge, but "casting out from the community": a very strong expression, but one not used after the fashion of party orators to strengthen their *language,* but to proclaim the simple fact, recorded in the Mining Law, that discharge was a right neither of the proprietors nor of the colliers, but a league concern, something rare and terrible—exactly what the expression signified, a casting out from the community of brotherhoods.

Accordingly, the hiring of a workman was called "reception into the community," another expression that sounds strong to our ears, but exactly states the fact; for according to the Mining Law the hiring of any person employed in mining must be exclusively a concern of the league, because the applicant had to swear to support the "Rule," and to be ranked in the community by the "Committee for the Ceremonies."

One might, incidentally, have supposed that this committee would be cautious in accepting a member, weighing and testing him carefully, since, once employed, he could not be discharged again, but only cast out. This, however, was not the case—quite the contrary! Admission, including the colliers' oath, required ten minutes; casting out, as many weeks; and anyone who resisted could drag out the process almost as long as he pleased, always supposing he had not been convicted of crime. After the smaller mine proprietors had taken oath under the League Ordinance, admission was everywhere the same: anyone who came to a pit head looking for work was simply searched for weapons by the gatekeeper, and directed without so much as a single question to the "House of Ceremonies," which must not be imagined as a splendid edifice, but as a three-room wooden shack, where (if we take the Johanna Mine as a model) two Carpenters were at work: one representing the proprietors, the other a collier or pit inspector, and both together constituting the Committee for the Ceremonies. The applicant was asked his calling; if he had none, no matter. His papers were taken from him; if he had none, no matter again. No matter whether he were ragged, sick, one-armed, an escaped convict, or a fugitive from the hills, he took the oath, the two league functionaries (at the Johanna Mine, Heinz, the office manager, the son of the commander of the Federal Police South Section, and the old pit inspector, Lange) congratulated him on being received, and said the rest would follow in due course. If he was not a miner, the Home and the employment office of the Carpenters awaited him, and under constant observation for at least a fortnight he learned the "Rule" and the "Life"; not until then did he choose his occupation, and the league, with branches all over the country, found him a job. To begin with, however, and for at least a year—until the "Feast of Initiation," the day when he was permitted to don the black costume—he had to content himself with a novice job, that is, work in a plant employing at least thirty hands; and he knew that his fellow workmen were Carpenters who were trying his heart. Accordingly we see that the Carpenter whom Mrs. Wenzel supplied as a farm hand to Alexander Kersting in an earlier chapter cannot have been a novice, since he was allowed to work alone.

The blithe way in which the Committee for the Ceremonies accepted new members was, obviously, no accident, but a matter of rule most vigorously insisted on by Andrew Zorn: "He who applies, knocks," say the secret rules for admission, "and no matter who may knock, to him it shall be unquestioningly opened come what may. There are no reasons for rejection of an applicant. The moment that you directly or indirectly put obstacles in the way of acceptance, let alone make them depend on the applicant's qualifications or fees, the league of brotherhoods will begin to decline."

The very wording of this rule, the "knock" and "it shall be opened," indicate its religious origin: a free and unlimited welcome is to ring out for him who knocks. You, an aspirant, are sick and crippled? Come, you shall be occupied. You, an aspirant, are a murderer and burglar? Come, you shall be cured. You, an aspirant, would rather beg than work? Come, beg for yourself and the brethren!

This was what Andrew Zorn meant, and this was what the Carpenters understood; but for the Conservatives the "negligent" method of reception also had a political background. They were playing for the runaways from the south. If nothing was required of the aspirant, no personal history, no profession of faith, not even personal identification; if the poorest and dirtiest could be received, solely on the basis of the promise whose terms we have already stated, into a brotherhood that all the provincial governors and the President himself belonged to; then the harvest workers brought across the frontier every year by Lienhardt's and Oriola's agents were offered a very strong temptation to seek the hills and make their way to the region of Geisenheim. For the great agricultural estates in the south were still fortresses, arsenals, recruiting areas quite impossible to keep track of, for Urban's civil-war army; and Gregory William Lienhardt, the middle brother and chief heir to the huge fortune after the shameful death of John Theodoric by Kate's hand, the same Gregory William under whom Urban had begun his career as an estate manager, showed an unexpected skill as a military organizer. His managers did not carry riding whips; there were no more beatings in the south, and armed employees no longer lay in wait at night for those who took to the hills: wages in kind and the food and lodging, on the other hand, were improved, the free beer flowed during the "jolly evenings," and the chief went around shaking hands, surrounded by affably smiling officers of the Sports Troop. More than this, the village police departments, now taken over by the Carpenters, had ascertained that the foreign harvest laborers did not go home at the expiration of their contracts, but stayed here and sent for their families. Anyone who could not or would not find work on the estates was placed in the plants engaged in the eastern food industries, which were favorably inclined toward Urban—or Borstel's armament and munition factories! There was at that time no legal means of preventing unwanted immigration, and a bill introduced for that purpose had no prospect of success with the Senate constituted as it was after the second general election. The son of the cousin whom Bishop Oriola hated now held the rank of general under Urban. What was there left to do except to grab away the customers from him and Lienhardt? Every police headquarters in the south had posters on the wall the year around: "The League of Carpenters accepts everyone! Nearest induction station, Homeland Tavern, Geisenheim."

The Carpenters regarded lightly the danger of thus accepting numerous secret agents and terrorists of Urban's into the mining communities and brotherhoods, so great was their confidence in their own ability either to transform or to unmask the novice. The Academy of Twelve, asked for a report, gave the following opinion: among the Urbanite agents who crept into the "league of autonomous brotherhoods" disguised as runaways, two categories must be distinguished, the very large one of the "convinced," and the numerically weak but extremely dangerous one of "natural Yellows." By natural Yellow was understood a man who had not been driven by circumstances or his so-called environment, much as he might talk about the latter, to join the Urbanite movement, but rather by his inborn and ineradicable character. "In the character of the natural Yellow, malice predominates —that is, pleasure in the suffering of one's neighbor, and a craving to inspire fear in him, as well as to witness the fear inspired; it predominates so strongly over all other spiritual characteristics that one may say, even if the malicious person never falls afoul of the law, that malice nevertheless governs his behavior throughout life.

"The Scriptures refer to this character when they speak of the 'children of darkness,' and the opposite one when they speak of the 'children of light.' For by comparison with malice all other bad characteristics pale into ridiculous insignificance: it is the primal evil, and cruelty is not worse, but simply malice in action. Consequently the average man is more terrified of malice than of anything else whatsoever, and the natural Yellow, i.e., the man born with malice (religious ages would have said, *of* malice), in order to escape being killed, must deny his own nature throughout his life, and constantly wear the mask of contemplation, of disinterest, even of kindness and pity. Hesse's address to the squadrons describes the natural Yellow, or primitive evil, with absolute accuracy: the scream of the victim is indeed the paradise of malice, and the man of malice himself is the evildoer who—for the reason just cited—'does not commit his crime,' but who keeps on his mask.

"For eighteen years Christian education, first of the high officials and army commanders, then of the whole people, has kept this one goal constantly in view: to teach people to see through the masks of malice. Accordingly, the Academy believes that the Carpenters will be able to discover the natural Yellows among the Urbanite agents who creep in as novices. They are to be delivered up to the lunatic villages.

"We regard the other categories of traitors, those who are merely *convinced* of Urban's 'paradise of the future,' as harmless. Life in the brotherhood will soon overwhelm them, and they will then be useful in disclosing Urban's methods."

Thus the Academy. But the poor population of cottage workers, weavers, and small farmers on the mountain slope beyond our southern frontier, although they swarmed in upon us, were too thoroughly humble and crushed to abandon the Lienhardts (now that they had hidden the whip and brought out the sugar candy) and follow the call of the Carpenters. They re-enforced Urban's army by a quarter of a million men, and in the days of decision they paid for the free beer, the bands, and the jollity with their blood.

A change had taken place in Adam Faust himself, and in the generals, provincial governors, and judges of Andrew Zorn's school, though not until the second Senatorial election which had proved so advantageous to Urban. Once they had confidence in man's nature, which they thought Christian in spite of all—*Humana mens naturaliter christiana* had been Frohwein's and Bishop Hesse's unshakable conviction. Now, however, they believed that Daruhi's "fog" sprang from the mistrust of neighbor for neighbor, that is, from forlornness, while the misery was due to liberalism and its base watchword, *"Laissez faire, laissez aller!"* It would therefore be necessary only to set an unmistakably serious example of Christian behavior, through state and government, and the simple man would enthusiastically follow, proving his "Christian nature." No one, they thought, could resist the Christian captain who protected the weak and showed a mailed fist to the insolent and unscrupulous.

If this calculation was correct, then the most defenseless of the poor, the farm laborers who were being transported across our frontier, must take to the hills in swarms and join the league of Carpenters, which latter was after all merely the conservative ideal commonwealth in daily practice, or "the Faust system in action."

But the very opposite took place: it was not the poorest, but rather the best-paid workmen, the printers, compositors, precision mechanics, machinists, and turners, those who were closest to craftsmanship, who formed the heart of the Carpenters' league, or at least supported it when they could not bring themselves to join outright a Christian brotherhood on account of their dislike for "horse collars." As "independents" under Hildebrand's leadership they made common cause in peace and civil war with the Carpenters, and it may truthfully be said that the long-organized aristocrats of labor were the first to understand the idea of brotherhood or the Faust system; the very poorest, on the other hand, fell a prey to Urban. The same was true of the middle class; an intellectually honest and courageous minority followed Faust and his Archbishop; the majority longed for the tyrant.

Had the optimists been wrong in dreaming that the soul of man, though "enmeshed in the bonds of Satan," was Christian at the core, that is, capable of recognizing and hating evil? In the eighteenth year of the President's term, pessimism spread among his intimates: blood must flow, was their opinion, and Frohwein, profoundly as he loathed civil war, gave Generals Kaempf and Hesse a free hand in their preparations for the conflict.

Jacob Willert remained an optimist to the last, through deep repugnance for civil war; his appeal to the ruling class of the country, spoken before the Senate in defense of the "reactionary extension" of the Mining Law that he had brought about, went as follows:

"When freedom disappears from men's hearts, which is the only place you find it, not in printed labor decrees, wage contracts, and constitutions, then, and in fact before then, candor disappears; and if a candid man does say something, people stare at him stupidly as if he were talking Chinese. Since he is not understood, he becomes the object of hatred. Thus there was stupid staring in the high-toned papers and magazines when a poor man, the miner Lewis Lange, speaking on behalf of the miners and colliers at Geisenheim, replied to my motion requiring all disputes to be brought first before the Proprietors' Court: 'We approve the motion of our brother in the league, Jacob Willert, because it gives to the gentlemen who excel in wealth an opportunity to distinguish themselves by their justice.'

"In reply to the vituperation that was immediately unloosed upon me and the supposedly terrorized Lange, I would say that my 'preferment of the Proprietors' Court' was meant exactly as the spokesman of the miners understood it.

"Yes indeed: sure, as I am, that justice is even more attractive of emulation that injustice, I put the proprietors in the front rank so that they alone, segregated and thus the more plainly in the public view, might testify before all men that they are resolved to survive the coming deluge of blood. That is the meaning of the so-called 'reactionary extension' which I introduced into the Marienhall Labor Decree. The proprietors are not to have some dispute presented to them only after the colliers and conciliators have chewed it fine. That would imply that our own justice has dull teeth. No, the matter must be flung to us fresh, raw, and hard, so that we shall not get out of practice, shall not fail to practice a selfless—no, not selfless, very selfish —conservative kind of justice: a justice aimed at our own preservation. 'For if a power or an order does not sanctify itself, how shall it hope to survive?'

"That, then, is the meaning which the unschooled pit inspector, Lange, grasped at once, whereas the 'high-toned and deep-thinking gentlemen' never grasped it at all.

"And there is in it another meaning, which Mr. Lange also understood, but omitted to mention out of politeness. For if I, being appointed to judge and decide, that is, to rule, in a circle no matter how small, do not look beyond that circle, do not hear the hanging bell, but stand with both feet on things of this world, weighing my own advantage and loss, I cannot preserve my earthly gains; the flame of justice will devour them tomorrow or the day after.

"By now I have already uttered this thought so often that I am beginning to desire the arrival of the day of justice lest I appear a fool. Yes, if some day the sky should turn red, and the force of justice should devour my house, still I would rejoice: 'Didn't I say so? How can a house stand that is founded on guilt? How can a family survive that wants only to live, caring nothing for the survival of its own family and its own business?' The blockheads have always believed they would survive if they smashed justice for the sake of a calculable advantage: but justice smashed them, and their indestructible stupidity was all that they saved from the ruins. For if you ask them who smashed their happiness, they can invent endless accusations, but they themselves are never at fault; many unfortunate circumstances, they say, contributed; but I have never heard them say that justice contributed.

"There is, then, a second meaning: the meaning that I fear the punishment to come. I fear that God may seek out some hand, red, yellow, or colorless, to punish me for neglecting justice. I am saying this so that in case I should be chosen for destruction my Red or Yellow friends may not think it was they who struck the blow. These gentlemen will never be victorious, unless by my own behavior I provoke their victory and my own annihilation."

At this point in the speech Mr. Susemihl, on the Urbanite benches, unable longer to restrain the flow of poetry, interrupted the head of the Conservative Party, crying out:

> For still the new transcends the old
> In signs and tokens manifold;
> Slaves rise up men: the olive waves,
> With roots deep set in battle graves!

Jacob Willert went on as if he had heard nothing: "For the inscrutable God looks upon the guilty, with fixed eyes He gazes upon the guilty; but the weapon that He wields to strike them down He does not look at. More than once He allowed the people He called His chosen ones to be struck down—by criminals a thousand times worse than the stricken people. Did He mean to lift up the criminals? No, He never saw them: He saw only the guilty that He had lifted up, and He cast them down.

"So He is looking upon me, for He has lifted me up: and if in His eyes I am guilty, then even a Communist or Urbanite hand may lay me low, a hand so dirty and so bloody that beside it my own is white as snow.

"How ridiculous, then, Mr. Susemihl, to suppose that the dead of battle fall so that the olive may wave above them! No: because they were ripe for His wrath He smote them down, and He would have smitten them down though He had known that the pestilence would spring from the graves.

"For thinking of advantages or losses—that is, of the consequences springing from an action—may be proper for a man who is only a merchant and nothing more, whether he sells stockings or opinions: but it is proper for the great man to think of the punishment!

"That is why I nominated Hans Simon, the banker, as a candidate for the Academy of Twelve and secured his election—because he alone was mindful of the punishment to come. By the fact that he punished Perlotta without regard for the natural consequence, namely a loss to himself of almost 200,000 thalers, by his incorruptible eye for what has happened, and by his contempt of the future, Hans Simon has shown that he is qualified to rise to the rank of the inner council. Looking into the future instead of the past is the wisdom of the salons and their moralists still wet behind the ears, of the sensation-hungry who must adorn their inconsequence and boredom with a touch of class struggle and revolution before the curtain falls.

"A word about the attitude of the papers toward the case of Roland Perlotta. It is just like our *Town and Country Intelligencer* to assert that Mr. Simon drove the 'pioneer of progress' and 'father of the oppressed' out of town because he himself wanted to enter the Academy of Twelve, not because Perlotta had behaved dishonorably. That is the ageless recourse of punished fools to wash themselves clean: they denounce the hand that punishes them. But there can be no washing clean. He who is cast down into the abyss does not prove that someone was lying in wait for him, but only that he has committed a crime. If *I* should be cast down—it may be that I shall not have strength to rejoice at the onset of justice, but this much is sure: whatever time I may have left to think, I shall not think about the little dodges and tricks by which I might have warded off the blow, but of the crimes committed by me!

"Not that I wish for my own downfall! Oh, I can wait. I will gladly wait a thousand years, and in my desire to postpone the vengeance to come I address this appeal to my peers. I would like to forestall Providence by thinking of my crimes before I commit them: I would like to think of the wrath before I provoke it. I see no other way of post-poning the punishment.

"I too am a reader of the Scriptures. It appears to me that the Lord God cannot wait to overthrow those whom He has lifted up, and that He never takes His eyes from them, whereas He pays less heed to the poor. My friends and companions in the rank of masters, of em-ployers, of the exalted—for he who can arrange his work as he pleases, who can give himself holidays and pay, *is* exalted, there can be no doubt of that—let us take thought for self-preservation, confronted as we are with the perilous nearness of God or of just retribution. It was not to overreach anyone, rich or poor, but to forward the survival of the accustomed order, since this order is the last that still has an interest in freedom—that was why I introduced the 'reactionary extension' into the Marienhall Labor Decree."

This speech, regarded as a warning from the President's party to the steel- and ironmasters, who were wavering toward Urban, created a panic on the stock exchange. Civil war, people said, was at the door. Not until six months had passed without any alarming occur-rences, except the Simon calumniation trial, was tranquillity restored.

BOOK TWO

TWO PERJURIES

XII

AT THE legal proceedings conducted by the President's favor-ite jurist, the dry, thin-faced, bespectacled Holzkopf, there was an outcry worthy of a kindergarten. The witnesses accused one another of having been coached in the halls, and also of bribery, perjury, domestic vices, or dipsomania; the de-fendant yelled at the State's Attorney, and the counsel for the litigants exchanged spiteful repartee. And all this without any objection from Supreme Court Justice Holzkopf for impairing the dignity of the court.

Abruptly he would order silence, break off the proceedings, with-

draw to his chambers with the assessors or the jurors, and try to discover whether his colleagues or, as the case might be, the jurors had
learned to interpret the behavior of the defendants or the litigants, dis-
tinguishing the "false shouts" from the genuine ones. He said this
technique was the only possible one in times when oaths were despised
and every defendant was aiming solely at "swearing his way out": he
had learned it himself in those most difficult of all trials, paternity and
support suits, when the truth is obscured by veritable squadrons of
lies. In order to get at the truth, he said, either the oath as evidence
or the dignity of the court had to be sacrificed; and the latter was
grievously damaged in any case by the innumerable perjuries as well
as the outcry of the parties. A judge, he declared, who allowed himself
to be confused by the noise and gesticulations of the quarreling parties,
instead of catching the glint of truth precisely in these spontaneous
outbursts, had no true gift for the judicial office.

Holzkopf did not preside over any legal district of his own, but
was employed as presiding justice all over the country whenever a case
seemed particularly complicated or likely to excite public interest.
Hence his appearance in Simon's trial for calumniation (although
Adam Faust was originally against it, and had to be warned by the
Twelve not to overdo his concern for the future). Holzkopf himself
had told the Academy the case was perfectly clear and perfectly hopeless; all he could do was reduce the minimum penalty by a few
months.

On the last day of the court proceedings the great Hall of Assizes
was so overcrowded that law students stood on the broad window sills
of the long hall to listen. By the windows in the long wall at the left
of the judges' bench sat the defamed Mark Antony Perlotta, near his
lawyers, Tadd and Pole, and the State's Attorney, a man still young
who reputedly belonged to Urban's party. The trial indicated that he
was not actually in any camp.

As Holzkopf was presiding, the parties had to be separated, prefer-
ably so far that they could not see the whites of each other's eyes, lest
their "outbursts of truth" should take a violent form. Accordingly, the
Perlotta tribe sat along the wall by the windows, where their witnesses,
Diana Rose, Mrs. Professor Habermann, and the former merchandise
inspector, Emil, were also seated. Opposite them, along the wall running into the hall, with the sun shining disagreeably in his face as he

sat on the defendants' bench, was Hans Simon; close beside him on the witnesses' bench was Elsie Ackermann, with Simon's attorney, Odo Sparangapani, the splendid Elizabeth's brother. The hall was paneled in brown clear to the ceiling.

In the space for spectators, shut off by a wooden barrier, a silence as tense as if the thunderstorm were already over their heads had prevailed during the testimony. Holzkopf seemed inclined to evade this by passing over, not seeing, and not taking the testimony of Emil, the enormous witness for the defense, who had on a freshly pressed suit.

Finally the presiding judge rose, asked the two chief witnesses to come forward, and addressed them thus: "It is my duty, Mrs. Professor Habermann and Miss Diana Rose, to draw your attention to the sanctity of oaths and the punishment that will befall the perjurer. For the purjurer, though he may triumph at first, will not escape his punishment, Miss Diana Rose; and a hand hidden from the outset has already fixed the time and place of punishment. If you wish to revoke or alter your testimony, this is the last moment. For that reason I will recall the main points to your minds; but you still have time to say, 'No, it was not like that.' You, Diana Rose, during the time in question, two years ago, were the manager of the theater department at Koenig Publications. You occasionally, but rarely, came in contact with the magazine department of the same firm, of which Mrs. Professor Habermann is still manager. You, Miss Diana Rose, bought Perlotta's comedy *Secretary Kreisler* as early as March sixteenth for the theater department; you, on the other hand, Mrs. Professor Habermann, did not acquire Ackermann's comedy *In the Middle of the Night* until two full months later, on May sixteenth, and in view of the similarity between the two plays you would have been put off buying Ackermann's work if you had had any idea that Diana Rose had already purchased Perlotta's drama. Do you, Mrs. Frieda Habermann, want to make this statement under oath?"

"Of course," replied that stately lady.

"And you, Miss Rose?"

"I do, Your Honor."

Then came the first flash of lightning: "Is this here a madhouse or a court of justice?" Elsie Ackermann shouted at the judges. She was wearing the high-buttoned costume of the female Carpenters, with her confirmation cross hanging around her neck; her pretty face was gray, beads of foam clung to the corners of her mouth, and she clutched the railing of the witness box.

The State's Attorney's pince-nez fell from his nose: "Unheard of! The witness Ackermann dares——"

"This is contempt of court," interrupted lawyer Tadd, and Pole added: "For which any other witness would get three days!"

Tadd, in turn, with a sidelong glance of scorn at Holzkopf: "Naturally the wife of the police poet can do anything she likes——"

"Under this particular presiding justice!" added Pole.

The State's Attorney's mind was made up: "I move that the witness Elsie Ackermann receive some nominal sentence for repeated misconduct in court."

According to regulations the presiding justice should have said something to this, but he was standing perfectly quietly, watching the jurors to be sure each one was trying to distinguish the genuine cries from the false. The silence grew so unbearable that a derisive voice was heard from the spectators' benches:

It's raining, it's pouring,
The old man's snoring!

A true Holzkopfian tumult immediately ensued. Elsie Ackermann, recognizing the songstress among the spectators as a particularly odious enemy of hers, screamed at the presiding justice: "That's Ruth Westen —she means you, Mr. Justice! That public woman meant you!"

Lawyer Tadd: "Public woman? That's a suit for defamation! If this goes on, the witness Ackermann will talk the shirt off her own back!"

"I could show myself without a shirt, but you couldn't, you unwashed pettifogger!" screamed Elsie.

Pole: "That's enough. The whole court has heard the witness Ackermann call counselor Dr. Tadd a dirty pettifogger."

Elsie: "Want me to say it again, you abominable guttersnipe?"

At last Holzkopf reached for his bell: "That's enough, now, Mrs. Ackermann!"

"No, it isn't enough," cried Lawyer Pole, outraged at the presiding justice; "it isn't enough for her! For a sense of honor is battling on our side, impudence on the other; the idealism of a great civilized nation on this side, the money-grubbing of a great bank on the other; the freedom and justice of a world dramatist on our side, yonder the dirty ambition of a schoolteacher named Ackermann who was thrown out of the profession for immorality; here is the Iron Phalanx of our intelligence, yonder the infernal pit of hatred for progress, and the mercenary scribblers of the Hesse police corps!"

There was loud clapping. Pole bent down to Tadd's ear, and asked: "How's that for telling them?"

"Beautiful!" replied Tadd, rocking his head from side to side.

The presiding justice and his two assessors put on their caps, and all those present rose from their seats.

Diana Rose and Mrs. Habermann were sworn as witnesses; Elsie Ackermann sobbed like a child with the hiccups; Hans Simon reached across the low barrier of the defendant's seat to stroke her hair: "Head high, Mrs. Ackermann!"

But Tadd heard him: "The defendant is attempting to influence one of the witnesses!" Pole: "What a state of affairs!"

At very long last, Simon's attorney, Odo Sparangapani, arose: "I move that the court question the witness Emil, to whom the witness Diana Rose made a confession while she was still living with him."

Again the Ackermann woman cut in, and a quarrel ensued: "He beat the confession out of her!"

Diana: "I guess you got a worse beating from your husband, you old slut! She couldn't go out of the house for three days!"

Elsie: "That's a different matter, because the law says: 'It is permissible for a husband to administer moderate chastisement.' Was Emil by any chance your *husband*, Miss Diana? He's a little thick, of course, but not as thick as that!"

Holzkopf: "That really doesn't concern us here, Mrs. Ackermann."

Diana: "It certainly does concern us, Your Honor, because a confession that anybody beats out of me is surely not worth the paper it's written on."

"Please put an end to this exchange," said Holzkopf. "The witness Emil!"

Emil, impressive in his fresh suit, got to his feet: "Gentlemen! May it please the court! In the campaign of the Perlotta brothers against Banker Simon I wish to declare my neutrality."

"You are not here to declare anything, witness Emil," the presiding justice instructed him, "but to give your testimony—or refuse to give it."

This, however, was Emil's moment to be pacific: "I lift up my voice on behalf of peace. Peaceful, peaceful, we adore thee, as the poet says. Man's striving is wicked from childhood onward. He who cannot forget stands condemned out of his own mouth."

The State's Attorney said in a sharp voice: "I request that the court put an end to this vaporing."

"You will have observed, Mr. State's Attorney," replied Holzkopf with great courtesy, "that I never put an end to any vaporing, so that the jurors may make up their own minds as to the true character of those concerned—that is, as to the value of their testimony. For true character emerges from vaporings."

At this Elsie Ackermann screamed for the last time, pointing in Emil's direction: "That fellow's been paid!"

The State's Attorney, pale with rage, and smiling: "The person who shouts admits himself in the wrong, Mrs. Ackermann. The person who shouts is trying to shout down justice. The person who feels himself in the right is perfectly quiet, does not constantly interrupt, is courteous, modest, and sure of himself. For justice is triumphant."

The author's wife gave him a good answer: "No, Mr. State's Attorney: dissimulation is courteous, hypocrisy charms by its modesty, thievery whispers. But wounded justice roars!"

There was applause, and the presiding justice turned to the witness: "If I'm not mistaken, Mrs. Ackermann, you wanted to ask the witness Emil a question."

"Yes, Your Honor, a very important question," Elsie said, and leaning toward the Lion of Afghanistan: "What do you mean, 'He who cannot forget stands condemned out of his own mouth'? Does that by any chance mean that you have forgotten Diana's confession?"

"Yes, that's what it means, Mrs. Ackermann," replied Emil, not looking at her. "I refuse to testify because I've forgotten the confession."

"But she hasn't forgotten the beating, you blockhead," roared the writer's wife, "nor that you threw her out on the street with one suitcase in the middle of the night. She's vowed vengeance upon you, that I know, and no matter what else she may forget, like paying for

what she buys at stores, she won't forget her revenge, not if she lives
to be a hundred. If you had any sense, you'd testify here, and smash
her with twenty words—but you haven't any sense, and this is going
to end badly."

Elsie had apparently exhausted her strength. She huddled down on
her bench and wept. Holzkopf, indicating regret with a motion of his
forearms, arose and announced: "The taking of testimony is completed.
There will be a recess of fifteen minutes, and then the pleadings will
begin."

The court attendant opened the doors to the public part of the courtroom.

In a little room for counsel on the corridor, meanwhile, Jacob Willert
was awaiting his brother-in-law. Odo came in, said, "Nothing to be
done!" and sat down by the table.

"Can we make his stretch in prison any easier for him?" asked the
banker.

"That we can. Holzkopf is by no means stupid, and he's a good
fellow. You should make him director of the Penal Bureau."

"Who can do it?"

"The President, on application from the Senate Judiciary Committee."

"I'll see to it. Will they arrest him right away?"

"I don't think so. Holzkopf will give him from three to five days
to put his affairs in order."

"See you later!" Jacob went out. Lawyer Sparangapani plunged into
a brown study, and did not hear the shrill sound of the bell summoning him to present his arguments before the jury.

Lawyer Tadd stuck his head in at the door: "It's time for you,
Counselor."

"Yes. Mr. Tadd, would you be good enough to tell the court that
I'm not going to sum up? I don't want to hold up the machinery.
I shan't hold it up again." And, after a long pause: "I'm going to
retire."

"Quite crazy," thought Tadd, closing the door.

A REAL GOLD WATCH

XIII

IT WAS a very ordinary, gray, foggy-smelling fall morning. The bells jangled through gray corridors broken by iron doors, corridors so long that the walls finally met like parallels at infinity. This meant "Get up!" for the convicts at the Federal Penitentiary: on with trousers, on with shoes, clean the cell. If the cell isn't shining like new by seven o'clock, there'll be no breakfast.

The lazier felons, indeed, thought, To hell with breakfast! Those fat gray slices of bread and marmalade, and that slop that they call coffee—it was never even in the same bed with coffee. And speaking of beds, if my old woman had give me any breakfast like that, I'd have pounded her good and proper! But when they have an inspection here, and some swell asks me, "How's the food?" I have to answer, "Good and plentiful," or the guard busts me one afterward!

Such were the thoughts of Theodore Engel, the senior inmate of Common Cell 19, who had kept watch during a burglary. "Oscar! Henry! Get up off your ears," he shouted. "Cell duty!"

They sat up, the gray, unshaven faces yawned, the feet of those in the top bunks thumped on the floor; they scratched themselves, for despite the semiweekly bug hunt there were bedbugs in the old walls.

"Morning, Teddy!" cried several voices, and Theodore Engel replied, as custom demanded, "Morning, boys!" Blankets, sheets, and bolsters hurtled to the floor, for the straw ticks that you slept on had to be shaken—that was the first step.

Cell duty was always performed by two men, one of whom did the sweeping and dusting, the other the wet scrubbing, with a brush, rag, and a liquid disinfectant that was added to the water. For the moment, all hands were burrowing in the straw ticks (made to open at one end), turning the hollows into mountains, and making the dust fly in all directions; the two on cell duty had no reason to hurry, for until the beds were made, the sheets taut, the woolen blankets freshly tucked in, and the blue-and-white checkered coverlets beveled off at the edges, but as smooth as a table top in the middle, and enough to rejoice the heart of an old top sergeant, there was no use in picking up a broom.

The fat burglar called Oscar was working at the window. He was a gray-haired safecracking specialist, a graduate of many penitentiaries, celebrated for his skill at the cant language and signaling through the cell walls; his need for exercise and activity was so great that the doctor had moved him from solitary confinement to the common cell, where he surpassed all others in bed making, bug hunting, and floor scrubbing. He was respected for his bodily strength, and looked down on because he would do anything for money and had always lived in the lower depths. Whenever his two neighbors, one below and one beside him, talked about some educated subject before going to sleep, his stomach would rebel, and perspiration would break out on his forehead—Borstel the millionaire was in the same situation one step higher up the scale. For a few pence he would do cell duty or wall cleaning for anyone who had got hold of money.

His two neighbors were Long Henry, a swell who was always powdered and smoothly combed, a jewel thief, receiver of stolen goods, and former member of fashionable clubs; and Tobias Witt, the bashful lad, snatched by Hesse's summons, "All hands on deck!" from his recent childless marriage with the dovelike Veronica Froehlich to do his duty to the Order of Carpenters as an "inconspicuous one" for two years. He had eighteen months already behind him; the Federal Penitentiary was his third position. Although he could recite the "story of his crime" without stumbling, his companions mistrusted him and suspected the truth.

In addition to Theodore Engel, the humorous lookout, and the fat burglar with his two educated neighbors, there were only two convicts in the cell: the mail and bank robber, Serge van Panhuis, the Terror of the Night (probably so entitled by his own vanity), somber-looking because of his low forehead, heavy eyebrows, and black hair; and the little "skip," or runaway, Arnold, a pitiable product of an orphanage, whose cheek had been disfigured by the bite of a police dog. Without ever knowing it, this Arnold had reformed both the welfare system and the Penal Bureau; for after he had told his ghastly, story frequently and at great length to Tobias Witt, the agent reported it to Captain Schwann, the head of the secret service, and it was published with the names of the guilty parties in the *Pensive Watchman*. Arnold himself, on his discharge from prison, was given a job as a railway trackwalker. The poor unfortunate had grown up in a world where the showering of slaps, not symbolic but genuine whistling slaps, was a law of nature; in fact, his world was like a hall with no doors, inhabited by slapping men and their victims. Every time he escaped from one slapper—and he slipped out innumerable times from the welfare orphanage where he had been put because his unmarried mother was a drunkard—it was all in vain, for the moment he escaped he would fall into the hands of a still more muscular slapper, as if the Muse of Slaps had been his godmother, or as if Charlie Chaplin had taught him the trick.

All six, stripped to the waist according to regulations, had already washed chest, neck, and head; they had drunk the brown coffee at the battered table, washed their dishes, and the fat burglar was desperately tapping the walls to implore aid, since the entire cell possessed not so much as a penny or a single crumb of tobacco. Just then the familiar keys jingled outside, the warder opened the door, and everyone froze into a posture of salute. Theodore Engel reported: "Common Cell 19, twelve beds, occupied by six convicts, senior inmate Theodore Engel."

The warder tossed a fat bundle of bedclothes, blankets, and dishes into his arms, pushed a tall, asthmatic, and terrified man into the cell with the words, "Just you go on in there now," and shut the heavy iron door.

Hans Simon, already clad in blue prison garb, blinked at the bare, gray-walled room, beds on the right, lavatory, table, and benches on the left: was this what they called "preferential treatment"? Before him stood the men with the chin stubble whom he had only read about in books heretofore; was he to live with these men for a year and a half? Engel tossed the bundle on a vacant bed, and, offended by the fear that was written upon the "educated man's" face, he barked at him: "Don't just stand there like a dummy, man, as if you'd never seen a cell before!"

The fat burglar, over by the cupboard, put down the brush with which he was about to blacken the stove, scrutinized the newcomer from head to foot, and opined ironically: "He's innocent—you can see that to look at him. He came by his three years as innocently as the Virgin came by her baby."

"You're quite right, sir," replied Simon naïvely, at the same time committing a breach of manners, for prisoners never use titles of respect.

Henry, the swell fence with the gleaming hair, raised his brows high, nodded, and said: "Looks like he was a great boor, and never learned no manners. It's still customary for decent people, my man, when anyone comes into the social rooms, he introduces himself by name, profession, and previous record."

"I beg your pardon," whispered Simon.

"There's nothing to pardon here—there's only an *in with you!*" cried the Terror of the Night, as if carried away by fury.

Thereupon Theodore Engel, as senior inmate, restored the honor of the cell: "Shut up there, you dopes! Can't you see the man's afraid? Of course you can't because you've got no eyes in your heads, and no knowledge of human nature in your bellies, and you there, Long Henry, put that scrubbing brush and broom in the cupboard, like they ought to be!"

"*Mr.* Henry!" corrected the swell fence. "Please keep to the subject, and no coarse familiarities!" He put the utensils back in the cupboard, and bowed punctiliously to the newcomer: "Waldo Henry, international jewel thief, former member of the Atlantic Club."

There was resounding laughter as the banker returned the bow. Arnold with the scarred cheek, already losing interest in the reception ceremonies, beckoned Tobias Witt to the table, and took a dirty pack of cards from his pocket.

Now Theodore Engel drew himself up before Simon to instruct him: "I'm the senior inmate here, that's supposed to keep order and everyone has to obey him, see? Anyone doesn't obey, he gets busted one."

"Pleased to know you; my name is Hans Simon," said the banker, bowing for a third time, and by his "swell ways" bringing upon himself the displeasure of the Terror of the Night: "Look here, Hans Simon, you look pretty much like a God-damned swell; going by your mitts, you're one of them fellows that made up the saying, 'There's nothing like work as long as somebody else does it!' Right?"

"I was a trader," Mark Antony's defamer replied cautiously.

"So was I," said Serge. "I traded bank notes. My name is Serge van Panhuis, mail and bank robber, also known as the Terror of the Night."

Suddenly Engel, acting like a desert wanderer who sees the Fata Morgana, uttered a cry: "Trader?" He pushed aside Serge, the burglar, and Long Henry: "Quiet, there! It's important for the man to be questioned and his financial situation investigated, which"—to Simon —"has reached a highly low ebb with us. Question one: What did you trade in?"

The banker felt entitled to save himself by a lie. If it came out who he was, he would have to suffer the envy of the dispossessed, the hatred of the antisocial for the privileged: "In lemons, apples, grapes, plums; I had a wagon," he answered.

"It ain't so—look at his hands!" cried the little runaway, jumping up from the table.

"Don't talk nonsense," said Engel, pushing back the lad with a wink. "The man had his people to do the work." And, to Simon: "Can you do any work at all?"

The banker grew even paler than before, and his tall figure shriveled. The lie had not helped him ease his way into the community of those whom he was condemned to live with.

"Whose turn is it to make the new fellow's bed?" cried Engel. "He can make it for himself tomorrow, and he's got to do it perfect."

Tobias Witt got up from his stool by the window and unfolded the blankets.

"There, now take a good look at the way he makes your bed and folds the edges," the senior inmate continued in pursuance of his duties. "At right angles, ninety degrees by the steel square; you'll do it alone tomorrow, but good, and if those manicured nails of yours break off——"

That was envy, Simon felt. He was very tired; he looked at the stool before his bed, but remained standing.

Tobias beckoned to the fat safecracker to help him fold the woolen blankets and slip them into the linen covers. While the two were at work, Long Henry whispered in the banker's ear, indicating Tobias: "Look out for him, boy! He ain't one of us! A stool pigeon, so keep your trap shut! One of Hesse's boys!"

Serge van Panhuis and Arnold, the runaway, began to play cards; Engel, an incorrigible blowhard, such as our capital produces many of, went on with his instructions: "You see we got solidarity here, and nobody has no privileges over the others, not even if he had a store, which you may have had. The blankets got to be turned over ten inches; later you can sew in the fold, if you've got the money for needle and thread; if you've got still more money, you can even hire someone to sew them in, though that ain't allowed on account of the general equality among all the convicts without any exception——"

At this moment the incident occurred. For the fat burglar, unwrapping Simon's dishes from the linen pillowcase, heard something jingle, and raised and turned over the cup, whose precious contents would have suffered from the fall if the agile Engel, leaping like a tiger, had not saved them. It was the banker's gold watch with its double chain, at whose other end was a flat medallion, while in the middle was another with a solitaire. The cardplayers jumped up and gathered around Engel.

Arnold: "Must be gold, ain't it?"

Simon: "It looks like it."

Engel: "Is that your watch?"

The burglar: "Jesus, look at that! With a medallion!"

The fence: "And the imitation diamonds!"

Arnold: "What's it made of—silver gilt?"

The fence: "Go on, it's pinchbeck!"

Engel: "Cat got your tongue, or what kind of metal is it?"

The poor banker's blood froze in his veins. Was he to admit that he was the "capitalistic money-grubber"? Never! So he said: "All that glitters is not gold."

Tobias Witt took a magnifying glass from his pocket, laid hold of the watch, which Engel surrendered to him, looked at it carefully, snapped open the lid, looked at the inside of the lid, and started the repeater action. The convicts were struck dumb with astonishment at the sound of eight silvery strokes. Tobias Witt looked smilingly at the banker, who felt obliged to justify himself: "Pinchbeck watches have repeater movements, too."

"Wrong, brother," said the young secret agent in so decided a tone that the tormented man took heart. "Around here you're among human beings. Around here you can tell the plain truth that that's pure gold, and the diamond alone worth five hundred thalers."

"A thousand!" The words slipped out of the financier's mouth.

There was a roar of triumph, and the inmates ran about like madmen in their delight. "Up and at 'em!" cried the fat burglar, rolling up his sleeves and tearing apart the banker's bed to remake it. The runaway dove at the straw tick: "I'm going to make your bed from now on. I was first!" He began shaking up the straw. Long Henry took his toothbrush from his pocket and brushed off Simon's long smock with gestures of devotion; the jewel thief fetched an old clothes brush from the wall cupboard and brushed the banker's thinning hair; the fat burglar snatched the blacking brush and began to black Simon's brown shoes. Serge van Panhuis, the Terror of the Night, regarded the newcomer with satisfaction.

"Don't be pleased in too much of a hurry, you crazy fools! What good is the watch to us if he ain't got no money?" yelled Engel, but did not himself believe what he was saying. The good fortune of having a rich man in the cell was too great for that.

Serge enlightened the speechless newcomer: "You see one time there used to be a butcher here, and he was allowed to spend fifteen thalers extra for food every week. Remember how we used to live in those days?"

A moan of longing for the golden age went through the cell.

Little Arnold: "Lard and bread and sausage all the time! And a bottle of beer for everyone on Sundays. The *guards* didn't live as good as we did."

The fat man: "Shut up, for God's sake, or I'll have to eat something! And cigarettes, and tobacco!"

Engel: "And matches!" To Simon: "Speak up, now: Are you as rich as the butcher was?"

Simon: "I don't know how rich the butcher was."

Engel: "You *won't,* then?"

Tobias Witt now intervened again, soothingly: "Don't be such an ass," he said to Engel. "You can tell by looking at the new fellow that he's a man with no experience of life. And you use your head, too, Simon! Jail is just the same as anywhere else. Anybody that has made money, and *still* doesn't wind up in prison with lice and bedbugs, is just lucky. Are you ashamed of being rich?"

"Not exactly——"

"Well, then! Anyone that's been lucky is popular—that's the lesson of experience. Now you take me, just look at these six fellows—they all think I'm a stool pigeon——"

"So you are!" Arnold interrupted.

"—and even so they don't hate me. Why?" He pointed to his breast pocket. "Because I was lucky."

"For God's sake do stop!" cried Long Henry. "He's got a picture of his girl in that pocket. Fit to melt in your mouth—and her name's Veronica! Makes my heart go pit-a-pat!"

The senior inmate put an end to these ironies: "Let's get down to it. Simon, are you as rich as the butcher was?"

"Yes."

"That's the first sensible word you've said," the burglar approved, and the others applauded.

Engel: "Can you spend fifteen thalers a week for all of us together?"

Tobias Witt: "If you're poor, and have small children at home, nobody'll even ask a penny from you."

Simon: "I could spend twice that much."

Engel: "Fifteen thalers is the most that's allowed for one person. It's enough, too. Ring that bell!" he ordered the fence.

Long Henry ran to the wall, rang the bell, and Oscar, the burglar, walked over gravely to Simon: "Now listen here while I explain the custom around here. When the butcher was here, Arnold and Long Henry had to make his bed together, and I cleaned the butcher's things—clothes and shoes every day, but perfect!"

Arnold nodded in agreement: "Maybe Engel didn't give us a kick in the rump if there was a speck of dust on the butcher's things! You don't have to get your hands dirty, no fear about that!"

The key rattled, and the warder's assistant, himself a felon in prison garb, appeared at the door. The convicts stepped back to the window, allowing the senior inmate to come forward and snap into a military attitude: "The inmates of Cell 19 wish to report that all the prisoners have a unanimous religious desire to attend church services on Sunday morning, the day after tomorrow. Accordingly we request to have the barber sent to the cell at once, so he can shave the occupants, because experience shows he don't have no time on Saturday."

"Is that all?" asked the warder's assistant.

"No. The prisoner Hans Simon requests to exercise the right of boarding himself. He wants to spend the maximum amount of fifteen thalers a week."

"Write down what he wants, and give the paper to the barber," the assistant instructed.

He slammed the door, and the prisoners, already beside themselves with hungry imaginings, drummed in concert on the table top. Theodore Engel ordered quiet: "Everyone up!" and turned to the bewildered banker: "In the name of the occupants, and in my capacity of senior inmate, I hereby solemnly declare that brother Hans Simon is accepted into the order of Cell 19."

THE CASE OF STEPHEN WENZEL

XIV

MRS. WENZEL, employment agent for skilled and unskilled help, married, prosperous, feared by the twelve maids in Jacob Willert's household, whom she "exchanged like Christmas presents that didn't suit," received a postcard summoning her to Eastern Police Headquarters, and signed: "Albert Schwann, Captain of the Federal Police."

Well, she knew it was a matter of their squeezing something out of her capacious person. As the old easygoing times were disappearing, with even the lace shops burning electric light, and the pleasant horsecars, rustic *pommes de chemin* between the rails, being electrified to fill the President's pockets, she decided at least to take a cab, and instructed the driver to "roll up in style" before the local headquarters of the black-garbed brethren.

"I'd like to talk to the captain about this postcard he sent me," said Mrs. Wenzel with the sauciness of a good conscience to the two Carpenters who sat face to face at a double desk in the anteroom, with their filing cabinets beside them on the floor. They were wearing the old green uniform of the Federal Police, and on office duty they even had their tunics open, revealing waistcoat, tie, collar, and watch chain dangling across their stomachs. In their upper vest pockets, held by metal clips, were red and blue pencils.

"Better not make trouble for yourself, Mrs. Wenzel, by calling a police summons disrespectful names," one of them warned her after a glance at the postcard. He got up and knocked at a double door so imposingly decorated that one might well have thought the house had once been inhabited by "the gentry."

"Mrs. Wenzel has come to call," reported the sergeant, opening the door, and the voice of the easygoing Schwann replied: "Please come in."

The room that the employment agent entered was more like a fashionable living room than a public office. At the left, seated with his back to the arriving visitor so that the light should fall over his left shoulder, at a desk between two double windows, was the head of the secret service, in mufti. By the second window, at a desk covered with papers, sat his secretary, Mrs. Haas, the widow of a Carpenter who had fallen in battle. But these were the only signs of officialdom, and the sofa with the plush armchairs and the oval table in front of it dominated the room. The gay checkered tablecloth was still on the table from breakfast, and a nickel-plated alcohol burner kept the coffee hot. On the wall above the sofa hung enlarged photographs of Schwann's parents and a picture of the murdered Kate in a gold frame. The big mahogany desk, surrounded on three sides by a little gallery, was so crowded with pictures of his children, his wife, his friends, and with souvenirs of travel, that there was barely room to write. Atop a marble slab between the inkwells a bronze stag, tremendous antlers laid back, was trumpeting into an imaginary autumn morning. On the side wall to the right, between the bookcase and the glass door giving a view of his private quarters, hung an autographed portrait of the President.

Mrs. Wenzel, whose eyes rested on the gleaming alcohol burner and the plump coffeepot over it, was observed by Schwann in a mirror fastened to the wall; he invited her to be seated beside his desk.

"I wrote to you," said the captain, "that your husband, Stephen Wenzel, yard master at the South Station, has been delivered up. That, I take it, is sufficient."

His official tone exasperated the woman: "I should think compensation and the payment of the legal pension was the least I could expect."

"You won't get a penny from us."

"But Mrs. Schulze is getting twenty-five thalers a month."

"Her husband was a switchman, and she's sick."

"I'm sick too."

Schwann seemed to be looking for something on Mrs. Haas' desk; she prepared to write.

"Have you lived together happily with your husband, Mrs. Wenzel?"

"Oh, well enough, yes. Why?"

"Why don't you put in an application saying you're willing to accompany your husband? We've been allowing that lately on principle. Married couples are allowed to stay together, and even engaged couples, because continence sometimes shortens life."

"Oh, I'm not so keen on that, Captain."

"Your husband will be there too, Mrs. Wenzel!"

"And what about my business if I go to a lunatic village?"

"It isn't a bad life in the lunatic villages at all, Mrs. Wenzel. In fact, for the past two years you might even have heard loud cries, though I must admit it's babies' squalling. Millions of people on this earth, and not the worst of them, at that, would like to live so if they were only allowed to."

"But I've got a business."

"Yes, a dangerous one."

"Does that mean I've placed Gas-House Boys?"

"Not knowingly, or you'd be with your husband by this time. But one of Mr. Urban's employees recently lost his handbag in a chance street brawl."

A smile of self-satisfaction spread over Schwann's face, and the employment agent burst out: "Chance street brawl? We know how those are managed! First two drunks yell at each other, and then the curious make a crowd—no wonder if somebody mislays something in the push!" she laughed out loud.

Schwann went on: "Do you know what the donkey had in his bag, among other things? A list of all the menservants, cooks, and servant girls that you had placed in the last two months."

Mrs. Wenzel was so horrified that Schwann seized her hand: "Listen to me! Your husband is a Gas-House Boy, but he's not old enough yet to live without a wife. He has applied to have you live with him in the lunatic village."

"I guess he would! Let him pay up for what he's done."

"You're going to visit your husband, Mrs. Wenzel, and if you won't do it willingly, we shall employ compulsion."

"Visiting him is another matter. Why not? But for how long?"

"Until you get out of him what the so-called 'antimobilization order' means."

"How am I supposed to find that?"

"I'll tell you. Would you mind going out for a minute, Mrs. Haas?"

The secretary departed through the glass door.

"Your husband is a vigorous, normal man . . . you understand?"

"If that's so, why didn't you say to him, 'First your confession, and then you can have your wife'?"

"What we need is not a false confession, Mrs. Wenzel, but the truth. You can tell by your husband's face whether he's lying. So you go out there and say to him, 'If you don't tell me the truth, just like that, the Carpenters will take away my business, and I'll get a divorce from you. And then you can just see how you get on without a wife!' Like that! If he tells the truth, he can have you visit him for three days every month—that's sufficient in the doctor's opinion— and you can keep your business. Do you understand all that?"

"What am I to ask him?"

"Well, you'll have to listen carefully: every Gas-House Boy is given a verbal antimobilization order. That is, if the government mobilizes the army, he has to go to this or that place and do this or that thing. 'What' is not pertinent at the moment. I want to know whether the antimobilization order given to your husband applies only if our whole army is mobilized, or whether it applies also if just part of the army is mobilized—for instance, one or more army corps, but not all. Furthermore, whether the order is valid only when the army is mobilized for war, or also when there are maneuvers coming. It will all be explained to you carefully later; now tell me if you're willing."

"What can I do?" she said, but the head of the secret service could tell by the look of her that she was very willing indeed.

"You aren't the only wife, Mrs. Wenzel, but one of hundreds, who are at present pumping their husbands. From the reports it will then be evident which ones among the ladies are themselves agents of Mr. Urban. We shan't treat them gently, you may be sure of that!"

"And what about my business?"

"You will take into your business, both in the West End office and the branch near here, a girl whom I shall send you, and whom I shall pay."

Mrs. Wenzel sobbed into her handkerchief: "I always said to my husband, 'Don't keep running to those meetings!' But pride goeth before a fall."

"That's how it goes in life," said the easygoing Schwann, terminating the interview.

Through this channel the government learned that Peter George's antimobilization order was effective for Gas-House Boys of all ranks in every corps area whose garrisons and reserves were mobilized, no matter for what purpose.

Adam Faust immediately ordered the mobilization of the First Army Corps, stationed in and near the seaport of Neuhafen. But the expected sabotage, for which the Carpenters were prepared, did not materialize. The silence of disappointment prevailed at the generals' tables in the Golden Eagle Hotel on Cathedral Square: the great man was not to be caught, they believed.

Actually the case was quite otherwise: the Gas-House Boys, exhorted by Peter George Lienhardt to do their duty, had balked. Weisse was the first among Urban's intimates to conjecture that the spirit of the saboteurs might have been broken by years of hunting down and "delivering up" the bravest—for instance, Koehler, the director of the electrical plant. The Ordnance Master and Justus Thomas contradicted, as in duty bound, and the former advertising solicitor, Dr. Grau, a very demon of persuasion, was assigned to Peter George Lienhardt as an assistant.

At the end of that year Adam Faust promoted Otto Hesse and the police commander of the south, fat Heinz, to be generals; Police Captain Schwann to be a lieutenant colonel; Captains Lindequist, Lorenz, and Stark to be majors; Generals Kaempf (in the north) and Laurenti (in the south) to be colonels general. The blond-bearded Charles Froehlich, secret agent and painter's model, brother of the horribly murdered Theresa, uncle of the dovelike Veronica Witt (née Froehlich), and ringleader in the bloody night of Carolswald, received a pension of two hundred thalers because he, with the help of the beautiful and dissolute Marie Klingenberg (the daughter of the man who had organized the bakers), had delivered up Director Charles Emil Koehler, the most dangerous Gas-House Boy of his time, to Hesse's men.

BOOK TWO

THE IMMORTAL DEAD LADY, AND THE BULLET IN THE CEILING

XV

I N THE nineteenth year of our Adam Faust's presidency everything remained quiet, but certain changes in personnel were interpreted as storm warnings. At the War College, the training school for higher officers, the director, Count Bessonoff, the President's favorite, resigned because his wife Ida had been seen standing beside the great man at an Urbanite parade in the Eastern Province, and wearing the uniform of a Sports Troop inspector. Bessonoff retired to private life and moved into his house at Mittelburg, without getting a divorce: the marriage could not be dissolved because the count belonged to the Order of Carpenters. Ida Bessonoff moved into the city mansion opposite the Willerts' on Lady Square. The fact that the most exalted favorites of Dr. Urban frequented the great house was interpreted by some as weakness in the government party, by others as willingness on the part of Jacob Willert to "recognize" the Yellow League Leader. Henry Willert, the son, was entering upon his thirtieth year, and beginning to get himself talked about. He was secretly associating, the story went, with Dr. Merckel, who had been sent to spy out the Urbanite camp and was Beyer's presumable son-in-law; accordingly, Henry must want to be on the side of those who were preparing for a sanguinary conflict with the Yellows.

At this time the Academy of Twelve was constituted as follows: Andrew Zorn; Dr. Daruhi; Jacob Willert; Matthew Brandt, the Teller of Great Deeds; the Archbishop; Bishop Kessel; Justice Holzkopf; Generals Frohwein, Kaempf, Hesse; and the labor leaders Lindbrecht and Hildebrand—the latter as head of the "independents." These were the Free Unions, which, like the Catholics, were not connected with the Carpenters except by a coalition.

Outstanding among the candidates were the miner Lange, an employment inspector after Anton Koerner's death; Hans Simon, released from prison after eighteen months; young Henry Willert, Jacob's heir; and two generals: Leugenfeld, the calculator of trajectories, and lanky Spitta, the learned theoretician of defense, Bessonoff's successor at the War College, and military governor of the capital.

Among the labor leaders the head of the Free Unions, Hildebrand, was the most highly respected; and indeed so independent a character was seldom to be met with. Astonishingly enough, his maxim, almost proverbial among the Faustites, "I won't be made a fool of, and I won't be made an accomplice of," remained his guiding rule throughout life; and his slender book, *The Forms of Concealed Bribery,* delivered a veritable rain of metaphorical slaps in the face to the Urbanites. "Among those who have helped me restore civic pride to the workingman," said Adam Faust, "he's in the front rank." The steadiness of his behavior, the fact that he never got drunk and that he had a flock of children by his fat wife, were highly respected virtues. His cigar merchant in Pioneer Lane, Mr. Bick, has recalled: "I could always tell for sure whether Senator Hildebrand was buying cigars for his own use or for distinguished visitors. His own were cheap Mexican, so-called sandy leaf; he couldn't stomach anything better." He was a veritable monument of Protestant sobriety.

A cleavage runs through the life of Lindbrecht, the leader of the "Christians." After the Geisenheim disturbances he helped old Hesse revive the Order of Carpenters. Then he was summoned to the capital for his lecture before the Natural Science convention, fell among orthodox Catholic working circles, and suddenly announced his resignation from the Order of Carpenters and his willingness to accept the governing post offered him by the so-called "Christians," that is, the Catholic workers' associations. In a letter so interlarded with foreign words and learned phrases that the two Geisenheim bishops felt he was hiding his true motives or did not know them himself, he defined the Order of Carpenters as "the incarnation of Christian unionism." The latter, an attempt to bring the two Christian confessions together in one, he said had been undertaken with a noble motive, and had failed. Nor could it succeed: any combined Christian church, adjusting all confessional differences, was always bound to be Protestant. The Order of Carpenters was Protestant; the capital city unionism of the Archbishop, who had restored monasticism and the confessional, was Protestant. In fact—he was sorry that he could not spare this reproach to the highly respected Bishop Oriola—even the unionist's wish to restore the "one and indivisible" Church was Protestant, and the uneasy conscience of the schismatic was evident in unionism. He had no thought of creating bad blood: probably the present condition of the world requires pluralism and a decentralization of Christianity; this opinion prevailed, at any rate, in the President's circle, and even sects of insignificant membership enjoyed tacit support. He for his part, having gone through battle and put the uncertainty of youth behind him, was returning to the peace of Catholicism.

Yes, he returned indeed; the curlyheaded ecstatic turned his back upon the thin-lipped warriors of the Lord and the Order of Carpenters, and reverted to the splendor, incense, and gaiety of the Catholic trust in God. Childhood memories' had come to life in the thirty-year-old with such force that they and not the years of his young manhood overshadowed the pathway of his life.

Adam Faust, growing weaker now, sat on his veranda above the river, and passed in review the men who might be able to carry out what he had prepared for. The statesmen, the Hildebrands, Langes, Kaempfs, Spittas, and the bishops went swiftly by; those whom he dwelt on were the nervous men of ingenuity, who might possibly add something new to his "system," and would corrupt it. No danger threatened from the health and the knife-edged sense of justice of Hildebrand or Kessel, the Bishop who had been called to the capital: it did threaten from young Henry Willert and Hesse, two morbid dreamers.

Now, Otto von Hesse, although he suffered sometimes from a twi-

light condition, nevertheless always seemed to be of sound understanding. The world of Henry Willert, on the other hand, would be
distorted for hours at a time to such a degree that he would talk,
not nonsense, but "trance logic," in Dr. Kuttner's phrase. Both doctors,
incidentally, sought the cause in an injury to the soul during childhood; but Dr. Daruhi was perfectly familiar with the case. It dated
back sixteen years. The bodies of Anne Mary Willert and her child
had just been laid out in the forester's house when the young doctor
was called away from Melchior's sickbed: the thirteen-year-old grand-
son, Henry, his grandfather's guest during the summer vacation, had
been dragged unconscious from the pond at the same spot where
the Beloved had drowned. Daruhi brought him back to life; and as
the boy, making a quick recovery, did not remember what he had
done, the incident was kept from his parents. But in the coming
years, until he was nineteen, he would frequently wake up screaming.
Later, in his twenties, after his shrewd mother had turned him over
to Madame Kittelsen, nothing disturbing happened. The matter seemed
to be quite forgotten, and then, just recently, "trance speech" in broad
daylight had begun to be observed. Once again Daruhi, convinced
that the injury was incurable, concealed the connection from the
alarmed parents. Jacob Willert, who had himself become head of
the house at twenty-six, put off turning over the business to his son
by a whole year. Finally the doctor's hypothesis was proved correct
by a conversation he had with Henry, proceeding from literary to
personal experiences.

Henry disparaged the celebrated "realistic" conclusion of Gustave
Flaubert's novel, *Éducation sentimentale,* as unrealistic. "Throughout
the whole admirable story, the great master is actually a realist," said
Henry Willert. "Suddenly, as if he were blinded by some silly bio-
logical or environmental theory, or perhaps because he had never
experienced such a thing himself, he regarded it as the summit of
realism that the hero, when his beloved finally comes to his room
after thirty years of being courted in vain, is repelled by her white
hair, lights a cigarette, looks out of the window, and thinks: 'Too
late!' How untrue, indeed how improbable! What a lack of con-
sistency!"

He shook his head, and fell into a brown study.

Daruhi wondered how he might encourage the confession: "Did

you ever hear the Greek legend, Henry," he asked, "about the tyrant
of Corinth, who came to such great misfortune along with his city
that he asked the oracle in Delphi what he had been guilty of? The
oracle answered: 'You put bread in a cold oven.' It was true, there
was no denying it: he had mated with his mistress after she was
dead."

"Yes, that's realistic," said Henry. "That's what happens. For white
hair, wrinkles, and death are no obstacle. Only I don't like the oracle:
in reality the dead woman herself told him what he was guilty of,
and begged him to burn her jewelry and clothes, everything that still
bore her scent, so that she might have peace from his pursuit. The
fable might have added that he afterward had several wives, and
deceived them all with the dead woman, every one of them with the
dead woman, because there is no such thing as forgetting."

Now Daruhi felt encouraged to ask directly: "Does your stepgrand-
mother, Anne Mary Willert, still come to you in dreams? You know
I'm not asking out of curiosity."

Henry, blushing for a moment, said: "Yes."

"But no longer in such a way that you're terrified?"

"No. Why should I be terrified?"

"One last question, Henry: they call you a misogynist. But supposing you should fall in love with a woman and get married—both
of your parents want you to, as you know—do you think you would
deceive your wife or mistress with the dead woman?"

"A question in return: Does that depend on me?"

The doctor made a vigorous gesture of denial: "Certainly not!
I'm not reproaching you. What I as a doctor want to know is something that only you can know, but that you know definitely: is the
dead woman growing . . . weaker, or is she growing stronger?"

Henry searched his memory: "Stronger," he said at last. "Though
sometimes I must say the features are vague, and resemble the statue,
so that I have told her several times not to disguise herself—that I
knew what she looked like, and that she was a shopkeeper's wife!"

"What does she say to that?"

"She smiles." And young Henry, remembering the dead woman as
a safe and indestructible possession, smiled himself.

He never doubted for a moment that the Beloved had taken leave
of life because the three Lienhardts in the garden had spread the story

that she did not know where her child came from. Accordingly, there could be no wavering for him, even though he was so anxious to agree with his own father that he would rather have left home than have opposed him overtly or secretly. As his life, like Lindbrecht's, was overshadowed by a childhood experience, he could never be in doubt as to who was Enemy Number One in our country: obviously the murderers of the Beloved, and Urban, who was supported by them.

For this reason—because young Henry's personal destiny allowed him no considering and balancing between Reds and Yellows—the old President, informed about the case by Daruhi, had made note of him along with Beyer, Merckel, Hesse, Hildebrand, Ackermann, and General Laurenti (whose son had been killed as a color sergeant by the Yellows), for some high state post, in case Adam himself should die or the armed conflict should break out first.

There was not even any need for secrecy; Jacob was informed that his son was to prepare himself for the post of Foreign Secretary. Only the real reason for the confidence that Adam showed in the young man was naturally withheld.

About that time it became necessary to suspend Otto von Hesse for six weeks because of a grave impropriety, whether committed in a trance condition or while he was of sound mind remained undecided. He took what went by the name of "arrest," a vacation cruise on a steam yacht hired by von Brick, in company with Alexandra—"a bit of woman makes one sleep better at night," the Federal Commissioner said to his presumptive son-in-law.

The citizens of the capital, it is true, laughed at the impropriety, and called it *the bullet in the ceiling;* but the Reds and pinks, ten months before the general election, shouted, "Tyranny!"

This was what had happened: the capital, serving as a model of all things to the provinces, had presented Mark Antony's "Revolutionary Party version" of *King Lear,* "modernized and made interesting"; accordingly, the provincial theater managers, not wanting to be behindhand, and anxious to "do homage to progress," unloosed a veritable plague of classical masterpieces made interesting upon the culture-hungry classes, the *bourgeoisie,* and better-paid workingmen. It was precisely the People's Theaters of the Free Unions, established on a common basis and supported by almost a million regular subscribers, that led the van, since "no one can escape progress." The attraction of these wretched perpetrations was twofold: firstly, the celebrated titles, such as *Macbeth, King Lear,* and *Richard III,* gave a semblance of ingenuous effort to serve art alone, following the maxims of the Iron Phalanx:

> *The many for culture, culture for the many,*
> *This is our purpose and aim above any.*

And secondly, the housewives thought, it must be far more interesting to see King Richard III playing his part not in solemn poetry but in what Mark Antony considered the "language of the people," and in Jacob Willert's clothes. Not all these plays were political; in fact, the most dangerous, quite nonpartisan, were calculated solely to cast contempt upon the past and soften up the public conscience.

The scene in *Richard III* that "bore witness to a moving and courageous love of truth," for example, consisted in having the leading man sit at a rude wooden table in Jacob Willert's clothes and mask; the table was covered with shiny gold pieces. Hands and head uplifted, eyes turned heavenward so sanctimoniously that only the whites were visible, he kept pouring the gold through his fingers, and cried out (while a beauty lying under the table made motions of an unmistakably obscene nature) in a piously saccharine, oozing voice: "For if a power or an order does not sanctify itself, how shall it hope to survive?"

"The amours, the wealth, and the cold-water sermonizing of Richard III, the winebibber," Nicholas Edwin Schiele wrote, "are pilloried with splendid and significant symbolism."

This time Jacob Willert was not alone in his protest. The Archbishop had depicted in his *Gospel of the Sunday Mortal* (Simon Library Publication No. 42) the proper desire of a mortal, when freed from the cares of every day, to hear the truth unadorned, and also the deceit that was practiced by the demagogues upon the "Sunday Mortal." But his cry found no echo. Adam Faust, instructed by his Academy of Twelve to put an end to this mischief, sent for the chairman of the Free Unions, Hildebrand, and shouted at him, demanding how he dared: "As honorary president of the People's Theater Societies you will forbid this obscene business, or out you go on your ear out of the Academy!"

"I'm no dictator," replied Hildebrand. "All I can do is enlighten people about what this drama means, and who's behind it."

"Can't Bart Plambeck be given money to write something?" asked the President.

"Yes, that he can."

This was the end of the interview; but even the crown jurist, Holz-kopf, could discover no remedy, and the presidential party thought it inopportune to infringe the constitution ten months before a general election.

Hesse burrowed in forgotten police ordinances: if modern drama could be shut off in the capital, it would lose its attraction in the provinces. One evening, on his way to the *première* of *Timon of Athens* in a Revolutionary Party version for the groundlings at the Municipal Theater on Augustus Square, Otto stepped into the big Café Opéra across from the theater, intending to have a cup of tea, as coffee was forbidden him. The large café was full of newspaper readers, and smoke was floating toward the ceiling. The waiters, however, seemed to be either Urbanites or malicious sprites: hurrying past Otto's table, shrugging their shoulders or brandishing their napkins, they pointed either to other waiters, and the number on their badges, or to the number of the table where the young general had sat down; or else mopping the sweat from their brow, they dashed on with a "Haven't got time, haven't got time!"

The door of the café was open, and Otto could already hear the shrill bell announcing the start of the play from across the street; he clutched a waiter, but the man tore himself free. Overcome with thirst or going into a trance, Otto snatched his pistol from his holster, cocked it, aimed straight upward, and fired. There was such a tremendous bang that the familiar life around came to a startled stop; but about Otto's table stood some fifteen waiters, perfectly placid, gazing upward to see how big the hole in the ceiling was. The manager, in black frock coat and white waistcoat, was instantly on the spot: "What does this mean, sir?" he demanded severely of the police general in mufti.

"Just take a look at these fellows!" said Otto, indicating the waiters who surrounded the table. "But a moment ago, protesting their honesty, they declared they had no time, and like time itself they flew by. Now here they stand, and have been, quite peacefully, for five

minutes past, gaping at the hole in the ceiling. Isn't everything a lie?"
And he went out with a dreamy smile on his face.

A TOAST TO PROGRESS AND JOLLITY

XVI

IT WAS fall, five months before the election; the perfume of
transition was still steaming in the clear woods, rising from the
paths, the mossy forest floor, the shrubbery around Madonna
Pond. It was so overpowering that Henry Willert did nothing
more, but laid aside his book and looked upon the water, upon the
beginning and the end. And then came the downfall from on high
that Matthew Brandt describes as follows.

A broad-branching tree, tall, with tapering crown, stands in the
midst of a meadow. The winter winds have shaken it, it has withstood
the storms of March; it is not old, but mighty to look upon. Now
it has nothing to fear, for this is summer, and the fat white cotton
clouds stand immobile in the blue sky. Then comes a zephyr so
gentle that it does not ruffle a feather of the little bird sitting in the
crown; it is not a breeze, a mere infant breath upon the little bird:
and the tree goes down with a crash.

Equally causeless and unjustified, in the eyes of contemporaries,
was the collapse of the Revolutionary Workers' Party in every province
of the country during a single week of September. Mass resignations;
shifts of entire party and Red Front organizations, newspapers, and
Red cultural and sports associations to the camp of Yellow Urban!

Naturally the Yellows held giant meetings to celebrate this welcome
accession so shortly before the election, and predicted "assured final
victory in the course of the coming year." John Henry Merckel's
prestige rose; the mistrust of the intimates, Justus Thomas and Weisse,
for this ambitious man who was crowding into the League Leader's
confidence disappeared. For Urban, as a materialist and apostle of

enlightenment, did not believe in chance or in trees uprooted by zephyrs; and since, despite his surpassing intelligence, he despised Matthew Brandt's fairy-story manner, he explained the downfall of the Reds as a natural consequence of the revelations continued year after year in the *Sunday Evening Post.* The capital invested in Frank the Printer began to pay interest, a triumph that was due to the rewriter of Bart Plambeck's stuff, this very Dr. Merckel; for the most outrageous truths, clumsily, importunately, directly, and un-symbolically put, will create a sensation that does not outlast the day. To give even the most righteous indignation any permanence, the artist must be called on. Dr. Merckel, a pupil and imitator of Hil-genfeld's at once childlike and solemn manner, was appointed a member of the Leader's personal corps. At the reception held in honor of the washerwoman's son, Urban said to his intimates, pointing to the newly promoted writer with that lack of envy that his com-panions repaid with faithfulness unto death: "Look at him! The artist has defeated the Reds. The arrows from the ivory tower are deadly."

The head office of the Revolutionary Workers' Party celebrated its own collapse by boasting that since the defection of the liars, slan-derers, spies, and syphilitics it had stood forth as an "unshakable rock of progress," strengthened by inner unity. Dr. Merckel, his coun-sel now respectfully heeded, advised the great man to take the Reds' ridiculous excuse seriously, and even to emphasize it by asserting that the Reds had staged the defection in order to go underground and let loose armed rebellion. The watchword of the election could then be: "Do you want Red rebellion, destruction, and murder? No? Then vote for the Leader toward peace, Dr. Urban!"

The greatest meeting ever known took place in the newly dedicated indoor arena on Cathedral Square. Three bands from the capital city Sports Brigade played simultaneously; in a gallery above the speakers' platform sat the trumpeters of the bodyguard regiment, who rose when the party symbol was carried down the middle aisle, put one hand on their hips, and set their long, straight, brass trumpets to their lips with the other hand to blow the party flourish, while the entire audience stood up and sang it. The flourish was the party program, simplified and set to music: *A Toast to Progress and Jollity.* This program was indubitably a stroke of genius, since there can be no criticism made of our nation's three ideals, toasting, progress, and jollity, which the millionaire joins with the beggar in doing honor to. The party symbol, also known as "The Greeter," was a male figure, fully clothed, built of light wood and papier-mâché, thirty-five feet high; at such important moments as the entrance of the Leader, or even in the middle of a speech, it was carried down the center aisle of the hall by twenty-four noncommissioned officers of the bodyguard regiment, to the accompaniment of a flourish, a welcome, and singing. The symbol (or idol) wore gray striped trousers, a white waistcoat, and a black frock coat, like the manager of one of our great restaurants. Willie Gaedicke, the inventor and maker of the figure, had very rightly thought that the restaurateur was our universal ideal, which, being equally popular everywhere, also embodied our national unity. On the monstrous papier-mâché head a small black bowler hat perched saucily, with a broad white ribbon on the front bearing the other beloved slogan:

Just stuff yourself and drink your beer;
And politics—don't talk them here!

Only at the first superficial glance does this saying seem an unsuitable watchword for a political party: it was precisely people's weariness of the belligerency and cocksureness of party speakers that had driven so many millions into the arms of the Leader, who allowed no parties.

The fat, purple cheeks and upward-twirled mustaches of the idol implied toasts and jollity; his mouth was opened as if proposing someone's health, and the party badge in his buttonhole indicated that he was not withstanding the spell of progress. Inside the hollow figure sat the manipulator, who could move the symbol by means of wires so that it would turn its head and tip its hat to right and left. He also sang the flourish, *A Toast to Progress and Jollity,* into an amplifying tube, and at least for great occasions the party insisted on hiring the first tenor of the state opera as a manipulator, so that the song would sound the more resonantly from the mouthpiece, inviting popular emulation.

Dr. Urban, already by this time a mythical figure to the masses, no longer appeared at meetings at all, but only in small gatherings, and in rooms too low-ceilinged to admit the party symbol. This he hated, at the same time realizing that he could only improve it, not take it away from his followers; it was already too popular, expressing as it did with such perfect vividness the altogether understandable yearning for toasts, progress, and jollity. Urban exhausted the resources of his imagination in efforts to refine the symbol; he discarded his own designs and those submitted by others, and almost despaired of finding a beautiful expression for the "idea."

The chairman of the meeting was Weisse. Next to him at the long speakers' table on the platform sat Countess Ida Bessonoff, in the uniform of a chief of the bodyguard regiment, on the right, and Lieutenant Colonel Justus Thomas, on the left. Then followed women on the right, men on the left—particularly those party members from whose appearance as speakers Urban promised himself a smashing success.

On the right of Ida Bessonoff, then, was Comrade Henrietta Koehler, the divorced wife of the electrical-plant director; Diana Rose, thrown out by Emil, and now secretary to Felice Gasparra, the painter; and Augusta Hoppelkopf, who always swooned. On the left, newly recruited comrades Dr. Grau, Bart Plambeck, and Emil, the Lion of Afghanistan, were looking down into the hall. Dr. Grau had been a member for two years, but had never been publicly presented; he was regarded as the successor to Peter George Lienhardt (who had fallen into disfavor) in directing the secret service.

Behind the speakers' table, helmeted, guns slung over shoulders, legs astraddle, motionless, stood a file of the bodyguard regiment of the Sports Troops.

When Dr. Grau, the former advertising solicitor of the *Intelligencer*, got up, shadows and shudders rippled through the hall, so completely did the man recall depictions of the Evil One. Smooth hair of a nondescript dirty color hung over a low, tormented forehead; but the pale, pockmarked, dissolute, oratorical face with its deep grooves around nostrils and mouth, the little slant eyes and cleft upper lip, seemed to belong to a principle incarnate, not a person. All he said, in a hoarse voice, clearing his throat frequently, was that the people must rise from the depths of commercialism to idealism.

Bart Plambeck too was a failure, though in his case it was due to stage fright. He had been spitting upon "those fellows" for eleven years, he said, and had believed they were drowning. But as they had now been seen to escape into the rathole of underground activity, the struggle against those who had not yet drowned, the swimmers in spittle, must be resumed.

The feeble applause showed that abuse alone could not satisfy even a green and unspoiled gathering. To offset the lack of enthusiasm, Weisse sent forward Emil, the Lion of Afghanistan, whose mighty figure was pleasantly conspicuous in the uniform of a sergeant of the Sports Troop. After Oscar Koenig's hush money was gone, he had arrived in Mittelburg, and had been hired as bath attendant and personal bodyguard to the Leader.

"My friends in the party," said Senator Weisse, "I now present to you our party comrade, Mr. Emil, in his youth a nurse and wrestler, later a merchandise inspector and registered member of the Revolutionary Workers' Party. Mr. Emil!"

As the tall, fat man stood up there was loud applause, and indeed he justified very handsomely the confidence that had been placed in him as a speaker.

"Esteemed party comrades," he began, "whenever I have visited my friends or acquaintances in the last few weeks, and told them I had gone over to our Dr. Urban, their opinion was unanimous: 'That's sensible!' For this simple reason, that a normal man who isn't crazy, and is living in a collapsing house, has the right to move out."

More applause.

"If I asked you now, my esteemed audience, who or what is this collapsing house, where thousands have canceled their leases just in the last few weeks, I suspect that you will unanimously reply——"

Emil had taken hold of his audience. They cried: "The Revolutionary Workers' Party!"

Emil: "Quite right, and you, my friends, show your intelligence by the way you recognized it. The Revolutionary Workers' Party is falling apart, the word has got around—and why? Because it can't hold together. For instance, if there's a party leader that's got enough money to build a splendid theater to advertise his firm——"

From the midst of the gathering came a shout: "And what is his firm?"

And the thousands answered: "The Revolutionary Workers' Party!"

They were well schooled. Emil went on: "Quite correct, and if this rich man is smoking a fat cigar and talking with ladies in low-necked dresses, and I come up to him in party uniform and say civilly: 'Evening, Comrade, how about a cigarette, huh?' and the stinker turns his back on me, why, I say to myself, this here is no party for me, and I go in with our Dr. Urban, who has spared no personal sacrifice for our uniforms and caps and boots, so we can make a decent impression."

Shouted salutations and hysterical screams. Emil went on: "Yes, sir, they can't keep on gluing together the cracks in the wall with talk, and in the next few days and weeks there's going to be a tremendous rush to the party of our Dr. Urban. Because even if it's true that voluntary expression of opinion belongs to a forgotten epoch, and the age of progress and restricted expression of opinion has dawned, so to speak, why all right; but in that case, while there's still time, I'm going to take a look at the gent whose opinion I have to think. There's got to be a limit even to lying; but the leading gentlemen in the Revolutionary Workers' Party must think no one is watching them when they make up to the workers in meetings, and then afterward, at the first street corner, they take a good look around to make sure no one sees them, and then whoops! up and away from the dirty working quarter to a first-class wine restaurant, to booze away our dues with low-necked ladies."

Booing and hissing.

"For that reason, my dear party comrades, hundreds of thousands of members of the Revolutionary Workers' Party have gradually waked up and come to the same realization as me, namely, all right, if we've got to march, better to do it in Urban's hunting boots than in the worn-out shoes of the proletarian, or imaginary patent-leather pumps that are just on paper. Yes, if we've got to obey orders anyway, better from regular officers that can take a joke and a drink now and then, instead of eyeball rollers, dames, flatterers, lawyers, lapdogs, pale-faces, and the literati with their horn-rim spectacles!

"The Revolutionary Workers' Party, a party of man-women and literati——"

Emil had lifted his right arm; like one man the crowd, numbering thousands, sprang up, and their rhythmic shouts echoed back from the walls:

"Boo! Boo! Boo!"

Emil: "The League for Enlightenment and Economic Peace of our Dr. Urban——"

No one with the exception of Augusta Hoppelkopf, who had swooned on the floor in her enthusiasm, was still in his seat. Two thousand arms were stretched upward, four thousand eyes fixed on the bandmaster of the bodyguard regiment, who had raised his baton, and directed the shouts as the idol was carried through the hall:

"Hurrah! Hurrah! Hurrah!"

Now the brass band too blared out, and the flourish was sounded: *A Toast to Progress and Jollity.*

That same evening Emil the tremendous and Countess Bessonoff made friends; Diana Rose, however, resolved to punish the faithless scoundrel.

BOOK TWO

THE PARADISE OF THE TORMENTOR

XVII

ON CHRISTMAS EVE the farm, buildings, and mansion of the original Lienhardt family estate of Moenckeberg, in the extreme south, bordering on the great solitude of the mountain forests, were surrounded by Federal Police. Fat Heinz barked at the bushy-mustached old man who opened the yard gate: "Where is Gregory William, the swine?"

The doorkeeper replied that there were seven hundred swine living in the barns of Moenckeberg. "Look out for your toes," cried the general, with Hesse's angry telegram burning a hole in his pocket; followed by his mounted men, with dark lanterns hanging from their saddles, he rode into the farmyard. The search for Gregory William Lienhardt proved unavailing, but on promise of protection an old stablemaid, the same one who had succeeded in giving information secretly and undiscovered, led the southern district commander and his retinue to the stable. With her lean brown arms she shoved aside sheaves of grain from the rear wall, revealing a door in the light of the dark lanterns. Inside, she bared the back of her fifteen-year-old son, who was resting on a tick in the coachman's room. The boy, lying on his stomach, raised his head; he was a handsome youngster with brown curls, a little pale from the soothing medicaments; he begged pitifully with clasped hands that they should not pull off the bandages covering his back. Fat Heinz, having been instructed to photograph the maltreated boy, scratched his head; but the battalion doctor reassured the lad that he would be taken to the Carpenters' hospital in the city, and given very good care there, with meat for dinner every day. He said aside to Heinz that by administering a small amount of ether it would be possible to take off the boy's bandages and photograph him without causing him any pain.

His mother testified that after lunch when almost all the farm people had gone out into the fields to work, leaving only the stable boy behind, two neatherds had gone after the boy with whips in the stable, two others had held him, and Gregory William had looked on, positively groaning with delight. Finally he had whispered quite faintly, "Enough"; but modesty forbade her repeating what he had done to himself during the torturing. Afterward "the master" had stretched out in the straw of the stable, and gone to sleep, and the doctor had been summoned to apply ointments and put on bandages.

What the boy's mother had been unwilling to say came to light nevertheless: for one thing, that the using of the young farm help, boys and girls, was a century-old custom, and nothing forbidden in the minds of these former serfs, but rather a right of the gentry; for another, that Gregory William had given "large presents," and besides, the lad had offered no resistance. At length, however, on going to confession, he had been forbidden to hold sexual commerce with his master. He had then thrust him away in the stable, and been chastised by the farm hands.

Owing to the suspicion of the other farm people because she had rebelled against custom and the gentry, the stablemaid was now in danger of her life, although it was urged in her favor that she had been egged on by the newfangled clerics, who in turn were egged on by the Geisenheim bishops. "Dismal state of affairs," said the Catholic priest, summoned by Heinz. As the priest muttered something about "being in God's hands," and about a white cross that the farm people would

soon be chalking on his door, Heinz left at the parsonage a guard of
three noncoms who had taken the Carpenters' training course. For
stories had already begun to leak out about the caves, subterranean
chambers with stalactite and stalagmite formations, with brooks running through them, and so tremendous in extent that whole cities had
found refuge there in forgotten days long past. The entrances, which
had been widened, were supposed now to have tumbled in and been
overgrown with brambles. There, not far from the ridge of the wooded
mountains, quantities of ammunition and arms, even Urbanite field
artillery and howitzers, were said to be stored; the foresters and woods-
men, housed in a hamlet near by, were serving as instructors to the
"sports artillery."

Accordingly, Heinz took the maid with him to the county town,
where the son was photographed and cured; then she went to Geisenheim, so that she could repeat her suspicions and accusations before
the provincial governor, Bruno Zorn, and General Laurenti.

These two, although suspicious of her fantastically embroidered tales,
equipped a "scientific expedition for the geological exploration of the
dripstone caves."

Meanwhile the President's eighty-first year was drawing near; only
six weeks still separated us from the general election. Hesse presented
to the Academy various inacceptable proposals for "intensifying" the
election campaign, and the doctors dared not hope that old Adam
Faust would outlive the winter.

The Reds had either given up hope, or had no money, or were depending on word-of-mouth backstairs propaganda; they ceased to appear in great halls. The business of the realistically-minded proprietors
of halls was all the better when the broad bands with Urban's slogans
shone from the walls, or the party symbol of progress and jollity, the
Greeter, swayed up the middle aisle. The voters of the presidential
coalition, beaten six years previously, were also not behindhand when
the "big guns," the Archbishop or Kessel, Andrew Zorn, Jacob Willert,
Daruhi, Brother Henry of the Franciscans, Hildebrand, or Lindbrecht,
were announced as speakers. In the south old Oriola, Lange, the conciliator, and General Laurenti, all of them speaking the local dialect,
were popular with audiences. For the first time in Adam's twenty years
the clergy took a hand: it had been as long as that before the prohibi-

tion of unnatural speech, mere quotation, and sanctimonious gesture could produce a race of great pulpit orators. Matthew Brandt records that these men, many of them still young, made by nature for preachers, trained in Zorn's school, and never letting an empty phrase leave their mouths, had surpassed all expectations.

The low ebb to which any hope of preserving civil peace had sunk, however, was shown by Hesse's proposals during the argument in the Academy of Twelve at the start of the campaign. For this and another reason, we will briefly review the debates. For it was not long before voices were heard saying that if John Henry Merckel was right, and governing required nothing but obedience to the Ten Commandments and "remaining a true and upright man," then—always presupposing upright intentions—governing would be the simplest thing in the world, and any honest blockhead could be a ruler, indeed the best of rulers. "Seek ye the kingdom of God," says Scripture, "and all these things shall be added unto you." Well, one thinks, this is really perfectly simple, and Leo Tolstoy's stupid Ivan, supposing that he existed anywhere, would be the ideal figure for a ruler.

This is unfortunately not so. In reality it turns out that to execute God's so plainly revealed will, and withstand the forces of evil, is a task so complicated that even the qualities of "clearheadedness and hardheadedness" praised by Merckel are seldom sufficient.

Thus the opinions of the President's followers were in sharp conflict even during the discussion of Hesse's first proposal, which seemed so simple and so well calculated to overthrow Antichrist. During the election campaign, the police general suggested, the photograph of the tortured stable boy, or rather his bleeding back, along with a brief description of the awful incident, should occupy the front page of every paper in the presidential coalition day after day. At the foot of the page they could put an appeal to surrender to the law the sadist Gregory William Lienhardt, who, like his brother Peter George, was hiding out in the country, and being used for secret assignments by his patron, Dr. Urban. Jacob Willert approved, and so did the bishops and the generals.

Daruhi objected, was backed up by the labor leaders, and gained the upper hand; cruelty and sadism were nothing new, he said, nor even anything that particularly distinguished our age from the past. The part which was really new and unheard of, however, was the fact that a popular leader and liberator could surround himself with sexual criminals and sadists without his reputation's suffering. "If you publish the picture, gentlemen, I can tell you in advance that you will be carrying on propaganda in Urban's favor. You won't win over a single one of his followers, but on the contrary will make them enthusiastic for Urban. The wavering ones will deny the crime; they will call it atrocity propaganda; but the smile with which they deny it shows their desire to follow the criminal's example, and their hope that the day of revenge and delight may be near. Mr. von Hesse seems to have forgotten his own address to the squadrons, where he explains that the era of progress, seen from within, is the era of the tormentor triumphant, and the cry of the victim the paradise of the tormentor. Let us not, after the fashion of the weak, try to conceal the downfall of the human race from ourselves: the more atrocities this Urban can perpetrate unpunished—unpunished, I say—the more godlike he will seem to his contemporaries!"

Hesse thereupon presented his second motion: Let Dr. Urban be required to turn over the sexual criminals Peter George and Gregory William Lienhardt to the police. If he refused, let his party be dissolved and legally prohibited.

When this motion was rejected as unconstitutional, Otto suggested that he might set a city on fire, lay the blame to the Gas-House Boys, and arrest 20,000 of them who were being carried on the list as suspicious. This would break the back of the Urbanites.

The Academy did not reject the motion, but tabled it. First they would see how the elections came out.

Finally Hesse moved that the military command should be instructed in case of civil war to ignore Urbanite acts of sabotage—that is, not to hasten to the rescue of a burning and waterless city—but to employ all available military force against the rebels. The Academy decided to leave the generals a free hand "to behave in accordance with the particular circumstances."

Once more all the right-thinking heaved a sigh of relief when the election results were made public in mid-February. True, Urban lost only one seat, but the Reds had none at all, and the intervention of the pulpit orators, already mentioned, made the Archbishop's Middle-Class Party the second strongest in both houses, with eighteen seats. The presidential coalition won a splendid victory, as is evident from the following table:

Urbanite Party   28
Christian Middle-Class Party
　　　(Leader, the Archbishop)   18
Conservatives
　　　(Leader, Jacob Willert)   15
Democratic Reform Party
　　　(Leaders, Hildebrand and Lindbrecht)   12
Liberals
　　　(Leaders, Oscar Koenig and Kuehn)   2
　　　　　　　　　　　　　　　　　　　　　　　　 ——
　　　　　　　　　　　　　　　　Total   75

Even if the two Liberals joined Urban, he was in a hopeless minority with his thirty votes against the presidential coalition's forty-five. On the other hand, there was no denying that he had for the second time united more than a third of all the votes.

There was uneasiness mingled with the joy of victory. Adam Faust, now in his eighty-first year, had lived out his life. The President's affairs were conducted by the Secretary of State, Count Savoya, called Brother Henry. The old man believed he had arranged for the succession; his "Instructions, to be Opened After My Death," listed by name the next President, Augustus Beyer, and his colleagues in the government. The Academy had approved of these instructions, and the general election had put the presidential coalition back into the saddle.

And so when he awakened from his half doze, in the gray dawn and again late in the afternoon, the President devoted himself to Bible interpretation, as if all business affairs were disposed of. He well knew that the preachers of both persuasions had brought him the victory, and he received them individually and in delegations; but he never asked any questions or made any inquiries. They sat still and listened, while he taught them until he fell asleep and the visitors tiptoed away.

About this time von Brick began to urge the intimates to pension him off and appoint Otto von Hesse Federal Commissioner, so that Alexandra's wedding could finally take place: there could be no further doubt of the Senate's giving the necessary confirmation.

The Academy declined, feeling that the opportune moment for smashing Urban had not yet arrived. So at last Hesse, out of pity for the forsaken old man, gave up his stipulation; the wedding was celebrated with great pomp at the von Brick mansion; Dorothy Kersting, née Thiess, shut herself up in her bedroom and wept, for which this was not the only reason. The public, however, regarded the event as "fair weather," an augury of peace, since Hesse's ambitions seemed to have been bought off with a dowry of three million thalers and a military promotion.

On the same February day the President's adjutants, Messerschmidt and Bogatzki, were promoted, the first to be a major, the second to be a lieutenant colonel; Schwann, the head of Hesse's secret service, was made a colonel; General Kraus took command of the First Army Corps, with headquarters in the seaport of Neuhafen. Marie Klingenberg, Charles Froehlich the secret agent's beater, married, after the death of her father, a gardener named Fred Uhl, employed at Jacob Willert's country estate. And at the Women's Hospital, in the arms of Peggy Witt, Jacob Willert's Geisenheim Roman lady, there died Cornelia Heide, wife of Bernard Sebastian Heide, supervisor and head of the kitchen-furniture department at Senator Kuehn's furniture factory. She died after giving birth to her third child, having asked Head Nurse Margaret to look after her husband and the children.

Our Emil, the Lion of Afghanistan, moved into the city mansion of Countess Bessonoff, who was not old enough to live the life of a widow. During those months he grew together with that completely dissimilar character, Frank Jaeger, the Caucasian Oak, to form the "Heavenly Twins," at least in the eyes of the public, because the two tall, preternaturally stout figures stood behind the League Leader wherever he spoke, in uniform and with legs astraddle. Emil, however, had become one of Urban's permanent entourage, as a male nurse; Frank, on the other hand, was only fetched occasionally from his printing shop for the sake of ornament.

True, not even Emil (although he was far more courageous than Frank) or the squad of twenty-five lined up before the speaker's stand could effectively protect the "great man" if Hesse should get permission to arrest him: but this permission was not forthcoming. And indeed what reason could have been given? He had committed no crime. That he was helping two criminals, Peter George, the murderer of the girl, and Gregory William Lienhardt, the violator of boys, to escape from punishment was a mere suspicion of the Carpenters, not susceptible of proof. And Adam Faust had declined to offer a bill that would allow an evildoer to be arrested because he was "definitely *preparing* for his misdeed."

Seen through the eyes of foreign countries and our own educated middle class, Urban was our greatest party leader, and personally impeccable. If he could be arrested, then no public speaker was safe from persecution, and the constitutional guarantee of liberty was abolished.

BOOK TWO

EUTHANASIA

XVIII

O N FEBRUARY 25, a Saturday, at noon, Jacob Willert and Beyer, some young clergymen who had distinguished themselves in the campaign, the two senior generals, Frohwein and Kaempf, and Albert Ackermann were summoned to the President's mansion.

"It looks as if the old man had got over the hill," said the adjutant, Major Messerschmidt, to those assembled in the anteroom. "He's feeling strong, and wants to see you all together." Well, if things had been looking bad, or if solemnities had been intended, the suddenly summoned callers felt that the sick man would certainly have demanded the presence of the bishops, and of Andrew Zorn, Daruhi, Matthew Brandt, and Hesse. What could he want?

Adam Faust was sitting by the window of the sun parlor, his back to the brightness that streamed in, his feet on a pillow, in a deep upholstered armchair. He invited his friends to be seated near him, and immediately addressed Albert Ackermann, the writer.

"You'd better take care," he said with surprising vivacity, "that the same thing doesn't happen to you as what happened to my long since dead and rotten favorite, who perished at thirty, nobody knows where. He wrote the finest stage scene that was ever thought up, the last in a play called, I think, *The Soldiers*. Do you remember?"

Albert Ackermann did not read much, was familiar only with our native writers, and did not remember.

"Of course you know the scene where a high-spirited girl, a jeweler's daughter, is seduced by a lieutenant, runs away from home, falls all the way to the gutter, becomes a whore, and finally invites her own father, who has been traveling around searching for his favorite child, to come up to her room. Is there such a thing as a misery too deep to know its own father?"

"Certainly!" nodded young Ackermann.

"There was a great deal of moralizing done in those days," the old man went on, "and the play bore the alternative title, 'Mothers Take Note!' Because the author of the play was a true moralizer, I mean not one of your modern parlor moralists, who digs up and displays filth because he's in love with it, they summoned him to the prince's court. This was bound to turn out badly, because though he was a moralizer, he was also a poet. What crime he may have been guilty of at court I don't know—probably let his tongue rattle on, and clapped ladies-in-waiting on the behind. They chucked him out, because they never dreamed that a poet is something that grows behind garden fences and in gypsy carts. Now you know why I didn't summon you to court and make you Clerk to the Government when Hilgenfeld died. I didn't want pride and a wrinkled nose to heave you out, so that you could perish like Raymond Lenz. I haven't given Rudolphi any title, for the same reason, because you're both gypsies. Now go on home!"

Ackermann kissed the old man's hand, and went home, wondering what the gossip about him had been this time. Ought he to play the indignant husband when the strawberry-blonde Hilthofer girl smiled at him? If a man is constantly portraying himself, how is he to control "himself"? What does controlling oneself mean? Does it not mean suppressing self-portraiture? Incidentally—Albert's thoughts ran on—that business about the garden fence and gypsy cart would have applied much more to Rudolphi.

"Are you still annoyed at me for that book *Against Overrating Externals* that I had Hilgenfeld write?" Adam asked the generals.

Both replied that they had never been annoyed.

"Don't tell falsehoods! You thought I wanted to take away your houses. Besides, you were annoyed that I made the pamphlet a subject of examination at the officers' academy."

"The middle classes live more luxuriously than the officers," said Frohwein.

"You shouldn't have deep mirrors in your homes," the President went on as if he had not heard, "or gaming tables, musical clocks, bric-a-brac, and dancing girls. The Carpenters drink no alcohol, and their wives wear high-buttoned dresses with broad linen collars around their necks, so that no one shall be tempted to lay hands on them. You must put every citizen of the country through your school, and set the nation an example in living the simple life that it needs to keep from putting on fat. A nation that puts on fat will grow too lazy and soft to defend itself, and will surrender one outpost after another—ostensibly as a humanitarian matter, but actually from obesity. Marriage is better than lust, and a piece of bread and sausage is better than starving; but a luxurious nation cannot resist, and offers itself to the conqueror like a cheap girl. Why, the Iron Phalanx all over the world has been abusing me as an enemy of equality—ridiculous when you remember that our staff officers have had to study the addresses and opinions of an unschooled turner before a regiment was ever entrusted to them. Why, actually, do they abuse me? It's because I have raised up two professions, yours"—he pointed to the three young clergymen—"and yours"—he pointed to Frohwein—"above all others. For I want the nation to be able to look up; and if it no longer believes in God, then at least it can look up to you; because where there is no looking up at all any more, you have not a human nation, but a bog full of toads. Do you think people will look up to you if you guzzle and stuff yourselves? By rights soldiers and teachers should be one profession, remember that—not two, one of which teaches and the other risks its life. That's wrong. No: he who wants to teach must be ready to risk his life for his teaching; he must be a soldier of instruction. On the other hand, anyone who wants to be a professional soldier must know what he is risking his life for, and that he is not risking it for such preposterous trifles as fine houses or comfortable carriages or electric light or progress and jollity and the poesy of Madame Kittelsen. When I'm dead, Urban will march on the capital, because when he gets that, the hinterland will break out in disorders and strikes. There's a man you can't satisfy, Frohwein, because he can't be bribed, I'm sorry to

say, and if you give him your little finger, he'll take your shirt. Have
you re-enforced the garrison?"

"That I have."

"Give me the figure."

The Chief of Staff wrote a figure on a piece of paper and handed
it to the old man. Adam put on his glasses, read it, gave a contented
smile, tore the paper into tiny pieces, and put them in the pocket of his
dressing gown. "You can go," he said to the generals. "Tomorrow I
want to see Spitta, Leugenfeld, and Hesse.

"Now I'm going to talk to the 'regents,' but you can listen," said
the President to the preachers, with a smile at the word "regent," after
Frohwein and Kaempf had left the room. "There mustn't be any quarreling between you two cousins," he went on after a while, "although
you're very different. But dissimilarity, after all, is humanity, good old
Anton Koerner used to say, and so you two together are conservative
humanity—you two together, because I would have you know, Augustus Beyer, that it isn't sufficient to be made of brittle steel and to strike
the enemy dead before he cozens you. As a stout yes-or-no man, whom
even the sirens could not have tempted, you are the right person for
the job when I die; but a deaf man needs someone by his side who
will yell in his ear. No man with an open ear, not even Odysseus, has
enough strength of character to resist the temptations; that was why
he had himself lashed to the mast. But he didn't close his ears; he
wanted to hear. You make it easier for yourself by saying, like Lindbrecht and Merckel: 'Never deal with an Urban!' You can't manage on
refractoriness and severity alone, Augustus Beyer; you will have to
lend ear to a man who can be tempted; you will have to lend ear, as
I do, not only to a knife-edged sense of justice, but very often to a man
of mercy. Maybe your cousin Jacob's ears are too delicate: he's sure to
hear suffering and a cry for help even in the shout of the pitiless. Your
deafness is a useful weakness as long as you are at the helm between
Scylla and Charybdis; later, on the open sea, you need a man with an
open heart. That is why, now that Andrew Zorn wants to retire, I have
appointed Jacob Willert President of the Academy as of today's date.
Let me rest a minute, but don't leave."

The old man must have pressed a button, for at that moment the doctors, Daruhi and Kuttner, came in through the hidden door on the
far side, the latter carrying a bag of instruments; after them came the

chef, with a covered bowl. The anteroom was now crowded: around a table at the rear sat the sons, Augustus Adam, the head of the machine factories, and Bernard, the mining man, with their married children; the generals had not gone, but were standing talking with Hesse and Spitta by the window; in the middle of the room Lindbrecht and Hildebrand were talking with Andrew Zorn; his son Bruno, the Archbishop, Justice Holzkopf, and Henry, the Franciscan and Secretary of State, were listening. Beyer approached them, Jacob Willert greeted his son, who was sitting against the wall with Leugenfeld and Bogatzki, and Bishop Kessel beckoned to the three preachers in order to question them.

Jacob inquired what the old man was being given to eat. Bogatzki took him down a winding stair to the basement kitchen. The spacious stove with a fender of shining brass stood in the middle of the room. The two cooks and the girl wore white linen dusters and white caps. "The Senator would like to see how the bouillon is made," said the lieutenant colonel, who belonged to the household. The senior cook lifted the lid off one of the copper casseroles, in which something was stewing: two chickens floating in rich soup. With a little kitchen towel he picked up one by the leg and put it on a flat dish; if it had been quite done, the drumstick would have let go. A press resembling an orange squeezer, but much larger, was fixed to the wall; into this the cook dropped the chicken, followed by a piece of beef still pink inside. The boy began to work a lever; Jacob watched steel cogwheels tearing the meat and grinding the bones. The liquid flowed out at the bottom into a china vessel; it was beaten up with egg yolk, and spiced with strong medicinal wine.

Jacob tasted the bouillon, thanked them, and learned that Daruhi was using camphor injections and champagne in small doses to keep the patient's heart going. "But you can't inject a desire to live," Bogatzki added.

Just then a manservant reported that the President wanted to see his visitors. When the five came in, the two cousins and the preachers, Adam was sitting upright, propped up on cushions. His eyes had an unnatural brilliance; he pounded the arm of his chair with feeble impatience, asked them to come closer, and said to the Senators, as if one particular thing were worrying him, "I'm sorry I snapped at Ackermann because of that loose Hilthofer woman, but his wife asked me to, and this whoring around has got to stop. I'm sorry: let him be appointed Clerk to the Government, at once."

Beyer promised to notify the Secretary of State.

The old man immediately heaved a deep sigh, as if feeling relief, leaned back, and looked at the young preachers with an expression of joy. "I do want to thank you for not folding your hands, rolling your eyes upward, and putting on an act for people. I really would never have thought that the present age could still produce prophets. Or was it perhaps I, in conflict with this age, who produced you—at last, at last? In my youth I thought the age of true prophets was past, and we were living in an age of false prophets. Later I discovered that even the age of false prophets was long since gone, and that those who now call themselves prophets—that is, the writers and artists—do not even want to prophesy anything, true or false, especially since they cannot tell the two apart, as everything is relative or 'determined by history,' as the fools like to say. In other words, they want to do something quite different from prophesying or teaching: they want to *sell* prophecies! Our age, then, is not that of true or false prophecies, but of prophecies for sale; or, as the Bishop said, we are living in the age of venal teachers. The man who 'teaches' today doesn't want to teach at all, and can't possibly want to, because if he did want to he would fall, be trampled in the mire, and sold down the river by the Iron Phalanx."

Adam Faust's breath began to rattle; Daruhi, coming in, gave him an injection, and he went on: "Accordingly, he doesn't want to teach, but to sell a doctrine, and live in a villa on what he sells—that's what he wants. Well, then, you three, if you hadn't had me, what would the sellers have made of you the moment they discovered that you didn't want to sell, but to teach, and that you weren't augurs simpering at one another in associations and conventions? What? I'll tell you: they would have forced you either to become sellers or to die. Before God, when the accusing angel names off my sins, I shall boast that I cherished you, bore you and brought you up, so that you did not have to sell yourselves; and then we shall see whether my guilt is not crossed off, whether the scales will not hang level on the balance of justice. I now command every officer and noncommissioned officer to carry the Bishop's *Gospel of the Sunday Mortal* in his knapsack, and there is to be religious instruction twice a week: do you understand, Augustus?"

"It shall be done as you say," replied Senator Beyer.

"Then give me your hand, and tell Messerschmidt outside to bring me my glasses and the newspaper."

They filed past the old man, touching his hand, and heard him whisper, angrily shaking his head: "Good God, how much I've still got to tell them!"

When the President was alone, Major Messerschmidt put his glasses on for him, put a page of newspaper clippings in his hand, and was going out when he heard the paper fluttering to the floor. He spun around, cried out loud, "Dr. Kuttner!" and tilted back the body as it sank forward.

Adam Faust, the fox of God, was dead.

BOOK TWO

HOMAGE TO JOHN THE FAT

XIX

THERE was a funeral such as even the oldest citizen had never seen; Augusta Hoppelkopf swooned again and again; the fragments of the Liberal Party, Senator Kuehn, who had furnished the modern kitchens in the suburb of East Luisenhof, and Oscar Koenig with his "idealistic bellyache," were seen in the funeral procession; and even Urban's own *People's National Times* appeared with mourning bands, a portrait of the deceased, and a caption that the well disposed called "magnificently objective," the others, "tricky":

> *He was a man, take him for all in all,*
> *We shall not look upon his like again.*

The thought behind it was obvious from the second line: if "his like" were not seen again, whose turn must it be to rule? Surely the other "great man" of our country—the same who had pushed aside the Reds, and who now remained as the only serious opponent of the system.

In a night session of the Senate, convened on March 1, twenty-four hours after the funeral, Jacob Willert announced in the name of the coalition of episcopal, conservative, and reform parties—the majority, that is—that since an election had just been held, and the mechanical facilities for voting had not been dismantled, the presidential election could take place within the next fortnight. In the interest of business and industry it was highly desirable to restore quiet throughout the country as soon as possible.

Weisse as the leader of the Urbanites, the strongest single party in both chambers, demanded to know what the term "restore quiet" meant. Adam Faust's coffin, he declared, had not yet been put into the vault when the Minister of War had called the last two classes of reserves to the colors, ostensibly for spring maneuvers, General Laurenti had equipped a "scientific expedition" to go marauding on private property in the southern frontier mountains, and at least fifty thousand Carpenters employed in industry and agriculture had received their green letters, that is, their orders to be ready for police duty.

To this, Henry the Franciscan replied on behalf of the provisional government that Urban's secret service had not even waited for the President's death, but had caused three carloads of parts for fieldpieces to be sidetracked and removed on the day before the event; whereupon Weisse shouted to the chamber, asking in what well-ordered state field artillery was so badly guarded that it could be stolen. If this disappearance were a fact and not mere clumsy propaganda, certainly the people would cause those responsible to be sidetracked and removed.

The Franciscan monk replied scornfully that if Mr. Urban were to offer his celebrated secret service for sale, he would get sixpence for it, no more: the removal of the guns (perfectly simple and safe to do by night if the railway management consisted of traitors) had been beyond their powers to keep secret even for twelve hours. Those responsible had already reached the lunatic village on Tuch heath by way of the interrogation depot.

As the tone of the two indicated that for the present there was no honest will to reach an understanding on either side, and that the Urbanites, furthermore, contrary to previous agreement, were presenting their leader, the Senate voted that the presidential election should take place on the second Sunday following, March 12.

One day later, on March 2, the Academy convened, and the fifth article of Adam's instructions to his successor was read aloud. Albert Ackermann read, and the twenty-four members and candidates listened, standing.

Homage to John the Fat

Let me devote a few words to my predecessor, old John, whom the people called "the Fat"—a nickname, incidentally, that would never have been given to an unpopular President, for we are fond of fat people.

John's love of peace was so great that he never inspected a troop division, but allowed our military institutions to decay. It took me seven years to build up a real army out of the comfortable ruin that John had left behind. His dislike of soldiering sprang from a fatal weakness, the optimism that leads a person to suppose people and states are kindly beings who will kindly refrain from ever attacking us, so long as we give them no provocation.

I was still a young man, about forty, when I got into an argument with him for that reason. "Look here, do you claim to be a patriot?" I yelled at him. After meals you could safely yell at him; he was always occupied with enjoyment and his silver toothpick.

"A patriot? No, my lad," he said perfectly calmly, "I'm a Christian ruler."

This surprising, I might even say stunning, reply led me to reflect upon John and his system, so different from the system established under my presidency.

John, as you know, removed from school and college textbooks all anecdotes calculated to arouse or increase patriotic pride, and prohibited all patriotic celebrations in memory of military successes. Such things spread pride, he said, the begetter of bloodshed. At the same time his popularity was so tremendous that he could always intimidate the Senate by simply threatening to call the nation to the polls for a direct referendum. In his day no officer was chosen for the Academy of Twelve, and as every patriot was suspected of trying to goad us into war, John himself held the portfolio of Foreign Affairs. He made no alliances with foreign powers: "Anyone who wants to make an alliance with you," he said, "wants to use your strength for his own purposes." He restricted treaties with foreign nations to five years, and in his excessive caution he always included a *rebus sic stantibus* clause.

"But we need alliances," I said to him. "Quarrels can't help arising, because this country is short of raw materials."

"Quarrels haven't anything to do with raw materials," he said. "Quarrels are always artificial fabrications of ambition, lust for glory, or arrogance. Because if you don't cheat the country that produces raw materials, it will be even more eager to sell its surplus to you than you are to buy it."

John was fortunate; the sunlight of peace shone upon us for all the thirty years of his presidency. Not until he was drawing near to death did the horizon darken, and Daruhi's "cosmic fog," a monstrous vapor of stultification, magniloquence, envy, rage, and hatred, descend to poison the race of men.

I cannot agree with Matthew Brandt when he says that the causes of this "decay" should be investigated. Instead I agree with Andrew Zorn, who says that this age is not one of decay, but merely the normal condition of mankind, a race altogether subject to Satan, whereas the interludes of peaceful happiness are abnormal, a sort of feeble and temporary victory of God over the Lord of the World.

Looked at in this light, fat John or any advocate of disarmament behaves like a gambler trusting to something wholly unmanageable and unlikely, his own good luck. Furthermore, I don't believe in the pacifists' peaceable intentions that they proclaim, but rather in the far from peaceable ones that they conceal—or their subconscious knows of. I shall curse my pupils and successors if they neglect army, navy, or police.

Conceding all this, still it is my wish that if a monument be erected to me anywhere, my predecessor John shall have his monument facing it not far away, and certainly neither smaller nor of poorer material than mine.

For while I was spending the first seven years of my presidency establishing an army better trained and more quickly mobilizable than what any of our neighbors had, the life and teachings of John the Fat, the true pacifist (as distinguished from the hypocrites), bore unexpected fruit.

I was sixty when I took office—not a silly boy fond of playing with fire, and not contemptuous of the little man who pays with his blood for the pride of the great. I was quite aware that in building up the army and administration I would also cultivate a bloody vice—indeed, the bloodthirstiest among all the subtle vices: national pride. That was why I favored the churches, the sects, the Order of Carpenters; that was why I pounded Christianity, the religion that humbles pride, into army and government; that was why every officer had to show familiarity with the opinions and utterances of an unschooled pietist, Anton Koerner, the turner, before he was promoted to be a battalion commander; and he whose life ran counter to these teachings was cashiered from the army. This was why no prelate was permitted to roll his eyes or recite theses that he was not willing to repeat before a jeering crowd in the prosaic daylight of the streets. This was why I kept reiterating my predecessor's decrees against refreshing the memory of victories, or including patriotic anecdotes and adulation of our country in schoolbooks and works of instruction.

I had been in office for about seven years, and was beginning to believe that my Christian endeavors were responsible for the weakness of national sentiment that struck every foreign observer in our beloved nation and fatherland; then something happened that snatched the dead John from oblivion and made my own merits dwindle as if a flash of lightning had lit up the nocturnal countryside.

Urban the agitator had made his appearance: what he preaches is peace; what he produces is hatred; what he tries to accomplish is degradation. To put it more exactly, he did not beget the hatred—it already existed; he stirred it up and whetted it until it was razor-sharp. How? By giving it an object. For it is not true that the object is there first, the subject or cause of hatred. On the contrary, the hatred comes first—just as hunger appears, followed by eating. True, man eats beefsteak and is satisfied; but hatred, devouring its own cause, grows ever hungrier. To put it less metaphorically: if I know exactly what I hate, and it exists in quantity, my hatred constantly grows; whereas if my hatred remains long without nourishment, so that I don't know what I really hate, Satan grows weak and eventually impotent, as in Tolstoy's story of stupid Ivan.

So Urban had to find an object for the existing hatred, a worthy and "just" cause, as durable as possible, that hatred could keep gnawing on, recruiting its strength. He tried his luck with the wholesale hatred called nationalism, and he failed.

My predecessor and friend, John the Fat, attempted to support his theory that man is good by nature (a theory which unfortunately still has many adherents) by a witty argument. He used to say: "If hatred were a quality as natural to man as being hungry or remembering, why would the demagogues rack their brains to think up as durable an object of hatred as possible? Why are whole philosophies elaborated and whole libraries written so that hatred may be kept alive and prevented from dying out? Nationalism, or national pride, for instance, is an awful vice because it is practiced not to exalt one's own nation, but to lower others; to the nationalist his own nation is only a means of humbling other nations. He wants his own nation to be strong as one wants a weapon to be strong that one means to use. Nationalism evokes the slumbering thirst for blood in a good-natured people, and transforms men into devils. If man were diabolical by nature, as the pessimists say, nationalism would surely fit human nature as perfectly as the perception of pain or the sexual instinct. No effort is needed to persuade a normal man to feel the sexual impulse; but tremendous effort, incessant exertion, filling whole libraries, is needed to persuade him of nationalism or other objects of hatred. Not even love of country, as different from nationalism as water is from fire, is natural to man, for he is descended from nomads.

"Man is no angel, but he is good, because he enjoys doing good. To make him do evil, to make him hate and despise other people or nations, you must educate him, stimulate him, goad him on."

Thus John the Fat, whom we might also call the Fortunate, because all his life was a Sunday, and he never knew the normal condition of humanity. True, his train of argument is correct from *A* to *Z,* but it proves far less than he meant to prove. It proves only that God is at war with the Lord of the Globe, and that God is constantly exerting His influence upon man, the child of Satan, with his "slumbering thirst for blood."

It is impossible to establish Christianity unless national pride is first broken down. This view is shared by John Henry Merckel, for in his *Dictionary of Splendid Phrases* he says of *nationalism* that it is the mask of malice in our time, chosen by Satan a hundred and fifty years ago from among the abundance of masks, when the true visage was beginning to show through the older disguises. And further, Merckel well says: "The hundred opportunities that Antichrist makes use of, the masks he puts on, the excuses he utters, no longer interest us. We no longer ask the murderer who shows us his victim's purse whether he was merely bent on robbery—for we know perfectly well that the robbery is an excuse of Satan, who wanted to hear the cry of the victim and see his blood flow.

"The psychological gentry cannot tell us that the murderer was really only a robber, or that the murderers of Bishop Hesse were actually nationalists who did murder for patriotism: we have learned in the training courses that they became nationalists to hear the cry of the victim, which may be a very faint cry. Indeed, an unpretentious malice may be satisfied with the silence and the fear of the person humiliated."

As I say, it may have been in my seventh year as President, or it may have been earlier, that the Academy told me Dr. Urban, unquestionably the shrewdest demagogue of his age, had put his agitation on a wholly new footing, since (in his own words) "National pride has perished beyond reviving in this nation, completely corrupted by the bloated John." So far Urban had been a nationalist: his first organization was called the League of Patriotic Farm Laborers (as if other farm laborers were men without honor or country), and his paper was the *People's National Times* (as if other papers were antinational). But his exhortation to national pride—that is, the hatred of other nations—found no echo in this country. None of our fellow countrymen thought it a privilege to have been born in this particular country; no one now despised any foreign nation. Therefore Urban had to devise a new doctrine of hatred, since nationalism had proved worthless: this, as you know, was the doctrine of world salvation through him.

Thereupon I gave orders to set up a marble monument in front of the Senate building to the dead John, with the inscription:

> *To John the Fat*
> *Beloved of the People*
> *Because he shattered national pride.*

For this much, my friends, I recognized even then: with all my efforts to reawaken some slight love for Christianity, I would have failed miserably unless my predecessor had devoted thirty years of his life to snatching from the degrader's face the (momentarily) final mask of Satan—nationalism, which is nowhere else recognized for the mask it is.

As this part of the "Instructions to My Successor" is meant for publication, and the uninitiated too will read it, I must add some explanation to what I have already said.

Many of the uninstructed believe even now that nationalism is actually an elevated patriotism, harmful because elevated (as elevated drinking is harmful), but otherwise deserving of honor. What about this?

In Greek and Roman antiquity patriotism was a party affair, and by no means deserving of honor in our eyes. Hardly a single ancient patriot hesitated, if an opposing party governed his native city, to summon foreign foes into the country, and with their help to destroy his homeland. In the late Middle Ages the Florentine Dante, a patriot and adherent of the Imperial party, implored Emperor Henry VII, a foreigner, to destroy Florence because the Pope's party, the Guelphs, held power there. These ancient and medieval patriots behaved just like our modern nationalists: they were partisans—plebeians or patricians (like Coriolanus) in antiquity, Guelphs or Ghibellines in later Italy. If they themselves could not rule their fatherland, they preferred to have it perish. That was how much they loved it.

Present-day nationalists, when they believe that their hour has come, never hesitate for a second to summon foreign nationalists into the country in order to establish their own dominion by this foreign help. To the international party of nationalists the term "high treason" has lost all meaning. They constantly betray their own countries without any consciousness of guilt.

The nationalist wears a double mask, one outside, the second hidden under this. The outer mask says: "I love my fatherland passionately, and want to raise it above other fatherlands." Only very stupid people believe this by now. But even the clever trust the second and better hidden mask, which says: "I hate other fatherlands, because they are different from mine." The speech of the second mask sounds much more probable, because it admits the hatred that is evident in everything a nationalist says; hatred, after all, is unquestionably his mainspring. But hatred for whom? For other fatherlands? No, my friends: the nationalist cares as little for other fatherlands as he does for his own. We must realize, on the contrary, that he is an international party man, whose fellow members are scattered the world over. It is them he confers with, them he trusts, to them that he betrays every secret of his own "fatherland," even in wartime, without feeling any guilt. *Because*—and here is his moral justification—the international party of nationalists is *his fatherland;* his own homeland, on the other hand, he hates as long as it has not a nationalist government, and he will slander his own national government more bitterly than any foreign one.

If Urban has too much trouble seizing power in his own country, he will try to seize it in our neighboring country, through his partisans there. If he succeeds in this, our neighboring country will declare war on you, and our native Urbanites will join the enemy. Therefore you must help our still peaceful neighbor, the government of the Southwestern Republics, to suppress the Urbanites before they get too strong, and so must you help any other government, no matter how remote, that is harassed by Urbanites.

For we too, my friends, are partisans—let us be honest. We too, my friends, we Christian conservatives, are, *let us hope,* an international party; and if we are not as yet, we mean to become one. The difference between the Urbanites and us is not, then, that they are international and we are national. I hope not: a national party in our day is about as important as a bridge club or an association of canary breeders. No, the difference is that we are the party of God, while they are the party of Satan, the Lord of the World. Because we are the party of God, not a single soul and not a single government need fear us, for we hate intermeddling unless it is forced upon us. We are glad to live in isolation if people will let us live in isolation. We do not believe that we have a mission, or that salvation will originate with us. We do not believe that God has created individual men and nations equal; therefore they cannot be ruled in the same way. We believe that equality is of the devil, and that the Lord our God delights in multiplicity.

I have written this homage to John the Fat so that his teaching about nationalism may never be forgotten, and so that you may exterminate the last remaining traces of this bloody vice by persuasion or force. For I believe it possible that the Iron Phalanx, in order to confuse vocabularies and stir up the people against you, my friends, may import from abroad to our peaceable country such ruinous doctrines as the optimism that would smile Satan out of existence, the pacificism that would disarm the soldiers of God, or the nationalism that would turn you into devils.

THE CRITICAL MONTH OF MARCH

XX

IN VIEW of the dangerous candor about Urban embodied in the fifth section of the "Instructions," publication was postponed. And as if at a preconcerted signal a torrent of pacifist propaganda swept over the country, bringing even to the small towns confusion and arguments that wound up as fist fights.

"Peaceful, peaceful, we adore thee," the Iron Phalanx wrote. "Now at last thou art here." For, they declared, the nation that would go to the polls on the twelfth demanded peace; it was weary of intrigue, guile, and violence. Both candidates, Beyer and Urban, were invited to make written statements about how they meant to safeguard peace.

Urban replied at once in the *People's National Times* that his program was peace for all humanity. There followed some very pretty phrases about the blessings dispensed among the nations by peace.

No one in the Faustite camp answered at all—neither Henry the Franciscan, head of the provisional government, nor Beyer himself.

The Iron Phalanx thereupon offered to come to the aid of the "ailing textile magnate" if he found himself embarrassed by the public posing of this question. For if he became President he could very easily assure peace by simply governing in the spirit of the constitution, and not trying to establish a veiled dictatorship. And the spirit of the constitution demanded that the greatest party leader in the country, who had gained more than a third of the entire popular vote scarcely a month before, should have a share in the government.

Beyer replied in *The Conservative* that if elected he would continue the work of his teacher and friend, Adam Faust. Not a word about peace or the spirit of the constitution.

Dr. Urban began to feel uneasy. The mass of voters is not volatile enough to revoke immediately a verdict given after six months' intensive propaganda; the man who had voted against the League Leader on February 11 would not vote for him on March 12. This calculation of the Faustites in preventing postponement of the presidential election seemed correct. So the great man, a calculator quite without illusions down to his dying day, saw only two expedients: a quite new, at once surprising and horrifying element had to be injected into the election campaign, and at the same time the unsuitability of the Conservative candidate must be proved.

On March 7, five hundred thousand copies of Urban's election leaflet were distributed. It asserted, quoting alleged eyewitness reports and sworn testimony, that Beyer, the textile magnate, had lived the life of the Roman Emperor Tiberius for seven years on an island in the Adriatic, with the children of the poor fisherfolk as his catamites. As he was already quite incapable of serious work, it declared, the cabal of generals—led by the blood-drinking Hesse, the well-known madman, who had shot three waiters at the Café Opéra—had put forward the diseased and palsied dotard for President, so that they might the more easily commit the crime of a foreign war against the Federation of Southwestern Republics. The reserves had already been called to the colors—"All in vain! For our peace-loving nation will elect the leader toward world peace, Dr. Urban!"

But "our peace-loving people" (not so imaginative as Willie Gaedicke, author of the above-quoted Urbanite campaign leaflet, and now restored to favor) preferred to believe the police reports that were immediately published showing the textile magnate's domiciles and removes during the past seven years. Hildebrand at a public meeting called the Urbanite leaflet bum-wad.

On March 12 Augustus Beyer was elected President of the Republic by an overwhelming majority. The following day the Iron Phalanx changed its tactics: the pacifist propaganda was backed up with Christianity. It was asserted that the people had elected the ailing spinner with confidence in his election promise to continue old Adam's work. Therefore the Christian commonwealth must now be established, the brotherly fellowship wherein swords would be beaten into peaceful implements, the police force reduced, and the mobilized troop units returned to a peace footing.

"No one shall reproach us," wrote Nicholas Edwin Schiele in *Freedom and Culture*, "with requiring Christianity from the government while we ourselves are backward in Christian conduct."

And indeed the Iron Phalanx was not backward, it took the lead:

the populace was inundated with a flood apparently long dammed up
—vast quantities of editorial leaders, popular articles, and Utopian
short stories in which souls were reconciled, armies flung away their
weapons, magnanimous industrialists forged their guns into plow-
shares, whole police forces abolished themselves amid wild cheering,
and prison warders embraced murderers after flinging wide their cells.

Innocent Isabella Rex, not giving another penny of his income now
to the impotent Reds, had been recognized since the appearance of his
novel, *The Life of My Grandma, Asleep in Christ and the Catholic
Faith,* as a specialist in Christianity. He was doing very well for himself by collecting twenty per cent of the author's fee from the innumerable brothers-clasp-hands articles, which were submitted to him
with a marginal note, "Everything in Except Religion," and then received a dash of religious flavor, sometimes even after they were in
type. For two hundred and fifty thalers apiece he wrote the two chorales, *Be With Us, Holy Ghost* and *Whom Did God's Son Cherish
First,* for the Disciples of Emmaus, a body that he founded; thus he
felt sure he had made provision for his family, even supposing that
Christianity should gain the upper hand after Urban's defeat.

Mark Antony Perlotta bought cheaply from an unspecified source a
dramatic choral work called *The Passion of the Lamb;* but he joined
neither the Disciples of Emmaus nor the Penitent Congregation of the
Last Judgment, founded by Schiele and Hoppelkopf.

The Christian propaganda, enormous in extent, spread confusion
and rebelliousness among the Federal Police Corps. In kitchens, on
back stairs, over garden fences, at groceries, in butcher shops, excited
policemen's wives in wide linen collars discussed the imminent dismissal of their husbands from the federal service, and said they would
have to take to beggary, for word had already got around that Augustus Beyer's "Christian commonwealth" would immediately reduce the
army, disband the Federal Police, and order the lion to graze on clover
along with the lamb. With such nonsense as this the policemen's wives
poisoned their husbands' minds; and since Hesse, turning over the
conduct of affairs to Colonel Schwann and occupying himself with
plans for defending the capital, was not available to callers, an impression was created that the government was avoiding an unequivocal
statement. True, to put down the suspicion that the Beyer government
was pacifistic it would have been necessary only to publish Faust's

"Instructions," which were known to nobody except the twelve of the Academy. The Preamble expressly stated that a Christian captain must above all strengthen the army and police. But the publication was not undertaken, because of the dubious reference to dictatorship as an expedient.

On March 20, Police Majors Stark, Lorenz, and Lindequist arrived at the presidential mansion to ask assurance that there would never be a "Christian commonwealth."

"How much more are you going to want?" the textile magnate, now growing nervous, snapped at them. "Do you by any chance mean that if I don't eat out of your hand you won't fight? Almost the entire economic system of production and distribution is passing into the hands of the industrial leagues, fellowships, and brotherhoods; they will also have the last word about the use of the taxes they raise. But the state, protecting the function of the teacher, is going to take on a religious character—you can just make up your minds to that!"

With this unsatisfactory statement the three had to return to their companions who were assembled in the chapel in the No. I Barrack yard. Like almost all Faustites they were backward people, who had to be spoken very plainly to; it was the harder for them to see through the deceitful leftist propaganda that called Christianity pacificism, or nonresistance, because their own brother in the order, Beyer, seemed to be playing the same tune with his demand for a "religious commonwealth." If a leftist like Nicholas Edwin Schiele had announced to them that the religious commonwealth meant rule by prelates, they would have believed him without more ado, and would have been quite satisfied so long as the "ruling prelates" allowed them to continue as police. But they did not want to listen to the outcry of the women any longer, and if things were going to be altogether "Christian," then they would hold everything up to Brother Hesse: the severity and grave hazards of their duty, their battles, wounds and losses in the encounters with the Sports Detachments; how little they contented themselves with, and what he had promised them if they risked their lives for the Faust system; and also that they excelled in honesty, took no bribes, and thus had amassed a fund of public confidence such as the police had never enjoyed before their time.

On March 21 the Iron Phalanx newspapers spread it around that the President had driven Hesse's corps to rebellion; thus, owing to the

incapacity of a government controlled by sick men, the state was beginning to dissolve from within, and the danger of bloody disturbances
was imminent. If only the two houses of parliament, to save the fatherland, would at last remember their right to vote lack of confidence in
the President by the necessary majority!

This impudence went too far. The Academy convened.

Meanwhile the League Leader had harmed his own standing by an
exchange of letters with the President.

Just as the gods first drive mad those whom they would destroy,
Urban, defeated in the election, and not awaiting the start of the next
round, approached Beyer in a letter of congratulation; he made fun of
his own leaflet instead of allowing it to be forgotten, described it as
a forgivable, because traditional, trick of propaganda, and demanded
the three cabinet seats that had been promised him—War, Public
Safety, and Justice.

The President immediately published Urban's highly compromising
letter and his own reply: Before he could enter into negotiations, the
Sports Detachments would have to be dissolved, uniforms and small
arms destroyed, the artillery and ammunition dumps handed over unharmed to the proper garrison commanders, and the sexual criminals
Peter George and Gregory William Lienhardt, as well as the munition-
maker Alois Borstel, who had furnished the Sports Detachments with
their new field artillery and at least a thousand army instructors, must
be delivered up to the Federal Police.

Urban could now see that the new ruler was more narrow-minded,
unimaginative, and dangerous than the old one, and that if he could
not manage to win over Jacob Willert, the peace-loving president of
the Academy of Twelve, he would have to fight. Without delay he prepared for both: the bloody conflict and a friendly alliance with Jacob
Willert.

At the white palace of finance on Lady Square, Weisse handed over
a respectful communication in the League Leader's own hand to the
president of the Academy of Twelve, in which Urban declared that
he had wrestled in prayer with God Almighty as to whether he, a tired
man, should accept the mandate of the people and bear one third of
the burden of responsibility. Still undecided, he was addressing himself
to Senator Willert for impartial counsel. He would not have troubled
him, he said, if it had not seemed likely that his own followers, dis-

gruntled at their leader's inactivity, might be led to take ill-considered steps.

At the same time the Sports Detachments of the entire country received verbal orders through special officers to be ready for immediate war. Dr. Grau, head of the secret service, the general, and Justus Thomas went on a tour of inspection to co-ordinate the activity of the Gas-House Boys with the military operations. The southern branch of the secret service was instructed *to prevent General Laurenti's "scientific expedition" from trespassing upon the forests and caves, the Lienhardts' private property.*

In the large and medium-sized towns of the Federation of Southwestern Republics, our peaceful neighbors for a hundred years past, meanwhile, streets and public halls were echoing with the war cries of the Urbanites. "Forward!" they cried. "Drive out this cowardly government, which is handing over our beloved nation and fatherland to barbarians already prepared to attack! Forward, to arms against the interlopers who are showering incendiary bombs on the flourishing industry of our eastern provinces in order to possess themselves of the globe! Remember our forefathers! Long live progress and jollity! Down with the sons of bitches! Down with the prelates! Smash them in the face and send their teeth flying! Down with these men of darkness and their system ripe for death!"

Beyer, asked for an explanation by the terrified neighboring government, advised them to silence the impudent liars, whereupon our Iron Phalanx accused him of "unauthorized intermeddling in the domestic affairs of a foreign state." But the foreign Urbanites shouted in vain: negotiations still went on.

For Jacob Willert, although he had burst out laughing at Urban's statement that he had "wrestled in prayer with God," did not turn away this request for counsel, but advised accepting the conditions made by the President, at least in part, as an earnest of good will. With more than a third of the electorate behind him, surely Urban could give up playing soldier, and use the money that the Sports Detachments cost him for some more useful purpose. Why did he not prefer to make himself useful to the country as the recognized leader of the opposition? He, Jacob, and his son were ready to mediate between the government and the leader of the Yellows if the latter would disband his "army" and surrender his arms.

In his second letter Urban expressed his thanks for the advice and his esteem for the president of the Academy. He said he would consult with his friends.

This was the state of affairs on March 22, when our Academy of Twelve, anxious to vindicate the honor of the head of the state, decided to arrest the Iron Phalanx in a body when all the writers, journalists, and publishers' readers were gathered for the next monthly meeting at Oscar Koenig's house. Such a resolution, taken in normal times, requires an executive order from the President for its execution, and Augustus Beyer asked for an expert opinion from Dr. Merckel by the usual circuitous route. Young Willert reports that Merckel, horrified, cried out, "No, for God's sake, don't!"—the Academy must have been blind to divert public attention from the enemy five minutes before the battle started. For, once *he* (Urban) had met his downfall, the Iron Phalanx, a perfectly harmless company of pompous nonentities, could be wrapped around one's little finger.

Merckel's memorandum, received on March 27, said: "Certainly the Iron Phalanx has commercialized intellectual life, and either smothered the average man, the 'Sunday Mortal,' or turned him into a seller. Certainly our nation has been demoralized by the discovery that it can depend on no one, because its 'teachers' can be bought. But I ask you: did any of the Iron Phalanx ever set up a naked girl as a target, and kill her by inches? Did any member of the Iron Phalanx ever have a stableboy flayed in order to send himself 'to paradise' during the procedure, through the agony of the victim? Has it ever been shown that malice, delight in the humiliation and torment of a victim—that essential attribute of Satan—is a characteristic of the Iron Phalanx? No member of it has ever been guilty of a crime of violence. No: these petty literati have none of the dreadfulness, the energy and grandeur of Satan. Diana Rose, too, often swoons; but does she own an umbrella at the end of which a dagger is mounted under a leather hood? Have you ever seen flashing in her eyes the white enthusiasm of the murderer who imagines his bleeding victim, as I have seen it at Urbanite meetings in the flashing, murderous eyes of bashful young girls and chaste blonde housewives —the same housewives who seem interested in nothing but scrubbing and recipes, and who teach folk songs to their tender, murderous children at home, perspiring the milk of human kindness and playing the lute? Why does murder glow in those gentle blue eyes; why do I seem to hear the victim scream when that red mouth smiles? Am I deaf? Yet I hear their teeth grit, I hear their daggers crunching into the victim's body as they coo 'good morning' outside the church door on Sunday; I can hear their orgiastic cries as the executioners march into the hall, and the commander in chief of murder lifts his hand. Instead of welcoming even the dirtiest man who is ready, no matter from what motives, to fight Dr. Urban's international murderers' association, you are apparently thinking of smashing an utterly flabby association of opinion peddlers, who furthermore are harmless because they can be bought, whereas the Urbanites would refuse all the treasures of this world in order to savor their delight in the agony of their victim. If you have forgotten what Adam Faust realized and saw and expressed in his last letter to Jacob Willert, I will pack up my things and my old mother, and emigrate to some nation that can still tell a tiger from a louse."

Merckel's shrewd advice brought it about that the Iron Phalanx, bewildered by the silence of the Academicians, and secretly convinced of the government's strength, showed its willingness to fall in with the Faust system by various religious eccentricities. The rats were now leaving the ship that they had long held suspect; Urban, on the other hand, damned "the *bourgeoisie,* so cowardly they stink, licking the boots of reaction."

Augustus Beyer, equipped with a delicate nose for changes in public feeling, began to think of continuing the dead President's work of cleaning house. The old man had elevated the clergy by ejecting from the theological seminaries first the ecstatics and the unctuous, then the born office clerks, and finally those who wanted to lead a slothful life with money and honor; he had thus produced a generation of great preachers and seekers after God. Just so Beyer proposed to create a Council of Censors to eject from the educational system those writers who conveyed nothing, but merely wanted to sell something. In this way he hoped to elevate the artistic profession at least to a point where the people, feeling itself besmirched by the monstrous filth of the Liebenau Statement, would regain confidence in the "teachers."

"Adam Faust was smothered," said the President to the Academy on March 29, "by the pants peddlers who called themselves artists:

not one of his measures could win popularity, because the 'teachers'—those who presumed to a teaching post—distorted everything. The Perlottas were bound to smother Ackermann: invariably, and of course under the most genteel pretexts, the pants peddler pushes aside the honest man who is able to express his own honesty, for even in these days such a man is dangerous as a competitor to the cheap scoundrel. I use the vocabulary of the training courses, which calls the man who *can* express himself an artist, and him who *wishes* to profess a faith, a prophet.

"So I say that the artistic prophet or teacher of the people is in need of protection, since the Iron Phalanx will either smother him or corrupt him by taking him into its own ranks and making him its accomplice; and as Adam Faust devoted his life to protecting the priest, so I shall devote my life to protecting the teacher from smothering and corruption. I must shield the writer by the same means that Adam used to shield the priest, and that the law uses to shield the honest tradesman. Unfair competition must be suppressed, that is, and an incorruptible Council of Censors must segregate the honest from the dishonest, those who have something to say from those who have themselves to sell or display. The amusement industry need fear nothing; it does not touch upon the field of the censors at all. But anyone who pretends to a teaching post must be put under the magnifying glass to see whether he means to teach or to sell. Thus the nation can regain a little confidence."

So spoke Augustus Beyer on March 29, after seventeen days in the presidency; his tone was sharper than the fox of God had adopted, but the spirit was the same. And he moved the introduction of pre-censorship for printed matter and theatrical performances that professed to be art and instruction; not for those that professed to be recreation and amusement. There was great surprise and a short debate: those members of the Academy who belonged to the Senate and were party leaders, like Jacob Willert, the Archbishop, Lindbrecht, and Hildebrand, withheld their views, for the measure was unpopular, and might be helpful to Urban.

A few hours later Hildebrand, his cheap Mexican cigar in his mouth, arrived at the presidential mansion to say that he could not join in: censorship was suppression.

"Political life is made up of compromises, and everyone must know how far he ought to yield," replied the lank Beyer. "The Council of Censors will not be made up of power seekers or mad dogs, nor of people with wounded ambition, but of such gentle and open-hearted men as Hans Simon, Dr. Nessel, Police Majors Stark and Lorenz, former teachers, and old Lange. You can be a member of the council yourself if you're afraid that proletarian grievances will be suppressed. This much I will say by way of preamble, and something more: I shall not offer the bill to introduce the censorship until Urban and his party have been eliminated from political life. Then, however, I shall present it, and shall consider myself in your debt if you accede to it; for I hear you are not fond of acceding. What do you want from me in return?"

The leader of the "independents" was accustomed to this direct talk, and he gave a direct answer: "It's a fact that thousands of employers, particularly in the east, are making labor contracts with the Urbanite League, but they won't sit down around a table with us, although we Free Unions are strongly represented in the plants. A wave of strikes is about to begin—on our part. We shall demand that the employer cancel his Urbanite contracts, and negotiate with us, or with the Christians where they are in the majority. I've made a deal with Lindbrecht."

"When are the strikes going to start?"

"April first, in the afternoon."

"Where?"

"Here in the capital, beginning at Kuehn's. We require that the government shall support us in the provinces through the provincial governors, the clergy, and possible sympathy strikes by the Carpenters, and here in the capital through the Archbishop, whose mediation we have invoked."

"You realize that you will thus be provoking Urban to go the whole hog?" the President inquired.

"We realize that, and don't care; the man is tremendously over-rated," replied Hildebrand.

Nothing could have suited the President better than this offer by the workingmen themselves to put the slow match to the power keg. "All things come to him who waits," he thought, smiling, and inquired: "Then if I instruct the Carpenters, the provincial governors, and the Archbishop as you wish me to, you'll agree to censorship over works of art and public instruction—a very liberal censorship,

of course. I've already explained the meaning of the thing to you.
You will agree?"

"Yes. For two years to begin with."

"That's enough. When things start at Kuehn's, let me know. I'll
speak to the Archbishop meanwhile."

Hildebrand informed the presidents of the various craft unions,
who were met in the capital at the time, that he had the President's
approval. What he had bought it with he did not say. Disagreeable
things should be let lie; stirring them up immediately is harmful.
And since the censorship was only planned, not yet a fact, he was
withholding from his companions not a fact but only a scheme, which
is less reprehensible. Naturally there was great joy, and the trusted
representatives of the workingmen cheered "good old Hildebrand."
The high spirits that Beyer thus managed to work up among the
"independents" created an irresistible impetus that swept everyone
with it at the great meeting on the night of April 1.

On April 1, Henry Willert took over the family banking business.
Here, at 11 A.M., the pleasant ceremony at the white Willert mansion
was interrupted by terrible news. General Laurenti's scientific expedition to "explore the dripstone caves" had perished with all hands in
the mountainous forests along the frontier. Details were lacking.

In the midst of the bouquets and salutations that welcomed young
Henry as head of the banking house of Melchior Willert, a carriage
rolled up before the main entrance. Major Messerschmidt got out,
and summoned the guest of honor to the presidential mansion, where
the Academy was in session, Merckel having arrived from Mittelburg.
The Academy had already decided to lay its cards on the table. Within
thirty minutes the cabinet proposed in Adam Faust's "Instructions"
had been appointed by the taciturn Beyer:

Interior and Deputy to the President	Merckel
Foreign Affairs	Henry Willert
War	Kaempf
Finance	Andrew Zorn
Justice	Holzkopf
Public Instruction and Worship	Henry the Franciscan
Public Safety	Hesse
Labor and Welfare	Hildebrand

At the stroke of noon, Federal Police encircled Urban's headquarters at Mittelburg, took the League Leader prisoner, and transferred him to the central prison at the capital, at the same time announcing the arrest and its terrible cause. A few hours later they suffered two simultaneous disappointments: the Leader, at Mittelburg five hundred miles away from the place where the expedition had vanished, admitted acquaintance with Alois Borstel and his Professor Bock, and denied all connection with the crime. Interrogation was still going on when an unforeseen counterattack by the Urbanites was announced from the east: the great foodstuff and transport enterprises there, supplying the capital with meat, potatoes, sugar, and grain products, went on strike, and threatened to destroy their stocks if the military should intervene. The day and the following night were spent securing information and conferring to decide whether the capital could be safely enough provisioned from elsewhere. The enemy's possible plan of cutting off communications with the capital, surrounding it, and starving it out had to be taken into consideration. The capital and the provinces heard nothing of the difficulty confronting the newly installed government. There were merely whispers that the great man was in prison for a crime that was not a crime but a natural catastrophe, and that he could not have committed five hundred miles away if it were one.

What had happened?

Professor Bock, a world-famous industrial chemist and director of the Borstel munition works, had caused one of the great dripstone caves to be filled with gas.

Ten hours later, when the celebrated specialist evacuated the gas by a process used in the mines, replacing it with fresh air, he found his suspicion that the "scientific expedition" had been looking for concealed artillery and ammunition confirmed. The dead, in civilian dress, had the Kate Schwann emblem embroidered inside their jackets. They were left lying where they were, and everyone went home, pleased with the thought that the well-known madman had been "given his come-uppance."

THE DOCTRINE OF THE LAMB AND THE TIGER

XXI

WHEN Henry Willert was driving hither and thither through the city on the afternoon of the first in order to feel out the sentiment of the people, he should have noticed the disturbance that had broken out at the gate of Kuehn's furniture factory: closely packed crowds deep in argument, pickets with placards, yelling women, and green mounted policemen, overtopping the knots of people. But the fabulous distortion of the outside world that was his special ailment deprived him on this particular day of all interest in reality.

Toward evening Arthur Kuehn was sitting over the coffee table with buttered rolls at his pretentious villa on the Park. (He hated soft, gooey cakes.) He was explaining to his spouse: "That swine Gasparra—devil knows I always thought that love-lock was suspicious; I'm no reactionary, God knows I'm not, but free love—no, take it away!"

Mary Kuehn, née Susemihl, said with mockery in her voice: "And of course you've got such firm principles!"

"Just one; want to hear it?"

"I know: 'When the bad boys try to tempt you' . . . !"

"No, it's this:

If this is a pot of baked beans
And this a pot of stew,
I'll leave the beans and stew alone
And take my Mary true."

"The bell's ringing," said Mary Kuehn, turning her head. "It can't be Betty Ann."

"How I hate to be interrupted at meals!" groaned the manufacturer, snatching away the napkin that he had tied around his neck, on account of the coffee dripping from the dunked rolls.

Bernard Sebastian Heide, the factory superintendent and foreman of the kitchen-chair plant, was shown in and invited to sit down at the table, and not to get excited, because that affected the gall bladder.

Well, said Heide, eating a roll, the strike had broken out contrary to expectations, though there was no danger, and everything was orderly, because the Federal Police, apparently warned beforehand, had arrived so promptly that the Sports Detachments, already on the way to protect "their plant," had been ordered to return to quarters. "Encounters are to be avoided," the League management had decided, probably in consideration of the negotiations that were going on in prison between the League Leader and the government.

The "negotiations in prison between the League Leader and the government" were a legend circulated by the Urbanites in an extra edition.

"Nothing smashed up?"

"Nothing," Heide agreed, "but the Archbishop is expecting Senator Kuehn this evening at nine—for negotiations looking toward an agreement."

"Who's negotiating for the strikers?"

"Hildebrand."

The manufacturer, with a sidelong glance at his wife, laughed peevishly: "You might as well say negotiations looking toward extortion! What do those two want to 'compromise'—Hildebrand, a Secretary of State of ten hours' standing, and the Bishop? They want to blackmail me, that's all."

"Don't go over, Arthur," said Mary.

"I wouldn't dream of it. My business is my business, which I built up. If the Bishop doesn't like it, let him take it over: we'll see who goes broke first. I'll show 'em who Arthur Kuehn is, ha, ha, ha! Ridiculous! They have no notion of practical life, but over the conference table they talk big—no, no, gentlemen, you aren't going to get at my till, he isn't going to get at my till, no one's going to get at my till; we'll see who's master in my house, me or that ridiculous Mexican-cigar man, seven children in one bed, and they all want to sleep next to the wall, and Grandma sleeps in the coal bin with the *Pensive Watchman* for a blanket. That's what you look like; I'm Arthur Kuehn by my own efforts, president of the Association of

Furniture Manufacturers, honorary president and so on—we'll see!
You look it!"

The length and violence of the monologue convinced both his wife
and the experienced factory superintendent that Kuehn would drive
up to the Archbishop's door promptly at nine, and would sooner sign
a contract with the devil than go through a strike of his best and
best-paid workmen at a moment when he was swamped with orders.
After all, one's fidelity to Urban could scarcely go so far as that;
besides, if he was so strong, why did he let himself be locked up?

It took place as expected. Hildebrand and the Archbishop were
waiting. Kuehn, having exchanged bows, started a carefully rehearsed
address that his wife had approved in their dressing room: "I have
come, Bishop, not only as the head of my own firm, but also as the
president of the Association of Furniture Manufacturers——"

While Hildebrand, disgusted by the magniloquent preamble, was
wondering how he could humiliate this braggart, the Archbishop was
fetching cigars and matches out of his desk, and pointing to a green-
leather armchair: "Won't you sit down, Senator Kuehn?"

The manufacturer—already displeased, since he had rehearsed the
speech in a standing posture—sat down and went on: "I have come
since the strikers, not to say the rebels, have invoked your mediation
—successfully, I am sorry to say!"

Kuehn declined the proffered cigar; indignation rose within him
as the Bishop, glancing at the grandfather clock, hurried the speaker
on, and held out the cigar box toward Hildebrand.

"Light or strong?" asked Hildebrand, as if the question were very
important.

"Light for Secretaries of State," said the Archbishop with a smile.

"You won't get me to change at my time of life," replied the
president of the "independents," taking a cigar and looking at Kuehn.

"This intimacy is just charming," thought the manufacturer savagely as he sat between the Archbishop and the infidel; and his plan
for breaking up the alliance of the Christian and the man who never
set foot in a church suddenly did not seem so promising any more.
As if the rectitude victorious in business could be a failure in any
other kind of life—but they would see!

"Successfully, I am sorry to say," remarked Kuehn as the two accomplices elaborately lit their cigars, carefully keeping the fire away

from the wrapper. "I say I am sorry, as a devout Christian and faithful member of the church. For things are bound to end badly when the Church or Christianity, which is the most sacred thing in the human bosom, allows itself to be dragged down into the mire of struggling interests, nay, when it deliberately descends into the tumult of the street where those treasures are fought for that moth and rust doth corrupt, Matthew 6, 19!" Grasping the arms of his chair, he nodded several times with outthrust chin toward the Archbishop, as who should say: "Well, there you have it, my fine friend!"

The clerical gentleman, momentarily surprised, for the manufacturer was considered to be an Urbanite, remembered the elastic phraseology; he recalled that Urban himself, in speaking to Christians, asserted that he "wrestled with God," and no one took it amiss. The Bishop, then, behind a cloud of smoke, was considering his answer. The impudence of these moneymakers is anything but small, he thought, nor should we despise the rottenness of our salons, where religious phraseology is even welcomed, provided only that it is frivolously meant.

"Yes, sir, Matthew 6, 19," repeated Kuehn in the teeth of Hildebrand, rebellious despiser of religion that he was.

"Well, if you're a Christian, Mr. Kuehn," the Archbishop said at last, "of course that's a very different matter."

"Me, no Christian?" said the manufacturer, jumping up.

"Oh, please sit down," the clergyman soothed him. "I was simply going to say, if you're a Christian, I shall recommend that the police disperse the strikers."

Hildebrand took a long pull at his cigar.

"Excellent," said Kuehn with a sigh of relief. "Our pastor at St. Andrew's Parish will confirm me when I say that the Kuehn family has never missed a church service, not for storm or snow, and that there's never a Sabbath we haven't kept holy—hell's fire, that would be a fine state of affairs! Nevertheless, I'm a sinner, naturally—I say it with all humility before God."

Hildebrand and the clergyman simultaneously remembered the celebrated "Kessel's warning." Almost seven years previously Bishop Kessel, then Hesse's successor in the mountain province, had had all church doors closed to such Christians as the Kuehn family, and on the doors he had posted the "warning against church attendance," because "churchgoing was conceived of as a social duty like parties, teas, tennis, New Year's calls, and baptisms." When "the Christians of the mountain province" petitioned to have the Bishop removed from office, Adam Faust promoted him by calling him to the capital.

But Count Savoya (which, as will be remembered, was the Archbishop's name) did not want to humiliate this captain of industry whom twenty years of the Faust system had passed by quite out of sight and hearing. This self-made man, unlike the Iron Phalanx and the intelligentsia, was by no means an envier, hater, and disdainful smiler at a higher form of intellectual life. He was only a stranger, unacquainted with it owing to an existence filled up with success and progress; it would be rude, spiteful, and cheap to insult him, whereas it promised to be a useful endeavor to lead him by the hand like a child.

Hildebrand, on the other hand, felt a smug pharisaical satisfaction that he had not allowed himself to be made a fool or an accomplice of by Kuehn's Christianity.

"Excellent, Mr. Kuehn," the Archbishop praised him, "or, to put it plainly, better than nothing." And upon the Senator's opening his mouth as if to let in some understanding of such contradictions, the clergyman went on: "There are a hundred and sixty-eight hours in a week. At least you have sacrified four or five hours to churchgoing, hymnbook carrying, listening to sermons, and singing. Better than nothing. But what about the other hundred and sixty-four hours? Have you dragged Christianity, the most sacred thing there is, over into weekdays, into the mire of conflicting interests and the tumult of the streets? No! Let me tell you, then: either there *is* a Christianity in the mire of conflicting interests and in the tumult of the street, or else what professes to be Christianity is a babbling and an abomination before the true God!"

"That's a new doctrine!" declared Kuehn, thinking he was uttering a threat.

"No, it's Matthew 5 to 7. But let's talk about business. You, Mr. Kuehn, have refused to agree on a wage scale with the Secretary of the Free Union of Woodworkers. For that reason part of your force has gone on strike. You want to establish wages entirely alone, without giving the workmen a hearing?"

"Not at all; I want to do it by agreement with my factory union, the Arthur Kuehn Workers' League. My workmen belong with me, and I with them: union is strength."

"I won't inquire *whose* strength this union means," the Bishop replied, "but I'll explain to you forthrightly that according to the natural Christian law the workmen in your plant do not belong with you, Mr. Kuehn, but with the workmen of other plants in the woodworking industry, and indeed rather to the workmen of other industries than with you."

"It is said, Bishop, that you have actually expressed this view in writing. By your leave, I think that is unheard of."

"Quite true. It was in a magazine article opposing the mingling of dissimilar callings. For what you are creating, Mr. Kuehn, with your workers' league, organized by Dr. Urban, is not unity but a mixture, a mixture and corruption of two natural and dissimilar occupational classes, that of the workingman and that of the employer. But dissimilarities should not be wiped out, and individuality should not be needlessly rendered unrecognizable for the sake of a gray monotony. Isn't it hard enough to get the workman to stick to the workman, the employer to the employer? You should let them both live, each for himself and within his own circle, rejoicing in his individuality and his existence, and remembering that God created us mortals not alike but unlike."

"But my workingman belongs to me, and I to him," Kuehn protested, genuinely knowing no better.

"You belong to the workingman?" interrupted the Bishop. "Five minutes ago you said yourself that you belonged to the Association of Furniture Manufacturers, and in fact were its president: that means that you, Mr. Kuehn, belong to an association about which no workman has anything to say, which I think is right and proper."

"That *would* be a pretty state of affairs!"

"Very well, but in that case the woodworkers should belong to the woodworkers' union, about which no industrialist has anything to say."

Kuehn shook his head indignantly: "What business have my workers with the workers of perfectly unconnected plants? To talk against me, I suppose."

The Archbishop: "*Your* workmen, Mr. Kuehn? If you say, this is my coat, these are my trousers, you are speaking the truth. But if you say, this is my worker, pressing him to your bosom as you do so, you are speaking not only incorrectly, but mendaciously. For the workingman is not an inanimate object, but a father of a family, a citizen struggling for his daily bread, just like yourself—no more, no less."

"I won't have the socialists stirring up my workers," Kuehn defended himself.

"Is the woodworkers' union socialistic?" the Archbishop asked Hildebrand, the labor leader.

"Politically the unions are neutral," he answered, "but we can't prevent the individual members from thinking their own thoughts about the blessings and advantages of the profit system."

The Archbishop raised a forefinger: "Scarcely a single soul has thoughts of his own nowadays, Mr. Hildebrand; ideas are served up either by individual interested parties or by interested cliques."

"Certain ideas come of their own accord," retorted the Secretary of State, "when a family with eight children must live in two little rooms, and literally has no butter for its bread, while another family with two children lives in a mansion and feeds chops to the lapdogs."

"You mean to say, Mr. Hildebrand, that if there were no profit system there wouldn't be any mansions?" asked the Bishop, realizing that Hildebrand in his rage at the Yellow leader was recalling socialistic phrases from his youth.

"No. I don't mean to say that."

"It would be wrong if you did, because there would still be mansions then, but the people who lived in them wouldn't call themselves capitalists, but representatives of the people, leaders, deliverers, heaven knows what. Now about the family with the eight children, or, in other words, the misery of the poor—is *that* capitalism's fault?"

"Whose else?" asked Hildebrand, staring the rich braggart in the face.

"No, my dear sir!" the Bishop shook his head vigorously. "Whenever capitalism prevails, great, bitter, outrageous poverty has given way to petty and bearable poverty. And hundreds of workers' associations like your woodworkers' union are fighting and winning every day, assuring a better life for the poor. The poor aren't so poor as they were even thirty years ago—that much is certain."

"But the rich are richer than thirty years ago—that much is certain too," said the union leader quietly. He was no longer talking in a fury. The socialist in him was coming out.

"If you deny the rich man's right to wealth," replied the Bishop, "we can't negotiate, Mr. Hildebrand. The right to wealth is a natural right: anyone who denies it is denying nature."

Hildebrand thought he could not have heard aright: "Does that mean, Bishop, that the rich man is foreordained to wealth through his nature, through his natural inclination or endowment? Do you mean to say there is a capacity for growing rich, which one person has and another has not?"

The Bishop: "You have taken my meaning exactly. Just as one man has a natural right to be a musician, because he has brought into the world with him a capacity and craving for music, another man will bring into the world the capacity and craving to be rich. And as the musician bestows melodies upon the world, so the rich man bestows wealth upon the world."

"I am a simple man, Bishop," said Hildebrand, quite without sarcasm, "and you can make me believe a good many things; but one thing I know by experience: to compose a tune a man needs an ear and imagination. But to fill his pocketbook, all a man needs is impudence and greed."

Arthur Kuehn got up, affronted: "I must really request that you refrain from such language, or——"

"Please, please, sit down, Mr. Kuehn! Have a cigar?" the cleric requested. His eyes shone with pleasure at the conversation. Again he addressed the leader of the unions: "Perfectly true, Mr. Hildebrand. Wonderfully true! Then the rich man does need something in order to get rich. You call it impudence and greed. Now let me ask you: are impudence and greed the qualities that a man needs in order to compose a tune?"

"Of course not!" smiled the union leader.

The Archbishop: "But in order to fill his pockets those are the right qualities?"

Hildebrand: "That's just what I said."

The Archbishop: "Accordingly, it is after all true, Mr. Hildebrand, that one man comes into the world with an ear and imagination, another man with impudence and greed—that is, with a natural right to wealth!"

Arthur Kuehn rose for the fourth time: "In the name of the governing committee of the furniture manufacturers, as well as of the entire woodworking industry, I must reject your statements, Bishop, as inacceptable for negotiation."

The Bishop rose and bowed with perfect courtesy to Kuehn. Kuehn returned the bow with the consciousness of having done his duty as a member of the governing committee.

"That isn't the question, Mr. Kuehn," said the Bishop when both had sat down again. "It isn't the question whether Mr. Hildebrand has given the proper name to the natural human tendency that produces a capitalist. I personally believe that impudence and greed are very inaccurate terms for the genius of the capitalist; but there *is* a genius, there is *actually* a special natural bent of the employer, just as there is a natural bent of the musician, the engineer, the teacher, or the inventor. I couldn't be a capitalist—could you, Mr. Hildebrand?"

Said Hildebrand, with considerable disgust: "No, thank God, I couldn't!"

Kuehn shrugged to indicate that these insults left him cold. The Bishop, noticing the industrialist's annoyed, almost contemptuous motion, strove to mediate: "Please don't be offended, Mr. Kuehn."

"Not in the least!" protested the injured manufacturer.

"But I've got to find some common road," cried the Bishop in candid despair, "some highway that all three of us can follow. How else can I mediate between you? I have proved to you, Mr. Kuehn, the natural right of the workingman to unite with his fellows, and to fight for a better life with all the energy that the consciousness of his numbers and indispensability can give him. If you don't recognize the natural right of the workingman, I can't negotiate.

"To you, Mr. Hildebrand, I must prove the natural right of the capitalist, or rather of the employer—the natural right of the employer to wealth: if you don't recognize this natural right, I can't negotiate. I'm taking the hard way, gentlemen, because I don't want to persuade you, I want to convince you.

"But ask yourself in your own experience, Mr. Hildebrand, if I'm not right. You can make an employer (let us say, Mr. Borstel or Mr. Kuehn) into a bishop—perhaps not into a good one, but at least into one who performs his duties somehow. But you can't make a proper employer out of a bishop: not unless the bishop has missed his vocation. You can make any employer into a turner, perhaps not into a good one, but into a fair one: but is every turner suited to be an employer?"

Hildebrand, contemptuously: "I hope not."

The Bishop was fighting desperately to gain recognition for his creed: "That sounds insulting again; but you must please remember, Mr. Kuehn, that our adversary is coming closer to us now. He's coming to meet us, actually admitting that the employer cannot be replaced haphazard by a random bishop or turner or workman.

"Allow me, therefore, in turn to go to meet Mr. Hildebrand. It may be bad qualities that make a man suitable for an employer—fierce, egotistical, and dangerous instincts. Perhaps, indeed probably, Mr. Hildebrand. But they are qualities that occur much more rarely than our qualities, the qualities of a bishop or union official. The heart of the wage earner, the humble, smoothly beating heart, *our* heart, Mr. Hildebrand, is of much more frequent occurrence than the restless, careworn, because insatiable heart of the employer. We need not hesitate to say it: the employer is a rarer phenomenon than you or I, and because he is rarer, he must be better paid." He laughed aloud: "Yes, we must even pay off his children and grandchildren in his own lifetime, because if we don't he will disappear off the face of the earth. Oddly enough, this—shall we say species of lion?—is extremely sensitive, and of a more nervous temperament than we."

Hildebrand smiled: "And supposing this—species of lion—*should* disappear?"

"My dear Mr. Hildebrand," replied the Bishop, while Kuehn got to his feet, "perhaps we, you and I, are two people who don't care what they eat, where they sleep, and how they are clothed. We can eat bread, drink water, sleep in our coffins, and be happy like the monks of Tibet. But is that everyone's choice? I don't believe so. And if the majority of mortals need wealth, then they need the rich man, for the rich are the ones who produce wealth. We, the carefree wage and salary earners, can consume wealth; but to produce it we need the careworn, restless, dangerous heart of the gentleman who stands there, and whom not chance, not blind luck, but nature itself has made a natural employer, a richer man than we two, Mr. Hildebrand."

Hildebrand stared into space. Kuehn, standing, thought it was about time to talk business. What was he to do against two bandits who were discussing in a foreign tongue how they might best empty his pockets?

Just then the Archbishop was called out, and Hildebrand, dipping into the cigar box, turned to the capitalist: "Brilliant speaker, the Archbishop, isn't he?"

"I should say he was," replied Kuehn, a trifle relieved. "I always say if a man has nothing to do all week but read books, he's bound to get some crazy ideas. Am I right? How's the cigar?"

In the next room, meanwhile, Lieutenant Colonel Bogatzki was informing the Bishop that he had been requested to make a reassuring speech on the relationship of the clergy to the unions at the evening conference of the Democratic Reform Party. The President himself, and probably also Merckel, would make statements on behalf of the government.

"Well, have you reached an agreement?" Count Savoya, coming back into the room, inquired of the dominant figure in the furniture industry and his adversary.

"If two men say to me, 'Your money or your life,' what can I do?" replied Kuehn with a loud laugh.

"It's all right, then?"

"I'm willing to talk, provided that those abominable shouters, the pickets, are removed at once. That one stipulation I must make, Bishop."

Kuehn, like many manufacturers, had a morbid antipathy for pickets; he would gladly have shot, trampled to death, torn limb from limb, and drunk the blood of these innocently marching men with their placards who kept strikebreakers out of the plant. The Urbanite movement derived great advantage from the employers' nervous dislike for strikers; indeed, the whole movement was actually built on that antipathy.

"How many men have you got patrolling there?" asked the Bishop.

"Two hundred," replied Hildebrand.

"I'd like to talk to the men, but not outside the factory; I'd rather have it at the Union Building before the evening conference; can you arrange that?"

The newly appointed Secretary of State for Labor and Welfare promised that the strikers should be on hand.

"You won't suffer any harm, my dear Mr. Kuehn, no practical harm at all," the pleased Archbishop assured the manufacturer, "just wait and see."

Downstairs, on the sidewalk of Henrietta Avenue, all was so still at this hour of the evening that the two bays hitched to the brightly lit town carriage pricked up their ears as a squirrel clambered through the branches across the way; Kuehn came to a halt beside his carriage. "I don't know, Joseph, I feel awfully funny," he said.

"The horses are restless too," said old Joseph, the coachman, and the manufacturer made up his mind: "Do you know what? Let's drive to the Union Building. I want to hear the complaints the rascals have to make of me, and what that book-reading fellow will answer."

And Arthur Kuehn got into the carriage and drove to the Union Building, brushing aside the coachman's objection that the horses were restless with the remark that he could stable them somewhere near by, since the damned gab would go on half the night anyway.

BOOK TWO

THE THREE MUSKETEERS

XXII

MEANWHILE resolutions had been made that assured peace, at least for the moment.

Late in the afternoon Merckel persuaded the President to discharge Urban as soon as he should have consulted with his confidants and telegraphed orders to restore quiet in the east. Accordingly, the League Leader, who was housed not in a cell but in the home of a prison official, received his three intimates at ten o'clock at night; at the same time, not far away, a squadron of mounted police were keeping open the entrances to the Union Building, which was awaiting its first visit from the head of the state.

Naturally the wife of the prison official, a local votary of the scrubbing brush, had made everything pretty for the great man, Urban, although she was a Faustite. What difference did that make? A League Leader is a league leader, certainly a man who has gone far; and when we look closely at our battles we discover that they are fought on top, above the level of the prison officials and little people who sacrifice their blood and lives.

There were embroidered covers on the plush armchairs; a pink paper shade had been put over the hanging lamp; on the desk were a pen, a pad of note paper, and sharpened pencils arranged parallel to the table edge; there was even a lace coverlet on the bed, and the floor glistened with cleanliness.

It is a good quality of our nation not to hate the great personage, even if he is a political opponent. The woman came in every two hours, bringing the prisoner coffee, poached eggs, applesauce, cigarettes, fresh water to wash in, and *The Three Musketeers,* by Alexandre Dumas, from the prison library to read.

It is easy to say unkind things about prison walls, but by enclosing they also give protection. Urban felt himself well taken care of, treated with respect, and while his companions were starting strikes to secure his liberation, he was enjoying the pleasure of being out of harness. He slept for two hours, asked to be taken to the shower, donned a comfortable dressing gown, and wished *The Three Musketeers* had had a thousand sequels, and he a thousand months of undisturbed peace to read them all and hear nothing but the helpful voice of the gentle prison official's wife.

Instead, the annoyances of life invaded his cell at ten o'clock in the evening under the light of the hanging lamp, as he was consuming lentil soup with pieces of meat in it and drinking half a bottle of red wine.

The three, Justus Thomas, Weisse, and the general, came in silently as etiquette required, and silently sat down, each one apparently occupied with something, for the great man refused to be "harassed by purposeful silence." Urban finished his meal, leaned back, and inquired when he could ever get a little undisturbed peace and quiet.

Weisse now disclosed the government offer. He was to be released "for want of evidence of his complicity in the Moenckeberg crime" as soon as the disturbances and strikes in the east had stopped.

Dr. Urban said nothing for a long time. Finally he asked: "Is everything ready?"

"Yes," they said.

"Then the government isn't to free me, you are to." He set forth the plan that he had formed during the moments of silence, while he enjoyed his peace and security: "I'll stay here. Tell Grau to deal with the Willerts, and demand three government posts, while you're getting everything ready. If he can't make a deal for any post (but he's really to try), I don't mind if everything stays as it was in Adam Faust's day, because the next election will give me a majority. That's perfectly sure, because as the world grows progressively more civilized, a reactionary and devout clique can't dominate a modern industrial nation—that would be illogical. There's just one thing we can't agree to do: disband or disarm the Sports Groups. Anything else we'll do. And that's the very thing that they'll demand, that we throw away our arms—I know Beyer. For that reason I'll stay here, as a pledge of peace, if the government wants it. You, however, are to say that you have no control over the strikes in the east, which will stop immediately upon my personal order if the government recognizes the *status quo*—you understand. No one could be more peaceably inclined; I am, because time is working on my side. Go shout from the housetops that I've offered peace, unconditionally, and that of our forty million countrymen all are in favor of peace except three: Hesse, Henry Willert, and the traitor Merckel. Any questions?"

"Peter George and Gregory William Lienhardt ask to be reinstated in the personal corps of the Leader," Weisse reported.

"First let the stupid swine prove they are capable of anything but nonsense: let them cut off the three heads that are in favor of war, but in such a way that no one can prove anything on them afterward. Give them any assistance they need; money doesn't count. Put a label on Merckel: 'This is the death for traitors.'"

"While you stay here?" asked Justus Thomas, who could take any liberty he pleased. "If one of the three assassinations succeeds— even one—I can see them cutting off your head right here in this little room, and tossing it to the Sports Detachments, which will then very probably break up for fear of their own heads, thus assuring peace."

"Very possible," replied Urban, not a timid man, but for the sake

of the cause he yielded when Weisse and the general made repre-
sentations. It was decided that the Leader should call off the strikes
in the east on the following morning, and leave the prison.

THE NIGHT OF BROTHERHOOD

XXIII

MISTRUST of enthusiasm is not exclusively a Protestant
heritage: Bishop Oriola and many Catholics felt the same
uneasiness at demonstrations of mass passion. It was said
of Adam Faust that at his family services, which in his
younger years he had held every Sunday for the whole family and
staff, a verse had been sung:

> *Put no trust in the people's cheers;*
> *They change from day to day:*
> *Where now Hosannas reach your ears,*
> *Tomorrow they cry slay!*

The old man would never have set foot in a meeting hall, let alone
the one at the Union Building, which accommodated three thousand
people. Lindbrecht and Hildebrand knew this; when invited to the
Staff College to deliver guest lectures to the future generals they had
seen on the walls the Conservative mottoes, many of them taken
from the works of a Danish Protestant named Sören Kierkegaard,
others from the Bible, Pascal's *Pensées,* and Plutarch. One saying of
the Dane's had impressed itself on their memories: "Lo, there was not
a single soldier who dared lay a finger upon his general, Cajus Marius;
but three or four women, imagining themselves a multitude, and
with a sort of hope that no one could tell for sure who had started
it—*they* would have had the courage."

Accordingly, in order to weaken the impression that a "multitude" had assembled, Hildebrand had tavern tables with colored tablecloths put in the hall, thus transforming it into a restaurant, and throughout the night the white-aproned waiters kept running among the tables with hot dishes and the wooden mugs containing the weak, sour beer of the islands, even during the speeches of the Secretaries of State. Just once, immediately after the announcement that the President was going to speak, the gathering shouted, "Get the waiters out of the way!" put down their napkins, and rose from their seats for a second ovation, which raged for more than five minutes.

The first ovation, one such as no statesman of our backward country except Urban had ever received, had taken place when the nine members of the cabinet came upon the stage of the hall, and the secretary of the "independents," Krueger, called out: "Gentlemen! The President of the Republic and the members of the government!"

There was no telling from their faces what the nine representatives of a system that demanded isolation of the individual, with a non-logical sense of life averse to figures and statistics, felt during the long minutes that they stood unsmiling, gazing at the hand clapping and huzzaing. One of them, Henry Willert, the Secretary of State for Foreign Affairs, felt ill, and Dr. Kuttner inconspicuously removed him to Melchior Willert's Women's Hospital, where he took a sleeping potion and spent the night.

The nine wore rather a look of surprise, then, as they stared at the hall and the unending shouts. Why should people who had not, like the Urbanites or the Reds, been drilled in cheering and jeering or indeed in any "spontaneous outbursts of emotion" show such wild enthusiasm for a brand-new government that had as yet done nothing except make one mistaken arrest?

At the center of the long, green-covered table on the stage, behind which the members of the cabinet, Augustus Beyer, Merckel, Willert, Hesse, Kaempf, Andrew Zorn, Henry the Franciscan, Hildebrand, and Holzkopf were standing, was a bronze bust of Adam Faust, with a green wreath of laurel on the brow. On the dais in front of this, lower down than the stage but above the floor of the hall, the table for the chairman of the meeting formed a bridge between the remote, ill-lit stage and the body of the hall. On the dais, closer and in better view of the audience, sat the heads of the Presidential parties, Jacob Willert for the Conservatives, the Archbishop for the

strong Middle-Class Party, Lindbrecht for the Democratic Reform
Party; the head of the Liberals, Kuehn, had joined them in response
to the Archbishop's courteous invitation, and joined, standing, with
the rest of the hall in the ovation to the government.

The sound of the bell wielded by Secretary Krueger had just
quieted the applause sufficiently so that the members of the government above could sit down, when the two hundred pickets from
Kuehn's marched in with their placards, as if to lend adornment
and meaning to the occasion. Marching along the sides of the hall,
while silence fell, they could be heard singing, not loudly, even rather
pleasantly, and not provokingly to anyone but their employer Kuehn:

> *Let the world slide, let the world go;*
> *A fig for care, and a fig for woe!*
> *If I can't pay, why I can owe,*
> *And death makes equal the high and low.*

As few people knew that the men with their placards had been
summoned by Hildebrand, general astonishment prevailed; chairs
were shifted, and even the waiters, carrying great serving platters
over their heads, read the inscriptions. Kuehn, beside himself with
rage and shame at the insolence of *"his* workers," yelled: "Impudence!
You hold your tongues in the presence of the cabinet!"

Almost the entire assembly, the workingmen included, were of
the same opinion; shouts of annoyance at the strikers were heard,
and the unsuspecting Krueger snapped at them: "I must say Senator
Kuehn is damn well right about your being so brassy. Who let you
in anyway?"

"The Archbishop!" came Hildebrand's voice from above. "The
Archbishop wants to make a statement on the labor question in his
own name and the name of the clergy."

Bravos, clapping, shouts of "Quiet for the Bishop!"; the pickets
stood their placards against the walls of the hall, and crowded forward
to hear better.

The Bishop, in ecclesiastical vestments with cross and chain, stood
up: "Let me say a few words to the pickets, you people, and you
too, Mr. Kuehn. It may happen that an employer feels himself damaged by the natural right of the workmen to join his equals. It may

even happen, and has been known to happen, that an employer will offend against the divine commandment: 'Thou shalt not muzzle the ox when he treadeth out the corn.' If, then, an employer withholds from the workman his natural right, or even his daily bread, the workman must lay down his work and prevent others from doing it for him—or else his own children will despise him.

"For my part, whenever I see pickets, I am glad that liberty and honor and battle and tension still exist on earth. When I see pickets, I feel like saying to them: Good, men! Even though you're poor, you're showing the world that poverty has not killed your honor or the intrepidity of your hearts. It is well that your children can say to you: 'See, our father is fighting for our bread.' For a man's honor and a father's dignity depend upon his readiness on the one hand to endure with humility before God sufferings and the blows of fate, but on the other to fight with open, honest weapons against ignominy and contumely put upon him by his equals—and before God there is no distinction among us. And further I would like to say to the pickets: it is not merely because of a few pence in wages that you do well to stand in picket lines, but because of the self-respect you show. For as long as self-respect and courage are present, brightness and joy will still be on earth: let our life be like the whirring arrow, sped by the tension of the bow. But"—the Bishop raised a warning finger—"now listen to these words also, you pickets: do not break the bow that creates the tension. Do not break down this order that allows you to form a picket line, this capitalistic order, as you call it, the order of dangers, of tautness, of courageous hearts: the only one that will allow you to form picket lines, because it is the order of personal freedom and dangerous living.

"Do not demand too much. Beware of your own defeat, which would make you trembling slaves of an overweening capitalist. But beware yet more of the defeat of the capitalist, which would make you and him trembling slaves of a socialist state!

"Against an all-powerful state you cannot strike: it would annihilate you with a clear conscience—more coldly and pitilessly, that is, than any capitalist ever did. On that account you must keep the scales in balance, for omnipotence belongs to God alone. That is what I wanted to tell you as my opinion and the opinion of the clergy."

The people looked at one another, and applauded. Was this the

"Christian commonwealth" presenting itself? The applause was courteous and controlled, and quickly over; the chairman plied the bell:
"Our fellow member Lange has the floor."

Rough old Lange, employment inspector in the mountain province,
rose to confirm his reputation: "We thank the Archbishop for his
assurance that the strike law is not to be interfered with. He did not
need to say it; we are certain that good old Adam cast a careful eye
over the gentlemen who are to succeed him and hold to his course;
and I'd like to say here in public that I am very confident, if it comes
to the point, that they won't leave us up the creek without a paddle,
nor on the other hand we them."

This time the applause was tinged with merriment: Lange's final
words had captivated all hearts. He was an initiate, as everyone knew,
and was not talking "through his hat." Accordingly, there would be
no prelate rule, as was evident from the words "he need not have said
that at all"; furthermore, it appeared that the government had given
or was about to give a promise to hold to Adam's course. Therefore—
and the men in the hall began discussing the possibility—an extension
of the mining communities and brotherhoods, which meant a conflict
with the Yellows, was to be expected. This was the significance of
Lange's words, "if it should come to the point." One man here knew
more than Lange, and could say whether the conflict was only threatening or actually planned: the prompter up above next to Faust's bust,
with his stiff academic collar and a face as if butter would not melt
in his mouth—Adam's secret agent, Beyer's illegitimate son-in-law,
John Henry Merckel. That he was the son of a washerwoman made
no impression on the gathering; they were usually inclined to distrust
a man risen from their own ranks more deeply than one who was
born rich. In addition, he was being kept under cover, he published
learned books, and he had never spoken to simple people. He was
living in secret concubinage with Beyer's youngest daughter, Kate,
the consumptive, whom Kuttner had forbidden to marry, it was whispered; and curiosity rose to such a pitch that his name passed about
from table to table: "Merckel," "Merckel," "Have Merckel speak."
Finally a striker, a youngster next to the wall, shouted at the excited
hall, as if he were the chairman: "Dr. Merckel has asked for the floor!"

First they laughed; next there was clapping and a brief whispering
from the Senators' table to the stage. Then he was on his feet, and

Krueger announced: "Secretary of State John Henry Merckel." The women in the hall clapped: a handsome man, and how touching to be engaged to an incurably ill girl!

"Ladies and gentlemen," he began. "Our inhabited world falls into two hostile camps, and very soon there will be no one left, whether he knows it or not, whether he will or no, who is not fighting in one camp or the other. Time was when you could wrinkle your nose, creep home, and draw the curtains; very soon you can't even wish to do so.

"You, my friends and countrymen, who have welcomed us with loud applause as pupils and emulators of Adam Faust, will become aware tomorrow of an applause even louder, longer, and equally honest, rising from the other camp to welcome the release of Dr. Urban."

Aha! The first surprise: heads turned hither and thither in the hall. So he was going to let Urban loose—but why? And it turned out that he *could* speak.

"And just as it is the duty of the countryman to keep an eye on the weather, the duty of a mother to keep an eye on her child, which, in the due order of this world, must survive her, so it is your and my and everyone's duty to keep an eye on the camp he lives in, which must survive him. And in fact everyone does keep an eye on the camp to see whether it is his, the proper camp for him, or whether he is in the wrong place. And since the disintegration of the world has just begun, there is still pondering and a pouring back and forth between the two camps. Not until almost everyone has recognized and occupied the proper camp for himself will the speeches stop and arms give the reply."

The women remarked behind their hands that Merckel was "a darling" and talked almost as philosophically as Lindbrecht—"Philosophically, I admit, but very nicely."

"Our camp is familiar to you, gentlemen, as is obvious from the fact that you have honored this brand-new government with your applause before it spoke a word, simply saying to yourselves: Well, these are the people whose names good old Adam wrote down on a piece of paper and said, let them go on when I'm dead. For that reason what we say doesn't make much difference, because you have learned from twenty years of Adam Faust what we shall do, whether we say so or not. As we live in this world, our words may not always be clear, they may sometimes be as ambiguous as the old President's words; but what we do is familiar to you, my countrymen, before we do it, because we are successors."

"Lindbrecht all over, didn't I say so?" whispered Krueger's daughter-in-law to young Lange.

"The other, the hostile camp, is also familiar, or rather recognized. By recognized I do not mean understood by scientific methods, for Urban can never be recognized by science, as I shall at once show you. For twenty years a thousand clever minds, businessmen, labor leaders, scholars, journalists, the entire intelligentsia of our intelligent nation have been trying to destroy Urban by recognition; they have criticized him, refuted him, convicted him, condemned him, pilloried him, torn him limb from limb, laughed at him: yet he grew incessantly, seeming not even to see his adversaries, and when he did see them he toyed with them as a lion toys with mice. And yet the presupposition of our intelligentsia that Urban could be destroyed by 'recognizing him' was perfectly correct. But it is the curse of the intelligentsia of our day that it can recognize only something similar to itself, something measurable, visible, statistical, capable of being counted—something superficial. Our intelligentsia cannot, however, recognize anything so dissimilar to itself, so deeply hidden, so superior as Urban is. Therefore I do not mean by 'recognizing' what the intelligent people, and particularly the highly intelligent people, mean by it; Urban can only be recognized as one recognizes an acquaintance on the street—instantly, without consideration; or as one recognizes instantly, without consideration, whether a man is friend or enemy. Thus in the bloody night of Carolswald, thirteen years ago, the Carolswalders recognized Urban and took to arms without a word. Thus, that same night of recognition, young Lieutenant Hesse, with a shadow falling upon him as long as his life, recognized Urban without pausing to reflect, and described him for all time, without understanding what he said, in the words: 'The cry of the victim is the paradise of the tormentor.'

"So make no mistake, my countrymen: the primal deed took place that night, the original deed of which all the deeds of Urban and his millions of followers, no matter what they may say or think about themselves, are but copies, but pale imitations, striving back toward the original, ideal deed, the primal deed—nailing mortal men to the cross. You as poor people know yourselves that the cross need not always be of wood, nor the nails of iron. A man can cry out without being noisy, and be degraded while eating rich food. Indeed, even the man who is fond of eating cares so little for food that a true Urbanite will starve and die if only he can contribute to the degradation of the exalted and the humiliation of all under the arbitrary authority of the leader. Food makes so little difference that you, my countrymen, true Faustites, will starve and die for the exaltation of all into individual human beings, citizens and inspectors of the government, and for the humbling of all beneath the universal, unalterable, and thus not arbitrary old law.

"That which we Carpenters, from President to beggar, wear embroidered inside our jackets, the picture of the woman slowly murdered at the martyr's stake, is the primal deed, the ideal deed, the murderous gleam in the millions of ecstatic eyes that will welcome their great man tomorrow, the final goal for whose sake they will die because we will not have it—for we will not sit by and watch the degradation of everything bearing a human countenance beneath arbitrary authority.

"We are already familiar with the murderous gleam of the eyes and the ecstasy of the other camp: with the same orgiastic cries the Urbanites five hundred years ago stood around the burning victims of the autos-da-fé, having paid much money for the best seats; with the same frenzy of enthusiasm they watched the Maid of Orléans burn. We, the Faustites, existed then too; we stood mistrustfully outside our houses, wrinkled our noses, and asked: 'What do I smell burning?' 'The criminal is burning,' cried the Urbanites, rushing past lest they miss her cries. 'What criminal?' 'It doesn't make any difference. Listen to her scream—come on!' And then we, fearfully, shivering with horror, crept away to our rooms. Today, five hundred years after, there has been one forward step, just one: we do not creep away, and we may be stronger than Satan."

Not a hand stirred, not a sound was heard as the President's deputy finished his speech and sat down. Instead, Henry the Franciscan in his dark-brown cowl arose and said, motioning to the band leader: "The Carpenters will sing stanza five of song number four hundred and ninety-nine: *Though all the demons gory.*"

And the whole hall, rising, began to sing as the orchestra played, even the Hildebrandites who remembered the words, and the women loudest of all, for their darling had really spoken too wonderfully:

Though all the demons gory
Should bid defiance now,
Our Lord will march to glory
Although we know not how.

What He has set before Him
And that which He would see
Shall come: all men adore Him
For done His will shall be.

Fresh beer was poured into the mugs; it was hardly necessary for anyone to say anything more—the President's prompter had told what people had wanted to know. Urban would be released and urged to submit; if he said no, then "The Lord would march to glory." The tension was relieved, and a great deal of beer was drunk, because the central committee was host tonight. Many of the wives were urging that it was time to leave, for midnight approached; and then the storm of enthusiasm already mentioned burst out, seemingly endless, so violent that all the doors to the hall were closed, and the historian despairs of recording the causes. Krueger shouted into the hall: "Ladies and fellow workers: the President of the Republic!"

Even so, while the lean, gray-haired man with his black tie and black frock coat is standing up there awaiting silence, and perhaps considering a chess move to make against his opponent Merckel in a blindfold game, we may mention two or three reasons for the enthusiasm.

He was the choice of the dead man, so he would be faithful; he emulated the inscriptions, and had reprimanded the fashionable people who hated everyone and never said good morning; he had arrested Urban, and was releasing him again; therefore he was strong.

But unquestionably the main reason was our native backwardness. A backward man is distinguished from a modern man by the fact that a much smaller number of events force themselves or are forced upon his attention, and that he seldom sees unaccustomed things. Naturally it is easier for him to distinguish the important from the unimportant. He is like a child with few toys, who pays more attention to each individual one, and can distinguish it more readily from the others than a child with too many presents can, since the quality of the individual object remains almost unknown to him, as, toying briefly with one thing after another, he pays no real attention to any. But before long everything goes into the attic, a new box is greedily opened, and for a day the child is busy trying out each game—for a day, and no more. The quality of the particular object, buried under the quantity of the many, is scarcely noticed; and that which is not new is tiresome. Thus the modern man becomes familiar with nothing, because he hears too much; his power of judgment, which after all is built upon careful distinctions, withers like an unused limb; the soul, growing dull, incapable of studying any individual object carefully and at length, craves novelties served up en masse. If you ask him, "What's new?" the "man of tomorrow" will list a great many things in a jumble, important and unimportant, large and small, temporal and eternal, all unrecognized and undistinguished together; and by tomorrow he has forgotten everything. If you ask one of the old Geisenheim herb women in the apothecaries' pay for the news, she will list a few events, from seven to fifteen years back, but of each she knows every detail; and strange it is, but the events are so well chosen, so important and typical of city and countryside, that you never forget one of them, and are abashed at having asked what was "new."

Thus, unimpaired by novelties and quantities, the soul of the backward man preserves its capacity for choice and for long remembering. The important, the lasting, the symbolic stands brilliantly clear before an eye not yet blinded by glittering abundance, an eye that keeps studying what little it sees from every angle, marking the details.

Our native backwardness has a long memory; the Carolswald murders took place yesterday, the stripes of the stableboy are still bleeding, and the old-fashioned people will never forget Urban's assertion that Augustus Beyer was a sexual pervert. They would have forgotten it in a moment if Urban had afterward said he had been misinformed. But they will never forgive Urban because this grievous defamation was "politics" or a propaganda dodge; and as a still-rustic people they are not able to take it lightly or to blow it away "from their horrified souls." Oh, no doubt Urban if he had won would have flogged them forward under the lash of enlightenment into the world of quantities and things indistinguishable (because all things are equal and all alike), on into the wave of the future where you are a drop, into progress and world records and towers of Babel. He came too soon. The leader of progress was wrecked upon the reef of our native backwardness.

At last those in the hall, clapping and cheering, had washed away from the man standing above them the defamation that they had not brought upon him, and the President addressed the meeting:

"My esteemed audience, ladies and gentlemen!

"Anyone today who takes over the government promises to solve the social question. Accordingly it seems—I say it *seems*—that a governmental program must start with the social question, with the question: How can I abolish want? In respect to this, I would say that our state is neither an economic enterprise nor a supervisor of economic enterprises, and the task of abolishing want is not incumbent upon it, but upon the productive people, made up of workingmen, employees, and employers, in whose everyday affairs our state will interfere only for the protection of the weak. In addition, those who shout loudest that they would abolish want if they were in power are actually demagogues and liars. In the first place, they know perfectly well that the state or its leaders, the government, cannot abolish want; in the second place, they do not even wish to do so. For what they want to abolish, if you could see into their souls, is not poverty but wealth.

"If there were even the tiniest spark of truth in the assertions of Dr. Urban and the revolutionists that they mean to abolish want, those parties would be made up of persons suffering want—of the poor. Actually, however, they embrace both rich and poor, and are instructed and directed by people who either have never known want, or no longer know it. But what have rich and poor in the same party got in common, since it cannot after all be want?

"They have two things in common: *envy* of a better, higher, bolder nature and accomplishment, and secondly a craving to oppress and to be oppressed—a common yearning to cringe to those above and trample those below.

"That which drives Dr. Urban's columns to overthrow existing things is not resentment at their own want, but resentment at the opulence of their neighbors. Not the satisfaction of hunger but the satisfaction of envy is the commandment of our age.

"If Dr. Urban is victorious, a new age will dawn, the 'World of

Tomorrow,' whose substance is the satisfaction of envy, or the establishment of equality among all men.

"They have trained their guns on wealth, fellow countrymen, not because it is useful to few and harmful to many, but because it is a symbol of distinction.

"They have trained their guns on art and beauty, not because art and beauty are useless things, but because they are symbols of distinction, and thus stand in the way of equality.

"They have trained their guns on God, not because He cannot be proved, but because He is a monument to the heights man has risen to—because, therefore, He stands in the way of equality.

"And because you, fellow countrymen, poor though you may be, share in every distinction and elevation at those moments when you want to be human—as mortals, that is, 'Sunday Mortals,' as the Archbishop put it—you have an interest as great as any millionaire in preserving this system that we live under. Despite its monstrous failings, it is the last remaining system with any interest in freedom, which includes the freedom of the exalted and outstanding. Why the exalted and outstanding (for instance, the teacher and his teachings) require freedom and even protection, I ask you to read in the *Gospel of the Sunday Mortal*.

"The unions have made it their aim to correct the monstrous failings I speak of, and accordingly they call themselves the Reform Party. Anyone planning reforms who appeals to me for help will not knock in vain at my door, for that is what I have undertaken to do, and that is my personal plan of life as President of the Republic: at the end of my career I want to be entitled to say of myself the same thing that my teacher Adam Faust said of himself in his *Incomplete Accounting*: 'I have never been a hypocrite, and so I am merry in my old age. For since the people know that I have been childishly and mortally in earnest in my intent to create respect for the Ten Commandments, they have gained confidence in me; and when I call them they will take up the position I order, instead of submitting to the tyrant.' "

The meeting lasted from ten-thirty until an hour after midnight. The birth registers showed that many men must have loved their wives in the dawn and in the nights that followed; for they were expecting the command to occupy the position assigned to them.

FLIGHT FROM THE BRIDEGROOM

XXIV

A T THIS same time, i.e., March 31 and April 1, events occurred at Liebenau that had a welcome effect upon the destiny of the Willerts.

When Dorothy Kersting, née Thiess, wrote a letter to the splendid Elizabeth saying that Jacob Willert must no longer tempt her Alexander into drinking and squandering money, or else she would leave the house, she had not foreseen the disastrous results. The Senator, however, kept his word, and did not go to Liebenau again, so that Caspar Schmalz, the young son of the mayor, gained the upper hand altogether at the regular patrons' table at Wernicke's inn. And if Alexander Kersting appeared at the bank building on Lady Square in any sort of predicament, "the elder Mr. Willert could not see him." He was indignant at Dorothy's ingratitude, resolved not to let her perish, and sure that she would come crawling once Alexander had sold the last thing he owned, his daughter Elspeth, to some rascal.

Matters turned out differently. Elizabeth Willert replied vigorously to Dorothy, by that time a woman in her fifties with two grown children, that from now on, in accordance with her wishes, Jacob would not meet Alexander again. Thus the loose-living farmer, braggart, and cardplayer lost the rail to which he had so long been able to cling; and while his way of life grew more circumspect, quiet, and serious, for want of Willert's subsidies the farm began to slip. He dismissed the Carpenter, worked alone with his son and two maids, and managed, with Elspeth's help in the house, to gloss over the collapse for more than two years. In the President's last summer he sold his harvest on the stalk, not frivolously but under pressure of necessity, and actually not on unfavorable terms; in March of the following year, during the days of mourning for Adam Faust, he was finished.

Dorothy, in turn, buried her hope that General Hesse (who had so often chatted with Elspeth of an evening outside the door in company with the tall Spitta) would propose marriage to the girl, especially as she was beautiful and educated, and generals rank so high that they often marry poor girls. This hope she buried on the wedding day of the slightly damaged Alexandra.

Two windows of the old-fashioned best room in the Kersting house give upon the yard and stables, two on the garden. On the thirty-first of March, a cloudy day, the long-legged Alexander, haggard, graying, was pacing the room, considering what shift might possibly be attempted still.

On the first of October of the previous year Mayor John Schmalz had called in his second mortgage of five thousand thalers with the stipulated six months' notice because Alexander could not keep up the amortization payments. And tomorrow was the first of April. Make no mistake: he had always paid the five per cent interest, but not the amortization, and so the whole sum was due. They must have been conspiring against him: neither Willert nor Simon nor the Farmers' Bank nor the Accommodation Fund of the Unions would take over the second mortgage, and of course everyone knows what a friend says when asked to go surety for a ridiculous five thousand on the real-estate register. If Alexander did not have the money in hand by April 3, he and his wife and children would be ejected from the farm with protestations of eternal devotion by the bloated Schmalz, that dreadful plebeian, who tossed the chicken bones under the table at Wernicke's, and who had once complained, throwing up after over-eating, "Too bad about that wonderful roast goose!" This swine of a village mayor would put him off the premises, and Caspar Schmalz would move in, Caspar with the flourished mustaches, who stood treat all around; he was the village mayor's second son.

Elspeth Kersting, the model of Praxiteles, now twenty-one years old, had heard from her brother George, six years her senior, what was the state of the farm, and why her mother had as it were driven away the wealthy patron of the house by a letter. The brother and sister, however, regarded the behavior of their parents in very different lights, and their discussions ended in reciprocal abuse when Elspeth emphasized her academic education with a shrugging "You don't understand about such things."

George did not accuse his father of sloth or slovenly management: the fault lay twenty-seven years back, when the farm had changed hands, and Alexander had acquired it with far too small a capital. He charged the old man with dishonorableness: "How could he buy a sixty-thousand-thaler farm on ten thousand thalers without being able to depend on a backer who would help out later? Why did he depend on Jacob Willert? He didn't even know him. He only knew him through our mother, because Mother said to him: 'Jacob Willert is giving me ten thousand thalers. Do you want to marry me?' 'Yes,' says Father, because in the first place Mother was already pregnant with me, and in the second place ten thousand thalers doesn't grow on trees. So far so good. But why didn't he buy a smaller farm, with at least fifty per cent down payment? There were very nice farms to be had for twenty thousand thalers. Why this big one? Because he said to himself: 'After all, I've got Jacob Willert,' instead of saying, like a man of honor, 'Anything within reason, Senator, but now she's *my* wife, and that's the end of it.'"

"Oh, I really do feel like spitting in your face!" cried Elspeth, actually spitting on his shoe. 'It's no disgrace to have a Jacob Willert, but to have a village slut like yours, with varicose veins, who doesn't brush her teeth, *is* a disgrace!"

"But suppose a woman is married?" he yelled back.

"Why, you aren't accusing Mother, are you?"

"Not in the least, but why did she write that letter to Mrs. Senator Willert?"

Brother and sister agreed that, conceding the original mistake, the letter to the splendid Elizabeth was the root of all the difficulty; both were sure that Dorothy had not seen the banker again since her marriage; that George was Alexander's son was proved by the resemblance. But George said: "Mother was defending her honor," whereas Elspeth said, "She grudged Father a pleasant life."

Alexander Kersting could not believe that his luck had forsaken him, and when he discovered that his Dorothy was meeting secretly with old Mrs. Schmalz, he was pleased. If the village mayor let the five thousand thalers run another two years, he could find a buyer.

Now Elspeth came in: "Put on your coat, Father, the two Schmalzes are coming—Caspar and the old man."

He offered no resistance as she helped him on with his coat; he dipped into the stone jar of smoking tobacco to keep the girl from seeing how pale his face was, and when there was a knock at the yard door, he called in a loud voice: "Come in!" Elspeth fled.

John and Caspar Schmalz looked like one person photographed at different times of life. The same trousers tucked into high boots, the same dark-blue frock coats, white waistcoats, gold watch chains dangling over prominant stomachs, the plump cheeks equally reddish brown, the flourished mustache white in one case, dyed dark in the other.

The mayor preceded, with a sweeping gesture of his top hat: "Good day to you all!" He saluted the room, as if already occupying it. Caspar copied his father's gesture.

What does he mean, "All of you"? thought Kersting, only now turning around; just then Dorothy came in, offered seats to the men without looking at her husband, and sat down herself. She was wearing a citified dress and an amber necklace; her graying hair was done up, and if (as in the fairy tale) the richest man were to get the most beautiful wife, she would have been fit for Jacob Willert.

"Well, well," said old Schmalz with an expression of beaming good will, having first put down his top hat on the floor beside him. For the moment this was all.

Dorothy, her hands in her lap, choked back a sneeze, and took her lace handkerchief from her little breast pocket. The two Schmalzes must have used some kind of pungent soap. From out in the yard, at regular intervals, could be heard the squeak of the pump, the splash of water, and deep mooing from the cow barns. The boughs of the old walnut tree outside the garden windows bent and creaked in the March wind, and the blinds rattled against the wall.

The mayor, first glancing at his son, studied Dorothy's amber necklace, as who should say, "Very grand people!" He raised his eyebrows as if to announce an important decision, and turned to Alexander: "Well, well, things cannot always remain the same here under the changing moon."

Kersting nodded to himself, and old Schmalz raised his voice: "Generations pass away and die that inhabited the earth before us."

"All right, say what you've got to say, John, but cut it short," said Alexander with a look of disgust.

"Tomorrow is the first of April. Can you pay?" the mayor asked.

"No."

"Even if you had the five thousand you wouldn't be any better off.

What are you going to use to pay for seed, fodder, repairs, and taxes?"

"That wouldn't be your worry," said the unhappy Alexander softly.

"But it would be yours!" cried Dorothy unexpectedly. "And the one we'd have to borrow of then would run all four of us off the farm, you and me and George and Elspeth! But John Schmalz isn't going to run us off the farm; we can keep three rooms—two for us, one for George."

"And Elspeth," asked Alexander, "can sleep with the cows, I suppose?"

At this Caspar Schmalz, the young man, pounded on the table: "Elspeth will sleep in an English brass bed nine feet long and nine feet wide, that cost a hundred thalers!"

"Indeed, indeed," growled the ruined farmer scornfully. "And out of what—no, *with* what—is my daughter to pay for the bed? You needn't explain to me, because I can tell you beforehand: better the cow barn than that!"

Now Caspar burst out with his dreams; his face became fine, for he was in love, and a strange voice seemed to be speaking from his mouth: "In six months your Elspeth won't even know what a cow looks like. And if she does go into the cow barn to remind herself of her childhood, the milkmaids will jump up from their stools, and the dairyman's voice will call: 'Attention! Mrs. Caspar Schmalz is inspecting the cow barn!' And the high heels of her patent-leather shoes will tap the well-scrubbed flagstones."

His voice trembled as if it would fail him at any moment, tears ran down his cheek, and Dorothy handed him her handkerchief. He put his face in his hands, and sobbed brokenly, with heaving shoulders, overwhelmed by the anguish of unrequited love.

John Schmalz's gaze, directed at the Kerstings, said: See that? Do you think *he* would take advantage of you?

"He's gone crazy," said Alexander with a sidelong glance at his wife.

She, however, looking at her lap, whispered: "I wish you'd been as crazy as that once."

To her immense surprise he leaned over and said: "I was, Dottie! Only I just didn't have the money."

"Then at least don't grudge your daughter the happiness we never had," she replied quietly.

Caspar was quiet now; he handed back the handkerchief, and sat upright by the table, pale, his mustaches tangled.

Alexander, fighting down the revulsion caused in him by Dorothy's remark, put on a businesslike air: "Then you propose to me, John, that I should sell my farm to you for fifty-five thousand thalers before there's a forced sale. You wouldn't have to pay a penny in cash, and while your eldest son inherits your own farm, your second son, Caspar, is to take over my place. In return for that Caspar is to marry my Elspeth. Is that right?"

John Schmalz shook his head: "No, Alexander, part of it's not right. In the first place, no member of your family need leave the farm, as your wife has already told you; and, in the second place, I haven't forgotten your son George. George would be in the same position you were in twenty-seven years ago. That is, he shall have ten thousand thalers from me so that he can marry into a farm. So your farm won't cost me fifty-five, it'll cost me sixty-five thousand thalers, five thousand more than you paid for it."

"Don't take it amiss, John Schmalz," said Alexander with unfriendly civility. "You meant well—by your children. A farm for each son! I mean well by mine, so I shan't sell my daughter."

"Just listen to the boaster!" cried Dorothy. "No shirt on his back, and he acts like the Emperor of China!"

"Quiet, Dorothy," old Schmalz warned, repressing her zeal with one hand, "your husband is right. A free man can sell everything, but not his freedom. Do I understand you, Alexander? Are we friends? One heart and one soul, hey? Just imagine us sitting of an evening on the bench outside there, with our grandchildren on our laps, philosophizing about the way of the world. Ah, what a life that will be!" he added with the air of a connoisseur.

But Alexander Kersting laughed at him: "For you, you old rascal! My daughter is a free woman, remember that! As long as I'm alive my daughter can decide freely according to her own judgment"— with a menacing look at Dorothy—"uninfluenced, do you hear?— whom she wants to have children with. Elspeth!"

"Don't yell so," said Dorothy, putting her hands over her ears.

Elspeth, quite unsuspecting to judge by her looks, appeared in the door to the living room and asked: "Father?"

Alexander hitched his chair around toward her: "Do you want to marry Caspar Schmalz of your own free will?"

The mayor's son opened his mouth as if awaiting his death sentence.

"Yes, Father," said Elspeth.

"Is that right?" her father asked again. "You've agreed with Caspar that you want to get married?"

"Yes, I have, Father."

"Is that so? Who talked you into making such an agreement?"

"Nobody. I made up my mind of my own free will."

This was too much; Alexander sprang up: "Have I fed you for twenty-one years, you silly goose," he yelled, "to have you make up your mind of your own free will behind your father's back? I'll give you something with a switch, you misbegotten brat! Get out!"

As Elspeth ran out, Dorothy took in the heavily breathing Caspar and his father, both of whom had risen, with a conciliatory gesture: "Better go now—go on, John, go on, Caspar! Come back tomorrow. You know Alexander. But he'll be sorry soon." Then, putting her hand on his shoulder: "Are you sorry, Alexander?" she asked in a soft voice.

After John whispered to his son: "She'll work on him all right," the two Schmalzes slipped out of the room. Dorothy, however, in terror lest all should be over, left her husband and caught up with the Schmalzes on the village street.

Half an hour after midnight Alexander Kersting, sleeping on the sofa in the best room, was awakened by a whisper: "It's me, Elspeth!" The farmer raised his head; his daughter, in an old raincoat, knelt by his pillow. "Caspar came—he said it was all arranged. I thought it might be possible to get engaged—without doing it; because you said you wanted to gain time."

"Didn't you lock your bedroom?"

"I couldn't; the key had been taken out."

"Aha! Get dressed and pack your bag. I'll take you to Uncle Charles' in town."

"At night?"

"Yes. Get dressed and help me hitch up."

As the farmer was leading the two dapple-grays in their harness out of the stall, while Elspeth polished the glass of the carriage lamps (it was a clear, windy, moonlight night), Dorothy came out with an old cape over her shoulders, and showed her husband in the lamplight two large sheets of paper clipped together: the marriage contract signed by both Schmalzes. He was sorry for his wife, she looked so pale: "Go on to sleep, and lock the papers up carefully," he said, and to Elspeth, "Hook up the traces."

Dorothy now mentioned that Charles, her brother, was sick. Charles Thiess, the grocer, in his basement at the corner of Canal and Broad Streets, dairyman to Professor Rudolphi and the officers in Police Barracks I diagonally across the canal, had caught cold among the milk cans in the darkness of early morning, and Aunt Augusta had written to Liebenau, something about pneumonia; but Alexander pointed out Augusta Thiess' inclination to "show a profit": "If Charles has a fever of a hundred, she'll say a hundred and two; she's got to take a profit of at least two degrees. If a neighbor had a higher fever than her husband, she'd take it as a personal affront."

And so, with an "All is not lost that is delayed," and a "No marriage contract requires that the bridegroom may visit his betrothed at night," father and daughter drove out into the night.

Arriving just as the stars paled, they slept at the inn where Alexander usually stopped; but when they went to the Thiesses' about nine, Aunt Augusta had shown no profit. The grown son in the basement shop said: "It's hopeless; but don't show it!" They went through the best room into the bedroom; nothing could have seemed more natural than a visit to the sick man from his brother-in-law and niece.

Beside Aunt Augusta at the head of the bed sat Jacob Willert; further down, the couple's second son, a sailor; at a table by the window, the doctors, Kuttner and Daruhi, were drinking coffee and being waited on by Kuttner's head nurse and assistant, Peggy Witt. The patient had gone to sleep.

"Well, I never, Alexander! Have you got leave?" said Jacob as Kersting leaned toward him, and Aunt Augusta asked: "What did you come for?"

"On account of circumstances," replied Elspeth's father, taken aback.

"And Dorothy? Or didn't she need to?" Augusta Thiess went on. "When did you come?"

"You'll wake your husband, Mrs. Thiess," Daruhi warned. The customary hatred between sisters-in-law prevailed between Augusta and

Dorothy, intensified by Alexander's "genteel front with nothing behind it."

Jacob Willert had got up; as it was to be presumed that Augusta would start a quarrel with Alexander, he put his finger to his lips, and said almost in a whisper: "Sit down here, Elspeth, in my chair. I'm going into the next room with your father."

"Would the young lady like a cup of coffee?" asked Peggy, beckoning Elspeth to the doctors' table. Angry at her aunt's behavior she sat down beside Daruhi, whom she knew from his lectures at the Liebenau interrogation depot.

Next door, meanwhile, in the Thiesses' living and dining room, Alexander Kersting was explaining his predicament, omitting nothing. Concealment would have been a mistake. If you wanted help from Jacob, you had to talk as if he were a father confessor, and in the tone of a military report, as Alexander knew from long experience.

"It's some time ago," Alexander concluded, "that you made me promise you I'd send my Elspeth to your house before I sold her in a moment of stress. You've probably forgotten."

"I haven't forgotten a thing," replied Jacob, "but your wife has forgotten that I brought up her daughter."

"You can depend on a good dog, but not on women," Alexander philosophized.

"What kind of work can your daughter do?"

"Any kind. She can feed cattle, hook up and unhitch, or even curry a horse."

Jacob Willert remembered that his own mother, the Englishwoman, had also been able to do this, although she was a millionairess. His father, however, had had a hundred horses, and his mother had been killed by a fall while steeplechasing. And the banker thought of his son, whose strange ailment Daruhi had explained to him. Everything comes around again, just like a carrousel.

"How much is Schmalz willing to pay for your farm?"

"Sixty-five."

"Then I'll take over the second mortgage. Schmalz can have his money, and you can have a spring loan, to get you through this year. I'd send your Elspeth to my wife, but she hasn't got time today. We're giving a soiree to celebrate my son's taking over the business. I'll send a message and the money to your inn. I'll give your daughter some easy job until she can make up her mind. Anything else?"

"Do you want Elspeth to start today?"

"No, let her go to Meyer, the second house steward, about ten to-morrow morning."

Meanwhile the sick man had awoken, and asked in almost incomprehensible words for the "Interrogator of the Tribunal."

Jacob got up and looked through the glass door. He saw the room being darkened and everyone except Daruhi (who had stepped over to the sick man) going into the shop, and he whispered into the ear of Alexander, who stood beside him: "He'll start imagining things in a moment, but all utter nonsense. Utter nonsense, do you hear? Take your daughter to the inn—go on, at once!"

He showed him the way through a dark hall into the shop. "It's all right, Alexander, you can thank me later," he whispered as the rescued farmer shook his hand, and returned to the sickroom.

One of the uncanny results of the Faust system, uncanny because it could not be reflected in statistics, was the rebirth of the guilty conscience. In our most recent historical literature it first occurs in the pages of Matthew Brandt, in connection with the story of Melchior Willert's later life, where it says he consulted Dr. Daruhi as a spiritual (i.e., conscientious) adviser, and advised his son Jacob to do the same. But it was not until the appearance of Hilgenfeld and Rudolphi's picture book, *Man's Journey Home,* that it made itself felt as a sort of epidemic. For in the book two diseases of the lunatic villages were described, the pharisaic disease and terror of conscience. For the former there was a special hospital in each delivery precinct, with an inscription on the gable: "To them that are without sin," and the people were brought back to a normal spiritual condition by derision and cold water. The second disease was regarded as so salubrious and beneficial by the Academy of Twelve that when Beyer afterward offered a prize for an answer to the question which one of Adam Faust's accomplishments had been greatest, first prize had been given to the reply: "The reawakening of the guilty conscience." For it had vanished from the world, like true nobility, architecture, Greek fire, and Chinese lacquer, and only such verbal traces as "idealistic bellyache" and "private and civil bellyache" had remained.

The phenomena of this "unearthly terror" are the same inside and outside the lunatic villages. A discomfort lasting for weeks turns to inflammatory fever: an uninitiated doctor will diagnose typhus, malaria, pneumonia, or pleurisy. After delirium—the fever having gone down somewhat—the sick man demands "the Interrogator of the Tribunal," a figure made popular by Hilgenfeld's book, actually the same whom Melchior Willert called a spiritual adviser. Now Daruhi, the man of longest and widest experience on the subject, causes the room to be darkened, not completely, but enough so that a greenish gleam comes feebly in. The sick man, propped up on pillows, sits up, staring fixedly into the greenish darkness and feeling for the hand of the interrogator, who sits by his bed; the patient answers the questions put to him, sometimes intelligently, sometimes senselessly stammering. He is replying not to the interrogator, but to a tribunal of Carpenters in their black costume ranged before his window in the form of a triangle with the apex upward, pyramid fashion. An examination of the sick man's eyes at this point will prove that he knows nothing of his true surroundings, and perceives neither the interrogator nor the room; the medical anomaly consists in the fact that he hears the questions put to him—not by the Carpenters, obviously, but by the interrogator. This is in the severe cases; the light ones resemble hallucinations.

At the time when Kuttner and Daruhi steered the visitors out, leaving Daruhi alone to darken the room, Charles Thiess, Dorothy Kersting's brother, was suffering from his third such attack. If the treatment is to be successful, the interrogator must either suspect beforehand or uncover through the statements of the feverish person during the attack the burden that is weighing him down. For otherwise there can be no interrogation; the patient wanders, and daylight has to be restored. Daruhi says that the patient very quickly betrays himself to any not altogether unseasoned interrogator as soon as the first command, "Recall your memories, miserable creature," has been spoken. Although all classes suffered from the disease, the presidential party called it the aristocrats' disease; anyone who was immune, on the contrary, passed for one of the rabble, and, in Hilgenfeld's phrase, belonged under police supervision.

During the first two attacks Charles Thiess had told very little, but that of such a painful nature that Daruhi now compelled all the visitors to leave not only the room but the shop and the house itself.

A sign, CLOSED, BACK SOON was hung on the shop door, and Augusta Thiess, her two sons, Alexander Kersting, and Elspeth went to the inn; Professor Kuttner, whose carriage was at the door, went back to the Women's Hospital with his head nurse, Peggy. Only Jacob Willert, thoroughly annoyed that his son's love for a dead woman had been concealed from him for seventeen years, was allowed to hear the grocer's confession.

"I have spoken to the judges, and all will end well," said Daruhi to the patient, who had sat up. On the bedside table were the doctor's stethoscope, ophthalmoscope, ampoules, and hypodermic needles. He injected a sedative. Jacob Willert was sitting in a wicker chair by the wall, in the deepest darkness. The patient, pointing to the imaginary judges, seemed to ask a question, and Daruhi replied: "They say you should have confidence in the tribunal. Your guilty conscience is your fear of God, and the fear of God is the beginning of wisdom. Repeat your life!"

The injection took its effect; Charles Thiess recounted, though with interruptions: "I was born on a farm. There were only two children, my sister Dorothy and me. Nevertheless, my father couldn't keep up the farm; he sold it, moved to this city, and opened a dairy. When other children were going to school, Dorothy and I were delivering milk, because in those days there were no milk carts. So we grew up, and when our father died, there was no inheritance, nothing but debts. Then the great stroke of good fortune came to us, for the rich Willert, Jacob Willert, took our Dorothy into his house. He kept her with all honor for two years in his little place by the river. Melchior, the old man, was still living in town; he made no objection to Dorothy, and set me up in this dairy, where I have been living for thirty-two years."

As there was a pause, Daruhi asked: "Who did make any objection to your sister Dorothy?"

"Melchior's lady, Alice, a racing rider. That was Jacob's mother, who got killed falling off a horse. 'I'm looking after my son,' she said to me; 'you look after your sister. Jacob can't marry her because he's betrothed himself to Elizabeth Sparangapani. If you can find a husband for your sister, he shall have ten thousand thalers from me, and you shall have five.'"

"So you sold your sister to your friend Alexander Kersting for five thousand thalers. You must tell everything: the tribunal is mercy itself," whispered the spiritual adviser.

"Yes."

Jacob Willert crept up and breathed in Daruhi's ear: "Ask whom she would rather have married, Jacob Willert or Alexander Kersting."

The patient, madly supposing one of the judges had asked him directly, answered: "Jacob Willert, of course, because he was her lover. How could she want to marry anyone except her lover?"

"Didn't you tell her," whispered Jacob from behind the bedpost, "that she would forget her lover and come to love her husband?"

"I did."

"What did she say?"

"She answered with a proverb that our minister gave her at her confirmation."

"What is the proverb?"

"Love is unending."

Daruhi snatched the dark-green curtain from the window. March sun poured into the room; the patient turned his head and fell back.

BOOK TWO

SECRET SUMMONS

XXV

THE following morning Elspeth Kersting set out upon her way. At the garden gate of the Willert mansion she encountered Marie Klingenberg, who gave a glance to the house steward who opened the door; on the wooden back stairs she asked her whether she was the celebrated Marie Klingenberg who had delivered up the electrical director.

"The same," the other agreed, giggling, and said she was now Mrs. Marie Uhl, the wife of Uhl, the gardener, who looked after the grounds at Willert's estate by the river and around Madonna Pond. The sleepy house steward, in ill-humor because he was to accompany the two to the attic floor to show them their room, observed that at the Willerts' there were no women, only maids, who were called by their first names: "There; and now shut your unwashed traps!"

"Meyer!" whispered Marie with a wink; and, as the man of might turned around on the wooden stairs, she said straight in his fat face: "At your service."

Putting up her hair in the bedroom upstairs, Elspeth asked her fellow worker how she had managed this.

"My God, you're green," replied Marie, an overblown, coarse-boned blonde. "I was Koehler's girl for a whole year. It wasn't only him I turned in, it was his accomplices too."

"But the Carpenters say you were the mistress of Charles Froehlich, the ringleader at the bloody night of Carolswald, who's a secret agent."

"I've been a lot of people's girl, you little ninny," laughed the other; just then there was a knock at the door, and Meyer's voice called: "You're to go to the Madam."

"I've got to help do the old lady's hair," whispered Marie, slipping out.

Elizabeth Willert's dressing room with its mahogany furniture and Indian silk rug had not been changed in thirty-one years; like all the couple's rooms it looked out on the quiet yard with the cobblestones and the statue on the fountain with the garden beyond. The mistress of the household, sitting in a peignoir before her wide mirror, was reading, allowing her hair to be worked on, and for probably fifteen minutes she said not a word. Finally she put aside the book, glanced indifferently at her coiffure, and said: "There's never anything but annoyance! Is it true that Andersen went to the hospital and slapped Peggy Witt, the operating-room nurse, in the face?"

Andersen was the third house steward, the handsome lad who had been taken on out of pity, before whose protestations of love Jacob's Geisenheim Roman lady, Peggy, had fled the Willert household.

Marie Klingenberg, although she lived with her husband and widowed mother two hours' drive out of town by the river, knew all the scandals of the Willerts' maids.

"Yes, but it isn't Peggy's fault," replied Marie, a great connoisseur of human nature. "It isn't true that she seduced Bernard Heide, the widower and kitchen-chair manufacturer; incidentally, they say he isn't a manufacturer at all, but only a factory foreman for Kuehn.

What happened is that Heide's wife died in childbed, and when she
was dying she saw her husband was in love, so she said, 'Nurse Peggy,
you marry my husband, but be good to the children,' after which
she died."

"Peggy is coming to complain today," said Elizabeth Willert; "we've
got to keep Andersen, the stupid thing, from giving her another
whack out of love. Or for that matter she may just be coming for
money, because Sebastian Heide wants to set himself up in business.
There's never anything but annoyance."

"It really would be criminal if he hit her again," Marie rejoined,
"I mean if Andersen hit Peggy. Why, she's pregnant by Heide."

Just then there was a knock, and a soft voice beyond the door whispered: "Meyer."

"Do you know Meyer?" asked the mistress of the household. "Oh,
no, you couldn't possibly. You've never worked here in the house."

Mrs. Uhl, née Klingenberg, knew the man perfectly well, but said
no, she did not know him.

The fact that Meyer was standing inquisitively at the door, and
probably spying through the keyhole, seemed to amuse the splendid
Elizabeth enormously: "He's the second house steward," she said.
"You must obey him—he's specially for the girls, but to tell the truth
he isn't really for girls at all, he's . . . you understand. After all, that's
why we put him over the female staff, just as you don't put a normal
man over a harem, nor an old one either, because as the saying goes,
there's no fool like an old fool; you take a eunuch."

There was a second knock. "Just a moment, with your permission,
my dear Mr. Meyer," cried Mrs. Willert, "you don't mind my putting
a shawl over my breast, do you?" and she added in an undertone, with
a twinkle, so that Marie giggled: "I'm being ironical, do you see,
because whether he sees your breast or not doesn't make any difference,
it doesn't do you any good."

"I was coming to introduce the new girl," said the voice on the
other side of the door.

"All right, all right," replied Elizabeth, "wait a minute," and to
Marie: "Listen to me: he'll take you out now and give you instructions
on the landing. You don't need to listen at all—he always says the
same thing every day, like all men—but stand still and lower your
eyes like an obedient slave. Eunuchs need slaves." Elizabeth turned

to the door: "Come on in, Meyer, or must I send you an invitation in writing?"

The second house steward, who, it will be remembered, was a plump-cheeked, beardless *bon vivant* with an unhealthy complexion, wearing a threadbare black suit and the low wing collar of a butler, came in, bowed, and waited for Mrs. Willert's permission to make his report. Behind his back he was concealing a girl.

Meyer's exaggerated obsequiousness annoyed Elizabeth: "I can hardly wait, my dear fellow," she said mockingly.

He stepped aside so that Elspeth Kersting could make her curtsy, and reported: "I have the honor to introduce the girl that the Senator engaged yesterday himself."

The lady of the house, who asserted a fortnight afterward that she had never been fooled for a moment, inspected the newcomer with the aid of a lorgnette: "Come over here. So you're the one that Rudolphi, the painter—what was it Rudolphi called you?"

"I don't know," said Elspeth, with eyes downcast.

"You know perfectly well, but it's sweet of you to pretend you don't. Go on, now. Everything will be taken care of."

Meyer, who could make no sense of the lady's talk, observed that there was nothing for the new girl to do. "The work has been assigned," he added proudly.

"Well, thank goodness that's *your* business, Meyer," cried Elizabeth, "and if there isn't any work left in the house at all"—she privately nudged Marie to call attention to her irony—"although you must have lots of practice in managing girls, why please ask Jacob Willert."

Going out on the landing of the famous staircase, and glancing upward to see whether the girls were watching him from the Belle Vue Gallery (but they seemed to have hidden), Meyer lined up the two new girls side by side, and administered his instructions: "Now, over here to the rail, please. Not so close together. No feeling of materials—no false intimacy of any kind. Intimacy is falsity, as our great poet says. Everyone for himself and God for us all. Now listen! No—not like that! Drop your shoulder, Marie, and pull your right ear down. Elspeth, put your left foot forward. There. For the time being you're to move into the guest room upstairs; your bag has been taken up, Elspeth, and a second bed is being set up, but I must request not to have any complaints. You're in a fine house now, where discipline, order, and morality prevail, morality above all in word and deed. This isn't like the country. Are you even virgins, as a matter of fact?"

"Yes indeed, Mr. Meyer," replied Marie promptly, whereupon the house steward turned to Elspeth, who was speechless with astonishment at the saucy fellow. "Aha, then *you* aren't," he triumphed. "Just what I thought, seeing you're from the country, where progress hasn't penetrated; but you'll have to give it up here—and about coming around some fine day and saying that Andersen (he's the third house steward, a hot lad—you'll meet him later), about coming and saying Andersen has led you astray: get that out of your heads. That was once upon a time, but today morality prevails. Now you know what's what."

Elspeth, after a glance at Marie, shook her head, and the butler barked at her: "What does that silly head shaking mean?"

"I didn't understand, Mr. ——" Kersting's daughter started to retort, convinced that the manservant was abusing his power.

At this Meyer laughed scornfully: "I can imagine, ha, ha, ha! Hard, isn't it, when you've only been to the village school?

"Point two: you aren't to go into the family's bathrooms and dressing room except when you're assigned to clean up. You have your own bathroom, where you can satisfy your urge for cleanliness, the fourth door on the left from the guest room, but about sitting in the toilet by the hour and smoking cigarettes, that's out of the question. You do that, and I'll have no hesitation in sending and having you fetched down by Mrs. Willert's first chambermaid, Emily, who stands before you all as a model of morality and devotion to duty."

Marie recollected hearing that Emily the moral, the Madam's lady's maid, had spent the whole night with Andersen and overslept the time to wake everyone up, at seven o'clock.

Down from the Belle Vue Gallery came Augustus Huebner, the head house steward, down the winding stairs with a toolbox hung over his shoulder, rule and pencils in the left breast pocket of his jacket. Meyer went toward him, snapped his heels together as if he were still a noncom with the Neuhafen Uhlans, and reported: "Instructing the two new girls."

Huebner the younger, a broad-shouldered, two-fisted artisan of some thirty-seven years, stopped and lit his cigar butt with deliberation.

He was wearing an overall suit of blue peasant linen, and no collar, so that the collar button was visible at his neck. His thin brown hair was parted, his angular face clean-shaven, but in contrast with the other two house stewards he wore a thin, clipped mustache.

"Did you wake up Emily?" he asked his subordinate.

"Certainly."

"Emily, the head coachman, and Andersen are to go out to Madonna Pond with the young master," he went on. Then, turning on the stairs: "Miss Kersting is to have some kind of easy work. She's to have a care of Andersen. Tell her that."

"I shall give the appropriate instructions," replied the former N.C.O. Returning to the girls and relishing his superiority with repeated nods: "Well, now, this can't go on, see?

> *For still the new transcends the old*
> *In signs and tokens manifold;*
> *Slaves rise up men; the olive waves,*
> *With roots deep set in battle graves!*

"I don't mean to say that the new life is a better life; in fact, for Andersen it's worse, and he's beginning to shrivel up, because the supply of tender new greens has been checked on account of the strict morals of young Mr. Henry. I, at any rate, have no desire," he went on, addressing Elspeth directly, "on account of a young thing like you to be thrown out of this house, where joy forever dwells, as the poet says. I therefore give you express orders—are you listening?"

"Certainly, Mr. Meyer!"

"Express orders as follows: if the third house steward on the stairs or the landing should stretch out his hand with seductive intent, you are to bust him on the snoot so that his false teeth scatter in all directions, quite without regard to what feelings you yourself may cherish toward him. Voluntary renunciation is the handmaiden's noblest virtue. Do you hear me?"

"Certainly, Mr. Meyer," smiled Elspeth.

"Then break step, march!" he ordered in a voice as soft as if his overexertion early in the morning had robbed him of his strength. He preceded the girls, who followed hesitantly down the winding stairs to the broad corridor on the second floor. Here were the double doors of the managerial offices, white and high, and the doors of the higher employees' offices, more modest, with panes of milk glass; the parquetry floor was in need of constant cleaning because confidential clerks and foreign commercial correspondents are too philosophical to scrape their shoes.

It happened that fifteen minutes previously a maid who was jealous of Emily had whispered into the door of Andersen's bedroom that his "star of the south," Peggy Witt, having strolled pensively around the lobby for a while, had gone into the office of the head of the house, and was negotiating audibly with Jacob Willert and the confidential clerk, Mr. Mueller, to get a bank loan of 22,000 thalers for her fiancé, Sebastian Heide, who wanted to set himself up in business with Kuehn's assistance. Handsome Andersen, first drying his tears and wishing "that damned money-crazy slut" a miscarriage, crept forth, overwhelmed with love, carrying a dust cloth to shine up the door-knobs; arriving before the chief's office, he heard the beloved voice, in reply to questions from Mr. Mueller, explaining the financial situa-tion, prospects, and business connections of the factory foreman, whose first wife, Cornelia, had died in childbed. She was already finishing, and apparently thanking Jacob Willert, for the latter replied: "This is a perfectly regular business deal, Peggy, and you needn't thank me; you shall have your trousseau besides, and the baby things, blue rib-bons *and* pink, because, after all, you never can tell——"

Andersen shuddered: on top of everything else, the slut was preg-nant by that dirty cabinetmaker fellow! As she might come out at any moment and catch him eavesdropping, he crept back to the stair-way without noticing Meyer, who was unlocking a broom closet on the landing, and also without noticing Marie and Elspeth coming downstairs, Elspeth by the banister, so that she must necessarily bump into him unless someone stood aside.

At that moment there appeared over the Belle Vue Gallery, like seraphim reclining on clouds, ten girls' heads, peering down at the lovelorn swain as he tottered up the stairs; a subdued and melodious tittering was heard beneath the skylight. Andersen, stretching up his arm to fend off this mockery, took hold of something soft and luscious. As he started to see what it was, Elspeth, well warned, took a swing and smacked noisily in the face the man who had accidentally touched her bosom, so that he flung up both arms and toppled headlong down the marble stairs.

Help, at any rate, was instantly forthcoming; Meyer rushed down from the broom closet; old John Huebner came from the ground-floor lobby, and his son Augustus arrived with the medicine case; the red plush stair runner and the bristly foot scraper at the bottom of the stairs had broken the fall. The victim of the accident was taken to his room to await the doctor, Meyer was upbraided for the excessive severity of his instructions, and Elspeth, crying with fright, having sat for a time on the lowest marble step listening to the consolations of the two Huebners and Emily, the lady's maid, started to work polishing the floor. Marie Uhl, however, was summoned to the mistress.

Andersen, awaking from a brief faint, saw his star of the south leave the chief's office and go downstairs to the lobby after a quick glance at the injured man and a long one at the weeping Elspeth. "I shall never regain consciousness," he thought, closing his eyes and wishing himself dead.

Henry Willert, meanwhile, slightly intoxicated—he supposed by the sleeping draft he had taken—had left the Women's Hospital in order to listen to the songbirds in the neighboring Henrietta Park and ponder the question why the world always gleams afresh in the early morning sun as it must have done on the first day of creation. As he fell asleep on a bench and dreamed, probably the strangest, probably the most portentous dream of his life, the first day of creation took flight before carriages, dust, nursemaids, *rentiers,* and strange old ladies with shawls and hats from past centuries, on which stuffed humming-birds waggled. . . .

Henry Willert, pursuing the dream of an endless carriage drive, and gay as a boy at the start of vacation, thought that he could now go home. And in fact it was nobody's business, and no one detained him until he reached the remote corner of Lady Square, where old Cath-arine, the flower seller with Grandfather Melchior's diamonds in her ears, had her stand. And just as was to be expected, she was standing there with a giant bouquet of roses.

"For the young master's happy day," she said; Henry had to accept the great bunch, and—with a frown because it was not proper to go without paying—to put back in his pocket the thaler he offered. Instead, recalling the endless carriage ride, which, dreamed or not, was too incredibly probable, he asked the street sweeper: "Since when have you been a coachman?"

"Oh, a person takes things as they come," replied Catharine on be-half of the dumfounded fellow, as if she knew the answer better. "I hope there'll be good things for the young master and the family on the young master's happy day," she wished him as Henry left and went into the house.

He whistled his way slowly up the stairs to the second floor, heed-lessly, for he kept tapping the bouquet rhythmically as it hung down beside his leg, and the rose petals spread over the stair runner and the freshly polished landing.

Naturally Elspeth Kersting cried out: "But, sir, you're shaking the flowers off that lovely bouquet!" When he turned and looked at the girl she regretted her hasty exclamation: good God, it was the head of the house; it was even the Secretary of the State for Foreign Affairs! The previous evening her father had shown her his picture in the *Illustrated News,* which printed the pictures of the new cabinet mem-bers, as well as the Clerk to the Government and the Teller of Great Deeds, including two of her former teachers, Ackermann and Merckel. But that was nothing: the others might be dismissed and sink to in-significance, but he never could, because he was the head of the house of Willert.

He must be somewhat taller and slenderer than his father, she thought, not daring to look; the barber had rubbed him with eau de cologne, and he wore his mustache clipped in the English fashion, of course, because Lady Beyer was the arbiter of style. Now she was study-ing him very closely—why did he stand there and let her look at him? She wanted to say something, something like, "Why don't you go, sir, into the chief's office, for instance?" but that was impossible. He had his hat in the same hand as the bunch of roses. Embarrassment made her breath come quickly, and she met his eyes, which regarded her. Now he would say something—he was making ready. His eyes were gray, and his face was pale—they were said to have been conferring all night. . . .

Henry, who had never seen Elspeth, recognized her at once: she was the Eve and the Rebecca and the blonde maidservant before the Palace of Pilate in Rudolphi's pictures. The model of Praxiteles was lovely! And with such speed and impact that nothing, not even a raising of the eyes, could come between, the distortion of the world that he had al-ways known departed; clearness and daylight spread about, and the meaning was plain, for this was the face in the water that had melted together with that of the dead woman; this was the one that had pushed aside the dead. He remembered down to the tiniest detail the dream he had dreamed early that morning:

Justice Holzkopf wanted to buy two acres of land out of the Willert estate on the riverbank, which spread uphill for ten thousand acres, almost to the western suburbs; he meant to have a country seat by the river, not far from the "big house," which was now heavily braced in case the Urbanites should attack the river line. Holzkopf, then, arrived in an antiquated coach with the white-bearded street sweeper as coachman, and two white horses from Jacob's stable, for an "inspection of the land" where he proposed to build his villa. But the rogue of a street sweeper, in order to increase the carriage hire, drove the proud purchaser of real estate not to the river, say in the neighborhood of Hinrich's garden at the Liebenau bridge, where, looking from the north, Willert's land begins and the big house is ten minutes away, but to a tumbledown park gate far up-country on the heights, where the riverbank is miles away, and a sea of green treetops rustles as if the forest had no ending. They got out, the judge and Henry; Holzkopf said to the wily coachman: "Now just you ask at that house over there whether I can have a look at the land. I'm the highest judge in the country, and want to buy."

"Where's any house?" said the aged man. "Get in, gentlemen!" And they had to leap quickly into the carriage, for the coachman was already racing downhill, swinging his whip, and singing a song with a voice that sounded as if he had a pipe organ in his chest:

Into the forest unending and green,
Sunlight and shadow and rustlings unseen!
Meadows pass by us; a stag, antlers high,
Harks on the hill to the soaring hawks' cry.
From balsam-crowned heights the brooks tumble and come
To reach the bright lake where the dragonflies hum.
In the whispering woods, warmed by golden sunbeams,
I would sleep as a changeling, wrapped up in my dreams.
Oh let me not know what the Sisters mete out,
But make me a drowsy child cushioned about.
Color and form blend where thy sweet light gleams.

When they reached the riverbank it was night; the ripples clucked against the retaining walls, the classical statues were shattered and cast aside, white marble bodies lay under the shrubbery, and the horses shivered.

The boat landing was built out into the river near the "little house"; there sat the broad-beamed fishing skiff; moon and stars glittered on the river, and Emily sat on the edge of the boat, watching Andersen, with whom she was spending the night, drawing a marble goddess out of the water and reeds with the long boat hook. The goddess was making herself light, and he had her in his embrace when Henry, who had been lying in wait upon the landing, sprang into the boat. It was him she smiled at, transforming her face as she had done in times past: but her first face passed by, her second, that of the monument, likewise, and a third took shape and was looking at him searchingly. Then Emily, mad with jealousy, flung up both arms and hurled the marble statue back into the water.

It was only a dream, but one had to distinguish meaning from unmeaning dreams, and Henry could not deny that this face had been foretold to him. Incidentally, his father had had the girl brought up, as he knew from his mother—whether for sheer charity he now began to doubt. But all other questions yielded to one alone, which he must ask unobserved and at once, no matter what the outcome. It was impossible to hold it back or becloud it longer, and he looked overhead and down the stairs to see whether an eavesdropper was posted anywhere.

"I have a question, Miss Kersting," he began, drawing his eyebrows together with the effort, "which I'm entitled to ask because I have known you for a long time."

She was so astounded that not a word escaped her. An awful pause ensued; he hesitated; she thought he had not said enough, and turned suddenly pale.

"Miss Kersting," Henry went on, his eyes flickering, "I have a question that I have never asked any girl, and I shall perhaps never ask it again, but if you don't want to answer at once I will give you three days' time to consider." He lowered his voice almost to a whisper: "Will you have a baby with me?"

Elspeth bowed her head as if to indicate a curtsy, and said yes without a moment's consideration. "Yes, Mr. Henry," she said. "Thank you very much."

"Give me your hand on it!"

She gave him her hand, and he said quickly: "We'll move into the little house by the river this afternoon. I don't want my parents or the staff to know. All right?"

"Yes, of course, Mr. Henry," said Elspeth.

A bank apprentice came up the stairs with a telegram. Henry, undecided whether he could offer the damaged bouquet to his betrothed, tossed it over the balustrade into the front lobby, bowed, and went toward the chief's office.

BOOK III

GOLIGHTLY'S
JOY
PREVENTED

With might and justice harnessed to the car
Was ever chariot more nobly drawn?
AESCHYLUS

DR. GRAU, A VERY DEMON OF PERSUASION

I

ABOUT noon, immediately before moving out to the river-bank with Henry's household goods in vans borrowed from Kuehn's, Andersen, Emily, the head coachman, Marie Uhl, and the two youngest maids, Olga and Ursula, gathered in the office of the young head of the firm.

He addressed them as follows: "You will lead a pleasant life out there, and not a monotonous one, for it is spring, which means variety and April weather. The detachment of sappers and miners that are fortifying the riverbank don't concern us; they are feeding themselves. Their instructions are of course to be followed, except when they demand something that might damage a young girl's reputation." Everyone smiled; young Henry's gaiety was infectious. "One thing more: there has been a mistake, quite natural in the excitement of yesterday; perhaps my mother made it, which is why I want to ask you all to maintain silence about the matter today and in future, to everyone. Miss Kersting, a young lady brought up by my father, was never hired, but is my guest, and will live in the rooms of Mrs. Anne Mary Willert, my grandmother, on the upper floor of the south wing in the little house. She won't need much service; who wants to see to that?"

"I will," said Emily, and no one objected, since she had hitherto been the confidante of the Madam, so that the easiest work was her prerogative.

Henry shook hands all around, and went to take leave of his parents. He had known for a long time (and suspected Daruhi was behind it) that neither of them would ever say a word of advice or interference in his daily life.

In regard to Henry's and Elspeth's life in the budding springtime around Madonna Pond from April 2 until the young lady's flight, accounts differ: while the servants whispered that they had come to an agreement very quickly, Matthew Brandt says they disagreed very quickly owing to Elspeth's inexperience and her pride, which apparently made her ready to stake everything, and also because Merckel's doctrine of the "love of the noble woman" had poisoned our unripe young beauty. Henry, enlightened by Hesse, did not believe the poisoning story, but thought she wanted to gain dominion over him and make him the plaything of her whims; but the von Brick tragedy, he said, should not be repeated in the Willert household.

Others put the blame on Dr. Grau, secret agent and peace negotiator for his Leader Urban: he tried, they think, to intervene between the Faustite Elspeth and the banker's son, who leaned toward an agreement. Others again, even including Jacob Willert, laid the entire responsibility on Henry, who, they said, spoiled by inferior women, left the woman with whom he was sharing his bed and board uninformed of the nature of his negotiations with Grau, and did not tell her what she asked to know. By thus withholding his confidence he alienated his helpmate, who quite rightly considered herself more than a concubine.

Elspeth herself, being asked in later years, talked of the "happy days." She roamed from early morning through the park and the woods on Cat Hill, shooting with a pistol at crows, and with a small rifle at rabbits that Andersen drove toward her into a grove from the copse. What she bagged she skinned herself, hung to her hunting bag, with blood dripping down her leather breeches, and delivered to Mrs. Klingenberg in the kitchen. Mrs. Klingenberg served the haunches and backs baked, in a thick cream gravy, at the table set for Elspeth and Henry outside the gardener's house on the terrace that looks upon Madonna Pond. "You can tell what a person feels like," she said, "by when he gets up. A happy person is early up and about; an unhappy one hates to see the day." And with a fervor that brought tears to her eyes she recalled the fresh, dewy meadows, on whose edges deer appeared in the morning mist, coming from where they had been grazing, and slipping back into the sheltering thicket; she recalled the starlings flying out of the poplars before the gardener's house, and the intoxicating aroma of the forest soil on rainy days when she hid and listened to Henry's conversations with Dr. Grau near the old wood road that runs parallel to the river behind the tumbledown park wall. On the second day Emily confessed to her that she had been "led astray" by

Andersen, who had afterward vowed he could not marry her because of his "undying love" for another. "The rascal shall marry you if I have to smack him again!" Elspeth said she had offered by way of consolation, whereupon the chambermaid had become her most devoted slave. Incidentally, handsome Andersen, who had hitherto been fit for nothing, showed excellent capacities as a forester, could soon shoot as straight as Elspeth, and won obedience from the two Scotch terriers.

In the smoky dawn of one of the first days, at the edge of a clearing in the evergreens on the ridge of Cat Hill, gently sloping toward town, Andersen discovered game snared, killed, and mutilated—a year-old hind and a she-hare. The kind of mutilation indicated sexual sadism, but a poacher, say, from the farms in the tilled valley would not have left the creatures for foxes to eat, but would have skinned them, taken out the entrails, and carried off at least the back and haunches. Elspeth pledged the young man to silence by promising him a green uniform, a hat with a heathcock feather, and a triple-barreled gun; for it was to be feared that Henry, who had inherited his love of the forest creatures from his ancestors, might leave the little house and the region itself in disgust at the vicinity of murderers. She could never carry a gun when he went with her; he took field glasses and a knotty stick, and lowered his voice with ingrained reverence as they entered the forest preserve beyond the park wall. The sight of an animal in the open preserve stirred him to a mysterious and panic joy; his hands would tremble so that Elspeth had to hold the field glasses for him. It was as if no game could ordinarily exist where city dwellers went walking, and as if that which still existed must flee in terror wherever the assassin of grass and trees appeared. For twenty years not a tree had been felled in the Willert preserves except dead trunks, which were cut up by the tenant farmers for fuel; and a forester, an old woodsman, was allowed to shoot twenty head of deer a year so that the damage they did to the fields might not get out of hand; nevertheless, the bills for damage done by game that the tenants on the scattered farms annually presented to the Willert estate were far from small. Jacob was willing to pay for having the game abundant and undisturbed, and never checked the bills; the first books that young Henry read were animal and hunting books, and the first rhyme that he learned to stammer out by heart, to his grandfather's delight, was:

> 'Tis credit to the hunter's name
> To cherish and preserve his game.
> The sportsman honors in the beast
> Of heaven's creatures not the least.

The old keeper declared that it could not have been any of the tenant farmers or their children: they did indeed shoot at crows and magpies with noiseless air rifles, and sometimes with small rifles at rabbits in winter, when the pelt was good for something, and they went after songbirds with nets—regrettably an ancient trade in the region; they would scarcely take venison as a gift, saying it required too much bacon or cooking fat, and as for mutilating innocent game and allowing it to rot—! In view of the keeper's honest puzzlement, Henry had to be informed that strange poachers were molesting the preserve. Of the sadistic mutilations Elspeth said nothing, but spied out Henry's rendezvous with Dr. Grau, and armed herself with a pistol in order to eavesdrop under the neighboring shrubbery. Two hundred Carpenters searched the preserve—too late; not a trace of the poacher was to be found. Taking quarters with the tenant farmers, fifty men remained under the command of Lindequist to watch, from well out of earshot, the wood road and the bench by the tumbledown park wall where Henry and Grau sat to negotiate.

The park wall included thirty green-bedded acres of dwelling houses, servants' quarters, gardens, and stables forming a quadrangle open to the river front. Its structure of solid brick and the iron spikes and broken bottles on the top had formerly afforded protection enough; and the wrought-iron double gate farthest inland, as well as the birch-lined approach to the front slope of the mansion, had always been kept in repair. But along the whole southern length of the wall, Melchior's first wife, the steeplechaser, Jacob's mother, had espaliered her fruit trees and planted exotic trees and shrubs familiar to her English homeland some sixty years before. And the south wall had been damaged by this very vegetation, growing along and penetrating the masonry, and later by badger and mole burrows. Bushes and brambles overgrew the destruction; with your bare hands you could take bricks out of the wall, cut your way through the brush with gardening shears, then go back and replace the bricks. For such considerations the herald and defender of "inspired office management," Lindequist, was not the right man; as a replaceable bureaucrat, he was merely the one among the high police officers who could most easily be dispensed with. Elspeth, in turn, imposed silence in this matter also upon Andersen, who, in boyish enthusiasm for adventure, had been the first to recognize and demonstrate the danger of the ruined wall. She was too much afraid that this beloved residence would be spoiled for her Henry, too confident of the former house steward's circumspection and devotion, and of her own eyes and steady hand. So it came about that the police guard was restricted to the wood road, cool in the shadow of the beeches, which ran outside the park wall and divided the dwellings from the open forest preserve—a favorite walk and drive for Melchior and his guests in an earlier day, and a bit of paradise to Elspeth, who would have refused nothing to the owner in order to possess what her eyes drank in. How much she herself was worth, and what she could demand, was something she realized in those nights when her partner, beside himself with love, twined his hands in her hair, bit her lips, and promised his beloved houses, park, and forest.

But in the morning at breakfast on the terrace looking down upon Madonna Pond, the night was forgotten, as if vows and embraces had been all in a dream. And while Mrs. Klingenberg and Marie Uhl served coffee, they would talk about Andersen's forester's uniform, the shooting range they would set up in the park, a roofed bowling alley outdoors, how they ought to go looking for plovers' eggs, and about everyday matters at the tenant farms.

Not until the fourth day, after Elspeth had overheard two conversations, was the name of the Dr. Grau, the negotiator, mentioned; and then began the embittered dispute between the lovers, never explained by anyone, not even Matthew Brandt.

"What does that Dr. Grau want here, the disagreeable fellow?" Elspeth asked.

"He wants to negotiate peace terms," replied Henry.

"Oh, you don't want to fight?"

"We'd rather not, Elspeth."

"That's a lie."

"It isn't a lie. It's simply that General Frohwein, the commander in chief, doesn't want to fire on his own countrymen."

"Why not? Out of cowardice in face of evil?"

Young Willert suppressed a smile. "Cowardice in face of evil" was an academic term in the Carpenters' training courses, around which Andrew Zorn had built up a whole doctrine, namely that we deny the influence of the demonic—including primal evil—upon our daily life not from intelligence but from cowardice.

"Let's understand each other, Elspeth: cowardice in face of evil doesn't mean that I'm afraid of evil, say, for instance, of Urban. On the contrary: cowardice in face of evil means that I laugh at Satan because he does not exist, but is an outworn superstition. Naturally Frohwein doesn't deny the existence of demons, or he would have split with us. But he thinks they have the upper hand; he's sure that we're lost."

"Ridiculous! All the provincial governors are Carpenters; so are Frohwein, Kaempf, Hesse, Merckel, and you too."

"All front and mere appearances, says Frohwein. People call us reactionaries; they call Urban progress, so he is the winner; and Frohwein is already seeing himself as Gelimer, King of the Goths, in the snake tower. Man can't fight against rats and snakes, he says. What was that story about Gelimer?"

Elspeth's face beamed. She was extravagantly fond of recalling school memories: "Gelimer, King of the Goths, was vanquished by the Romans, and they locked him into a damp dungeon with snakes, but left him his harp. So whenever the serpents started to bite, he sang, and they fell back. This went on for three days, and then he weakened, and the poem says:

> *When he had sung the third night away*
> *And sunrise proclaimed the break of day*
> *The serpents bared their fangs, they say,*
> *And Gelimer the king fell dead."*

"Frohwein thinks that's our fate," said Henry, ending the conversation.

Dr. Grau was genuinely a peace negotiator. For Urban firmly believed that he could weaken the body of civil servants and the army if he were given three cabinet posts. If not, still time was working on his side, provided that his Sports Regiments retained their arms. They had the most modern of equipment. So he mobilized in secret and offered peace in public, sending his agents to urge the "sensible" members of the government, like Willert, Frohwein, Hildebrand, and Holzkopf, to recognize the *status quo*.

The government, in turn, had to gain ten days' time to provision the capital. If Urban struck at once and surrounded the capital, things might end as Frohwein feared.

Beyer had instructed Secretary of State Willert to delay and put off Grau, Urban's most adroit agent, at least until April 12, and if possible to drag out the negotiations beyond that date.

The agent, Dr. Grau, was an interesting figure. His name was not Grau, and neither was he a doctor; he had grown up in the country, the son of a shoemaker, maltreated because of his small stature, his crooked shoulder, his matted hair and pockmarked face. Because of his fondness for reading and his fine memory, the village parson drew a philanthropist's attention to him, and he went through the city high school. Just before the final examinations the rich man died. The boy gave up his studies, tried his hand at journalism, and found himself able at barely thirty to make as much money as he pleased by selling advertising for Koenig Publications: no one could resist his powers of persuasion.

Then he fell in love with the daughter of Winkler, the wine merchant, one of Urban's backers. Instead of the bought love of whores and the bold impudence of the gadabouts whom he pursued every evening, gripped as he was by an insatiable craving for women, he began to dream of the reciprocal love of a decent woman. Biting his pillow, he would murmur the name of her whom he was devoted to: Louise Henrietta Winkler. Louise Henrietta stood for decency, a sense of shame, a settled life, advancement to the ranks of patricians, old established families, the honored personages whom people bowed to on the street. More than this, Louise Henrietta would not refuse her love even to a man with a crooked shoulder; she was extremely shortsighted, wore one pair of glasses on the street and two for reading, had an injured hip suffered in a fall as a child, and wore false teeth at the age of twenty-nine; so Dr. Grau calculated that the girl was scarcely marriageable, according to the view of the time, for four reasons—age, teeth, lameness, and near-blindness.

Her unexpected opposition fanned his love to the point of frenzy. "An advertising salesman? Never." She would sooner remain in the house of her beloved Papa. Or, of course, she might not say no if he could offer her her picture in the *Illustrated News* and social celebrity, which Ackermann was giving her school friend Elsie, a perfectly vacuous goose who had not even read Scott's *Ivanhoe*. And her father, under his aging daughter's thumb, made this condition: so gifted a man as Grau, he said, must try his hand at politics. The betrothal should be celebrated on the same day as his appointment to personal corps of the Leader, Dr. Urban.

So Dr. Grau left Koenig Publications, and in barely two years made himself indispensable to the Leader. When Urban left the central prison on the evening of April 2, Grau had a definite promise of promotion to the rank of Weisse and Thomas if by persuading the Willerts, powerful as they were in Senate and Academy, he could succeed in restoring the *status quo*.

Every day on the wood road at the southeast corner of the park wall Dr. Grau pounded away with his arguments at the young Secretary of State. The arguments were the strongest Henry had ever heard: the weariness of humanity after four hundred years' supreme effort to endure freedom; the longing for the man who would take upon himself the worry about daily bread and the torments of conscience; the daily dishonesty of those who damned progress, but sold their horses in order to plow by steam, and were incapable of sustaining a tooth extraction without a local anesthetic; the daily dishonesty of such religious persons as Bishop Hesse, whose *Practical Instructions* forbade asking a Carpenter his faith, thus showing by his own words that science had taken the place of religion, for a religion without belief in a commanding God was a mere moral doctrine, a mutable work of human hands. What could possibly be the feelings of Henry and his "highly esteemed father" as they watched the turning and twisting of the Christians and their retreat from one position to another before the spotlight of science? Surely the two of them, who as Conservatives were after all concerned for the survival of their power and their business, must begin to pursue a long-range policy in sheer self-preservation —that was to say, a policy of compliance with the desires of humanity. "You, Mr. Secretary, and your esteemed father are clinging to Faust's wish dream, according to which every single human being is supposed to be an individual, connected with his neighbor by brotherhood, meaning a generous recognition of earthly differences."

"Yes indeed," said Henry, "for that would be a community of saints or the kingdom of God, which the Apostle expressly recognizes will not come by outward gestures."

"But that wish dream is the exact opposite of the modern man's wish dream, Mr. Secretary," cried Dr. Grau, "as Adam Faust himself admits by his fantastic 'Instructions to His Successor' to defend freedom, that is, the brotherhoods' cult of the individual, even against the people. You gentlemen in the government may have a momentary success; but who do you suppose, my valued host, will be the victorious survivor—Adam Faust's wish dream, the individual; or the collective, the wish dream of the people?"

"What do you call a collective?" asked Henry.

"A good question. I can never tire of negotiating with such people as you, Mr. Secretary. The collective is the community freed of the individual, creeping to the leader's feet without anguish or care; the soldier singing in ranks; the happy patient under the doctor's orders; the child in his mother's lap. The collective is the form of life taken on by an intellect made humble through knowledge, an intellect that has seen through all the heavens, and desires nothing but to live—that is, to savor whatever can be enjoyed. It is the end of human presumption, the victory of the innocence that distinguishes the animal, because it desires no more than nature offers—food and mating."

"You must admit, Mr. Grau, that this 'wish dream of humanity' did not exist a hundred years ago."

"Certainly I do, Mr. Secretary."

"Well, then how did it come into being so quickly?"

"What a profound question! A pleasure, as aforesaid. I shall strive to be brief and clear. For the first time in the earth's history, the masses or the man of the masses or the 'spirit of the masses' has awakened, arising and overshadowing all that has gone before. That spirit is the world of tomorrow. Let us compare the spirit of former times with the spirit of tomorrow, matter-of-factly, calling the one 'Smith' and the other, the modern spirit, 'Brown.' Smith, or the past, has always wanted to rise and be something more than his neighbor; equality has been odious to him: thus we have the individualistic age. The modern man, Brown, or the world of tomorrow, in contrast to anything in the past, demands the equality of everything wearing a human countenance. Brown, that is, requires the collective, in which no one counts for more or has more to say than he himself. Brown, since he no longer *can* rise himself, wants to prevent anyone else from rising. But, weak as he is, he cannot himself accomplish the humbling of everyone: he needs the leader, the despot, who will lower all men to the same level. Thus we have the age of collectivism: for in the collective no one counts for anything, no one has anything to say, no one is responsible, no one has to make a decision—except the leader! Discovered at long last, the collective is the proper form of life for modern man, the form where everyone can be replaced by anyone, and no one has anything left that would allow him to rise above his neighbor and be something on his own account. The collective is the organized equality for which the man of tomorrow will offer his blood and all he has. The collective, as the organ and form of equality, is the future of the human race. For the last time, Mr. Willert, I invite you and your esteemed father to join the gods of tomorrow, who are organizing the collective of mankind."

Henry, sitting on the bench and leaning against the wall, replied most courteously that he held the negotiator's frankness very highly, and that the "iron truths" he had cited, the weariness of mankind and its desire to be dominated, were indisputable. Only there was still the question of whether those who ruled must not keep running their heads against the wall of fact before they abdicated, until, like the royal lizard in the fairy tale, they fell down dead.

"Even in primitive times, Mr. Secretary," replied Grau, "no human being was regarded as strong enough to beat his own head against a wall, and among animals only the oldest had such strength. How can a present-day man, who cannot stand having a tooth pulled without a narcotic, run his head against a wall? And surely the facts I have mentioned, the longing for security in a collective, the disgust with the perils of freedom, are comparable to a strong wall."

"Certainly they are," replied Henry, inviting his fellow emissary to dinner, as evening was falling.

The Urbanite, smiling with a childlike and incredulous gleam in his eyes—at any rate, he thought, I've gone this far: what will Louise Henrietta say?—regretted that his collar was soaked with perspiration from his efforts; awkwardly he displayed his wrinkled neck, whose furrows were pouring with dirty sweat.

Elspeth, hidden behind the wall, from which she had removed two bricks, was able to see through; she shook herself with disgust.

Henry offered him a bath and fresh linen, and to this the other could not say no.

But the young lady? Where could the young lady be? The day before, when General Spitta arrived to inspect the river fortifications, and stayed with two companions at the house, she had assisted the master of the house in receiving and waiting on the guests, wearing the gown and jewelry of Anne Mary Willert, the Beloved. And her arrangements, attentiveness, and smoothness had won such admiration that the slightly tipsy general proposed a toast to the lady of the house, calling her "a true daughter of Alexander Kersting"—no small praise if the old toper's popularity among his companions and kindred spirits be taken into consideration.

Dr. Grau, shaking his head at such magnificent hospitality, was bathed, shaved, sprayed with eau de cologne from an atomizer, and provided with fresh linen, which was available in all sizes, though the cut was old-fashioned; Andersen yelled at Emily, asking if she hadn't told Miss Elspeth that the guest was staying for dinner; Emily declared that two estate agents from Justice Holzkopf had taken Miss Elspeth with them on a tour of inspection in Jacob Willert's shooting cart. This was possible: for weeks now Mrs. Holzkopf, as attested by Henry's anxious dream, had been disturbing the quiet landscape with her real-estate brokers. She said there were water rats by the river, swarms of gnats in the meadowland, high winds on the heights, with rheumatism thrown in, for her Louis always threw open all the windows; in short, the city lady was dissatisfied with everything, as if she were doing the Willerts a favor, not they her, by invading the peace of the great estate with her project of building a country house.

For the first time Henry felt a rising anger with Elspeth: it really did not require much imagination to satisfy tall Spitta's alcoholic gullet; he drank gin with N.C.O.'s, slapped waitresses on the behind, and goggled at Anne Mary Willert's diamonds as if at a higher world. But the young Secretary of State's first mission, to delay the outbreak of violence until Kaempf gave the signal, depended for its success or failure upon the little man with the dissipated face and the dirty wrinkles; he must be patted, wrapped in cotton wool, chained to the house night and day, enchained with eyes, lips, and hands so that he should not depart, like the bewitched Odysseus in the house of Circe; and here she had run off because the man was not handsome enough for her!

True, she had uttered a warning at the coffee table that morning: "I simply couldn't stand that face"; but Henry, for fear she would pump him about his mission, which even his own father must not get wind of, diverted the conversation to Merckel's three-volume *Dictionary of Splendid Phrases,* now printed and withheld from the public, which had been delivered to the house an hour before.

"A revolutionary work, a textbook of the future Christian commonwealth," he tried to explain to his beloved; but Elspeth, weary and inattentive, went away.

"Have Mrs. Klingenberg wait on table," Henry ordered the butler, who inquired what she should wear. "Dark dress and an apron—good God, did I come out here to give costume parties?"

He was sitting in the old billiard room on the ground floor, so that he might hear Elspeth's footsteps overhead in case she had told an untruth and locked herself in. There was not a sound, and he realized that out of defiance she was letting the brokers take her driving and entertain her at a tenant farm. But no Willert's wife or mistress had ever had the right to choose her own guests or be unable to stand some ugly face; and anyone who is proud of his beauty no longer possesses it, because pride makes faces vacuous. This was how things had started at von Brick's, with unpermitted excursions—or perhaps in some other way: things always start some other way, so that you can't guess what's coming in the next installment.

Dr. Grau, in an often-laundered linen wrapper, sat in the bathroom waiting for his suit, which young Ursula was going over with a carpet beater, brush, and flatiron; he studied his own powdered face. "Really I'd call it a face of strong character," he flattered himself: if Louise Henrietta could have seen how he was being honored, perhaps the wine merchant's daughter's pride would have melted away.

He approved of his tactics of intimidating the adversary with "brutal facts." Simply to present the Leader's ridiculously modest demand for the *status quo ante* would have required only a messenger, not a negotiator; but the messenger would have been thrown out, because the Beyerites of course were feeling their oats after the nocturnal demonstration.

Tears of pity for himself and anger at the injustice rose to the little man's eyes: they sent *him* out into a desperate situation, and on his genius depended the existence or downfall of a vast social movement;

yet Weisse, a dry executive official without imagination or agility, was the party leader in the Senate, garnering all the honors, and to him Louise Henrietta would have rushed with open arms. Because he was handsome? Not at all: women are no aesthetes when it comes to choosing a husband—"Long hair, short brains," says the proverb; and a woman doesn't look at her husband to see what kind of children he will give her, but what kind of clothes he will buy her. Otherwise the human race would be handsomer. He spat with contempt, and rubbed it over with his foot, looking around anxiously: she would find herself mistaken!

If he vanquished the Willerts, he could wallow in women like a millionairess in gowns. If he did not vanquish them, there were two possibilities: Urban would overthrow the government, and then Dr. Grau would be a Secretary of State, and immaculate beauties would crowd his anterooms, snatching off their own corsets on his divans. For that, my dear ladies, would be dictatorship, and she who was reluctant should have what would make her sorry she had ever been born—perfectly simple. The second possibility, which he considered with a frown, was that Urban might be defeated and exterminated—a likely possibility if you attributed any prophetic acumen to the speculators on the cultural exchange, who had suddenly veered from Urban worship to religious ecstasy. Incidentally, the highest-paid fortuneteller in the city—a friend of Kittelsen's, it must be admitted—had rocked her fat bosom doubtfully to and fro when Grau had got Urban's fortune told for a goldpiece before starting on his mission; and though the woman might be a stupid goose, the cards, a new pack that he had just bought and shuffled himself, were disinterested and seldom lied. But only a silly little fool, says the poet, imagines his doom the moment he sees no way out; and he who stands behind the door and peers through the crack can let revolutions roar safely past him. Had he less wit than Innocent Isabella Rex, whose "religious seasoning," or Mark Antony, whose drama, *The Passion of the Lamb,* was insurance against the worst eventuality? Take this Henry, the third member of the Merckel-Hesse-Willert alliance: had not the force of "reality" already seized him, shaken him, flung him to the mat? "You can't take me in with those banker's eyes!" thought Grau. "I could see well enough that whenever I speak your heart trembles, and your house rocks as if the foundations were being snatched from under it. Among the honest

men of today the banker is the most honest, because he knows that
dishonesty no longer shows a profit. If I come out from behind the door
after the revolution has roared past, and accost him, saying, 'Here I
am, as a realist, in your camp. Admit that I'm useful!' will he deny it?
No, not he!"

Augustus Huebner brought the freshly pressed suit, and led the
guest into the dining room. Only two plates—what an honor! The millionaire was already so impressed that he dared not present his concubine to the secretary of the Leader, a member of the Leader's personal
corps. Only keep this up, and the world was his!

As the two sat down, Henry anxiously studied his guest's face for a
moment to see whether the absence of the fair one, whom he must have
noticed the day before, offended him. Thank goodness he was beaming his gratification!

"This is Mrs. Klingenberg, the maker of good things," said the host,
indicating the white-haired woman who brought in the soup.

"Honored, I'm sure," she said, while Grau bowed in his seat, noticing
that the grander the master, the more white-haired his servants. A very
dark soup, with eggs, mushrooms, and chunks of meat floating on it,
according to the recipe of John Christopher Laemmle of Geisenheim,
won the guest's admiration, which the banker passed on to the cook.

In reply to Grau's remark: "Well, I should hardly think they'd have
poor soup at the Willerts'!" she protested that even rich people might
sometimes have very poor soup indeed.

"Your own experience?" asked Henry, laughing. Conversations with
old women had always been a mania of the Willerts.

"Money makes a great deal of difference, Mr. Secretary, no doubt of
that, but it don't make much difference if there isn't no taste to go
with it. I can tell you a story about that, gentlemen, where you'll admit
yourselves that there's a deep meaning hidden in it."

"Another spoonful, Mrs. Klingenberg. You too, Mr. Grau?"

The widow refilled the little soup cups.

"All right, now, out with the truth!" said the master of the house.

"Naturally there's got to be money there; money makes the soup
bones, the soup bones make the stock," said the old woman, "but stock
isn't soup, and even if you chucked in a whole pound of butter it still
isn't!"

"Excellent," Henry interrupted. "What do you as a materialist think of it, Mr. Grau?"

Grau laughed, feeling flattered, and the old woman went on: "You see, when my late father was still alive, by the name of Vogel—my maiden name was Vogel—at first he was a waiter and then a theater doorman, always very grand with his gold buttons and gold braid and gold epaulets on his coat—well, maybe he didn't have good taste, that he learned when he was a waiter! But the money, now, that was just so-so. So naturally when our mother put the soup on the table, with us being seven children, not even counting the dead ones, why naturally Father looked funny, and Mother said: 'Like money, like soup. Of course if I had ten thalers' housekeeping money a week, like Mrs. Sandrock next door has, I could make good soup too.' 'That so?' my father says, lifting his voice way up. 'All right, then, next week you'll have ten thalers.' No sooner said than done. But when my mother brought the soup on the table the next Monday, or was it Tuesday—it was beef broth—and stood there with arms akimbo, like a person does when he's in the right, or maybe he just wants a row, and when she asked Father, 'Huh? Is the soup any better this time?' he shook his head and said, 'There's just more gobs of fat floating on it!' "

"That was very well said of your father," the guest agreed.

"Let me tell you it certainly was well said, Doctor! There's a deep meaning behind it that fits anyone: you see, if you compare a lot of rich men that have a great deal of money with poor people that have nothing, you feel like saying about the rich, 'There's just more gobs of fat floating on them!' "

Over coffee and a long cigar the government negotiator invited the Urbanite to stay overnight, so that they might reach an agreement on fundamentals: "When the Archbishop is negotiating, he always says there must be a common highway that both parties can set foot on, or else there's no getting ahead. I think that's right, always supposing one wants to get ahead."

Dr. Grau, looking at his interlocutor's honest face, thought: "If you want to get ahead, you're lost," and aloud he said: "Precisely my opinion. In fact, I even know of a common highway."

"So do I," smiled the other, "but first I'd be glad to know what you think of the chances if we *don't* get ahead."

For a moment the negotiator seemed to be thinking intently; his thoughts were quite simple: No hostility now, for God's sake! Accordingly he said: "With pleasure. Urban is so strong in the north and east that he will crush the government troops like pasteboard boxes. In the south it's anybody's race, because we don't know how the runaways will fight, and Laurenti is the most dangerous of the government generals. The west doesn't count, being too far away from the capital; before the Urbanites can force the broad stream, the decision will be made. *Voilà!*"

He had a pleasing way of speaking, leaning back with eyes open, displaying his palms to his interlocutor as if nothing were to be concealed from man to man.

Henry mopped his brow, horrified—why, the man was speaking the truth! The generals saw the situation in just this light. Could he have been telling the truth before—the belief in his heart? If Urban's messenger persisted in telling the truth, the government negotiator would be faced with an unforeseen difficulty. He had taken the Carpenter's oath to open unto him that knocks, and was obliged to give an honest answer to a man who spoke honestly, for he who speaks honestly to you is knocking. This is the supreme rule; he who sins against it will do wisely to report himself to the Joint Court. If he fails even to report himself, things may go hard with him.

"But if I tell the truth," thought Henry, not looking at Urban's agent, "I shan't be carrying out the job they gave me, to gain time by dragging out the negotiations. I'd better do my job," he thought, "because if the situation is as threatening as Grau says, I've got to gain time or we're done for. Incidentally, admitting the picture is so black for us, why doesn't Urban strike? Why does he give us time to arm?"

Grau guessed what his host was thinking, but to answer the expected question, "Why don't you strike?" was the hardest thing imaginable, for he could only have told the truth: "We want peace." But to make this very truth, this honest truth sound probable was impossible; any untruth was more credible than this. How would it be, though, to tell it, and then send two other truths after it, swelling it into an avalanche, a roaring avalanche of truth? There was nothing to be accomplished by petty dodges and pinpricks anyway against these pachyderms that had resolved to defend their freedom even in spite of the people.

"Why don't you strike?" whispered Henry.

"Because we want peace, for if we can keep peace our victory is sure. It won't be much longer, I am sorry to say, my truly esteemed sir, it won't be much longer that you can keep on swimming against the current. I say I am sorry, because it was a heroic spectacle." Grau too had lowered his voice to a whisper.

"But conversely," retorted Henry, leaning forward with both fore-arms on the table, "if you can't keep peace, that is, if there is fighting, you are done for, and this is why you want to keep peace."

"That's not so: if there is no fighting, then you, Mr. Willert, may be lost because time is working against you. But if there is fighting, you are certainly lost because, supposing we are defeated, then after your victory you will have to establish your system—the system of hypo-critical orthodoxy and pitiless war on everything that the multitude desires. How long can that go on—three years, five? I honor the Faust-ites, Mr. Secretary, I honestly confess my astonishment and admira-tion; you cannot charge us with a single disrespectful word against the dead President—us, whom Ackermann, Merckel, Daruhi, accuse of all imaginable vices. Not a word of disrespect to you, sir, either, but the old saying is still true, many hounds are the death of the hare, or, there's no fighting against the multitude."

The government negotiator almost caught himself saying, "It may be too late even for truths." He checked the sentence, and said instead: "It would be easier for me to talk to my colleagues if Urban could get along with the Archbishop, as leader of the second strongest party."

"What pain you cause me!" replied Grau, and the wrinkles in his dissipated face seemed to have increased by hundreds. "I really did believe in the common highway, but you're demanding submission. For it would indeed be possible to retire the Archbishop on a large pension, but never to take him into the firm, as I shall immediately show you."

"First one question: what do you call the common highway?"

"The security of the householder," replied Dr. Grau, opening his eyes wide like a merchant tendering an unbelievably good offer to a competitor. And as Henry made an interrogatory gesture, he went on: "Now why do the masses come pouring in to Dr. Urban? Not simply, or not chiefly, to satisfy their malice, vengefulness, or cruelty. Inciden-tally, you yourself didn't originally make that claim; Daruhi spoke of a cosmic fog, Held and Hilgenfeld of the forsaken heart, Zorn and Adam Faust of the anxiety of the father; but they all meant the same thing, namely that the householder does not know today whether he will be able to pay the rent tomorrow. This system of unbearable insecurity has brought the masses to the Faust system and to us as well; that is, the same cause has made us both, friend and foe, great, because both, Adam Faust and Urban, promised to put an end to the insecurity."

"The insecurity of the *householder,* you say?"

"Yes—for the young, unmarried man still loves variety and adventures, but the married man wants stability."

Henry nodded.

"Accordingly, the Faustites and the Urbanites, the Christians and the Yellows, are steering toward the same goal: the security of the householder. For even to you, my dear sir, the doctrine that we want to satisfy our envy and enjoy the scream of our victim is undemonstrable, mystical, and furthermore quite new, an invention of old Hesse's, spread among the people by his son in his address to the squadrons. Merckel has recently taken it up—why, judge for yourself, my excellent host, why? Because he will not admit that we have the same goal, and could march on the common highway for the salvation of the world, instead of hearing the scornful laughter of our common enemy—ah, yes, we are so closely linked that even our enemy is shared, dear God, our goal and our enemy we hold in common!" He covered his face.

Steps were heard on the upper floor. The runaway had come home.

"Finish what you were saying, Mr. Grau."

"—instead of hearing the scornful laughter of the Iron Phalanx as we annihilate each other."

The mahogany grandfather clock in the corner struck eleven, and Henry, troubled by longing for Elspeth, said: "Tempting, very tempting, Mr. Grau."

"Surely you believe me?"

"Without restriction. But the night is advanced, far advanced"— again the banker was strongly tempted to give away too much symbolically—"and what you say challenges reflection. Let us sleep on the matter; as a point of honesty, because I see in you an opponent I can respect, I will say this much: there is no common highway in sight yet, and only outwardly a common goal. For what you call 'security' you want to bring about forcibly through organization. We seek security in brotherhood."

"I am empowered, Mr. Secretary, to inform you that the Leader is ready to recognize the brotherhoods, and to give the title of brotherhood to every one of his organizations."

Henry changed color: one more frank word, and this negotiator—not a bad man but a beaten one, a runaway from the mountains but not a Carpenter, humble it was true, but slavish through self-contempt—would leave the house, acknowledging the failure of the negotiations, and by tomorrow the guns would be crackling. This must not be; the government man must not tell his adversary that the Commission to Investigate Phrases would never let Urban—the Faustites would sooner let themselves be killed and plowed under—would never let him call his associations brotherhoods. Sooner than this the "Decree Against the Use of Splendid Phrases," ready prepared in Merckel's desk, would withdraw the word "brotherhood" from circulation by a general prohibition, as had already been planned for nine hundred other great words because of their easy availability for hypocritical speech.

"This concession," said the Secretary of State, getting up, "perhaps, nay probably, creates a new situation, so I would like to request that we discuss the new situation tomorrow, on a new day."

In his bedroom Grau found standing on a side table mineral water, a bottle of red wine, a corkscrew, crackers, a box of sugar, lemons, and a lemon squeezer; in a cupboard were a white shirt, two handkerchiefs, shaving gear, eau de cologne, and a small tin of sodium bicarbonate. The nightshirt lying diagonally across the pillow of the open bed was folded back below, so that one could slip straight into it. On the bedside table were cigars and cigarettes in a Chinese cloisonné box, matches, the evening papers, and a light novel. The butler had half opened the matchbox invitingly, laying one match on top of it. The negotiator, comparing this assiduity in guessing the needs of a guest with the chilliness of many guest bedrooms that he had been offered in his travels, thought of Mrs. Klingenberg's story. He was yet more astounded when he opened the paper: it was the *People's National Times,* official organ of the Urbanite party.

Meanwhile the head of the house was knocking at the door of Elspeth's living room; Emily slipped out to meet him, and whispered through the half-open door that Miss Elspeth had gone to bed with a bad headache, taken a sleeping powder, and was already asleep. Emily would tell Miss Elspeth that he had been kind enough to inquire after the patient.

"Dr. Kuttner will call tomorrow morning," replied Henry, departing. If he had stayed for a moment he would have heard the giggles of his loved one, who was sitting up in bed eating stewed fruit, monstrously amused at Emily's notion that she would "tell Miss Elspeth that he had been so kind," just as if Henry had intended only to "inquire after the patient."

Nevertheless, Elspeth had not been party to a lie, in respect to either the real-estate brokers or the headache; the sleeping powder did not take effect, and her heart ached because she was not being honest to her lover, nor he to her. But could she tell and not have everything over with—not have the landscape, Cat Hill, the broad valley whose eastern sky gleamed reddish at night in the lights of the capital, not have river and forests fade away like a dream? If any meaning should be discovered in the sequence of her remarks, either Henry would have a close guard and this peace would be destroyed, or he would be ordered away.

The two real-estate brokers, men with full beards, had arrived in an open landau, most smartly got up with a liveried coachman, white horses, red harness, and gilt lamps; they drove up to the main entrance at five o'clock, and asked the gatekeeper to call some member of the family. They wanted to be driven around the inside of the valley, as that was the likeliest place to find a spot for Mrs. Justice Holzkopf. Where was their permit from Major Lindequist, the gatekeeper asked. They produced it, signed and stamped: "Commission of Public Safety, Guard Department," said the stamp, with Lindequist's name scrawled below.

As Henry was ending his conference with Grau, Elspeth came out in an old raincoat; she noticed that the gray-bearded gentleman, top hat in hand, who introduced his companion had his eye fixed on her coat pocket, where she carried the pistol; for as she buttoned up the raincoat (her hair being confined in one of Anne Mary Willert's plaid kerchiefs), the outline of the butt and lock protruded.

Would she be inclined to accompany Mrs. Justice Holzkopf's envoys on their tour of inspection, giving occasional directions to the driver, since no one could be better able than she to point out the "secluded dells" on the edge of the valley? The extraordinarily elegant diction of the bearded and gray-haired man who gave his name as Broker Hahn, and his fat and gigantic companion's as Broker Schmidt, did not accord with his demeanor: he scratched his chin as if the beard itched, and made a face. Elspeth, as yet by no means accustomed to the role of mistress of the household, and incredulously enjoying her good fortune, smiled, inflating her long nostrils and twisting her mouth as is the way of a beautiful woman unsure of herself and smiling when offered something irresistibly tempting. A drive of at least three hours in an open landau drawn by white horses with gilt bells jingling on their red harness was something Henry had not yet offered her; so she lied, saying she knew every nook and corner of the valley, and would also gladly take the ribbons now and then, being a practiced driver.

Broker Hahn, with a magnificent sweep of the arm, pointed the way to the carriage, whose coachman saluted; squinting after the beauty as she got into the carriage, he licked his lips with such abominable lasciviousness that the other rascal, in sheer high spirits (the gate-keeper had departed), lifted up his false beard for a moment, and stuck out his tongue behind Elspeth's back. He resembled Emil, the Lion of Afghanistan.

But the exploit of which the two were quite capable, which at least the gray-bearded Mr. "Hahn" had dreamed of—getting the woman drunk at a tenant farm when they stopped for a rest, and then when she had to step outside in the darkness stopping her mouth behind a stall door, and prying those long thighs apart ("It's enough to make your mouth water," observed Mr. Hahn to the Lion of Afghanistan when Elspeth had taken the coachman's seat, and the carriage was rattling off along a stone roadway)—neither this adventure nor any other took place. For if the graybeard and his powerful companion were to pursue their private pleasure today instead of preparing for the execution of the Leader's orders, by tomorrow they might be floating beardless, with throats cut, along some stinking roadside ditch, down toward the river and the sea.

Their continence, however, was richly rewarded. For Elspeth, whose hands fairly itched to drive, had at once taken the coachman's place, and she waved her whip in salutation as Police Majors Lindequist and

Lorenz, who alternated in command of the guard detail, came riding along the southeast corner of the wall toward the carriage from the south. No more welcome encounter could possibly have taken place. Elspeth, proudly enthroned on the box, and knowing both policemen from the training courses at Liebenau, naturally introduced the two brokers, Hahn and Schmidt, as Mrs. Holzkopf's emissaries who were "looking for a little place"; so they were not even asked to show their permit, and were vouched for in advance, so to speak, for future visits to the region, and safeguarded against police suspicion. Accordingly, the drive, with the pipe-smoking coachman sitting next to Elspeth, passed off in perfect harmony; the fact that Mr. Hahn, when they drank champagne to "all I love" at the inn in Little Rose, several times came rather close to Elspeth's bosom she excused on the grounds of masculine weakness and his eagerness to do business.

Miss Elspeth, not returning until ten o'clock at night, had Emily serve her supper in bed, and began to forget what she had told the brokers in casual conversation, a bit at a time, about the loopholes in the guard, the times when the guard was changed, the crumbling south wall, the old gate rotting on its hinges, and the location of the neglected park paths.

Incidentally, she was offended—not at Grau, however, but at Henry's changed behavior when the sun was shining: at his lack of demonstrativeness by day. Did he ever sit as familiarly on the bench with her as he was doing with this fellow? Did he listen with such interest, laugh with such delight, when *she* said something? It was not the fact that he was an Urbanite and quite obviously Satan himself that hurt her feelings, but the fact that Henry enjoyed him more than he did her during the hours of daylight and common sense.

Thus, by way of a feminine false conclusion, namely that "the fellow was taking away her sweetheart," she began to hate Grau, and at the same time to condemn Henry, thinking that the banker was seeking peace out of cowardice. She instructed Emily to turn away Henry, and cried herself to sleep when the maid left her.

At six o'clock in the morning Dr. Kuttner and Benjamin Werner, the President's stenographer, were fetched from their beds and driven out to the estate by the river. At half-past eight—it was raining, and the breakfast table was set in the dining room—Henry, Dr. Grau, and

Werner sat down at the table, and Urban's secretary agreed with delight to having the morning's conference transcribed.

Professor Kuttner, meanwhile, found Elspeth suffering from nervous depression and nothing more. At this, bursting into tears, she asked him to relieve her of her pregnancy; her sweetheart, she said, was showing contempt for her, so she did not want his child, she wanted her freedom.

The high-society surgeon heard such complaints every day, and gave the usual prescription: not to let her sweetheart notice anything, for goodness' sake not to turn him away; to explore the causes for his behavior tenderly, without abruptness or hardness, and to consult the doctor again in a fortnight, or sooner if necessary. Pregnancy could not be determined for a matter of weeks, and sunshine ordinarily followed after rain.

Would he terminate her pregnancy as soon as it could be diagnosed? Elspeth asked.

"If circumstances require it, yes," replied the doctor, kissing the young lady's hand, and went back to town.

Scarcely had a cup of coffee been drunk, a roll been eaten, and a cigar lit, before Henry, giving a sign to Benjamin Werner, asked the negotiator to resume the subject of the day before, the security of the householder; the argument developed in a quick series of questions and answers.

"Whence does security derive according to your theory, if I may ask such a direct question?" Dr. Grau began.

"From justified mutual confidence."

"And the mutual confidence?"

"From a reinstilled belief that the main thing is common to everyone, rich and poor alike."

"What main thing?"

"There is only one, which is why there is only one common highway, too. Adam Faust called it 'the old law,' and he called it 'the last public opinion,' or 'the succession of the Apostles,' but it all means the same thing; or you may say the epistles of Paul, or Isaiah, or one of the Psalms, which after all are teachings for kings, for example, 'The Lord preserveth the strangers; He relieveth the fatherless and widow; but the way of the wicked He turneth upside down. The people will *never* let *anyone* take this common law away from them so long as it is meant in deadly earnest by the governors, and not brought into contempt by babblers and hypocrites."

"You talk about the 'old law,'" Grau interrupted. "Where is the lawgiver?"

"I don't know; and it doesn't make any difference anyway," replied Henry.

"But, my esteemed host, what about the security of the law if the lawgiver is not secure—in fact, if he is nowhere present, as Daruhi maintained thirteen years ago at the Natural Science Congress? If the law is to offer security, the lawgiver must be the securest of all, the most tangible—nay, he must be omnipresent in order to strike a blow wherever he is despised, just as the police are present everywhere, striking immediately when the lawgiver is despised."

"The mills of God grind slowly . . ."

"No, my dear sir, they don't grind at all, because the Miller doesn't exist. Even Bishop Hesse—just think: *Hesse* admitted this by forbidding anyone to ask a Carpenter—think of it: a Carpenter, a servant of the Miller—whether he believes in the Miller."

Young Willert, suppressing a smile, poured out a cup of coffee for his guest. It is hard to withstand a mind that has a sense of humor.

Grau thanked him with shining eyes, and, his first onslaught having been successful, flung in fresh reserves: "Besides, it isn't true that the people will go to their death for the law; they go to death for the lawgiver, for the visible, existing, all-powerful lawgiver, because he cannot only promise security to all, but—actually present and all-powerful as he is—also can afford this security. What security do you, Mr. Willert, afford to your employees if even the slightest possibility be conceived that you may go bankrupt the day after tomorrow? What security is afforded to the nation by a government that in the first place is a beggar, since it possesses nothing except the taxes it begs; and in the second place tosses like a nutshell on the ocean, to be swamped tomorrow or the next day by some ridiculous ripple, I mean the whim of a clique or parliamentary majority? How can the householder expect security from a government that begs for his favor with speeches and leaflets, that humbles itself before him, the insecure, the man craving security, to re-elect the whore he has been supporting?

Naturally he does not re-elect her, because if one must depend on whores—I am not speaking from personal experience—one at least elects to have a variety!"

Even if this fellow is Satan, thought Henry, he would be a more interesting neighbor than the righteous Holzkopf!

"Here too, although you deny it," Grau began.

"Not in the least," smiled Henry.

"Deny me in your heart, there is no difference, no abyss between us; on the contrary, there is a *common* highway; for Adam Faust said that democracy was the form of government which compels the teacher to tremble before his class and flatter them."

"Adam never said that."

"Because he was a fox; but honestly and truly, my excellent host: might he have said it?"

"I should think it was possible; one says a good many things."

"Correct; but many things that one says are a giveaway, allowing deeper insights. Please let's go back to the starting point: the only serious problem of a modern government, the *only one,* is the security of the householder. Do we agree in that?"

"Completely."

"Therefore a householder needs a government that is itself the most secure, the most powerful, the most unshakable thing that he, insecure and craving security, can imagine even in his wildest dreams. Therefore the householder, or the nation, longs for the tyrant, for he can do everything, has everything, is everything, and no control can touch him. Therefore uncontrolled tyranny is the modern form of democracy. Am I talking demagogy or logic?"

"Logic," said Henry; and Grau, concentrating fiercely, forgot that the Faustites were at daggers drawn with the calculable.

"One thing you will admit, Mr. Secretary: as long as the least, the stupidest, the most unskilled of laborers is not absolutely certain that every Friday evening all his life he will be punctually paid his wages, or the substitute for wages, the dole, mankind will know no tranquillity. Are you of a different opinion?"

"No."

"Then I will come to the conclusion, the final conclusion, by a necessarily circuitous route—I ask your pardon for this. For the people demand more than assurance of their daily bread: even the *promise* of this security must be secure, trustworthy. Have you noticed with what disgust the simple man listens to such phrases as 'election promises'? Not another word about that democracy, but my compliments to you, sir: one thing we have learned from Adam Faust. Do you remember the interview that our Leader gave to a foreign journalist some ten years ago? Do you remember his contempt for the smilers, for those who are in earnest about nothing, and his respect for the late President? That interview is memorable, for it reveals the secret of how a ruler maintains his rule. Adam Faust got the people behind him by a promise. He did not promise anything so deeply desired and reasonable as what we promise, security. No, he promised something unwanted, senseless, dead and buried—Christianity. But half the people followed him blindly—fantastic as it is—toward what they did not want: for thirteen years our Leader stared at this spectacle, struck dumb with admiration. It is proved, my dear sir, that the people are tired of one thing: lack of earnestness, sneers, election promises—in a word, politics! This we know now, and so much you can be sure of: security, the reasonable and desired promise which we hold out, is a matter about which we are as literally, childishly, and mortally in earnest as Adam Faust was with his 'old law.' And here is the conclusion: at least half of the people know that when we have promised security and been victorious, the poor people will embrace one another and weep with joy, for paradise will have arrived. Yes, security will be at hand, because our government will no longer flatter and tremble, but will have *everything* at its disposal, men and materials. Thus it can distribute everything to everyone. Security will be at hand, secondly, because our Leader has learned from Adam Faust that the people will submit to the man whose promise is childishly serious—to him who loves his wish dream more than life. Urban's wish dream is the security of all through submission to the Leader, a security so great that if a hair on the head of the humblest factory workman were harmed, the factory would instantly go up in flames, and the manufacturer would be hanging on a gallows beside it.

"I am done. The aim, Mr. Secretary, our common aim, is the security of the householder. The road to it, the only one—in other words, our common highway—is the tyranny desired by the people, and therefore democratic."

Dr. Grau wiped the perspiration from his face and neck with a handkerchief soaked in perfume; Henry asked the stenographer: "Got everything?"

"Everything," Benjamin Werner declared, shuffling the sheets together to make a fair copy in the next room.

"Mr. Grau, I shall now spend three days trying to explain your arguments to the Faustites, and to assure peace through concessions on both sides," said Henry Willert, getting up.

The former advertising salesman was already captivated by this splendid hospitality, the bath, the perfume, the shirts, and the frank eye and cordiality of the millionaire, who listened to everything and seemed to believe it all. Poor Dr. Grau was past noticing that Henry's words had no meaning except perhaps the pitiful one: "Come back in four days." Even forgetting to sign the transcript, he got into his carriage and drove to town, where the much-envied Weisse awaited him.

"You missed meeting an interesting man," said Henry to Elspeth, sitting on the edge of her bed, "perhaps rather a tragedy of a man." And when she continued to keep silent like an obstinate child, he asked: "Why do you want to meddle in these rude and awful struggles? You should be glad you can keep your hands clean." She held out her hands to him with a smile; he kissed them, kissed her mouth, and they loved each other, but confidence was not restored.

Benjamin Werner's neatly written fair copy, dated April 9, suffered ignominious treatment. When Henry drove to town that afternoon, Elspeth found the document on his desk, read it, called Emily, and ordered: "Into the stove with it!" As the girl was opening the stove door, she changed her mind, saying: "No, it's too dirty for the fire— cut it up and hang it in the servants' toilet!" And so it was done.

HE WHO SEEKS SECURITY SHALL FIND IT

II

SEVERAL circumstances combined to cast a shadow over the spirits of the Yellow League Leader: the menacing growth of the Laurenti army-group swing to the authorized partial mobilization; the insufficient report from Dr. Grau—five days' negotiation and nothing accomplished!—and finally the unfaithfulness of Countess Bessonoff, who, whenever she spent the night at the mansion on Lady Square in the capital, had the enormous Emil sleep with her.

At Urban's headquarters in Neuhafen the high functionaries crept about as if in a house of mourning; Thomas, when Grau asked why he was not admitted to the presence, advised the little man to leave at once, and to disappear altogether for a time unless he could bring peace with him on the thirteenth. Had anything been decided against him? Grau asked. "It's a matter of mood—who can tell?" replied the Chief of Staff. "Urban believes that instead of simply demanding the *status quo ante,* you made some nebulous demands."

"But, good God, you always have to demand more, so that your opponent can beat you down," the negotiator defended himself, feeling a wave of fear-inspired nausea. He went back to the capital, struggled through the streets for another day and through the House of Dreams for another night, and drove out at daybreak to the estate by the river. Being known to the policemen, he wandered around Madonna Pond unmolested, for an hour, looking up every ten minutes at the windows of the little house. Invited by Mrs. Klingenberg to come in, he took coffee with the old woman and her daughter, and at half-past seven in the morning was shown into Henry's study. The Secretary of State, coming in unshaven in his dressing gown, asked what went on.

"I can't wait any longer," Grau replied. "The Leader will surrender any post in the government, but he won't let his Sports Detachments be touched."

Young Willert asked leave at least to take his bath and shave, which the other granted with a smile so sad that Henry suspected he was trading now not for Urban but for his own life.

He sent for Andersen, and had the cipher telegrams that were lying ready dispatched. There were only two: one to the President, one to Hesse, who already had authority to cause the arrest of 20,000 suspicious characters all over the country, under the circumstances that now prevailed, before Urban could be informed of the government's intentions. There was no other way to terrorize the Gas-House Boys and forestall their sabotage. It was eight o'clock; the arrests, prepared down to the last detail, would require from four to six hours; by noon the Urbanites might strike back, and the "operations" might begin. . . .

So Henry had to take his guest for a drive as the sun began to shine on Cat Hill and the valley. To drag out the interview, he asked whether Grau was fond of nature.

But Grau, already past the state of mind where one speaks flattery, and arriving at the bravery that sees bridges burning behind, replied that the flowers of the field had smelled bad through the door of his parents' peasant hut when his mother lay dying without medical care because there was no money. "When the house begins to fall down, nature crowds in, and the city man, instead of assisting the helpless inmate of the house, calls the devastation picturesque. The only person who can think nature is beautiful is the man who expects nothing of it, and pays for it besides."

Henry remembered the bills for damage by game: "And flowers, Mr. Grau—roses, violets, carnations—don't you think they're beautiful?"

"Oh, very beautiful—in the florist's shop where they really belong, cut, sprinkled, tied into a bunch, and presented to a woman who exists in your imagination."

Sitting in the grass on the crest of the hill they looked down into the valley, where the second smoke of the day rose from the red roofs of the hamlet. The woman must be pushed back and cut off too, thought Henry, so that she doesn't grow through the window of one's soul. Dr. Kuttner had informed him and warned him against betraying any state secret to her: "She's testing out your ability to resist her now," said the doctor. "If you love her, don't give in, not even if she runs away. A woman wants to know that her bounds are set—that's quite natural. She is herself the protecting wall around the child. Can anyone who readily softens and yields be a protecting wall to *her?*"

"Mr. Grau, you said that the bishops couldn't be taken into the firm. Why not?"

"If they behaved like the bishops abroad, they would fit in wonderfully. All over the civilized world—not in this country, that is—Christianity is a serious social institution on Sundays; during the week it means nothing, because on weekdays calculation, objectivity, and practicality predominate. Irrationality is reserved for days of rest. Are you really willing to have this childishly seriously meant absurdity dominate our workaday world?"

"Yes, as a matter of fact," Henry returned.

"Very clever, or to be more precise, very rich," said Grau. "Anyone who is rich enough so that he can pay for nature without expecting anything of it has Sunday every day. He eats caviar with a spoon, and absurdity is his daily bread." He laughed a dry, coughing laugh, and Henry thought of the wheat field that grew into the bedroom of the sick woman who had been this bitter man's mother. "But the poor man needs assured wages and stable prices: that is, he needs the tyrant, and he in turn must be the most secure of all things, and therefore above criticism or control. I proved that to you three days ago."

A cloud of dust arose along the country road between lines of plum trees in the valley. Ten Federal Policemen, their carbines hung over their shoulders, were galloping toward the hamlet of Little Rose.

"Look at that," said Henry, "someone's being arrested."

"Now if our bishops were real bishops, educated society men who were pious or graceful, as the case required, how useful they could be to us! But these here are themselves absurdities, either by nature like the Archbishop and Kessel, or made crazy by Adam Faust, like the younger ones."

"You mean to say the bishops are a threat to the security of the tyrant?" asked the Secretary of State.

"Our bishops, not the civilized bishops. Ours are an insupportable threat, if only as aristocrats: tyranny has never endured an aristocracy.

We need watchdogs, but not inspectors to keep their eye on the ruler. All the tyrants in history have risen from the masses and been men of the masses; all the tyrannicides without exception have been aristocrats."

"There aren't any more aristocrats in the world, Mr. Grau."

"In the civilized world, you mean: thank goodness that's true. But if your dead President had had his way, he would have made the whole nation into aristocrats with his crazy 'old law.' Do you remember the anecdote about 'That's nothing to me,' where he made fun of his own workman for relying on the kindness and justice of his employer? Do you remember Anton Koerner the turner's impudent address on equality at the patrician banquet? Adam Faust wanted to make the dirtiest street Arab into an aristocrat, for anyone in the 'Christian commonwealth' who can read a Bible is by that fact an inspector of the government. That means he's your superior and dangerous to you, Mr. Willert."

"Obviously, because—what does it say on the pediment of the Staff College: 'If there is no God, what sort of captain am I?' Putting it differently: if I don't follow the 'old law,' and don't win respect for it, by what right am I in the government?"

"And security, the security of the householders—what about that, if the ruler is not secure? Would you deny that a dominion has feet of clay if any devout blockhead with a Bible in his hand can call it to account? My dear sir! To build an earthly kingdom on God is truly to build it on sand. For the multitude, the man of tomorrow, wants to worship its masters, but not to call them to account. Naturally, so long as a man has God, he is free, since with the Bible in hand he can sit in judgment upon his masters. But does he want that? Honestly and truly: does he want to be free?"

"It isn't what a man wants that matters, Mr. Grau—especially since he wants something new every twenty years—what matters is his freedom, which you yourself quite rightly derive from the 'old law.' The ruler must defend his 'freedom derived from the old law,' and if men do not want it, then he must do so against men."

"Then you do insist on running your head against the wall. Is that a refusal?" asked the negotiator; but he was no longer afraid. Thomas' warning opened up the possibility, of course, that if his mission was a failure he might be shot in front of a sand heap. But he did not want to die, and fear of death shook Grau's confidence in Urban as the guarantor of universal security.

Henry Willert looked sidelong at the little man who lay stretched out in the grass: "Let's go down to Little Rose and see who's been arrested. We can have breakfast at the posting inn—white cheese, hard sausage, country bread, and island beer." And as the negotiator looked up mistrustfully, he added: "We're perfectly safe here in the preserve. There's a double guard every two hundred yards."

It was afternoon by the time poor Dr. Grau knocked at the door of the office of the Carpenters' Induction Commission on the canal bank. As railway communication to southwestward had not yet been cut off, and the mountain province was safe from uprisings, Major Stark, informed of the situation by Henry Willert, shipped "the man who had knocked" to Marienhall, where he was assigned a temporary residence on the Geisenheim highway, guarded by police. In the streets of the capital the newsboys shouted: "The Leader's private secretary surrenders to the government"—and that evening Laurenti's advance guard on the Moenckeberg heath came in conflict with General Oriola, and was beaten back after three hours' fighting.

BOOK THREE

THREE OUTRAGES

III

THE rich landowner, Oriola, friend of Lienhardt and patron of Urban, whose "Christianity" was derided by his namesake the Bishop as a monument of hypocrisy, will be remembered from the first part of this account. So will his lame daughter, Frederica, whom "iron necessity and unforeseen circumstances" had compelled to become engaged to John Theodoric Lienhardt, the eroticist and defrauder of Kate.

The old man died, and Frederica retired to a country house by the romantic Mediterranean to devote herself to poetry and love. Her brother Ernest Oriola took over the estate, and assumed command of the Urbanite army in the southern province. He was a brave and circumspect military leader, and sure he could beat Laurenti on the field of battle and break through into the central provinces, whose loyalty the government was depending on.

For his part General Laurenti, father of the color sergeant shot at Dammerkerk and the first lieutenant who was serving as Kaempf's adjutant, could have broken off the engagement in an hour, or thrown back the hastily advancing enemy by bringing up reinforcements. He was sitting in a camp chair behind two batteries of field artillery firing at the enemy artillery position from a slightly rising open spot in the pines. As he watched the thin skirmishing lines of the Urbanites through his field glasses, occasionally giving an order in a soft voice and chewing on a straw, his thoughts were in no way different from those of the staff and his colleagues in the west and east of the country, who were directing similar initial operations.

Planes and tanks, the dreadful offensive weapons of the present, were as yet unknown. Victory could be gained only on the offensive, by a break-through, an encirclement, or a combination of both; but still—granting equal troop morale, equal armament, equally skilled leadership—victory required a numerical superiority of at least two or three to one, and the attacker's losses were tremendous. Laurenti, therefore, quite sure of himself with the inexhaustible reserves that were advancing after him from the mountain province, dragged out the encounter in his curiosity to see how the Urbanite runaways would behave under fire. When night fell and the tumult had died away, he sent a warning telegram to Frohwein, the commander in chief of the army: "The Sports Divisions are fighting like tigers."

In reply he was told that the orders were to remain unchanged. These orders, a system of arrangements for the civil war, had been communicated to the army leaders as much as eighteen months previously; they gave a general view of the probable situation when the rebellion should begin. The capital, the central provinces, and the mountain province in the southwest, the orders stated, would be in government hands. Urban would attempt to advance from the south and northwest toward the interior, and from the east and north toward the capital. This way the government could use the advantage offered by the strategic interior line as well as by the superiority (other things being equal) inherent in defense. It was, however, to be observed that the insurgents' blood was the blood of citizens just as much as the government soldiers' was, and, accordingly, the greatest possible moderation was indicated. Thus ran the general orders, which were followed in the open field more than in the cities.

Not only was the "greatest possible" moderation not employed, but there was none at all in thickly settled districts. Pistols, carbines, bayonets, and hand grenades raged with implacable savagery in the hand-to-hand fighting for the police stations, government buildings, post and telegraph offices, provision warehouses, powder magazines, gasworks, railway stations and tracks, waterworks, and electric-power lines.

It was a fact that not only the officer but the private soldier received two hundred hours' instruction every year; the principles of the Carpenters' Rule were part of the curriculum; and malice and cruelty—pleasure in the scream of the victim—had been characterized as original evil or Satan, and made such an object of popular contempt that very few cases came into court any more in times of peace. But now the reverse of the medal was surprisingly revealed: the private soldiers, even the Carpenters, were unshakably convinced that anyone who destroyed engineering facilities, thus cutting off water, light, and power from the hospitals, must certainly be Satan, and deserved to be killed. And, defying the humane orders, they proceeded to kill every saboteur they found, not bloodthirstily, not joyfully, but simply because he was "original evil."

They it was who perhaps saved the state: after the third day no sabotage took place, and the auxiliary troops went rolling over the hastily repaired bridges and tracks from the central provinces toward the capital, which was threatened on two sides.

It was high time. Urban's Master of Ordnance in the north and General Susa, a previously unknown Sports Detachment commander, in the east drove the weak government forces before them, and by the eighteenth of April were only two days' march from the capital. Our General Baer, of the Western Army Corps, could not hold the river line. Now Laurenti finally received orders to attack regardless of losses, and to fling his army northward after his victory, leaving behind a contingent sufficient to hold his gains.

During those days, with life lines, betrothals, marriages being cut off, things sadder, funnier, and grander than we have to tell may have happened a hundred times in bedrooms and on the edges of the fields. Since it is usually the things happening in close proximity to governing personages that are recorded, we turn to the capital.

By the twelfth, when Dr. Grau's capture—which it actually was not, as he had surrendered of his own accord—became known, Urban had already left Mittelburg, and the Carpenters advanced into an empty nest. The League Leader, watching the tremendous fires and listening to the explosions by which his Gas-House Boys were destroying the eastern part of the seaport of Neuhafen, beyond the river, repeated his orders issued from prison. Peace might still be preserved, he said, if the reasonable wing of the government were straightened by removing the three morbid bloodhounds, Hesse, Merckel, and Henry Willert.

So his courageous retainers went to work. The infernal machine with a time fuse that was planted in Hesse's study, looking out on the canal, exploded punctually, destroying the sofa over it, the side wall, and the plaster ceiling. The general, however, had gone to the stable to look at a newborn foal.

Merckel may have had some premonition, but the mansion of the Secretary of State was much more strongly guarded within and without than Willert's houses by Madonna Pond. At seven in the evening he sent two papers to his mother by his housekeeper, Mrs. Haas (who had given up her job with Schwann), as if they were not safe in his own desk. These were his "Political Testament" and the unpublished papers of Adam Faust, which had been put in his hands for publication. The woman had scarcely been gone ten minutes before the Gas-House Boy came through a hidden door behind Merckel's chair and clapped a wet pad of cotton over his victim's face as he turned. The Secretary of State, struggling against unconsciousness, overturned the heavy chair as he fell; the murderer, kneeling, opened his victim's shirt, and drove a three-cornered dagger up to the hilt in his chest. A tag inscribed "This is the death for traitors" was attached to the dagger handle.

As the crash of the oak chair had been heard, the murderer, pursued by a patrol, fled into the basement kitchen, whence a secretly dug passageway led down to the sewers. He was shot on the narrow iron ladder. But the President's deputy died.

Elspeth Kersting's conscience was not easy. Nocturnal footprints in the park, clumsily obliterated, reminded her of the mutilated forest creatures and the not entirely mercantile behavior of the two real-estate brokers, who came back with their grand carriage—not one of Willert's, it appeared—and picked out one "secluded spot" after another, protesting that the justice's wife would be overjoyed.

As chance would have it, just at the moment when Dr. Grau was sitting in the train that took him to the quiet town of Marienhall, an old museum guard and gossip, Caspar by name, was showing his drinking companion, Charles Froehlich, a dirty piece of folded paper. "Strictly discreet and confidential," he said with momentously uplifted forefinger, as if the two words meant different things. It was a military drawing, a sketch, showing an attack upon the capital from east, west, and southwest. When the old fellow went to the toilet at the inn, the secret agent abstracted the map from his coat pocket. Going away, he appeared after sunset at the main entrance to the Willert estate by the river. Major Lindequist, summoned by the gate-keeper, asked what he wanted. To him Froehlich showed the sketch, whispering in his ear, as one friend to another, that this was the chance of his life.

Major Lindequist was a man who would go with his friends through thick and thin; at all events he was certainly not of an envious disposition, and was heartily glad of the three thousand thalers that the ill-paid agent would extract from the rich Henry Willert for the worthless scrawl of a barroom strategist; so he showed him the way: five hundred yards down the central promenade, then turn off to Madonna Pond on a side path to the south; on reaching the end of the pond and the south wall, he was to turn west, where the path runs straight toward the little house.

His heart beat higher with joy when he saw the water. Just then two fine gentlemen, one gray-bearded, one black-bearded, came toward him along the straight pond promenade, twenty paces from the south wall. That they themselves were being observed by a trembling woman who crouched behind the shrubbery in an old hooded cape, brokers Hahn and Schmidt did not know. But Elspeth Kersting had seen them coming from a direction that took her breath away. They were coming not, as usual, from the city and the forest and the wood road where the carriage was waiting, but from the river; accordingly, since there was no further guard along the bank now that the work of the

Pioneer detail was finished, they must have made their way in across the ruinous wall by the bank. Hidden in her recess, she took the pistol from her coat pocket and released the safety catch.

"Attention, please—secret police. Please show your identification," said broker Hahn to Charles Froehlich.

"Don't bother me—I've got permission from Lindequist," Froehlich urged them.

At this the black-bearded Mr. Schmidt suddenly had a revolver in his right hand, and removed his hat with his left: "You need not disguise your voice, Mr. Henry Willert; nor will your false beard avail you anything."

"But, my dear sirs—" Charles Froehlich tried to explain, but was instantly interrupted by Mr. Schmidt. "Shut up!" ordered the Lion of Afghanistan. "Mr. Hahn, please read the sentence."

"Henry Willert is sentenced to death because he gulled Dr. Urban by eleven days of protracted and pretended negotiations," broker Hahn read off a piece of paper.

Broker Schmidt, formerly known as Emil, had fallen back a step during the speech of his accomplice, behind and to the side of Hesse's secret agent, whom he shot through the back of the head. Charles toppled forward and fell on his face, but the crack of the pistol, reverberating along the wall, had caught the ear of the police, and already horses' hoofs were echoing up the main promenade. As the two stopped and listened to make sure of the direction whence danger threatened, Elspeth fired at the murderer of Charles Froehlich and grazed his coat collar. The stout man sprang into the underbrush with incredible agility, but Elspeth's second shot went straight into the open mouth of Mr. Hahn, who was so maladroit as to look back. He gurgled, spitting blood, fell against the trunk of a birch, and his face plopped into a mud puddle.

Why did they want to murder Henry? Miss Elspeth wondered, pistol in hand, but not venturing out. There might be more real-estate brokers lurking in wait hereabouts; perhaps at this very moment they were murdering the real Henry in the little house—and she was pregnant by him! But of course Emily would testify that it was not by anyone else. One hand washes the other: if Elspeth compelled Andersen to marry Emily (failing which, his comfortable job would be but a memory), then Emily in turn could testify to Henry Willert's nights of love with Elspeth, particularly as she had eavesdropped at the door. The other witness—if two should be needed—was Andersen himself, such a hot lad that if you let him sleep with you once ("Once doesn't count," says the proverb), he would swear to anything. "But I *am* pregnant by him; good God," she thought, "it's undoubtedly true—why must I prove it? Dear God, he mustn't be dead!"

By now the mounted police had arrived: "The little house!" she yelled. "Henry Willert's being murdered—this here's the wrong one!" And when Lindequist looked at her blankly while two policemen rolled over broker Hahn, she cried out again, "The little house!" so frantically that Lindequist motioned the four horsemen who had not yet dismounted to follow this madwoman. She sprang into the saddle of the commander's bay and pelted off along the pond.

Little Sergeant Werner, Benjamin's son, meanwhile, had been looking at Mr. Hahn's dirty face through a magnifying glass; he uttered an exclamation of surprise, pulled off the broker's false beard, and stood up while Lindequist came over.

"So it is after all!" said the major, recognizing the dead man. It was Gregory William Lienhardt, the violator of the stableboy.

Thus died the second of the Lienhardt brothers, three of whom had laughed at Anne Mary Willert in the garden seventeen years before. Emil, the Lion of Afghanistan, made his way to the river and then to the capital, because Elspeth Kersting had led the mounted police in the wrong direction.

THE POLITICAL TESTAMENT OF
DR. JOHN HENRY MERCKEL

IV

I. OF SALVATION

ALTHOUGH the unhappy race of mortals, unhappy through its own malice and cowardice, has thrust away the hand outstretched in Holy Writ, that hand will remain outstretched until the end of time.

God has declined to seize mankind by the collar and thrust it forcibly upon His road. But He has pointed a hundred times, in words that a child can understand, to the road of salvation. He has pointed to it in the books of both Testaments, so that this road lies before us now, smooth, passable, every corner lit up by an unsetting sun. By refusing to give us compulsory salvation, God has hinted that we must decide of our own free will whether to follow His command or not: therefore our freedom of decision is part of the divine road. *Either you shall travel the road of salvation,* God would tell us, *of your own free will, or you cannot travel it at all.*

The obstacles that barred the road of God or the salvation of man have been cleared away by His simple word. The traveling of the road, or salvation, is something that mankind must accomplish for itself. If man attempts of his own free will to seize God's outstretched hand, that hand will grow toward him; if man *wishes* to set foot on God's road, the road will spread out; if man wishes for salvation, he will be saved. If he does not wish it, no one can help him, not even God, as is plainly evident from the prophetic books.

To live according to the word of God is salvation; and as this word has been spoken, recorded, and handed down, plainly enough for the understanding of a child, indisputably man is already saved—if he wishes to be. Whoever, then, may rise up today and say he is a rescuer or savior is obviously scorning the salvation that has come about, blocking up the road, and leading the weak astray: he is the Antichrist of prophecy. This is a sign that I give you by which to recognize Antichrist: he will say that he is a savior, perhaps even *the* savior.

2. OF HITHERTO HARMLESS AUTHORITY

A few scattered spirits, frequently straying, have traveled the road that was marked out for them. And a few will travel it in the future, undiverted by what may go on around them, and beyond intimidation by authority. But until not long ago all the authorities of this earth, though they might be neck-deep in vice and the pomp and circumstance of the world, nevertheless showed their reverence for the word and the road of salvation; at least they did not deny their good will, and did not prevent their individual subjects from seeking the ancient fount of happiness.

Never, until lately, has any earthly authority (no matter how far removed itself from the road of God) displayed itself as a savior. Until recently Antichrist had not succeeded in appropriating the government of whole nations or continents. The moment he starts to do so, mankind is at the crossroads.

3. GOD BADE ME STEP IN

Let me repeat, my friends: until now authority has been harmless; it was not of God, but neither was it of the Devil; it took your money, but not your soul. It sometimes sent you to misery, often to your death; it never sent you to perdition. Thither you alone could dispatch yourself. For this reason, because authority was harmless, quite like an average mortal making himself comfortable in life, the Saviour and the Apostles said that we must obey and pay our tithes.

If these matters had remained as they have been for nineteen hundred years, then I, a washerwoman's son risen by luck and persistency, would have led the peaceable life of a schoolteacher. But instead I was alarmed at the age of twenty by a monstrous spectacle: educated as I was in apostolic indifference toward the state and everything to do with public life, I saw the foe, the worshiper of power and external splendor, creeping into the national government.

Thereupon God bade me step in. And I stepped into the swelling army of Satan to search out his muster rolls and use them against him. When I had searched them out, I stepped into the national government. Today I occupy the second highest post in it. I am trying to drive out Satan—not out of the world, for that is impossible, but out of the government of the world, so that authority may once more become what it has always been: harmless; not of God, but not of the Devil either; quite like an average mortal making himself comfortable in life; not holy, but not unholy either, and at least worthy to demand your money and your mortal portion.

4. OF THE FOREMOST TASK OF A NATIONAL GOVERNMENT

He who would govern any state today needs no expert knowledge of the many individual matters that the state looks after (and it looks after far too many). He will have around him experts who will give him reasonably honest advice if he himself is honest.

But he does need one capacity so rare that only two or three in a million human beings possess it: the capacity to recognize Antichrist. I personally incline to the belief that the capacity to recognize Antichrist has existed on this earth for no more than a hundred years or so—possibly because the foe, long as he has been carrying on his machinations, had never attempted until our time to crowd out God's influence from earthly affairs, making himself sole master of the globe. And as the task of keeping the foe from power makes all the other tasks of any authority pale into ridiculous insignificance, a state must install to rule it those who are capable of recognizing the enemy.

5. SATAN THE NAÏVE AND ANTICHRIST

When our forefathers portrayed Satan, he was always made to look something like the mercenary captain of the Renaissance who used to have his victims seized naked by the legs and smashed dead because he took pleasure in the cracking of skulls, in the brains and blood of infants and young girls splashing the walls. A gold plate on a chain hung down upon his chest, and on it were engraved the words: "Foe of God and mercy." Thus everyone was more or less invited to beware. With such innocence did past ages depict Satan! And of course he actually was just as he was portrayed: in those happier days there was truly nothing more satanic than cruelty. But there was no such thing as Antichrist; otherwise our forefathers, with the keen eye and honest courage to which their art and writings testify, would have depicted him.

True, our Antichrist is also Satan, and certainly his malice, his vengefulness, his masterfulness, his pleasure in the sufferings of others, are no less than those of the mercenary captain. But—and now please notice the difference—have you ever heard a modern Satan say he had killed women and children because he was a foe of God and mercy? The plate on the mercenary captain's chest, after all, surely meant that he denied nothing—neither the murders nor their cruelty. If anyone asked him, "Why did you do that?" he simply pointed to the inscription on the plate. He could do murder, but he could not argue a murder away. He simply could not, because he could not imagine that there was no God. His plate proclaimed that God *was,* and that he was His foe. Therefore he was not Antichrist. In Satan the naïve, God is alive; in Antichrist, God is extinguished.

Because God is extinguished in him, Antichrist is not a foe of God; he is the foe of mankind.

God was aflame in Satan the naïve, as the plate on his chest shows. Antichrist, however, has heard of God as one has heard of a name or an address or a forgotten book.

6. THE MACHINE AGE AS THE PRECURSOR OF ANTICHRIST

Never since history has been written has man ceased to lie, steal, rob, and murder. But until recently men knew that a lie was a lie. They knew the difference between lie and confession; that is, they knew shame when they lied, and they feared the contempt that hung over the liar.

The lie is still with us; but we know nothing now of the liar's shame, so often equivalent to a confession, nor of contempt for the lie. If we do, it is only as one knows of a name or an address or a forgotten book. Once upon a time shame and contempt had a dreadful strength that often struck down the liar. Today the strength is on the liars' side. Not the liar is despised now, but the one he lies to; and if the victim is struck down by the power of the lie, the onlookers spit in his face.

How has this come about? In all the ages that preceded progress, man lied and murdered as he does today. But the liar and the murderer in the old days were terrified at lies and murder; they could not fling off shame and terror from their own souls, because they could not imagine that there was no God. Accordingly, Antichrist had not yet appeared. Before Antichrist could arise, science and machinery were needed to enlighten man and inform him that there was no God.

If man can imagine that there is no God, what is a lie then? Mere sound and fury; or, if effectual, a means of influencing people. What is murder? An unconsidered action, or, if Urban causes it to be perpetrated, a means of influencing people. If there is no God, before whom should I be ashamed; of what should I be terrified? Before him who is powerful enough to punish me? But if the supreme power itself is a power that knows no shame or terror, because it no longer knows God, then I, the subject, may still fear blows, but not shame or horror.

The man of past centuries had constantly before his eyes as the most ominous of facts not want or some other discontent, but God and himself—in short, sin, especially lying and murder.

So long as sin is within man's field of vision, Antichrist can have no power over him. For it is not the sinful man, knowing sin and wallowing in sins, who has departed from God, but he for whom "sin" is a religious anachronism.

To the man of progress, the word *sin* belongs in a book of religion. In our modern practical life, where there are errors, missteps, and possibly "victims of society," "sins" are no longer to be met with.

The science of dialectics has abolished the difference between truth and falsehood. Of the uncanny and boundless region that our forefathers called "lying," only a legal term remains: deliberately false testimony.

Everything is enlightened and explained; no lie and no murder now cause shame or horror anywhere on earth.

After all, some of our contemporaries are already so abysmally stupid that they confuse the building of railroads and telegraph lines, the invention of flying machines, the popularization of great teachers' and writers' lifeworks, and even the increased effectiveness of weapons, with the intellectual progress of the human race. It appears that undreamed-of speeds and undreamed-of deterioration in the human intellect must have come into being on this earth simultaneously so that Antichrist might arise.

7. SWORD, GO FORTH!

I wrote my *Dictionary of Splendid Phrases* so that you might recognize the danger of the verbiage your orators speak, which you repeat like parrots. For it is cowardice in face of their own phrases that brings nations to servitude. Out of cowardice in face of the word "tolerance," which blinded you to the enemy, you listened for twenty years to Urban, the "great popular leader," while he made God and freedom seem contemptible.

Enslaved by your own fine talk about "freedom," which includes tolerance, you—like women under the spell of an adventurer—would have succumbed to the destroyer of all tolerance and freedom unless you had been rescued by the clearheadedness and hardheadedness of an upper crust that despised fine phrases.

Therefore, my friends, if in future an Urban of the right speaks to you of "honor and the fatherland," if an Urban of the left speaks to you of "freedom and culture," and when both of them speak of "social justice," then close your ears and keep the handcuffs ready.

If an Urban says it is fine weather today, two times two makes four, hunger hurts, or that the sun rises in the east, do not believe him, but keep the handcuffs ready.

For that has been his trick now for ten years: he would string out a thousand stale truths, and then slip in the lie that really counted. To lend color to the lie that will enslave his listener and extinguish his conscience, he begins with a thousand truths. Our forefathers would have listened to him for two minutes and then struck him dead with their clubs, offering no contradiction, with unmoved faces, and silently crossing themselves.

My friends and I have treated Urban as our fathers did, which will be counted to our credit on Judgment Day. We lured him from the cave of his dissembling on to the field of battle, and struck him down as God had bidden us.

Never forget, you king, president, or senator: if you entrust your fortress to an Urbanite wearing the uniform of your army, he will deliver it up to the national foe—not for the sake of the fortress, for fortresses do not interest him, but in order to destroy good faith. If you entrust God's church to an Urbanite in the vestments of a priest, he will deliver it up to the defamer of God—not from enmity for God, because God does not interest him, but in order to destroy good faith.

Perhaps Urban was not Antichrist at all; probably he was a precursor. Certainly others will come after him, in officers' tunics, in priests' vestments, in the frock coat of the burgess, in the working-man's jacket; and they will be fiercer, wilier, more dangerous than Urban.

And this sign I give you that you may recognize him. Each one of them will say the same thing, namely that *you* are rightly dissatisfied, that *you* are being oppressed, and that *he* will deliver you.

And I give you this second sign: the masses will cheer him who speaks in this fashion. But if any one of you, my friends, goes to a meeting and asks this deliverer whether he is ready to harmonize his words and acts with God's commandments, and to lead along the road of salvation, the one asking this question will be made mock of.

No matter when this takes place, remember that the hour has come when the Lord God speaks: "Sword, go forth!"

BOOK THREE

THE PRESIDENT OF THE IRON PHALANX CAPITULATES

V

ON APRIL 15 the *Capital City Intelligencer* and hundreds of its offshoots in the provinces printed an editorial leader by the editor in chief, Dr. Daniel Hoppelkopf, who was celebrated as the oldest staff member and intimate of his chief, Oscar Koenig.

The article deduced, from the reports of trustworthy correspondents, that the government was fighting with but half its strength, since it had not mobilized for war anywhere except in the mountain province. If it were to make an effort, Urban would be flattened in three days.

The cabinet members racked their brains trying to think how they could have earned such tremendous assistance; for now, after all, the newspaper reader's confidence in Urban was done for.

On the other hand, the same paper printed a heartbreaking two-column boldface story that the millionaire families of Professor Bock,

Borstel, and Susemihl had fled in terror across the frontier, and were
suffering penury in second-rate Paris hotels because in their haste, and
fearing search at the frontier, they had left everything behind, even
their jewels. Once again, the story said, Oscar Koenig had proved
his humanitarianism—he who gives quickly gives doubly—by promptly
creating the Society for Ameliorating the Condition of the Rich with
a capital of five million. Everyone who still had a human heart in
his bosom was urged to join, with monthly dues of only a thaler.
For if even the poor man mourned any loss of position, how indescribable must be the anguish of the rich man, unaccustomed to privation,
when some blow of fate befell him!

The ink, one might say, was hardly dry before Beyer summoned
a cabinet meeting in order to suppress that member of the *Intelligencer*
and get the whole edition pulped. Not for two hours, the President
cried, would he sit still under the accusation of having helped increase
the misery of the rich. All his ministers except Hildebrand (Henry
Willert was absent) agreed with him; but not one was willing to
countersign an order suppressing the paper, which had printed Hoppelkopf's editorial leader with equal prominence. The latter, they
pointed out, would shake the confidence of the entire nation in Urban,
whereas Oscar Koenig's society would only weaken the confidence of
a minority—the Carpenters and Lindbrecht's Catholics—in the dis-
passionate justice of the government. And even this weakening of
confidence in the government could be made good, and yet greater
confidence earned, by immediately banning the new society, while
satisfying the financial claims of the fugitives.

At this Hildebrand, the leader of the independent unions, objected.
All of Urban's large backers, he explained, had made twofold preparations, foreseeing that neither Faust nor Beyer would surrender power
to them without a battle: they had prepared for victory by arming
Urban's troops, and for defeat by an unconscionable accumulation of
jewels, particularly diamonds. Countess Bessonoff alone, he said, wore
jewels sewed into her undergarments to the value of ten million gold
francs.

"And who can forbid her doing so?" the President wanted to know.

"The law concerning the Social Reserves," Hildebrand retorted.

For ten years, he asserted, these rogues had been cheating the
workingmen and clerical employees of their share in the reserves by

falsified balances; they had thus filled their vaults with light and easily concealable valuables. So far as the motions before the cabinet were concerned, he hoped that the very number of the *Intelligencer* now under criticism would have the widest possible distribution, but agreed with the majority that Oscar Koenig's society should be banned "for damned impudence"—for he would like to see the man who had ever suffered penury in second-rate Paris hotels!

To avoid emphasizing the conflict between the "independents" and the "Christians," Augustus Beyer closed the meeting, and went off alone with Hildebrand to the presidential mansion. Inviting him to sit down at the desk, he pushed toward him, with a twinkle of intimacy, a box of cigars that he had just pried open especially for this smoker of Mexican sandy leaf. Obviously they were expensive cigars, impressive in stature, of an even, pale, brownish-gray sandy color, the wrappers rough, knotty, and like a sandy floor.

In his delight at such perfection the labor leader waited a moment before helping himself: "Too grand for the likes of us, almost too grand," he said with a giggle deep down in his throat, took out one of these splendid objects, lit it, and began to puff.

The textile magnate, to be closer to the spectacle of the enraptured smoker, sat on the table, letting his long, thin legs dangle; leaning with one hand on the table top, he searched Hildebrand's face.

"Yes, sir, this is the right kind—for Sundays," said the labor leader. He could never get over acting as if he were still a poor man and a "workman," who had no business with expensive luxuries.

Suddenly Beyer turned his head, slid off the table, crept to the door, stepping high, and listened through the keyhole—"like a stork in a lettuce bed," thought Hildebrand as he watched the bony, gray-haired eavesdropper.

Evening was falling. From far away came a groaning as if someone were suppressing a cry under the surgeon's knife; then doors banged, there were soothing voices, objection from the patient, and silence once more. The textile magnate stood up and leaned against the door. Thus he stood for a moment with bowed head, his hands in his trouser pockets. His caller knew it was Kate Beyer who had cried out; she was quieted with opiates every evening at about the time when the Gas-House Boy had murdered Merckel. It was only three days ago, of course; but she had lived with him for seven years, without any quarrel or cooling of passion, relishing the secrecy, since the doctor had forbidden them to marry. She had begun at eighteen; now she was twenty-five, and might live to be old, for her lungs were beginning to heal.

It was perfectly silent; she must have fallen asleep. Hildebrand thought of the Society for Ameliorating the Condition of the Rich.

He knew, incidentally, what the President wanted of him, and was wondering how to say yes without rousing the suspicions of the "independents." The office of Henry the Franciscan, who had taken Merckel's post, was already at work on a proclamation inviting the fugitive families to return. If they still preferred to stay abroad, the government promised not to enrich itself at their expense, but to pay their fortunes over to them without deduction in whatever foreign currency they might ask. Real property was to be honestly liquidated, or else the income might be transferred like the cash.

The Franciscan had promised to submit a fair copy of the proclamation to the cabinet before nightfall. Hildebrand too was expected to make the President's signature valid by his countersignature; if he should refuse, he would have to resign, and Beyer would immediately find a substitute.

Hildebrand knew just as well as his cabinet colleagues that this generous proclamation had not sprung from "humanity" or pity for the fugitives, but was founded on the intellectual system of the Faustites. The tall, dry man at the door, still listening for his child's moans, had no need to waste a word upon his reasons.

Of course, thought Hildebrand, wreathed in smoke, of course one might sign the proclamation as if it were an odious but necessary war measure, and print it so in the workingmen's papers. Only this was of no service to the President: it was precisely for the newspapers of the poor, who were now being expected to "take up the assigned positions," that he required plain, forthright, and approving comments.

But the Hildebrandites were not stupid; they knew perfectly well that the millionaires' families had fled abroad not in fear but through hypocrisy, as propaganda for Urban.

But they didn't take along their jewels! Correct: do you mean to say it was through fear or precipitation? Not at all; in the first place, it is because they were sure the government will not deprive them of a single pin, and the diamonds could not be safer than they are in the vaults at home; in the second place, it is to pretend poverty, arouse pity, and lament the tyranny that has "driven them from their homeland." Besides all this, the workingmen still remember certain suits, suits that Hildebrand himself and the trustees of the Welfare Reserves brought against the fugitive scum for concealment of assets.

"These are the facts, Mr. Augustus Beyer," the leader of the "independents" felt like saying, "and the workingman wants *facts* in the commentary you need, not soft and dubious phrases composed by the former journeyman cabinetmaker and present Secretary of State, Hildebrand (salary twelve thousand thalers), who is sharing the millionaires' feelings lest he be obliged to resign."

The longer poor Kate's father allowed his caller to think, the more impossible the latter found the transaction.

Finally the gray textile magnate—everything about him was gray, his hair, his suit, even his patterned necktie—stalked back to his seat behind the Empire desk with the bronze trimmings, bronze edging, and glass top. "Well, now you've said what you think," he said to the smoker of Mexican sandy, "so please let me say what I think."

Hildebrand had not, it is true, said a word, but he had known the man for thirteen years, ever since the Geisenheim disturbances, and he replied, "Glad to."

"We can stand up under a great deal," the President began—"poor mobilization, defeats, quarreling among the generals, threats from abroad; we can stand up against Urban and hold him off for twelve months before we give him the *coup de grâce*. But one thing we cannot stand up under for twelve hours—the distrust of our own people."

"Very true!"

" 'Because see here,' people will tell themselves—they may not even say it any more, but just think it. No, I guess things'll never go that far—they'll tell themselves: 'Adam Faust governed for twenty years, and he wasn't always very particular; but did any family ever flee the country? What does a family flee from that has been guilty of nothing—otherwise they could have been stopped at the frontier? From the tyrant, my dear fellow, as the whole history of mankind goes to show. Other countries have Borstels, Susemihls, Bocks, and Koehlers too, and they belong to and support the political opposition. Why don't they flee? Why do they sit calmly at home? Could it by chance be because they enjoy the protection of the law, while here

the tyrant makes his own laws, with the support of slaves and para-
sites?' Such, obviously, will be the thoughts of our people whom we
are requiring to take up the assigned position instead of submitting
to the tyrants."

"But the scoundrels didn't flee at all!"

"I know, I know; but what are the scoundrels to us? What we
care about is what our people think; and for the present they believe
what they read, namely that those who have left are fugitives. If we
start to wrangle and maintain that those fellows fled as a trick, as
propaganda, what will the whole world and our own people answer
us? That we are flinging mud after the *émigrés*—doing just what
every despotic government does. Do you think we can stand up even
under that, just because our conscience is clear? No, we cannot, because the conscience of our followers will no longer be clear. Now if
we were just a regular government . . ."

"First time I ever heard we weren't a regular government," Hildebrand remarked.

"I don't say we made any promises, but our life and behavior have
been a promise; twenty years of Adam Faust have been a promise.
We can't fall back, or Urban will rush into the gap; he will rush
after us into the 'space denuded of force,' and we shall be swamped.
For there can be only Adam Faust *or* Urban; there is no third party
who is marching along the road to Utopia. Why can't the Iron Phalanx
fight? Why does it look so silly, staggering like a drunken man,
laughed at on every hand? Because it has no Utopia. Honestly, now,
Hildebrand, if Urban's Utopia of silk stockings every day, lipstick
every day, and beefsteak for all, I say if this wish dream of the enlightened were stronger than ours, then certainly what Dr. Grau
predicted to Henry Willert would happen: we would certainly be
lost. Our Utopia is to have mankind regain confidence, to let no single
wretched pilgrim to the grave tremble before another. And whatever
we do or do not do, the nation marching with us sees each step we
take as a step on the road to Utopia. Therefore no one must tremble
except him who has been unmasked as Satan. Therefore no one must
flee; if nevertheless he does, *we* cannot wrangle or call names, but
must fling his property after him, and if possible something more
besides as compensation for his mistaken fear. True enough, man
must live in fear and trembling, and also, it seems, in suffering: I

have more than a hundred millions, and I couldn't spare Kate this, not for any money. But he should not live in fear and trembling before his own pitiful peers."

Hildebrand took another cigar. "Help yourself, help yourself," cried Beyer. "They were specially made and exported for you by my friend Rio Grande del Norte in Mexico!"

The leader of the "independents" looked at the President. He saw how he was prevaricating and thinking up some name at random. He also saw how the man's long, lean hand trembled as it held out the cigar cutter to the guest. He cares as much as this about my signature with approving commentary, he thought, and said: "What you've just mentioned, that about fear, might do for our news service, though of course I couldn't use anything about Utopia; that's a dangerous word, not very far removed from *chimera.*"

"Leave it out, for God's sake, do it however you like!" cried the textile magnate, almost speechless with joy. Then, with hand outstretched across the table, almost in a whisper, he revealed "a secret and a great stroke of business."

"I know you'll say it's all superstition and an invention of the prelates. Agreed: why shouldn't I make some concession? But some things have been proved true; here, oddly enough, dispute ceases. The sentence has been proved true: 'But seek ye first the kingdom of God'—please note the *'first,'* the most important word in the whole verse; 'first the kingdom of God, and His righteousness; and all these things shall be added unto you.' Do you know who has been added unto us?"

"Dr. Grau?"

"Someone much greater."

Hildebrand laughed: "Not Urban, by chance?"

"No. Those rivers don't flow uphill."

"Well, then?"

"Oscar Koenig!"

At this the smoker of Mexican sandy actually put down his cigar. "When?" he asked.

"Two days before Grau, on the tenth."

"Did he knock?"

"Not at the Carpenters'; at my door. No one knows it yet except Henry the Franciscan, Jacob Willert, Holzkopf, Zorn, and Schwann," the President explained, handing a folder of transcripts across the table.

From the transcripts it appeared that the following had taken place: at noon on April 2, before Urban's release, Oscar Koenig, age seventy, requested an audience in the presence of the Minister of Finance, Andrew Zorn, and Jacob Willert the banker. He said he wanted to sell his business at once.

In the interview granted a week later between him and the other three, the old man presented a summary statement of his property and the balance sheets of the last few years. What he modestly called his "business" proved to show an average annual profit of eighteen million thalers, making it the largest family concern in the country.

Jacob Willert and Zorn, first going into the next room to check Koenig's figures, declared that a thing of this sort could be sold only very slowly.

"If the business isn't sold in three days," replied Koenig, "I shall give it to anyone who will pay off my three children—the two daughters and my son Benjamin."

"How much are they to get?" asked Zorn, and the publisher mentioned a sum so small that Beyer wanted to call on a psychiatrist for an opinion. If the old man were not of sound mind, the contract might later be upset. But in the test of intelligence (conducted not by Daruhi but by Supreme Court Justice Holzkopf, whose duty it was to work out the contract) Koenig proved to be normal, and to have an excellent memory "for the outrages committed by and upon him." He said he wished to be removed to a lunatic village and was expecting his punishment. He had already informed his relatives, friends, and employees that he was leaving for an unknown destination. He declared that his business managers and editors were innocent and had done nothing to deserve losing their positions.

What punishment did he suggest, Holzkopf inquired of the old man.

"That's not my business," replied Koenig.

The judge upbraided him for first ridding himself of his property, and then trying to rid himself of his punishment as well. The state could not punish him, because he had violated no law; nor could the Order of Carpenters, because he was not a Carpenter. "Have you no one, Mr. Koenig, of whom you could make inquiry concerning the suitable punishment?"

At this Koenig remembered a Carpenter who had appeared to him during a recent illness: "I have made inquiry," he said.

"What did your friend say?" Holzkopf inquired.

"Call back the memory, degraded man, of your happy years!"

As he did not want to go home, the president of the Iron Phalanx remained under medical observation at the presidential mansion for the following two days and nights. No sign of mental derangement was observed. A quick exchange of cipher telegrams between Schwann and the commandant of the Guldenberg Delivery Precinct reached a pleasing conclusion when the splendid Elizabeth's brother, Odo Sparangapani, the lawyer and spiritual adviser of those quartered in Guldenberg Valley, to which he had removed, invited the old publisher to stay at his house.

It may be remembered that Odo had forsaken temporal courts and "the world" during Hans Simon's trial for defamation.

BOOK THREE

THE BLUE BOOK

VI

AMONG the mitigations, we cannot say of punishment (for the Carpenters claim no authority to punish the criminal, but only to "deliver him up to God")—among the mitigations of delivering up, then, that have been introduced in the course of years was the institution of spiritual advisers. At least one Carpenter familiar with the civil law had to be on hand at every one of the enclosed precincts or "lunatic villages"; and a captive who had spent six months in the colony was allowed to "ask advice" by appointment on Wednesday and Saturday mornings. Before long, the adviser's house was besieged by such a press of people that he needed an office, and finally many offices. Those seeking advice no longer saw the adviser himself, but only his hundred secretaries and their dossiers, which, however, were kept up with a care unknown in the outside world—quite naturally, for he who did not open to him that knocks for advice was punished by the Joint Court.

Such institutions, once allowed, spread out as it were organically; thus the spiritual adviser gradually broke through the wall of isolation from the outside world. Because the prisoners were forbidden to correspond with their families, he had to assume the task, and report to the "applicants for advice" on Wednesdays and Saturdays whether their wives were well, and the children in school had been promoted. Fathers of families were not alone in seeking advice. Single men, even if they required neither advice nor information, came simply because the prohibition of loud speech had been revoked in the Counsel House so that secretaries and applicants could understand each other more easily.

Finally matters went so far that only the "Blue Book prisoners," the segregated ones or "those with bad records," had access to Odo Sparangapani in person. These were the prisoners guilty of malice or cruelty, among them a few who had taken part in the murders of Kate Schwann and Theresa Froehlich at Carolswald—fewer than three hundred altogether. They were segregated from the other prisoners, and decimated themselves in bloody quarrels when they came home to their quarters from work. "A burden upon the earth" in the opinion of the Carpenters, they were not restrained from killing one another; their graves were obliterated, and when they were dead their records were cut out of the Blue Book and destroyed. Not ruffians and killers alone belonged to the category of the segregated, but also swindlers and usurers in whose cases it had been found that they committed fraud and usury not from greed but to delight in the anguish of their victims.

Hesse's address to the squadrons, "The Cry of the Victim Is the Paradise of the Tormentor," can never be forgotten among us, even though the Blue Book, the never-ending dossier of all crimes of malice, is kept strictly secret. Even to members of the cabinet it is opened only by special request, after a vow of silence.

A person visiting this country, reading our papers, and attending court might easily fall into the mistake of supposing we had uprooted malice and violence. This of course is by no means the case; these vices are merely excluded from public discussion and gossip, whether in courtrooms or in newspapers, and they are therefore actually on the decline. Even in Adam Faust's time a paper that gave so much as a single line, no matter how well hidden, to any crime of malicious violence would have been ruined by a long suspension. It must not be forgotten that under our constitution the President is not a puppet of parliament, but an "elective republican king" with wide executive powers. For in his book *On the Character of My Countrymen,* Andrew Zorn, old Adam's most confidential adviser, had asserted that crimes of malice, which is to say the truly satanic (for the Carpenters regard greed not as satanic but as "complementary to vitality"), flourished in an atmosphere of publicity. Cut off from this, they would wither away. A crime committed from delight in the torment of the victim, which is equivalent to malicious pleasure, disgraced not only the criminal but the whole country, putting it in need of atonement. But since the word "atonement" in the age of progress is only a splendid phrase or an empty boast (for where there is no God there may be beatings, but no expiation), crimes of malicious violence must be kept secret. The second reason was that the exposure and vulgarizing of something shameful through news stories and editorials do not wipe away the shame, but on the contrary spread it abroad and even make it interesting. The third reason was that the malicious criminal in his vanity desires nothing more eagerly than to find his picture and life story in the papers. This, after all, is the only possible way for him to attain celebrity. Many of them would be deterred from their crimes if they knew with certainty that no one except the judge would ever hear of their crimes, and that they themselves and their very memory would disappear beyond recovery even in the grave.

The Blue Book prisoners, then, are worse off than the others—not, however, because they are intimidated or driven at their work; this is never done. If one of them should choose to lean on his shovel and gaze for half an hour at the sky, the bushes, or the furrows of the fields, no one would disturb him. No Carpenter could depart so far as this from his own doctrine that work is a curse, and man a reflective wanderer toward the grave. The discrimination against these people consists, rather, in the fact that they must live among themselves, segregated from all others, and that the rule of whispering is never suspended, not even on the Saturday mornings when they fill the garden and ground floor of the mansionlike building that Odo Sparangapani built with his own money and occupies alone.

As aforesaid, Odo reached an agreement by telegram with Jacob Willert, and invited Oscar Koenig, the peace-seeking president of the Iron Phalanx, to stay here in a comfortable apartment on the third floor. And so, having received the payments demanded for himself and his children, the great publisher disappeared from the bustling world and from our story, although everyone thought that he, like the Bocks, Susemihls, and Borstels, was living in Paris. For ten years more he watched rabbits and fox cubs playing around their burrows in the forests of Guldenberg Valley. He heard the cries of Elspeth Kersting as she bore her first child, and three weeks afterward, as a guest invited to the christening by the Kerstings and Willerts, he had to hold the ridiculously tiny girl on his outstretched arms. For the Joint Court meanwhile condemned Henry Willert to twelve months in the land of whispers (the smallest permissible atonement) for violation of the Rule.

BOOK THREE

ON THE EDGE OF THE KNIFE

VII

THE daily defeats of our "doughty troops" in the east and northeast, although they were led by Kaempf, Spitta, and Leugenfeld; the immobility of Laurenti in the south; and in the west the retreat behind the broad barrier of the main river, running exactly north and south; all provoked laughter among the indifferent groups that regarded the civil war as a fight for booty among sharks. They also provoked the President's displeasure.

Augustus Beyer knew anguish enough during those days: at the grave of his son-in-law he had seen his invalid daughter collapsing and reaching out her hands for her beloved. "Egypt," said Kuttner; but Kate demanded to die at home. Behind the coffin of Charles Froehlich walked his niece, the dovelike Veronica, and her husband, Tobias Witt; behind them, leading the Carpenters, went Hesse, not from religious scruples or because he admitted to having known the dead man, but because he had fallen in love. It was the first time, he confessed to her—yes, he was in love with Veronica.

For Bernard Faust, the younger son, the mining king, had offered Tobias Witt a post as head bookkeeper in the capital in recognition of his activity as an agent (the Carpenters were reproached with "sticking together like glue"). When the young couple moved, therefore, from quiet Marienhall to the roaring capital, Veronica thought she had come up in the world; and—with no child to take care of, furthermore—she allowed the swarm of salesmen to talk her into making installment purchases: cherry furniture, rugs, pictures (copies, it was true, but expensive ones from the shops of the Government Printing Office), clocks, floor lamps, even a piano with an embroidered cover for the keys, and potted palms adorned their dwelling in the modern colony of Charlottenhof. To her alarmed spouse she said: "It's all right, Tobias, I'll make some money, never fear." Wearing her broad linen collar over the high-buttoned dress, she reported to the labor office of the Carpenters, where she was given the post of secretary to Colonel Schwann, which Mrs. Haas had found "too nerve-racking." Later, because of her charm, she got a better-paid job at the Induction Commission of the Carpenters in Police Barracks I on the canal bank.

There General von Hesse, already married to Alexandra von Brick, first saw her. She was twenty-four, he thirty-eight. That which followed can be recounted, but not explained by listing the causes. It was mysterious and terrible.

On April 18, it will be remembered, Laurenti had been ordered to feign a frontal break-through, and then by the aid of the reserve army, which was to be brought up unknown to the enemy, to crush Oriola's right flank and hurl "the whole nonsense" into the marshes and swampy forests on which the left wing of Urban's southern army was supported. Laurenti executed the maneuver with his wonted circumspection. At dawn of the second day, however, when the reserve army assaulted the right wing, he found himself faced with a solid front. During the night Oriola had regrouped his forces, crowding some low pieces of rising ground on his right with artillery, which in turn flanked the attacking enemy. Nevertheless, the Urbanite general felt by the afternoon of the second day that he was defeated and would not long be able to withstand a frontal thrust. Then, to his utter astonishment, the enemy began to retire. Laurenti, satisfied with the exhaustion of the Sports Troops, attested by prisoners, had changed his plans. For toward evening—it was April 28—Frohwein reported the crushing defeat of our main army near Mittelburg, two days' march northwest of the capital, by the Master of Ordnance and General Susa. Tall Spitta was slightly wounded, and Kaempf had been recalled to the capital to organize the arming of civilians. If General Baer could not make a final stand in the west, said Frohwein, all was lost. He himself with a hundred thousand men from the capital garrison had brought Kaempf's beaten army to a standstill, and taken it into a fortified defensive position in the hilly country of Neumuehle and Niederwesel. He said he could hold out there for 'five days: five days would be enough to fling into the capital all the troops that could be spared from the south. The victory or defeat of the government now depended on the resolution and devotion to duty of Generals Laurenti and Baer. Leugenfeld in the east was holding off the enemy (who had advanced alarmingly) from the marshes and the alder woods growing in the water.

Thus far the report of the Chief of the General Staff, from which it was evident that the daring Susa had detached a large part of his forces to the west under Leugenfeld's very nose, and had fallen upon the flank and rear of the government army at Mittelburg, while Urban attacked from the front.

Laurenti did not suspect the state of dissolution prevailing in the enemy forces, even though they had held their position; but he was convinced that Oriola could not think of making an attack himself in the next few days. Therefore, emulating Susa's daring by requisitioning the undamaged railways and every usable vehicle, he started two thirds of his army on their way northward—more than 200,000 men.

Old General Baer in the west, on the other hand, sent a report to the President charging his old schoolmate Frohwein with the responsibility for most of the defeats through his order to exercise all moderation possible. So long as this order was in force, the troop commander was prevented from making legitimate use of heavy artillery.

In consequence Beyer countermanded the order for "humaneness" in the jurisdiction of the western army. Baer telegraphed his thanks: "Now I will show the Urbanites what's what."

On the evening of the twenty-eight, after what was loudly proclaimed as the "decisive victory" over Kaempf and Spitta, Urban marched into Mittelburg, cheered to the echo by his old friends, welcomed with flags and deputations from the students at the Technical Academy. While his victorious men were advancing on Neumuehle and Niederwesel, he took up his quarters in Bessonoff's big house on the market place. The count, faced with the threat that traitors would be strung up, had to act as host, and even sit by while his wife (who wore a uniform as "Head of the Political Troop Inspectors") was summoned to spend the night with the Leader and Willie Gaedicke. This performance was so much the more scandalous since Countess Ida had appointed for her bodyguard Emil, the Lion of Afghanistan, who had succeeded in escaping to Mittelburg.

We learn from the reports of the patrols in- and outside the house that two hours after midnight a strange spectacle was seen. From the great man's bedchamber three strange characters emerged: a country pastor dressed in old-fashioned clothes, a fussy little old woman, her dress and hair those of the heroine's mother in a play of the fifties, and a youth with a high choker collar, preposterously tight trousers, and a gray tailcoat, the very image of the Biedermeier. As the sentry in the anteroom knew who the three were—Dr. Urban and his nocturnal companions—he informed his fellows of the guard, and followed the disguised personages into the market place, where no one was allowed to be at night. With affected motions and unnatural speech they walked along the sidewalk surrounding the broad square, each one by himself as if rehearsing a part. The League Leader, like the party symbol called the "Greeter," constantly doffed his hat, smiled his thanks, and bowed in every direction as he walked, although there was no one there to see him.

Despite the splendid victories, his heart was filled with grief and bitterness. Unless the western group, the strongest of his armies, could push aside General Baer and come forward by forced marches to join hands with his right wing, the carefully planned capture of the capital could not be accomplished. True, the distance was great, and through his agents he had spread the erroneous view that the fighting in the west was merely a delaying action, fought with half strength in order to immobilize part of the enemy forces. In reality, however, the western army was being urged to haste by threatening orders. Urban had no notion of wading through marshes and lakes, which fringe our city on the east and south. Instead, Susa's men were unexpectedly to scale the blunt cone of Cathedral Hill, never before attacked, at the point where the river forks; they were to occupy the Old Town, which appeared safe from artillery fire owing to the national collection of art treasures that was kept there. At the same time an overpoweringly superior force, the main army combined with the western group, was to cross the river, penetrate the city, and grip the enemy in a pincers movement from the west and southwest, while Susa thrust forward from the Old Town and the Inner Boulevard into the center of the city.

The word "bitterness" is too feeble to describe the Leader's state of mind when he thought of the Iron Phalanx. Oddly misapprehending the world and his own path, he had flung himself upon the bosom of Nicholas Edwin Schiele and the opinion-mongers after the night of brotherhood on April 1, which that fraud Beyer had improvised. Was not he, Urban, the incarnation of progress, culture, objective science, the security of the householder, the League for Enlightenment and Economic Peace? The medals bestowed on him by medical societies, art associations, and natural scientists were displayed. What was he asking except to be left unmolested and to enlighten the people about the "more glorious future" with the help of "our great standard-bearers of civilization"? Just before the outbreak of hostilities the Urbanite papers teemed with the phrases coined by the Iron Phalanx and unmasked by Merckel in his dictionary as "the adornments of modern thieves' slang": freedom, culture, civilization, responsibility, patriotism, intellectual life, fraternal, solidarity, one for all, collective, onward and upward, Christian tolerance, humanity. One might have supposed that Urban's editors had steeped themselves in Mark Antony Perlotta's style.

But what Elsie Ackermann had said about Diana Rose, that she forgot everything, for preference the paying of her bills, but she wouldn't forget her revenge, could also be said of the Iron Phalanx. At last it repaid the insults that the League Leader had heaped upon the Schieles and Perlottas from the time of his Blendheim address on; it repaid them, and, as befitted its character, took vengeance with ladylike smiles and impeccable gentility. No unfavorable judgment of Urban was permitted so long as the battle was undecided; but the recognition of undeniable merits was proclaimed "scientific objectivity," spiritual engineering. The Iron Phalanx descended to depths that Frank Jaeger had had in mind when he asked young Albert Ackermann to write "so as not to give anyone grounds for unkind thoughts, or better yet to not give anyone grounds for any thoughts at all, but to simply fascinate them with the beauty, the sweep, and the depths."

The historian, remote from the struggle, can understand the boundless rage of the League Leader that is to be seen in his last five addresses. If there were such a thing as logic and justice, the Iron Phalanx must have stood as one man behind the leader of progress and a world organized by reason, against a caste that bore the irrational upon its escutcheon. Instead, some of them scattered entirely, pointing out that the Muses are silent in wartime; such others as Innocent Isabella Rex, Mayor Heidemann, and Professor Schiele established the Disciples of Emmaus, the Penitent Congregation of the Last Judgment, and sang hymns, thus licking the boots of the government, as Urban put it.

For three days the Urbanites stormed Frohwein's defensive position, laid out at right angles to the line and the river; for three days a hundred and twenty guns thundered from the big and little redoubts in the hilly country outside Niederwesel. On the evening of May 1, Frohwein decided to withdraw across the river to the capital and to hold off the superior enemy force with a rear guard of only three divisions until Laurenti's arrival should be reported.

For many years afterward fathers told sons about the battles during the first few days of May, about the loss of contact with the enemy, the "fight for the Stoop," and the crime of Professor Bock, which was in reality a crime of Countess Bessonoff. For the wooded chain of hills that the good Lord bestowed upon His church village of Niederwesel as a protection against an enemy advancing from the west does in fact go straight north for fifteen miles to fulfill its destiny, but then sweeps eastward to include the village of Neumuehle. From the point where the curve begins to where it ends, seventy-two guns are mounted, their barrels thrust out to west and north, whence the Urbanites were making their onslaught. This is the Big Bulwark, twelve batteries (for our batteries have six guns—not four, like those of our great neighbor to the east). The lowland at the foot of these fortified hills is planted to potatoes, turnips, and oats—a light clay soil, mingled with sand and occasional gravelly hills, not very productive, and therefore forested with pine in spots. In this lowland the battle raged to and fro for days beneath an overcast sky with thin rain that soaked the fighters to the skin in the flat trenches that they dug with their entrenching tools. Both sides knew the method of elastic defense in which a position is given up when it could still be held, in order to thrust with machine guns, hand grenades, and bayonets at the enemy as he advances in disorder, punishing him until he retreats, while one reforms one's own ranks under the screen of fire, and advances again in turn.

In this fashion "the Big Stoop" had already changed hands three times—but here it must be explained why the name of that corpse-strewn terrain had such a friendly sound and was so deeply beloved. For if you, reader, should ask one of my countrymen: "What do you say to a big stoop?" you would find joy lighting up his face, quarrels being forgotten, and you would hear him reply, taking you by the arm as a brother and fellow traveler, "Now you're talking!" For a big stoop is a plump beer tankard holding nearly a quart; and as our intestines are not constructed to receive so much liquid without previous preparation by a number of brandies and a large pork chop and applesauce (which Marie Uhl, née Klingenberg, in her happiest days called "the foundation"), a big stoop is equivalent to three hours' good entertainment. For never will your heart swell more gloriously with generosity and great thoughts than when the drink flows down, putting care to rout, after the foundation has been laid.

The word *stoop*, a drinking vessel, is what the philologists call a "homonym" of *stoop*, front steps.

A flat oval depression about a thousand yards long and half as wide in the middle of the battleground, for whose quite worthless possession the hostile countrymen fought like lions, retreating and advancing, was originally called the Big Stoop, perhaps from some fancied suggestion of the steps before a public building, and later also in honor of the first glass that the returned warrior drinks at home. It is not hard to imagine that this beloved name was what really caused a bramble-covered hole in the ground to exert upon both parties an attraction otherwise inexplicable.

The eleven divisions that had been ordered back to the capital were already pouring eastward along the highways, unseen in the shelter of the hills; crossing the river by the Liebenau, Florida, and three pontoon bridges, they reached the positions prepared for them outside the city. Then, about noon of May 3, while the camps at Goerz and Christopher and the quarters in the southern suburbs were filling up with Laurenti's infantry, the mysterious atrocity took place in the Stoop.

In an access of hysterical enthusiasm Countess Bessonoff, the Chief of the Bodyguard Regiment, had the Stoop flooded with gas by Professor Bock. A hundred and ninety-eight wounded, including General Spitta, stifled under the tent roof of an emergency hospital set up in the hollow.

This outrage, unusual even in civil wars, and committed, furthermore, upon wounded prisoners, forthwith circulated with all the speed of rumor. Although publicly denied by Urban's intimates, who secretly demanded the deposition and death of the countess, it changed the situation of the insurgents for the worse.

As early as the evening of the third, without consulting the Council of War or the Academy, Beyer telegraphed Baer an order to attack regardless of losses, making use of the howitzers. Because of their terrible effect, the latter, which could smash whole blocks of houses into atoms, had not been used by either side. In this the government sacrificed its advantage, for Urban's howitzers, kept in the south, could not be transported in time after the surprise arrest of 20,000 Gas-House Boys on April 12. On the night of May 3-4, while the Urbanites were crowding closer to Frohwein's right-angled hill position outside Neumuehle and Niederwesel, and the rescued main body of the Kaempf army was coming across the river into the suburbs, the Council of War was summoned. The bishops and Jacob Willert, president of the Academy, objected to the "barbarous use" of the howitzers mounted on the western slopes of the capital hill to defend the river line. Kessel, famous and notorious for his "Warning Against Church Attendance," displayed copies of paintings by a Russian war artist in which pontoon bridges were being destroyed by explosive shells, while the limbs of human beings (which the Carpenters' Rule called "irreplaceable children of God") were flying in fragments through the air. Both bishops and Jacob Willert declared that they would immediately resign their offices if a professedly Christian government should do such things.

Beyer, profoundly irritated because he could not take back his order to General Baer without losing prestige in the army, retorted that in the first place the government did not profess to be Christian, and never would, and in the second place the Carpenters' Rule, so far as he knew it, permitted even worse harm to be done to a fellow man: it permitted lying, so long as the person lied to was unworthy of trust. And lying, he declared, damaged not the mortal body, but the very soul.

Daruhi, leaping to the President's aid, offered the opinion that the bishops' horror at the miseries of battle rested upon an overrating of externals. The decay of the physical body was painful even in bed. The whole world was raising an outcry at the murder of the 197 prisoners and General Spitta; yet they had died more easily than any lung or liver patient.

General Kaempf, with a glance at his friend Hesse, asked whether the clergy had any objection to the destroying of inanimate objects such as works of wood and stone (Exodus 20) by heavy howitzers. Being asked to speak more plainly, he disclosed that the Susa army, fringing the marshes east of the capital, had been moving northward for two nights as if to attack the blunt cone of the Old Town hill, never assaulted before, where the river forked. The observations of our outposts could be depended on, since Susa's men did not hide their lights with sufficient care.

Both Kessel and the Archbishop knew Kaempf's schoolmasterly garrulity. If they dropped another groat into the music box, it would grind out a military address lasting at least two hours and tending to expose them as military incompetents. Accordingly, both said they would not object to cannonading at inanimate objects like bridges or houses, provided the passers-by and inhabitants had been removed in time.

The generals expressed their thanks, and asked leave to depart from the conference. If the howitzers were not allowed to attack transports, columns, and ferries, they said, Urban could not be prevented from crossing the river and closing in on the suburbs. And with a touch of mockery that the clergymen made note of in silence, Kaempf added that his respect for religion was so great that he would allow Urban to march undisturbed up the old Blue Griffin Road, since that seemed to be the customary triumphal lane of our enemies, as far as the Outer Boulevard. Now, however, he and Hesse would get to work, as the old plan for defending the city had been rendered worthless.

So it'll be street fighting, thought the members of the gathering, departing. Among those present at the Council of War, only Beyer knew that the generals' confidence stemmed from favorable reports that had been trickling in from the headquarters of the western group since early that night.

There was great debate in later years about Frohwein's foolhardiness in drawing toward him, like what one might call a magnetic hedgehog, an enemy seven times his own strength from the evening of May 2 to the evening of the fourth, while he had only two divisions—for the third, under General Schroeder, was also dismissed on the morning of the second. Whether this foolhardiness of the seventy-year-old general, assuring time for the main body of troops to withdraw and for the city to prepare for street fighting, saved the military situation has been much argued and written about; but the final victory has usually been attributed to General Baer. If Baer, in the three days' battle from the second to the fourth, had not halted and thrown back the Urbanite western group, finally encircling it and pushing it against the broad river, so that it surrendered on the afternoon of the fifth, who could have forced Urban, people asked, to make his premature entry into the capital? He could then, in accordance with his plan, have waited unmolested for the arrival of the western army; accordingly, the palm should go to old Baer.

Matthew Brandt, the Teller of Great Deeds, ascribes the victory to the dead President, our Adam Faust. The decadence in which our country was then languishing, says Brandt, was the spiritual state that knows nothing higher than the enjoyment of life, even of a miserable life. The Biblical words of wisdom, "A living dog is better than a dead lion," says Brandt, constituted the deepest wisdom of which this decadence was capable. Adam Faust, says Brandt, snatched our nation out of this spiritual state of the sleepily blinking, overfed crocodile, into which mankind falls beyond escape if it worships mechanical progress. Frohwein's heroism would have been useless to a decadent nation, because he could not have found thirty thousand men willing to join him in sacrificing their lives. And, the teller of the May battles goes on to say, Adam Faust's gravestone very properly bore the antidecadent inscription from the great Greek, Aeschylus:

With might and justice harnessed to the car
Was ever chariot more nobly drawn?

On the evening of May 4, with every fifth man of the two divisions
dead, and only three out of the thirty-six guns he had kept with him
still firing, old Frohwein capitulated in Niederwesel ravine. Lying
on a stretcher himself with his arm bandaged, he was transported
back to Mittelburg in the carriage of the Urbanite chief of staff, with
his pupil Thomas, who tried vainly to start a conversation with the
old man. There he died, ostensibly of wound fever, in which he raved
about Gelimer, King of the Goths, about singing in the snakes' tower,
and about rats that man could not fight against. Some doubt has been
entertained of the wound fever. The Federal Police discovered on the
list of "traitors" condemned to death at Mittelburg who were to be
hanged after Urban's victory, among the names of well-known Carpenters, that of the nurse who had cared for the wounded general
on the night of the fourth. The reason given for her sentence was
"failure to follow doctor's orders." She herself testified some weeks
later that the general ordered her to loosen his bandage. Death had
come kindly to the old man, she said, though he had half sat up, his
eyes feverish, and had audibly repeated, smoothing the coverlet, the
following verse:

> *When he had sung the third night away ·*
> *And surprise proclaimed the break of day,*
> *The serpents bared their fangs, they say,*
> *And Gelimer the king fell dead.*

The nurse was brought before a court-martial on suspicion of
murder, and acquitted when Hesse remembered having heard the
same verse from Frohwein's lips years before.

When the surrender and capture of the government commander in
chief became known, as early as the evening of the fourth, the territory occupied by Urban resounded with a jubilation more than a little
offensive to all the well disposed. Common report, exaggerating as
always, charged our side with 45,000 prisoners and as many again
dead and wounded; it did not mention the losses of the Urbanites!
Leaflets and newspapers named May 5 "the great man's day," and

announced epoch-making addresses to the Women's Social Service, the "Old Friends," a delegation of students from the Technical Academy of Mittelburg, and the Augmented Corps of the Leader. The Bodyguard Regiment, being held in reserve, was also to have the honor of a speech from the Leader in connection with the great day.

To the intimates, however, it was already abundantly clear that Frohwein had deceived the Urbanite leaders and saved Kaempf's army. They said nothing of this to the League Leader, who was in Count Bessonoff's paneled study at Mittelburg, reading addresses of homage, now and then making note of a sentence that he would speak that evening at the victory banquet in the great banquet hall before the wives of the highest party functionaries.

The shriveled James Unger, former cashier to Roland Perlotta, now secretary of the secret service, came in and presented a list of traitors condemned to death. After him came Justus Thomas.

"Why aren't there any reports here from the western army?" Urban asked the lieutenant colonel, reading the attached explanations of the death sentences.

"The western group has been detained."

"It was beaten; why aren't you telling me the truth?"

"General Baer has attacked; nothing more is known," Thomas prevaricated out of pity.

Urban pretended to be absorbed in the papers. He was ashamed before these people who reproached him with having "nourished a viper in his bosom." Everyone on the staff had hated Countess Bessonoff since the moment when her idiotic "hecatomb" had turned public opinion against Urban, spurred the government to desperate resistance, and destroyed the hope of a peace conference, which had been growing day by day with his military successes. Now not even General Susa believed in victory; Oriola's army, weary unto death, was stalled opposite Laurenti, while the western group could indeed slowly push General Baer back, but not thrust him aside or put him to flight; and so the Leader had agreed with his intimates to invest the capital city. When the food shortage began to trouble the inhabitants, he would offer the government an honorable peace, demanding no more than he had asked before being forced to fight: that his military units should remain intact.

In order, therefore, to show the world that the 198 prisoners had been murdered without the knowledge or desire of the League Leader, Countess Bessonoff was condemned to death, and along with her, for the sake of the Leader's followers, the count as well. This was merely in outward appearance, to reassure the faithful: in reality he had already been made prisoner and taken to safety at Neuhafen. But Ida herself, because she had been mistaken only in her choice of means to carry out her "noble intention" of honoring the Leader, was to know nothing until the moment of her execution on May 6. Professor Bock and his assistant Emil, the Lion of Afghanistan, were entrusted with the swift and painless execution of the sentence.

"Not so much as a cat, not so much as a cat," the Leader hissed, hurling the death warrants across the room. James Unger caught the list, while Thomas realized that Urban was thinking about the encirclement of the capital. If the western group joined the operation, the ring could be drawn so tight that not so much as a cat could sneak through.

James Unger slunk out, first bowing, to arrange for the erection of the gallows. The League Leader vented his hatred to his familiar friend, as he did daily until all those who listened were weary. Tormenting himself, he stabbed at the wound of his hatred for the Iron Phalanx, which pursued him even into his sleep: "If I win, those opinion-mongers will be dead, as they well know; but if the government wins, the word 'dead' is sheer flattery for what they will be then. Not even a flea squashed by a child twenty centuries ago would be so dead, which also they well know. If neither side wins, though, and reason emerges triumphant, so that I can make a peace of reconciliation, the Iron Phalanx will not only be alive, it will be honored and courted for its casting vote; it will constitute public opinion, intelligence, and culture. Well, the intelligentsia have always been stupid, but never so stupid as they are today—admitted, my dear boy. But even supposing they were still stupider than they are today; supposing they were as stupid as they will be day after tomorrow, which is beyond the power of the human imagination to conceive—even in their day after tomorrow's condition, how could they help straining every nerve to bring about a peace of reconciliation and the *status quo ante,* in which they were so powerful?"

"They think the government is going to win," Thomas returned, "and are buttering it up in good time. Isn't that understandable?"

"Perfectly understandable, perfectly, Thomas! But you can't butter up the Carpenters by earning their contempt."

"Everyone does what he can."

"You say 'understandable,' but is any intelligence understandable that is too stupid to know how to butter someone up?"

The lieutenant colonel laughed aloud.

"Did you know that the dead Hilgenfeld, who of course was a great man, reprinted parts of my Blendheim speech in *The Conservative*? That shows how wonderfully well those people like me, without my meaning to butter them up. Man, what madness to fight a life-and-death struggle with the very government that likes me as well as that!"

That evening in the brilliantly lit banquet hall, before the bejeweled wives of his high functionaries, the Leader made his "speech on the intellect," which overflowed with hatred for the Iron Phalanx. Only two listeners, Thomas and Weisse, could feel that it was also overflowing with abashed love for Adam Faust and a yearning for reconciliation with the dread Carpenters: they saw this by the way it denounced the Liberals to the Carpenters as the common foe:

SPEECH ON THE INTELLECT

"To you, ladies, so that the rattle of arms may be drowned out for yet a little while, I will speak of a delicate matter, something that I am not supposed to have, and yet that I have always been: the intellect.

"Now, I must say I do not think that unmanliness, *laissez faire,* liberalism, and tolerance have ever been the way of the man who can rightfully call himself an intellect, or that an 'intellect' is anyone who can be talked to. What I, the so-called Antichrist, reproach the creator of Christianity with is not that he was no intellect, but on the contrary that he laid upon the average man, with the mercilessness of an intellect and with all-too-intellectual extravagance, a burden he cannot carry.

"So an 'intellect' does not mean chattering in newspapers, not even when you can write beautifully. Intellect has nothing to do with emotion or education. An illiterate—yes, an illiterate—may be an intellect, and is so more often than the educated.

"The intellect has nothing at all to do with democracy, as people keep bellowing in order to harm my cause. Well, yes, once upon a time long ago intellect had something to do with democracy—three hundred years ago, when democracy existed in a very few scattered places. That was when the settler from across the water, with his pitiless Book, the Bible, in one hand and a pistol in the other, defended against his enemy the plantation he had won from the wilderness.

"So intellect, which is another way of saying the spirit, ladies and gentlemen, whether it be the spirit of evil or the so-called spirit of good —one looks damnably like the other—the intellect, the spirit, signifies hardness and contumacy. Yes, contumacy; or at least the will to resist —to be one-sided, hard, and fanatical, sacrificing one's life if need be. That and nothing else is what the intellect signifies—a fact that must be recalled in these days when writhing, eel-like pants peddlers, smiling at everything and upon everyone, making material success their God, talk about a threat to their 'intellectual' work, which they perpetrate with impunity in newspapers and magazines—no, not with impunity at last, since I am threatening their freedom!

"Of course the man who does not want to fight because he has nothing to fight for can easily be liberal, tolerant, pacifistic—in short, something that we, my friends, do not fear or even combat, but wipe out of existence with a single police ordinance—with a sweep of our coat sleeve! *We* have only the intellect to fear, and only our peers to fight against: I mean the spirit of Christianity, hostile to us, remote from mankind, contemptuous of it—but nevertheless a spirit, an intellect, that will give us proofs enough of its guile, hardness, and brutality in the days to come. Against those who invoke 'intellect' against us, however, which they confuse with impudence and cowardice, against the tolerant, liberal, hand-shaking traders, we need not fight, my friends. We have only to step over them as one steps over corpses—holding our noses, I mean. I ask the ladies' indulgence and pardon."

At midnight, whether from pity or sadism, Urban ordered Countess Bessonoff to his bedroom to spend the night with him.

THE SECOND FLIGHT OF ELSPETH KERSTING

VIII

WHEN Dr. Grau drove off in the carriage from the posting inn at Little Rose in order to knock at the Carpenters' door, Henry Willert went to the stable and asked to see the saddle horses that were being boarded by the postmaster, a belated remnant of his grandfather's famous strain. Enameled plates showed the names, racing records, and birth dates of the ancestors of each animal to the fifth generation.

"Never mind this family-tree business! There's got to be an end of it some time," said the Secretary of State to the young stableman who accompanied him and said, "Yes, sir!" without asking why. Henry, meanwhile, was thinking that he might equally well have said it would have to start again some time.

Dr. Grau's cry of anguish had thrown Henry so completely off his usual form and balance that he had no doubt of being himself a "last man." He vowed that his children should never be Secretaries of State, Senators, or worst of all, Carpenters—not that, under any circumstances. Better for them to be what their fathers had been: bakers, tailors, shop assistants, mariners, restaurant-keepers, carpenters—no, that was what they mustn't be: better for them to be mechanics or muscular journeymen blacksmiths, starting over at the beginning.

Then he sat down in the cool best room of the posting inn; the postmaster brought him paper and writing utensils, and he reported himself to the Supreme Joint Court of the Order of Carpenters.

When he received and accepted his orders to postpone the outbreak of hostilities by deliberately dragging out negotiations, Henry wrote, he had not dreamed, nor could he possibly have dreamed, that his interlocutor would speak the truth in the sense of the Carpenters' Rule— the honest belief of his heart. This, however, contrary to all human foresight, was the very thing that Dr. Grau had done. He (Willert), on the other hand, out of consideration for the interests of the state and his orders, had been obliged to violate the Carpenters' Rule, which required that an honest answer be given to him who speaks honestly. For this damage to his interlocutor as well as this infringement of the Rule, proceeding from his official duty as Secretary of State, he wished to lodge the prescribed denunciation of himself.

He gave the letter to the stableman, changed his mind, took it back, drove to town himself, and went to the Joint Court. Holzkopf, whom he had meant to ask for advice as to whether the self-denunciation might perhaps be unnecessary, was busy as an assessor in court. Andrew Zorn, the commentator on the Rule, was not at home either when Henry called; so he took a bridge across the canal to Federal Police Barracks I. Brother General was on the winter riding school, the sentry informed him, but Henry had scarcely stepped into the half-darkened hall before he turned back. A little bit aside from three young officers who were watching the riding stood Hesse, Hesse and a sandy-blonde woman.

That's all I needed, to have the Schwanns be celebrating a birthday, thought the forsaken Henry, and such of course was the case. To avoid blundering into a birthday in the family of the secret-service chief, you would have had to keep seven dates in your head. Furthermore, not even the constant celebrations had dulled the anticipation of the five children or the husband and wife; there were callers big and little, hot chocolate, whipped cream, home-made cake, dancing and piano playing in such abundance that a visitor with worries preferred to slink silently away from such a noisy profusion of vitality. Henry, with a long road behind him, did not want to turn back, and the colonel took him into the garden, where his wife served coffee and cake to the guest.

Well, said the easygoing Schwann with a smile, the self-denunciation had been correct, but the trial might be delayed for a fortnight; when a member of the government was accused, the judges' bench had to have its full complement. His own opinion of the matter was that the Carpenters' Rule had a gap in it. The law, springing originally from the thirteenth century, was intended for free men, but not for governing men, and consequently the present conflict of duty between the oath of office and the Carpenters' oath was not provided for in the Rule at all. Surely an acquittal must result, since it was quite impossible to imagine what would have happened if Dr. Grau had reported to his Leader on April 3 that all was up.

Henry had dinner with the Schwanns, played folk songs for the birthday child, a confiding four-year-old citizen of the world, on his new harmonica, and finally went home late at night, accompanied by mounted police. From Andersen, drunk with sleep, he heard a story that did not please him, touchy sobersides that he was.

Elspeth, after missing stout Emil and shooting Gregory William Lienhardt, raced up in front of the little house, screamed to summon the servants, and made them and the mounted police search every room from attic to cellar for Henry, dead or alive. She herself, as if overwhelmed by a sort of terror after the act, sat on the stone steps before the terrace and sobbed with pity for her own fate. Enlightened a few moments later by Major Lorenz, while Lindequist was having the two dead men laid out in the barn by the forester's house, she seemed to be ashamed that her sweetheart had concealed his whereabouts from her all day.

Then, to make good her own disgrace, she invited the officers and patrol leaders to dinner. She got out the damask tablecloths, crystal bowls, champagne goblets, and heavy silver candelabra that were reserved for occasions of great state. She appeared in the evening gown and with the jewelry of the dead "Beloved"; the speechless Carpenters, who thought all this had been done with Henry's approval, toasted her as the "happiness and splendor of the house"; if one is to believe Andersen, he called her attention half an hour afterward to the fact that she was drunk, and led her to her apartments, where, being undressed by Emily, she at once fell asleep.

Now any informed layman, even Alois Borstel with his ejaculation, "Yes, you know, her nerves!" would have given the proper name to Elspeth's condition; in the second place, she was her father's daughter, and celebrating "escapes" with carousals was a local custom. But this pretentious and senseless function outraged young Willert. She had indeed shot Lienhardt, which was quite in order; but she had saved no one, nor had she any right to fill up the house with guests except with his permission. Henry's mother had had her face slapped so that the powder flew thirty years before for a very similar extension of her own personal sphere. That quite aside, she got drunk when admittedly pregnant!

When Henry Willert went into his living room, slamming the door in the face of the house steward, who remained standing in the hall, that ladies' darling thought he must have said too much. His master, however, had already forgotten the story; undressing in the bathroom, he let the lukewarm stream of the shower pour over his head and back. Obviously, everything Schwann had said about the conflict of duties and the "gap" was a mere attempt at consolation. Before the Joint Court there were no excuses, no apologies, and also no acquittal and no fine; the smallest punishment was a year of prison or lunatic village. The shame of standing in the iron barred cage for defendants, gaped at by a thousand spectators, was the only thing that the accused could escape from, by simply requesting that the trial be conducted in his absence. But two examples proved that it was better not to make this request. A provincial governor and the president of the Supreme Chamber of Accounts, both of them being requested by the presiding justice to expose themselves to the gaze of the spectators, had stood on their right (a constitutional right of the defendant) to absent themselves from the trial. Both lost their posts.

True, the defendant was not subjected to express humiliation; the judges and official defense attorneys discussed the case as if the chief personage were absent. They were even forbidden to *look* at the man in the cage; neither his name nor any reproach ever passed the lips of the judges. For the commentators on the Rule regarded the punishment not as something that followed the trial, but as a part of the trial, and the trial itself as reconstituting the Rule, broken by the violator. This is plainly evident from a custom formerly smiled at, but now easier for us to understand: after sentence had been pronounced, the presiding justice stepped up to the cage, and the following invariable exchange took place between him and the man under sentence:

"Brother X, do you accept the punishment?"

"I accept it gladly, Brother President."

Thereupon the presiding justice would say: "I congratulate you, Brother X, on having reconstituted the Rule by trial and punishment."

Henry amiably begged Elspeth's pardon for having been away on business all of the preceding day, and told her the latest scandal from the capital.

Alexandra von Hesse, née von Brick, had wanted her husband to give her an amethyst ring that was on display in Levin's show window—"A bargain, not cheap, a gift," she declared. Otto had retorted: "A Carpenter's wife doesn't wear rings on her fingers; she wears a broad linen collar around her neck." "I'd sooner wear a rope," Alexandra was supposed to have replied.

"Is the amethyst ring worth as much as that—I mean is it worth more than your grandmother's solitaire diamond ring?" asked Elspeth.

"Anne Mary Willert's solitaire cost a thousand thalers," replied Henry. "The amethyst at Levin's is scarcely worth half that. Do you want it?"

"No. I'd like to know why they hate each other—Otto Hesse and Alexandra."

"She hates him because he won't spend any money. He hates her because she can't have a child. He didn't know that before."

Now, on one of the last days in April, Elspeth's distrust poured out like a river, winding up in the flight of which Dr. Kuttner had had a premonition. Just at this time a scandalous high-treason trial was putting the officials of the diplomatic service all over the continent in terror of their lives, for it revealed the negligence even of ambassadors in guarding their correspondence. Accordingly, the Secretary of State arranged a secret compartment in his desk, for which only he and Augustus Huebner, who had to handle the mail, possessed keys.

On the afternoon of the twenty-ninth, Henry came back from a walk through the preserve to find an official communication in a large envelope with three seals broken and open on his high desk. Elspeth, being summoned, made no denial: she had taken the letter from the messenger, and opened it because the words *Joint Court* were plainly to be seen on the red sealing wax. That meant it was not diplomatic correspondence, and she had long been curious to know what he was concealing from her.

Henry, beside himself with indignation, roared at her, demanding to know who had given her permission to open his mail.

"Your mother," said Elspeth as softly as if she were uttering a dangerous threat, "opens all the letters your father gets."

Said Henry, utterly amazed, "Well, that's really rather different!"

"Oh, so that's different!" whispered Miss Elspeth, her face as gray as an old wall, and walked out.

Don't call her back! Don't go after her, for God's sake! The lover remembered Kuttner's warning. He sat down on his couch, the letter

in his hand, and fell asleep as he had done in childhood when sorrow
and shame had driven him into some dark hiding place.

In the capital, meanwhile, the trolleys were jingling, horses' hoofs
were clopping, the newsboys were racing, the strollers were strolling,
the housewives were doing their marketing just as they did in the
tranquil days of peace, and not even buying larger quantities than
before. For the government, relying on its emergency powers, had
threatened the merchant or manufacturer who raised the price of any
of these goods with two years' "land of whispers."

When the first street lights were being lit, General Otto von Hesse
and Alexandra stood outside Levin's jeweler's shop studying the glittering display. The stout gentlemen with the too-tight overcoats, turning their backs on the couple, regarded the front of the houses opposite
as if they were thinking of renting a floor.

Hesse looked tired; probably from weariness he passed over Alexandra's veiled allusions to the amethyst ring, which, ridiculously
enough, was still on display, and actually at a reduced price.

"If the price has been reduced, I don't suppose it's a good one," the
general offered.

"For you, for your *wife,* I mean, it'd be good enough!"

This allusion too Otto passed over; he had been passing over a good
deal recently. Pointing to a costly brooch, he said: "Nice piece, that
diamond butterfly. But the setting seems to be silver. Why shouldn't
it be gold, if the diamonds are real?"

"But it's platinum, man!" she retorted scornfully. Sometimes she felt
he was like a parvenu.

"Do you think it's expensive? More expensive than gold?"

Why, you impudent swine! thought Alexandra. She could no longer
control herself: "What do you care, my continent Carpenter? Tell
me, is it true that you're personally giving riding lessons at the winter
riding school to your secretary, the alleged Miss Veronica?"

"Is it more expensive than gold, platinum?"

"Because if you think you can get away with anything with Dad's
money, you don't know me!"

Not looking at her, the general weighed her truly pitiful chances
of avenging herself upon him. A marriage with a barren woman who
had concealed this "important circumstance" from her suitor was not
a proper marriage according to the custom of the country. Even a

Kate Beyer had not been allowed to marry her Merckel because she had not the strength to bear children. If Alexandra put it to the test of divorce because someone else was expecting a child by Otto, she would be held at fault, and her husband would retain the dowry.

"I tell you, don't you dare start carrying on with that placid cow!"

"Surely I may ask if platinum—" said Otto, breaking off and looking around. Alexandra, boiling with anger, had left him standing and gone on alone.

"There's no harm in asking," he called after the furious woman, and was just starting into the jeweler's shop when a closed carriage rattled up. He recognized the chestnuts and the high, old-fashioned vehicle. As the footman was about to jump down from the box to open the door, a very stout gentleman who had inconspicuously emerged from the doorway motioned to him not to leave his seat; a second stout man, turning over the lapel of his overcoat, seemed to be displaying something to the coachman; the third, coming from the far sidewalk and twirling his mustache in high spirits, or perhaps because in imagination he was already spending the reward that had been offered for the apprehension of a "gentleman real-estate broker," put his plump hand on the open carriage window on the street side: "Let's see your papers, Miss Real-Estate Broker!" he said through the window.

"What do you think you're doing, you insolent creature?" yelled Elspeth Kersting, getting out of the carriage as Hesse removed the three stout men. She was rather pale, broader, and a trifle taller than the boyishly slender Otto, who held out his hand, apologizing for the guards.

"Oh, it's you," said the startled Miss Elspeth. The general, with the truth of the popular saying, "Love lost, life lost," running through his head, did not let go her hand. His eyes fixed upon her, he made an unexpected reply: "Do you still remember how you repeated those verses at Merckel's, with your hands folded like a schoolgirl's?"

"They weren't verses."

"What were they, then?"

"The story of the love of noblewomen."

"I asked you then if you would marry me. Why didn't you say yes?"

"Goodness, General, I was sixteen years old."

"I'd always have been faithful to you. We'd have lived modestly in a little valley, and had a flock of children, one smaller than another, like organ pipes; and when we came to die they'd have stood in crowds around our bed, with their own little children."

Elspeth seemed rather pleased by this flattery. She took the glove off her right hand, and removed a diamond ring from her finger: "All that may still be possible, and possibly I shall be at your disposal if you'll go in now and pledge this ring for me. I need five hundred thalers. It's worth twice that."

Hesse took out a brown leather wallet, and counted five hundred-thaler notes into her outstretched hand: "You can keep the ring," he said, but she thrust it into the flat leather wallet.

So it happened that the great solitaire of Anne Mary Willert, the dead Beloved, changed owners: for later the dovelike Veronica would not surrender it, but Hesse gave Elspeth one so much like it for her wedding that she thought it was the old one, and asked him: "Now have I got to give back the five hundred?"

At the Women's Hospital Professor Kuttner tore his gray hair when the head nurse reported that a Miss Kersting was demanding first-class accommodations and "to be relieved of the child at once." She said she had money and could pay for herself.

"What did you tell her?" the director asked.

"That what she wants isn't paid for in money, but with two to five years."

Kuttner had the most expensive of the private rooms assigned to Miss Elspeth. He went up, pushed the excited girl down on a couch, and, in order to gain time, let her bewail her sorrows; he withheld from her the fact that he knew about the case; as medical adviser to the Joint Court he had read Andrew Zorn's and the President's opinions on the case of Henry Willert and Dr. Grau.

Interrupted by tears, she poured out protestations and complaints of the two men and of Henry's lack of confidence. What, must even the enemy be trusted if he told the truth—the enemy, but not she? A single word from Henry to her about the negotiations with Grau, and she would immediately have advised the Secretary of State to break off the conferences, give up his mission, and suggest a government negotiator who was not a Carpenter and thus not bound by the Rule. This was just what the President wrote in his opinion, which Henry might have heard from her, yes, from Elspeth Kersting, before he made a fool of himself and laid himself open to punishment; with the permission of Hesse and Spitta she had attended the Carpenters' training courses at Liebenau. But she did not care to be worn out for a while yet as a bed pillow and brood mare to revivify an old city family. So away with the child, and an end of it! "I shall have half a dozen children yet, never fear, Professor, and by a man of equally high position!" she concluded her hysterical bragging.

The doctor pondered ways of smoothing out the quarrel. In the last few days he had already lost one patrician household—in fact, the most distinguished of them all: Kate Beyer screamed and scolded him out of the room when he called at the President's house, because for five years he had prevented her marriage, so that after the murder of her sweetheart she was still Miss Beyer, and not, as she properly should have been, his widow.

Accordingly, ostensibly preparing for the operation, he prescribed hot and cold baths, showers, and massage for Miss Elspeth, which consumed time and distracted the patient from her fantasies. Meanwhile he gave a medical description of the case to Jacob Willert.

"Is she pregnant?" Jacob asked the doctor.

"Beyond doubt."

By eight that evening the splendid Elizabeth was sitting in the hospital room of Miss Elspeth, who had been worked over by bath attendants and masseurs for two hours. Elizabeth said: "You're crazy. Haven't you heard about the trial where they're throwing the diplomats out of their jobs because other people opened their letters? Jacob would have broken every bone in my body if I'd opened a letter and he was Secretary of State! But you see he hasn't risen so far as your Henry. Or is all this just an excuse, and you have something else against Henry, such as a woman might have against a man who didn't satisfy her, for instance?"

Elspeth declared she was satisfied, and the two women agreed that the betrothal should be celebrated on May 5 in the house on Lady Square. Young Willert, awakened from sleep and summoned to the phone, learned about the reconciliation from his mother. His surprise and delight were so great that he felt inclined to write immediately the letter to Dr. Grau that the Joint Court had ordered him to send —the trial itself was not to take place until the uprising had been put down. He felt that the poor man should enjoy some of the new courage and vitality that now inspired him.

And Henry wrote: "Dear Dr. Grau: I thought it would be easy to postpone the outbreak of hostilities because I expected you, not indeed to make outright false statements, but dishonestly to conceal the aims that Urban was fighting for. In this case—supposing that you were not frank—you would not be 'knocking,' and so I would not have to open to you, in accordance with the Carpenters' Rule.

"You, however, by speaking openly, quite plainly knocked at the door of your interlocutor's soul as early as April 5. Therefore the Joint Court, postponing consideration of the case for the time being, until communications are restored, has charged me to make good in a letter what I failed to do, namely to explain the Faustite wish dream as against your vision.

"If Urban the materialist were right, the present civil war would be a class struggle between the well-to-do, living in security, and the poor, craving material security. Yet ninety out of a hundred Faustites are poor men. For the mad, the absurd-sounding truth, my brother, is that men have no craving whatever for security—particularly since they are going to their death readily as never before—but only for their lost honor. And this cannot be won by 'silk stockings and beefsteak every day for everyone,' and certainly not by degrading the human race to 'equality,' which means an organized herd with the tyrant as shepherd.

"About the way to regain honor, the honor of every individual as a unique, irreplaceable child of God, there can be no doubt. For a man's honor rests not upon wealth or gentility, but—as it always has so long as mankind has existed—upon the confidence that he inspires in others. This confidence in turn depends on the honesty of heart that he shows to every honest man, without so much as a single exception (as you can see in my case).

"By the reports of Hesse's secret service I know that your former leader, Dr. Urban, has laid stupendous plans of organization and production, embracing the whole world and extending for from five to twenty years, which will 'absolutely guarantee' security. We, on the other hand, regard the Tower of Babel as a perpetual warning to mankind. We have, I freely admit, no plan. In Adam Faust's literary estate, repeated a hundred times over with senile obstinacy, is the commandment: 'Do not believe in the future!' Surely this means, 'Sow the seed, and weed out the weeds. The harvest is no affair of yours.'

"We are sowing the seed by restoring man's honor.

"As soon as Urban is defeated, we shall weed out the weeds by three prohibitions:

"1. A prohibition of 'splendid phrases.'

"2. A prohibition of the corrupt teacher.

"3. A prohibition of cowardice in face of evil.

"How these prohibitions are to be understood will soon be evident in practice.

"General Heinz has received orders to allow you freedom of movement in Marienhall, Geisenheim, and the surrounding country. Please transmit to him, a trustworthy brother, your wishes and my kind regards.

"Henry Willert."

BOOK THREE

HE CREEPS AS THE GRASS GROWS, UNSEEN

IX

WHEN Urban's General Susa left his army group, taking with him forty thousand picked men to inflict the severest defeat of the campaign upon us by the above-mentioned flanking thrust at Mittelburg, he left his second in command, Bruns, with almost impossible orders. By means of sand heaps, stone roadways, and felled trees Bruns was to cross the moors and the alder forests growing in the water, so as to have a broad front drawn up on the evening of the fourth along the branch of the river that embraces and safeguards the whole length of the "egg," the oval hill of the capital city.

"Almost impossible," a glance at the terrain tells us. It extends for two days' march, marshy terrain intersected by waterways, wooded and trackless, but glorious in spring with the scent of growing things, brilliant in fall with a thousand hues. It is the home of eels, pike, a delicate small kind of turnip, parsley, and cucumber salad.

But Susa and his General Bruns were not given to wild imaginings. It has become evident from orders since discovered that they were depending on the help of the impoverished marsh dwellers as guides and road builders, and in particular on co-operation with the Urbanites who had remained in the capital itself, in the poor eastern quarters, and had escaped Hesse's pursuit. For, after all, the northeastern industrial region does not stop at the river branch, but goes across it by bridges, footbridges, and ferries to spread upon the far bank. All night the peasant carts and the fishermen's box carts come rumbling in from the east to the capital, which is eager for fresh vegetables, lettuce, and fine river fish. So long as carriage and pedestrian traffic across the east branch of the river, therefore, was not interrupted—which did not take place until the last day of April—there was an exchange not only of goods and money, but also of whispered and written news in the open market places and the market halls of the East End, up to the very edge of the Old Town. Fishwives and their helpers could not be distinguished from Bruns' emissaries, nor could plain citizens going shopping be sorted out from agents of Urban's secret service. So it was that in the traditional Council of War, when the bishops and old Willert restricted the "barbarous fire of howitzers" to inanimate targets, General Kaempf gave up at once and without regret the old plan for defending the city—first, because it was highly probable that the plan had already been betrayed to the Urbanites; second, because the old man thought it useful to spread confusion in the ranks of the enemy by the news that "the defenders are changing their plans." The following day Hesse, as deputy of Spitta, the city commandant, halted traffic across the eastern branch of the river; thanks to government purchases the capital was safe from shortage for the next four weeks.

On May 1 Schwann got a report that light signals were being exchanged by inhabitants of the Old Town and the East End, on the one hand, and Bruns' troops, camping in the woods beyond the river, on the other. Efforts to apprehend the culprits were unsuccessful, particularly since the search was given up on the second. Kaempf put no faith in the signals: he thought they were being shown in order to make him believe Bruns would attack the city from where he was, that is, from the east, forcing the river branch. This would have been madness: the eastern branch is twice as wide as the western, toward which Urban's main force was hastening from Mittelburg. Therefore Kaempf and Hesse stuck to their original assumption, subsequently confirmed by our outposts, that Bruns with all his force would storm the blunt cone of Cathedral Hill from the north, where the river forks, and simply conduct a sham battle across the river in the east.

So far, so good. But if the enemy suspected that we knew his real plan, he would change it after all, and upset our arrangements a second time. He must have no idea that we had seen through him.

Just then that undependable and suspicious character, Mr. Heidemann, Mayor and President of the Art Commission, half Urbanite prophet, half Iron Phalangist, and for some days past also an ecstatic worshiper of the pacifist little Lord Jesus, arrived and was announced with fluttering coattails, top hat, and accompanied by Felice Gasparra, Suspicious Character Number Two. With a "highly important request concerning the city" he burst in on a conference of the generals. It was nine o'clock on the morning of May 4; the reports from Baer's group in the west were already beginning to have a flavor of victory, and Frohwein was fighting his last fight, leading a forlorn hope against a force seven times his own at Niederwesel.

The generals' humor was far from bad, and Hesse indicated to his colleagues that the matter must surely be highly important, or else it could never have routed Professor Gasparra out of bed "in the middle of the night"!

"It is indeed of national importance, concerning the national art treasures housed in the cathedral and the Town Hall on account of the emergency!" agreed Mr. Heidemann, mustaches bristling.

"Oh, just a moment," Hesse broke in so hurriedly that there was not even time for a traitor twinkling of the eye, "just a little moment, Mr. Mayor! You came rushing in here as if there were a fire; we, with hearts pounding, were expecting something terrible—and then you start to talk about art! No, my dear sir, urgent matters have to be attended to here; the decision as to what is most urgent lies with me. You will please have the kindness to come back in fifteen minutes. *Inter arma silent Musae,* I believe the proverb says!"

As an orderly simultaneously opened the door, Heidemann and Gasparra went out, checking the word "barbarians" behind the barrier

of gritted teeth. The twittering of starlings and robins was heard
through the window in the small conference chamber of the War
Ministry, with the smooth table in the middle, the antiquated chandelier, and the smooth oil paintings on the papered wall. Little Kraus,
the artilleryman, found himself for the hundredth time unable to see
why scores of tiny lyres and ribbons had been painted in gold or
bronze on the dark-red paper, as if the conference chamber were a
music room. Messerschmidt, the younger brother of the late Minister
of War, was tossing white bread crumbs into the garden.

Hesse too had been slightly alarmed, and while General Messerschmidt sat down at the table again, Kaempf asked: "Isn't it right
in the beginning of the Bible, in the first few pages, 'It shall bruise
thy head, and thou shalt bruise his heel'?"

There was general surmise as to where the passage could be found.
Hesse vowed it was in the Revelation of John or the Book of Daniel;
little Kraus declared it was not in the Bible at all, but in a pamphlet
of Hilgenfeld's, as was obvious from the language itself; whereupon
Messerschmidt indicated the possibility that there might be a third
and much older Chinese source, from which both Hilgenfeld and
the Bible had drawn. Messerschmidt was an admirer of the Chinese
popular philosopher, Confucius; without making any converts, he had
asserted that Urban was a caricature of Confucius' adversary, Lao-tse.

"Don't let the bishops hear you saying," Hesse warned him, "that
God has been plagiarizing from Confucius!"

They spent ten minutes on this pleasant discursion. One minute
would have been enough to fetch a Bible and have the orderly open
it to the passage; but it is not the way of the Carpenters to throttle
conversation by dogmatism, or unnecessarily to pass over from digres-
sions to business and facts. In testimony of this, remember how
Lindequist went off from his offices in a doctor's carriage to see what
was behind some fence; he occupied a high position in the brotherhood. They believed and still believe unshakably that work is a curse
of God—something imposed on us by God, which has to be done,
but still a curse. Hence their treatment of beggars and tramps, in
contradiction to modern ideas.

At last Kaempf looked at the clock and asked Otto von Hesse for
his opinion. This fellow Heidemann, he said, was an emissary of the

Iron Phalanx, and his hissing was a preparation for the fangs in the heel. "What are we to do?"

"Nothing," replied Otto, and the generals thought the singing birds in the garden sounded friendlier. This accursed national art treasure of crumbling canvas and ancient oil might cost an honest officer's fortune if a Madonna should be harmed through his fault.

The others nodded. For Mr. Heidemann, and his employers listening backstage, were worried not about the national art treasures but about the use of the seventy-two heavy howitzers, with their barrels capable of turning in any direction, which were hidden under concrete domes in the western slope of the city hill. Obviously, the voice of some general or Academician, rendered expansive by a bottle or so, had let slip that the howitzers might be trained on inanimate but not on living targets; and a guessing game must have ensued to see what inanimate target Leugenfeld and Kraus, the artillerymen, would choose. If the Urbanites had discovered only this much, the expansive voices had still done harm; for now Thomas, Susa, and the Master of Ordnance knew that the western river arm and suburbs were undefended before their superior force. But more than this, they were positively invited to suspect that in order to hold off their attack from the north we would make the blunt cone of Cathedral Hill, the slope, and the forking river impassable by a barrage from the heavy guns, so that their expected gathering place, "the northern base of operations," the Old Town, including cathedral, Town Hall, and Courthouse, would perish in a sea of flames.

"So that's why Heidemann came," Hesse finished his brief lecture. "If we admit to him that the national art treasures, which he himself sent to the Town Hall in order to safeguard the Urbanite base of operations, are in danger and should be removed, then he will tell Bruns how we mean to use the howitzers, and that his, Bruns', attack on the blunt cone is hopeless."

"Finished?" inquired the didactic Kaempf.

"Not quite. If Heidemann has even the slightest hint of a suspicion of an idea that within a few days there will be nothing left to admire of his residence, the Town Hall, and the Old Town except ashes and rubble, he'll run to the bishops. They'll run to Beyer, and we shall be forbidden to use the howitzers against Cathedral Hill. Then what?"

"Then let the government do its own dirty work," said little Kraus.

Kaempf, forgetting that he belonged to the government himself, concurred.

Thus Heidemann, standing in the doorway with Gasparra listening over his shoulder, was dismissed with the brief statement that the art treasures were nowhere safer from harm than in the cathedral and Town Hall.

As the generals had conferred for twenty minutes, the mayor mistrusted them now more than ever; by flattery and promises he induced Rudolphi, the painter, to sign a petition to the government from the educated classes of the fatherland, protesting against the "barbarous destruction of the cathedral and the art treasures."

At this same hour on the afternoon of the fourth, the civilian volunteer army that had answered the call of Hildebrand and Lindbrecht, the Catholic leader, to "take up the positions assigned to them," were being shifted from the western slope across the width of the city to previously prepared positions on the near side of the eastern river branch. From that quarter, the east and the marshes, only a sham attack could be expected, as we have seen; the whole force of the Urbanite onslaught would fall upon the western suburbs and Cathedral Hill in the north. Accordingly, the regular troops of Laurenti and Kaempf and contingents arriving from the central provinces occupied the largely uninhabited region along the river and in Florida and Blumeshof. They had been provided with such knowledge of the terrain, and were in such force, that if Urban had been "reasonable" he would have preferred not to set foot in the suburbs at all, but would have surrendered on the open field. The very fact that he was not reasonable, however, but had what he himself called "intellect, or spirit"—in other words, the will to resist, sacrificing life itself if necessary—was what distinguished him from the Iron Phalanx and swept the millions with him.

The clergy at this time had but slight confidence in the humanitarian assurances of the generals, although the battle was being fought not ostensibly but actually for the clergy's and God's honor. "My field and that of the Minister of War are too divergent," the Archbishop justified his doubts. Uneasy about his sheep, he was on a tour of inspection through the city in company with Kaempf, Hesse, and old Willert, when a workingmen's regiment marching east through Augustus Square attracted criticism by their incomplete uniforms.

In my native country almost everyone is a soldier, and therefore a critic of soldiers.

"Half goldfish, half canary," cried Jacob Willert, pointing his stick at the marching men, who were in civilian dress, carrying carbines, with leather sword straps, cartridge pouches and entrenching tools, and wearing old, peakless uniform caps.

"Halt and right face!" Hesse yelled at the commander, who saluted from horseback. There was not the slightest reason for such an order, which furthermore was hard to carry out because the regiment was marching with other detachments before and behind it. Long-drawn commands of "Halt!" passed to the rear by the file leaders, echoed down the street. They lost contact with the troops marching ahead. The "independents" and the "Christians" stood still, facing toward the gentlemen on the sidewalk.

"What do you think you're doing? You're holding up the whole business!" objected old Kaempf in a whisper. Even if Hesse had heard, he would not have understood: apparently at this moment in late afternoon the nervous collapse that Daruhi called "temporary impairment of consciousness" took place. As will be seen, it continued throughout the night, interrupted by sleep; but it did not distort, only darkened, his view of the outer world, with snatches of dream.

"Why are these people only half uniformed?" Hesse asked.

The commander, an old major of infantry, accustomed to naïve questions from generals, thought to himself that City Commandant Hesse should know, if anyone did, why the men were not in uniform. But he replied: "No order has been given, Your Excellency."

"Is that so—no orders?" said Otto. "Then why those abominable peakless recruits' caps?"

"They just happened to be there, and were issued to the men so that they could give a military salute."

In spite of himself Jacob Willert laughed aloud: "So that's why? Is that what we're fighting for? I bet nobody knows what the fighting is for."

Hesse turned to the file before him: "All those that know what the fighting is about, raise their right hands!"

Not a man raised his hand, and Kaempf asked: "Has the leaflet been distributed?"

"What leaflet?" Hesse inquired. While the major was replying, "No, there hasn't been time," he learned that it was an excerpt from the Bishop's *Gospel of the Sunday Mortal*.

"I want the men completely uniformed and the leaflets distributed within an hour!" Otto ordered. "Any other complaints?"

Tobias Witt, pale, slim, and terrified, a full-blown red rose in the buttonhole of his civilian jacket, was in the front rank; he raised his hand and said: "The quartermaster sergeant told me I ought to be shot because I was sick."

"What's wrong with you?" asked Otto, coming closer to the edge of the sidewalk.

"A weak heart."

"That's no sickness. What's your name?"

"Tobias Witt of Geisenheim, age twenty-eight."

"Right. Any other complaints?"

Once again Tobias was the only one to raise his hand: "The quartermaster sergeant gave me this ugly cap, although he could see it was much too big."

"Throw it away!" ordered Otto, putting his own gray silk cap with its gleaming black visor on the head of the dissatisfied soldier. Tobias Witt beamed.

"Are you satisfied now?" asked the general.

But whether from fear or from a premonition of death, the young man's face shriveled, his wide eyes begged mercy, and he shook his head: "No, General. My young wife is crying because I'm away. This rose is all I have left of her." And, after staring at the ground for a moment as if to gather courage, he added softly: "I used to be a secret agent of yours, Brother General."

The armed men, standing at ease, suppressed a grin. "Well, playing soldier and not playing soldier at the same time is impossible," replied Hesse. "It's impossible because it's a contradiction. A complete contradiction. March!" he added, taking leave of the infantry major with a gesture.

"Attention! Left face! Break step, march!" cried the commander. The file leaders, looking over their shoulders, passed on the commands, the regiments started off, and Tobias Witt, who had sworn thirteen years before at the meadow's edge never to become a soldier, marched off into the evening to his death.

The Iron Phalanx had already begun to stink with every color of putrefaction in Matthias Grünewald's palette; that same afternoon it rose up out of its gentility and deep thought—though not awakened by Jesus, and certainly no Lazarus—to play its next-to-last prank.

For the household of Rudolphi, the sculptor and painter (whom Adam Faust had hired to make reliefs and statues, Melchior Willert to do the Madonna statue of the dead Beloved), was in just such a state of slovenly extravagance as von Brick had described to young Hesse some thirteen years before: "The women can't get along on the money they have, and if you were to give them a thousand thalers extra, they could get along on it even less."

Then Adam Faust died, and a dozen cities commissioned Rudolphi to do monuments to the great President. Thus at last splendor, even if not happiness, returned to the neglected household. And in the retinue of splendor came overweening pride, the ruination of many a good fellow ere this. The whole house was refurnished, and the reception room was lined with mirrors from a royal castle, bought at auction by Clara Rudolphi. On the day of his death Adam Faust had warned the generals against these pier glasses that reached to the floor; the devil seizes upon the soul of him who looks in them often, says the proverb. He crept as the grass grows, unseen, tempting the professor to sleep late, to have a barber come to the house, to look upon the new maid—the interest was "purely artistic," of course—and to reply with flattery to the flattery of his colleagues, whose duplicity he had formerly despised. For "living costs money," and the art of making friends takes study. He creeps as the grass grows, raising up the original hardness and vanity in the downtrodden soul of the housewife.

On the afternoon of the fourth the coffee table was set in the pier-glass-lined reception room. Mrs. Rudolphi, looking in these witnesses of splendor, was showing eight-year-old Sylvia how a society lady receives guests: "Why, Mrs. Holzkopf, how well you are looking! In the summer? Oh, no, I can't stand those starchy watering places! A cottage, a bathing hut by the sea—that's what I enjoy." And Clara made her sea-green taffeta rustle; little Sylvia curtsied in the mirror.

Just then in came her father, a whole hour late, slightly exhilarated, apparently in glorious humor, and wearing his light silk-lined summer topcoat, gloves, and top hat. Tossing his outer garments on a sofa, he shouted, rubbing his hands: "Cawfee!" He imitated the dialect of the capital.

"You really must get out of these habits," said Clara Rudolphi loftily. "In the first place, it isn't cawfee, it's coffee, and, in the second place, you ring the bell."

"I will, I will!" cried Sylvia, pressing a white button, and whizzing into the kitchen to see if the bell had really rung.

Rudolphi, noticing from his wife's tone that she intended to put him down, countered her gentility by playing man of the people: "Waddaya mean? I was over to Hesse's doin' some painting. Now I gotta go over ta Gasparra's."

"I *must* go *to* Gasparra's, you stupid vulgarian!"

Ursula, the fresh and blooming-looking maid, came in to ask her mistress what was required, tossing a glance to the celebrity: "Yes, Madam?"

"One more such look, you trollop, and out you go!" screamed Clara. "Coffee!"

Ursula fled. "And as for you," the tormented wife went on, "kindly don't play irresistible! It's really *too* cheap in these surroundings."

Rudolphi sat down and tucked a napkin in his collar: "Trying to start a fight?"

"No; but you behave yourself, and when Ursula brings in the coffee, don't look at her like a love-crazed mongrel!"

"You always used to say we had fights because there was no money in the house. Now there is money in the house, and we fight just the same."

At this moment Ursula rolled the rubber-tired tea wagon into the room, with coffee, cream, sugar, and pastry. The painter, carrying out literally his instructions not to look at the young maid, covered the side of his face that was toward her with both hands, so that the girl hastily departed, running before the storm.

"I'd really like to slap your face properly," yelled the mistress, "you utterly vile creature, you!"

"How so?" he asked, helping himself. "You told me not to look at her."

Clara gnawed her lips with fury: "No, you put up your hands to let the girl know what I said, because you have about as much shame as a sixpenny whore, because you have to be always showing off."

"Is that so? Who was playing the *grande dame* in front of the mirror, if I might ask, and actually with that innocent child Sylvia?"

"That's different—we were alone. But you show off before *people;* to millionaires, but to servant girls too, because you can't help it; you're halfway between a player, a talker, and a dissembler—in other words, a tomfool."

"Success is what counts; you wouldn't try to deny that, would you?"

At this her anguish and disappointment found vent: "Oh, if only I'd married some respectful man, a master baker or a teacher, whom you could respect! Even fifty feet under ground, you'd still be a tomfool making the worms laugh, you wretch!"

But the master had heard this condemnation so often before that it no longer offended him. "Make me a sandwich, will you?" he said, reaching soothingly for her hand. "I've got to go to Gasparra's. We've formed a committee."

She turned pale with terror lest he should have done something stupid again: "Good God, what business have *you* on a committee?"

"Now be sensible and listen to me," he said gravely. "Professors Heidemann, Schiele, Innocent Rex, and Habermann have retired, and are to some extent in a state of religious conversion."

"In a state of religious conversion . . . ? Do you seriously mean that?" gasped Clara.

"Surely I do," he assented. "Well, now the position of president of the Art Association is vacant, and if I join the Committee for the Protection of the Art Treasures, I'm to be president. Gasparra promised me that on his word of honor. I'm not the poor devil I once was."

"Goodness, don't puff out your chest any more than it is now!" she jeered.

Leaning over the table, he whispered: "If I'm the president of the Art Association, I can sell anything, don't forget that."

"It's all a lie, you liar! You can sell any picture you want to now, without the Art Association. Tell me what you're lying for!"

"Why shouldn't I be president for once?" asked Rudolphi, now obviously offended.

"Aha! To show off. I see. It's all right with me. Feed candy to the monkey! But what is this Committee for the Protection of the Art Treasures? What art treasures?"

"The Christian paintings from the early Renaissance that have been transferred to the Town Hall—because the old museum has been condemned."

"Is it those you want to protect? From what?"

"From artillery fire. You just don't know anything."

"Well, my goodness, who's going to fire at the paintings?"

"The government," replied Rudolphi, getting up, putting on his coat, and reaching for hat and gloves.

"All nonsense," cried Clara with awful premonitions, "thought up by Gasparra so that you'll make an impossible fool of yourself. If there are Urbanites in the Old Town, and the government shoots a couple of shells at them, are *you* the one to interfere with the government?"

Probably she would have stayed him by force, or perhaps by threats. But reasonable considerations, even such weighty ones as Clara was urging, offended his manly pride. *He* let himself be taken in? Preposterous!

Walking very erect, high hat on his head, the artist of the Faustite faction departed without a word.

He got into a cab. Slightly tipping his top hat, like the President of the Republic when the sentries present arms, or the members of the Academy in reviewing a parade—slightly tipping his top hat, I repeat, for which there was no reason, as the coachman was not looking at him at all, Professor Paul Rudolphi, painter and sculptor to the Christian government, blond, obese, a person exhilarated and unsuspecting, climbed into the cab. As president of the Art Association, made a fool and an accomplice of by the Iron Phalanx, he would sign at Gasparra's house a petition against letting the government generals shell the "precincts of the Old Town, sanctified by irreplaceable treasures of Christian art," with howitzers.

He was unsuspecting, for he knew nothing of the already historic struggles in Academy and cabinet between the radicals, who regarded Urban as Enemy Number One of the state, and Jacob Willert's followers, who so regarded the Iron Phalanx. Nor did he know anything about the shifting fortunes of these struggles, and how the ranks had been jumbled. Just about this time the outline for a speech before the Academy had been found among the literary papers of the assassinated John Henry Merckel; it was the washerwoman's son's last work.

If Rudolphi had been acquainted with it, he would have behaved differently.

The speech, unfinished, read as follows: "We have no program. We shall attempt no conspicuous change, no overt or covert act of violent innovation, except for the three prohibitions of splendid phrases, corrupt teachers, and cowardice in face of evil. These three prohibitions, however, we shall issue without preamble, without explanation or justification, without a word of comment. They are bound to cause offense, shaking of heads, nay horror; and even a faint gleam of understanding of what we intend can hardly be expected for years from the present generation, whose educated young people have deserted in swarms to the demagogues. They are blind with enthusiasm for the demagogues' splendid phrases; stultified to the point of animality by overestimating externals; like women in their slavish delight at arbitrary despotism; cowards and masochists in their desire to eat the bread of charity; but unruly in their urge to trample the weak and be trampled by the strong.

"Where, may I ask, are Mr. Borstel and his seven hundred draftsmen, designers, engineers, directors, the inventors of modern rapid-firing guns, the builders of our machine miracles, the discoverers and drivers of the modern vehicles propelled by internal-combustion motors? May I ask if Senator Borstel and his heroic pioneers have rushed to the colors to defend the fatherland against the rabble?

"Well, my dear sirs, I should guess that among the seven hundred pioneers of machine civilization—or, to put it differently, of progress—there are perhaps twenty who have *not* gone over to Urban, being as it were seduced into clinging to tradition by birth and upbringing and a thousand freaks of chance. But these few exceptions do not count; I might almost say that they have missed their calling. For he who has wholeheartedly made a calling of machine civilization or progress was on Urban's side before there was any Urban, and must therefore be ready to fight for the world of thoroughgoing progress, 'the world of tomorrow.'

"But we, who on hearing the word 'progressive' immediately think of paralysis (which is also 'progressive'), we, who are convinced that the intellectual destruction of the human race will follow unless someone opposes the progressive paralysis of our time—we regard even the martyrdom of Laurenti's expedition to Moenckeberg as a small sacrifice if it will halt for an appreciable time the machinations of the machine worshipers and their demagogues.

"What is the aim of our three prohibitions? They aim to restore the dignity of man and his freedom of decision, which proceeds from the old law.

"How, by what means are we to accomplish this? By regarding machine civilization as what it is—an incidental; by putting it in the humble place that rightfully belongs to it as a servant of the lowly desire for comfort. Whereas it is natural now for a simple person to consider machine civilization (or progress) sublime, in ten years we want children to be saying in their sleep: *Progress is barbarism!*"

BOOK THREE

THE DISCIPLES OF EMMAUS; AND THE FALL INTO HELL, ALSO CALLED THE AFTERTHIRST

X

LATE on the evening of May 4, Urban's advance guard was approaching the riverbank; Colonel Bruns, feigning a heavy attack, was shelling the capital from across the eastern branch of the river; one shell exploded before the trench of Tobias Witt, translating him to a better world. Hesse was on a camp cot in the basement of Police Barracks I, and Urban was sleeping for the last time with Ida Bessonoff, candidate for death.

Late that evening, then, the Iron Phalanx assembled its elite in the grand house of Professor Gasparra to impart momentous news, recruit members, and hold divine service for the Disciples of Emmaus in the lecture hall on the second floor.

When Rudolphi entered the big salon on the ground floor of the artist's villa, he found it furnished with two corner pulpits, an altar, Bibles, crucifixes, and silver candlesticks; but the prayer benches had been removed, and in their stead propaganda literature was spread out on two large tables in the center, while two beautiful young girls, coming to meet each caller, held out their collection boxes, curtsied, and praised "the new Christian organization" with eyes, voice, and splendid teeth.

"The Christian League for Sunday Mortals, an Association for the Recreation and Amusement of the Poor, requests your support and valued membership, sir," said one of the pearly-toothed girls, leading Rudolphi to her table.

The artist, in high spirits after his champagne dinner at noon and his triumphant resistance to his spouse, could not say no. His eyes on the fair one's lips, he heard her say: "The League of Sunday Mortals, sir, in accordance with the principles that the Archbishop has expounded in his *Gospel of the Sunday Mortal,* will undertake the expense of amusing the poor on holidays, and work for the transformation of large private gardens and parks into places of public amusement. Thus those who live on the shadowy side of life will be refreshed by nature and entertainment, and will return the more joyfully to their weekday work. Will you not enter your valued name on this list, sir? At its head you see the leading personages of our society, Oscar Koenig with twenty-five thousand thalers, Senator Kuehn with fifteen; if you please!" The beauty handed him a pen and held a leather armchair for him.

"See here, my child," said the affable artist, while Mayor Heidemann and "Professor" Innocent Isabella Rex closed in from the windows and a green-topped conference table behind his back, "you do talk very nicely, but it isn't so. A good friend of mine who was unfortunately shot by accident has read me parts of the *Gospel of the Sunday Mortal.* It doesn't say anything about the poor, and certainly nothing about recreation and amusement."

"Just a moment, Professor," Heidemann interposed, "the Sunday Mortal, I believe, is a mortal who seeks recreation."

"Not according to the Bishop and his *Gospel,*" Rudolphi contradicted.

"Because what the Bishop proclaims is all theory; we go by considerations of actual practice . . ."

"The practice of Christian humanity," added Innocent Rex, offering the painter his hand with a bow.

"Your valued name, sir, please!" the young lady employee requested, bringing her bosom close to him as he sat. The painter, reflecting that she was a poor wretch working on a percentage, signed his name, put "ten thalers" after it, and got up to go over to the other table. Here he looked into the eyes of a long-legged brunette in pale make-up, beaming at him—a model for Judith who might be summoned to the studio when his wife was away. "One of those that screech," thought the master, "because she promises more than she keeps." Her emaciation would have delighted a necrophile. The Ballet of the Lifeless Brides occurred to him as the pale brunette recited her piece: "Actions speak louder than words, says the proverb. Everyone who joins our great Christian society, the Association to Restore the Honor and Fortune of Sufferers from the Old Regime, proves not by words but by actions his devotion to the victorious Christian government. Let us therefore put aside the works of darkness and gird on the armor of light! Twenty-four branch associations, already established in the peaceful central provinces, demonstrate the unceasing activity of the presiding committee, and touching letters of thanks from those compensated prove how many tears have been dried. It is our task to wipe away the tears from the eyes of the despotically humiliated so that there shall be no more death, neither sorrow nor crying, neither shall there be any more pain: for the former things are passed away, Revelation 21, 4!"

Heidemann and Rex, protesting their devotion with repeated bows, called the government painter's attention to the interesting letters from those compensated. Rudolphi leafed through them; they were written in the style of *North's Love Letters* and the various "Letter Writers for All Occasions." He found the same name, Dolores McCarthy, five times.

"It is not the committee," declared Heidemann, "that was guilty of this deception." He said the greensick girl had traveled around, and actually received the sums she spoke of from five different branch associations. The tenderheartedness of the pious governing committee, added to the fact that she had actually been a victim of injustice, outweighed her transgressions. Innocent Rex wiped both eyes with a multicolored bandanna the size of a table napkin.

The painter, who was getting hungry again, cared nothing about the wily McCarthy girl, whom he had painted as a gleaner during the

months of her fame—the less so since his attention was now attracted
to three other objects: the dark-haired saleslady with the beauty spot
on her white-powdered cheek; a rhythmic stamping with musical accompaniment on the second floor, which made the glass chandelier
shake; and the sideboard, covered with choice edibles, that occupied
the whole long wall on the left.

Finally the claims of the flesh triumphed. Standing at the sideboard,
most respectfully assisted in the choice of dainties by Rex and Heidemann, he ate three rolls spread thick with caviar, sardines, Russian
sturgeon, a substantial slice of roast beef, and was unable to resist when
the butler offered him boiled eggs whose yolks had been made into
mayonnaise stuffing in the northern fashion. So that these heavy
victuals might be the more readily digestible, he drank some very old
aquavit and several French cognacs. For alcohol properly refined, the
painter declared with scientific nicety, dissolves adhesive substances,
particularly the greasy ones, breaks up their heaviness, and draws the
walls of the stomach together; therefore our forebears were perfectly
correct in saying that one should not eat without drinking.

"Exactly my principle," agreed the barrel-shaped Innocent, taking
a quick one himself. "Nature must always be our guide."

"Your very good health, Professor—and do we understand each
other?" cried the ecstatic Rudolphi, touching glasses with the com-
poser of chorales. "Do we understand each other? Are we, then, to be
friends?"

"One heart and one soul!" said Innocent Isabella, and was obliged
to take out his bandanna once more.

But Mayor Heidemann, who had not been drinking with them,
urged him to sign, and all three went over to the green-topped conference table, where Felice Gasparra had the petition ready, engrossed
on costly parchment, and sealed with the seal of the Art Association.
The butler, followed by a footman carrying a three-legged silver cooler
full of ice, brought in bottles of champagne.

Rudolphi, having embraced Felice Gasparra as a friend and fellow
worker, signed in the indicated space, appending (to signalize his
resolution) a flourish so emphatic that the pen broke. The butler had
already filled the glasses, and the alliance was confirmed with bows
and clinking of glasses while Gasparra tossed in an elegant *"Quod felix
faustumque sit,"* and Rudolphi toasted the noble Muse of Art.

"If art and life come in conflict, I always say, 'Long live art!'" declared the government painter, growing truculent.

"General von Hesse unfortunately feels otherwise," Heidemann whispered cautiously.

But Rudolphi brushed the police commandant aside with a sweep of the arm: "Ridiculous. In the dispute between Mayor Heidemann and General Hesse I'm altogether on Heidemann's side—matter of course, fully understood! Do you hear?" He was beginning to yell so loud that Professor Habermann, coming downstairs from the religious services, went over to the conference table to make peace.

Innocent Rex introduced him: "Professor Habermann, editor of the *Monthly Review for Art and Life,* a first-class publication in gentility and deep thinking."

"Then you're the man for me, sir," cried Rudolphi, delighted. "Gentility has always been my ideal. Decent tablecloth, Sèvres china, footmen behind each chair, hot plates, cold beer glasses—always my ideal, I've accomplished it at last. Do we understand each other?"

"Perfectly, Professor," declared Habermann.

"Now read it out loud, the whole petition!" Rudolphi requested of his former competitor. "Lesh hear ever'thing good old Felice has cobbled together thish time!"

Obsequious mirth rewarded the government painter's witticism.

Seizing the parchment, covered with signatures, Gasparra read out: "To His Excellency, Secretary of State and Deputy of the President, Henry, Count Savoya."

"Splendid! Marvelous formulation!" Rudolphi interrupted.

Gasparra went on: "The art lovers of the entire country and the Committee for the Protection of the Christian Works of Art in particular make outraged protest——"

Once again enthusiasm carried away the government artist: "'Outraged protest'! Marvelous! Absolutely my opinion! Brother Gasparra! Your very good health!" He drained his glass and hurled it to the floor.

"—outraged protest against every attempt to bring destruction by bombardment with heavy howitzer shells to the irreplaceable relics preserved in the Old Town. We would point out that the heavy guns have a dispersion of a thousand feet even in a slight wind, so that limitation of fire to military objectives is impossible.

"A cry of indignation echoes throughout the civilized world, and causes the hearts of the undersigned to tremble . . ."

"Magnificently formulated—not a comma needs changing! Why, the thing will hit like a bombshell!" cried Rudolphi, beckoning to the butler to refill the glasses.

A special messenger in green uniform with a big yellow-leather pouch by his side had been summoned meanwhile. To him Gasparra handed the letter: "My carriage is outside. You're to have this letter at the President's mansion in ten minutes, and get a receipt."

"Nonsense!" said Rudolphi. "Go straight to General Hesse, Police Barracks I! Do you hear?"

"Police Barracks I, General von Hesse," repeated the young man.

"Yes, sir! And you tell him: 'Professor Rudolphi is waiting for an answer!' "

"Professor Rudolphi is waiting for an answer," replied the messenger, and was dismissed.

On the second floor, meanwhile, Diana Rose, who had forsaken the Urbanites again out of hatred for her insulter, Emil, was conducting the service of the Disciples of Emmaus jointly with Professor Schiele.

The two of them stood on a spacious platform against the long rear wall of the hall, the lady to the right of the crucifix, to the left old Schiele, who had condescended to become the reciter of prayers in order to save his family and position. Diana, "in religious ecstasy," had raised both arms, and was dancing in place, humming, and sometimes giving little cries. The musicians, three flautists from the opera orchestra, were striving to produce religious music worthy of the ecstatic gestures and hip twistings.

As long as Diana was at work, emulated by the worshipers, some standing, some sitting on the long benches before the platform, Professor Schiele remained immobile, as if God's presence could be compelled by a supreme concentration of will. His eyes were fixed on a black spot that Gasparra had painted on the opposite wall. It was the ancient, easily learned ritual for invocation of a deity, and Diana could already point to great successes in the first two rows. It is easy to transport the middle class into ecstasy; thus a tall lady bookkeeper in the first row had undone her hair and her blouse, scattered her black hairpins all around, and was holding up her old face and dry bosom to God. Another nameless one, with spectacles, shapelessly fat

and dripping perspiration, put her hands on her hips and was execut-
ing a trampling dance of her own invention in the open space before
the first row of benches. Others in the first two rows were following
the ceremonial only by lifting up their arms, smiling ecstatically, and
uttering a chant of little cries. Nicholas Edwin Schiele had hung his
jacket over the bench, rolled up his shirt sleeves, and stretched both
bare arms perpendicularly upward; he remained in this position as
rigid as an Egyptian saint on a column.

While the flautists redoubled their efforts, Diana Rose sang:

> *To my dear Lord I sing: I am*
> *Surely a white and spotless lamb.*
> *Let thy mercy still increase,*
> *Oh Little Jesus, Lord of Peace.*

But she was able to fascinate only the front rows; further to the
rear, where sliding glass walls gave a view of the staircase leading up
from the ground floor, worshipers had broken up into anxiously whispering groups, and were spreading the news: "Five thousand arrests!
Hesse's raging like a mad bloodhound."

"The lunatic villages are belching forth dead men. Urban has released Electrical Director Koehler and three hundred other men. A
ship is waiting for them at Neuhafen to carry them to the western
coast. They're like corpses."

"Hesse's had a row with the Bishop, because each one wants to be
boss. The Bishop has fled or been killed!"

"Why with the Bishop?"

"The Bishop demanded the dissolution of the Penitent Congregation—you know, they call themselves the Penitents of the Last Judgment."

"Is that the sect that's always attacking the churches and saying
that anyone who goes to church is of the devil?"

"Right. That's why the Bishop demanded that General Hesse
should dissolve the Penitent sect. 'Dissolve the Penitents,' he said.
'Who's giving orders around here,' Hesse yelled, 'you or I?' 'I am,'
said the Bishop. He hasn't been seen since. You know—the way Director Koehler disappeared, and Dr. Grau."

"Well, have the Penitents been dissolved?"

"Listen to what I'm telling you! When the Bishop disappears, **Henry** the Franciscan goes to Hesse: 'Dissolve the Penitents!' he says. 'No!' yells Hesse. 'As long as *I'm* in command of the police, no Christian is going to be touched!' 'So you call *them* Christians,' says the Franciscan, 'when they insult the Church every day?' 'All sectarians are Christians,' Hesse shouts; 'Christianity has taken refuge in the sects!' 'Is that so?' says Count Savoya in his monkish cowl. 'In that case I guess I won't be needed after today.' 'So you won't,' says Hesse, and has him arrested."

The glass partitions were pushed back. Professor Habermann, Innocent Rex, Felice Gasparra, and Rudolphi came into the hall of prayer; Diana Rose, soaked with perspiration from her devotions, gave Professor Schiele a glance asking him to take over her task.

"Take your seats, my dear votaries," cried Professor Schiele, handing Diana an open book. "We are to hear the words of the prophet Jeremiah in the Ninth Chapter." And with carefully rehearsed singsong voices Professor Schiele and Diana Rose read in unison, while the flute music faded:

Yet hear the word of the Lord, O ye women, and let your ear receive the word of his mouth, and teach your daughters wailing, and every one her neighbor lamentation.

For death is come up into our windows, and is entered into our palaces, to cut off the children from without, and the young men from the streets.

Professor Schiele raised one arm. They all rose, and Diana sang: "This is the will of the Lord. His will be done. Hallelujah!"

The congregation: "His will be done. Hallelujah!"

Professor Schiele: "His will be done. Hallelujah!"

The congregation: "His will be done. Hallelujah!"

While Diana and Schiele recited alternately, the congregation repeated the verse fifty-five times, as the rule required. Bodies grew weary, brains grew weary, and resistance to the coming of God flagged also.

Rudolphi, still sober in his drunkenness, thought that Urban might perhaps have learned from these sects his technique of catchwords repeated a thousand times over. Then, sinking down upon a bench, he fell asleep.

Now Diana Rose said: "Listen, dear votaries, to the Lord's words
to Jeremiah in the Ninth Chapter.

" 'Thus saith the Lord, Even the carcasses of men shall fall as dung
upon the open field, and as the handful after the harvestman, and none
shall gather them.

" 'Let not the wise man glory in his wisdom, neither let the mighty
man glory in his might: But let him that glorieth glory in this, that
he exerciseth lovingkindness and righteousness: for in these things I
delight, saith the Lord.' "

Professor Schiele: "His will be done. Hallelujah!"

The congregation: "His will be done. Hallelujah!"

This time they varied the repetition, taking turns with Schiele, with
only the hallelujah repeated, but a hundred times.

A blissful smile overspread the votaries' faces when Professor Schiele
proclaimed after allowing two minutes' rest: "As our first song we
shall sing today *Be With Us, Holy Ghost.*"

The flautists changed their sheet music: the wild, jolly rhythm of
the song made the singers ecstatic:

> *Be with us, Holy Ghost! Be with us, Holy Ghost!*
> *Let our hearts to thee be host, to thee be host!*
> *Be with us, Holy Ghost, let our hearts to thee be host,*
> *'Twould be sad that life is fleeting*
> *If we could not hope for meeting!*
> *Hallelujah, Hallelujah, Hallelu-u-u-u-jah!*
>
> *Lo he rides before us now,*
> *Exalted of visage, so it seems,*
> *Drawn by noble steeds, see how*
> *They walk upon his radiant beams.*
>
> *Summoned by the swelling sounds*
> *Hallelujah, Hallelujah!*
> *He burst forth from heaven's bounds*
> *Hallelujah, Hallelujah!*
> *And came to those far gone in sin.*
> *A blaze of glory frames him in.*
> *Hallelujah, Hallelujah, Hallelu-u-u-u-jah!*

Ah, this time to hold him fast
Let your shouting never end.
Shout ye, young and old, at last,
For great glory He shall send.

Like wine, swiftly as an arrow
The Holy Ghost speeds to my marrow.
The Holy Ghost is here, aha!
Hallelujah, Hallelujah, Hallelu-u-u-u-jah!

Hallelujah, Hallelujah!
Hallelujah, Hallelujah!
Hallelujah, Hallelujah!
Hallelujah, Hallelujah!

The singing was drowned in uproarious shouts of *Hallelujah* and uncontrolled screams. The uplifted arms, shaken like twigs in a thunderstorm, seemed at once to beseech and to threaten the Deity; five ladies sank down upon their benches, foaming at the mouth; others rolled on the ground; others again, heads and arms held heavenward, emitted a long-drawn roar, like that of patients after an operation as they come out of the anesthetic. Rudolphi was snoring.

When the enthusiasm died down a little, Professor Schiele arose and distributed "the second chorale of today's services" to all the votaries: "Brethren and sisters, we will now sing the household hymn of the Disciples of Emmaus, composed for us by Brother Innocent Isabella Rex."

Perhaps owing to the exhaustion of the votaries, this song did not stir the enthusiasm that the song of the Holy Ghost had done:

Whom did God's Son cherish first?
To whom are His arms flung wide?
Whom does He keep from hunger and thirst,
Gladly, as through this vale we stride?
Whom does He call? Let none gainsay us—
The assembled Disciples of Emmaus.
Hallelujah!

Who strolls the length of heaven's walls
Yet never tumbles overboard?
From the way of grace who never falls,
Upheld by angels and His word?
Whom does Jesus bid be gay? Us,
The assembled Disciples of Emmaus.
Hallelujah!

The sinners are parted from the good
By the Lord's unbending law.
Who goes with us, the lamblike brood,
Who'll toss himself in Satan's maw?
Heavenward march—He'll not betray us
Assembled Disciples of Emmaus!
Hallelujah, Hallelujah, Hallelujah!

Hallelujah, Hallelujah, Hallelujah, Hallelujah!
Hallelujah, Hallelujah, Hallelujah, Hallelujah!
Hallelujah, Hallelujah, Hallelujah, Hallelujah!
Hallelujah, Hallelujah, Hallelujah, Hallelujah!

As the mill wheel, brought to a standstill, rattles on for a few more beats; as the lover surprised by a knock on the door cannot at once leave off; as the thoughts in the lonely thinker's brain wing their way onward when he lies down to sleep beside his spouse—so, starting in the hindmost rows, the hallelujahs faded away, drowned out by rapidly spreading cries of terror. Fervor crawled away and hid, the garments opened to God were buttoned up again, jackets were put on, arms lowered. Some one of the disciples must have looked around and given a worldly cry quite different from the prevailing ecstasy, for in an instant they were all facing about, except for the reciter on the platform and Professor Rudolphi, who was snoring.

Federal Police were lined up all along the rear wall and in front of the side doors; escape was cut off. True, they had their helmets in their left hands as regulations required when in rooms used for religious purposes; but their dangling right hands grasped pistol handles, and forefingers curved over triggers. Anyone who had thought of whisking through the hidden door, calling out God's name, would have been in paradise sooner than he intended. Nor was much time allowed for the sober second thought that there was no danger whatever, since after all Hesse had told the Bishop that Christianity had taken refuge in the sects, and woe to him who laid hands upon a Christian. However, something must be wrong, for the man standing before the broad glass door was one of the intimates, Lindequist, now promoted to lieutenant colonel, the "inspirer of the office."

Now he spoke, helmet in hand: "Who is in charge of the services?"

"Here!" said Professor Schiele loudly, giving his name.

"I beg your pardon, Professor, for having disturbed your devotions," said Lindequist. "You can go on at once if two gentlemen whom the Federal Commissioner of Public Safety wants to see will come with me of their own accord."

Gasparra, as host to the congregation and master of the house, now stepped forward: "Who are the two gentlemen, if I might ask? My name is Gasparra, Felice Gasparra."

"You're one of them," cried Lindequist, beckoning to two N.C.O.'s. Between them, the artist of enlightenment vanished through the glass door. A noise was heard, as challenging as a tree trunk being sawn through amid this mute dismay: Rudolphi's snores.

"Who's snoring so loud?" cried Lindequist. Old Schiele replied with a smile of pride: "Professor Rudolphi, the painter and sculptor to the government."

The lieutenant colonel cried out, "He's the other!" Two N.C.O.'s grabbed Rudolphi, and although he resisted and yelled, "Guess you don't know me, huh? I'm Rudolphi!" he was dragged out amid the laughter of the Carpenters, who thereupon holstered their pistols and left the prayer meeting.

"Thank you very much, Professor," Lindequist called upstairs to Schiele. "Do please go on, and permit me to share in your devotions for a few moments."

Relieved and beaming, the Disciples of Emmaus lined up before the crucifix, clapping their applause for their courageous reciter, the fatherly shepherd of his poor flock, who had defied the armed multitude while Diana crawled away under a prayer bench.

"Dearly beloved," he cried, spreading both arms, and signaling to the flautists to begin, "we will sing the invocation to the Holy Ghost." Amid the sobbing and trilling of the flutes, arms upraised, with

jubilant little cries from feminine throats, they invoked their God a
second time:

> *Be with us, Holy Ghost, be with us, Holy Ghost!*
> *Let our hearts to thee be host, to thee be host!*
> *Be with us, Holy Ghost, let our hearts to thee be host!*
> *Hallelujah, Hallelujah, Hallelujah, Hallelujah,*
> *Hallelu-u-u-u-jah!*

Otto von Hesse lay on an army cot by the wall next to the yard
in the hall-like basement of Police Barracks I, formerly the uniform
room, now cleared out and transformed into the central command
headquarters of the supreme command. As he lay there he had the
following dream vision.

Civilians were being uniformed—quite naturally, for an order had
been issued; and this was where the uniforms were being given out.
The basement windows were barred, and oil lamps hung swaying
from the ceiling; the clerk was distributing pay books and identification tags to workmen from the industrial quarters, moving awkwardly
in heavy uniforms. Standing before open lockers the soldiers traded
misfit caps and sword straps. They sliced off fat slabs of bread, spread
on drippings, and then a slice of bacon—all very wisely, since there
was a hard march to the trenches in the eastern lowland ahead of
them. Indecent postcards, gaudy, bare bosoms and feminine posteriors,
were tacked up on the inside of the locker doors, beside photographs
of General Spitta, who would scarcely be still alive, because some bitch
of a woman had killed him. She must have been mad at him; perhaps
he didn't give her what she wanted.

The sergeant, the ugly, square-faced fellow whom the men called
"Pig-cheek," came up to the clerk's table with Tobias Witt, to whom
for sheer spite he had given trousers that were too long and an over-
size cap: "Put down that this malingerer is to go in the front lines
on account of mental disease, by the general's order. The mentally
diseased ought to be exterminated."

"But the general gave orders that mental disease isn't a disease at
all," Tobias Witt defended himself.

"And furthermore," said the sergeant to the clerk, "furthermore we'll report this impudent swine for punishment because he had the impudence to complain to the general."

The clerk handed Tobias a red rose, which he fastened to his lapel as an identification tag. Then all at once privates Frank and Emil, Urban's bodyguards, were standing beside him with a mastiff as big as a calf between them, confirming the sergeant's diagnosis.

"He's a very dangerous madman," said Frank.

"Very dangerous," nodded Emil.

"I'm not dangerous, gentlemen," Tobias protested.

"Didn't you bite my dog in the leg in a fit of progressive paralysis?"

"Are you gentlemen," Tobias smiled, "condescending to have your little joke at my expense?"

"He's pretending amnesia."

"Head up, so that we can look you in the eye. An honest man looks others in the eye."

Said Tobias, tossing his head in rapt ecstasy: "Let us be comrades and friends! If we are friends, the boots will not pinch, and the ill-smelling boot grease will be like roses!" But the comrades had already gone off, first opening Tobias' cartridge pouch, abstracting cigarettes, chocolate, and matches, and distributing them among themselves.

With a cry of horror Tobias rushed into the corner of the room, which was now not the barracks basement, but the rear transept of Geisenheim Cathedral. A milky light came in through the tall Gothic windows, and the pious General Hesse was standing at a table beside the paneled wall, with the closed side portal at his left hand, a simple wooden door leading into the vestry at his right. He kept signing one large blank sheet after another, and thrusting it with his left hand through a hole made to serve as a letter slot in the wall, whence the papers were snatched one after another by a strong wind, and blown away.

Tobias, taking off his peakless cap and wiping the sweat from his brow, reached for the general's arm, panting from his run.

But the general shook his head: "Just a minute. I've got to sign the death warrants. Caught in the wind, they are fluttering overland like birds."

"Why the humiliation of this cap," the young soldier complained, "these far too heavy trousers, these stinking boots, and the sweat of disgust on my skin, a white gull crying out for wind and water? Do you hear me, Brother Hesse of Marienhall? I was in your secret service for two years."

"Any more complaints?" asked the general.

Tobias lifted Hesse's silken cap with its gleaming visor to his lips and kissed it: "You've given me your cap already; it's soft and smells like early morning. So I think I'd better go; otherwise someone will take the rose away from me."

He opened the Gothic side door and stood amazed by the splendor of the view. Close before the door rose a steep, wooded hill, crowned by a simple chapel gleaming in the sunrise. A winding forest path went up the hill to the chapel. Wooden Madonnas under little roofs, places for contemplation, stood by the wayside.

Tobias' glance wandered: "Where is she? I walked along this path with her at daybreak, hand in hand, before work, and neither hand let the other go. No, neither hand let the other go."

"The light is reddening before Colonel Bruns' gun barrels. Come back!"

"First they said we were to volunteer. My wife said, 'You shan't go!' I didn't go. Then they said, 'Anyone that's ever served in the army is going to be called up,' and they snatched me from my wife. Do you want to see her?"

Tobias opened the door into the vestry. It led into a bright, sunlit bathroom. A gentle young woman, her nut-brown hair in thick braids, rose from the tub, wrapping herself tighter in her bath towel and looking at Tobias in surprise.

Then the wrath of God rent the cathedral roof with one whistling blow. Tobias flung up both arms and fell over backward. He had scarcely touched the ground before the woman was beside him, while the bath towel dropped off; embracing his body, she picked him up with one vigorous beat of her wings, and shot up like an arrow in the fire of the broad, blazing lightning, into the opened heavens.

A howitzer shell fired clean over the Old Town had exploded in the yard of the police barracks. "Where did the scoundrels get the cannon?" said General Kaempf, stepping to the barred window. The glass, shattered into a thousand fragments, lay scattered on the floor. Orderlies hurried up with brooms. Lieutenant Colonel Lindequist was standing before Hesse, who sat up, awakened by the noise. From the open door of the telegraphers' room the telegraph sent its ticking into the command headquarters.

"Orders carried out," reported Lindequist. "The two painters have been arrested and brought in."

Hesse could not remember: "What painters?"

"Gasparra and Rudolphi."

"What did you arrest them for?"

The Lieutenant Colonel took the order for arrest from his cuff: "Here. Because of their treasonable petition to the government."

The Federal Commissioner for Public Safety pushed the paper aside: "Oh, you and your papers, man! How *could* you arrest Rudolphi, our own man for the past twenty years? Have you gone quite off your head?"

"This is too much!" Kaempf intervened. "This fellow signs, and on the top line at that, a petition whose meaning and intent is to let General Susa march unopposed into the Old Town."

"But that isn't why he signed it! That isn't why, you simpleton!" Hesse yelled at the Minister of War.

"Why else? Can you explain?"

"Because his heart bleeds, you bumpkins, when he thinks of those precious works, the irreplaceable paintings and statues from a day that will never return. Orderly!"

Two lance corporals rushed up and got Hesse ready to go out.

"You don't know Rudolphi. *I* know him—oh, I'm utterly ashamed. I shan't sign anything more. Sign your own dirty work!"

"He paints wenches too, in fact, very worldly ones—even that Mc-Carthy tart . . . just to help you keep your shirt on, my son," said Kaempf.

Hesse donned his cap, pulled on his gloves, and spoke in a voice of such shame, reverence, and suffering that no one contradicted: "Certainly he paints worldly pictures, too. But when he sees the work of a great master, I know from my own experience that his heart quivers with a longing for a world which is gone. Merckel writes in his diaries, 'Rudolphi's art is never timely or interesting, because it is never merely skillful imitation: it is always worship, an inquiry into the meaning of life.' I've seen Rudolphi standing before a painting by an old master that he has a copy of in his studio. Other people ignore such things. When *he* looked at the picture—it's called the

Fall into Hell, by Roger van der Weyden, the Dutchman—his face was full of joy and anguish: joy at such masterly painting, and anguish at the fall into hell; that is, the question of the meaning of life. Did you take everything away from him—knife, scissors, belt, suspenders, so that he can't do himself any harm?"

"Not his suspenders, Brother General," replied the N.C.O. who had taken Rudolphi to his cell.

"I'll go over there and release him myself. If he's done himself any hurt, heaven help you!" So saying, Hesse went out, slamming the door behind him.

"You're completely covered," said the Minister of War to the alarmed Lindequist. "I can testify that Hesse signed the order for the arrest when in full possession of his faculties."

"Sometimes I'm inclined to doubt whether he still has all his faculties," replied the lieutenant colonel, shrugging his shoulders.

On the far side of the police barrack yard, separated from the winter riding school by greenery, was the unpretentious white, one-story "Strong House," the lockup for political prisoners being held for examination. It had two hundred cells for solitary confinement; there were no common cells. At morning exercise the prisoners walked in a circle twenty paces apart, and the supervision was stricter than in the prisons for "ordinary" criminals. Tortures, however, have never been employed, and if the contrary is nevertheless asserted, the reason may be found in Zorn's and Daruhi's teaching that a judge who employs torture can get out of the prisoner under any circumstances whatever he wants to hear—the truth if he cares to learn it, but also untruths, no matter how fantastic and improbable. For the victim of the torture will say whatever will make the judge terminate it. It is, then, granting a just judge who wants to hear the truth, a sure method of reaching a verdict. Our government has never employed it, and has confined itself to withholding hot dinner from the most refractory prisoners. Within a week they will accuse themselves of the most monstrous crimes for the sake of a hot beefsteak and two glasses of cognac—quite understandably when the nature of my countrymen is taken into account. We are unable to endure hunger for long; how the matter stands with thirst will be seen in a moment.

When the warder opened the heavy iron door and bellowed: "Attention!" Rudolphi was lying on the wooden bench with no blanket, fast asleep in his suit and hat. Before him stood a clay pitcher of water. Toilet facilities for the prisoner were in the cell itself, outdated though this arrangement is. The guard brought the general a chair, took the sleeping man by the shoulder and shook him, and shouted "Attention!" again. It was ten o'clock at night; Rudolphi had slept quietly for two hours. Groaning, he raised his head, put his feet on the floor, and regarded Otto, his admirer.

"Has the Professor asked for anything?" Hesse inquired of the guard.

"Yes, something to drink, fifteen minutes ago; I brought a pitcher of water right away, but he was asleep again."

"Yes, for sheer anguish," Rudolphi murmured. His face was the yellowish gray of the wall, and as crumpled as his clothes.

The police general, unutterably ashamed to see the genius thus maltreated, sent the guard away: "That's how things go, Rudolphi," he said. "Again and again saviors are crucified, or, if they're lucky, cast down among the damned. The fall into hell happens over and over again."

"Do you know the *Fall into Hell* that hangs in my studio?"

"Yes. Naked figures, faces and limbs distorted in anguish, falling into the infernal abyss, with the flames already licking at them."

"The torment of those damned is what I'm suffering now."

"I know," said Hesse, looking at the floor. "It'll all be over tomorrow morning. I can make arrests by myself in an emergency; to release a prisoner I need the signatures of the Secretaries of State."

"The picture is to be taken symbolically," replied the painter, not noticing his friend's consolation. "The fire is the consuming dryness that gnaws at the vitals of a thirsty man. I don't mean an ordinary thirst——"

"Naturally," Hesse interrupted.

"—I mean the scientifically determined thirst that begins a few hours after partaking of alcoholic beverages, because the alcohol draws the internal organs together, and dries them out so that they send forth flames like the jaws of hell—I mean the pangs of thirst. That's the deeper meaning of the picture called the *Fall into Hell,* which is why *I* call it *The Afterthirst,* because it depicts the hellish torments of the thirst that comes afterward. And—here is the interesting and terrible part of it for a man like me, and even for Roger van der

Weyden—it isn't a water thirst, as one of your ignorant guards may suppose, but a beer thirst. I'm speaking the pure truth, which of course one ought not to do; but so learned a man as General Spitta has been known to say the same thing in the presence of witnesses. Good God, how I'm suffering!"

Mr. von Hesse got up so suddenly that his chair crashed to the floor. He pressed the button; the prison warder, who had probably been listening at the door, appeared at once.

"Bring the professor a quart of Pilsner and two herrings!" he said, and left the Strong House without another word, accompanied by the inspector.

"That's what I call talking!" Rudolphi shouted after him, and turned didactically to the warder: "You see how they honor an artist, my dear fellow! Be off with you, and bring *two* quarts of Pilsner! At my expense—we'll drink it up together!"

BOOK THREE

THE DAY OF THE GREAT MAN

XI

THE exact moment when Dr. Urban became deranged can no longer be fixed. All witnesses agree that he was still normal on the afternoon of May 5, a clear, sunny day of the kind that lovers pray for. And, in fact, on the very day of the collapse his mind sparkled more brightly than ever before. This is proved by his speeches, except for the last, which he made at night before the Bodyguard Regiment, drawn up in an open square behind Jacob's hotel and posting inn by the river.

Just before this, Weisse and Lieutenant Colonel Thomas maintain they caught the unguarded words of a major standing directly behind Urban; in this way they believe he discovered the surrender of his western army group to General Baer, which had been concealed from him for twenty-four hours. From this he must have concluded that the fighting was being continued for the sake of honor alone, but no longer with any prospect of victory. Then came the terrible bombardment of the blunt cone, during which he stopped his ears with wax because "the uncivil noise interfered with his reflections." He began to draw the "great figure," and his madness came upon him.

Others maintain that his memory was impaired as early as the afternoon of May 5; he had slept very late at the Bessonoff mansion at Mittelburg. As a matter of fact, he allowed Countess Ida, under sentence of death, and Emil, her guard, to escape to Neuhafen, where the two boarded an emigrant freighter. Clinging to each other in a corner of the cabin, they fled to a Breton port, whence they made their way to Portenuovo with the help of the jewels sewed into corsets and petticoats.

But if we are to believe General Messerschmidt, the doctrine of the "new Lao-tse" is unfolded as clear as a sky-blue day in the five speeches: to the students of the Technical Academy at noon, to the "Old Friends" two hours later, to the farmers at four, to the staff officers by torchlight beyond the river bridge, and to the Bodyguard Regiment at eleven that night. Anything he said all day is perhaps excelled in clarity and prophetic foresight by what he confided at midnight to his private secretary and friend, Weisse, while drawing the great figure; "Golightly's joy," or "the longing for what is cheap and attainable to every human being," is precisely the image of the universe that Messerschmidt calls Laotsian. Never did any of the Iron Phalanx's flowery orators, who after all were reeling down the same road, foresee its end so clearly.

How are we to reconcile with his proved keenness of intellect the fact that he was already unbalanced when he made his midnight confession? We do not know. But it is easy to smile at those now covered by the sod, the honest burgesses of Neuhafen and Mittelburg, for making May 5 a festive day for themselves and their Leader. They celebrated with gay pennants, streamers across the street with the slogans of progress and jollity, tiny flags for the children, and regular flags flying from houses or carried flapping in the May wind by standard-bearers, with brass bands, drummers marching with "echoing tread," with lemonade and sausage stands, far more beggars than usual (but if Urban won they were done for, as everyone "is worth as much as he accomplishes"), with congratulatory delegations and speeches of thanks, and of course all the ladies in white; for the government commander in chief, Frohwein, had been taken prisoner with the rest of the beaten army at Mittelburg.

And so matters really seemed to stand at the time; our own subalterns held the same view, and the younger men could not grasp Frohwein's master stroke in concentrating a ridiculously small rear guard under the protection of the two artillery positions, the Big and Little Bulwarks, drawing the full enemy strength upon himself, so that the main body of his army could escape across the river—an operation that works if you are lucky.

The Leader, awaking about two, discovered by a sidelong glance that his bedfellow had departed; he never mentioned her again. For the rest of his life he never said a single word about any person whatsoever, himself included, for the "great figure" is neither a living being nor a dead body. Nothing but ideas still survived in him. Stepping through the curtain, he went to the window, and looked out upon the sunlit market place, swarming with students in gala dress with flags and standards, and with women and children. The schoolboys clung to street lights and the trees around the monument; roofs, balconies, open windows were crammed with cheering throngs.

"Whom am I supposed to speak to?" he asked in the shower bath.

"To the students of the Technical Academy," replied Weisse.

He pondered. When the bath attendants were dressing him, he said: "To students you have to talk on two subjects, cowardice and heroism, which is to say on the bourgeois—and us."

"Wasn't Adam Faust a bourgeois too?"

"No, Weisse, unfortunately he wasn't. He was an adventurer, like us. The bourgeois sees himself, or possibly his wife and aunt; an adventurer sees visions. You know who the bourgeois is in our day, the archbourgeois? The Iron Phalanx—*that's* the bourgeois for you. He sees himself, he puffs up when the audience claps, he wishes it were always his birthday, and that his wife could always sit on her perch like a parrot, gaped at by the passers-by. He's the center of the world; he has no center outside himself, because he has no vision. I shall be talking about him, or the Iron Phalanx, or Mr. Hoppelkopf (which is all the same thing) when I speak of cowardice. And did you know that cowardice has deadly weapons? So I shall speak to the students about the weapons of cowardice, the weapons of the bourgeois, which incidentally is quite easy. It's easier to talk about baseness than about heroism, because you have more words available."

The footmen opened the glass doors, and the League Leader went out on the balcony. When the outcry of salutation had died away, he made his speech "On Heroism":

"Students of the Technical Academy! I ask that you, who are to be the nation's teachers, shall throw overboard the old concepts and terminology, and bring new concepts of instruction to the new life of which my life is an example. It is a matter of course that the cultivated classes of yesterday, whose intellectual livelihood is breaking down today, should have given pretty names to their frailty. How many pretty names there are to cover up cowardice: tolerance, Christianity, seeing both sides, humanity, democracy, and freedom! If a man doesn't want to fight, he can find pretty names, but he can't fool the people, at least not in the long run. For when the people hear these words, they unfailingly hit on the right answer: Ha-ha! This fellow is making excuses for not fighting. He wants to cover up his cowardice. I could mention a dozen such humanitarian phrases that are used to keep off the subject; but of course everything pretty-sounding is simple cowardice. We haven't been cowardly; we've stood up and taken it. The people aren't so particular what it's for, but they demand that you should stand up and take it.

"But what did the *bourgeoisie* do? First they tried to meet us with a conspiracy of silence. They thought if they pretended we didn't exist, we were sure to perish. You can put down the superfluous in that fashion, but not the necessary.

"So we kept growing stronger.

"Then they made jokes about us. They poured out derision in the newspapers. But he who would be a successful derider must have something he does not deride, something he will go to his death for. Because the crowd not only wants to jeer, it also wants to worship.

"Our friends the *bourgeoisie* who made fun of us had nothing to worship and nothing to defend.

"So we kept growing stronger.

"Finally they told the people that what we had to offer, what we were going to our deaths for, was slavery, violence, and brutality. And the people replied to these well-fed burgesses that they were too cowardly to employ brutality and violence, because they were too craven to fight. The people love a fighter, and forgive his violence and brutality. But they despise the noncombatant, and hate the coward.

"So we kept growing stronger.

"And then, with the world of tomorrow already dawning before our eyes, while others were still sleeping or wavering, one single man rose up against us. Adam Faust was his name, and he realized the great truth that the masses are not to be won by peaceful speechmaking, but by acts of violence and brutality. He had something that he would go to his death for. We have something too—the future of humanity, the world of tomorrow. What he had was . . . the past! Which is the stronger?"

"The future!" said Senator Weisse softly.

"Let's not fool ourselves, Weisse. The past is stronger, if—yes, *if*—it is defended by force of arms. Then, however, it is the strongest power there is, almost unshakable. After all, how could that which the human mind and blood have nourished for tens of centuries help being stronger than the insubstantial fare of 'the future'? If we win today, we shall be able to boast that we have vanquished the strongest force in creation, something almost unshakable: the forcibly defended past."

The Leader's voice did not change to the very end; it had the moving music and powerful resonance of a great bell.

The substance of the speech was criticized for not being calculated to rouse enthusiasm, as the functionaries who remained behind put it. And in fact Urban had scarcely left town in his carriage drawn by white horses to address the oldest party members, the so-called "Old Friends," assembled on the football field of the captured village of Niederwesel, before criticism, disorder, nay debauchery, began. Gold and silver vanished from the Bessonoff mansion, and there was masquerading; the masqueraders departed with loot in their bags for Neuhafen, there to secure steamer tickets by collusion. And as if the Judgment Day of pleasure had dawned, the maids in the mansion allowed the soldiers of Urban's garrison to lead them into lewdness instead of cleaning up the rooms; singing resounded from the dives, drunks lay in gutters and doorways, and housewives abused each other from windows across the street, threatening each other with the gallowses that were being set up in the market place as night fell.

The room in which Countess Bessonoff had been locked up when

she left Urban's bed was opened by Emil, the Lion, with a false key.
She fell upon his bosom: "Save me! He has told me all, I think out of
perversion. I've got my jewelry with me, worth a million francs."

"It's worth six times that. Why don't you tell the truth?"

"How am I to know what it's worth? You'd be my last romance.
I'm getting old—not yet, but soon: my poor heart craves rest."

He showed her his passport: "See my new name? Emilio Branconi,
revivalist preacher."

"Revivalist preacher?"

"Yes, and Vicar General to the South for the Penitent Congregation
of the Last Judgment. A very steady trade, absolutely safe, under the
patronage of His Excellency, the Federal Commissioner for Public
Safety. Want to be my secretary?"

"No! You'll wear me out the way Urban did, only faster. No. I'd
sooner have you give me the pill or the injection you were supposed
to give."

She wept. At this the great, stout man knelt down. "Ida! You must
believe what I tell you now. I could very easily polish you off and
skip out with your diamonds. But . . . I love you."

"Not now, Emil, tonight, I promise you."

"I'm a poor wretch, Ida, a plebeian, I know. But I have a feeling
for higher things. I always used to declaim poetry, even as a child,
and look up at the windows of the mansions, not from envy but in
adoration; and when they play *La Paloma* on the phonograph, I can't
keep back the tears."

And he sang. Freeing his head, taking his arms from around her
hips, his eyes uplifted, his hands uplifted, tears running down his fat
face, he sang: "A white dove wings across the sea."

Ida made one last attempt: "Couldn't we look quietly out of the
window, as married couples do look down on the street of a Sunday,
with our elbows on a pillow, contented and carefree, simply saying,
'Good day, neighbor! How wags the world?'"

She brought her face close to his, and licked his lips with her pointed
tongue. Emil surrendered: "Maybe you're right. Maybe quiet is better
than honor."

So the pair escaped by way of Neuhafen to Portenuovo, the great
seaport of the Southwestern Republics, and thence, thanks to the

jewels, eventually reached the quiet market town of Belrigardo, where
we shall meet them again.

On the football field at Niederwesel, the hills in the background,
the plains before him, his eyes turned eastward, where the dull rumble
of field artillery foretold the crossing of the river, the Leader found
himself reminded of the Blendheim meadow. There, after the defeat
of his partisans in the bloody night of Carolswald, on his way from
old Lienhardt's funeral, he had made the speech that had pleased
Herbert Hilgenfeld so much that he had reprinted it in *The Conservative*. Those were the days! Was the situation worse today—would one
be done for after a few more breaths? Was one not, on the contrary,
better off? One was not the young stripling of yore; one had gathered
experience, and watched old Adam rallying the people around him
with a doctrine absurd from *A* to *Z*. It had been done not by the
doctrine, nonsensical as it was, but by nonsense itself: by the incredible,
the irrational; miracles, and the smile of the Sphinx. Have I seen
through you, old boy? Such were Urban's thoughts. "Oh, Adam Faust,
water preacher and wine drinker," he thought as he stood next to
Weisse on the dais that had been set up, while a white-bearded idiot
droned out something or other. "Water, no mirrors, and abstinence
from dancing girls; you preached law and justice, old Adam, but you
stole the mines; and when dusty mathematicians, the most harmless
of men, defended their axiom of parallels, you were the one who
yelled for a police force 64,000 strong—as if the public peace and good
order were disturbed by mathematics! That was madness, but the
people gaped admiringly; for the people did not want to understand,
but to gape and admire. It was your courage in proclaiming a miracle
as if it were an arithmetic example for children that made you 'the
great President,' causing you to live on in the schoolbooks. There is
nothing more you can teach me, Adam Faust!"

The veterans of the League, bareheaded under umbrellas, with long
frock coats, stood in the meadow in the afternoon glare. The white-
bearded man on the dais between Weisse and the League Leader
made the introduction: "You will certainly feel with me, comrades,
that we would sooner let ourselves be torn in pieces bodily than that
we would see any harm come to our Dr. Urban. Howsoever and in
spite of the fact that no one can ever tell what the future will bring,

and the banner must be held high, though the man may fall, our noble chief has accordingly decided to announce his principles of government to us old fighters and provincial leaders, so that we can do like they say if he himself should be overtaken by a mortal bullet in the victorious struggle ahead. Our Dr. Urban!"

Unfortunately, thought Urban, there are moments when one is out of action, and a pig of a long-tongued female spoils in ten minutes what it took me twenty years to build up. It's because she murdered Spitta and the 197 that Beyer declined my offer. "What was the name of that other hero who fell on account of a woman?" he asked aloud.

"Hercules," replied Weisse; and, the huzzas and shouts of salutation having died away, Dr. Urban finally had to bring himself to speak.

"Silence!" cried the man with the white beard, and the object of their adoration, frowning, commenced in rather a low voice, so that the old fighters crowded closer to the wooden scaffolding. Soon attaining his wonted volume of sound, he opened the second of his speeches that were not calculated for the listener, the speech "On Saying and Doing."

"The past century was the century of calculation and realism; but a modern political movement must be built up entirely on imagination and the incredible. The crowd admires nothing so much as what it itself lacks: wealth and imagination—which is to say, the fabulous. In soberer times it was expected that a statesman's words would roughly coincide with his actions. The present day requires of a politician inscrutability and the smile of the Sphinx.

"And never forget that the people dread nothing so much as the uttering of the truth. We live in a harsh age. But the harsher the reality, the more highly is the illusion esteemed, and the more agreeable the language of dissimulation. If you talk to people, then, tell them pleasant things, and say what they expect. Never be so misguided as to do what you say, lest you be despised as Philistines, flatheads, and bourgeois nincompoops.

"Always say what they expect, and always do what they don't expect. The middle classes expected that we would found athletic clubs, for that they thought was sensible. So we said we were establishing sports associations, but we *did* the fabulous thing that makes people believe and carries them away with admiration: we started an army.

"The crowd wants to *understand* what you *say,* but to *gape at* what you *do.*

"Whenever some prattler let out in the newspapers that we were gathering arms and hiding them in cellars, we always made the same answer: we laughed, shouted *boo!* and said: 'Look at Dr. Urban, the wizard! He can conjure up soldiers out of straw!' By this reply we accomplished two things. We denied the truth which the crowd is too cowardly to listen to, and we elevated the Leader to the rank of a wizard. The people publicly believed what we said and secretly admired what we did.

"For the world always believes what it wishes, and does not believe what is unwelcome. The *bourgeoisie* wish for an orderly state; therefore they believe they have one. This bourgeois faith, which springs from fear of truth and change—in other words, from cowardice—is what has made *us* great. We have grown by our own undismayed insight, and through cowardly reason, which has no insight.

"Therefore you must always preach reason to others, but be at home among miracles yourself. If the bourgeois asks you what you mean to do with that dagger, tell him, 'Peel potatoes,' and he will believe you even with the blood already spurting from his jugular vein. For cowardice has been his companion through life; why should it forsake him in death?

"So you will preach respect for law—for others; likewise love of peace, humanitarianism, and respect for civil rights. But to our men you will preach naked nature, and to our elite a desire to do the unpredictable.

"No man can know who will carry off the victory in this struggle, the more so as the enemy has put himself under a leader whose strength is similar to ours, because it stems from the irrational. If we should win, while I die, do literally as I have just told you—and remember that the natural man is bloodthirsty. But the most natural of all human beings, the human being of naked nature, is woman. Therefore, when the public executions take place on bright, quiet afternoons, the most comfortable front seats for spectators are to be reserved for women of all classes. For they want to hear the cries of the tormented; the great jet of blood from the neck whose head has just been severed will console them for the loss of their husbands; they want to give little cries of horror when punishment overtakes their hated next-door neighbor, while they themselves go on crocheting.

"Thus, my old fellow warriors, in this spirit, if anything should befall me, you are to carry on my work to final victory!"

On the way to Forest Marsh, whose innkeeper, Stramm, was an even fatter pig than Fred Ritter at Liebenau, the Leader's friend chid him. It was true that Weisse, soldier and civil servant by nature, had heard such things said ere this in the intimate inner circle; to him they were witty boasting, fit if need be to amuse a threesome in Bacchic high spirits. But a meadow is not a taproom, and there should be no extravagances in the very face and eyes of the underlings. The abominable decoration of Mittelburg market place with gallowses was the work of the secret service (Section IV), in order to "put down the counterrevolution." Weisse and Thomas protested in vain. The Senator said with his accustomed and permitted frankness that the erection of the gallowses was a "beery notion," and that mentioning it in the address had been a miscarriage of oratory.

Urban made no reply. The suspicion of his Section I, Party Organization, headed by Weisse, and Section III, Military Forces, set up by Thomas, toward Section IV, Secret Service, was as old as the Urbanite movement itself—and as vital to it as salt and leavening to bread. Except for the secret-service agents in their midst, all of Urban's soldiers would have turned into mercenaries, deserting in mid-combat to an enemy who promised higher pay, and the party organizations would have become middle-class voting bodies. Furthermore, according to Urban's doctrine the ruler must not combat the "natural instincts" of envy, malicious pleasure, and vengefulness, but give them a guarded but wide field, whose boundaries are rendered invisible. The secret service was such a field.

"You're going to talk to the big farmers at Forest Marsh," said Weisse as the carriage slowed down (for the road had been ruined by the fighting), "who won't understand a word of what you said to the Old Friends. Farmers are natural people—I don't call a love-crazed female natural—which means they want to shake off the burden of understanding and ruling. If any class ever craved security through submission, it's the farmers. So do tell them what they want to hear! Philosophy and bitterness are what they don't want to hear."

"You mean give 'em sweetness and the poetic touch?" asked the Leader, his lips curling ironically.

"**Certainly**, if you're capable of it today," replied the truthful Weisse. "By which I don't mean to say that you should tell untruths."

"Then you want truth, sweetness, and the poetic touch, all in one! It isn't an easy thing you're asking."

Over the rough village cobblestones they had to drive at a walk; shouts of salutation shattered the air. Mounted military police from the rear guard filled the village, and were fed from mobile soup kitchens, popularly known as "goulash guns."

When the Leader entered mine host Stramm's big dance hall, the faithful Urbanite farmers of the country stood up. To the number of about a thousand they were armed and divided into companies to put down any rebellions that might rise in the rear of the army. The Master of Ordnance in person was teaching them their duties. By this time, at four in the afternoon, the assault on the river was going full tilt; if it were beaten off and a siege became necessary, the provisions and munitions supplies must be safeguarded. The general, ordering "Attention!" made his report to the League Leader, and then conducted him to the stage of the hall, decorated with garlands, red paper streamers braided with silver, and a bust of Urban.

"Stand at ease, or better yet sit down, my old fellow workers," Urban began with a smiling sidelong glance at Weisse as if to recall his half promise, made during the drive, to dispense truth, sweetness, and the poetic touch. "Permit me to tell you something about my life. In my younger days I was an estate foreman, a poor devil who supervised the farm laborers on a great estate, under the supreme command of an estate manager. The morning breeze was blowing; I was twenty years old. Before us were the gray quarters for the help, and leaning against the wall stood farm hands and reapers, then known as mountain runaways, who had come across the frontier from the south for the harvest after having got their wives and the village girls with child. Above us was the monstrous sky, as blue and carefree as we. Out of the arbor of his house came the manager, wiping the last drops of coffee from his beard. Morning greetings were exchanged, the columns were divided up, people clambered aboard, the carts rolled off, turning sharp left around the corner of the long building for the help, and thundering over the wooden bridge across the brook. On the other side the village began. As we drove along the sandy summer road, with dust flying—the first dust of the day—we in the first wagon struck up a song.

"But for my part I was beginning even then to do what I have done all my life, namely to ponder. I pondered why we were so happy, and discovered that we were happy because we were carefree. Sure enough: no responsibility weighed us down; no blame was ours, no harm befell us if the birds ate the seed corn or hail ruined the harvest. We were assigned to duty and under orders; hence, then, our freedom from care, and hence in turn our happiness. So I hit upon this recourse: if all mankind were assigned to duty and under orders, it would sing and laugh as we did. The old earth, which today echoes with the cries of the terrified, would be a paradise. So where there are duty and orders there is no fear, as you, my friends, can see for yourselves if you look around. Where there are duty and orders, there are confidence, health, joking, and laughter; if I'm hungry the great kettle comes swaying up, the canteen dangles from my belt, there are girls standing in doorways at evening, and even death amongst one's comrades is easy.

"Five years afterward I began to talk to people, and whenever I expounded our aim, I had this sight before me: the walls of the gray building for the help; the vigorous men with the wooden pipes, waiting cheerfully for duty and orders; above us the blue of the sky.

"Fear is our ancient enemy. If, however, there is no more fear where you find duty and orders, but only freedom from care; and if almost all men without distinction agree that freedom from care is the one essential condition for happiness; then happiness depends on submission and obedience. For duty and orders imply that the masses, hungry for happiness, will obey some will that assigns duties and gives orders. The people shoulder off their fear upon the commanding will: it now bears the fear; it is the one to be apprehensive lest birds eat the seed corn or hail ruin the harvest. Thus fear and care are the portion of the ruler, carefree bliss that of the subject. Are you ready to fight to attain that goal?"

"Yes, my Leader," cried the thousand farmers, rising.

"Are you ready to go to your death to win a life of freedom from care, based on submission and obedience?"

"Yes, my Leader!" they yelled.

"Do you believe the lies of the revolutionists, who say that any kitchen maid can govern the state and free you of fear?"

"No, my Leader!"

"Then listen to the general's orders."

The shouts of salutation were quite endless; the Leader shook hands with Weisse and the general, and the cheers were redoubled again as dispatch-bearers from Thomas reported victory upon victory: "The river crossed with slight losses; the outskirts of Blumeshof, where a halt has been made, reached in the northwest, the suburb of Florida reached in the southwest. Troops are now feeling their way cautiously forward so that the divisions can maneuver in echelon formation. General Susa, reinforced by Bruns, and unopposed by the enemy, is approaching the assigned position in the north of the Old Town hill. The general assault has been set for nine o'clock."

This was the state of affairs at six in the evening. Urban ordered General Susa to take command of the strongest of the three attacking columns, the southern one, which had penetrated Florida, and to surrender command of the northern group to Bruns. A misfortune had befallen the latter: in a three-hour artillery duel that morning across the broad eastern river branch, the government generals, Leugenfeld and Kraus, exploiting their better knowledge of the terrain, had not only silenced the Urbanite guns, but also spread panic and death among the infantry columns approaching the eastern river by flanking fire from the islands of Goerz and Christopher. Support from the east was no longer being counted on for the general attack on the inner town—hence the remark that Bruns had "reinforced" Susa's force in attacking from the north.

From the sober account of Thomas and Susa (both of whom survived the butchery of the night), published two years later, we learn that as early as noon Urban's military leaders, the Ordnance Master included, had put the correct interpretation upon the silence of our howitzers by the river and the withdrawal of the government detachments into the then uninhabited meadowland beyond Florida and Blumeshof. They had even had some foreboding of the "metaphysical background" of our action. Judging by this it seems as if down in their hearts they actually approved of the "bloody purging of the nation"; for a man seldom has premonitions of that which he does not approve, but fears and hates.

Whether Urban correctly judged the "news of victory" we do not know, as he withdrew soon after midnight into the world of his own visions.

But on the drive through the villages of Molkenberg, Maraun, Rehberg, Rosenthal, Tann, Liebenau, Baerwald, and Grafenstein to the river, and beyond it to Jacob's Beach Hotel and posting inn, he was full of gaiety and gratitude for Weisse's words of praise.

The Senator begged him to speak to the commanders as he had spoken to the farmers, combining truth, sweetness, and the poetic touch; and the Ordnance Master, riding in the same carriage, added that these old officers, faced with a difficult task, had deserved and would continue to deserve to know the true intentions and ultimate aims, without poetic trappings, of the party they might be going to die for. They had no illusions, and were not old women, so by all means let the Leader come out with the unvarnished truth.

Complete darkness had fallen. Standing on a table outside the inn, in the uncertain light of the torches, occasionally outshone by rockets set off by pioneers farther forward, beyond the captured hills along the river, Urban addressed the commanders of the rear guard. The batteries were silent; the general attack had been postponed for half an hour while the southern group felt its way forward into nothingness. The west wind carried away the rattle of skirmishing, and it was so still that the Leader could hear the slap of the ripples against the planking of the riverbank on his left. With eyebrows slightly raised, as was his way when something humorous occurred to him, his right hand at the clasp of his silver sash, he began his speech "On Submission." Smiling, he said to the men under the trees in the beer garden before him:

"The general has ordered me to enlighten you, my commanders and fellow rulers, about the 'true intentions and ultimate aims' of the party. This sounds almost as if I had never given you a candid accounting until now, at the last moment, but had kept the unvarnished truth from you hitherto. Truth, however, is rather like a pyramid of steps or a building with many stories, each of which can hardly be lit up at the same time with equal brightness. To our simple farmers I spoke from a lower floor, as it were, about restoring the joy of life. To you, however, I speak from the topmost platform, and my subject will be our aim, which is only now dimly seen on the horizon. Thus if I should fall in this struggle, you will still be able to keep your eyes in the right quarter during our advance, which no defeat can check.

"Our aim is the peace of all humanity, which we shall accomplish by persuasion toward everyone, by violence toward the powerful if persuasion should not suffice. We urge everyone to submit, and by submission to lay aside the heavier part of his burden through obedience to the inscrutable decrees of the Leader. The comman man can lay off that part, I mean to say, which a merciless megalomaniac Christianity has called 'conscience' or 'responsibility' or 'personality.'

"*Your conscience, tormented mortal, shall weigh you down no more!* is the first article of our creed. Your instincts, which Christianity has called 'animal' because in its megalomania it imagines that an average man can rise above the animals—your instincts are to be appeased so that they will slumber like a she-tiger after eating and mating.

"The Leader will decide what shall be good and what evil; and you men already know his very simple decision: 'Good' is submission, 'evil' is rebellion.

"In this way—I mean by joint subjugation of all those who yearn for submission, because they can no longer endure the uncertainty and perils of freedom—we shall finally realize the old ideal, the 'equality of all those who wear a human countenance.' As for the revolutionists' lie that we do not even want to think about equality, because we allow wealth and the rich to go on living, we could pass over this ancient calumny except that many people still believe it. It is true enough that we, like the revolutionists, have promised to abolish poverty. But the difference is that we mean it honestly, while they mean it dishonestly. For wherever they have temporarily attained power, they have proved that they wanted by no means to abolish poverty, but only wealth. And wealth they have indeed abolished wherever they could. Poverty, however, wretched, crawling, subservient poverty, they have deliberately kept alive so that they could rule the more surely. For a mind like theirs, bereft of imagination, merely babbling the ideas of a vanished century, cannot see that rich and poor are growing ever more alike, so much alike that they scarcely differ even in clothing, and not at all in thoughts and feelings. The headwaiter of the fashionable night club dreams the same dreams as the millionaire he waits on; the elegant lady worships the same prize fighter as her maid. Where now is the difference? For people are distinguished not by the wool or cotton that hangs around their bodies, not by the veal or pork they have eaten, but by thoughts, feelings, and intentions. In my childhood a maid would have been fired if she had not emphasized the difference in classes—which is to say, her remoteness from the gentry—by very thick hand-knitted woolen stockings summer and winter; today mistress and maid borrow each other's silk stockings, and the Bishop has said—against me, but quite truly—that the rich have strewn forth a wealth our fathers did not even dream of.

"We have no notion of abolishing this wealth, for precisely the wealth that the rich disperse among rich and poor is what has broken down the barriers and shaken the last apparently impregnable bulwark of inequality. The mistress of the house who exchanges silk stockings with her maid exchanges not stockings alone, but thoughts, feelings, yearnings. They worship the same prize fighter: both wish they might sit in costly furs and paste diamonds like gaudy birds upon a perch, gaped at by the passers-by. You know that the same thing may be said of the millionaire's son, and to a greater degree of the millionaire's daughter, the creator and pillar of modern culture.

"It is obvious, then, that wealth cannot be what stands in the way of our ideal, the equality of all men. On the contrary, increasing wealth is the greatest leveling force of our age. But *we* know what bars the road of equality; it is the arrogant will of the individual to judge his own actions, to be responsible for his own life, to prepare for his own death, to stand alone like a tree in a meadow. It is 'personality' that stands in the way of equality; personal conscience declines to be ranged in the mass. Calling itself 'Christianity' and proclaiming itself as a model that must be followed on pain of public contempt, it has betrayed the masses, yearning for security, into the peril of freedom. Not the rich man but the solitary man who claims to be irreplaceable, the unmanageable, self-willed *individual,* is the one who scornfully refuses you, my countrymen, who casts you out, poor wretches, from the realms of faith and carefree happiness. Therefore, the individual will either adapt himself to the justified desire for universal security or perish. For we have discovered at last that personality, Christianity, or conscience (which all mean the same thing) is an invention of the megalomania that would elevate the crowd above the animals, and the individual above the crowd, thus rendering equality, the happy dream of the masses, forever impossible.

"For mortals will never keep peace among themselves, or feel peace within them, until they are all equal; and that means until they are all equally subject to one arbitrary will. Out of this insatiable craving, in ancient times, they invented religion, which has now lost its force because it is exposed as a mere invention. Thus robbed of the arbitrary will that they had set up over themselves, because they cannot live without stretching their arms upward—in their terror and forlornness, then, they cried out for us, and millions of voices joined as one in a single cry of terror: God is dead! Whom shall we submit to?

"Just then, 'at the last possible moment—for they had already begun to point the finger of scorn at each other, to rage and destroy one another—*we* hastened to their aid. We were more merciful than Christianity, and more understanding too, for we saw that man is an animal being, craving peace through submission and equality, now that fruitless suffering has taught him that the burden of personal freedom and conscience imposed upon him is unbearable.

"There, my friends and corulers, you have the truth of the topmost story; now that I have given you an accounting at your general's express wish, let us mount our horses and ride into the night against the past, which is already giving way."

BOOK THREE

GOLIGHTLY'S JOY

XII

AT TEN o'clock, when Bruns in the north, Thomas in the northwest, and General Susa farther to the south in Florida had reported "Ready" to the Ordnance Master, the northern column crossed the river that forks just short of the blunt cone. Thomas' line, running due east on both sides of Blue Griffin Road, advanced from Blumeshof into the uninhabited territory, which was overgrown with rank meadow grass, sparse oats, and nothing at all. Raked by a barrage it lay bright as day in the flares, between outlying villages and the edge of town.

Shouting "Hail to the Leader, victory or death!" infantry and machine-gunners bounded across the two-thousand-yard interval to plunge into the trenches abandoned by the government infantry along the Outer Boulevard. They were half mad with the hum, roar, and slap of the small-arm fire, the howl of the shells, the screams of the dying, and the yellow light of the star shells bursting over their heads. Facing them across the two roadways and the bridle path were the little houses that Hesse had once said were built by farmers with no talent for city dwelling; these were still burning, and beyond them in turn was a damned open stretch, the so-called Mayfair Meadows, used in the old days for trials of markmanship.

"Do not advance any further," was the order; "assemble at the Outer Boulevard." But no bugle call would have roused those who lay stretched full length in the bottom of the trench, or sleeping as they sat, scattered, jumbled, leaderless, and horrified through and through.

On the dot of eleven-thirty, silence fell in the northwestern sector, silence as complete as if the government were inviting the lieutenant colonel to try his luck a second time at charging across the Mayfair Meadows and the People's Park.

At that moment came a roar as if the earth had opened, followed by a crashing and splintering like mountains being catapulted at each other. The Old Town hill seemed to burst asunder. Roaring fires under a black sky hurled walls and spark-spouting timbers about. The cathedral towers, whirling like arms, the domed roof, the Gothic Town Hall, Courthouse, museum, and armory went down in a sea of flame.

"Well, I guess we can go home now," said an elderly N.C.O., who had been cooling his face in the muddy water from the bottom of the trench at the Outer Boulevard. "Bruns is done for."

"I'm not going," replied a humorist who was lying full length on his back in the muddy water, "I'm going to stay here until Judgment Day." A moment later he actually was asleep.

Bruns, with the northern group, was actually done for, although he had suffered slight losses in crossing the fork, the meadows, and mounting the blunt cone. The bombardment of the howitzers began with awful suddenness, and the heavy shells burrowed in the slope; more people were killed by scattering masonry and falling fragments than had been by missiles. The attackers fled back to the river meadows, found their pontoon bridges destroyed, their retreat cut off, and so surrendered at dawn to some government machine-gun companies, already followed by ambulance trains.

The highly esteemed General Susa was fighting unsuccessfully in the southwest. In the course of two hours he sent five divisions out into the night, where they were so cut up by artillery and machine-gun fire from hidden nests that the general sent patrols to establish contact with the main body and ask the Ordnance Master for reinforcements.

At about this time, half an hour after midnight, the Supreme Command at Jacob's hotel and beer garden by the bridge found it had no choice, particularly since two bull's-eyes had destroyed the pontoons, but ordered retreat southward, in order to join Susa's forces. The plan would have been practicable if they had set out for Florida, not too far away from the riverbank, moving the length of the Willert estate and keeping out of contact with the enemy. Instead they made for a colony of villas northeast of the Botanical Gardens, a point that Susa had never reached; this group, which had already lost a third of its strength in the attack on Outer Boulevard, was caught on the left flank and afterward on the rear, and annihilated. The remnants—the Master of Ordnance had fallen, and Thomas was gravely wounded—fled partly into Willert's woods, more largely into Florida, where they surrendered along with Susa's survivors to the government on the following morning.

We have exact information of Urban's demeanor during the terrible night when his divisions were being crushed. At about eleven, perhaps three quarters of an hour before the bombardment of the Old Town hill, Thomas decided to send in the Bodyguard Regiment, the beloved parade unit. The Leader, who lay on the black oilcloth sofa in the lounge, silently brooding, was asked to make a speech and spur on "his" regiment, which consisted entirely of equally tall twenty-year-olds.

He made his last speech, "The Reward of Victory," outside the rear entrance of the inn, from the top step of a projecting, old-fashioned outdoor staircase, in the light of hurricane lanterns. He spoke in a sharp voice that sometimes cracked, as if he were trying, not to fire the young soldiers' spirits, but to tell them off. "He saw no one," Weisse said later, "thrust his head forward, and barked into the night."

"Let me tell you, my young soldiers of the Bodyguard Regiment, what you were yesterday, and what you will be tomorrow! You were slaves. You will be masters! No later than tomorrow you will be pointing a finger at the dishes you choose to enjoy and the women who are worthy to share your couches. And the women, the greater half of mankind, will rejoice aloud, freed of two thousand years' unnatural and repellent compulsory continence. The women will file out in a long line from the cathedral, where deliverance from the unnatural and the natural right of the strong will be preached henceforward; the women will file past you, I say, calling attention by evolutions of their limbs to the charms that ridiculous convention had bidden them conceal. And the impeccable ones, so long condemned by the base necessities of life to serve weaklings and graybeards, will fall down before you, arms outspread, breasts taut, eyes already swimming with ecstasy, swooning with anticipation, carried away with desire. The elder ones among you too—I mean your officers—will have their day. Let him that is past forty leave the young ones to the young who are satisfied with a hasty and unstudied coupling; let him instead rejoice in the gratitude and subtle arts held ready by the man-crazy girls and women in their riper years.

"Now go out into battle; win; and snatch these defrauded victims of a system ripe for death from possessors enfeebled by Christianity and capitalism. You are to push across the Outer Boulevard into the city, which will open to you like a woman's arms, and to join hands with your brothers moving toward you from the Old Town. Ready, march!"

The Bodyguard Regiment was lucky. Half an hour later General Kaempf, in the basement of Police Barracks I said, "Enough of this massacre!" and Messerschmidt, the detachment commander, ordered the firing to cease.

When the regiment had gone, Urban's face relaxed, softened, grew gentle and seemingly younger. Everything about the place pleased him: the yard, surrounded only by a fence, the vegetable garden beyond, the lights, torches, the whicker of horses hitched to fence pickets, eating oats from nosebags. With a smile he asked to have the tables carried out, the night was so beautiful. He was obeyed. He patted his bay mare on her gleaming hindquarters, tugged at a stirrup to make sure the girth was tight, and then suddenly turned and went with arms outstretched toward Weisse, who sat idly on the edge of a sand pit. In it some dismounted dispatch-bearers had started a fire. That has always been the way in my country: wherever we see a dry sand pit, we cannot help lighting a fire to watch the life of the flame, and, when it goes out, the glowing coals.

Urban put both hands on the shoulders of the Senator, who was shorter than he, and regarded him with a look of infatuation: "Let them manage their own business," he said, pointing through the buildings. From the front garden and the highway the rattle of munition carts, signal whistles, commands, and the hiss of rockets could be heard. "Go into my bedroom, but don't touch the clothes cupboard— that's my secret!"

He turned his head toward the Master of Ordnance, who was sitting at a table by the wall next to the adjutant, dispatching orderlies with instructions; before him he had a map of the city hanging down from the table to the ground. The spacious courtyard was already filling up with dismounted horsemen, pickets outside the toolsheds and stables, hurricane lanterns and torches.

"Where's Willie Gaedicke?" cried Dr. Urban.

"The smell of powder made him sick," replied Thomas with a loudness that was beginning to show rather a lack of reverence. In reality the barber, odious to the staff officers, had denied the treachery of which he was accused by a "court-martial" at Mittelburg, confessing, however, that he had never been an Urbanite or Faustite, but "an artist first and foremost." Thereupon he had been condemned to death, but had slipped away along with a good many others to Neuhafen in the debauchery that then began to run riot. "That's it, with a stomach-ache, and his sensitivity offended by loud noises," added Thomas as if anything were permissible in this night of disaster.

"See, they don't understand at all," said Urban tenderly to Weisse. "Go on in, without looking at the cupboard, and get me my drawing

board with the drawing tacked on it, and some drawing things—
they're in the desk drawer."

The Senator went in and rattled the door of the forbidden cupboard. It was locked. Then he took out the drawing board and kit.
Urban moved his own table to the staircase, beneath the tavern lantern, and began to draw. He erased, improved, squinted this way and
that, and raptly scoured his upper lip with the tip of his tongue, meanwhile giving occasional explanations: "The Greeter, blue-cheeked,
bloated party idol that he is, is abolished—*I'll* give them a surprise,"
he said with a crafty sidelong glance at the officers. "That toper,
glutton, and blowhard is your countryman, but not mine, and don't
forget it!" He worked tensely and in silence for a while, with Weisse
watching him. The adjutant, at the staff table, tinkled on a mandolin
that had been found in the fugitive innkeeper's family living room.

Then the earth trembled, the howl of the howitzers drowned out
every other sound, and the officers leaped up to watch the suddenly
reddened sky.

"So they did after all!" said the Ordnance Master, tugging at his
nose.

Urban spun around in a fury: "Can't you silence this uncivil noise,
Thomas, that won't let me think? Time was, if you will kindly remember, when silence was supposed to prevail if I started to speak.
If that isn't possible now, I'll go into town and continue my conversation in the Town Hall, in the quiet of the garden salon."

But he isn't conversing, the officers thought. To avoid unpleasant-
ness the Ordnance Master took some yellow beeswax out of his pocket,
warmed it in his hand, and stopped both the Leader's ears, first asking and receiving permission. "Can you still hear anything?" he
asked, and as Urban sat down and resumed his drawing, the adjutant
said boldly: "Why, he's beginning to talk sheer nonsense! Did you
hear what he said about the Town Hall and the garden salon?"

"Poor Bruns!" said the Master of Ordnance, going to a field telephone now repaired for the dozenth time.

The League Leader showed his confidant the almost completed
figure: "See, this is Mr. Golightly."

Weisse shouted in his ear: "Who's Mr. Golightly?"

"Mr. Golightly, secretary or clerk," said Urban softly, in an intimate,
happy tone, as he regarded the drawing. "There he is, going walking

with his walking stick. This is the colossal monument I shall set up to him, and under it the inscription: 'Golightly the clerk,' no, better 'Golightly the secretary'—or, quite simply, 'Golightly the stipendiary.' Of course you will ask who he is, and what his name means. He's the ideal of humanity and, as I am a humane human being, also *my* ideal."

The generals came back, and Thomas asked: "What's this he's babbling about ideals? His ideal, Ida, has left, and is sleeping tonight with her friend Emil!" Remembering the Hofer woman's silvery voice when she was invited to an evening function at the Senate, he tinkled out and sang her oft-heard *Oh, Promise Me*.

It was quarter of twelve. The eastward crossing of the Outer Boulevard had become useless, and Leugenfeld's howitzer fire must have hurled the northern group down the slope. The Ordnance Master ordered assembly.

"You ask what an 'ideal' is?" said Urban to his confidant, who was looking at the drawing. "Ideal is a Greek word, and means a tremendous figure standing at the end of a tremendous road, and it's called an 'ideal' because you have to approach it. So, undismayed by the tremendous distance, you keep approaching it all your life, faithfully striving. At last—the shadows grow longer, evening is falling— you believe you are close to it, within arm's reach. And then it falls back on the road you have traveled; the road spreads out before you, covered with footprints—*your* footprints. You fall on your knees to make sure the footprints before you are yours. Yes, unhappy man, you have traveled the road before you, and you are tempted to stand still." Urban covered his face with his hands as if in pain.

Lieutenant Colonel Thomas shook his head: "Is he talking sense?"

"If we were winning, it would be divine sense," replied Weisse, "but as things stand, it's the sense of the vanquished."

"But fortune smiles on the persevering," Urban began, awakening from his pain, and now with the look of a victor. "You stand erect, you fix your eyes upon the retreating ideal, and it cannot resist your will: it congeals, begins to have edges, takes on an outline, approaches, floats toward you. It is Mr. Golightly with his neatly brushed hair, dandruff on his coat collar; the cut of his coat is a little old-fashioned, nor is his waistcoat new, with the steel watch chain across it—but what matter?"

He pointed to the drawing, circling the various parts with his pencil.

"The stout boots under the too-long trousers have been to the cobbler at several points; there are bits of tobacco in the bristly mustache, and the rows of teeth below are not white and perfect like a mincing actress'. I have shown all this in the drawing. But what I could *not* show, and what you, my Weisse, my Peter—for the others will sell my clothes before cockcrow—what *you* must know, what you must see every moment of the day and night, is the life of Mr. Golightly, the stipendiary, the light-footed, the contented. For if a man is contented, will he stamp heavily? It is of this life that you must speak in a tone of invocation to the remaining mortals until, magically transformed by your will (for, after all, nothing can resist the will), they take on the shape of Golightly, thus carrying out my last will. For this is my last will and testament: *Golightly is to be humanity.*"

Weisse nodded his agreement.

"How does he live? For you must never preach abstractly; always give examples and anecdotes. He wakes up in the morning, looks at the clock, says to his wife, 'Time for coffee!' and gets dressed. He dips the rolls in the coffee—you know, on account of his teeth; the coffee drips from his mustache, and he wipes it off; he reads the paper and knows what he is supposed to think. I suppose you think *somebody* must have written the paper, so that there's a flaw in my calculations?

"Not at all: he who writes the paper is himself a Golightly, and knows what he is supposed to think, although naturally it is a part of his profession to write in such a way that people will think he means to give them something to think about. There must be freedom of the press, never forget that. If you don't supervise or limit the papers, they will always write in such fashion that Golightly will nod his head and not cancel his subscription. And *if* an issue—I mean a subject about which there is a dispute—should turn up, a gentle hint to the papers will be enough. Tell them to support both sides of the question with equal conviction, because that is justice. This will confuse Golightly so much that he will drop the matter, since both sides are right. Follow his life, no matter whether he goes to a factory or an office: the wheel he turns, the piece of paper he writes on and hands to the Golightly next to him, neither is any concern of his. It is not his business. Nothing is any concern of his, nothing burdens his heart, no life, no death, no struggle, no opinion; and as surely as the leaves fall in autumn, as surely as dawn breaks and night darkens, Golightly the cashier will pay Golightly the secretary his salary. This is the ideal, the ultimate aim: Golightly's joy."

The Master of Ordnance and the lieutenant colonel, standing a step from the table, looked at the drawing.

"Does he suffer from want of anything?" Urban went on. "In the afternoon his wife calls for him at work; they go arm in arm across the bustling market place in ripe strawberry season: 'Good day! How do you do?' you hear on all sides. 'You know what?' says Golightly to his wife. 'I have an idea.' 'You shouldn't do that,' says Mrs. Golightly. 'Ideas give you a headache.' 'Is that so?' says Golightly. 'Well, I guess it isn't necessary then,' he adds. 'It isn't *necessary*,' says his wife, 'but you'd better tell me your idea, so as to get it out of your system, and then you won't think about it any more.' 'Well, it was just an idea,' says Golightly, 'but a good one, and if I were to tell it to our friend Fred Ritter, he'd be sure to say: "That's sensible!"' 'What idea do you mean?' 'I mean,' Golightly answers, 'I'd like to drink a bowl of strawberry punch.' That's his idea, and you must remember, Weisse, it has occurred to him in view of the tremendous cheapness of all the strawberries rotting in the market baskets. If there weren't any cheap strawberries, the idea would never have occurred to him: because longing for what is cheap, that is, for attainable objects, and disdain for what hangs high—these are the foundation of his character and the essential of his happiness."

Exhausted by his great exertion, he leaned back, closed his eyes, and smiled in apology for his weariness.

Meanwhile everything was in motion: the telephone lines were dismantled, the horses led out, the fires extinguished. As the Old Town was on fire and General Susa had asked for help, the Ordnance Master had ordered everyone to march south—the disastrous order that dragged Urban's main group down with Susa's defeat, for want of sufficient cover on the flank and because it veered to south-southeast.

The Leader did not heed the sounds of departure, nor his calash with its four bays, standing under hurricane lanterns in the yard with a file of mounted military police, powerful fellows in bright-green jackets with silver lacings, before and behind the carriage.

Open-mouthed, as if remembering something he had forgotten, Urban bent over the drawing again: "It's fall. I'm going to put an overcoat on him, and behind him a figure, yes, *behind* him—Fortuna, the goddess of luck, following him and reaching almost humbly for the hem of his garment. For that is the glorious thing about Golightly (although his figure and appearance, actually, are short of beautiful). The glorious thing about Golightly is that he's not chasing after Fortune, but Fortune is chasing after him."

"Beautiful," said Weisse, while Justus Thomas gave orders to the commander of the escorting military police: "We don't know where we shall stop. So you're to take the League Leader through Willert's property, keeping close under Cat Hill, to the posting inn at Little Rose. Or Willert's houses by the river would be safer still."

"Those are pretty likely to be shot to pieces," the commander of the military police warned.

"All right, then Little Rose."

"Yes, sir, Little Rose, sir!" the M.P. repeated.

But Urban, beaming with joy, clapped his most intimate confidant on the shoulder: "Would you like to see me? Would you like to see me as Golightly?" And not waiting for the answer he unclasped his sash, dropped holster, sash, coat, and cap on the floor, shouted for an orderly, sprang up the stairs, and vanished into his room off the hall. Weisse could not help thinking of the forbidden cupboard and the mummery that the sentries had seen a few nights before at Bessonoff's mansion and on the sidewalk of the market place.

The Ordnance Master, meanwhile, yelled at the commander of the Bodyguard Regiment, who had sensibly turned back with his third battalion (since the Old Town was in flames), and was now detailed to guard the flank: "It's taking you a good while, Mr. Steinhoff," he yelled at the white-bearded colonel, "to gather up your odds and ends—or have you been getting your fortune told again?"

The old mercenary, a former army officer who made game of the Carpenters' training course although he was as superstitious as an herb woman, saluted: "No need, now," he said.

At that moment Secretary, Clerk, or rather Stipendiary Golightly came out into the yard. From his wig, false eyebrows, mustache, and the dandruff on the rather greasy coat collar down to his patched boots he was a very masterpiece of the quick-change artist. Neither the cheap old slouch hat nor the brown walking stick with its pedantically rectilinear imitation ivory handle was missing. Flourishing the slouch hat with rather theatrical triumph, he presented himself to

Weisse and the officers while the horns tooted, whistles trilled, and a regiment of mounted chasseurs raced out into the darkness to southeastward.

The old colonel turned away; the general, frozen with horror, stood open-mouthed. Weisse, looking around, seemed to be asking who had perpetrated this final scandal; Thomas the adjutant sat down at the table again, covering his face with his hands for shame.

"See them turning away, men of little faith!" laughed Urban, but his laugh was shrill and unnatural. "See them turning away, dazzled by the sun of an ideal!" He tossed his uniform trousers, which he was carrying over his arm, to the floor with the rest of the uniform. "There, take my clothes, let the soldiers cast dice for them! Thirty pieces of silver, what?"

Justus Thomas sprang up, and although he was gritting his teeth, tears ran down his tanned face. He embraced the Leader, whispering in his ear: "Good-by, old boy. We'll make one last attempt, for your sake!"

Urban shook off this man who was already a stranger, shouted, "Into the corner with you!" and, tossing his head back, assumed the slightly comical attitude of an indignant office manager. In this posture he walked to his carriage, got in, and waved his slouch hat; chromos show some fatherly reigning prince greeting his subjects thus. The Ordnance Master, to spare his officers and soldiers the sight of the madman, hissed "March!"; and the carriage with the hat-waving Golightly, his faithful Weisse at his left, the escorting squadrons ahead and on both sides, rolled out into the night.

THE CHAMBER OF GUILDS

XIII

THE following morning the President decreed a week's national mourning, during which not only all places of public amusement but also the churches were to remain closed, and newspapers might be published but once a day, with the news section reduced to four pages. Accounts of the battles were not allowed; but to avoid ruining the editors or publishers, the advertising section remained unrestricted. In fact, this department of the papers actually flourished, since much that was close to people's hearts—for instance, the whereabouts of their families—came out in the form of advertisements.

Augustus Beyer, it is true, immediately reassured the public with the rather strangely stylized announcement that he *would not be outdone by anyone in his solicitude for the burials*. From May 6 to 13, practically everyone was busy with the dead—the very few among the government troops and the enormous number of victims (never announced) from the massacre caused that night by Kaempf, Leugenfeld, and Kraus.

On the morning of May 13, an overcast day, the President mounted the stand of the South Luisenhof race track to address the captured officers and N.C.O.'s of the Sports Troops, who were lined up in the enclosure, already in civilian dress and furnished with railroad tickets.

"Officers and noncommissioned officers of the rebel army! You have fought for a bad cause. By that I do not mean to say that you are bad men, although you are—but more of that later. The man who fights is a good man, and even he who fights for a bad cause is better than one who does not fight at all. Nor do I condemn you for having set a master over yourselves, but only for having chosen one who had no idea what a master was; for your Urban was a degrader. He who would degrade all men to equality is a slaveholder, but no master. For that matter, you knew this, and chose Urban because you wanted to be slaves: so you knew that your fight was a fight to win slavery. For the first time in human history a host of armed men have marched out with insane determination to win slavery for themselves. This is not the first time that men have been brave enough to endure wounds and death; but it is the first time that men have been slavish enough to prefer wounds and death to the perils of freedom. Great efforts will be needed before the shame with which you have covered yourselves can be forgotten.

"You are in sad case. But we, your overlords from this day forward—not only through the power of the victor, but so that your dream of beautiful slavery may be forever dreamed out—have pondered what might be said in your defense. We have found two facts: firstly, that you fought this shameful fight bravely, or, in other words, were not cowards; secondly, that you remained true to your bad fight and your bad master even after he was lost, which is to say that you are not rats. Because you are not cowards or rats, you are to be dismissed unpunished to your native places, along with your surviving comrades from other Urbanite troop divisions who have fallen into our hands—except for a few criminals. We shall, it is true, expunge from the book and the memory of the living those employees of the water and electrical works who used the trust put in them to assassinate Secretary of State Merckel and threaten our cities with interruption of their vital functions.

"You will therefore go home as soon as your names, residences, and personal data have been recorded. But if, once at home, you should think of reviving the old dream and choosing a new Urban, you will vanish into the lunatic villages, and if this is not enough, very soon to a place where neither sun nor moon will light your days and nights!"

The President's address won the approval of my countrymen, and well deserved a friendly reception abroad also, for it contained what the peoples love: authority and justice. Instead of this, however, suspicion and insult awaited us, probably because the reshaping of our lower house had already been announced.

For the President was much concerned to launch the necessary changes while the impression of victory was still fresh. On May 6, with the hospitals filling up and everyone occupied with the dead, all the units of the Urbanite party were dissolved; its rosters, archives, and funds were impounded by the Federal Police; and the party treasury was provisionally incorporated in the Social Reserve Fund. In consequence Urban's smaller backers demanded their "contributions" back. Though not without lawsuits, they recovered their money in a year or so.

On May 7 the so-called Rump Parliament, the Senate and lower house without the Urbanite members, approved the Three Prohibitions —splendid phrases, to the number of about 900 (ten times the number, including compounds); the corrupt teacher; and cowardice in face of evil. The state was declared the protector of the teacher's calling, at the same time withdrawing from the economic sphere. Consequently we had for almost a full year to contend with widespread confusion; for as some mountain giant shakes down an avalanche from its shoulders, so the law by which our commonwealth "assumed a religious character" shouldered off upon private business and the fellowships all ordinances and decrees previously enacted by state, provinces, and parishes to further trade and relieve the needy. The petty private businessman, baker, tailor, barber, or delicatessen merchant, now had to unite with his fellows to consider practical everyday matters, since the same state that was no longer concerned with him—with his "weekday," that is—loaded upon him the functions of state. There was simply no one left to do it for him. Thus all chatter about sentiments stopped at once, while economic life, previously disjointed and largely supervised from above, promptly coagulated like milk into economic organisms the moment supervision was removed. These organizations were called production chambers because though each branch of trade was independent in matters of its own special concern, all branches had to unite in debating what they held in common— particularly taxes, hours, shop closing, and care of the sick, crippled, and needy. In these parish and provincial production chambers and in the Chamber of Guilds that replaced the lower house (which had dissolved itself) there was, then, no little argument about practical matters such as money and property. But there was no time or opportunity to vaunt sentiments or "convictions." Various as were the practical interests that emerged—for who does not want to live well?—still those strange minglings of sacred convictions and ruthless business that the nineteenth century knew as "parties" were no longer to be found in our new lower house. And very naturally too; after all, the lower house had become the parliament of production, to which the butchers delegated a particularly able butcher, the watchmakers an experienced watchmaker. The point, then, was to fight for the interests of the butchers or watchmakers; the hobbies or "convictions" of the individual delegate outside his calling were his private affair just as much as his Sunday suit, and no concern of the Guilds'.

But man lives not merely for the sake of business or for a bare livelihood. The reflective wanderer toward the grave, as the Carpenters call him, is not merely the weekday man, demanding bread, women, and merriment, as we shall shortly hear; he is also the "Sunday Mortal," with needs that no guild can satisfy.

For the world and man, dualistic through and through, consist of irreconcilable opposites—matter and consciousness, reality and dream, individuality and generality, mutable and immutable, motion and rest, God and Satan, trade and Sunday, eternal and transitory, simple and compound, time and space. One thing cannot be traced back to the next, nor one "united" with another, except by idle chatter.

We consist of opposites, of a multiplicity of opposites: so let them be, good people, multiplicity and opposites! It has cost us blood enough to wipe out Urban because he tried to wipe out the multiplicity of the opposites within our nation so that he might rule over a degraded monotony—over Golightly the stipendiary.

The convinced dualism of the Carpenters, then, explains the continued existence of the Senate and the Academy of Twelve, those old checks upon the state. They remained as always, bodies to check and balance the President and his Secretaries of State; the Senate was elected as before by universal secret ballot, while the Academy was constituted by appointments made on its own application. Only their field of activity could not remain what it had been, now that the state had shouldered off all care for daily bread upon those who produced it. Thus the government and its system of checks and balances came to be concerned with the *Sunday* life of man, of the mortal from whom hunger and thirst, guile and malice, fall away because, as the Bishop says, he "wants to be a human being for once."

And whereas lower house and Senate were formerly almost the same thing, one a duplicate of the other, a duality has now been established, as everywhere else in nature: so the activity of the Chamber of Guilds or "parliament of production" is man's weekday worry; but the Senate and cabinet have to uphold man's Sunday dignity. That which we have yet to mention, reaching the end of our account, concerns the state's efforts on behalf of the mortal who desires dignity, or (which comes to the same thing) to "be a human being." For we are not alarmed about the mortal who hungers for "necessities," food, shelter, women, and merriment: he does his job, oils the machinery, and there is no idle talk in the brotherhoods.

One of the mysteries, the very many mysteries, that we cheerfully accept as inscrutable and irrefutable facts is the cohesion of opposites. Opposites, though essentially different and incapable of union, do cohere, and many even influence each other: matter and consciousness, reality and dream, motion and rest, trade and Sunday, woman and man. Things essentially unlike and incomparable cling together. There are mysteries; we observe them, and let them be. What business of yours is that which is not your doing?

BOOK THREE

PERSONAL MATTERS

XIV

D R. URBAN, his secretary Weisse, and the half squadron covering their escape were apprehended on Willert property on the afternoon of May 6. The Leader's military police were treated like the rest of the soldiers; Urban was taken to the capital-city institution for the insane, and Weisse to the camp at Goerz.

As the daily reports indicate, the doctors took great trouble with the former Leader, and at first his condition did not seem hopeless. He died suddenly three years afterward of apoplexy, as completely forgotten as if he had never terrified and almost overthrown a powerful government that had been preparing for thirteen years to struggle with him.

In an obituary in the *Pensive Watchman* Ackermann declared that he had been a leader of the first rank, overthrown neither by his own overweening pride nor by the confusion and treachery of his subordinates, but by the unkindness of fate. He, like Cyrus and Alexander the Great, had seen, when almost no one else did, the impotence, the bloated vaporing decadence, of his contemporaries. And he rushed into the "space denuded of force," as he himself had said. Ackermann added that the great names of Cyrus and Alexander would never have been handed down, and the bearers of those names would have died under some anonymous headsman's ax after quite insignificant early successes, if they had been faced by a man whose vision was as strong as theirs. They were fortunate enough to find as adversaries mere orators, courtiers, and people ready to submit. Urban too judged his time correctly, realizing that it was composed of women in trousers, of smilers, courtiers truckling to a public opinion that did not exist, and quaking newspaper readers. But he met his match: he encountered the man with the stronger vision, who mobilized the "clearheadedness and hardheadedness of an upper crust that despised fine phrases" to fight the visionary of the rabble, the contented Golightly. He encountered Adam Faust, and was bound to perish. Thus Albert Ackermann.

Three hours' questioning of Weisse by Colonel Schwann brought to light various unknown facts, among others the piquant circumstance that Ida Bessonoff in Neuhafen—the turmoil by then was so complete that no one knew about the sentence of death upon her—had released her husband and their eldest son Alfred, the major, from arrest by the Urbanites, and sent them back to Mittelburg with an escort and instructions to restore order in the mansion. Thus early were Emil, or "Emilio Branconi," and his friend Ida firmly convinced of Urban's downfall. Weisse spent two years at the Guldenberg lunatic village, and was later appointed resort and social director at a watering place in the northern coast province because of his interesting past.

On the last day of national mourning, May 12, the Association to Restore the Honor and Fortune of Sufferers from the Old Regime brought in a bill to prosecute Dolores McCarthy for having accumulated from twenty-four branch associations a total of six thousand thalers' compensation for the damage done her by Roland Perlotta. But she had already left the country with her loot. Although letters found in the possession of her family indicated that she was living a

"pleasant life" as a cook's assistant at a hotel in the brilliant capital
of our southern neighbor, the criminal police refrained from delivering her up, owing to the "insignificance of the whole matter."

After the coffin of Tobias Witt, who was buried in the Soldiers'
Cemetery at the capital, walked his widow, the dovelike Veronica,
née Froehlich; beside her the dead man's sister, Margaret Heide, née
Witt, Jacob Willert's Roman lady of thirteen years before, and her
husband, Sebastian Heide, a kitchen-chair manufacturer with a flourishing establishment, for the great banker had a long memory. He
had forgotten neither John Christopher Laemmle nor the venison soup
nor the filet of young buck in the Upper Town Casino, and certainly
not the girl with the sea-green taffeta gown from old Stern's and
the gold-braid shoes. Had not Beyer told him in the train that the
Roman ladies of Geisenheim were loveliest at forty? After all,
although he was about to become a grandfather by Elspeth Kersting,
he was only fifty-four, not an old man; walking at Hesse's side in the
funeral, behind his old love, he tickled her ankle with his cane. "If
you're pregnant by your honest Sebastian, Peggy," his sinful thoughts
ran, "so much the better—no harm can come to you."

Yes, Hesse was walking in line too, because, after all, Tobias had
been his secret agent. True, he did not follow other secret agents
to the grave, but to this particular one he had given his cap, because
the man was a fellow countryman, and for no other reason; and the
police general's eyes hung upon the gleaming reddish hair that the
wind had loosened from the thick knot against Veronica's white neck
below her hat. His wife Alexandra, née von Brick, had of course
stayed at home with a headache—no wonder, when an operation had
deprived a woman of her most womanly part. Perhaps she had gone
out after some man, as her mamma had done in her day, or simply
because her own husband was going his own way; she would soon
be caught and haled before the Joint Court for a divorce—or possibly
not while the old man was still alive.

Peggy Heide, née Witt, had plainly noticed the cane against her
ankle: "Well now," she thought, "if I haven't caught him again, the
great salmon. If I have, you shan't get off so cheaply as you did before
with Stern and Miss Pauli; I know how prices run now. Dorothy
Thiess, the milkmaid, got ten thousand—I won't even count in the
fact that her girl Elspeth has captured Henry, because luck is blind,

perfectly blind! You can feel through your back how Hesse doesn't
see anything but Veronica; he scorns me, although I had honest
parents. She never even knew her father, and he may have been a
bricklayer or a strolling tinker that drowned in the buttermilk—luck
is blind!"

> *Oh God, our help in ages past,*
> *Our hope in years to come,*

the band of the First Foot Guard Regiment played as they marched;
the band leader was as fat as if he had swallowed the bass drum.

After the general and the president of the Academy walked
Rudolphi: he owed it to his commission, the five-thousand-thaler
commission that Hesse had given him. Hesse had suddenly decided
that the chapel in the middle of the police barrack yard was too bare.
A stray shell had smashed the bright stained-glass windows; but when
those were repaired, what should he want but a huge painting on the
long left-hand wall, facing the stone Magdalen—the *Resurrection of
the Soldier,* of the soldier Tobias Witt, no less!

Incidentally, the general had described very carefully the scene that
was to be shown in the space between the altar and the vestry of the
gutted cathedral (there was going to be enough work for the next
five years; Clara was already beginning to boast that her daughters,
twelve-year-old Charlotte and nine-year-old Sylvia, would have a dowry
of fifty thousand thalers each, and of course a six-room apartment).
Well, the soldier was to be lying on the ground floor, or no, rather
he should be already awakening as the strawberry-blonde angel came
sweeping from the bluish vestry and the sulphur-colored divine wrath
smashed the roof, cutting into the deep brown of the beams, the altar,
the vestry door, half a pew, the curving pulpit steps. And she, the
strawberry-blonde Veronica, God's own daughter, was to be coming
in with one mighty beat of her wings, whirling the dust from the
floor and causing a church mouse to spiral upward; her left angel
wing, overpowering, would touch the floor and draw the awakening
soldier toward it: "She would carry him up like an arrow in the fire
of the broad, blazing lightning, into the opened heavens." Hesse had
described the scene as exactly as if he had been there himself. . . . How
about putting him in, a dark minor figure, as the donors of paintings
had had themselves shown in former times? An extra thousand

thalers, particularly since Gasparra would be necessary as an assistant anyway—no one could ever do it alone in six months. What about putting in Hesse and his mastiff, as big as a calf, spotted, standing with its tongue hanging out in a spot of sunlight, watching the resurrection? He would hire Gasparra at once: in the first place, he hadn't run away, and, in the second place, he could paint; after all, he couldn't help it if he was stupid.

Further to the rear, at a respectful distance from generals and presidents, walked Frank Jaeger, the Caucasian Oak, and Bart Plambeck. At last he was on the right side—the honest seaman, president of the Revolutionists, author of the "Seven Cautions," outcast muckraker, John Henry Merckel's fellow editor—and now, if God was kind, editorial writer to the government. His superior, the printing-plant proprietor, did not wear sweaty woolen shirts now—there was no need for it; and the old worn cellar stairs had been replaced by a modern electric lift. The old business methods were forgotten; you could live on the plant without the paper, if it weren't a pleasant honor to have a "sheet of your own" to say what you thought in the language of people who had gone to college, signed, Frank Jaeger. Pale, fat, and tall in his good frock coat and top hat, he walked with measured tread, a successful man from whom you ordered announcements of bereavement. Between the two men, in black and white— white hair and a young spirit—walked Claire Mill, alone in Simon's house since Emil's departure, and therefore hired by Frank Jaeger in place of Ruth Westen (who had been fired at last), because Claire was "well acquainted" with Dr. Nessel, who could refuse her nothing —Nessel, editor of Simon's publications, and presumable president of the Council of Censors. The man-crazy Claire had perhaps drawn the long bow a little about Nessel, but it was actually true that she had seen him every day, waited on him at table, and made his bed.

"Frank," she said, "a man like you needs a wife that looks impressive and won't run off, or else his business will suffer. What do you think?"

Frank thought he might perhaps marry her, for she did look stately as she walked with him on the street, and maybe the others hadn't had gaudy pasts too!

The Iron Phalanx played dead. True, the government, meaning to exploit the mood of triumph, which is highly perishable merchandise, had enacted the Three Prohibitions; but a law needs an administrative ordinance so that the citizen may know what he must do and not do. The administrative ordinance had not yet been issued, and the Council of Censors was not yet appointed. Merckel's *Dictionary of Splendid Phrases* made three stout volumes, with copious commentary. How was any ordinary editor to read it in three days, and when he had read it, could he be expected to look up every word of an incoming manuscript in Merckel's dictionary to find out if it was a "splendid phrase"?

Most of them read nothing but the preface, because any right-thinking man who had read that would know that the author was an abnormal madman in the last stages; but could you say so without having that fellow Bart Plambeck pillory you as a defamer of the President's son-in-law? A pretty state of things—and this was what they called liberty!

"I don't suppose you'll believe it," said Nicholas Edwin Schiele to his colleague, the subeditor for locals and miscellaneous items, handing the preface across the editorial desk: "Here you are—help yourself!"

And the subeditor read:

PREFACE

I

No matter how often you, my contemporaries, may insist that the Christianity which I strive to recall to your minds is a figment of my imagination, and nonexistent in the world, whereas facts, not chimeras, are what count today—you are wrong! You are twice wrong: firstly, about the figment of my imagination; secondly, about Christianity. For it does exist; I have seen it, sat at its table when I was a little child, encountered it in my manhood, and I recall it to mind as I saw it, forgetting much and adding nothing.

You say it does not exist, although it lives perceptibly among you, held down by silence, put down by witticisms, looked at askance and hated by you, but still lives. By your nevertheless protesting that it does not exist, I can see into your hearts, whose secret wish that it did not exist you lack the bravery to express.

Nevertheless, vulgar as you are, I still prefer you who say, "All nonsense! There never was such a thing as Christianity—it was all sham and hypocrisy. I'm for something substantial!" to the churchgoers and eye rollers who confuse Almighty God with a bath attendant who scrubs away their sins between eleven and twelve on Sundays, thus entitling them to act like swine for the rest of the week.

But there is still a third sort; and only when they grow powerful enough will God's time be ripe to return and sit in judgment. I mean the sort in priestly vestments who have turned Christianity—the following of God's word—into worship of power and obedience to worldly leaders. On this I shall have much more to say.

II

Freedom and culture, democracy and the rights of man, personality, Christianity, humanity—why do we find these expressions used so often today and so seldom in the past?

They are used so often today because the things they express no longer exist. The essence of modern barbarism is that it has transformed mankind's great possessions into "splendid phrases"—into sheer vociferation. Perhaps it will be possible to revive the instinct for freedom or Christianity, now quite dead, by threatening the severest punishment to anyone who uses the *words* "Christianity," "freedom," and the others previously mentioned.

For my part, if I came into power anywhere, I would immediately destroy these phrases, the weapons of the vociferator, so that the things connoted by the words might be summoned back to the life whence they have been driven by the demagogues. If a person is not allowed to use the word "freedom," possibly a secret love of freedom, the violated thing itself, may burgeon in his heart. Perhaps if the *words* "Christian" and "Christianity" are withdrawn from circulation by a strict interdict, a person may shamefacedly remember the things themselves. For our great words are ceremonies that have lost their meaning. What such ceremonies are worth was revealed by the Lord of Hosts to the prophet Isaiah in the first chapter; and our Bishop Kessel has never ceased to proclaim to the nation the danger of ceremonies. So that you, my friends, you men of good will, may travel Kessel's road a little more easily, I have compiled this *Dictionary of Splendid Phrases*.

JOHN HENRY MERCKEL.

"Completely loony!" said the subeditor, shaking his head.

THE ONSLAUGHT OF THE PRAYING BRETHREN

XV

THE highest-ranking brotherhood of the League of Christian Carpenters, the Federal Police Corps, built up by faithful adherence to old Hesse's *Instructions Concerning Practical Piety in the Police Service,* was the first to rebel against Christianity. As early as the end of March, Beyer had dismissed Majors Lindequist and Lorenz, who had been sent to him to protest against the expression "Christian commonwealth," with the ungracious inquiry whether they would fight only if he ate out of their hands. And his further remark that the state would assume a religious character had not eased the worries of the policemen's wives about their husbands' livelihood, but rather increased them. And yet, as is so often the case, not the livelihood of the discontented ones was put in question, but their "honor among men": if through the reduction of the Federal Police Corps they were transferred to the standing army or to administrative positions, they would become second-class Carpenters, at least in their own view.

For they and their simple wives with the wide linen collars (which suspicious foreigners call our "court costume") naturally misunderstood the expression "religious state." Precisely such notions of Beyer's as prohibiting décolleté and short dresses for lady guests at receptions (do you remember Melchior Willert's fourth piece of advice to his son Jacob?) strengthened the Carpenters' suspicion that the "religious commonwealth" would be a clerical state and hostile to the police.

Accordingly, two days after Urban's defeat, they held an officers' meeting in their windowless chapel in the police barrack yard by the canal, while their wives and children looked on from the high gallery of the choir in the background. In order to make the "Christian commonwealth" impossible they passed the following resolutions:

Firstly: to request the Archbishop and General Otto von Hesse as members of the government to withdraw from circulation as a "splendid phrase" the expression "Christian" with all its compounds, as Secretary of State Merckel himself had recommended in his preface.

Secondly: since the Archbishop would be reluctant to take such a step, an important concession would be made to him as a well-known antisectary. If he should prove inclined toward prohibition of the word "Christian," the Federal Police Corps in every province would further the Bishop's wish to dissolve the sects, particularly the Penitent Congregation and the Disciples of Emmaus, by every means in its power.

During those days of national mourning Hesse was spending a furlough at his private estate by the lake south of the capital. When Lindequist and Lorenz drove out, for reasons of discipline, to present their resolutions to the general, they were ejected by the dovelike Veronica —politely and with apologies, but ejected: "Brother General has deputized Schwann to represent him."

Well, they guessed they were as powerful as Colonel Schwann, themselves; thus the matter was allowed to rest until two successive incidents in June came to their assistance.

On May 13 the state, having declared itself the protector of the teacher's calling and the "Sunday Mortal," abruptly unloaded its responsibility for the bodily welfare of its citizens—for the "weekday" —upon our capitalists and fellowships, that is upon the economic system as a whole. Four weeks later, after closing accounts in orderly fashion, state and parishes ceased to make any payments to the needy, unemployed, sick, crippled, widows, and orphans. The result was turmoil, and the poor on relief were in immediate distress. They rushed to the Federal Police stations, shouted one another down, mothers threatened to leave their children on the office desks—"You feed them, if you're Christians!"—and old people of both sexes sat all day on the benches in the endless corridors, beleaguering the offices.

In this first conflict of the religious commonwealth with the guilds, or rather with a dereliction of duty on the part of the guilds, Colonel von Lindequist once more demonstrated his skill as an "inspired officeholder." He suggested to the President that an emergency decree should be issued with a time limit, allowing the needy on relief to purchase food and clothing in suitable quantities at the shops near their homes, without identification beyond what they already had, and without money, simply for the signing of a receipt. The tradesmen could then take the receipts to their guilds and demand compensation. The same regulation would hold for landlords who had had no rent from the needy on relief. This decree was issued on the afternoon of the same day, with the unanimous approval of the Academy, and by evening the poor were taken care of. While the production chambers of the provinces, made up of guilds and parishes together, quickly reorganized the welfare system under pressure of the tradesmen's noisy demands for compensation, the receipts signed by the needy were accepted as readily as cash by banks and savings banks. The President's emergency decree, entitled "On Permissible Self-Help," was popularly called "the bullet in the ceiling" in memory of Hesse's shot at the stucco ceiling of the Café Opéra when the waiters, shouting "Haven't got time! Haven't got time!" did not bring him his tea. Thus, people thought, the guilds and corporations, occupied with themselves, had no time for the poor; but when the decree threatened their holy of holies, the till, they had brought tea like a flash so that the presidential decree could be withdrawn.

In reply to the reproach that this dictatorial emergency decree ran counter to the democratic spirit of a guild constitution, Andrew Zorn and Holzkopf retorted that the spirit built the body, and not vice versa. Therefore government and Senate, as representatives of the "Sunday Mortal," could claim a natural precedence over the Chamber of Guilds. After all, if soul and body, God and Baal, came in conflict, one did want the former to win, the latter to be subdued, regardless of the irreconcilable dualism and difference in nature.

Whereupon their adversaries said that on this theory our unwritten constitution was not a balanced democracy.

Beyer replied, in *The Conservative,* that the democracy of our opponents was a "splendid phrase," and would not even be that for long, because they knew Urban would rush into a democracy that had no authority, as into a "space denuded of force." He would request the gentlemen of the opposition not to complain of Urban when this happened, but to remember Beyer's prediction.

The Federal Police Corps, however, emerged from the affair covered with glory. The first few hours of the day of hunger showed what confidence the poor had in the "praying brethren"; the guilds owed the absence of disturbances, thefts, and mass robbery to a police colonel.

Naturally the police now grew too big for their boots. They made a regular deal with the two bishops at the capital, this time without asking Hesse.

Hesse had scarcely heard about this breach of discipline before he ordered a meeting of officers in the chapel at Police Barracks I.

The little church, built of red brick in humbler days, looked minute in the vast expanse of the barrack yard, and even the tiny steeple was lower than the main building that fronted on the canal. With its small portal, long nave, and the carved choir screen behind and above the altar (paintings by Rudolphi), it resembles a village church of the better sort; only the abundance of entrances and exits, to allow quick marching in and out, set it apart.

Early on the morning of June 20 the nave was filled with the officers of the police garrison, and the so-called upstairs choir in the rear with their wives. As there was no organ at the time, the musicians, a regular military band with fifes, flutes, and brasses, had taken their stand behind the altar.

The little bell in the steeple began to strike eight; the side doors were closed, and from the front portal the offended Hesse strode in, while the congregation rose; he walked the narrow red carpet that the brethren had laid along the middle aisle in his honor, mounted the two steps before the altar, knelt on a white silk cushion, and put his helmet down beside him. He turned his back on the congregation, his face toward the silver crucifix, holding his body erect and his hands on the buckle of his belt. The moment he kneeled, the men in the nave and the women in the choir sat down. Colonel Lorenz, in the center of the first pew, rose, hymnbook in hand, to announce: "We will sing the first stanza of Hymn No. 499."

The conductor raised his baton three times: toward the nave, toward the choir, toward his orchestra. They were all so well trained in the ceremonial that instruments and voices started at once, without preliminary:

> *Entrust thy footsteps quailing*
> *And that which grieves thy heart*
> *To him whose love unfailing*
> *In heaven shall take thy part.*

He who commands the breezes
And bids the clouds begone
Can point the path that eases
Thy soul and guides thee on.

Singing and music broke off short. There was not a sound as Hesse took his helmet, rose, and, still standing before the altar, turned toward the congregation. The place and the hymn had soothed his spirit; there was no anger now, at most perhaps surprise in his voice as he said: "Why, this is a military conspiracy. You go to the Bishop without my knowledge, and offer him your help in dissolving the sects, although I myself am the son of a sectary."

Colonel Lorenz rose to contradict; he had been chosen beforehand as spokesman: "General Frohwein was a member of the Revival Mission too. But he was no sectary."

"What's wrong with being a sectary? 'In my father's house are many mansions' says the Lord."

"That is true," replied Lorenz, already embarrassed, for the dancing and arm waving of the Disciples of Emmaus and the Penitents made no impression on the policeman, not even a bad one.

"So you went to the Bishop to make a horse trade: he was to forbid the 'Christian commonwealth,' and you in turn would help him forbid the sects, so that not a single soul could pass judgment on religious matters except the Bishop."

"That isn't the reason why we went."

"Not the reason, but the result!" cried Hesse. "Because if you make the Bishop a Christian arbiter, the judge in matters of conscience, do you know where you will end?"

"The Bishop doesn't want to be an arbiter of conscience," persisted the colonel.

"Then why does he want to prohibit the sects?"

"Permit me a few brief words, Brother Hesse," requested Police Colonel Stark, the former schoolteacher who had been chosen Censor, getting up. "In order to wipe out the Iron Phalanx, which still exists despite the Three Prohibitions, the government has enacted a 'Law against bartering with God.' Would you say that the Disciples of Emmaus and the Penitents were *not* bartering with God? Must the law against bartering with God not be applied to someone simply because he is also violating a second prohibition, that of 'splendid phrases'?"

The general silently noticed that there was too much irony in his subordinate's speech, particularly for a censor, who ought to avoid rhetorical questions and find the simplest positive form of expression, never batting an eye.

"Hard, hard!" said Hesse. He meant that simple speaking is hard, and remembered the endless debates in the Academy about commentary on the Three Prohibitions, and about whether Henry Willert was guilty or innocent of violating the Carpenters' Rule. Involuntarily he took his left hand from his belt buckle and put it below his heart, which hurt. Perhaps it was not his heart that hurt, but the violence of his desire to escape from the capital city of triumphant Pharisees and scribes to his quiet town of Marienhall, and to climb Castle Hill at daybreak, hand in hand.

Stark and Lorenz searched Brother General's face to see what he actually meant by "Hard, hard!" But he motioned to the band leader, turned his back on the nave without a word, and knelt upon his cushion.

The conductor raised his baton three times, to the men, to the women, to the orchestra, whispered three times, "Stanza seven," and the song began. Hesse had not even sung the first stanza; as he was facing the center altar painting, and absorbed in the commission given to Rudolphi, no one could see his mouth.

The women's voices came clear and jubilant:

> *Rejoice, and bid thy sorrow*
> *And pain a last good night.*
> *Rise upon the morrow*
> *And let thy heart be light.*

> *Not thine to be the master*
> *Yet captive of a throne;*
> *Enthroned on alabaster*
> *The Lord God rules alone.*

The general got up from his cushion, and all followed his example; Lorenz called out: "Attention!"

Silently, as he had come, Otto left the chapel.

BOOK THREE

THE REALISTS AND ULTIMA THULE

XVI

THE rye was harvested and haying had begun when the proclamation was posted on the walls of the police stations and church doors:

"In concert with the government and the national synod of churchwardens, the Archbishop hereby renews the former

WARNING AGAINST CHURCH ATTENDANCE

"Cease at last to roll ecstatic eyes, to wave your arms, and to run to church! For thus saith the Lord our God to the prophet Isaiah in the first chapter: 'And when ye spread forth your hands, I will hide mine eyes from you: yea, when ye make many prayers, I will not hear. Seek judgment, relieve the oppressed, judge the fatherless, plead for the widow. Though your sins be red like crimson, they shall be as wool.'"

The horse trade disdained by Hesse had been concluded nevertheless, and the proclamation on the church doors was the price the Bishop had had to pay for Hesse's signature to the decree dissolving the Disciples of Emmaus and the Penitent Congregation because they had bartered with God.

By now, also, the censors' offices were established in all the towns, even the small ones, and so the prosecution of the Iron Phalanx began. The hatred of our more civilized neighbors for this "recurrence of the Dark Ages" forced the government into various withdrawals and "crawling servilities" in the face of foreign threats. Dr. Nessel was appointed to the presidency of the capital-city Censor's Office as Claire Mill had predicted, with Police Colonel Stark as his official secretary. The first audience of the Iron Phalangists with Stark fell out so unfortunately that a second conference was attempted.

Yet the unlucky call on Stark was really quite unnecessary, springing as it did from the pompous pretension of the Phalangists, who might have maintained their position by a bit of shrewdness. The decree introducing precensorship of "literary products written for purposes of art and instruction" left many loopholes and lines of retreat open to those who wished to escape. For the government, in the unenviable position of a husband in the waiting room during the long birth pangs of the guild constitution, took good care not to add unnecessary difficulties to the inevitable ones. Furthermore, the government and Academy included such powerful private capitalists as Beyer, the spinner, the Archbishop (far from a poor man), the generals trembling for their wives' money, and Bessonoff, the country's largest sugar producer (whose post as Minister of War had been restored after the legal dissolution of his marriage, while Kaempf advanced to Frohwein's position); there were also Willert and Simon, the great bankers; all of these men naturally wanted to preserve, not lose, their fortunes through the guild constitution. They were neither weaklings nor masochists, as everyone knew.

Accordingly, the decree began by listing the industries *not* affected by the Three Prohibitions or "legislation to protect freedom of instruction": these were the news, entertainment, and amusement industries. No Ballet of the Lifeless Brides, no *Maid of Orléans,* at Madame Kittelsen's had to fear the censor; the naked girls in the "Piquant Nights" in Scottish Widows' Lane could cast off their veils unmolested. Perhaps the authors of the commentary were too old to be interested in such matters; even pornography went untouched.

In those first days the gentlemen of the Iron Phalanx need not have submitted a single dramatic or narrative manuscript to the censor if they themselves had described it as entertaining or amusing literature, and printed it under that heading: the decree, after all, had left this recourse open. But they wanted to be "creative," and believed they were so—hence their downfall.

From the middle of July on, the serious articles in the magazines (except, of course, for *The Pensive Watchman* and its like) and the "cultural" sections of the newspapers were unreadable, such were the numerous and gaping holes in the text punched by the censor.

"But we can't take out all the splendid phrases," cried Habermann and Schiele to Stark, the Censor. "What would be left?"

Stark shrugged his shoulders: "Write anything you please. But anything prohibited will be cut out."

"Why?" they asked.

"Because you aren't teachers. If you were, you wouldn't ask such stupid questions."

At this they and Innocent Rex implored the colonel to see reason. Goodness knew there was no reason for enmity; they were not Urbanites, and if they had to be "teachers" now, why not? They proposed that the Censor should hold a conference once a week, and tell the creative writers and editors just what they were permitted and expected to teach at the moment. The authors had always been accustomed to ask the publisher what they should write. In the present state of affairs, therefore, they would be gladder still to ask the Censor.

This was when the regrettable outburst took place: "Just one more word," Stark yelled, "and you'll go to jail for defaming the teacher's calling! Do you think a *teacher* is enough of a rascal to ask the Censor or anyone else what he's to write? Or that he asks permission? A real *teacher*—but anyway you're peddlers, opinion-mongers, profaners of the Sabbath—out with you before I get you arrested! If I cut out a comma of a real teacher's, he'd come in here and bust me in the teeth, and *I'd* go to jail for having cut out a comma of his, and he'd bring charges against me before the Carpenters' Joint Court for infringing the freedom of instruction! Get out, you ruffians!" And the three, thus ignominiously used, departed from the office of the capital-city Censor. The law firm of Tadd & Pole was instructed to bring charges before the Carpenters' Joint Court against Colonel Stark for infringing the freedom of instruction. The bill of complaint pointed out untenable inconsistencies on the part of the Censor. On the one hand, he had insisted that writers who declined to join the fellowships of the amusement or entertainment industries must be "teachers." On the other hand, he had said, according to the record, "If a man honestly *wants* to be a teacher, but isn't, owing to incapacity, I daren't molest him. In fact, if someone maintains he has written an original composition, and all he has done is to write a hundred times over the sentence, 'The Censor is a pig,' I shan't touch a single letter, not even the dot on the *i* —if the man really means what he writes. It doesn't make any difference whether it's right or wrong or stupid or clever—who's to decide that? But whether a man means what he says, whether he's revealing his own heart—that's what matters, and nothing else; that is, the dignity of the teacher's calling depends on honesty of heart."

Abroad, meanwhile, tales were being circulated that we were destroying the theaters, our churches were closed, Christianity was abolished, and socialism was on the march.

At Portenuovo, the great commercial port of the Southwestern Republics, the rabble screamed, "Do like they did!" smashed the mayor's windows, and burned three grain vessels.

Hereupon, in order to put an end to the dispute, Henry the Franciscan, Merckel's successor, summoned the editors in chief, Schiele, Habermann, and Hoppelkopf (Mark Antony had already fled) to the prior's cell. By his side sat the president of the Censor's office, Dr. Nessel, and the latter's secretary, Colonel Stark.

Nessel conceded that the prohibition of splendid phrases had destroyed eighty per cent of the local culture. He admitted the truly deplorable state of several hundred theatrical and operatic producers, who had indeed always cynically maintained that they served the public and the box office, not art; but now that they were compelled to admit this and describe themselves publicly as "establishments for recreation and amusement," they were losing weight and showing signs of melancholy despite excellent business. In fact, dramatic works of art hitherto suppressed by the Iron Phalanx and rejected everywhere as financially hopeless were now being dug up, described as pornography or comedy to evade the censorship, and performed without regard for profit and loss. This therefore made it evident that under threat of censorship the art entrepreneurs, hitherto frivolous, had reverted to honesty and dignity.

"Ninety per cent of culture is destroyed," whispered Professor Habermann, repressing a tear.

"What does he mean?" the monk asked the secretary of the Censor's Office.

"Because we have forbidden bartering with God," Stark replied, "intellectual life is beginning to die out. It is expiring with a last sigh, so to speak."

Brother Henry, little pleased with the cheap irony of the victor, turned amiably to Hoppelkopf: "Surely you must have had someone in mind, all of you, I mean, in your strange activity."

"The people!" replied Habermann, interrupted by Stark, who ejaculated: "He means the customers!"

"Hairsplitting!" Habermann went on. "We dealt with the entire nation, all classes and professions! But we *served* them, make no mistake! We didn't govern. We never forced any taste or opinion upon anyone; on the contrary! We listened reverently to the pulse of the nation, to discover its taste and its opinion. . . ."

"Do you mean you had no taste or opinion of your own?" the Franciscan probed.

"That's what I just said: we were servants from conviction. For a writer and poet can indeed mirror reality, but never instruct it. What is a wretched little man in his attic, thinking his thoughts, by comparison with tumultuous reality? What are a few cubic inches of brain matter compared to the vast sweep of practical life?"

Professor Schiele, editor and writer, grown old but not hardened in the culture trade, shook hands with the speaker: "Ah, my dear co-worker! You speak from our very hearts! Yes, humility and modesty befit the intellectual: one man cannot be wiser than ten thousand. Therefore our ear was pressed to the heart of the nation: 'Nation, instruct us!' we said. We were not megalomaniacs enough to try to instruct tempestuous life. The masses were our teachers. To put their needs on paper in comprehensible terms, to keep their cultural requirements alive with exciting news and stories—this is service to the nation."

"Service to customers!" Stark interrupted.

"Certainly, since we are realists. What would you do with a culture for which there were no customers? Whom can such a culture serve, if I may ask? The producer? But he can't sell it, and Hilgenfeld went mad. The publisher? He loses his money on it, can't meet his payroll, and his workers lose their jobs. That is downfall. That is decay."

"Ninety per cent of culture," whispered Hoppelkopf, most difficult to down of the three, but now shaken in his turn.

"—annihilated, yes, say it," Schiele finished. "We were the servants of the public, and the mirror of the age. Hence our flourishing——"

"Trade!" cried the pitiless police colonel.

"Well, oughtn't it to flourish?" asked Habermann. "If the publisher's trade doesn't flourish, what are writers to live on and support their families with? Government subsidies? That would be tyranny, the end of the intellect! Or do you mean to say that the writer is not obligated, like every husband and father, to support his family? Is he to be the sole exception? If, however, as is obvious, he *must* support his family, then he like any other producer must produce salable goods. And whether or not his goods are salable is decided not by him but by the buyer: is that clear?"

"Undoubtedly," agreed Henry the Franciscan, and Habermann went on: "So he can't set up to be wiser than ten thousand; he must listen to the pulse of the nation, and seek out its needs. For the nation is the buyer; the nation decides whether the manufacturer's goods are salable, and whether the writer is writing what will support his family."

The President's deputy nodded agreement: "That is a logical, consistent philosophy, Stark, perfectly reasonable, and in my opinion not punishable."

"Mr. Secretary," Schiele burst out, overpowered by true emotion, and bowing as he sat, "I hope Your Excellency will allow me to speak as a poet: wisdom flows from your mouth! For we as realists know perfectly well that in human history there are periods of freedom and periods of unfreedom. Freedom lies behind us, it lies buried: as realists we take note of this fact, and only a madman can gainsay accomplished facts with the tongue of folly. Only a fool can oppose himself to the superior force of tumultuous life. But life strides over the prostrate forms of fools. In times of freedom the writer must speak out the needs and the pulse of the people; in times of unfreedom, the pulse of the government."

"That's what realism is—the recognition of accomplished facts," Hoppelkopf agreed. "And not only that. It's the truth. A hundred times we have asked Censor Stark to consider our talent, our experience, our good will at his disposal: we want to be close to the heart of the government, listening to its pulse, putting its desires and needs on paper in comprehensible language. But how are we received?"

The Secretary of State looked first at Nessel, then at Stark, then at his fingers, blew some dust off the table, sighed deeply, and said at last to Hoppelkopf, Habermann, and Schiele: "Gentlemen, this is a hard thing for me to say, but I must inform you that you will be granted your full salaries as a life pension, and retired from the former firm of Koenig Publications. We recognize your good will, but it will not go far enough toward giving effect to the Three Prohibitions, since you do not and cannot understand any one of the three. I wish I might have given you a word of consolation and encouragement. What we are doing here seems harsh, I know; it looks like unfreedom. I dislike to let you go with this bitterness in your hearts. But did you not say yourselves that in times of unfreedom we must listen to the government? Do that: listen for just a year. It may be, gentlemen, that with good will you can discover the country for which we have set our course: *Ultima Thule."*

BOOK THREE

THE GOSPEL OF THE SUNDAY MORTAL, OR THE RELIGIOUS COMMONWEALTH

XVII

A T THE end of September, after lying apparently dead for three months, the Iron Phalanx rose up for one last attempt. Its "League of Sunday Mortals for the Recreation and Amusement of the Poor" held meetings all over the country; and as the Three Prohibitions did not prohibit anyone from telling the truth, i.e., the honest belief of his heart, they asserted that the government was suppressing Adam Faust's last will. The latter, they claimed, required the Archbishop's *Gospel of the Sunday Mortal* to be not only taught but followed. In reality, however, it was not being followed, for the poor had too little recreation and amusement on Sundays; they were begrudged their right to "be human beings for once" on Sundays. Therefore the League of Sunday Mortals had presented a bill to expropriate the park and forest lands of the rich for the benefit of the people, and appropriate a sufficient sum to establish popular Sunday entertainments with free beer in every parish.

The government and Senate forthwith prohibited the name, and the name only, of the League of Sunday Mortals, as the term opened the door to momentous errors. There could be no objection to philanthropy, and if the guilds wanted to ruin their innkeepers by furnishing free beer on Sundays, that was the guilds' business. But where, in what passage did the Bishop's *Gospel* mention philanthropy?

Four weeks later, the mob of Portenuovo having rebelled a second time, the League itself was dissolved for disturbing true doctrine.

On November 1, Adam Faust's birthday, the Church of the Saviour in the capital was jammed full. The papers had announced that the Archbishop himself would defend his prohibition and also explain what the *Gospel of the Sunday Mortal* really signified.

The old man's sermon was as follows:

"A crowd of fools have spread a rumor that by the Sunday Mortal I meant a mortal who wanted to rest from work and have a little pleasant amusement on Sunday. So that even the poor man might be a 'Sunday Mortal' of this sort, a League of Sunday Mortals was founded. We studied it for a while, and then merely forbade the name of the association, because we did not yet know whether it was a society of harmless or of dangerous fools. We hesitated a long time before issuing even this interdict, and we argued long in the Academy—you yourselves, my dear friends, will know why. Woe to the government that drives folly and merriment from its realm!

"Meanwhile, however, the police have learned that folly and malice hand in hand were deliberately obscuring my picture of the mortal who 'wants to be a human being for once,' and that these malicious fools were *intentionally* misunderstanding my *Gospel,* and dragging it down to the low estate of philanthropy. Accordingly, we forbade this league of fools.

"Why do these fools glare at us so savagely? Well, behind closed doors and among themselves they are today conceding that they went too far. If they had given the mortal who 'wants to be a human being for once' just a little air to breathe, they would still be in their editorial and professorial chairs, dominating the people with printer's ink.

"They carried it too far.

"And we, since no other way was open, finally established this religious commonwealth, so that freedom—suppressed, sneered at, and odious as it has been—might once more dare to appear on the public street.

"And what is 'freedom'? The right of assembly? No. Freedom is not a right at all. Freedom is a way of life: it is the life of the mortal who 'wants to be altogether a human being for once,' or, as I put it, the Sunday Mortal. It is him I would speak of, and this time so plainly that even the Iron Phalanx can understand me if it will.

"Let me start with his opposite, the weekday mortals; but you must realize at last that these expressions are symbolic, and not literally meant. The one tremendous fact that dominates the life of almost everyone is the struggle for survival. We call this practical life, and the man who manages to survive, a practical man. But we no longer produce for ourselves what we need to live on; and in order to purchase we must first sell something that was our property—silver spoons or old trousers or knowledge or our bodily strength. Buying is easy and selling difficult. Therefore the simple formula for practical life is, 'Offer what there is a demand for.' Possess something that will bring either pleasure or satisfaction: 'Bread, women, and merriment are always salable,' said Hilgenfeld the poet. And this is the right way to speak to a practical man, for he speaks so himself. But some fine day, when the practical man has supplied himself with bread and a wife and merriment, he will wash his neck, comb his hair, put on a clean shirt, and when his wife asks him what he wants, he says he wants to be a human being for once. 'Good God,' says his wife, 'you aren't sick, are you?' She quickly sends to the drugstore for an ice bag, because she realizes he isn't normal. All at once he begins to smile a silly smile, to hum, to be absorbed in himself, to express a desire for solitude—in short, he gets into such a state that his wife turns away with apologies his friend in the leather line who had come to close an advantageous deal. The practical man is, as they say in court, legally incompetent.

"What kind of creature is this that is not satisfied after eating? What kind of creature is driven by an unrest inherent in him alone among all God's creatures, a purely human unrest, to peer up at the stars, search books, create shapes and tunes, stammer out prayers or tales, roar blasphemies, and apparently to forget all useful things—buying and selling, hunger and satisfaction, survival, reproduction, gains and losses: everything that goes to make up practical life?

"It is the mortal who 'wants to be a human being for once.' And what is this unrest that comes upon him alone of all animate creatures, lifting him above all creation? It is the question of life's meaning: not the meaning of life in general, but of his own special individual life; and again not the meaning of the individual life of a human being in so far as he is a manufacturer or seller or useful citizen of some kind, but on the contrary in so far as he is nothing at all—except a human being.

"For the meaning of the producer's or seller's life is a question as easily answered as that of the meaning of a wine drinker's or a mother's life; the wine drinker is to drink wine, the mother to bring up her child. The producer, the seller, the cabinetmaker, the cobbler: the meaning of their lives is exhausted in the one fact that they know their business, and this life is spent between working and resting from work. The meaning of a cobbler's life can be expressed in two words: cobbling shoes. But just ask him if he himself thinks he is really no more than a cobbler, and if his whole existence is compassed in work, rest, and amusement!

"Surely it is impossible to suppose, a mother says, that the meaning of my life is exhausted in bringing up a child, simply so that when the child is grown up he can do the same thing that I, damn it, have already done, namely to bring up a child!

"Surely it is impossible to suppose, says the peddler of old pants, that the meaning of my life is exclusively pants peddling, and that I am nothing more than a link in an endless chain of pants peddlers!

"And even the tavernkeeper with his face taking on a purple flush from practical life, and the fat veins standing out at the temples to give warning of apoplexy—how often have I heard him say, as he wound up the squeaky phonograph, that he was really not a tavernkeeper but a musician—at least in his heart. Conversely (this is irrelevant here) I have known musicians who said they were really tavernkeepers. But this was never the fact; for the musicians who were in truth 'really tavernkeepers' carefully concealed the fact, and talked like the man with the purplish flush and the thick veins.

"In short, no one, no matter how practical, will ever surrender his claim to being a 'human being.' Some fine Sunday you will be overwhelmed with longing for the totally useless, for that which cannot be bought, which was not made for sale or for anyone's profit except perhaps that of the 'human being.' Some fine Sunday, after damning the world of success and pleasure, and putting on a clean shirt, you will depart for the *region of monuments,* which either the Creator himself or his pupil, the mortal who wants to be a human being, has put up. For the answer to your ageless question about the meaning of your life must surely be found in nature or art, if anywhere.

"Out you go to the region of monuments. For, avid though his endeavor to find the answer to the ageless question, the average man, when he wants to be a human being, requires a fellow seeker, a helper in his search, without whom the mere asking will confuse, exhaust, and discourage him, flinging him back into his easier weekday existence.

"And he finds his fellow seeker: the Sunday Mortal whose whole existence has been charged with the joy and anguish of asking and seeking after the significance of being human. This Sunday Mortal it is who has left behind the monuments, which are simply a record of revelations from an unknown authority that must know more than any mortal. We call the recorder an artist or a man of religion, thus indicating that his record, even if apparently it springs altogether from earthly observation, nevertheless does not come from here, like the report of an accountant or a soldier. Where the report really comes from we learn in Anton Koerner's speech on equality, made thirteen years ago. The atheists, trying to explain the derivation of the monuments from the weekday, have found an excuse that they call "imagination": an empty word, my friends, unless it expresses the capacity to receive revelations.

"Now, my dear listeners, let me speak of the helper in seeking and questioning, the setter up of monuments, whom we encounter in two shapes—the artist and the man of religion. The latter is sure he has found a final answer to the ancient question; the former is not. Millions of human beings turn for help to the man of religion, seeking the tranquillity that he alone can give. For the answer of the artist, always probing into the question, and ending as a question itself, leaves the seeker rejoicing and exalted, but not at rest.

"How does an artist live, I ask, and how must a government behave toward him? Since his life is filled with seeking and listening, the people, the healthy common people, have always rightly supposed that he was not created or able to amass riches. Therefore he must live in poverty, but honored and respected because he is the teacher whom a mortal turns to when he would be a human being. And the common people, still healthy, still clinging to their humanity, have always realized that they honored themselves in honoring the teacher who helped them ask the ancient question. The healthy common people have never required that the priest or artist should earn his bread by weekday labor. They have always been ready to give him what he needed for his seeking and listening: bread, meat, shelter, and solitude. The common people who still bear the future within them have been glad when he was content; they have frowned when he lived in luxury—not from envy, but for fear he would be corrupted.

"For the healthy common people know that they themselves will be corrupted if the monument builder is corrupted.

"And of course they, the people, want to live, to live on into the future. And they know perfectly well that it is not the statesman, the officer, the moneymaker who transmits the memory of the people; it is Homer, Plato, Isaiah. The humblest interpreter of omens, the least of prophets, transmits more of the people's life than the conqueror of the world.

"I have already said that the healthy common people strive to give their teacher everything he needs at the moments of his seeking. Just one thing they demand of him: that he utter the truth, even if it be in screams and blasphemies. The people demand that he be *free*.

"When John the Baptist was in a cage underground, he did not cease to teach. To make him stop they had to cut off his head. When John the Baptist was locked up, few people heard what he said, so his effectiveness was diminished in prison; *but his freedom was not diminished*. Nor are we told that his freedom gradually faded away like the health of a man in torment: we hear nothing of that. An hour before his death his freedom was as great as when he was giving baptism in the Jordan. It fell from him at a blow, at the blow of the ax.

"What then is freedom? The life of the teacher! What must a government do to restore freedom? It must restore the teacher. For he who has the teacher's calling can have no choice: he must endure freedom. No emperor, no prince, no government, can offer him directions or advice, but he can give these to everyone. And precisely because he does this, not concealing what he has seen, the people honor him and give him what he needs.

"The healthy common people know all too well that he who follows the teacher's calling holds in his hands the honor, the strength, the future of the people. If he becomes unfree, whom are they to ask in their hours of seeking? To whom shall they turn to purge their souls and 'be human beings for once'?

"There is no one whom they can turn to if the teacher is not there. And if he is not there, but in his place are a pack of wily swindlers, what then?

"What, my friends, becomes of that nation whose moments of want-

ing to be human beings grow ever shorter, since the helpers in the
search who thrust themselves forward are all frauds, flatterers, pussy-
footers, windbags, and traders, unctuously truckling to a nation that
really desires to be instructed by a high authority? And yet, oh filth
and rottenness, this gang comes crowding long-eared upon the nation,
trying craftily to spy out the message it would wish to hear, to find
out what it will pay highest for.

"What becomes of such a nation, my friends? It ceases to be a
nation: it disintegrates into cliques, parties, and communities of interest.

"A nation that accepts the teachings of swindlers grows blind and
deaf. A blind, deaf nation cannot distinguish the teacher, the interpreter of signs, the kindly or awful seer, from the swindler. Such a
nation no longer has any Sunday. And a nation with no Sunday lives
in the bog.

"Our nation was ready to perish in the bog. It was still alive, but
not as a nation. Who can help us become a nation once more?

"The man who creates arrogates to himself the teacher's calling.
Therefore he must have something that he has heard to communicate,
and he must be able to endure the freedom that goes with being
honest. If he has not this freedom he is a fraud, calculating profit
and loss: let him peddle pants!

"As long as *we* live, there will be no barter with God in this country, no huckstering with monuments, and an artist who arrays his
monuments for sale will lose his civil rights and wind up in a
department store as the salesclerk he is.

"But the hasty covering of paper with comprehensible phraseology
has stultified mankind to such an extent that you, my neighbors, even
you, thought I meant recreation and amusement when I issued the
Gospel of the Sunday Mortal! Oh, I fairly quailed with chagrin and
disappointment. For recreation and amusement are breaks in work;
that is, they belong to the weekday, to business. Every workingman
is allowed his recreation, just as he is allowed to go to the toilet or
sleep with his wife: for he is meant to recruit his strength for work.
In fact, the shrewdest among the industrialists even offer recreation
and amusement for the workingman at their own expense, because
relaxation and laughter increase strength and good will. Recreation

and amusement make the workman more of a workman. But where is it written that they make him more of a man?

"Certainly it is true that the question of life's meaning, or the desire to be a human being for once, may be choked by long and excessively hard work. But surely you don't suppose long and excessively hard work is the only way to choke off being human. If that were so, the rich and idle would be more 'human' than the workingmen. For the life of the idle consists exclusively of relaxation (from what, I always wonder) and amusement. But Scripture itself says that the slothful man who amuses himself all night and relaxes by day from his amusement is stupider, dirtier, and more bestial than any workman.

"And they accuse *me* of despising the masses!

"But it is precisely the man who goes to concerts and the theater because he would otherwise have to hang himself for sheer boredom who usually talks contemptuously about the 'masses.' He never dreams in his stupidity that he is more 'masses' than any masses whatsoever, and less of a human being than any mortal.

"Certainly a blessing flows from recreation and entertainment, as anyone knows who works hard; but the profit-maker into whose pocket the blessing flows knows it better yet.

"How can you fools put me, your bishop, in the ranks of the utility worshipers who would give recreation and amusement to the poor man so that he may work better and more willingly? What are your sordid interests to me? What are recreation and amusement to me? What concern of mine are the industries that give excitement to the idler? Reach for the rope if you suffer from boredom; I shan't cut any of you down, or babble a prayer over your grave. I help the living, not the dead!

"When General Hesse proposed to us, his colleagues, that the Municipal Theater should be leveled with the ground for massacring Shakespeare's masterpieces, I offered a counterproposal: it would be enough, I said, to chisel off the name 'Municipal Theater' from the façade, and carve instead the words, 'Recreation and Amusement Shop.' But at the same time, I said, there must be monstrous posters hung on the walls of the building, kept fresh constantly for ten years, proclaiming that the voice of the mortal who wants to be a human being for once, the voice that is heard in works of art and religion, must never be raised in this building, not a word, not a syllable, not a

note of music, as punishment because the proprietors of the building
had maltreated the Sunday Mortal.

"For the money-changers belong in the market place, not in the
temple.

"Since then my proposal has given rise to the federal law against
bartering with God; this interdict, as is well known and thank goodness, has forced over a hundred theaters and opera houses to change
their signs and call themselves what they are.

"Thank goodness, I say. For none of you, my friends, believes deep
down in his heart that the monstrous bog from which the swamp-
flower Urban sprang can be drained by 'denouncing conditions,' or by
patting and pretty talk.

"In conclusion, my friends, I will betray a secret. Not I, not Willert,
Hildebrand, or Lindbrecht, not one of the Senators belonging to the
so-called first team, paid any attention in earlier years to the literati
and their associations; we smiled and took Ackermann's and Hilgenfeld's excoriations of the Iron Phalanx for clever magnifications. That
was an error. Now, since I as a censor have gained an insight into the
cultural trade, all the Urbanites who were still in prison have been
liberated at my instance, except of course for the Gas-House Boys.

"For while I am sure that if Urban's followers had won a victory
they would have built an inferno of idolatry, hypocrisy, and thralldom,
still General Kaempf testified that they fought like lions, and died
tight-lipped. They were devils, they were hell, but they were *not* the
bog. And as for our countrymen who streamed to Urban's banners—
well, friends, I cannot despise the man who says in his heart: sooner
hell than the bog!

"And now let me reply to the charge that we drove the Federal
Police Corps to rebel.

"The truth is that the officers of the capital-city police garrison committed not rebellion, but an error.

"They supposed that no nation could assume the title of 'Christian'
until it had put aside sinfulness. The very opposite is true. The nation
that knows nought of sin has fallen bodily into Satan's clutches, as we
can plainly read in Merckel's 'Political Testament,' Article Six. And
in the same place, throughout Article Four, the nature of a Christian
commonwealth is established: the one whose governing personages are
able to recognize the enemy, i.e., the satanic element.

"For the good, my friends, cannot be bred: it grows in freedom, and withers in a greenhouse.

"But be of good cheer: very shyly at first, then more boldly and bravely, the tiny blossom will look up from God's earth and spread among you the perfume of its gladness, if only you will root out the weeds."

BOOK THREE

EMIL AND IDA

XVIII

I. THE ENCOUNTER

TWO hours' drive from the splendid capital of our neighboring country, pleasantly bedded in woods between the railroad right of way and the hill, lies the prosperous little *rentiers'* community of Belrigardo, where citizens of the capital, grown well-to-do, have long built cottages and cultivated their gardens.

One of the most respected families in the place, whose imposing house often gathers in a circle of elbow-bending friends, is the Branconi family, consisting of Mr. Emilio Branconi and his wife Ida. There are neither children nor cares; the well-kept property fronting on Horse-Chestnut Street and Copper-Beech Avenue (both of which do honor to their names by stands of old trees) was bought cheap from a bankrupt previous owner, and the Branconis' livelihood is assured by a plump account in the National Bank of the Southwestern Republics.

As the couple have been living in Belrigardo for ten years, word has got around that the unpretentious Mrs. Branconi is a countess. "Splendid people, the Branconis," is the accustomed phrase of Mayor Louvain, who grew rich by improving Camembert cheese, "with her a countess and yet always perfectly simple," whereupon he adds that food chemistry is opening up unlimited vistas.

The second main street of the village, a countrified thoroughfare with low cottages and little shops, opens out near the railroad station into the quiet Place des Trois Soeurs Provençales, which has in the middle a patch of green turf with benches. A few trees give shade; asters and mignonette are in bloom. In the corner building, one side fronting on the street, the other on the little square, is the shop where Mr. Donohill, an immigrant from Ireland, has his grocery and delicatessen shop. A special sign on the street side adds, WINES AND COAL. Facing the shop, with a front lawn, is the village church.

One glorious fall afternoon we find the Branconis upon the square; Emil is sitting on a bench, Ida stooping to pick a sprig of mignonette, when along comes the portly mayor with a bespectacled young man, his secretary.

Seeing the Branconis, he gave his enthusiasm free rein: "Life is wonderful, sir, say what you please. Food chemistry is opening up unlimited vistas. I don't say that because of cheese, but as a humanist. Look there. Who is standing there at the corner, outside Donohill's shop, by the bed of mignonette? The Branconis: she, once a countess, is putting a sprig of mignonette in her husband's buttonhole. And see how she looks at him, with her hair snow white, but fresh and youthful! Pessimists are blind, blind to beauty! Ida, Countess Bessonoff, a millionaire's wife, but love cares not for law, justice, or might. And so she married the poor officer in the secret service, and was happy with him. Splendid people both, the Branconis!" And, passing with raised hat, the sterling citizen greeted the couple: "Madam Countess! Mr. Branconi!"

"Why, Mr. Mayor! How about Saturday dinner for a roast chicken?" Ida returned, while Emil the tremendous bowed in his seat.

"It will be an honor and a pleasure!" Mr. Louvain agreed, and with that the village dignitaries were on their way.

Ida knelt down by the mignonette as if to drink the sweetness of the perfume: "This is summer's end—heartbreaking: can you smell it? You feel like taking the earth in your hands, like sleeping on every stone. . . . You wish time would stand still at this very moment, and everything would stay just so—forever, always."

"Exactly so," observed Emil from the bench. He had taken off his slouch hat, and was making marks in the sand with the point of his cane. "You know, Ida, I've got an idea."

Ida had arisen, a branch of mignonette on her arm; she breathed heavily, from stooping, and sat down with a happy sigh: "Do you remember ten years ago when they were putting up the scaffolding at Mittelburg? Would you ever have thought then that we could be happy some day, as happy as we are? I wish everything would stand still, and nothing would change. You've turned into a gray-haired man, universally respected, and cultivating your garden. And I'm a lady, which I never was. I never used to believe in God, either; now I'm beginning to, because on a fall day like this I can feel something saying to me, 'Give your consent!' Can't you?"

"After all, we've earned it, Ida," replied Branconi. "I always say, he who fights in his youth will find a haven in his old age. Do you feel like going into that church yonder for a little while? I mean, you see I had an idea."

"What was it?"

"Well . . . since you ask, young Susemihl over in Depot Street has got a new phonograph record of *La Paloma*—you know that was always my favorite song . . ."

"Oh, my dear man, do go on and have a quick one," smiled Ida. "I'll go take a rest in church; the air has made me tired."

Emil, getting up, searched his pockets: "Haven't we forgotten something?"

She shook her head, surprised: "No. Tomorrow's Friday; we'll go in town early to get fish."

Mr. Branconi arose, twisted his mouth peevishly, and tried to swallow: "Damn it, I did forget the sodium bicarbonate. Well, Susemihl's got some. What were you saying about tomorrow morning?"

"Getting fish—you know perfectly well. In the Rue St. Thomas."

"Oh. Has it absolutely got to be there?"

"Of course. Why do you ask?"

"I just don't like the street," replied Emil, hand on heart. "Damn this heartburn!"

"All at once?"

"I saw a woman there . . . You know, one of these religious fanatics, pretty awful."

"Well, and . . . ? Getting restless again? I've seen old acquaintances too—and they me. You bow and pass on. That business with the hundred and ninety-seven wounded was the act of a crazed chemistry professor, the world knows that."

"That isn't what I mean. That was during the war. War is war, people say."

"Well, whom *did* you see in the Rue St. Thomas?"

"Diana Rose."

Now the white-haired woman was standing close beside him: "Did you look into it?"

"Yes. She's living on the sixth floor of a building not far from our fishmonger's. She seems to be a religious maniac, and has a small income. I was in the same prayer-meeting place, in disguise of course; I saw her frothing at the mouth."

"What kind of prayer-meeting place?"

"The Chapel of the Brides of Christ, on the same street."

"Why are you afraid of—Diana?"

"Because she was frothing at the mouth."

"Do you owe her money—or something else? Be honest, now, Emil!"

"Nothing. She got enough pickings and stealings in Oscar Koenig's great days for her to live on."

"Well, then! We can't emigrate to the moon. We'll stick to our fishmonger—and if you meet her, you'll soon see if she wants anything. After all, anyone deserves a hello and a kind word, even your friend Diana. And if she doesn't want anything more than . . . *that?* Good God, Emil, before you'd let yourself be killed for it? 'Once doesn't count,' the proverb says."

"Never." His mouth twisted again, with disgust or heartburn.

"All right, all right!" laughed Ida. "See you later, my dear!"

And Emil, first kissing his wife's hand, stalked off on his long, stout legs to young Susemihl, restaurateur and wine merchant, where you could hear the latest from home over a glass of Algerian Red.

So old von Brick was dead, and his celebrated son-in-law was divorced from Alexandra, who had gone her own way. The dovelike Veronica, owner of the chatelet on the hill at Marienhall, had pulled it off. And Claire Mill, the wily devil, was dressed in silks and satins as the consort of Frank Jaeger, the Caucasian Oak; and Louise Hofer, the Geisenheim nightingale, was openly living in sin with Hans Simon, Secretary of State for Foreign Trade. Odd that that fellow Lienhardt, the youngest one, Peter George, head of the secret service, didn't turn up anywhere: a smart lad in his day, you might say. Better give Diana some money so that she could buy herself a man; take up that old affair again? No: apparently she wasn't even washing any more; Christ himself would decline with thanks! . . .

As Ida got up to go into the church, Mr. Donohill came out on the street to close his shop, where you could buy anything, oranges, sausage, string—and, the sign added, VINS ET CHARBONS.

"Evening to you, Countess," said the portly man with the brown mustache drooping over his lip.

"Oh, Donohill!" Ida returned his greetings. "How's Dolores?"

Just then she herself came out of the door, her youngest in her arms —Dolores Donohill, née McCarthy, still thin, but the picture of health. Six-year-old Mary was clutching her mother's skirt behind.

"Want to come with me to church?" asked Ida Branconi.

Dolores was delighted: "Oh, yes, I'd love to sit down for a while. Martha," she called into the shop, "bring me my shawl and take the children!"

2. THE SHADOW GROWS

It was the depth of winter now, Belrigardo was covered with snow, and tomorrow was Christmas. But on the evening of the twenty-fourth there would be carp and red wine, the good Algerian Red, at the Branconis'; that was as sure as preaching. Louvain, the *mairc*, would not be missing, but good old Charles Emil Koehler, witty and amusing just as he had been in his days as electrical director, unfortunately could not come this year: he worked for the Northern Railway, and was on duty.

Very early, with dawn just breaking, Ida, well wrapped in furs, set out for Dolores Donohill's to buy a net shopping bag; hers was torn. It would also be interesting to hear the views of Donohill, the encyclopedia of information on Belrigardo's best society. Alarming tales of threats from a person who did not sign his name were circulating among the *émigrés* who put their heads together in Susemihl's back room.

Dolores had the shopping bag that Ida had just bought lined with care: "Put in oiled paper, Martha, the good kind, and fasten it around the edge with a darning needle. The Countess wants to buy fish."

As Martha started on the job, Donohill appeared in the shop, and of course he knew the whole story: "Well, yesterday the mayor got the second threatening letter, this time with exact details, but anonymous again."

Ida, though she was not asthmatic, clutched at her throat as if choking: "You mustn't think I'm frightened, Donohill! It's not that . . ."

"Why not?" returned the portly man with the untidy mustache: "If some anonymous swine goes and writes that there's a murderer in our parish, every man and woman is bound to be frightened, except possibly the infants. Because, after all, even the most honest person has had a moment of weakness at some time or other. Anyone that writes anonymous letters ought to be strung up, that's what I think."

"But there's a Statute of Limitations," Ida suggested.

"Of course."

"What does this anonymous fellow say? You can tell me, Donohill; it won't go any further."

"The first one was quite vague—like a bad smell that you don't know where it comes from. The second one, typewritten: 'Mr. Mayor, living in your community as a respected *rentier* is the Gas-House Boy who murdered Henry Merckel, the Secretary of State, ten years ago. If you don't arrest him yourself'—it ran about like that, but the idea is right—'I shall come to the assistance of your perspicacity.'"

"Well, well," said Ida. "Will you come to dinner tonight? Two lovely carp. The mayor's coming too; only the Koehlers declined. He's on duty."

Donohill, opening his eyes wide and pressing his lower lip to his mustache, so that his mouth quite disappeared, looked far from bright. He leaned across the counter: "I wouldn't invite those people in again, Countess. You see Koehler *isn't* on duty . . . But he may have some notion who the letter writer is—how do I know?"

3. PREPARATION

The medicine cabinet in the Branconis' lumber room was amply supplied; this was something with which Emil, as an old nurse and madhouse attendant, was thoroughly familiar. At eleven o'clock in the morning the couple stood ready to leave before the open cabinet; he was wrapping a narrow instrument case in a white napkin.

"I could lay her out with that box," said Emil, pointing to Ida's typewriter. "It's heavy enough; but it would make a conspicuous wound, and it would hurt. So you'll have to do exactly what I tell you now——"

Ida trembled: "But in the excitement . . ."

He seated her tenderly on a white enamel hospital stool: "Where's any excitement? It's all thought out beforehand, and no time to get excited. That will come afterward, or not at all. I know the layout of the two rooms and kitchen perfectly. When she opens the hall door, she takes her visitors into the room on the right, looking out on the yard."

"But you say she doesn't receive any callers between four and six, because she's praying then."

"That's when she cooks; but she'll receive *us*. You come behind me, carrying the shopping bag——"

"With the fish? That'll be hard."

From the medicine cabinet Emil took a bottle of clear, colorless liquid, possibly a pint, and tried the cork to see if it was in tight. He also tried Ida's overcoat pockets, which were cut like a man's, buttoning at the top. The bottle fitted in comfortably. "Now listen. As soon as you come in behind me, you quickly put the bag on the floor, shut the hall door, take out the bottle—just try the cork to be sure it isn't in too tight."

Ida twisted the cork out without difficulty: "It's in just right." Then she smelled of it.

"Cork it up and don't do anything foolish! There. Now I'll put the bottle in your right outside pocket; nothing but handkerchief and gloves in the other—nothing heavy. You'll have both hands free; you look at me, take out the bottle, uncork it, pocket the cork—and you quickly pour out half the bottle on the cotton batting that I'll hold out to you. That's about all. You keep the bottle in your hand—don't spill any, don't smell of it—you know ether can knock you out. You just stand there and wait for my orders. The whole thing will take seven minutes."

Ida nodded: "You can rely on me. What's that there?" She pointed to the flat package wrapped in the napkin.

"That's the case with the big hypodermic needle, which I've already filled. You'll see how it's used. Don't ask any more questions: you aren't to think about anything except the bottle of ether in your pocket. Now I'm going to put some thin gauze around the cotton batting, to hold it together better. You're to pour half the bottle on it quickly, but not hurriedly."

Ida began to sob.

"Are you going to weaken?"

"Now you listen to me, too, Emil, just for two minutes. Of course I'm going to help you, but you've got to answer my questions."

"Go ahead and ask, damn it; but a fool can ask more questions than ten wise . . . you know about that!"

"Are you absolutely sure it's she, and that the denunciation means us? How awful if it were a mistake . . . And we . . . We're committing murder."

"No, no. It's right enough, Ida. She put it to me straight."

"Diana? In the prayer-meeting place?"

"Not in the chapel. Right out on the street. And I wasn't disguised, either. 'You stupid donkey,' I tell her, 'you vengeful idiot, how could *I* have murdered Merckel? The Gas-House Boy belonged to Section IV, sabotage, and at that time I was in Section II, police and army. Besides, I can prove an alibi, and Susemihl can testify to it. When Merckel was assassinated I was in Susemihl's equipage five miles away, riding through the woods on Cat Hill.'"

"But if your alibi is a good one, can't we simply wait for her to charge us?"

"That's just it, the alibi isn't good. That was the afternoon, you know, I was two steps away when Elspeth Kersting shot down Gregory William Lienhardt, the lover of stableboys. She grazed my coat collar."

Ida had heard the story of Emil's nearly losing his life so often that she smiled: "She was a wild one, all right, a dangerous character. Look here, Emil, can't you convince Diana that her accusation is mistaken?"

Emil looked out of the dirty lumber-room window into the garden: "You can't ever convince a person who wants revenge. On the contrary, he'll convince everyone that *you're* guilty; and if his desire for vengeance is strong enough—that's what counts!—he'll even convince *you*. We learned that from Urban. No, no! He who cannot forget stands condemned out of his own mouth."

Ida looked at him wide-eyed: "Emil! *You* don't want revenge on *Diana*, do you?"

"Now I'm going to tell you something very serious, Ida," said he, sitting down on a box. "I've been looking forward so much to this evening, the carp, the wine, the Christmas carols, the jollity; and Diana would have been lying in the morgue, with peace in her heart. But if I find that you have the slightest suspicion of me, the faintest, in any hidden corner of your heart, then we won't go to town, and I'll put that mixture there in the hypodermic, which is meant for Diana, into my own veins" (he rolled up his sleeve) "right here—I've been taught how to do it; and I'll ask you as one last favor to help me until you can see by my eyes that I'm dead."

"What does this mean?" she screamed, quickly covering her mouth with her hands.

"This means that Diana Rose is more remote from me, and I care less about her, than about a flower withering on its stalk. I'm fighting off the disturber of our peace: I don't hate the disturber, but I did love our peace up to the moment . . . Until you said I'd take pleasure in murdering that old psalm singer!"

"Oh, stop it, don't be sentimental. I should think a person could knock down a burglar, all right." By his sleeve she pulled him to his feet: "Come on, my dear! I shan't make any mistakes—you'll see."

4. DEATH OF DIANA ROSE

At four o'clock in the afternoon Branconi, with his wife behind him, rang the bell on the shabby staircase outside Diana's apartment door.

A shriveled maiden lady opened it. "Criminal Police," said Emil, well disguised by a Gaedicke beard, throwing back his coat. "It's about your denunciation to the mayor of Belrigardo. The questioning may take five minutes."

"Oh, certainly, no reason at all not to," sang the maiden lady, retreating into the dark hallway, and opening the door to her living room. "Everything I do is public property, everyone knows that, I've never had anything to do with the police, oh, not at all! To God Almighty now confide thee; fear not, weep not, nor be sad. At His hands shall good betide thee, Bride of Christ, in glory clad."

While she was babbling, still holding the knob of the living-room door, Ida put the shopping bag on the floor, and looked at Emil, who was facing toward her with his back to the excited maiden lady.

"Get out your ink bottle. Out with the cork!" cried the police official.

"Miss Rose, this is my secretary; we've got to take down a little statement." He held out something soft and white into the darkness.

Ida poured ether on the cotton batting; Emil cried out: "Arm's length! Turn your head away!"

"Why, what are you doing?" asked the little bride of Christ inquisitively.

At this he flung his body around in a flash, just as he had done ten years before in Willert's park, embraced the slender Diana with his left arm, holding both her arms to her body, and with his right hand pressed over her face the large wad of cotton batting, from which two tapes dangled.

"Help! I'm choking!" whimpered the woman, while Emil now calmly whispered his orders, one after another: "Pour more on at arm's length, slowly; keep your head away . . . Through my fingers . . . Right through between my fingers—there. Nothing's going to happen to you, Diana, this is a precautionary measure; I'll lift the bandage—there!"

He lifted the cotton a fraction of an inch: "Take a deep breath . . ." To Ida: "Pour on some more—keep your head away! Diana, can you hear me? Take a deep breath!"

"A train—whistling—" said the maiden lady, her breath rattling.

Emil let the unconscious woman slip to the floor, and tied the tapes on the cotton around behind her head. "A train—whistling . . . Did you hear, Ida? How happy she is! Pour on some more. No pain, no struggle! Keep your head away! At arm's length! Pour more on, slowly. There, now I've got my hands free. I'll drag her into the kitchen; you come along, and pour on more, very slowly, drop by drop . . ."

The maiden lady was put down on the kitchen floor, next to the gas stove. "She's asleep," whispered Ida, adjusting Diana's clothes.

"Please put a cushion under her head," Emil ordered in a perfectly normal voice, emptying the rest of the bottle on the cotton pad.

"There, now she's resting softly." Ida pushed a chair cushion under the head, which was strangely heavy, and got up. "What have you got there?"

"To sleep, perchance to die—who said that? Splendid; Hamlet, of course," Emil philosophized, taking the napkin-wrapped case from his coat pocket, opening it, testing the hypodermic, squeezing out the air, and seizing Diana's arm. "Roll up her sleeve. That's enough. Hold on to that arm; I've got to find the vein—mustn't make any mistake in treatment, or the arm will swell up. There it is, a good vein. . . . She can't feel anything."

He jabbed the needle in: "See the blood coming back? That was the test of whether I hit the vein. . . . Hold on to that arm. This is a morphine mixture that makes her dream more deeply; I'll inject it very slowly: she's not wincing, so she's having pleasant, quiet dreams. A bad dream would cause convulsions. . . . There's a right way to do everything . . . slowly . . . *somnium frater mortis appellatur quia morti simillimum est* . . . Unfortunately, I never got much further than that. Where's your excitement now, Ida?"

"Is she really dreaming?"

"If a person has bad dreams, he resists. Now you take the arm and hold the hypodermic—in the same position. . . . There, now I'll look for the pulse. The pulse is gone. . . . But it might come back. . . . Let it go, I'll inject the rest. Five c.c.'s—that's enough for three Dianas . . . there. Please go out and lock the apartment door. . . . Where's my sticking plaster? I had a piece cut off."

Ida took the sticking plaster, wrapped in paper, from her pocket. He took a small piece, withdrew the hypodermic needle, put it in the case, and stuck the plaster on Diana's arm.

Ida sniffed the air: "It smells of ether."

"Very soon it'll be smelling of gas, from the gas ring. No fire or coals in the cookstove?"

As the stove proved to be cold, Emil tossed in the cotton pad, and burned it, watching the green flame and the glowing mass. Ida had gone out to fetch the dead woman's typewriter. If she killed herself, it was probable that she would leave behind a few lines of prose or verse—more likely the latter, from habit, although it would be quite different in sentiment from what she would have composed in her youth, when she was still writing:

> *The many for culture, culture for the many,*
> *This is our purpose and aim above any.*

Emil, meanwhile, was philosophizing into the cookstove: "It wasn't necessary, my dove! You could have gone on buying your vegetables for thirty years, eating your chops, taking a praying brother to bed with you to give your little heart peace, with a bit of sunshine like that. . . . You could have drunk a drop of wine and eaten a bit of fish. . . . How are you, my dove?"

"What are you muttering about?" Ida hissed at him, entering. She almost dropped the typewriter in fright: then people would have come, and the jig would have been up.

"I'm just thinking," Emil declared.

She put the typewriter on the kitchen table, and spun a sheet of paper into position: "Put the gas pipe into her mouth. Afterwards, when she's stiffened, we can't get it in."

Emil obeyed.

"And if you must think, try thinking what sort of message she left. Probably poetry, I should think. Can you write verse at all?"

Emil straightened up, tried the gas to see if it would flow, and turned it off again: "Write poetry? Naturally. Anyone who can't write poetry is a semibarbarian in my eyes."

"Come on, then! We'll stick the poem on her door afterward. Heading, 'My last request.' "

"Excuse me, that's wrong, or at least not humane," Emil corrected; "the neighbors have got to be warned. Heading centered, all capitals, spaced out wide: 'Caution! Gas!' "

"Caution, gas," repeated Ida, while Emil paced the kitchen, with his hands behind his back. This lasted for an agonizing minute.

Ida could wait no longer: "If you think it will do our carp any good to stay in that hot hallway for another hour or so, just take your time!"

"Listen! I've got it! But don't write yet—listen to it first:

> *Oh soich not for the luckless wight*
> *Who after all the storms of life——*

"But the rhyme is wrong, man," the countess criticized.

"How so?"

" 'Wight' doesn't rhyme with 'life.' "

"That's poetic license. Now:

> *Oh soich not for the unhappy wight*
> *Who after all the storms of life*
> *Toins on the gas to be the bride*
> *Of He who Pilate crucified.*

"And now all in capitals again: 'Caution! Gas!' That's perfect—and just right for the neighbors to understand. Of course they all know she was a member of the Congregation of the Brides of Christ, and besides there are other members around here in the neighborhood."

"How does it go, now? One line at a time!"

"Oh soich not for the unhappy wight—" Emil dictated.

"*Search* not!"

"—Who after all the storms of life . . . Toins on the gas——"

"*Turns* on the gas!" the countess corrected.

"—to be the bride Of He who Pilate——"

"Him whom Pilate!"

"Crucified."

Ida was finished: "Crucified?"

"Exclamation point."

"Thank God!" Ida whipped out the sheet and replaced the typewriter, while Emil took a careful look to make sure nothing was left behind, stowed the instrument case in his pocket, and turned on the gas.

They left the house unobserved. Half an hour later, neighbors noticed the smell of gas and the verses pinned to Diana's front door. The innkeeper on the ground floor telephoned to the police of the St. Thomas Quarter.

5. LA PALOMA

Night. Dinner was just being served by candlelight in the Branconis' cozy dining room, with the festive aroma of the Christmas tree, while Bessonoff family silver gleamed upon the table. Two maids, the Donohills' Martha and the Branconis' Josephine, were removing the remnants of a goose that had followed upon the carp. Between Dolores Donohill and Ida Branconi sat the resplendent mayor.

Now he arose, smiled cordially at the mustached Donohill and his host, bowed to the ladies, and tapped his glass. Everyone was pleased; things had been a little quiet, which was excusable with the carp, but a goose has no fine bones. Perhaps Mr. Louvain was at fault; he thought so himself, and apologized: "Carp and wine loosen the tongue, I always say, and it's true, too, although our little company is not inspired with the wonted merriment—and no wonder, since the suspicion of crime . . . no, does not rest, *has* rested, I hasten to add, upon our community. At the same time I would apologize because this evening, the night of the proclamation of the glad tidings, I have concealed my own glad tidings until dessert—because, and this is my apology, because when our dear hostess' carp, the best carp in the world, comes on the table, everyone must be silent and address himself to the victuals, even the mayor!"

The ladies laughed aloud; Louvain was able to chalk up his first success. The two maids, prettily dressed with tiny aprons, served two baked Alaskas. The *maire* took a paper from his pocket, slapped his pince-nez on his nose, and went on: "On the other hand, when I now read out the telegram that reached the mayor's office at three o'clock this afternoon, even the tempting frozen dessert may perhaps melt with delight:

"'To the mayor of Belrigardo, Union of Southwestern Republics.

"'Diplomatic telegram. Replying to your telegraphic inquiry of December twenty-third, P.M., we beg to reply that the assassin of our former Secretary of State, Dr. John Henry Merckel, was shot fifteen minutes after the assassination in attempting to flee down a subterranean shaft. Peter George Lienhardt by name, he was the youngest of three brothers, not one of whom died in his bed. The statement made to you that the assassin escaped and is now domiciled in the parish of Belrigardo is therefore not in accordance with the facts. With regard to your observation, sir, that we never denied the rumors indicating that persons in our republic suddenly disappear leaving no word or trace, we would reply that members of a treasonable sabotage service, so-called Gas-House Boys, do in fact disappear in our commonwealth in the fashion described by you. Having lived lawlessly, they suffer a lawless death, without judge, hearing, or notice to the public or their families, and the circumstances of their death are not announced. Peace to men of good will!

"'Alfred, Count Bessonoff,
Minister of War.'"

Both maids rushed over, or Ida would have cracked her head in her fall. She was set up again, chair and all, and her forehead was chafed with snow.

"It's nothing, it's nothing, my dear friends," she smiled, but everyone knew that Alfred Bessonoff was her eldest son.

"I must admit," said honest Louvain, deeply downcast, "that the telegram is not couched in very delicate terms. I was a boor in the presence of ladies—of delicate sensibilities—Madame Countess, I most deeply apologize."

At this Emil suddenly straightened to his full, enormous height, but what he said did not make any intelligible sense:

> *That telegram was like the voice of a dove,*
> *Or angels singing up above!*

"Sit down, Emil, don't talk!" Ida ordered, seizing his arm. In the midst of the ensuing embarrassment the maids brought coffee and cake; to break the awful silence, the two women praised each the other's skill at baking.

But the host was not to be ordered about. He was standing again, rapping his glass so violently that it broke. When the hymn, "Peace on Earth to Men of Good Will," was heard from the Protestant church across the way, he took up the subject in a strong, joyful voice: "Yes, peace! For peace is what matters. Peace to married couples, peace to families, peace to friends, peace to parishes, peace to men of good will, keep peace, says Holy Writ. But about men of evil will, who do not forget, do not forgive, who carry vengeance in their hearts and invade the houses of peace, long yearned for, painfully won, dearly bought, fondly loved—what says Holy Writ about them? Are they to have peace and satisfaction? No: as they have lived lawlessly, they suffer a lawless death, without judge, hearing, without notice to the public or their families, and the way in which they perished is not made known. Peace to men of *good will!* Peace to you, my beloved wife, my dear friends!"

Clapping, shouts of bravo, delighted handshaking by Mr. Louvain across the table: no one had expected so splendid an after-dinner speech from the usually taciturn Emil. Jollity prevailed; while Josephine and Martha, arm in arm, joined in the song, Donohill with his bristling mustache played the Christmas carol of his native isles.

But the mayor, as a humanist, could not refrain from putting his enthusiasm into words: "Didn't I say our Emilio was first-rate? You'll look in vain for such a dinner-table speaker in all Belrigardo! Usually there's just some gab that embarrasses everyone; but this, straight from the shoulder, clear from the heart, and—certainly we mustn't forget this—such choice phraseology, altogether different from everyday language."

Bicyclists in the street were crying the evening paper: "Evening paper! Final extra! Mysterious body in the Rue St. Thomas!"

"Interesting! Go get a paper, Josephine!" Ida requested, her face chalky gray, and leaning on Dolores.

"—altogether different from everyday language," the *maire* went on, "which isn't anywhere near so easy as the mere layman imagines, but takes practice, careful practice! Practice makes perfect, I always say—right, Branconi?"

Josephine brought in two papers. Donohill turned to the financial section, but Dolores read out loud from the front page: "No murder in the Rue St. Thomas!"

"*No* murder?" asked Ida incredulously.

Dolores: "That's the headline. Here, I'll read it to you: 'The state's attorney has released the body of Diana Rose, a pensioner, for burial, as gas poisoning has been definitely determined, and according to the neighbors the deceased often spoke of taking her own life. The mystical ideas encountered among the so-called Brides of Christ may have done their share toward motivating the act. An empty bottle that lay beside her on the floor must have contained a strong alcoholic liquid, from which she apparently derived courage for the act. Enlightenment is sorely needed, in respect to both medieval superstition and the menace of alcohol.'"

Ida put a hand on Emil's shoulder; but he did not stir. Sitting up to his full height, he gazed at the gaily lit Christmas tree.

The literary masterpiece that had just been read, combined with the good Algerian wine, rendered Louvain quite ecstatic: "Magnificent! Magnificent in matter and manner! What do you as a stylist think of it, Branconi? Our papers grow better every day—there's no halting progress. Life is really glorious, say what you please. Food chemistry—I speak as a humanist!"

But Donohill put aside the paper he had been reading. Christmas! He sat down on the piano stool again; Josephine at his right and Martha at his left said, "Ssh!" He was just about to strike the keys when Emil restrained him with a gesture: "Let's not have a religious song, Donohill—I know another one. For lo, there was not always peace. There was storm, and you take her, for example"—he pointed to Dolores, while the two maids stood hand in hand, open-mouthed— "I treated her like the devil when I was Roland Perlotta's merchandise inspector, and she was a seamstress. But *she*"—he pointed to Ida—"was actually condemned to death. I was supposed to carry out the sentence as an officer of the secret service; you have to obey, you know. I was supposed to carry out the sentence in her own mansion in Mittelburg. Instead—what did I do instead, Ida?"

With all eyes now upon her, the countess replied with loving mockery, "He kneeled down and sang a song, the song of his life."

"How true, how true to life your answer is, Ida! The song has even been translated into many languages, because it expresses the lives of many people—I mean storm and peace. Donohill, play that song that always brings tears to my eyes—*La Paloma.*"

Donohill played, and they sang the song, whose sixth verse, today as always, filled the stout man's eyes with tears—his first for today: "A white dove wings across the sea!"

ALPHABETICAL INDEX OF NAMES
AND
EXPLANATORY GROUP INDEX

READERS wishing to make sure of the group and family to which any character in the novel belongs should use the list of names, turning first to the alphabetical index. After each name will be found the serial number under which the person sought may be found in the group index.

ALPHABETICAL INDEX OF NAMES

A

Ackermann	43, 44
Andersen	74

B

Baer	40
Bessonoff	33, 34, 114
Beyer	2
Bock	110
Bogatzki	41
Borstel	106
Brandt	9
Bruns	113

D

Daruhi	5
Donohill	95

E

Eisenberg	68
Emil	139
Emily	75

F

Fallières	93
Faust, Adam	1
Faust, Augustus Adam	18
Faust, Bernard	19
Frank	138
Froehlich, Charles	62
Froehlich, Theresa	63
Froehlich, Veronica	64
Frohwein	28

G

Gaedicke, Willie	140
Gasparra	137
Gaul	87
Grau, Dr.	105

H

Habermann	126, 131
Heidemann	122
Heinz	54
Hesse, Bishop	7
Hesse, Otto	8

EXPLANATORY GROUP INDEX

I. Persons of the Ruling Classes

A. THE DEMIGODS

1. Adam Faust, President of the Republic, owner of machine factories and mines. He is sixty years old when the story begins.
2. Augustus Beyer, Senator, intimate adviser of the President, and his successor. Leader of the radical Christian and activist wing of the Conservatives. Rich textile magnate.
3. Dr. John Henry Merckel, chief assistant headmaster, son of a washer-woman, Beyer's reader and prompter, lover of Beyer's youngest daughter, Kate. Conservative whip, and secret agent in the service of President Adam Faust.
4. Professor Andrew Zorn, theoretician of the Conservatives, promulgator of the doctrine of the Christian commonwealth as a "perpetual league of autonomous brotherhoods."
5. Dr. Daruhi, personal physician to the President, professor of occult sciences, and, along with Merckel, Andrew Zorn's most prominent pupil. Experimental psychologist and criminologist.
6. The Archbishop, Count Savoya, pupil of Zorn. Protestant, but a Unionist, attempting to reconcile the Christian denominations.
7. Bishop Hesse of Geisenheim, also a Protestant and Unionist. Former revivalist preacher and head of the Revival Mission; later he and Andrew Zorn establish the League of Carpenters, the "ideal Christian commonwealth in vest-pocket form."
8. Otto von Hesse, the Bishop's son, first a police lieutenant, later organizer and commander of the Federal Police Corps, a Christian brotherhood. Friend of Merckel, and iron fist of the Conservatives, known to the enlighteners as "the well-known madman."
9. Matthew Brandt, the "Teller of Great Deeds," historiographer and archivist to the President. Does not play a prominent part.
10. Herbert Hilgenfeld, Christian-reactionary Aristophanes, familiar friend of the President. Does not play a prominent part.
11. Henry Willert, son of the banking prince, Jacob Willert, and friend of Merckel and Hesse, the radical hotspurs. Becomes prominent late in the story.

12. Adolf Hildebrand, journeyman cabinetmaker, later leader of the "independents," i.e., the free-thinking unions, whose members do not belong to any church. Establishes and conducts in concert with Lindbrecht (see below) the Democratic Reform Party, which supports the President through fear of Urban and hatred of the Reds. Finally a Secretary of State.

13. Theodore Lindbrecht, pit inspector in the Johanna Mine, Christian Unionist and helper in building up the Order of Carpenters, subsequently President of the Catholic Workers' Associations and propaganda speaker for the "Faust system."

14. General Kaempf, Director of the War College, afterward Minister of War. Theoretician in the strategy of attack, and hatcher of schemes. The only army officer with political influence.

All the above-named reject any peaceful solution of the existing tensions, and consider "bloody purging of the nation" an actual necessity. Thus it comes about that the demagogue Dr. Urban is able unhindered to establish and arm a strong force for civil war.

B. THE MINOR PLANETS,
MODERATES WHO HAVE LESS POLITICAL INFLUENCE THAN THE ACTIVISTS

15. Oriola, Catholic Bishop of the mountain province, friend of old Hesse and the President.

16. Kessel, Protestant Bishop, successor to old Hesse, famous for his "Warning Against Church Attendance."

17. Brother Henry, Count Savoya, nephew of the Archbishop, prior of the Franciscan Monastery, subsequently a Secretary of State.

18, 19. Augustus Adam and Bernard Faust, the President's two sons. Do not play a prominent part.

20. Jacob Willert, the country's greatest banker, spokesman of the Conservatives in the Senate; by far the most influential man among the moderates.

21. Elizabeth Willert, his wife, nonpolitical.

22. Little Elizabeth, their daughter, a child.

23. Eugenia Sparangapani, Jacob Willert's mother-in-law, a patrician old lady.

24. Odo Sparangapani, her son, Elizabeth Willert's brother, a defense attorney.

25. Maier Herschel Simon, the second banker in the country, an aged man. Does not play a prominent part.

26. Hans Simon, his son, book collector and publisher of the Simon Editions, leading fighter against the Iron Phalanx.

27. Dr. Theodore Nessel, Simon's secretary and librarian.

28. General James von Frohwein, Chief of the General Staff, pessimist, convinced that mob rule is inevitable. Dies after the Battle of Neumuehle and Niederwesel in a manner as yet unexplained. The alleged murderess is acquitted.

29. Edward von Brick, Federal Commissioner of Public Safety and grain merchant. Without influence.

30. Alexandra von Brick, "the damaged Alexandra," the Federal Commissioner's daughter, Otto von Hesse's first wife. Inconstant, like her mother; a beautiful brunette.

31. Old Radowitz, governor of the mountain province at the start of the story. Is deposed.

32. Mrs. von Radowitz, the governor's wife, whom "the rats have gnawed at."

33. Count Bessonoff, brigadier general, millionaire, friend of the President, but without influence because his unfaithful wife, Ida, has gone over "to the enemy," i.e., to Dr. Urban.

34. Alfred Bessonoff, son of the foregoing, eventually Kaempf's successor as Minister of War. Takes a prominent part at the conclusion with an interesting telegram.

35. Spitta
36. Laurenti
37. Leugenfeld } Generals. Without influence.
38. Messerschmidt
39. Kraus
40. Baer

41. Bogatzki } Officers. Adjutants and couriers to Adam Faust.
42. Messerschmidt, Jr.

43. Albert Ackermann, teacher and writer. Herbert Hilgenfeld's successor as "Clerk to the Government," and editor of the Federal Police Corps magazine, *The Pensive Watchman*. Friend of Merckel and Hesse. Prominent in Book Two.

44. Elsie Ackermann, the "high-spirited Elsie, who can't get along on the money she has," the writer's wife.

45. Professor Paul Rudolphi, Christian-Conservative painter and sculptor, favorite of the President.

46. Clara Rudolphi, his wife.

47, 48. Charlotte and Sylvia, their daughters.

49. Albert Schwann, originally a bookkeeper; occupies the Lienhardt mines after the bloody night of Carolswald, and becomes head of the government secret service. "The easygoing Schwann," eventually a police general.

50. Von Lindequist
51. Lorenz
52. Stark

} Police officers and Carpenters; the last-named finally Censor at the capital.

53. Bruno Zorn, son of Andrew Zorn, inventor. Does not play a prominent part.

54. Cavalry Captain Heinz, Commander of the Southern Federal Police.

55. Supreme Court Justice Holzkopf, the President's jurist.

56. Dr. Kuttner, the President's second personal physician, privy physician to the millionaires of the capital.

C. UNINFLUENTIAL ADHERENTS OF THE RULING CLASS

57. Arnold Mueller, confidential clerk to the Willerts.

58. Anton Koerner, turner in Faust's plant, later employment inspector in the mountain province.

59. Lewis Lange, miner, later Koerner's successor as conciliator and employment inspector.

60. Tobias Witt, of Marienhall, bookkeeper, secret agent, falls in the Urbanite rebellion.

61. Margaret Witt, of Marienhall, sister of the foregoing, Jacob Willert's "Roman lady," finally Mrs. Bernard Sebastian Heide.

62. Charles Froehlich, hedge lawyer, later secret agent of Hesse and model to Rudolphi; murdered by Emil, the Lion of Afghanistan.

63. Theresa Froehlich, sister of the foregoing, maidservant at the Lienhardt château; murdered in the bloody night of Carolswald.

64. Veronica Froehlich, "the dovelike Veronica," illegitimate daughter of the foregoing; later Mrs. Tobias Witt, and finally second wife of Police General von Hesse.

65. Kate Schwann, sister of the "easygoing Schwann," maidservant in the Lienhardt château, murdered in the bloody night of Carolswald.

66. Benjamin Werner, the Carpenters' shorthand reporter. His sister is Hans Simon's stenographer.

67. Wernicke, tavernkeeper at Liebenau.

68. Baruch Eisenberg, antique dealer.

69. Mrs. Klingenberg, née Vogel, Henry Willert's housekeeper after the death of her husband.

70. Marie Klingenberg, eventually Mrs. Fred Uhl, does not properly belong here, but among the Urbanites. *q.v.*

71. John Huebner ⎫
72. Augustus Huebner ⎬ House stewards in the Willert mansion.
73. Meyer ⎪
74. Andersen ⎭
75. Emily, first Elizabeth Willert's, then Elspeth Kersting's, lady's maid, finally Mrs. Andersen.
76. Charles Thiess, grocer in the capital; under the patronage of Jacob Willert.
77. Alexander Kersting, farmer, the "roué of Liebenau."
78. Dorothy Kersting, née Thiess, his wife, sister of Charles Thiess, sweetheart of Jacob Willert's youth.
79. Elspeth Kersting, "the model of Praxiteles," daughter of the foregoing; heroine of the chronicle.

II. *Nonpartisans*

80. Widow Mantels, Peggy Witt's employer at Geisenheim.
81. Mr. Stern, proprietor of a ladies' specialty shop at Geisenheim.
82. Miss Schiller, supervisor ⎫
83. Miss Pauli, salesgirl ⎬ At Stern's.
84. John Christopher Laemmle, restaurateur at Geisenheim.
85. Josephine Laemmle, his wife.
86. Postmaster Scholz ⎫
87. Dr. Gaul ⎬ Prominent citizens of Geisenheim,
88. Westphal, the architect ⎭ Laemmle's steady patrons.
89. The Widow Merckel, washerwoman, mother of the Secretary of State.
90. Madame Kittelsen, proprietor of the high-class brothel called "The House of Dreams."
91. Dolores McCarthy, prostitute and seamstress, heroine of Book Two.
92. Joseph McCarthy, her father, a cripple.
93. Madame Fallières, a governess
94. Louise Hofer, singer, daughter of Matthew Brandt of Geisenheim.
95. Mr. Donohill, from Ireland, grocer at Belrigardo, husband of Dolores McCarthy.
96. Mrs. Wenzel, employment agent in the capital.

III. *The Urbanites*

97. Dr. Urban, modern popular leader.
98. Old Lienhardt, mining king of Geisenheim, Urban's largest backer, an aged man. Leaves three sons:

ABOUT THE AUTHOR

Hermann Borchardt came to the United States in 1937, self-exiled from Hitler's Third Reich. Born in Berlin in 1888, he was brought up by female servants and a widowed father whose three chief hobbies were duck-shooting, chess, and clocks. The father, a monarchist and a patriot, wanted his son to become a professor of philosophy, and in consequence young Hermann Borchardt attended the necessary gymnasium and universities, receiving his doctor of philosophy degree, *summa cum laude,* as well as his degree as master of arts. His father died during the last war and the inflation destroyed the family fortune. Hermann Borchardt then turned to the teaching of philosophy and made his living as a *Studienrat*—which corresponds to our assistant professor—in Berlin. In 1927, the House of Ullstein published his first and only book, dealing with the basic principles of philosophy, and in 1933 Max Reinhardt accepted one of his plays for production. But Hitler's arrival in power wrecked all his plans. Dr. Borchardt moved to Minsk, in the Soviet Union, where he served as a professor in the State Teachers' College for two years. He also suffered imprisonment in one of the Nazi concentration camps. When Dr. Borchardt arrived in the United States in 1937 he brought with him his wife and two children and at once set about making a new life for himself. They had a third child in this country and Dr. Borchardt proceeded to write a long play which won the admiration of Franz Werfel and, although the two men never met, Mr. Werfel offered to write an introduction, but urged Dr. Borchardt to recast the story in the form of a novel. The advice was accepted and *The Conspiracy of the Carpenters* is the result.

123. Innocent Isabella Rex, chairman of the Iron Phalanx and novelist.
124. Mark Antony Perlotta, playwright of world freedom.
125. Roland Perlotta, brother of the foregoing, liberator of the proletariat and dealer in ladies' ready-mades.
126. Professor Habermann
127. Professor Schiele   } Oscar Koenig's editors in chief.
128. Dr. Hoppelkopf
129. Augusta Hoppelkopf, who always swoons.
130. Francisca Schiele, mother of the revolutionary Nicholas Edwin "with the hip gesture."
131. Mrs. Frieda Habermann, manager of the play department of Koenig Publications.
132. Nicholas Edwin Schiele, son of Francisca and Professor Schiele; the hero of the "Liebenau statement."
133. Diana Rose, secretary to the playwright of world freedom.
134. Ruth Westen, niece of Oscar Koenig, founder of the "Female Friends of Armed Rebellion."
135. Dr. Tadd   } Lawyers, counsel to Koenig Publications.
136. Dr. Pole
137. Felice Gasparra, painter and sculptor of the social revolution.

V. Wavering Figures, Bribable and Bribed

138, 139. Frank and Emil, the two monstrously tall, pale, fat soldiers of fortune, should not be confused. Frank is originally a printer, Emil a madhouse attendant. Frank is cowardly and loves poetry, Emil loves music and looks death in the eye. Frank is paid simultaneously by banker Simon and Urban; Emil goes over from the Iron Phalanx to Urban not for sordid motives, but for love of Countess Bessonoff. Both wind up as nonpolitical and prosperous citizens: but Frank does so after an unadventurous rise; Emil, after Elspeth Kersting's pistol shot has grazed his coat collar and he himself has committed two murders (Charles Froehlich and Diana Rose).
140. Willie Gaedicke, barber, mask-maker, catamite, traitor, and fighter for freedom. Dies abroad by the daggers of Section IV.
141. Bart Plambeck, revolutionist and idealist, finally editorial leader writer to the government; rightfully known as "the honest seaman."
142. Claire Mill, Urban's spy, later pious, eventually wife of Frank Jaeger, "the Caucasian Oak."

99. John Theodoric Lienhardt, the "eroticist," seducer of Kate Schwann. Killed in the bloody night of Carolswald.
100. Gregory William Lienhardt, the violator of the stableboy; shot by Elspeth Kersting in Willert's park.
101. Peter George Lienhardt, chief of Urban's secret service, murderer of Kate Schwann and John Henry Merckel; shot in the cellar of the Chancellery.

Dr. Urban's "inner council" consisted of his *three intimates:*

102. The Ordnance Master, former army officer.
103. Weisse, the Leader's chief secretary, head of the Urbanite faction in the Senate.
104. Lieutenant Colonel Justus Thomas, Urban's adjutant, organizer of the army units.
105. Dr. Grau, the Leader's second secretary.
106. Alois Borstel
107. Arthur Kuehn } Liberal Senators, but backers of Urban. The two last-named eventually abandon Urban.
108. Susemihl
109. General Oriola, son of the landowner, Urban's army leader in the south.
110. Professor Bock, industrial chemist, murderer of Laurenti's expedition and the 197 wounded.
111. Susa
112. Steinhoff } High officers in Urban's pay.
113. Bruns
114. Ida Bessonoff, unfaithful wife of General Count Bessonoff; eventually, as Madame Emilio Branconi, wife of the Lion of Afghanistan. Tall, strawberry-blonde beauty.
115. Charles Emil Koehler, director of the capital-city electric plant, friend of Madame Kittelsen; victim of his own vitality and high spirits.
116. Marie Klingenberg, later Mrs. Fred Uhl.
117. John Schmalz, village mayor of Liebenau.
118. Caspar Schmalz, his son; suitor of Elspeth Kersting.
119. Fred Ritter
120. Jack Stramm } Urbanite innkeepers in the country.

IV. The Iron Phalanx of Intelligence,
glittering with all the progressive party colors including the blood red of revolution

121. Oscar Koenig, newspaper and book publisher.
122. Mayor Heidemann, progressive windbag.